YOU CAN GO HOME AGAIN . . .

Spock's voice as he addressed the Guardian was clear and precise: "I wish to visit the planet Vulcan."

"TIME?" rumbled the Guardian.

"Thirty Vulcan years past, the month of Tasmeen, before—before the twentieth day."

"LOCATION?"

"Just outside the border city of ShiKahr."

By way of reply, the pastel mists that filled the circular Gate started to swirl and boil, until the blur of time pictures began to steady as the Guardian locked in to the requested time line.

Then, abruptly, the Gate was filled with a view so familiar to Spock that it immediately relaxed all inner tensions. A hot, dry, orange world—Vulcan!

"TIME AND PLACE," the Guardian shouted, "ARE READY TO RECEIVE YOU."

Suddenly Spock was running, running forward . . . and he took that short, final leap into the time portal . . .

By Alan Dean Foster
Published by Ballantine Books:

THE BLACK HOLE

CACHALOT

DARK STAR

THE METROGNOME AND OTHER STORIES

MIDWORLD

NOR CRYSTAL TEARS

SENTENCED TO PRISM

SPLINTER OF THE MIND'S EYE

STAR TREK® LOGS ONE–TEN

VOYAGE TO THE CITY OF THE DEAD

. . . WHO NEEDS ENEMIES?

WITH FRIENDS LIKE THESE . . .

The Icerigger Trilogy:
    ICERIGGER
    MISSION TO MOULOKIN
    THE DELUGE DRIVERS

The Adventures of Flinx of the Commonwealth:
    FOR LOVE OF MOTHER-NOT
    THE TAR-AIYM KRANG
    ORPHAN STAR
    THE END OF THE MATTER
    BLOODHYPE
    FLINX IN FLUX

The Damned:
    Book One: A CALL TO ARMS
    Book Two: THE FALSE MIRROR

STAR TREK®
LOG ONE
LOG TWO
LOG THREE

Alan Dean Foster

Based on the Popular Animated Series Created
by Gene Roddenberry

A Del Rey Book
BALLANTINE BOOKS • NEW YORK

A Del Rey Book
Published by Ballantine Books

STAR TREK® LOG ONE
Copyright © 1974 by Paramount Pictures

STAR TREK® LOG TWO
Copyright © 1974 by Paramount Pictures

STAR TREK® LOG THREE
Copyright © 1975 by Paramount Pictures

ISBN 0-345-38247-1

Manufactured in the United States of America

First Ballantine Books Edition: January 1993

Contents

STAR TREK® LOG ONE

CONTENTS

STAR TREK LOG ONE

Log of the Starship *Enterprise*
Stardates 5321–5380 Inclusive

James T. Kirk, Capt., USSC, FS, ret.
Commanding

transcribed by
Alan Dean Foster

At the Galactic Historical Archives
on S. Monicus I
stardated 6110.5

For the Curator: JLR

PART I

BEYOND THE
FARTHEST STAR

(Adapted from a script by Samuel A. Peeples)

I

Veil of stars.

Veil of crystal.

On the small viewscreen the image of the Milky Way glittered like powdered sugar fused to black velvet.

Here in the privacy of the captain's cabin on board the *Enterprise*, James T. Kirk had at fingertip's call all the computerized resources of an expanding, organized galactic Federation in taped and microfilmed form. Art, music, painting, sculpture, kinetology, science, history, philosophy—the memory banks of the great starship held enough material to satiate the mind of any civilized being. Satisfy and fulfill him whether in the mood for matters profound or trivial, fleeting or permanent, whether curious about the developments of yesterday or those as old as time itself.

Yet, now, in this particular off-hour, the man responsible for guiding the *Enterprise* safely through the multitude of known hazards and an infinitude of imagined ones that lay strewn throughout space—when he could have devoted his thoughts to little things of no importance and rested his mind—chose instead to study a smaller though no less awesome version of the same scene he was compelled to view so many times from the commander's chair on the bridge of the starship.

His eyes strayed idly to the lower corner of the screen. Gossamer thin threads of crimson and azure marked a spectacular nebula of recent origin—the flaming headstone marking the grave of some long vanished star, perhaps marking also a cemetery for a great, doomed civilization, caught helpless when its sun exploded.

Men in his position who would have deliberately chosen

to observe such a sight fell into three categories. First were those for whom natural creation was too small. Men who found universes of greater magnitude within—artists, poets, landscapers and dreamers of hologram plays, sculptors in metal and stone and wood.

The second group would be that now dwindling but still sizable number of individuals who also looked inward—but whose gaze was forever out of focus—the catatonic, the insane, the mad . . .

The third and last assemblage fell somewhere in between, not quite artists, not quite mad. These were the men and women who forsook the solidity of Earth, gave up the certain knowledge of a definite sky overhead and unarguable ground underfoot, to ply the emptiness between the stars. Starship personnel.

James T. Kirk was a captain among such, a leader of this kind—which made him, depending on which extreme you tended towards, either a frustrated artist or a well-composed madman.

He sighed and rolled over on the bed, temporarily trading the pocket-view of infinity for the cool, pale blue of the preformed cabin ceiling.

A visit to the Time Planet, where all the time lines of this galaxy converged—and who knew, perhaps those of others as well, for men knew nothing of other galaxies except what little they could see through their attenuated glass eyes—was their present assignment. A pity that time lines did not choose to make themselves visible to man's puny instruments of detection. Only one race had found that secret.

It hadn't saved them.

A visit to the Time Planet was always interesting. That wasn't its designated name, of course. But popular conceptions had a way of overwhelming scientific notation. He smiled slightly. There were enough new shocks, enough running discoveries taking place every time a new section of space was charted to cause the once unbelievable Time Planet to recede into the land of the commonplace.

Kirk was a starship captain, not a historian. So his prime interest in the Time Planet was from the standpoint of its curious chemistry and even more curious physics. The trip promised to be at least as interesting as previous ones. But it was no longer possessed of that special thrill.

The remarkable view of the Milky Way in the tiny screen was as complete a portrait of the galaxy as anyone was ever likely to see. Few probes, even unmanned ones, had flown further outside the galactic rim than the *Enterprise* was now speeding. Starships were too expensive to operate and too scattered for Starfleet Command to waste them on, say, just convoying experiments from world to world.

That's why the *Enterprise* had swung wider than its best course to the Time Planet, to enable it to take readings and star-map this section of the galaxy's fringe.

Kirk flipped a switch on the tiny console by the bed and was rewarded with the view out the starboard side of the ship—a view of almost unrelieved blackness. Here and there were tiny dots of luminescence, dots which were not individual stars, but rather distant galaxies—some vaster, some more modest than our own.

Thoughts uncommon to most men raced through the deepest pools of his mind as he contemplated that yawning, frightening intergalactic pit. Someday, he mused, someday we'll have engines that won't burn out at warp-maximum eight or nine. Someday we'll have engines capable of driving a ship at warp ninety, or even warp nine hundred.

Someday.

Of course, the spatial engineers and physicists were agreed that it was impossible for any form of matter to travel faster than warp nine. Kirk thought that this belief was simply a modern superstition. It had also been said that man would never be able to fly or, wonder of wonders, exceed the speed of light.

An inship communicator buzzed insistently for attention. Again. Kirk looked at it irritably, then remembered that he'd blocked off the channel. In effect, he'd hung out a *Do Not Disturb* sign. He sat up and rubbed his eyes. There was nothing for it but to answer.

There were only two men on the starship who were on permanent, round-the-clock call. Doctor McCoy was one. He was the other. He opened the channel.

"Kirk here."

"Spock, Captain."

It was only a trick of aural mechanics, true, but somehow the monotone of his assistant commander seemed less distorted by intervening kilometers of solid- and fluid-state circuitry than the voice of anyone else on board.

No, not completely monotone—for now he heard a definite hint of puzzlement in Spock's tone.

"Captain, I hate to bother you during your rest period, but we have encountered what appears to be a unique and extremely peculiar situation—"

That woke Kirk up. "An extremely peculiar situation" to Spock could be anything from just mildly serious at best to imminent disaster at worst.

"Be right up, Mr. Spock." He flipped the switch off, threw on his captain's tunic, dilated the door, and headed for the bridge double-quick.

Behind him, the miniature glowing panorama of the intergalactic gulf, forgotten, patiently awaited his return.

The elevator paused once, at B deck, where Spock joined him. At the same time, the lights in the lift car and in the disappearing corridor beyond began to flicker. An all too familiar uneven yowling sounded.

"General Alarm." He looked at Spock, who replied to the unasked question.

"Lieutenant Commander Scott should be the officer of the deck, I believe."

"Why didn't he call me direct?"

"He did not say, Captain. But I think, if I interpret Mr. Scott's actions correctly, that he did not feel qualified to interrupt the Captain's rest period for a phenomenon of as yet undefinable proportions. He left that up to me."

Kirk considered that as the lift halted once more at the last level below the bridge. Dr. McCoy joined them.

"Jim . . . Spock . . . what's happening?"

"I don't know yet, Bones," Kirk said honestly. "You know as much as we do. Something that Scotty felt strongly enough about to sound the general alarm for."

Seconds later the doors split, and the three walked onto the bridge.

Helmsman Sulu was working busily at the navigation station. Uhura glanced back and forth between her communications console and Sulu. And from the engineering station, Scott looked up at their arrival and let out a visible sigh of relief.

"Glad to see you, Captain. I wasn't ready for makin' too many more decisions. Not considerin' the nature of this thing, whatever it is."

Spock went directly to his library computer seat—the control station for the brain and nervous system of the *Enterprise*. As Kirk took his own place in the command chair, he noted that the alarm system was still sounding its howling warning.

"That's enough noise, Mr. Sulu." Sulu nodded. Lights and alarm returned to normal status.

"Situation, Mr. Scott?"

Kirk was already studying the projected vector-grid Sulu had thrown up on the main screen. In a lower right-hand quadrant, the white dot of the *Enterprise* was moving rapidly centerward—too rapidly, Kirk thought.

He envied the old sea captains of Earth's ancient days, when a vessel's energy came only from the blowing winds, envied a skipper who could feel a change in his ship's speed through his feet. Out here in the black, uncaring vacuum, there was nothing to push against, nothing to feel against you. Compared to a rambunctious sea or strong gale, artificial gravity was a poor stimulant.

Man's senses only operated here artificially, through enormous mechanical amplification—and the only waves one could get the feel of were in wave mechanics.

"We've picked up speed, sir," informed Scott, confirming Kirk's analysis of the situation depicted on the screen. "A great deal of speed!"

"Cut back, then, Scotty."

"I've already done so, sir—cut back twice—but we continue to gain momentum!"

"Now don't get excited, Mr. Scott—" The question had to be asked, despite any damage that might incur to the engineer's pride. "—but have you checked your instrumentation?"

"Aye, Captain, checked, and triple-checked. I'd prefer the instrumentation *were* off, than to have to proceed with these readings. No sir, the information is correct." He gestured in the direction of the vector-grid.

Kirk swiveled slightly in the chair. "Mr. Sulu?"

If anything, Sulu's expression was twice as worried and half again as uncertain as the chief engineer's.

"She's not answering the helm, sir! We're—" he paused to check his own readouts, "—two minutes right ascension off course." He hammered at the stubborn controls in front of him, as if that might have some naturalizing effect on the incredible information coming in.

"And drifting farther off every second, sir."

"Mr. Spock."

"Captain?"

"Do me an in-depth computer-library scan on all known major stellar bodies in this fringe sector."

"Yes, Captain."

"And put it up on the big screen when it's ready."

There was a brief, quiet pause. Nothing moved on the bridge except the white dot of the *Enterprise* on the view-screen. Then the vector-grid was replaced by another, an overlay star-map. Or rather, part of the grid was replaced. Three-quarters of the screen did not light up with the light blue of completed mappings. It remained maddeningly blank—except for one large word in yellow, a word Kirk had almost expected to see.

UNEXPLORED

A second later, information appeared beneath this first disappointing word in the form of the legend.

To Be Mapped—No Accurate Data Currently Available.

"That's what I thought, Mr. Spock. But there was a chance. Information comes into Starfleet's banks so fast these days."

"Evidently not fast enough, Captain."

"No. Not fast enough. That'll do, Spock."

The uninformative star-map overlay blanked out and the vector-grid dominated the entire screen once more.

"Captain?" The call came from the rear of the bridge.

"Yes. Uhura?"

She seemed confused. "Captain, I've been picking up strong, but very strange radio emissions for the past two hours. Both source and direction were at first far to the right plane of our course. But since our position has been shifting, the source of emission and the course of the *Enterprise* are lining up.''

Kirk considered this piece of news. It was not especially foreboding. Not yet, anyway.

''All right, Uhura, I'll keep it in mind.'' He looked back at the screen. ''At least there's something out there.''

The white pinpoint continued to move purposefully across the grid, drawn by . . . what? He could reach out with a forefinger and blot the great starship from view. At the same time he reached a decision. While whatever was pulling them off course had shown nothing that could be definitely interpreted as a hostile action—it was probably a natural phenomenon anyway—it still behooved them to put up some form of resistance.

''Mr. Sulu, stand by to back engines.''

''Standing by, sir.'' Sulu divided his attention between the screen and his bank of controls.

''Back engines.''

The helmsman's hands moved over the navigation console, flipped a last knob 180 degrees. A slight jar traveled through the bridge, followed by a distant but distinct rumbling. Everyone made an instinctive grab for the nearest solid object. But only the slight jar gave evidence of the tremendous stresses operating on the starship.

Kirk stared at the vector-grid intently. The white dot slowed perceptibly, slowed . . . but continued on its new path, moving inexorably forward.

''Mr. Spock,'' Kirk demanded, ''have you got anything yet?'' We'd operate a helluva lot more effectively if we had some idea of what we were up against, Kirk thought.

Spock had remained glued to the hooded viewer of the computer readout. Now he looked up and over at the captain's position.

''At this point, Captain, I can only say we are headed toward an unknown object—probably natural, probably of at least planetary mass—that is generating a remarkable amount of hyper-gravity. Hyper-gravity more concentrated than any we have ever encountered.''

''Well, if there's something like that out there,'' and Kirk gestured at the screen, ''that can put out that kind of pull

plus radio emissions, why aren't our evaluative sensors picking it up?'' He rolled his fingers against one leg. ''Open the
forward scanners all the way, Mr. Sulu, and close off everything else. Divert all sensor power forward.''

''All of it, sir?''

''All of it.''

There was a moment's rush of activity as Sulu hurried to
comply with the order. It left them uncomfortably vulnerable
to anything that might choose to sneak up on the ship from
any direction but ahead. But what could be sneaking around,
out here on the galaxy's rim?

The screen flickered. The vector-grid vanished. Extending
from the left side of the screen two-thirds of the way across
now was the outermost arm of the Milky Way. A distant,
ethereal packing of rainbow-hued dust. The other third, except for a few scattered, lonely spots of brilliance, was black
with the blackness of the intergalactic abyss.

But in the center of the screen . . .

In the center, something was taking a smooth, crescent-
shaped bite out of the glowing star-mist that formed the arm.
Something spherical, small—but growing. A globe of nothingness that was obscuring star after star.

No, not entirely nothing, now. As they moved nearer, a
distant, faint glint gave evidence of a solid surface. Fascinated, Kirk and the rest of the bridge personnel stared at the
unknown, dark wanderer. They tried to define, pin down,
regularize its maddeningly elusive silhouette.

Uhura finally broke the silence.

''Captain, that's definitely the source of the emissions.
They've changed considerably since I first detected them.
And they've also grown much stronger since we've moved
close.''

''Pipe them over the communicators, Uhura. Don't keep
it a secret.''

She hit a single control. Immediately the bridge was filled
with a shrill, piercing electronic hum. She smiled apologet-
ically and reduced the deafening volume. As the sound became bearable one thing was instantly obvious to the lowliest
ensign. That whine was too wild, too powerful to come from
an artificial source. It was as natural an extrusion of the ob-

ject ahead as a solar prominence or a man's arm. It was definitely *not* the product of a constructed beacon or station.

Everyone listened to the alien hum as the outline on the viewscreen continued to grow, eating away at the distant starfield.

"Mr. Scott, ready your engineers for a maximum effort."

"Aye, sir." Scott turned to his direct line back to engineering.

"Davis, Gradner, get off your duffs! The captain's going to be wantin' some work out 'o ye in a moment—"

"Mr. Sulu," Kirk continued, "stay on these back engines."

"Yes, sir."

"Mr. Spock," and Kirk tried not to sound desperate, "anything yet?"

"Sir, I've had the computers working since we first entered the peculiar gravity-well, but I hesitated to offer an opinion on preliminary sensor data alone. Now that we have achieved visual confirmation, I no longer hesitate."

Spock's eyebrows shot way up, which surprised Kirk. For Spock that was an expression of astonishment equivalent to an audible gasp from a human. Something unique was surely in the offing.

"It is a negative star-mass, Captain. Spectroanalysis confirms finally ninety-seven point eight percent probability that the object ahead of us is composed of imploded matter. Every reading on material composition records in the negative."

"Great! That means we're headed toward an immensely powerful aggregation of nothing?"

"That is rather more colloquial than I should put it, Captain, but it is effectively descriptive."

Sulu chose that moment to interrupt with additional happy news. "Captain, our speed is increasing again!"

That did it. "All engines, full reverse thrust!"

There was a long pause as another jar and a following rumble ran through the *Enterprise*. Then Sulu looked up from the helm. He didn't appear panicked—he was too good an officer for that—but he was clearly worried.

"It's no good, sir, we're still falling toward it."

"Mr. Scott," said Kirk tightly, "what's the matter with those engines of yours?"

"There's nothin' wrong with the engines, sir," the chief engineer replied evenly. "They're doin' their best, sir, but they're badly overmatched. They're designed to push . . . not pull against a gravity-well as deep as this! I'm not sure we could pull free now if we had ten times the power."

Kirk looked back at the screen, where the negative stellar mass now all but filled the forward view, blotting out the last visible stars. With the decreased distance, more of the surface had become visible. Dull black in color, it was pockmarked with ancient craters—uneven and clearly, inarguably dead. Occasionally a startlingly bright bolt of electrical energy would arc between high points on the surface, leaping from crag to crag like a stone skipping over a pond.

To be visible at such a distance the bolts must have been enormous.

"How much time do we have?"

Spock replied easily, evenly, without looking away from his viewer. "Impact in ninety-three seconds, Captain. Ninety-two . . . ninety-one . . ."

Stunned silence suddenly filled the bridge. It had all happened so fast. One minute they were in minor difficulty, experiencing some strange, slight course deflection, and then—

No one saw the strange expression come over Uhura's face— She flicked a long nail against one earphone, then the other. No, the instruments were working properly, all right.

"Captain, I'm picking up a new signal. Listen." She moved delicate fingers over the console.

The drone of the dead star filled the bridge. But sounding over it now was a second, distinct whine, almost a wailing cry. More importantly, the sound was clearly modulated, obviously emanating from an artificial source. It faded in and out at lonely, regular intervals.

"Forty seconds, Captain," intoned Spock. For all the excitement he exhibited he might as well have been reciting the time left on a baking cake.

"Thirty-nine . . . thirty-eight . . ."

Inside, Kirk was fuming. Time, time . . . ! They couldn't go forward and they couldn't go back. That left . . .

"Mr. Sulu!" he barked abruptly. "Flank speed ahead! Declension thirty degrees."

"*Ahead*, sir?"

"MOVE IT, MR. SULU!" The helmsman moved. Maybe the hyper-gravity helped.

"We've got one chance at this point. That's to make a safe orbit. After that, we can figure out a way to break away at our leisure. I need more than thirty seconds for that."

Sulu moved rapidly at the controls. His body became a soft, fleshy extension of the *Enterprise*'s navigation system. Like Aladdin, he had only to present his wishes in comprehensible form and the electronic genie would handle the details.

But would it have enough ability to counter the titanic black demon sucking them forward to destruction?

Kirk stared at the screen, now wholly occupied by the shape of the dead star. If their bid for orbit failed, no one would ever know it. The death of the *Enterprise* wouldn't even be recorded by an idle astronomer on some distant planet as a tiny flash in far space. The massive gravity-well of the negative mass would swallow light as well as life.

"Nine seconds," came Spock's calm voice. Only a slight rise in pitch betrayed any hint of anxiety, excitement. "Eight . . . seven. . . ."

It was absurd, Kirk thought, holding tightly to the command chair! That wouldn't prolong his life by the minutest fraction of a second. But his hands continued to grip the unyielding metal nonetheless.

An electrical discharge thousands of kilometers in length lit the screen for an instant, impossibly close. Then, it was gone—and so was the blackness. Ahead once again lay the friendly, fluorescing mists of the galaxy, and the honest darkness of open space.

But Kirk knew this vision of escape was illusory. A second later Sulu confirmed it.

"No breakaway, Captain, but insertion accomplished." He sighed in visible relief. "Details of orbit to follow. We'll have a low perigee, damn low, but—" he smiled, "not low enough to drop us out of orbit."

"Praise the Lord and pass the ammunition!" called Scott.

"I beg your pardon, Mr. Scott?"

"Nothin', Spock, nothin'."

"I beg your pardon again, Mr. Scott, but you definitely

said something, not nothing." Scott gave him a pained look, and Spock suddenly comprehended.

"Ah, I see. The use of nonreferential archaic terminology served to audibilize the otherwise inexpressible emotions you felt at that moment."

"So would a punch in the snoot, pointy-ears!" warned the chief engineer.

"Is that a further audibilization?"

Kirk looked away so they wouldn't see the broad grin spreading across his face.

"Give up, Mr. Scott, you're fighting a losing battle."

"Aye, Captain," acknowledged Scott disgustedly. "I've an easier time communicatin' with a number-four automatic welder!" Then he too smiled, but only briefly. Current thoughts were too serious.

"Speakin' of which, Captain, if we don't need the power right now, it'd be a good thing for the engines to go on minimum, after all the time they spent puttin' out maximum reverse thrust."

"Yes, of course, Scotty. Mr. Sulu, compute the minimum drive we need to hold this orbit without falling and feed the data to Mr. Scott for issuance to engineering."

"Yes, sir." Moments later, "Ready, sir."

"Fine, Lieutenant. Now activate rear scanners and put our stern towards the mass."

There was a wait while the view in the big screen seemed to rotate. Actually it was the ship that was changing position and not the universe. The star-field was gradually replaced by a fresh picture, a view of the ebony sphere turning slowly below them.

"Mr. Spock, final orbit confirmation?"

"We are holding this orbital configuration easily, Captain. Effectively standoff has been achieved."

"Good. Steady as she goes, then, Mr. Sulu."

"Aye, aye, sir." The lieutenant couldn't keep an admiring tone from creeping into his voice. Kirk glanced away, slightly embarrassed.

Dr. McCoy observed the captain's reaction and grinned. No one had noticed his arrival on the bridge. They had all been, to say the least, otherwise occupied. For his part, McCoy had kept quiet. He had had nothing to say that could have been of any help, and the situation when he had arrived called for anything but a dose of his dry wit.

Now, however, some idle conversation might have its therapeutic values. He had a degree in that, as well as in medicine.

"If its pull is so strong, Jim, how do we ever break out of its grip?"

"What? Oh, hello, Bones." Kirk turned his chair a little. "One thing at a time. If we'd known what we were heading for soon enough, I'd have at least tried a cometary orbit. But by the time we knew for sure what we were up against, it was too late." He looked over at the library console.

"But you're right—it's a question we'll have to deal with eventually. How about a slingshot effect, Mr. Spock? Have we got enough power to break out at the last second? We can run on maximum overdrive for the necessary time. We'll have to dive as close as possible to the surface before pulling out, to make maximum use of the gravity-well's catapulting power. If we don't make it, we'll end up so many odd-sized blobs on the surface. Don't forget, Bones, it's attractive force increases exponentially as we near the actual surface."

Spock didn't answer the opening query right away, instead stayed bent over the viewer and continued to work.

"I'll need some time for the computations to go through, Captain. Power, orbit, proper distance from the stellar surface, angle of descent, crucial altitude. Information is still coming in through our sensors at a tremendous rate. Our knowledge of hyper-gravity is woefully slim. This is the first time a starship has been so close to a negative stellar mass. At least, the first time one has been this close and survived.

"There are too many variables at this point for hasty calculation. I can't give you an answer yet."

"All right, Spock. Set the computer on the problem. We'll learn as we orbit. We've nothing else to do, anyway. Starfleet will go crazy over the data."

As if on cue, Uhura broke in. "Excuse me, Captain, but I'm picking up that secondary signal again. We lost it temporarily when we powered into orbit, but I've got it back." She paused. "Or else *it's* got *us* back. Nine seconds north inclination, dead ahead and closing fast."

"Is it . . . ?" he began, but Uhura guessed the question.

"No, Captain. We're coming up on it, not vice-versa. Still, I wonder."

"The universe is full of coincidences, Lieutenant. How soon till sensor contact?"

"It should be on the screen in a minute, Captain."

Everyone on the bridge turned full attention to the shifting view in the main screen. For long moments there was little change in the picture. Then a faintly luminous jumble of tiny lines appeared. It began to increase rapidly in size.

Even at this distance it was easy to see that the object was an artificial construct and not a natural body. But there must be something wrong with the sensors. It was too far away to appear so large.

"Can we slow enough to match orbits, Mr. Sulu, without dropping beyond the safe range?"

Sulu fumbled with the navigation computer. "Have the answer in a second, sir." He paused. "Yes sir, no difficulty, sir. We have a respectable margin."

"Then put us alongside as we come up on it."

The object grew speedily until it dominated the viewscreen as the dead sun had before. Sulu had to reduce perspective twice to keep the entire shape in full view. Suddenly there was silence on the bridge when it became apparent what the shape was.

II

The starship was beautiful.

All the more so in contrast to the stark dead giant that held them trapped in this isolated corner of the universe. The huge *Enterprise* was an insignificant spot, a parasitic white shape alongside it.

"A thousand cathedrals all thrown together and then they added star-drive," whispered an awed McCoy. "Tossed all together and lit like a Christmas tree."

"Can it really be a starship?" murmured Uhura softly.

Spock's reply was equally hushed. "The probability is . . . considerable."

Vast arches and flying buttresses of multicolored metal and plastic soared up and out, racing in and around metallic spirals and pyramids. Here and there, gracefully designed yet massive metal pods nestled at regular intervals amid cradling arms of silver and gold and iridescent blue. Faery arms of spun alloy.

The race that had built this vessel was a race of artisans as well as engineers, poets as well as shipwrights.

"Bring us in, Mr. Sulu. Mr. Sulu?"

The lieutenant seemed to shake himself awake. "Aye, sir." He touched controls, and the *Enterprise* responded. The intricate gleaming tapestry began to move closer and then past them.

Under Sulu's skillful hands, the *Enterprise* drifted deeper into the tangle of alien crossbeams and spars. He adjusted speed and they drifted towards what seemed to be a major pod.

"It's got to be a starship!" McCoy muttered. "But, Aesculapius, the size of it!"

23

"True, Bones," Kirk agreed and then gestured, "but it seems that neither size nor beauty renders it invulnerable. Or maybe to something else, it wasn't so beautiful. Look!"

As they continued their inspection, it became clear that despite its massive bulk, some time in the past the alien ship had undergone stresses and strains of as yet unknown but undeniably powerful origin.

Arches and soaring spans of binding metal were torn and scorched—bent unnaturally in some places, sliced in half in others. The huge pods exhibited the most obvious, ominous signs of disaster. They were lined with rows of odd, hexagonal-shaped ports. All were cold, dark.

Dead.

Every pod was damaged. There were no exceptions. The metal floated easily in space, bloated with ruptures and tears. Deep gashes split one pod like a chrome grape.

"She was probably pulled in like we were," murmured Kirk. He didn't voice the attendant thought. Had this total destruction taken place before the alien starship was gathered in by the negative sun's gravity—or after?

And if the latter, why? More importantly, how?

Two surprises from outside were enough for any one station, but Uhura was destined to get yet a third. Idly adjusting receivers and amplifiers, she suddenly threw the sound of the secondary signal—the signal that came from this dead enigma—into the bridge again.

But it was different now. More of a stutter than a moan. And while there were no reasons, no facts to support it, everyone sensed that the strange call was now more urgent, more insistent than before.

"Confirmation, sir, final," she said excitedly. "I *thought* that signal was coming from the alien. Not only is there no longer any question about it, but somehow the transmitter, at least, has reacted to our presence! That's the only reason I can think of to explain this sudden change in broadcast pattern."

"I have secondary confirmation, Captain," added Spock, his eyebrows rising again, "and I should agree. But—it isn't possible. That ship is utterly, unequivocally, dead. All life-support sensors read negative. All ship-support sensors read the same. No energy is present. Temperature on board the alien is identical to that of open space—absolute zero. I have no reason to even faintly support the contention that there is life aboard . . . biological or mechanical.

"Also, there is no evidence of any stored energy capable of generating these radio emissions. I read only a slight magnetic flux—probably normal for the vessel's metal."

"Yet you reconfirm Uhura's readings—that the signal is coming from the ship?"

Spock seemed reluctant to restate his position, but, "I have no choice, Captain. That is likewise what the sensors read."

"That doesn't make sense, Mr. Spock."

The science officer's reply was drier than usual. "We find ourselves in complete agreement, Captain. Yet," he paused briefly, "that is the case."

"You're positive?"

"Probability ninety-nine point seven, Captain."

"Ummmm." Kirk leaned back, drumming a mildly obscene ditty with his fingers on one arm of the command chair. Pursuing a confessed paradox was going to get them nowhere. Better try another tack.

"Can you identify the design of the ship or its composition, Mr. Spock?"

"Negative to both, Captain," Spock replied after a glance at the computer readout. "The readings I have so far on the alloy itself—barring actual analytical confirmation from a specimen of same—indicate a material both harder and lighter than any registered in the ship's library. As for the design, it is not a recorded type." He hesitated, glanced back at the readout.

"Something else, Mr. Spock?"

"Also, Captain, silicon dating or the vessel's spectra indicates that it has been floating in orbit here for . . ." he checked the computer figures one last time, ". . . for slightly more and not less than three hundred million terran years."

There was a concerted gasp from the bridge personnel. Everyone's attention was drawn back to the screen. Back to the delicate arches, to the dreamlike design—alien in both pattern and function to the solid, prosaic shape of the *Enterprise*.

"I should think, then, that that precludes our chances of finding any survivors aboard," Kirk murmured.

"I couldn't have put it better myself, Captain," agreed Spock.

"I just know that it's beautiful," put in Uhura, half-defiantly. "To have put such grace and perfection of form into something as functional as a starship—I wish I could have known the race that built it."

"Beauty may have nothing to do with it, Lieutenant," suggested Spock conversationally. "The design may merely conform to their own conceptions of spatial dynamics."

She turned back to her instruments, an expression of distaste coming over her perfect features.

"I might have guessed you'd say something like that, Spock."

"Don't give it a thought, Uhura," chipped in McCoy quickly. "According to his own system of spatial dynamics, Spock probably finds your form purely functional, too. Don't you, Spock?"

Sulu grinned, and even Kirk was distracted enough to smile.

Spock's reply barely hinted at mild distress. "It is very easy to tell when you are joking, Doctor—which is most of the time. It is when your statements make absolutely no sense—which is most of the time."

While the byplay continued behind him, Kirk let his attention drift back to the picture of the alien starship. He envied the long-dead commander. And yet there was a hint of unease back of all the admiration.

What could have happened to so totally destroy such a magnificent vessel, with all its unknown potentialities and abilities? Certainly it must have possessed defensive powers commensurate with its size. "A civilization advanced enough to build such a craft—three hundred million years ago! Man wasn't even an idea then in the mind of nature," he murmured.

"A second or two in the span of eternity, Jim," McCoy commented, switching abruptly from the silly to the sublime.

Sometimes McCoy's comments grew wearisome, even annoying. But when he was right, he was the rightest person on the ship.

Kirk sighed. "All right, Spock. There's got to be an answer to this. You read no power from the vessel now. Any indication what its power source might have been?"

"No, Captain. There is apparently something new and undetectable at work here, capable of avoiding even the most delicate sensor pickup. But this far from any star with a planetary system, it goes without saying that they possessed some form of warp-drive. A most efficient one, beyond doubt, judging from the size of the craft."

Kirk continued to study the vast alien ship. As usual, the sudden flash of insight that would solve all and make him appear the most brilliant spacer since O'Morion didn't occur.

He had no business ordering what he was about to order. Every second should have been devoted to extricating the *Enterprise* from its present perilous position. Still, the lure of the incredible vessel was too strong to ignore. He hesitated. At least he could make one last check.

"Mr. Spock, how is the computer coming on the computation for a slingshot course?"

Spock consulted his viewer. "It appears it will take some time yet, Captain, for all the variables to be considered and an optimum program to be devised."

That settled it. He rose and spoke firmly.

"We'll board her, then. Scotty, Bones—you'll come with us. Life-support belts, of course. Lieutenant Uhura, you're in command. Sulu, have the transporter room stand by."

"Yes, sir," Sulu replied as he moved to notify the transporter chief. The four officers were already heading for the elevator.

"Captain," said Spock, "may I inquire as to your reasons for boarding the alien?"

"Nothing extraordinary, Mr. Spock. We have the time. Curiosity. Plain old ordinary human curiosity."

"That is what I thought. However, if that expression of exclusivity is intended for my benefit, Captain, you ought to know by now that it's misplaced."

"Why, Spock!" McCoy exclaimed, rising to the challenge, "don't tell me that you're subject to an emotion like curiosity!"

"Your evaluation of the phenomenon is typically inaccurate, Doctor. Curiosity is a natural, logical function of the higher mind—not one of the baser emotions.''

"That all depends on how you choose to interpret it," McCoy countered. "Now . . .''

The argument was continuing full force as they entered the transporter room. Transporter Chief Kyle was at the console, waiting for them. The console itself emitted a barely audible hum, an indication that it was prepared and ready to perform its usual functions.

Kyle had also removed and checked four life-support belts from the nearby lockers. Kirk, Spock, McCoy, and Scott buckled them on, each double-checking his own and then throwing the activating switches. Each passed before Kyle's console for a last, mechanical check. Kyle's voice read out the results.

"Captain . . . check. Commander Spock . . . check. Lieutenant Commander Scott . . . okay. Lieutenant Commander McCoy . . . check.'' He looked up. "All belts operational, Captain.''

"Thank you, Mr. Kyle.''

"If you'll take your places, sirs. . . .'' A lime-yellow aura now surrounded each man—a comforting, vital field put out by the life-support belts. They stepped up into the transporter alcove and took their places on four separate transporter disks.

"Ready, Captain,'' warned Kyle.

"Ready, Chief,'' Kirk replied, then grinned. "Try not to materialize us inside any solid objects, hmmm?''

Kyle essayed a slight grin at the old joke. Safety overrides on all transporters made such occurrences quite impossible.

"Energize, Chief,'' instructed Kirk.

Kyle carefully brought the necessary levers up, keeping a watchful eye on the vast array of monitoring instrumentation. A familiar, part-musical, tinkling hum filled the transporter room as the alcove was energized. The bodies of the four men slowly diffused, as if seen through squinted eyes in early morning . . . until they became four cylinders of multicolored particles glowing on the platforms.

Kyle hit a switch, drew the four levers rapidly down.

He was alone in the transporter room.

* * *

Four pillars of speckled fire appeared on the cold surface of the largest pod of the alien starship. The pillars faded quickly, to be replaced by the frighteningly fragile figures of three humans and a Vulcan. Each stood bathed in soft lime-yellow light.

Spock was the first to survey their harsh surroundings. They were standing next to one of the huge, dark, hexagonal ports. Just beyond the port was an enormous, gaping hole, a black pit fringed with torn, twisted metal clawing at empty space. Clear indication that whatever cataclysm had ruptured the skin of the pod had come from within.

As soon as everyone had recovered fully from the effects of transporter dislocation, they began to move toward the forced opening. All paused briefly by the dark port. Spock ran the thin force-field of the life-support system under his heel over the black, glassy surface.

"The six-sided shape of the port suggests a similarity to the natural designs of certain terran insects. The honeycombs of bees, for example, where the individual bee cells possess a similar shape. Such a similarity is, naturally, purely superficial. To read any possibilities into it would be unreasonable."

Kirk knelt and tried to peer through the thick glass—which wasn't necessarily glass, or thick. In any case, it was like staring at an onyx mirror. If anything remained inside the pod, they'd never get a look at it this way.

Engineer Scott was standing near one of the torn flanges of metal, running his hands over it. He had his face so close to it that the force-field over his nose was nearly touching.

"Would ye look at this, now!" he whistled in surprise. His lifebelt radio carried the eerie disembodied sound to his companions.

"What is it, Scotty?" Kirk rose and moved towards him from the unrevealing port.

"It's this metal, sir. I don't know much about terran insects, but I do know metal. This stuff wasn't cast or rolled or flextruded. And it's got a faint but definite *grain* like fine grains in good wood." He looked disbelievingly at Kirk.

"I'm willin' to bet, sir, that this metal was made by being drawn out into long, very thin filaments and then formed into required shapes. There's layer on layer on layer of 'em right here in this one small section. Like laminating in plastics, only on a much finer scale.'' He tapped the metal silently.

"The way a spider spins its web,'' Kirk mused.

"If you will, sir,'' continued Scott. "Such a method of metal formin'—even with our own alloys—would make for material far stronger than anything known.''

Spock had his phaser out. The brilliant beam of the tiny weapon lanced across space and sliced free a small segment of the metal. Spock caught the sample before momentum imparted by the phaser could shove it away, examined it closely.

"Lighter and stronger than anything we have now,'' he whispered, echoing an earlier reading. Then he looked in turn at McCoy, Scott, Kirk. "If this can be analyzed, Captain—''

"And duplicated,'' Scott added.

"I know, I know,'' Kirk admitted. He didn't want to put a damper on their enthusiasm—he felt pretty much the same— but they were in no position to get carried away by *any* discovery.

"Providing, however, that we're not trapped here ourselves, for some other unfortunate starship crew to stumble across a hundred million years from now.''

Stepping back along the graceful metal beam that emerged from this section of the torn pod, he moved to get a better view of the rest of the alien vessel. Staring upward he scanned the fronds of the metal jungle, eyed the other shredded and shattered pod-shapes.

Nearby, one thin soaring arch, as delicate as the finest example of the wood-carver's art, dangled crookedly, distorted by unimaginable stresses in the far-distant past.

"Look,'' he instructed the others. "Every pod—every one. Notice any similarity?''

For a change, McCoy was the first to reply.

"They've *all* been burst open, Jim. Funny—there doesn't seem to be an intact one on the entire ship. Maybe on the other side, but . . .''

"Aye,'' acknowledged Scott, "and from the inside, too. But we already saw that.''

"Must have been some accident,'' the doctor added, "to get every pod.''

Spock replied without looking, choosing instead to speak while studying the ruins of the ship.

"Accidents seldom operate according to a system, Dr. McCoy. The destruction here is too regular, too obviously managed for 'accident' to be given as cause. No, I believe we must give serious consideration to the alternative possibility that the crew of this vessel voluntarily destroyed her—and, incidentally, perhaps, themselves."

Leave it to Spock, thought Kirk, to voice what all of them were thinking but none could say.

They stood there—four insignificant animate forms, on the skin of a starship tens of millions of years in advance of anything their own civilization could produce—and considered what threat might be serious enough to prompt her crew to suicide.

Dwelling on morbidity brought no answers. Kirk started off toward the beckoning black cave and the others followed, striding with the aid of belt-gravity across the smooth hull. Without breaking stride he brought out his communicator, flipped the cover back.

"Kirk to *Enterprise*."

"Enterprise," came the prompt reply. Kirk was gratified. That gal would make a fine captain someday. "Uhura speaking."

"Lieutenant, are you still receiving radio emissions from this vessel?"

"When did you develop telepathy, Captain?" came the startled reply. "I was about to call down when you checked in. It ceased broadcasting the moment you stepped aboard."

Kirk considered this.

"Whatever machinery is still somehow operating on board this craft, Captain," theorized Spock, "is also sensitive." Kirk nodded agreement, spoke into the communicator again.

"Thank you, Uhura. Inform Chief Kyle to lock on with the transporter and be ready to yank us out of here on a second's notice."

There was a pause while Uhura relayed the necessary information.

"Expecting trouble, sir?"

"No, Lieutenant. But we're going to try and enter the

ship. There may be surprises other than finicky radio trans-
missions, something of a less indifferent nature.''

Another pause, and then a second voice came over the
compact speaker.

''Kyle here. Don't worry, Captain; I've got all four of you
right on frequency. And I'm not budging from this console
until you're all back on board.''

Kirk smiled, closed the communicator.

''Sounds like the chief,'' smiled McCoy. Another few
steps had brought them to the edge of the gaping, metal-
fringed cavern.

Kirk spent a long moment examining the dim, shadowy
interior. Clearly nothing was alive here. He swung lightly
over the edge. Scott followed. McCoy stepped aside and
gestured inward.

''After you, Spock.''

''Why, Doctor, don't tell me that you, a man of science,
are afraid of the dark?''

''Very funny, Spock—say, that wasn't intended to be—no,
that's impossible. Vulcans don't joke.''

''Joke, Doctor?'' Spock's expression was unreadable.

''Oh, well,'' McCoy sighed. ''Hope springs eternal.'' He
followed the science officer into the abyss.

They moved slowly, carefully down the wide passageway.
If necessary, the glow of their life-support belts would have
been sufficient to see one another by. As it developed, that
glow wasn't needed.

Faint light issued from long panels of translucent, poly-
ethylenelike material inlaid in the walls of the airlock—for
such it clearly was. Or had once been. Both air and at least
the outer lock had long since departed—the air by natural
forces, the lock by apparently unnatural ones.

Spock studied one of the luminescent panels. He couldn't
see a tube, a bulb, or a strip beneath it. The light seemed to
come from the plastic material itself, but he couldn't be sure.

''Something in the ship is still, somehow, generating power
that our sensors were unable to record, Captain. Or else there
are other devices that somehow generate their own power—
as these light panels seem to do.''

''Don't look a gift horse in the mouth, Spock. It's a damn-
sight easier than moving with only belt-light to see by.''

They continued deeper into the tunnel. Eventually they came up short against what appeared to be a solid wall of metal. It blocked further passage very thoroughly. Initial inspection produced nothing but disappointment.

It was Scott who first noticed the slightly brighter stream of light up near the "ceiling." Sure enough, the metal there was bent. Some titanic force had wrenched at the very structure of this inner lock.

"Some kind of emergency shutoff seems to have been in action here," Scott guessed. "Energy was operating on a tremendous scale. It would have had to be, to bend this alloy like that." He nodded up at the revealing gap.

"This passage is big enough for one of the *Enterprise*'s shuttlecraft to fit in."

Kirk put out a hand and touched the dull metal. He couldn't feel it, of course—the force-field blocked the sense of touch—which was just as well, since the metal was as cold as open space. His hand would have frozen to it.

He knew the door was solid because something halted the progress of his palm. The gesture was more hopeful than anticipatory. As expected, nothing happened when he shoved. The enormous lock didn't budge.

"Let's try up near where the top buckled," he suggested. "If it's only jammed and not really locked, we might be able to jar it loose."

He and Scott took out their hand phasers. Two beams of incandescence began to play about the top of the lock.

Two minutes of concentrated beaming, however, produced nothing more than a slight red glow in the affected area.

"Useless," he murmured, watching the red glow fade along with all hopes of entering the ship.

"Captain."

The two men put their phasers away.

"What is it, Mr. Spock?" Kirk squinted. Spock was off on the other side of the passageway.

"I believe I may have had some luck, Captain."

"I hope so, Spock. We haven't. We may have to bring the *Enterprise*'s main phasers to bear in here. I'd hate to do that. Either we'll surely damage whatever's inside—the main batteries aren't as delicate as Bones' cutters—or else we won't be able to cut through at all.''

They moved over to where Spock was waiting. He said nothing, only pointed upward.

About three meters off the floor was a large square panel, recessed into the wall of the tunnel. Three hexagonal-shaped plastic plates were set into the recess.

''I think, Captain, that that may be a key. Probability would suggest some form of manual backup system to operate any airlock.''

''I agree, Spock.'' Kirk studied the panel, made an experimental jump. ''There's only one problem—artificial gravity seems to be in full operation here. For the moment, our key is out of reach. Someone can beam back aboard and bring back a . . .''

''I do not believe that will be necessary, Captain.'' Spock moved to the curving wall and braced himself against the metal. ''If you will climb onto my shoulders, you should be able to reach the panel.''

''Isn't science wonderful?'' murmured McCoy.

It took Kirk, a trained gymnast and tumbler, only a second or two. Then he was securely braced on the Vulcan's shoulders. Even so, the recessed panel was still over his head. But by straining his arm he could manage to reach all three hexagonal plates.

''I always said you were a supportive influence, Spock,'' ventured McCoy.

''And I've always felt your humor was in execrable taste, Doctor.'' Spock's voice barely hinted at the strain of keeping Kirk's weight on his shoulders. ''However I feel that in all honesty I must revise my opinion of your puns.''

''Well, it's about time! I always knew you'd come around, Spock.''

''They are,'' the science officer continued, ''not merely bad. They are atrocious.'' McCoy's expression fell.

Kirk pressed firmly on the nearest plastic hexagon. It sank inward under his fingers, but nothing else happened. Trying the one to its left produced a similar lack of results. When he hit the third panel, however, the plastic suddenly pulsed with a soft green glow.

The brilliant reaction from something three hundred million years "dead" was startling—so much so that Kirk nearly fell.

"Careful, Captain," Spock admonished, tightening his grip on Kirk's legs. "I can support you like this for a long time, but if you insist on shifting your weight, well, I'm not an acrobat."

"Don't worry, Mr. Spock. I'm the one who'll end up falling. I don't plan to, not even in this light gravity." He kept his hand on the depressed disk and was rewarded with a faint but massive grinding sound.

"It's movin', Captain!" shouted Scott.

Sure enough, there'd been a slight hint of motion from the massive lock door. And the space near its top admitting light from somewhere within had grown a little wider. But the grinding stopped immediately and the green light faded from the disk.

"Try again, Captain," Spock suggested. Kirk pressed the disk once more. The glow returned. So did the grinding noise. He kept the disk forced down, trying to watch the lock door at the same time.

He heard a deep and echoing ripping sound, as of ancient joints and bolts giving way. The massive door shuddered, started to swing wide on unseen hinges . . . then stopped. This time not all Kirk's jabs on the disk could move it.

But there was a gap between door and tunnel wall now wide enough for a man to slip through.

"That's good enough, Spock! Coming down." He jumped carefully clear of his second's shoulders and moved to the new opening.

They had seen nothing so far to indicate that any excessive caution was required. Nonetheless, Kirk stepped softly as he edged through the gap. Spock followed, with Scott and McCoy bringing up the rear. The captain's last real fear was eliminated when they were all inside and the gigantic lock door failed to slam shut behind them.

The interior of the chamber in which they now found themselves was built on an enormous, inhuman scale. The walls were the color of pale chalcedony, dull and waxlike whites and blues. They curved upward and outward, forming a room vaguely hexagonal in pattern. Apparently the six-sided format was repeated throughout the interior of the vessel as well as in the construction of the superstructure.

The walls and sections of floor were lined with shattered, smashed machines of unknown, indefinable purpose. It was unlikely their purposes would ever be divined. Even the smallest device partook of the same feathery, lacelike design as the great ship itself. It was almost as though the builders had selected the internal structure of a leaf as their pattern for interstellar craft.

Some shapes—more solid, less ethereal of form—were still intact. And still operating . . . or at least dormant. They pulsed with different shades and blends of the visible spectrum. Violet and umber, emerald green and deep maroon and a light, pastel pink—each seemingly too beautiful to be functional.

The men moved toward the center of the room, where a monstrous amorphous shape squatted like a jeweled toad. From its top, graceful appendages radiated roofward in all directions—wands of flexible crystal. The four men moved closer.

As they advanced, the crystalline strands began to move. Slowly, gently, swaying to the ebb of some unseen tide. As the strands moved they were accompanied by a strangely melodic, somehow nocturnal music.

McCoy murmured, "I heard something like that, once. Not exactly the same, but close. Ever hear electric cello, Jim?"

"Close, close," Kirk agreed. "I wouldn't swear to any similarity, though. You know me, Bones, I'm more partial to classical stuff."

They stopped next to the enigmatic structure. When they halted, the floating fronds also stilled, the haunting music fading out in a last, trilling pianissimo.

"What do you make of it, Spock?" Kirk asked. As he spoke, the translucent limbs fluttered slightly and invisible fingers ran ever so lightly over a faraway harp.

"Look here, Captain," interrupted Scott before Spock could answer. He was pointing to the upper surface of the stocky construction.

A thin, sparkling band of pink light had suddenly appeared

around the upper trunk of the main body. Spock made a quick reading with his tricorder.

"Captain, it's registering energy output. Quite weak, but definite."

"Still functioning, then," mused Kirk softly, "after all these millennia. The lock door I can understand—it *would* operate off any oddball, emergency power source. But this thing?"

Spock was circling the object, constantly consulting his tricorder. He was shaking his head as he rejoined them.

"I am still getting tricorder readings, Captain." When he spoke there was music and movement in the room again. "I would hazard an opinion that those strange appendages are accumulators, receptors that pick up any faint form of kinetic energy—motion, movement in the air from sound waves . . . our voices . . . anything.

"It absorbs this energy and metamorphoses it, returning it or 'playing it back' in at least two readily observable ways. As motion in its 'arms' and as music . . . if those sounds are indeed an alien conception of music."

"Yes, but what is its function?" Kirk pressed, staring at the wands. They threw his words back at him and added a lithe tune.

"As to that, Captain, your guess is as good as mine. This could be anything," and he gestured at the shape, "from an energy-acceptance station for the starship's engines to a recreation area for her crew. We do not have enough information to deduce."

"It gives me the creeps," announced McCoy firmly. It wasn't a flip evaluation, either. "I feel like something that ought to be dead is watching us." Scott looked equally uneasy all of a sudden. Machines were his province. He knew them better than most people, but this thing—

"Aye, Captain, I feel it, too."

"A standard physiological symptom of latent primal superstition," Spock said. "The fear of primitive peoples confronting something utterly incomprehensible to them."

Kirk was studying the rest of the silent chamber. He spoke idly.

"Compared to the beings that built this craft, we *are* primitive peoples. You too, Mr. Spock."

"I did not mean to imply otherwise, Captain. Merely to attempt an evaluation of—"

"All right, all right, never mind, Spock. Let's keep moving."

He pointed to the far side of the chamber where another door waited.

III

Whereas the inner airlock door had been a single massive plate of unadorned metal, this portal was both more elaborately designed and more formal-looking. It was decorative as well as practical. The flat surface was seamed by triple lines, forming three triangles, each engraved deeply with alien words and cryptography. To the men of the *Enterprise* they were so many scratches.

Spock located another recess with its three inserted hexagonal disks.

But when he depressed them, nothing happened. All four stared at the seemingly impenetrable barrier for a while.

"Of course!" blurted Scott suddenly, as the others turned. "The other door was bent, damaged, so only one disk was enough to operate it. Or maybe the circuitry was jammed together. But three triangles—three disks. Press them all at the same time, Mr. Spock."

"Quite so, Mr. Scott," concurred Spock, sharing in the chief engineer's revelation.

His hand was not quite wide enough to cover all three disks, but both hands managed the trick neatly. This feat gave them some idea of the size of the starship's crew members, or of their manipulative digits, anyway. Spock pressed in.

The three disks glowed green. Seconds later the three sections of door slid back silently, disappearing into walls, roof, and floor. Another huge chamber opened beyond.

The interior of the pod was circular in design, with huge rooms spaced around a common core, and they were walking around it. This particular chamber was lined with a long row of the dark, hexagonal ports they'd seen from outside.

Whether it was from starlight they admitted or the presence
of more of the ubiquitous plastic strips, the light here was
much brighter.

"No, Captain," mused Spock as they discussed the continuing puzzle of the strange illumination. "I think the light
has been on in here all the time."

"Why couldn't we see in through the ports, then, from
out—Oh, of course." Kirk answered his own question.
"One-way ports, to protect the observer from external light
and other radiation sources."

They moved deeper into the long, curving chamber. One
interior wall was dominated by a huge reflective shape. It
resembled a giant convex mirror and was also six-sided in
form, though greatly stretched-out. Objects with even
stranger patterns—weird instrumentation and peculiar machinery—lined all the visible walls and dominated rank on
rank of high, slanted consoles.

There was something else unusual, more unusual than any
individual piece of apparatus.

The destruction that had blasted the rest of the starship,
including the room they'd just left, was not in evidence.
Whatever catastrophe had torn the great vessel asunder had
passed over this room.

As they moved further into the chamber and close to specific instruments, lights began to appear, glowing, emanating from scattered dials and panels and hidden strips of
plastic.

"Proximity activation," noted Scott absently. "Huh-oh
. . . look there." They stopped, turned.

The gigantic mirror, which was doubtless anything but so
simple a device, began to exhibit a milky opalescence. Colors commenced to flow and drift and blend across its surface.
A moment later there was more music. But this was quite
different from the sounds produced by the octopoidal machine in the other chamber. They were more rhythmic, insistent and yet soothing.

They moved toward it, curious. Spock began to adjust his
tricorder, preparatory to taking some preliminary readings.

"A most intriguing phenome . . ."

The gentle light on the clustered console to Kirk's right
abruptly exploded in brilliant green. A lurid, blinding em-

erald flare bathed them all. Formerly stolid, calm music changed suddenly to an enraged percussive clamoring. An enormous outpouring of emotion that even over three hundred million years and unfathomable differences in shape and physiology still sounded unmistakably like an alarm.

Behind them the three segments of the tripartite portal slammed silently shut. McCoy took a couple of steps toward it, slowed, stopped when he realized the futility of the gesture.

The light dimmed; the music ceased.

They were trapped in the cyclopean cave.

There were the three familiar disks set in a familiar recess to the left of the doorway. McCoy sauntered over slowly and depressed the three plastic plates. Lightly at first, then with all his strength. Then he tried them in various combinations. All attempts produced equal results—none at all. The door remained resolutely closed, as obstinate as the dead star circling below them. Not even the faint light appeared from within the disks.

Various imprecations and comments on the dubious parentage of the door's designers also failed to have a salutory effect.

"Somehow I didn't think it would work, Bones." Kirk smiled grimly. "Analysis, Mr. Spock?"

Spock consulted the all-purpose tricorder once more, wishing instead for the mythical terran supercomputer JWG. Wishing was not logical, but under the circumstances, he permitted himself the tiny private deviation. The tricorder was singularly uninformative.

"Nothing available on whatever activated the door mechanism, Captain. But an atmosphere has been supplied now." He sounded surprised. "It approaches Earth-normal. Shall we deactivate life-support belts? We may be here for a while and this gives us an opportunity to conserve the power supply since we can't return to the *Enterprise* for recharging."

Kirk hesitated. Force-fields could be more of a problem than a benefit at the damnedest times, but . . .

"No, Spock. This is just a bit too neat, too easy. That door could open again as fast as it closed. Whatever established an atmosphere in here might not have had the foresight to do the same in the other room. No, we'll keep our life-support systems on." He flipped open his communicator, eyed the now ominous walls uncertainly.

"*Enterprise*, do you read me? Mr. Sulu?" He paused, tried again. "Lieutenant Uhura, acknowledge. This is the captain speaking."

A faint, rhythmic humming was the only sound the speaker in the compact unit produced—a normal blank receptor wave. That proved the communicator was operating.

"No use, Captain," said Spock, still working with the tricorder. "Some sort of blanket interference has been set up. Its efficiency approaches totality." He looked up from the 'corder.

"I do not like this at all, Captain."

McCoy had ambled back to rejoin them.

"You always did have this marvelous ability for understatement, Spock. A gigantic alien zombie could come crashing through the near wall, spewing fire and dripping venom from poisonous fangs, and you'd sum the situation up by declaring that its intentions were other than benign!"

Kirk noticed that Scott had his phaser out. "What are you going to do with that, Scotty? We can't cut our way out any more than we could cut our way in."

"No, sir," the engineer admitted. "Not exactly."

"You've got an idea, Scotty. Don't keep us guessing."

"Well, sir, these walls are tough. I'll give you that." He gestured towards the trisected door with the phaser. "But those control disks don't look like they're made of anythin' near as strong a material. If I can burn through the covering plates and short the controls—assumin' they're shortable—there's no reason why the door shouldn't release."

"It's a good thought, Scotty," Kirk confessed. "I don't like being destructive, but . . . Give it a try."

Scott walked over and eyed the recessed disks briefly. He lined up the phaser on the lowest one, carefully set the power level, and pressed the trigger.

Nothing happened.

He tried again, turning up the power all the way. This time he produced a very faint red glow which quickly faded and disappeared.

At a sudden thought Kirk pulled out his communicator

again. This time he didn't try to activate it. Instead, he turned it over and checked the power telltale set in the base.

"No energy rating. Something's drained them. Blanket interference my eye! Something's at work in here that drinks energy like a sponge." His eyes darted around the innocent-seeming chamber, saw—as expected—nothing.

"And whatever it is, it's selective. These panels and dials are still glowing, still activated. I'm surprised this even picked up a carrier wave, before."

McCoy had his own comm unit out, checked it and then repeated the check with his phaser.

"Mine too, Jim."

"And mine," Spock added. "But not the tricorder." He made his own survey of the silent room. "Odd."

"So we're stuck," said McCoy unsubtly. "No communications and no weapons . . . no way of telling Kyle to pull us out of this." He jammed the useless instruments back in his belt.

"Only for the moment, Bones. Things are happening awfully fast here. They might happen in our favor any moment. We'd better be ready to take advantage of them if we get a chance. You miss a lot mooning over current disappointments. For example, notice anything new?"

They all searched the chamber. Creamy opalescence still washed across the face of the convex mirror. Lights still flickered and stuttered from different instruments.

"I see. Everything's returned to normal." McCoy studied the mirror. "Or at least, what was passing for normal when we came in." He paused a moment, listening. "Even the music's back—if that's what it is."

Kirk noticed the large, hexagonal dais in the center of the room. They had just been passing it when everything had gone crazy. Now, staring at it intently for the first time, he kicked himself mentally for not noticing the similarity before. Despite its size and shape it bore an unmistakable, if faint, resemblance to another smaller, more familiar object . . . his own command chair.

Recessed knobs, oddly curved levers, and triple-disk controls lined the slanted face of consoles inside the "chair," along with a vast array of multicolored, winking dials and band indicators. There were markings over the transparent dials and plates that might have been instructions, directions. Whatever secrets they held were locked up in a long-extinct alphabet and mathematical system.

"Control and navigation instrumentation, maybe," he mused. He turned to scan the room, suddenly seeing it in a new light.

"I'll bet this was the ship's bridge." He touched the peculiarly formed seat. "The captain must have sat here, in this same chair—eons ago." He stood on tiptoes and let himself down gently into the seat. Whatever the nature of his long-dead alien counterpart, one thing was certain, their backsides had different configurations.

Spock was fiddling with the tricorder as he circled the command chair.

"I don't think so, Captain. The source of the interference is here, somewhere. Also, various aspects of construction taken together with certain readings lead me to believe that this was not a part of the vessel's original equipment. It seems much more like something that was made up for a special occasion—'jury-rigged' I think you call it. To handle an emergency, for example.

"One thing is certain . . . it's generating all kinds of energy patterns. I suspect that the signal which activated the door came from here, too."

"Sure some sort of automatics were designed to seal off this room," agreed Scott, suddenly uneasy. "But seal it off from what?"

"Not from us, obviously," added McCoy.

"This ship, despite its size and probable power," Spock continued, "has been all but totally destroyed. Even the last chamber we were in. But this room, these instruments, this console—especially this console—they remain intact.

"Something, gentlemen, once came aboard this ship. Something formidable enough to not only destroy it here, but enough to cause her crew to commit suicide . . . yet leave this one last room intact. As a precaution, I should think."

"But the door closed when we entered here," protested Scott. "Surely we didn . . ." He stopped and his mouth gaped. "Oh, come on now, Spock! No known form of life could survive three hundred million years of exposure to naked space!"

"Quite right, Mr. Scott," agreed Spock grimly. "No known form of life."

McCoy interrupted them all.

"Jim, Spock, Scotty . . . the door . . . !" They whirled as one.

In the center of the still tightly closed portal, lines of glowing emerald energy, shading occasionally to aquamarine, now to deep olive, were playing freely across the metal surface.

"No," McCoy whispered, taking a step backwards.

Spock studied tricorder readings and spoke without emotion.

"Something is trying to get in here, Captain. The interference energy put out and directed by this console is reacting with another outside energy source of unknown proportions and capabilities. The flux that is the result of this interaction is now visible on the surface of the door."

"Will it hold?" Kirk asked. Spock nodded slowly.

"If the energy involved holds at present levels and does not increase."

Kirk studied the door. It was hard to turn away from that threatening, shockingly silent conflict of energies. But he forced himself to, to look down and study the alien controls. Somewhere in the maze of dials and switches designed for digits other than fingers there had to be a clue to what was happening. Something, anything at all, to give them a hint of what they might be up against.

On a hunch and with a lack of any real information to proceed on (not a very promising base) he began pressing in disks, moving switches as best he could with clumsy hands. For a while nothing happened. Then, when he accidentally nudged a spiral-shaped knob, the lights in the console began to intensify. Spock murmured something, and Kirk glanced up at his science officer.

"The mirror-thing, Captain." Kirk turned so that he could see the huge, hexagonal reflector.

It was beginning to pulse softly. The rippling waves of diffuse color started to flow more rapidly across its shifting surface. The mirror shuddered, turned to face them on some kind of hidden swivel mounting.

For a moment the four of them were reflected in the gleaming, curved material, enlarged and grotesquely distorted.

"What is it, Jim?" McCoy demanded. "What's it doing?"

"I don't know, Bones." Kirk tried to watch the mirror and handle the console at the same time. Something had activated the mirror this far. Very well. His hands played over controls as yet untouched. After a few moments the colors started to fade, the mirror itself to brighten.

Then the chaotic display of color solidified, coalesced into blurred images fluttering across the screen. That's what it was, a screen! And sound emanated from it now, too . . . a husky chittering like the song of a gigantic cricket. But the sound was much more varied, much richer in invention. Somewhere behind those sounds there was a guiding intelligence.

A picture began to form in the mirror-screen. The image sharpened. In the background was a control room of some sort. A familiar control room.

The control room they were in now.

More interesting still was the creature that dominated the screen. It was insectlike but not ugly. Its surface features were smooth, streamlined—not spiky, boney, or sharp. It was difficult to get an idea of its true size because of the way it dominated the mirror-screen. It must have been sitting very close to the visual pickup. But it was clear that it was much bigger than any man.

Big enough to need the two huge doorways they'd encountered thus far. Big enough to make use of a ship this size. Big enough so that each pod might be quarters for a single crew member.

Not big enough to prevent its destruction.

Now they could match up the strange sounds coming from speakers behind the screen with the being's mouth movements. There was a definite tone of urgency in its peculiar, rasping words. It seemed—though it was hard to tell due to vast differences in voice-box construction—that some of its message was being repeated, over and over.

Kirk finally broke the silence that had settled over the little group. The creature on the screen didn't react to the sound of his voice. If there was any lingering doubt about that, there was none now. They were watching a recorded message, and none cared to think how old it might be.

"Could be the ship's log," he thought out loud. "Or a warning. Or a religious service, or instructions for game playing, or music lessons."

"I think not, Captain," said Spock. "This preparation and care hints at more than mere frivolity."

"True . . . there, there's that same collection of sounds again!" Kirk insisted. "It's repeating itself, all right—at least part of the time."

McCoy murmured, "A message from three million centuries ago."

"It is possible, it seems," nodded Spock. "That much of their amazing technology has survived." He was working with the tricorder again.

Kirk divided his attention between his busy science officer and the strange alien on the mirror-screen.

"Can you get anything out of this, Spock?"

"I may be able to affect a translation," he replied. "The basic voice pattern does not exhibit any impossible aural characteristics. Perhaps we are deceived as to its potential complexity by sheer age."

A sudden change seemed to come over the voice of the ancient speaker. His speech was louder now, more insistent. McCoy glanced back at the triple door. Scott followed the doctor's glance with a worried one of his own.

The green and light blue bands of energy sparking across its surface were thicker, less intermittent than before. Whatever was at work on the incredibly tough alloy was definitely working its way through.

"Hurry up, Spock."

"Patience, Doctor." He activated some switches on the tricorder. Leaving the compact instrument, he started to scan the console, examining switches and dials.

Eventually he seemed to find what he was looking for. He removed the tricorder from his shoulder and placed it carefully on the panel, setting it on top of a small six-sided grid set into the metal. A last switch depressed on the tricorder and then he stepped back, turning to watch the screen.

Instantly, the voice of the alien started coming from the tricorder speaker instead of from the mirror-screen. The chittering sounds began to seem less garbled, more comprehensible. Blank spaces in the speech replaced chitters, where the

tricorder's marvelous abilities were unable to translate deli-
cacies of alien syntax.

"Danger . . . (more chittering sounds) . . . star . . . drawn
to it . . ."

Spock reached up and made some final, fine adjustments
to the 'corder. The voice was suddenly clear and understandable in the huge chamber.

". . . Rather than carry this malevolent life form to other
worlds," came the voice from across time, "we have decided to destroy our own ship. The Thing had been trapped
here by the tremendous gravity-well of the dead sun. So it
must remain. So, sadly, must we. We have studied the problem quite thoroughly in the time remaining. There is no other
solution."

Kirk desperately wished he could read the expressions on
the face of the speaker.

"The others are dead. Only I am left, to give warning. If
you are understanding this message, comprehend that you
are protected in this room only for the moment. The Thing
. . . grows ever stronger . . . it wants . . ."

A spectacular flare of green phosphorescence erupted from
the region of the doorway. The voice of the speaking alien
was drowned out by a violent, hysterical flow of pure energy.
Then the three segments of the door exploded inward as
though struck by a small meteor.

The shock threw Dr. McCoy and Scott off the dais. Kirk
and Spock were knocked down, but managed to hold onto
the control chair and console. Fortunately, the splinters of
flying metal from the ruined door somehow missed everyone.

The great curved mirror-screen began to vibrate, shiver as
tremendous unrestrained power was played through it. A
wash of stunning olivine boomed across the surface, absorbing the milky opalescence, drowning out all other colors.
There was a deep rumbling.

The polished surface started to quiver at fantastic speed,
then to flow. A crackling sound followed, then another, and
another as shards of mirror material broke free, fell from the
screen to the floor. Another powerful explosion tore the remainder of the wonderful device into tiny pieces of shining

metal and blew a deep hole in the structure of the interior pod wall.

Clinging desperately to the unsteady, rocking console, Kirk and Spock watched as even the smallest fragment of mirror-screen was enveloped in soft green light. Each bit was then melted into a tiny, shapeless blob of hot metal.

At that point the command chair and console began to glow faintly green. Spock noticed it just in time.

"Off, Captain!"

Kirk was already jumping clear. Seconds later the temporary control center began to glow white-hot beneath enveloping green mists, then to run and drip like hot butter.

All around the great chamber, the other previously un-touched mechanisms and devices started to show the now deadly green fire.

Kirk had a supportive arm around a dazed but otherwise unhurt Scott. Spock aided McCoy, who likewise had only been stunned.

"Out of here!" Kirk shouted into space. "Hurry!" Several pseudopods of translucent green started to advance to-wards them from various melting panels.

The men froze. Glaring light played suddenly over their forms. They dissolved, became four small shapeless masses of colored particles.

". . . Located them right after you pinned down the area of that last explosion, Mr. Sulu," said Transporter Chief Kyle into the intercom. His hands were smoothly operating the transporter controls as he spoke.

"Locked on and beaming them aboard," he finished.

"Good work, Chief." Uhura's voice echoed back over the grid from the distant bridge. "I thought we'd lost them when we were first cut off. And then when the pod they entered started to blow . . ."

Kyle looked up into the transporter alcove, saw flashing pillars beginning to take on solid, familiar outlines.

"Piece of cake, ma'am. They're coming through now."

The gleaming cylinders continued to build and take bi-pedal form. Kyle studied his dials and indicators intently, moved the levers down the final notch.

Kirk was in the foremost transporter disk. He blinked,

took in the transporter room at a glance, and grinned in relief at Kyle. His expression changed fast when he noticed the chief's face. Kyle wore the strangest expression, of shock, perhaps. He was staring and pointing at Kirk—no, not at him, behind him.

"Chief," he began, "what's the—"

"Captain!" Kyle finally managed to gasp out, gesturing. "Something beamed aboard with you!" Kirk whirled, looked behind him. So did Spock and Scott and McCoy.

The fifth disk was occupied . . . by a glowing and pulsing shapeless green mass.

"Transport it back out!" In an instant Kirk was dashing for the transporter console where the chief stood frozen. He dove for the activating switch. He'd think about saving Spock and McCoy and Scott later.

Too late.

The entire transporter room was suddenly drenched in light the color of deep rain forests, in diffused energy that tingled and sent waves of terror over every man present. Then the walls seemed to suck up the light like a sponge.

Kirk recovered, his hand precious centimeters short of the activating lever. Might as well have been parsecs. Standing slowly he looked around and saw that Spock and the others were staring at the walls. Then he noticed it also. The walls of the transporter chamber were now radiating a faint, greenish glow.

At the same instant a roar of sound burst from the ship's speakers. A bizarre, untranslatable, somehow triumphant cry. It was repeated, once.

In space, the *Enterprise*—infinitely tiny compared to the giant alien starship—suddenly flared with a halo of pale green. Then the seething mist thinned as the ship's hull seemed to reabsorb the color into itself.

Kirk let out his breath slowly, trying to regularize his metabolism.

"Mr. Scott, are you all right?" The engineer was staring blankly at the no longer friendly walls. His gaze held hints of panic.

"MR. SCOTT!"

The engineer shook at the verbal blast, but it was what

was needed. He drew himself up, holding his right shoulder with his free arm.

"Yes, Captain. This is just a bruise. But what . . . ?"

"Bones?"

McCoy rose slowly from his kneeling position on the platform, brushed at his lower back and grimaced, then nodded.

"I'll be all right, Jim."

Two unrelenting forces flowed through the *Enterprise* then. A green something that had lived at least three hundred million years ago now permeated the entire ship, and a holocaust of thought racing through the mind of her captain, who had lived somewhat less.

IV

Kirk, Spock, and Scott moved toward the bridge. Despite his continuing curiosity, McCoy had left them at another level. His job was elsewhere now.

To their credit, the crew on the bridge had remained reasonably calm. Less highly trained personnel might have done something drastic. The three returning officers took up their regular stations. A glance served to pass command back from Uhura to Kirk. They had no time to waste on formalities.

Reports were starting to filter onto the bridge from the rest of the ship as different sections responded to Kirk's request for status reports. His initial nervousness relaxed, but did not disappear, as section after section reported neither damage nor loss of life—no harm done by the strange discharge of green energy.

Or whatever it was.

He sighed as Uhura relayed the report he most wanted to hear.

"Sick Bay reports, sir. Dr. McCoy on alert—no injuries."

"No damage to engines or hull structure, Captain," came Scott's report a moment later.

So the *Enterprise* was still healthy, organically and inorganically. That was something, at least. They'd been given some time.

But how much?

"Automatic bridge defense system activated and operating, Captain." This from Spock.

Kirk spared an idle checking glance up and behind. A small metal globe, looking rather like a child's toy ball studded with tiny pipes, now protruded downward from a small hatch in the ceiling. A tiny red light on its side winked on, showing that the automatic phaser mechanism was powered up and ready to deal with any intruder.

Kirk had seen the last-gasp defenses of the enormous alien ship fail in an attempt to halt the forays of the green light. He didn't pin much faith on the powerful phaser.

He nodded in acknowledgment and turned to study the main viewscreen. The now familiar shape of the ancient traveler, in reduced perspective, still floated against the vast blackness of dead sun, empty space. He thought a moment, then activated the chair comm unit, leaning slightly forward to project clearly.

"Uhura, give me all intership speakers. Open channel."

"Channels open, Captain."

"All sections are to remain on full alert until further notice. Section reports from Sick Bay indicate your companions are all unharmed. Engineering reports no damage to the ship. Nevertheless you will remain on full alert until told otherwise. All personnel will wear . . ." He caught himself. He'd almost said, "will wear sidearms."

What would they shoot at—green light?

"All personnel will wear clothes." Sulu and Scott tried to stifle laughs, failed. McCoy would have approved. He tried to think of something brilliant to conclude with, failed as usual. "Everybody do your job . . . be ready for developments . . . and relax. Further orders and information will be forthcoming."

He switched off the communicator and found that everyone was watching him expectantly.

"So—we're in great shape, aren't we? But whatever was on that ship—" and he indicated the floating alien starship, "used our transporter beam to come aboard when it was good and ready. I don't think there's any question but that it allowed the alien's defense system to jam our communicators, the transporter, and our phasers until it was prepared to board the *Enterprise* itself."

"This in itself says that it has some limitations, Captain," suggested Spock. "If it was forced to rely on our transporter, then it seems certain it cannot move freely through space."

"That's true. We may have occasion to hope it has other limitations, Spock."

"That alien commander, sir," said Scott slowly, choosing

his words with care. "At least, I assume it was the commander. His message confirmed that they had to destroy themselves. Why?"

Kirk didn't reply. He sat and stared closely at his left foot. It was as good a subject to focus concentration on as anything else. Staring at Uhura would be more pleasant, but would have the opposite effect. Despite his concentration he was aware that everyone was still watching him, waiting. As usual, they expected him to get them out of this. It was so goddamn unfair!

Kirk's opinion was not unique in the thoughts of captains. When he finally spoke, the words came slow but clear.

"Until we learn more about this creature, Scotty, perhaps we should be prepared to do the same." He paused, but Scott wasn't going to help him out on this one. He'd have to say the words himself.

"Take two of your men and arm the self-destruct mechanism in the engine core."

"Sir?"

"You heard, Mr. Scott. Carry out your orders."

Scott came erect, snapped off a sharp salute.

"Aye, sir!"

An interval of solemn, respectful silence followed as the chief engineer left the bridge. He could have delegated the task to his assistants, but that was not Montgomery Scott's way.

"Mr. Spock, any change in the *Enterprise*'s readings? Anything to indicate what this creature may be up to?"

"Nothing obvious or immediate, Captain. We are registering a slightly higher than normal magnetic flux. It's not dangerous—not as it reads now. However, if it should go higher . . . and the level isn't constant. It appears to be fluctuating irregularly. There is some slight pattern, some half rhythm to these pulsations, but nothing recognizable enough to . . ."

Kirk barely heard the rest. "Like the beating of a heart," he muttered, half to himself.

A light blinked on suddenly on Uhura's board. No one turned immediately to watch her. At the moment, private thoughts were of greater importance.

"Bridge here." She paused, listening. Her life-support

aura formed a lemon-colored nimbus around her, contrasting sharply with the red uniform of a communications officer.

"What?" The loud exclamation brought Kirk around. "Thank you, Lieutenant." She swiveled to face the captain. Her voice was grim.

"Sir, decks five and six report shutdown of all life-support systems." An anticipatory shudder seemed to run through the bridge. "They'd just gone over to life-support belts—there was barely enough time." She paused.

"If you hadn't given the order for full alert, sir . . ." She left the obvious unsaid.

"What about manual override?" Uhura shook her head.

"According to the officers in charge, manual overrides have failed to respond, and—"

The raucous blare of the general alarm drowned out her concluding statements and all other sounds on the bridge. Kirk spoke angrily.

"Cut that, Mr. Sulu."

Flashing lights and siren died quickly. He shifted in his chair. "Mr. Spock!"

"Still checking, Captain," came the science officer's calm, reassuring tones. "Here it is—trouble in the engineering core, Captain."

"Damn. Any injuries?"

"I do not know, Captain. Apparently the alarm was sounded, but no one remained at the engineering communicator to supply answers to queries."

Kirk shook his head in disbelief. Didn't *anyone* remember his training?

"Bridge to Sick Bay," he began, speaking into the communicator he'd been pounding for the last ten minutes. "Bones, get down to Engineering Central, on the double. No, I don't know what it is, but that's where the general alarm was sounded." Another call switch down.

"Life-Support Central . . . LIFE-SUPPORT!"

"Life-Support here . . . Lieutenant Crandall, sir."

"Get on those dead systems on decks five and six, Lieutenant. Draw any additional personnel you need from other sections, but get on them!" If the hard-pressed Crandall desired to reply, she didn't get the chance. Kirk was already heading for the elevator with Spock close behind.

The lights in the elevators ticking off the different decks seemed to pass with maddening slowness.

"What now, Spock?" he muttered tightly.

"I cannot say, Captain—but I venture to guess that the problems in engineering, as well as in life-support, are due to the conscious intervention of the creature that managed to beam aboard with us."

"Yes, of course—but what's it doing, Spock? Conscious, perhaps, but is it random or guided consciousness that's at work here? What's its purpose? Or does it have one?"

"Xenopsychology is not one of my specialties, Captain. At this stage we can only be certain that its intentions are both destructive and combative in nature—whether guided by intelligence we cannot yet say for sure, though its actions would tend to support such a hypothesis."

The light to the engineering core blinked solid green, inviting egress.

Kirk smiled sourly. "Bones was right about your facility for understatement. 'Combative!' " They stepped out.

This was the real heart of the *Enterprise*, just as the bridge was her "brain." Awesome energies worked quietly here, tremendous force was channeled, contained, kept domesticated. It was an awkward place to have trouble.

A number of engineers, technicians, and a few security personnel were clustered at the far end of the chamber. They shifted, moving wordlessly aside as Kirk and Spock approached. Dr. McCoy was already there, kneeling next to a partly opened hatchway.

The hatch leading to the maintenance tube that in turn led out to the central core was closed nearly all the way. Nearly, because Chief Engineer Scott was holding it open. He was pinned securely between the enormous weight of the power-activated hatch cover and the floor. It pressed against his waist, and the lime-yellow glow of his life-support force-field flared redly at the point of contact.

Another few steps and Kirk was able to kneel next to the trapped engineer. Scott looked up at him and smiled grimly. He was in no real pain, as yet. Kirk touched the smooth metal of the hatch cover—its engaged closing mechanism now humming softly, irregularly—and felt as helpless as it was possible for a starship captain to feel.

Spock had detached himself from the group and had moved immediately to the nearby control panel. Now he was conferring intently with the assistant engineer in charge. The assistant was a thin young man with a wisp of blond mustache and an earnest expression. Just now he was perspiring heavily.

Meanwhile Kirk managed to dredge up a smile, somehow. It wasn't much, but Scott apparently appreciated it. He smiled back.

"How are you doing, Scotty?" Kirk finally said to break the silence.

"I'm all right, sir." Kirk reflected on how adversity made liars of all men. Scott's voice was tinged with nervousness, if not pain. "There's a good side to everything, I suppose. If the general alarm hadn't been given, I wouldn't have been wearing my life-support belt. And if the belt hadn't been activated, well—" he grinned faintly, "there'd be two of me now."

"The force-field of his belt won't hold against that kind of constant pressure for long, Jim," noted McCoy softly. Kirk, who was about to admonish McCoy for mentioning it so loudly, reflected that if anyone knew the capabilities and limitations of the belt fields, it was Scott.

"I know that, Bones." He looked over toward the control panel. "Override system, Mr. Spock. Open the core hatch."

Scott shook his head slowly.

"It's no good, Captain. The mechanism's been frozen in the close mode. We tried everything."

Spock looked over from his position at the controls.

"Engineer Scott is correct, sir. Something has jammed all circuits. Very effectively, too."

Think . . . think . . . ! Kirk studied the massive hatch cover closely, sought ideas in the intermittent hum of the servomotor.

"Scotty, is there a manual device for handling this baby?"

"No, sir. Its designers never envisioned a situation where it might be necessary to move such a heavy, vital piece of machinery by hand. Security has something to do with it, too. Anyhow, the last command it received was to close. Only the computer can tell it otherwise, sir, and it's blocked, as Mr. Spock says. Nothin' mere muscles can do is goin' to force it backwards against that command.''

As he finished, a desperately bright flare of red came from the place where the cover rested against his force-field and waist. He squirmed uncomfortably. The brighter flare was the belt's way of warning its wearer that they were approaching a critical point.

''Gettin' a little weak, sir,'' he said unnecessarily.

Kirk spun and glared at the watching engineers and technicians. ''Well, what are you all mooning at? The *Enterprise* can survive without one hatch cover. We'll have to. Maybe we can jury-rig an emergency radiation shield. Get those cutter beams out. Move!''

''Yes, sir!'' replied one of the mesmerized engineers. Then they all seemed to be moving at once, like an army of toy soldiers.

Kirk studied his trapped chief engineer, and Scott smiled reassuringly back at him. Which was damned odd. It ought to be the other way around, he reflected. But that was the kind of person Scott was—always worried about others first. Quiet, more reserved than Spock in some ways, less ebullient than McCoy, Kirk tried to think of some way to make small talk, but nothing that came to mind seemed in any way appropriate.

Despite the fact that starship captains were not permitted the option of being maudlin, for the moment, at least, the alien invader was completely forgotten.

Two of the engineers finally returned and began setting up a complicated arrangement of spools and spheres and silicon spirals on a flexible tripod. Kirk backed away. One of the engineers gave a ready signal. Scott bent his head down to his chest and turned away as much as he could, covering his face with his arms. Both engineers wore thick goggles.

Kirk put his own hands over his eyes to shield himself. There was a soft click. An incredibly brilliant, seemingly solid line of violent, violet light lanced out from the tip of the heavy-duty cutter. It touched one of the thick hinges at the back of the hatch cover.

Immediately the hinge began to glow a deep red, shading rapidly to white. A moment more and the metal began to flow like gray milk. The hissing of the melting metal was the only sound in the engineering section.

What seemed like ages later there was a dull snap, and the hinge was cut through. The engineers instantly switched off the cutter. Now pressing shut with only a single activated hinge, the hatch cover was canted at a definite awkward angle. Scott was just able to struggle free, carefully avoiding the still white-hot area where the one hinge had been melted away.

Kirk gave him a hand up. The chief was unhurt, only badly shaken.

"Be nice to be able to be in two places at the same time, sir," he commented, "but I don't fancy managin' it in quite this way. In the final reckoning it's a mite too divisible."

Sulu's voice sounded over the open intercom before Kirk could reply.

"Bridge to Captain Kirk."

He moved to stand near the pickup. "What is it, Sulu?"

"Sir, something's taken over the ship's phaser banks! They're locking on the alien starship."

Now what? He dismissed the engineers and security men to their normal duties, then moved to the small wall-screen set close by the communicator. A quick touch and once more they were treated to a view of the magnificent, ancient vessel.

Suddenly, two thick beams of destroying energy licked out. They struck the alien, struck again. Huge sections of metallic lacework were blasted apart. Archwork and shattered pods disappeared as bolt after bolt of phaser energy tore at the helpless derelict. Bits and pieces vanished in a maelstrom of organized destruction.

Torn free and impelled by the force of the phasers' power, segments of the ship began to spin end over end. They dropped out of ages-old orbit, falling into the crushing gravity-well of the waiting dead sun. Kirk's comment came in a whisper.

"The creature has no respect for beauty, either."

"Or history, Captain," Spock added, equally shocked by the invader's actions. "All that knowledge . . . all those potential discoveries—lost forever."

"Perhaps even more, Mr. Spock."

Sulu showed obvious relief when the others reappeared on the bridge. He'd watched the dissolution of the alien vessel and experienced an unusual feeling of impotence as the phaser banks, usually under his control, failed to respond to repeated attempts to halt firing.

Kirk listened to his helmsman's comments as he resumed his command position.

"Phaser banks were off, Captain. They activated themselves. I tried, sir," he half-pleaded, "but—"

"Override systems refused to respond?"

"Yes, sir. How did you know, sir?"

"The same thing just happened in engineering, Mr. Sulu," informed Spock. "The same thing which has affected the life-support systems on decks five and six. About all that can be said in favor of our visitor is that it is not capricious. It is clearly about some private plan of its own. One which we seem quite unable to alter."

"If we only knew what it wants!" Kirk muttered through clenched teeth. The familiar hiss of the elevator doors operating sounded. He turned to see Scott and Dr. McCoy appear.

"No internal damage, Jim," said McCoy, nodding in the chief engineer's direction. "He's fine."

Scott's expression, however, was less encouraging.

"Let's have it, Scotty. Nothing you can say could really upset me any further—not now."

"Sir, we cannot get into the core. All exits are sealed. And that means . . ."

"That you can't arm the *Enterprise*'s self-destruct mechanism. What about cutter beams? They still seem to work. Can't you cut your way . . . ?" He paused. Scott was shaking his head slowly.

"They might've worked a little while ago, sir. They're drained of all energy now. Apparently this creature has to sense something in operation before it can drain that something of power, or counter its command source. I don't pretend to understand how the creature does it, but there isn't a cutting or weldin' or seaming tool in the whole engineering section putting out enough juice to rearrange a loaf of stale bread."

"Captain—" Kirk turned his gaze to Uhura.

"What new good news do you have now, Lieutenant?"

"Cargo holds three, four, and five report shutdown of life-support systems. They've gone to belt-support."

"Terrific—that's just marvelous!" He spared a glance for the emergency telltales located at Scott's station. Spotted among the normal greens and blues were an uncomfortably large number of flashing reds. Even one of the galley lights was winking crimson.

"What the hell would the thing want in the galley?"

"Sir?" asked Spock, failing to sense the irony in Kirk's voice.

"Power is now out on all but key levels, Captain," informed Scott. "I'm getting a strong magnetic flux reading on all out decks."

"Captain!" Uhura shouted. She was staring in disbelief at her instruments. "Something's going through every computer bank on board, every microspool, every tape, every storage bin—and fast!"

Spock had backed slightly away from his station, watching while his dials and checkouts gave back impossible readings. Sulu's hands hovered hesitantly over his own console. The telltales of all the bridge computer systems—navigation, library, communications, engineering—were alive with myriad flashing, sparkling lights. All indications were that information was being processed through them simultaneously at an unbelievable rate.

Then the double-red local emergency lights went on, and the bridge alarm howled. They had very little autonomy left—or time. If Kirk was going to do anything he'd have to do it now. His mind raced. One last computer was as yet uncontrolled, unread, by the invader—a delicate marvel that could also process information with more insight, if not more speed, than all the onboard ship computers put together.

"Spock," he murmured finally, "can you rig a temporary, low-frequency shield, like the one we found on the alien ship, for our own navigation console?"

Spock hesitated briefly. "It would have to be a very small field, Captain."

"That's all right, Mr. Spock. Just the navigation console. I don't expect you to be able to whip up a convenient, invader-proof, bridge defense system in a couple of minutes. We're short on time."

That was enough for Spock. He bent over the navigation console and started to work smoothly, efficiently, among the instruments. Occasionally he asked Sulu for help and advice on this or that particular piece of circuitry or had him depress this or the other switch at a certain time.

Meanwhile, the force-fields of both men flared and gleamed bright as Spock played with local but powerful energies. The resulting radiance and field interaction gave each man a satanic silhouette.

Scott was bursting to complain about the lack of adequate safety precautions for such work, but he managed to contain himself. They had no time to be careful anymore.

After an interval of minutes that seemed like years, Spock stood and walked back to his station. Scott eyed the critical meters on his board and let out a sigh of relief.

"It's activated and in operation, Captain—but only for an area three meters square."

"How's the flux reading there now?" Kirk asked. Spock took his tricorder off a rack and moved back to stand close by the shielded section of console. He played the compact instrument over the affected section.

"Negative reading, Captain. The shielded area is completely normal." He moved the tricorder randomly over other sections of the helm. "Especially now, compared to what the rest of the panel reads. Readings here are rising rapidly."

McCoy took a couple of steps forward and stared at the slightly lime-yellow section of shielded console in disbelief.

"Jim, you don't think this is going to help? Whatever this monster is, it's survived eons alone in a dead, empty hulk. All it has to do here is outlast us and take over."

Kirk's reply was rich with a certain morbid satisfaction.

"No, Bones. It is obviously trapped here by the gravitational power of the negative star-mass. We have already ascertained that it cannot travel freely in open space. Therefore it doubly needs a starship—this starship—to break free. And it must also need a crew to man it. Otherwise it would have left here long ago in the alien vessel we explored. Because—"

Further elaboration was cut off as the room suddenly was

bathed in shades of color as brilliant as cut emerald. Something . . . spoke—using the computer speakers. The phrasing was oddly rushed, childishly impatient. But it was not the impatience of uncertainty, for no voice was more self-assured, more fully confident than this.

This is what it said.

"YOU ARE CORRECT, CAPTAIN JAMES T. KIRK! I POSSESS A GREAT MANY ABILITIES, BUT THE ABILITY TO BREAK FREE OF THE PULL OF THIS GRAVITY-WELL IS NOT ONE OF THEM. SO I DID . . . I DO . . . NEED A STARSHIP. NOW I HAVE ONE."

The voice rose to a shrill, almost hysterical scream.

"A BODY . . . TO HAVE A BODY . . . TO HAVE FORM . . . SOLID, SENSUOUS, AGAIN! SO LONG . . . SO TERRIBLY LONG!"

The voice ended abruptly. The flashing lights on the computer telltales suddenly died. Only the normal blink of standard activity now registered. If anything, the panels were even quieter than usual.

Spock ventured back to his library station and tried the controls. They worked normally. Only their readings and the information they now provided were abnormal. He studied them a moment, then looked back at Kirk.

"It has absorbed the computer banks, Captain. All of them. Language was naturally but one small section of the total information it gleaned."

Kirk eyed the walls thoughtfully, trying to penetrate to the heart of the softly ominous green glow that pulsed there.

"All the information in all the worlds of the Federation won't give it what it needs, Spock. A manipulative digit. In going through your library, I'm sure it discovered that we carry no manipulative robots on board that it could control."

If the captain expected that statement to provoke the creature, he failed. The alien seemed to have only a single tone of voice. One continuous flow of nervous emotion. The voice was a mirror image of its actions—violent and quick. It ignored the mild sarcasm, if indeed it was sensible to such subtleties, and spoke with single-minded purpose.

"YOU WILL NOW REMOVE THE STATIC SHIELD FROM THE NAVIGATION CONSOLE, CAPTAIN JAMES T. KIRK."

Kirk considered his reply carefully. It might still be possible to reason with this thing.

"You've shut down life-support systems and threatened

the lives of my crew. I'll remove the static shield if you restore those systems first.''

As he half-expected, even that modest request was denied. No, not even denied. It was ignored, treated as unworthy of comment. For this being, nothing existed outside of self.

''ALL NONESSENTIAL SYSTEMS HAVE BEEN EXTINGUISHED IN THE INTERESTS OF SIMPLIFYING CONTROL. OBEY ME!''

That made his decision simpler, if not more pleasant.

''And if I refuse?''

A phaser beam darted out of nowhere as Kirk rose in the command chair. No, it issued from . . . the automatic bridge defense system! The beam impacted on his force-field squarely and knocked him stumbling into a bulkhead.

''OBEY ME!'' the alien thundered from all speakers.

Kirk tried to dodge out of the phaser's line of fire and searched frantically for cover. But he couldn't dodge the beam of the phaser anymore than one could escape sun in a desert. As for finding cover, the automatic defense system was very thorough. It had been carefully designed to permit a hostile intruder *no* cover.

The beam cut off for seconds, shot out again, and slammed him against a wall. It pinned him there like some shriveled, colorful insect. His force-field flared pink, then red, turning slowly to a deep crimson. Beads of sweat began to form on his forehead. Though it hadn't broken through, the intense concentration of heat was starting to hurt like blazes. He felt himself weakening, slumped against the wall.

''Captain!''

Spock ran toward him, stopped. The beam left Kirk for a split second, affording him little relief. It moved to Spock. But when the science officer remained frozen in place, it swung back to batter again at Kirk's shield.

Spock took a heavy, metal-spined reference manual from a shelf and stepped quickly toward the bridge defense module. As he threw, the phaser beam looped around and struck at his ankles. The thrown book fell far short, bounced over the command chair. Moving higher the powerful beam shoved Spock back against the base of the library computer. Then it shifted slightly and he was washed down the floor along the wall like a leaf in the grip of a powerful hose.

It finally pinned him upright against a far bulkhead, holding him there until his force-field also flared pink, red, and crimson.

Kirk put a hand to his singed chest and rolled over slowly. He staggered to his feet. The first thing he saw was Spock, pinned up against the wall. Swaying, he took a step toward the science officer. It was the shock of the near-fatal phaser assault that had affected him, more than any actual physical damage. He knew what an uncontrolled phaser of even mild strength could do to something as fragile as a human body.

At that moment there was a deep red flare, almost black, from Spock's life-support belt. Then his force-field was gone, overloaded by the concentration of energy from the phaser. Immediately the beam stepped down to low power. It continued to focus on the center of Spock's chest. Kirk could have continued to advance, but now dared not.

From somewhere in the depths of the ship, from all around them, the implacable alien consciousness spoke.

"OBEY ME!"

It was Kirk's turn to scream.

"You'll hurt him!"

"REMOVE THE STATIC SHIELD FROM THE DRIVE CONTROLS AND NAVIGATION PANEL! DO IT NOW!"

No hint of compassion—not even a mention of Spock. There was absolutely no doubt in Kirk's mind that the creature would kill Spock slowly, without thought.

The subject lying under that threat still had his voice, if not his mobility.

"No, Captain!"

The phaser beam intensified ever so lightly. No cry of pain escaped Spock's lips, but he writhed. A tensing in the knuckles showed what he was feeling. Inwardly, Kirk slumped.

"I will obey. Let him go."

As quickly as that, the phaser beam was gone. Spock stood leaning against the wall for a moment longer. Then his legs gave way under him and he collapsed to the floor. Kirk took a step in his direction, but that damnable, all-seeing voice interrupted again, bellowing.

"NOW! IGNORE THE FALLEN BIPED AND PROCEED WITH THE FIELD REMOVAL!"

He turned and started reluctantly to the helm-navigation console. McCoy moved to Spock's side. There was a small but neat hole in the center of the science officer's shirt. Mc-Coy dug out a tiny spray vial and began to work on the injury.

Kirk thought furiously. It was the end of everything—unless . . .

He looked down at his chest, where he'd been lightly burned . . . lower, to his stomach. His hand slipped slowly, ever so slowly, down to his life-support belt.

"It's too fast for us, Doctor," Kirk said quickly. "So don't try deactivating the defense module with one of your sprays." McCoy looked up, puzzled.

Had the alien learned enough to read a human expression?

It had not. McCoy's response was to look at Kirk. In doing so he automatically brought the spray vial away from Spock, and up. The phaser shifted to cover McCoy and the almost awake Spock.

In that brief, unguarded instant Kirk whipped free his life-support belt with one hand, hit a switch on the console with the other, and dropped the activated belt across a certain unshielded section of it. He jumped clear as the panel erupted in sparks and fiery flashes.

He'd been gambling that the creature wouldn't turn off the bridge life-support systems and risk killing them all. He was right.

But the phaser beam swung to burn an opening in the floor. Desperately he rolled to get away from it. It eventually caught up with him at the other end of the helm console. Stopping, the beam focused just a few centimeters to one side of his head. He could feel the deadly heat on his cheek. The beam had been raised to killing force.

V

"REPAIR THE WARP-DRIVE CONTROLS! OBEY ME!"

The now maddened voice had risen to a tremulous shriek.

Kirk got to his feet slowly, cautiously, making sure he made no rapid gestures that might be misinterpreted by the trigger-happy alien. As he rose the beam stayed centered parallel to his skull. He walked to the command chair.

"Mr. Scott."

"Yes, sir?"

"The warp-drive controls have burned out. Commence repairs immediately. Install the auxiliary bypass system."

If Scott suspected anything, he gave no sign.

"Aye, Captain." He looked around, his gaze coming to rest on the somnolent bridge defense mechanism. It was as good a point to direct his voice to as any.

"I'll need some cuttin' and repairin' tools." He pointed to a nearby locker. "I can get what I need in there—if you'll allow them to energize."

"YES, YES!" came the anxious voice. "BUT MAKE NO WRONG MOTIONS. I HAVE THE ENTIRE WARP-DRIVE AUXILIARY BYPASS SYSTEM AND REPAIR PROCEDURE FROM YOUR OWN COMPUTER RECORDS. HURRY!"

"Do as it says, Mr. Scott."

"Aye, Captain," Scott replied, keeping a determined pokerface. Not that he knew what Kirk had in mind, but he suspected the captain was up to *something*. And it was up to him to give Kirk as much time as possible to prepare for it.

He walked slowly to the locker, at the same time being careful not to move unnaturally and thus make the creature suspicious. There was a nervous moment as he energized the precision microwelder. Small as it was, it could still easily

67

burn a hole even in a bridge defense module—if given the time.

However, the alien apparently felt secure in its control. It permitted him the necessary small tool. He walked to the fused section of helm, examined it, and shook his head like a doctor clucking over a sick patient.

Then he moved to the back of the bridge, near Uhura's station, and a small wall panel that needed to be removed. Controls and switching points were revealed within. There were also several long coils of fine cable.

As he brought the activated welder close and began to make the necessary connections, the voice again reverberated around the bridge.

"ANY ATTEMPT TO SABOTAGE THE AUXILIARY WARP-DRIVE CONTROLS, CHIEF ENGINEER MONTGOMERY SCOTT, WILL RESULT IN IMMEDIATE DESTRUCTION OF ALL OTHER BRIDGE PERSONNEL. I WOULD RATHER NOT RESORT TO THE USE OF INFERIOR, SECONDARY PERSONNEL TO CARRY OUT MY COMMANDS—BUT I WILL NOT HESITATE!"

"I'll be sure to try and keep that in mind," Scott mumbled, concentrating on the delicate work at hand.

Spock was on his feet again. He touched his chest once, looked at McCoy.

"A fine, professional job, Doctor. Fortunately, your medicine is more effective than your jokes." For once, McCoy didn't feel up to a reply.

The science officer walked over to stand next to Kirk. Both faced casually away from the bridge defense system's video pickup. Apparently the creature's abilities did not also include mind reading. It had divined nothing of Kirk's series of delaying actions beyond their immediate practical effects.

The defense sphere's sound pickups were not designed to detect whispering. It was primarily a visual device. Normal ship noises would have drowned out soft talk and only confused an efficient mechanism. So the two men felt reasonably secure in conversing.

"Let's have it all, Spock. You've had enough experience with this creature's actions to have formed some solid opinions about it, at least. What are we dealing with?"

Spock rubbed his chest again. "Beyond its undeniable belligerence, Captain, we know nothing about its mental composition. We can theorize more thoroughly about its physical makeup.

"It seems to be some form of pure energy organism, without much actual mass, and it is essentially electromagnetic in nature. At the same time, it appears capable of a strong parasitic relationship with a solid host body. A starship could provide such a body, it seems.

"It appears to utilize the electronic network of the *Enterprise* the way a man on Vulcan uses the nervous system of his body. It has, in effect, become the *Enterprise*. We, on the other hand, are only marginally beneficial organisms in its structure, like the white corpuscles in human blood. That is, some of us are. Apparently it regards most of the crew as unwelcome growths—germs—simply to be disposed of as rapidly and with as little effort as possible.

"And, Captain, the computer library still operates. It has indicated that the flux readings are growing in strength. The longer this being has to adjust to its new body, the stronger and more secure it grows."

Kirk dropped his voice even lower. If the alien could somehow pick it up and understand it, then all was lost. But it had given no sign of being able to so far. And devilish subtlety did not seem to be one of its characteristics. They had no choice but to try. Spock was looking at him expectantly and Kirk remembered that he couldn't read minds, either.

"The slingshot effect, to throw us free of this gravity and out of orbit—can you do the necessary math in your mind, Spock? I've got reasons for not using the navigation computer."

Spock nodded. "I see. Yes, the alien would know. I believe I can, Captain. Soon I will have to aid Mr. Scott, but my mind and hands can operate on different projects at the same time."

Kirk turned and raised his voice as he addressed the rotating sphere of the defense mechanism.

"The chief engineer will need assistance from my first officer to complete repairs. Is this permitted?"

Circuits continued to open and close. Human diaphragms operated somewhat slower. Otherwise there was little motion on the bridge. Spock strode slowly, cautiously, to where Scott was working. Kirk kept a wary eye on the dormant phaser, but no punishment, no warning was forthcoming.

"I guess it is," he murmured.

"WHEN REPAIRS ARE COMPLETED," came the voice suddenly and, as usual, without any warning, "YOU WILL LEAVE THIS ORBIT AND PLOT A COURSE THIRTY-SIX POINT THREE TWO ONE FROM OUR PRESENT LOCATION."

Sulu spoke up.

"That's the heart of the galaxy, Captain!"

"Set the course, Mr. Sulu."

Sulu looked back at him incredulously and made no move to obey. Spock glanced over from his work and spoke.

"Captain, we've seen this creature separate itself into different parts. If it can divide and grow, it could take over every starship we meet. It could control entire computer centers—perhaps whole planets."

"I am aware of that, Mr. Spock. But we have," and he looked downcast, "no choice, I'm afraid."

"COMPLETE REPAIRS!" screamed the voice. "OBEY ME!"

"Set the course, Mr. Sulu! That's an order."

"Yes, sir." Sulu's reply held a hint of bitterness.

Scott and Spock unwound two small cables from the recess in the wall and ran them along the deck to the burned-out navigation console. Working with the microwelder and Spock's assistance, Scott proceeded to install a small metal box to one side of the melted panel.

The box's face contained a basic, simplified version of the ruined warp-drive controls. The engineer made a last connection, wiped his forehead with the back of a hand, and took a deep breath.

"Auxiliary controls ready to activate, Captain." Everyone on the bridge was staring at Kirk.

The Captain looked up at the sphere, hardly daring to breathe and yet forcing himself to maintain a normal tone of voice.

"The auxiliary controls can only be opened manually."

At that, the memory banks of Spock's computer-library station suddenly hummed into operation. No one needed to be told what was taking place. The creature was checking Kirk's statement against the operations manuals stored deep within the ship.

Eventually the lights at the computer station returned to normal. There was a short, screaming silence. Kirk willed himself not to sweat.

"THAT IS CORRECT. OPERATE THE MANUAL CONTROLS. OBEY!"

Kirk breathed an unseen sigh of thankfulness and offered prayer to all supernatural deities who looked after starship skippers. Then he nodded slowly to Scott.

The engineer moved back toward his own station. Kirk rose and walked calmly to the auxiliary control box. He placed his hands on the simplified device. It was only illusion, but the smooth metal controls and knobs felt hot.

"Control activated." He paused, started toward another set of switches. "Setting cour——" His hands moved in a blur.

The *Enterprise*'s engines slammed into emergency drive. Not away, toward the beckoning mist of the Milky Way, but down, down and in, toward the devouring black maw below.

Sulu jerked in his seat as the dark bulk of the dead sun grew suddenly enormous in the main viewscreen. He spun to face Kirk.

"Captain, we're falling out of orbit! We're falling into the star!"

"APPLY FULL POWER—REVERSE ENGINES!" shrieked the disembodied alien. "OBEY ME, OBEY ME!"

The bridge defense phaser came on, swung around to touch Kirk's back. He jerked and hung grimly to the controls. He had no force-field to protect him now, with his life-support belt fused to the original controls.

Picking up speed with every microsecond, the *Enterprise* rushed toward the destroying gravity below. The phaser abruptly cut off—and Kirk cursed silently. The creature had guessed what he was trying to do. If it killed him while he was hanging onto the controls and failed to cut his hands free in time . . .

It tried something else, and for a few seconds Kirk was forced to fall away. The entire console section and even the deck around the manual control unit began to glow with heat. At the same time the walls of the bridge began to fluoresce an angry, pulsing green. The vivid color deepened and dimmed in indecipherable, distorted patterns. The voice of the alien rose to a terrible, frightened scream.

"NO, DECELERATE! DO NOT DESTROY THE SHIP! OBEY— OBEY—OBEY!"

Kirk had glanced down at his hands, then back at the glowing console. If the alien realized that at any second it could now safely kill his him and induce another member of the crew to operate the controls . . .

He threw himself back on the metal box and its burning knobs and dials. There was a sizzling sound and the odor of burnt flesh filled the bridge. Uhura screamed. Tears streamed from Kirk's eyes, but his hands stayed frozen on the controls.

"Stand by to activate warp—drive!" he gasped. Spock instantly took the vacant assistant helmsman's place next to Sulu . . . in case.

"NO . . . DON'T!" came the terrified voice. The *Enterprise* dove toward the extinct solar furnace. It filled the viewscreen now, as complete a grave as any man could wish for. Its surface was alive with brilliant discharges of electricity.

The starship glowed all over with a soft green aura. This rapidly coalesced into a single, bright blob of beating, living light. On the bridge the green luminescence of the walls suddenly faded and seemed to sink into the metal. The phaser beam of the defense sphere abruptly cut off.

That was the first sign. Now for the final blow.

"Activate warp-drive!" Kirk managed to cough out. The white heat of the panel had vanished at the same time as the phaser beam, but the metal was still fearfully hot. If it was a last, desperate ruse by the creature to get him away from the controls, it failed.

"Activated, Captain," came Spock's prompt reply.

The ship shuddered briefly as the titanic warp-drive engines cut in. There was a last faint pulse of green radiance— then it was gone. A final, despairing cry, shrill and weak now, came from the speakers.

"PLEASE . . . DON'T!"

Suddenly the *Enterprise* seemed to leap toward the black sphere, toward the very horizon of the sun that was no more. It seemed impossible that it could miss that sucking, grasping target. It *must* strike, vanish in a blank flash of instant annihilation. The image of the starship wavered as it reached the critical point of that bottomless pit of gravity, seemed to flow like a liquid . . . and disappear.

An instant later the combination of emergency overdrive and the tremendous pull of the star had flung the *Enterprise* far beyond any threat—far beyond any clutch of its relentless tug.

For a few seconds the star wore a ring of incredible thinness. A tiny narrow band of soft green circled the black sphere, revealing a last, hopeless grab for a ship safely out of its reach. Forever out of its reach.

Then the green ring contracted, shrunk in on itself, to become a single bright, emerald blob of incandescent life— an amorphous mass of now harmless malevolence.

"You can let go now, Captain," said Spock gently.

"Let . . . go . . . ?" Kirk mumbled. His eyes glazed. Spock reached over and gripped the captain's wrists. They pulled easily but that death grip was not so simply broken. Spock reached around more firmly and pulled, pulled again, hard. This time both hands came free of the controls.

Kirk slumped in Spock's arms, unconscious. The second-in-command of the *Enterprise* carried his captain over to the command chair. Sulu immediately put the helm on automatic and took over the warp-drive controls, his hands safely encased in a pair of thick protective gloves. He brought the *Enterprise* down from emergency to normal cruising speed.

McCoy had been waiting. Spock watched him at his work. When he spoke, his tone was as emotionless as ever—and as lucid, curious.

"Well, Doctor?" McCoy was already working with a second kind of spray, then rapidly applying some white cream to Kirk's hands—those blackened, terribly burned hands. The cream hardened instantly to an almost plastic consistency. He smiled just a little.

"I don't find any serious nerve damage, Mr. Spock. Nothing that won't repair itself. As for the skin, that's easy to regenerate. Oh, someone will have to feed him for a few days, but other than that . . ." He smiled wider. "He'll be as good as new."

Sulu, Uhura, and Scott all turned away—so that no one

else could see how relieved they were. McCoy moved to the nearest intercom, which happened to be the one in the command chair, and thumbed the switch.

"Sick Bay? Doctor McCoy here. I want a medtable on the bridge, double-time."

Spock was watching Kirk. The captain's eyes fluttered as both anesthetic and stimulants took effect.

"Is it . . . it . . . gone?"

"Affirmative, Captain." At moments like this Spock almost wished he could smile—but only for the therapeutic effect it would have on Kirk, of course.

"It left the ship when it thought we would crash into the negative stellar mass. In the end it seems that the alien's instinct for self-preservation, even after all these millennia, was stronger than its analytic abilities. If it had gambled and stayed with us another few seconds it would still be with us. Now it is trapped back there once more.

"And now that we know it is there, we can enter its description, dangerous characteristics, and location with Starfleet, so that any other exploring vessels that visit this sector can give it a wide berth."

The elevator door dilated, and a pair of medical techs with a mobile medtable between them entered. Under McCoy's direction they lined it up parallel to the command chair. Both techs gave a little start when they saw that the patient-to-be was the captain, but McCoy reassured them.

"It's all right Darrell, Elayne—nothing too serious."

Kirk eyed the medtable and then shifted his gaze to the face of the good doctor.

"What's that for, Bones? I'm all right. You just said so yourself."

"I know, Jim. There's nothing wrong with you at all that a pair of new hands won't fix." He patted the table. "Be a good boy and climb aboard without forcing me to tranquilize you, hmmm? I will if I have to, you know."

"Okay, okay—! Don't threaten me, Bones."

"Threaten, Jim?" McCoy grinned.

With the help of the two techs and Spock, Kirk slid onto the table. The table was convoyed to the elevator.

"Wait a minute, Mr. Spock—Captain," Uhura broke in.

McCoy froze the elevator open. Her brows drew together as she fiddled with her controls.

"We're still picking up emissions from the area of the dead star. It's growing faint as we move away, but . . . ah, there!" She did things with the amplifiers.

A tremulous, desperate voice filtered through the speaker. A familiar voice, made harmless now by increasing distance and hopelessness.

"DON'T LEAVE ME ALONE AGAIN! OH, PLEASE, PLEASE!"

No one on the bridge said anything. There was a crackle of static as a different source of distant energy from another star announced its own presence. Then a final, faint piping.

"SO LONELY . . . OH, DON'T GO! DON'T . . . DON . . ."

The voice vanished, swallowed down and digested by distance.

"It doesn't sound so dangerous now, does it, Mr. Spock?" Kirk whispered.

"The creature? No, Captain. Not now. But the danger behind it remains."

"If only the alien had tried to cooperate, to communicate instead of threaten . . ." He shook his head tiredly, beginning to feel the side effects of McCoy's ministrations as they rode down the elevator. He stared at the steady light set in its roof.

"What makes a thinking, intelligent being act in such a fashion?"

"Who knows, Captain? We know not where it comes from. And we do not even know what makes certain men or Vulcans act the way they do. The creature's instincts, in the final analysis, are not so incomprehensible—or even alien."

"Now you're acting unnecessarily rational, Spock."

"To me, Captain," Spock replied, "that is a contradiction in terms."

"You know," said Kirk abruptly, "I think I can feel my hands again. They're beginning to tingle slightly."

He felt a pressure on his upper right shoulder.

"What was that?" Turning his head slightly he saw that they were entering Sick Bay. "Bones, what have you done to me now?'' McCoy smiled down at him reassuringly.

"You're coming out of shock, Jim. I just gave you a good dose of something to keep your mind off it. If I didn't, despite the local anesthetic, in a few minutes those hands would do more than just tingle slightly.''

"Shock? What do you mean, shock? I'm not in shock, Spock.'' McCoy had to grin. "And nothing you slipped me, Bones, is going to make me go un . . .''

PART II

YESTERYEAR

(Adapted from a script by D. C. Fontana)

VI

A world of silvery sky.

There seemed to be no oceans; but they were there, rolling and heaving under the shining clouds. There seemed to be no deserts; yet they existed, too. Dry, bone dry, and inhospitable, and old. There seemed to be no green forests or rolling hills. True, they were rare; but they too held a real existence.

There only seemed to be sky.

There was a peculiar atmospheric aura to this world—a kind of shimmer in the stratosphere that rippled and flowed with strange effects—other than merely meteorological.

Kirk finished his glass of reconstituted rombouton juice, prepared on a distant South Pacific isle on Earth itself, and studied the image on the viewscreen before him. He touched a button on the arm of the command chair and leaned over to direct his voice into the open grid.

"Captain's Log, stardate . . ." He burped, rather loudly, and looked around in mild embarrassment. Everyone on the bridge studiously avoided looking back at him. But at the helm, Sulu made a sound suspiciously like a stifled chuckle.

"You find our approach maneuvers amusing, Mr. Sulu?" Kirk was not in the best of moods. His newly regenerated skin on his hands itched something fierce.

"No, sir," deadpanned Sulu in return. He examined the readouts of the navigation computer most intently.

Satisfied that dignity had been maintained, Kirk hit the switch once more. "Erase that last," he muttered, then began again.

"Captain's Log, Stardate 5373.4." He paused, formed his thoughts.

"After an unexpected delay of some substantial awkwardness . . ."

"What was that I once heard you say about my tendency to understate, Captain?" came Spock's quiet voice from the area of the library-computer console.

"Quiet, Mr. Spock. I'm recording. Or trying to." He hit the unlucky switch again, irritably. "Cancel that last.

"Captain's Log, stardate 5373.4. After an unexpected delay of some substantial awkwardness . . ." he glared around, but this time no one saw fit to interpose a comment, ". . . we resumed our original course and are now lying in orbit around the planet of the time vortex.

"Commander Spock and I will land to carry out basic research for the Institute of Galactic History, in conjunction with and in support of similar research to be conducted by historians Jan Grey, Loom Aleek-om, and Ted Erickson.

"Dr. Leonard McCoy will also accompany us, as . . ." He held the panic button down and looked back to where Dr. McCoy was standing, idly observing the view of the planet rotating lazily below. "How do you want to go into the record on this, Bones?"

"What?" McCoy dragged his attention away from the fascinating image of the time planet. "Oh, might as well play it linear, Jim. 'Interested onlooker' will do. I'm not hunting for academic credits."

"Attaboy, Bones. I thought you'd say something like that." Kirk let the pause switch up. ". . . as interested onlooker." Satisfied, he switched off the log and thumbed a communicator switch.

"Historians Grey, Aleek-om, and Erickson report to the transporter room, please. We are ready for descent." He flipped the communicator off and rose.

"Lieutenant Sulu?" The younger officer glanced up from the helm. "You're in command in my absence."

"Yes, sir," Sulu replied. He hesitated, then spoke quickly, earnestly. "I sure wish I was going down with you, sir. I've heard a great deal about the Guardian of Forever."

Spock and McCoy were waiting at the elevator, and Kirk moved to join them.

"It can be very interesting at times, Mr. Sulu—that's true. It can also be infernally dull. Either way, you know the regulations. No one is permitted on the surface outside the reception stations except authorized research personnel and Starfleet officers with the rank of Lieutenant Commander and above.'' He smiled.

"You'll be there in a couple of years, Lieutenant."

When they'd left, Sulu looked back at Uhura.

"Somehow, Uhura, I get the impression the captain's not terribly enthusiastic about this expedition."

Uhura replied while taking the opportunity—now that the commanding officers were absent—to touch up her makeup. "I suppose even the most exciting of pasts can grow dull with repetition. Seeing a famous person or witnessing an important historical event could be offset by bad smells and unsanitary plumbing.

"Besides, who can blame him for being a bit blasé after what we just went through with that—that *thing* on the fringe?" She whistled. "Substantial awkwardness . . . wow!"

The three historians were already waiting in the main transporter room when Kirk, Spock, and McCoy arrived. All appeared outwardly composed, but their faces betrayed the excitement they were feeling. Two had made the trip to the surface once before.

Their anticipation was understandable—history was their chosen profession. The discovery of the Time Planet—and the subsequent development of the Guardian of Forever and the Time Gate as a research tool—had been to the study of galactic history what the invention of the warp-drive had been to interstellar travel. Kirk could empathize with their special excitement, even if he couldn't wholly share in it.

Of the three, Erickson and Grey were human. Erickson was a small, intense man in his mid-forties, with thinning grey hair cut in bangs in the front—Vulcan style. His limbs seemed to be in constant motion, like the legs of a millipede. The most noticeable facet of his personality was his finding everything, absolutely everything, to be "fine, just fine"—and said so.

Jan Grey was slightly younger, taller and she had a pleasant narrow face that was now glowing with inner anticipation. Both humans wore plain grey jumpsuits emblazoned with the crossed Ionic column and short spade of physical history. They carried elaborate tricorders in shoulder harness.

The third member of the official research party, Loom Aleek-om was neither human nor Vulcan. The native of Aurelia stood head and shoulders above Spock, though he was thinner and lighter than any of them, even Grey.

His wings he kept neatly folding along the line of his back. Short arms ended in a spread of delicately taloned claws, which could manipulate the extremely fine controls on his own, smaller tricorder.

Tattooed on his beak was an intricate scroll—sign of manhood—above which wide, black eyes shone piercingly. They were in startling contrast to his brilliant gold and blue-green plumage.

"Ladies and gentlemen," Kirk smiled, "are you ready?" A rhetorical question. Erickson couldn't resist waving his pudgy arms in reply anyway.

"Ready?" he chirped, feigning disbelief. "We've been ready for days, for months for this minute, Captain! First we encounter that terrible monster and I thought we'd never get here at all. Then more days of unexpected travel and waiting. And you want to know if we're ready?"

"I do not believe I shall ever understand this extraordinary affectation of humans," mused Spock as they took their places in the transporter alcove, "for answering a simple, direct question with half a dozen inane ones."

"Don't worry, Spock," replied Kirk, scratching at his newly grown right palm, "it's not contagious."

"I sincerely hope not, Captain," said Spock fervently.

Beaming down was convenient and quick, though uneventful. They missed the spectacular sights of shuttling down through the silver atmosphere.

No one would miss a descent to the dry, semidesert section they would eventually arrive at, however.

Oddly, very little was known of the early civilizations of the Time Planet itself. Nor of how its inhabitants were able to unite a seething infinitude of time lines and tie them to a single point on their world. Nor why.

Oh, the usual reasons were given . . . curiosity sparked them, and the spirit of scientific exploration. But Kirk and many others couldn't help but believe that the builders of such an incredible device as the Guardian of Forever must have had some other, unknown, more potent reason for constructing it.

There was irony on a grand scale present, too. For in tying together thousands upon thousands of time lines, the builders of the Guardian of Forever had apparently neglected to tie in their *own*. So historians could use the Guardian to research the reasons behind any great invention—except the Guardian.

A distant chance existed that this was not in fact the case, that the time line of the Guardian's inventors was in truth accessible. But if so, it had not yet been discovered. It's builders had covered their own past too well.

The research party materialized at the modest, clean reception station of the Historical Institute. The reception port was fully automated, proceeding on the logic that machines couldn't be bribed. Anyone attempting to beam down to another part of the planet, illegally, would have found himself materialized instead—thanks to elaborate transporter intercepts—inside one of the well-armed armored fortresses that circled the time planet with unceasing, never-tiring vigilance.

The station was near the southern sector of the best preserved portion of the massive urban ruins that rose near the Guardian. The city of Oyya, all two thousand square kilometers of it, was itself a formidable subject for historical and archaeological study.

Excavations had revealed that at one time the city was even greater in extent. And there were ruins of other enormous cities scattered around the planet, many even larger than Oyya. But none were so well preserved.

Had the Time Planet, then, once been severely overpopulated? Was the Time Gate a last, desperate means of finding a way to relieve population pressure before it overwhelmed its creators? There was evidence to support such a theory.

Most particularly, despite the unquestionably high degree of civilization attained on this world, there was no hint, no sign that its inhabitants had ever discovered a drive capable of carrying them from star to star. And there were no other planets, uninhabitable or otherwise, in the Time Planet's system. It didn't have even a single moon.

The Time Planet was alone in space. Its visionaries and explorers had been forced to go adventuring in time.

The automatic checkpoints at the reception stations were thorough and efficient. As soon as they'd cleared, they were met at the exit lounge by the head of the Institute's main station on the planet, Dr. Vassily.

Dr. Vassily was elderly, silver haired, scintillating of mind, very female, and built like a hockey puck. Notwithstanding, she had the voice of a pixyish eleven-year-old.

She invited them into the nearby central building, a Spartan yet comfortable facility, for a light snack and some heavy conversation. Visitors were still a rarity on the Time Planet.

Brandied tea, cake—the tea was good, even if reconstituted. Somehow, though, reconstituted brandied tea, in all its varied brands and types, never approached the real thing. Of course, the natural product was far beyond the financial reach of pioneer historians—however revered and respected.

Kirk forced himself to make easy conversation with the good doctor. It wasn't hard; she was fascinating. But before long Erickson was squirming like a jellyfish with the fidgets, Aleek-om was beginning to flap his wings nervously, sending feathers into everyone's tea, and even the normally imperturbable Jan Grey was showing signs of severe impatience.

"We certainly appreciate your hospitality, Dr. Vassily," Kirk said smoothly and honestly. "But as you can probably tell, my professional charges are anxious to be about their job."

"Of course," she nodded sagely. "Thoughtless of me. I've been working here for so many years I'd forgotten what the experience of a first trip to the Gate means to outsiders." Her voice turned brisk and workmanlike.

"There's a ground car waiting for you outside in the motor-pool hangar. Take the black and yellow one. I've had it pre-checked and fueled for you." She rose, her coveralls falling in shapeless wrinkles around her stout form, and walked them to the door. It stood open to the dry desert air. The climate here sucked moisture from unprepared bodies, but the temperature was not as severe as on other parts of the Time Planet.

She directed her attention to Aleek-om. "By the way, Loom, what time line are you going to search out?" Aleek-om's upper and lower beak clicked several times in rapid succession—a sign of humor among his kind.

"Why, that of the city Oyya's, of course—*cher-wit*!" Dr. Vassily smiled at the in-joke.

"It's been tried, believe me. With every semantic variation you could think of. Every play on words, every stretching of definitions. The Guardian's reply to such requests is always the same.

" 'There is no access through the Gate to the requested time line.' " Aleek-om looked suddenly serious.

"Dr. Vassily, do you really think the builders of the Guardian forgot to tie their own time line into the device?"

"No one can say for sure, of course," she replied, wholly professional now. "Personally, I tend to the belief that any race which could construct such an astounding phenomenon as the Guardian would not overlook something that affected them so deeply and so closely. I prefer to think that for their own unknown reasons they denied access to their own past— to themselves and to those who might come after them.

"We may never know the truth, and I want to!" She grinned awkwardly, a little embarrassed at the sudden outburst of emotion.

On the way to the motor-pool hangar, this was commented on. Grey found it unseemly. Aleek-om attributed it to too little fresh contact with others. Erickson thought it only human.

Spock, as usual, pinpointed it.

It was called dedication.

The ground car carried them easily and rapidly over the dry terrain. It was fifteen kilometers from the reception station to the site itself.

There was no Gate, no artificial barrier in evidence around the Guardian. It had value beyond measure, value that transcended mere monetary considerations. Anyone who wished to try and destroy it—if, indeed, it could be destroyed— might seemingly have free and clear access to it. It had been demonstrated time and time again that madmen would attempt most anything.

Nor was there any visible bar to potential misusers of the device. It seemed that anyone who could manage the time and expense necessary to reach the Time Planet and who shuttled instead of beaming down to its surface could make whatever use of the Gate he wished.

Of course, there was the small matter of slipping past the four superbly equipped orbital fortresses that covered every square meter of the planet in a ring of destructive power. Power reserved elsewhere only for protecting prime military centers.

It meant avoiding the gigantic phaser and missile batteries buried deep in the innocent-looking sands that drifted in low dunes around the Guardian itself.

But anyone who could get past that—well, access to the Time Gate was quite free to all such.

Such elaborate precautions were more than justified.

It would not do to allow the frivolous or unstable access to the malleable past. So the missiles that remained locked in their racks and the phasers that sat on their stores of ravening energy and did not disturb the desert bushes around them were occasionally publicized. Thus far no one had yet tempted them.

A well-mounted expedition might possibly have succeeded in seizing the Guardian by force, if it managed to avoid total destruction in the battle that would ensue with the planetary defenses.

But that would mean war. Access of a belligerent to an enemy's past, well, it was unthinkable. So three empires and two interstellar federations cooperated in policing the Time Planet. They were reassured by the certain knowledge that any one of them who dared try to make use of the Guardian for its own purposes would invite the immediate wrath of the other four.

It might not have been the most civilized of arrangements, but it worked.

Not that the setting of the Guardian was unimpressive, oh no. Hydrogen missiles might be larger, planet-to-space phasers more intricate, but none could match the nearby city of Oyya for sheer splendor. It stretched on and on, magnificent ruins dominating the horizon as far as one could see to east and south.

And of course, there was the Guardian of Forever itself.

Physically, it was impressive without being massive. Certainly in size it was nothing to match such awe-inspiring artifacts of ancient civilizations as the Temple of Halos on Canabbra IV, or the Aljaddean Wall on Qahtan.

In color it was the shade of rusty iron, spotted here and there with overtones of grey. In shape it resembled a lopsided doughnut. The central hollow of that doughnut was the actual Time Gate. It was always filled with luminous, shifting images of a thousand pasts, all racing by at speeds far too rapid for even scanning tubes to pick out and disseminate.

They left the ground car near a clump of some hearty green-brown desert bushes and walked up until they stood a couple of meters in front of the cut stone base. Kirk and Spock, having been here before, chose instead to spend a moment observing their fellow observers.

Grey just stood there quietly, her eyes shining. Aleek-om's wings fluttered gently and thin claws drew small preparatory beeps from his special tricorder. As for Erickson, he shoved both fists into chubby hips, blew out his cheeks, and beamed.

"Well, isn't this *fine*—just *fine*!" he said reverently. He turned to his companions. "Let's get a-move on."

Grey seemed to float back to reality from some distant place. "Yes, by all means. You know the rules." Aleek-om nodded, a thoroughly humanoid gesture.

"Only one of us is permitted to undertake the actual entry and journey with Captain Kirk and Commander Spock acting as supplementary observers and escort. The rest of us will remain here in the present time to record and interpret the subsequent flow of regularized time-sequences."

Then the three historians did a curious thing. They bent over and spent several moments searching the ground. When they stood, each placed his or her open palm face up towards a common center. Two pebbles of varying size lay in each palm.

"All right, get ready," Grey instructed. Hands were placed behind backs, Grey doing likewise.

"I beg your pardon, Captain," murmured Spock curiously, "but what, exactly, is happening?"

"We're going to decide which one of us goes and which two stay behind, Commander," Grey told him.

Spock considered this. "I see—no, I do not see. You will pardon me, Historian Grey. I am not familiar with the intimate interworkings of professionals in your field—so perhaps I should not venture to comment upon them—but this does not strike me as an especially scientific way of determining the composition of this expedition.''

Aleek-om shook his feathered head again, set brilliant gold plumes dancing. "If I live for a thousand mating flights, I'll never understand you Vulcans."

"Ready?" queried Grey.

"Ready," the two males echoed.

"Now!"

Each thrust a closed fist into the center of their little circle while Grey counted, "One . . . two . . . three!"

Three hands opened. A single pebble rested in Grey's open palm, another in Aleek-om's.

"Ah, that's fine, colleagues," announced Erickson, "truly fine!" He tossed both his revealed pebbles over his shoulder. They dropped their own, downcast. It didn't last but a moment.

"Well, good luck, old boy," said Aleek-om, and Grey concurred. "Yes, good luck, Theodore."

They proceeded to a solemn shaking of hands. Aleek-om curled his hand in a peculiar way so as not to scratch a sensitive human palm. Then the two unlucky historians began to prepare their tricorders.

"Captain," intoned a thoroughly puzzled Spock, "I confess I am still confused by this method of selection for such an important mission. I don't believe I have witnessed anything quite so arbitrary since . . .''

"I'll explain it all to you later, Mr. Spock," Kirk grinned, "in the future. Right now, Mr. Erickson seems impatient to be on his way."

"Yes, yes," insisted the little historian, waving his arms like a semaphoring turtle, "let's get going."

The other historians turned their tricorders' visual pickups on and aimed them at the flowing Time Gate. Erickson mounted the stone platform and took up a position just in front of it. Kirk flanked him on the right side, Spock on the other. Then his voice boomed out—a squeaky parody of an old-line politician's.

"Guardian of Forever!"

For a long moment nothing happened. Then, from somewhere out of the air in front of them, a ponderous, rolling voice replied. It was heavy with age and weighty with infinite patience. Was this an accumulated effect, from answering thousands of inquiries? Or was it the Guardian's original voice? Kirk wondered. It always responded with perfect fluency to any question, no matter what language it was framed in.

Regardless, the effect produced by those thunderous yet gentle tones was sobering.

The last vestiges of humor disappeared from the little assembly. Everyone was all business now.

"TO WHENCE DO YOU WISH TO TRAVEL, AND FROM WHENCE COME YE," rumbled that mighty voice.

"We come from elsewhere," answered Erickson formally, his words ridiculously inadequate in counterpoint to that stentorian thunder. "And we wish the elsewhen of the Empire of Orion."

The Empire of Orion! Kirk started. He'd never bothered to inquire which time line the historians intended to explore. They hadn't struck him as a particularly adventurous bunch. Erickson's request came as a double surprise.

He'd figured this group of academicians for something much duller and more mundane than this. Say, the Butterfly Wars of Lepidopt, or the ceramic- and porcelain-making era of Sang Ho Hihn.

But, the Empire of Orion!

He found himself getting just a little bit excited. This was going to be rather more fun than he'd anticipated.

There was a clouding effect obscuring the Gate. A creamy blue-green blur filmed over the hazy surface of the circular center. As it did so, the dizzying array of time scenes began to slow. It was like watching a projector gradually wind down from a high speed—the visual equivalent of a slowing tape.

Eventually only a single alien scene remained. It did not shift, did not ripple, but held steady and clear. The blur started to fade. As it did so it was replaced in the scene by natural colors.

When they passed through the Time Gate, their first task would be to obtain a change of clothing. In the barbaric Empire of Orion, two starship uniforms and the casual dress of Historian Erickson would render them something less than inconspicuous. No one knew what passed for casual dress in that time period. Kirk knew this was so because if they *did* know, the historians would have had their necessary costumes prepared in advance.

Fortunately, the medium of exchange was only gold, and Erickson was amply supplied. They'd have no trouble making any needed purchases. Erickson was probably pleased. It gave him an excuse to bring back three sets of the genuine article—for study, of course. It was forbidden to profit materially from a journey through the Gate. Otherwise, the most dedicated researcher might be tempted to travel back in time to, say Earth's past and return with some little valuable knickknack like Praxiteles' lost gold statue of Pallas Athena.

They could touch things, move about, and purchase, but nothing of real value could be brought back except for study purposes.

Once through, they would spend some thirty minutes objective time. That might be several days in the subjective time of the Orionic Empire. Then, wherever they happened to be in space in that ancient civilization, the Guardian would reach out and pull them back to the present, ejecting them once more on silent desert sands.

Thirty minutes! Even the great, still unexplained energies that powered the Guardian could not hold open a time vortex any longer than that. And the amount of power necessary to hold a time dilation for even five minutes objective time was nothing short of astronomical. It was generally agreed on that the Guardian somehow drew directly on the local sun for power—but exactly how this was accomplished was still a source of mystery and controversy.

"Captain Kirk, Commander Spock," piped Erickson, "if you're ready, gentlemen?"

"Whenever you are, Mr. Erickson," acknowledged Kirk. Erickson turned to glance back behind himself.

"Ready, colleagues?"

"Ready, short stuff," grinned Grey.

"Go get 'em, Ted," cheered Aleek-om.

"Then, gentlemen," he said importantly to Kirk and Spock, "if you will, on three—one, two, three . . ." They stepped forward.

Two seekers of knowledge . . . one human, the other

faintly so, stood alone on the sandy plain where a moment before they had been five. Two seekers of knowledge—and one interested onlooker. McCoy had chosen to remain quietly in the background.

The early Empire civilization turned out to be a maelstrom of colors and sights and fascinating detail through which Kirk, Spock, and the little historian moved like wraiths in a dream. The sounds matched the barbaric imagery—the unexpected and incredible exceeded the wildest expectations. They spent two and a half days, Orion time.

When their thirty real minutes were up, seemingly seconds later, Kirk was as sorry to leave as Erickson.

One moment they were changing clothes in the backroom of a disreputable inn in a gaudy bazaar, while meters away an equally disreputable personage was auctioning off modest examples of local feminine pulchritude. The next, they were standing once again on the stone platform facing the Guardian.

Grey and Aleek-om made no move to approach them as the three travelers swayed uneasily. There was always a moment or two of nausea that followed any passage through a time vortex. Then their systems had readjusted to the sudden change in climate and gravity and other variables, and they stood easily once again.

Both historians appeared excited and pleased by the stream of slowed time pictures from different time-sequences that they'd been able to examine and record. Apparently that had been exciting enough. No one seemed the least upset now at being left behind.

Erickson, for his part, was flushed with a glow that on a more imposing individual might have been interpreted as maniacal.

Kirk noticed McCoy staring at Spock. There was an expression of mild concern and some puzzlement on the doctor's face. Studious physician to the end, the Captain reflected.

Come to think of it, Aleek-om and Grey also seemed to be staring at the science officer. But in the first flush of excitement at their successful journey and return, Kirk didn't notice the intensity of their stares. For that matter, neither did Spock or Erickson.

"Relax, Bones, we're all fine. Usual upset stomach, and that's all but gone. Orion at the dawn of civilization, Bones! Just watching, not interacting significantly for fear of changing some tiny bit of history . . ." He paused. The others were paying absolutely no attention to him. Instead, they continued to stare at Spock.

For the first time, Kirk took notice of their odd fascination with his assistant.

"What's the matter?" He still smiled. "Bones, what's wrong?"

Dr. McCoy did a rather startling thing, then. He jerked his head in Spock's direction, then pointed at him. His voice was open, curious.

"Who's he, Jim?"

This outrageous comment took some time to register. Kirk looked over at Spock reflexively. It was the same old Spock, all right, down to his unwavering expression and peaked aural receptors.

For his part, Spock's eyebrows made an upward leap of Olympian proportions. In fact, the science officer looked as close to total befuddlement as Kirk could ever recall having seen him. The captain turned back to McCoy, mildly irritated. The excitement of their return had been stolen from him.

"What do you mean, 'Who's he?' You know Mr. Spock."

McCoy's nonchalant attitude and indifferent manner were much more shocking than his casual reply.

" 'Fraid I don't, Jim."

Spock's expression changed only slightly at that. Just the veriest hint, the merest touch of annoyance seeped through his otherwise stony visage.

Kirk, however, was much more expressive in his display of facial contortions. He started to speak further to McCoy, became aware of his imminent loss of self-control, and thought better of speaking just now. There was no point in getting upset, yet.

It was a practical joke. Yes, of course! Bones probably authored the whole thing himself. It would fall apart any minute, as soon as someone made a slip and said something relating to Spock. For now he would go along with the gag.

He pulled out his communicator, flipped open the grid, and glanced over at Grey and Aleek-om.

"You've both concluded your observations, then?" Jan Grey sighed reluctantly. That was the most blatant show of emotion she had yet displayed. Maybe she had Vulcan blood.

"Sadly, yes, Captain. It was all too short, too brief. But yes, our work here is finished."

They all climbed back into the shuttle car. Kirk, Spock, and McCoy rode in silence while the three historians chattered in the back.

"We should stop before we depart and thank Dr. Vassily for her help and consideration," noted Aleek-om when they'd returned the car to its stall in the main hangar.

Erickson agreed. "Yes, by all means." He nodded vigorously. Kirk interposed a negative as he toyed with his open communicator. He'd put off calling the ship. Erickson's call to remain here longer woke him from idle daydreams.

"Why not, Captain?" The stout researcher was pouting. Then he smiled shyly. "That brandied tea wasn't half bad, even if it was reconstituted."

"It's not the quality of the refreshments, Erickson. There's something else." Kirk looked around at the now curious faces.

At first they'd all stared with unconcealed fascination at Spock. Now they were studiously ignoring him. If this was a practical joke, then someone was carrying it off in style. Too much style. Kirk was starting to feel that any overtones of humor to the situation were becoming shaded in tones of black.

He activated the communicator. Anyone could beam freely up from the surface of the Time Planet. Getting *down* was the problem.

"Kirk to *Enterprise*."

"*Enterprise*," came a familiar voice with sharp vowel sounds. So Scotty was working with Chief Kyle on the transporter now. So much the better.

"Six to beam up, Scotty."

"Aye, sir."

Aleek-om had been thinking. Now he spoke delicately to Kirk.

"If you don't mind, Captain, I should like to remain here

a while longer, to record and study some of the artifacts Dr. Vassily has unearthed. If we have some time before departure, that is.'' The Aurelian's expression was hopeful.

"Me too, Captain," added Jan Grey. Kirk nodded, turned to the other historian.

"How about you, Erickson?"

"Oh no, I'm satisfied. All I want to do is put my tapes in a big viewer and play them back. I was so busy recording and taking notes that I didn't have half a chance to enjoy the journey.'' His blissful look turned momentarily serious.

"But you've got to understand, Captain Kirk, that this is a once-in-a-lifetime experience for most historians. We can't hold you up.'' Aleek-om and Grey indicated agreement. "I know starship time is precious. But if my compatriots could have even a few additional minutes . . .''

"All right, all right.'' Kirk grinned, spoke into the communicator. "Cancel that, Scotty. Four only to come up. Myself, Mr.—'' he hesitated, "and the others.''

The two historians who would remain a while longer thanked him profusely and then hurried off toward the reception station. They promised to be ready for the transporter pickup at the first call from the orbiting *Enterprise*.

"All clear, Scotty. Bring us up.''

"Aye, sir.''

There was a familiar feeling of disorientation. The four figures dissolved into four roughly cylindrical columns of luminescent particles.

In the transporter room, Chief Engineer Scott personally handled the delicate task of transporting while Chief Transporter Kyle, himself a master at the job, watched admiringly. Those calloused, practiced hands operated the transporter controls even more smoothly than his own.

The first thing Kirk noticed when he regained sight was the startled expression on his chief engineer's face. The first thing he heard when he regained hearing was the startled tone of his chief engineer's voice.

"Captain—'' Scott paused, unmistakably confused. "I was expecting two of the historians with you and Dr. McCoy. But a Vulcan—''

Kirk decided that was quite enough. If this was a practical joke, it was going too far.

"Explain yourself, Mr. Scott!" he snapped. Scott's mouth worked. His puzzlement seemed honest.

"S . . . sir?"

Kirk chewed at his lower lip and stepped out of the alcove, off the platform.

"I don't know what's going on here—but the first officer of this ship will be treated with respect!"

"Captain," came a strange voice from the elevator, "I assure you no one has ever treated me otherwise."

It was Kirk's turn to look dumbfounded.

His gaze snapped to the right. The humanoid who'd just brazenly laid claim to Spock's title walked easily into the room. He was an Andorian, clad in the blue shirt of a Starfleet science officer, and wearing the insignia of a full commander.

Like most Andorians he was slim, rather fragile-looking, and had the pale blue eyes and silver hair of most of his people. Kirk noticed the two slightly curved, flaring antennae which protruded from his forehead and ended in dull, round knobs. These were his organs of hearing. He had no shell-shaped ears as did human or Vulcan.

Where distance was involved the knobbed antennae had less range than other humanoid sensing organs, but they could pick up much higher and lower frequencies. The Andorian's slim build belied his agility and strength, characteristics which certain other races had learned about the hard way.

Kirk took a couple of steps toward this alien, and his jaw dropped in amazement. He looked the other up and down without fazing him, finally managed to blurt out his thoughts.

"Who the hell are you?" This time it was Dr. McCoy who replied, wryly.

"I thought sure you'd know Thelin by now, Jim. He's been your first officer for five years."

"Is something the matter, Captain?" queried the Andorian. His tones were soft, slightly accented. And he too seemed openly puzzled. Kirk could only stare at him.

Spock finally broke the silence, summing up both his own and Kirk's thoughts in his usual terse fashion.

"Captain, I have come to the conclusion that this is not a game."

"No—no," Kirk muttered. "I agree, Mr. Spock. But if

it's a reality—and everyone else here seems to think it is—then what happened?'' He stiffened.

"All right, I don't know what's going on here, but I'm going to get to the bottom of it! Spock, Mr. . . . Thelin. If you'll both come with me to the main briefing room. There's no point in upsetting anyone else on board.'' They started off.

"Me too, Captain?'' asked Erickson. He had no real part in the problem, but if something was the matter with Spock—well, he'd formed enough of a friendship with the starship officers to at least be concerned.

"Yes, by all means, Mr. Erickson, join us.''

VII

The command briefing room was small, with a single free-formed table of dark mahonganylike wood from the forests of IandB dominating the center. Holographic portraits of various alien landscapes decorated the walls, along with a framed copy of the Federation charter, and there was a musical rain sculpture shifting and chiming softly in one corner.

The seats were also free-formed, lush and comfortable, but they could do little to ease the tenseness of the four humanoids who now sat in them.

Erickson immediately set to work with his tricorder, keeping his verbal requests to the machine to a whisper. He had thought about the unbelievable situation, and decided that maybe the compact instrument had noticed something significant they had not remembered.

"I will pass over the obvious, gentlemen," began Kirk. "I can think of only one explanation for what seems to have happened, and I'm sure it has occurred to you also."

"When we were in the time vortex, something happened to change the present as we know it. No one seems to recognize Mr. Spock. And neither he nor I nor Mr. Erickson recognizes Mr. Thelin. The only answer must be that the past was somehow altered when we were in it. Instead of emerging into our own time line, Mr. Spock, Mr. Erickson, and myself have reemerged into an alternate secondary one as a result of that as yet unidentified change." He paused for breath.

"And if that sounds confusing, gentlemen, I assure you it's a fit description of my present state of mind."

Erickson chose that moment to interrupt. He shook his head and looked disappointed.

"Nothing, Captain Kirk. I've just done a double-speed review of our entire journey. The tricorder has no record of anything we did while in the vortex that could conceivably have affected the future. *Any* future."

"Please, Mr. Erickson," requested Kirk. "I don't doubt your readings. But could you . . . try once more? Take all the time you need."

"I don't need any more time, Captain. I've done this sort of review a thousand times before." He shrugged, bent over the tricorder once more.

When he looked up again a while later, after completing the second run-through, the stocky historian found all eyes were on him. The sameness of his expression was eloquent.

"Nothing, Captain. I've even run down any changes in the atmospheric content while we were present, and there's absolutely nothing."

Kirk slammed a fist down on the smooth wood. One of these days he was going to break a hand doing that.

"But, dammit—*something* was changed!"

"It seems, Captain," interposed Spock easily, "that I am the only one affected. The mission, the ship, the crew—except for myself—remain the same."

"Not entirely, Mr. Spock," Kirk countered. "I still know who you are. So does Erickson." The historian nodded vigorously. "But no one else aboard does. While we were in Orion's past, the time revision that apparently occurred here didn't affect us." He looked thoughtful. "I wonder how extensive it is?"

"If you'll pardon me, Jim," began Thelin. Then he smiled faintly, uncomfortably. "Captain, I might be able to answer that. While we were on our way down here, I took the liberty of placing an information request with the library. It should tell us how complete the time change has been."

"I didn't hear you put in any request, Mr. Thelin."

"You were in deep conversation with Mr. . . . Spock, at the time," the Andorian replied.

As if on cue, the bosun's whistle sounded in the room. Thelin looked pleased.

"That ought to be the reply now." Kirk pressed a half-hidden switch under the rim of the table. A three-sided viewer popped up from the center of the dark wood. He hit another switch.

"Kirk here."

The picture of a young, neatly turned-out ensign appeared on the three screens. The ensign started to speak, but Kirk waved him off.

"Just a minute, Ensign." He turned to Spock. "You know who that is, Mr. Spock?"

"Ensign Bates, Captain. Inexperienced, but studious, well-intentioned, reasonably efficient. Graduated OTS Starfleet with high honors but not the highest. Served one year apprenticeship on the shuttle tender SCOPUS. Transferred to *Enterprise* starda . . ."

"That'll do, Spock." Kirk looked satisfied.

"That would approximate my own evaluation of Bates' abilities at this stage, Captain," Thelin added casually. "Transferred to *Enterprise* stardate 5365.6."

"Ummm." Kirk's tone was noncommittal. He directed his attention back to the screen. "What have you got for us, Ensign?"

"Sir, we've checked Starfleet records as Commander Thelin requested."

Even though he thought he was growing used to the present impossible situation, Kirk still gave a little mental jump every time he heard the Andorian referred to by his own crew as "Commander Thelin." Deep down he knew that—in the original time line, at least—the Andorian didn't really exist.

Or was *this* the real time line, and the other merely a secondary copy? One problem at a time . . .

Yet McCoy, Scotty—everyone—seemed to know Thelin intimately, and not Mr. Spock.

He blinked, remembered Bates. The ensign was patiently awaiting Kirk's orders to report the researched material, destroy it, stand on his head, play dead, or do *something*.

"Findings, Ensign?" he said crisply. The ensign's reply had the directness of truth.

"There is no Vulcan named Spock listed with Starfleet in any capacity, sir. Neither as commander, nor cook—no listing whatsoever."

Spock's only visible reaction was the moderate ascension of one eyebrow.

"I see," Kirk muttered. He thought a moment, then, "You have your visual pickup on?"

"Of course, Captain. I was not told this was to be a closed meeting . . ."

"No, no, it's not. Relax, Ensign. Now, you can see the Vulcan sitting to my immediate right?" Bates' head and eyes moved. He showed no reaction.

"Yes, sir."

"Do you recognize him?"

"No, sir," responded Bates, who was one of Spock's regular science-library assistants. "I've never seen him before in my life."

Thelin leaned forward and addressed the screen. "Did you also research the Vulcan family history requested?"

"Yes, Commander," said the ensign crisply. "There are some related visual materials. I can put them on the viewer pickup, if you wish."

"We so wish, Ensign," Kirk ordered. Bates hit a button below screen pickup level and his image vanished, to be replaced immediately by a still hologram of a distinguished-looking male Vulcan clad in formal ambassadorial attire. Bates continued to speak.

"This is Sarek of Vulcan, ambassador to seventeen Federation planets in the past thirty t-standard years."

Spock broke into the Ensign's speech. "That is not correct."

Kirk only grinned sardonically.

"In this case—or this time, Mr. Spock—it seems that it is." Spock gave a slight nod of understanding and looked back to the tripartite viewer.

"I wish to ask a question."

"Yes, Commander?" Bates might not know Spock, but he could still recognize the uniform and rank of a starship commander, even if not his own.

"What of Sarek's family? His wife and son?"

The picture of Sarek disappeared, to be replaced by another hologram. This one was of a lovely human woman in her early thirties. She was fair-haired and slim, delicate—one of those rare women who you know instantly will retain her youthfulness well into old age. The young officer's voice—impersonal voice, doom voice, continued—

"Amanda, wife of Sarek, known on Earth as Amanda Grayson." Kirk gave Spock a sympathetic look as Bates droned on. "The couple separated after the death of their son."

That finally drew a visible reaction from Spock, though, as Kirk knew, ninety percent of it was still bound up tightly inside his first officer. Bates continued.

"The wife was killed in a shuttle accident at Lunaport, on her way home to Earth. Ambassador Sarek has not remarried."

Everyone was watching Spock now, and he was watching none of them. His eyes remained glued to the picture on the screen. When he finally did speak, there was a pause, a bare hint of a catch in his voice that could have been—no, ridiculous.

"My mother—" he whispered softly. Then he spoke—well, almost normally. There was no uncertainty in his tone, only a desire to satisfy perverse curiosity to the utmost, to draw out the thing to its ultimate mad conclusion.

"The son—what was his name and age when he died?"

"Spock," came Bates reply. "Age . . ." he seemed to be checking some off-screen reference, ". . . age seven."

"Sympathy is not among my race's primary traits, Mr. Spock," said Thelin, "but I believe I can understand a little of what you are feeling now. I'm sorry, truly I am." He gave the Andorian equivalent of a shrug. "But I am me and you are you, and there is nothing to be done for it."

"Not in this time line, no," mused Kirk.

"You are, of course, correct, Captain," Spock added. "But if we didn't change anything in the past—"

"We didn't!" insisted Erickson. "We didn't!" Suddenly his forehead creased and he repeated, softly this time, "We didn't!"

"Of course! Jan and Loom!"

"Surely," said Spock, "they didn't enter the Guardian while we were in the vortex?"

"No, no!" Erickson was nervous as a mouse. "They would never do a thing as potentially dangerous as that. But scanning—they must have been scanning! We might at least get some useful information from them if they . . ."

". . . were looking into my past while we were in Orion's.

Yes, I see what you are leading toward, Historian." Spock rose, looked at Kirk.

"Captain, we must go down to the Guardian again. And as quickly as possible. The longer we stay in this time line, the stronger our position here grows, and the less chance we have of returning to and correcting our own—my own."

"Certainly, Spock. Erickson, come on!" The four rose and left the briefing room.

"You're sure you don't recognize him?" Kirk asked Scott when they'd returned to the transporter room. They were mounting the transporter platform prior to beamdown. Scott studied Spock carefully, indifferently, and shook his head.

"There are few Vulcans on the *Enterprise*, Captain. I'm not likely to forget any, let alone a commander."

"Thanks, Scotty. Beam us down, please."

On the way back to the Guardian in the ground car, they tried to explain the situation to Grey and Aleek-om. Since Kirk was still confused himself, he wasn't sure they made things much clearer to the two historians who had remained behind. But they seemed to grasp the idea behind what had happened better than he had. Time was their business, space was his.

Of course, neither of them recognized Mr. Spock. And both seemed to know Thelin. The Andorian had insisted on coming along, as was his privilege both as commander and science officer.

By the time they had returned to the quiescent Guardian of Forever, mutual agreement had reached on an approximation of sequential probabilities. Nevertheless, Kirk continued to examine every salient fact with the three historians as they all made their way toward the Guardian. As always, the Time Gate was modest in appearance, overwhelming in capabilities.

Glowing cream-colored mists flowed and danced patiently, languorously in the central hollow, oblivious to the petty problems of the small knot of approaching humanoids.

"If we didn't change anything while we were in the time vortex," Kirk insisted, "someone or something else must have." He turned to Aleek-om and then Grey. "You were using the Guardian while we were gone."

"Yes, but it was nothing unusual," said Grey matter-of-factly. "We were merely scanning occasional sequences of recent histories."

"Any recent Vulcan history?" asked Kirk.

"Why, yes!" She smiled in sudden realization. "I see the way your thoughts have been going, Captain. I don't see what we might have done, but—of course it seems the only other possibility."

"What time period?" asked Spock as they mounted the last step leading towards the Gate.

"I'm not sure." She fumbled with the omnipresent tricorder. "Just a moment . . ." A quick recheck provided the desired information. "No specific dates listed—approximately twenty to thirty Vulcan years past." Kirk had a sudden thought. His question beat Spock's by a few seconds.

"Was there any notation recorded on the death of the son of a Vulcan ambassador named Sarek and his human wife?" Both historians looked thoughtful, glanced at each other before turning back to Kirk and Spock.

"I don't recall any, but there was so much information—" Aleek-om looked a little tense as he worked his own tricorder. Thin, powerful claws clicked over the sensitive controls, too fine for any human to manipulate. It hummed softly, then stopped.

Aleek-om jabbed a recessed switch, ran something back and played through it more slowly. The hum deepened. He stopped again and nodded, his crest bobbing and dancing in the dry desert breeze.

"*Cher-wit!* Yes, the death is indeed recorded."

"How . . ." Kirk all but choked on the peculiar-sounding words, "how did he die?" He still found it hard to believe he was living this nightmare. It was no consolation to know that it must be a hundred times worse for Spock.

Again, Aleek-om checked the instrument readings.

"The child is recorded as dying during some form of . . . maturity test. Yes, that's it. It is recorded only because the father was a notable figure in government and in Federation history."

Spock spoke absently. "The Kahs-wan—a survival test for young males. It is traditional, a holdover from less peaceful, less civilized days."

"The death is recorded as—" Aleek-om continued, but Spock finished it for him.

". . . falling on the twentieth day of Tasmeen." All but Kirk and Erickson looked at Spock in surprise.

"How do you know this?" asked Thelin. Spock paused, spoke slowly.

"That was the day my—my cousin saved my life when I was attacked in the desert by a wild animal."

But how could Spock know that that was the particular day and that that incident was crucial?

Inspiration hit Kirk then, without warning—at warp-eight speed.

"This cousin, Spock, what was his name?" Spock frowned, shifted his position on the rocky surface underfoot.

"That I do not seem to recall clearly. I was very young. He called himself—yes, Selek. A common enough name in my father's family. He was visiting us." Spock frowned slightly. "Odd, but I never saw him again after that—though I wished to, many times. Nor, I believe, did any of my family." The frown grew deeper.

"Captain, your expression, I believe you . . ." Spock seemed to hesitate.

Kirk looked directly at his first officer. Inside, Spock *knew*. But he was so close to the answer that it hadn't yet come to him.

"Spock—this Selek—did he by any chance look like you do . . . now?"

Even then, Spock was reluctant to accept the idea. Alternative lines of possibility, however, suddenly looked more barren than ever. He nodded slowly.

"I believe he did, Captain. And I see what you are thinking. That other time, it wasn't my 'cousin' who saved me—it was I. I saved myself."

"But this time," continued Kirk, pushing the thought forward, "you were in Orion's past with Mr. Erickson and me. At the same time, Aleek-om and Grey were here, playing back that section of Vulcan history. You couldn't exist in two time lines simultaneously, so you had to vanish from one of them. In other words, you had to die as a boy, since you couldn't be there to save yourself." He shook his head. Much more thinking along paradoxical lines like that and they'd all be candidates for the silly station. He spun to face the Gate.

"Guardian, did you hear that?"

The shifting colors seemed to flow a little faster, shine a touch brighter. When it spoke, the colors pulsed with internal light as each syllable was intoned. The words themselves were, as always, neither masculine nor feminine nor even machinelike—but instead a kind of strange sexless and timeless neuter.

"I HEAR ALL."

"We could resort to the *Enterprise*'s computers," Kirk murmured, as much to himself as to the Gate, "but in all the Universe, no one, nothing, knows as much about time as you. Tell me—is it possible for Spock the Vulcan to return to the period when he was not (God, this was insane!) and repair the broken time line so that all is the same as it was before our last journey?"

A pause, then, "IT IS POSSIBLE," the Guardian boomed indifferently, "IF NO OTHER MAJOR FACTOR HAS BEEN CHANGED, OR IS CHANGED IN THE CHANGING."

Kirk turned to his science officer.

"Do you remember enough, Spock? You heard the Guardian. You can't risk changing anything when you go back. You've got to repeat what happened when you were seven years old."

Spock shook his head slowly, the strain of recall showing plainly.

"I do not remember everything, Captain. There are vague memories, from a child's point of view. But as is common to youthful memories, a child's details are blurred and run together. The memory *is* there—but slightly out of focus."

"You'll have to try!" Kirk insisted. "For you—and your mother—to live." Spock nodded slowly, considering.

"Yes. I will need the following items: a Vulcan desert soft-suit and boots, and a small selection of plain streetwear accessories circa—8877 Vulcan years. The matching obligatory carry-bag should be of the same period and look well used."

"You've got them," nodded Kirk quickly. "I'll have quartermaster section drop whatever they're doing and run them off now." He flipped open his communicator and moved slightly to one side. The three historians were already engaged in animated discussion of what had become for them a fascinating socio-mathematical exercise in conflicting time lines.

This curiosity was touched with tragedy only for Erickson, since among the arguing historians only he had been intimately involved with the actual expedition into Orion's past. But his academic concern outweighed the desire to offer further consolation to Spock. He wasn't very good at such things, anyway.

That left Spock alone with his quiet doppelganger—Thelin. The Andorian studied him closely.

"This proposed modification of time lines will put you in my place on a different plane . . . replace another Thelin somewhere." He paused. "Yet, I am not aggrieved."

"Andorians are noted for many things," said Spock conversationally. "However, as you yourself admitted, sympathy is not one of them."

"True," Thelin nodded. "A warrior race has few sympathies and little time for same. Yet it is not a normal situation we find ourselves in. I, personally, do not feel threatened. Yet, in a way, I am actually contributing to the murder of a distant cousin."

"Who should not be there in the first place," concluded Spock evenly.

"Perhaps. Yet one empathy we Andorians do possess is for family. On this time plane, you will lose—and so would your mother. The knowledge that this will be prevented, at least, is acceptable mental compensation for me."

He gave Spock a smart Vulcan hand salute. "Live long and prosper in your own world, Commander Spock—in your own time." Spock returned the salute.

"And you in yours, Commander Thelin."

There was nothing to do now but wait for Spock's requested clothing and materials to be sent down from the *Enterprise*. There'd be no problem there—planetary defenses could recognize the difference between a suit of clothes and a photon torpedo. But it left them with nothing to do but think, and after a while that wasn't too comfortable for the historians, either.

The little group spent several nervous, awkward minutes

wandering around the base of the now familiar Guardian. Kirk studied it idly.

Certainly it possessed some strange unknown variety of organic/inorganic intelligence—witness its answers to questions in many languages. But no one knew if this intelligence lay dormant until evoked. Might it not be always alert, constantly observing? Was it even now looking down on them from some uncomprehensible alien Olympus and musing on their problems? He could ask, of course.

But the Guardian of Forever did not deign to answer any questions about anything but time.

As for other sights to study, they were too far from Oyya for the city's ancient and distant attractions to hold their interest for very long. The area around the Guardian itself was singularly barren.

Even the Time Gate was beginning to seem like no more than a pile of oddly hewn rocks and stone by the time a small transporter effect, a chromatic glow of atomic action, began to take shape nearby. As it faded, the glow congealed into the form of a Vulcan carry-all bag, a small pile of goods and knickknacks, boots, and a neatly tied bundle of sand-colored clothes.

"Nice to know that the crew in this time plane is efficient, too," Kirk commented appreciatively. He hesitated, then held out a hand to Spock. Words were unnecessary.

It took Spock a few moments to make the change of clothing. He stacked his uniform and boots neatly to one side, then turned and moved away from them, walking up to the base of the Gate itself.

Thelin moved to stand next to Kirk. Not wont to miss even a blurred glimpse of what might take place, the three historians activated their own special tricorders. Spock's voice as he addressed the enigmatic intelligence known as the Guardian was clear and precise, as always.

"I wish to visit the planet Vulcan."

"TIME?" rumbled the Guardian.

"Thirty Vulcan years past, the month of Tasmeen, before—before the twentieth day."

There, that ought to provide a reasonable margin of time in which to get reacquainted with himself.

"LOCATION?"

"Just outside the border city of ShiKahr."

By way of reply, the pastel mists that filled the circular Gate started to swirl and boil, flowing slower and slower, until the blur of time pictures began to steady as the Guardian locked in to the requested time line. Then, abruptly, the Gate was filled with a view so familiar to Spock that it immediately relaxed all inner tensions.

A hot, dry, orange world—Vulcan.

"Yes," was all Kirk heard him say—though there seemed to be other words, voiced too low to be understood.

"TIME AND PLACE," the Guardian shouted in tones as stable and final as the Universe, "ARE READY TO RECEIVE YOU."

"Yes," Spock murmured again. One word worth a thousand pictures. Then he was running, running forward, and taking a short leap into the time portal.

His body faded from view as though he were slipping into a transparent sponge. As soon as he touched the field, the picture began to blur from the temporary distortion of the time vortex.

For several moments after he'd vanished, Kirk stood staring at the now resumed blur of time-patterns racing across the Gate. Then he turned to one side, where the blue uniform of a Starfleet commander, science section, and a pair of boots—Starfleet standard issue, officer's—lay on the broken gravel, awaiting their owner's return.

In another, unknown time line, another James T. Kirk was staring at another set of clothes, thinking the same thoughts, hoping the same hopes. And on a different line, perhaps, yet a different Kirk. And another, and another—an infinitude of Kirks waiting for the return of a billion Spocks in a million variations of a certain awkward second or two in time. . . .

Spock stood on the sands of the world of his birth. Behind him, the land was desert, painted in harsh ocher-yellows and umber-browns—spotted only reluctantly here and there by an occasional winsome patch of greenery.

Further back, a range of forbidding black mountains clawed at the sky with great ragged talons of granite, basalt, and gneiss. The thin atmosphere inspired a roof of flinty orange-red instead of the soft blues of Earth. But the clouds that spotted it were just as cottony white.

Before him lay the city of ShiKahr, like a neat, orderly oasis in the wastes. A wide band of lush, landscaped parkland formed a civilizing barrier between urban environment and raw, arid sands. Flowers and other vegetation tended toward soft, warm hues of yellow and brown, with a few isolated sprinklings of pink or purple.

The park buffer zone was as modern as the rest of ShiKahr, which nevertheless was an old city. Buildings were geometric, regular, and aesthetically as well as architecturally sound. A logical city designed for relentlessly logical inhabitants.

A person standing next to Spock at that moment might have heard him mutter something vaguely like, "thirty years . . ." Or it might have been the wind rippling through a desert bush.

In any case, no one could have stood close enough to see what was going through Spock's mind. That mind was considering. From here on, he was quite aware that his very continued existence depended on repeating with as much precision as possible events he could barely remember, events that had taken place thirty years ago—now.

He shifted the carry-bag higher on his shoulder, ran his right thumb underneath the strap, and started off towards the city. At the city gate he experienced an instant of apprehension. There was always an outside chance that something else about him, something unseen but vital, had been altered by the interlocution of time lines.

If the automatic sentry defense systems which were designed to keep out fierce desert carnivores sensed anything suspicious about him, he would be, not killed, but immobilized and held helplessly tranquilized until the arrival of a detention squad from the city reasoning force.

That wouldn't be fatal. But subsequent questions and examinations could be embarrassing as well as time delaying. At the very least, serious alterations in this time line might be produced. That could jumble matters beyond repair.

They might be damaged beyond change already, but there was little benefit to that line of thought. Besides, it was very depressing.

He needn't have worried. Unseen radiation probed him, hidden sensors clucked approving mechanical tongues. His shape and composition were familiar—Vulcan. No challenge was offered as he walked through the park. No tranquilizing darts *phocked* out at him, no stun rays sought to bar his passage.

He experienced no difficulties whatsoever. His only barrier to progress was confusion of a mental variety. He'd forgotten the beauty of ShiKahr. The calm efficiency and palpable sense of security that made a Vulcan city so different from the hectic, albeit exciting urban hodgepodges of so many other humanoid worlds.

He passed by the last of the flowers, past a gentle fountain that dispensed a constant stream of fresh well water, and suddenly found himself on a walking street.

This pathway was broad and paved, but designed for pedestrian use only. It was quiet and tree-shaded. Every effort—every stone, every bush, all but the actual placement of the leaves on the branches—was predesigned and executed to enhance one's serene appreciation of podal locomotion.

High walls kept homes and gardens discreetly secluded from passersby. Delicate symmetrical blossoms on creeping vines trailed over many of the stone walls and brightened the rustic scene even further. There was a main artery in the distance ahead, busy with ground-car activity. Old-style, outmoded ground-cars, he noted.

That mechanical sound was distant. But soon, another clamor reached his ears. A group of young voices—male. Their tone was biting and sarcastic—a near-emotion to which even Vulcan youth were not immune. The words matched the tone of delivery.

"Barbarian . . . Earther . . . throwback . . . emotional, squalling, uncontrolled *Earther*!' "

He'd heard those same insults long ago, it seemed. Surprising how painful they could still be, after all those years. He moved to a corner, turned it, and looked ahead.

A high wall fronted on an intersection of several small pathways. He moved a few steps further, halting in front of a high, solid old gate of polished, engraved wood. Nearby, another lower gateway led to a flourishing garden. In front of this second gate stood a very young version of himself.

There was no question of who it was. Inwardly, he'd dreaded this moment—from an intellectual, not an emotional, standpoint. How would he react to the first sight of

. . . himself? Kirk had equated it to an old terran expression—being "on the outside looking in." Now that Spock was actually confronted with the experience, the result proved anticlimactic.

There was no abrupt sundering of mind, no shattering of preconceived images. No, no emotional damage. This younger, smaller version of himself was only a young boy who looked somehow familiar. But another person entirely.

After all, he'd met a universe full of aliens—and to an adult, children are often the most alien of all.

He blinked. Three other Vulcan youngsters stood in front of young Spock, taunting him. Old memories came drifting back, long-lost little pains that made small wrenching tugs deep in his mind.

That one, there, with the light-colored hair—that must be Stark. Then Sofek, next to him, and the tallest one standing between them had to be Sepek—a persistent childhood tormentor until later years, when they grew to become great friends.

But for now . . .

"You're a terran, Spock," shouted Stark. "You could never be a true Vulcan."

"That's not true!" yelled young Spock in reply, barely managing to keep a grip on his temper. "My father . . ."

Sepek's reply touched each noun, each syllable, with contempt.

"Terran! Your father brought shame to Vulcan! Marrying an Earther wom—"

That was more than enough for young Spock. Sadly, his physical reaction was more emotional than reasoned. He rushed forward blindly, arms flailing, to crush and rend his tormentors. Old Spock's first reaction was to observe that one against three—with one of the three much older, heavier, and more experienced—was an illogical arrangement to aggravate. Not to mention an unnecessary one.

But he'd been different as a youngster. Now the rather astonishing emotional outbursts of childhood rushed back to him. Had he really been so ready to react belligerently to mere words? Had he actually been so impulsive, so blind, so—so emotional? There was no denying the evidence of his eyes.

Any last concerns he might have felt about meeting his younger self disappeared. The child really was a different person.

Any mother could have told him that.

Sepek, the nearest and strongest, easily dodged young Spock's blind, angry punch. Sepek deftly tripped him backwards while avoiding the clumsy grab. Young Spock landed unceremoniously on his backside in the smooth dirt.

He didn't appear to be hurt—not physically, anyway. Sepek's voice dripped contempt.

"You haven't even mastered a simple Vulcan neck pinch yet!" he said nastily, concluding with the ultimate insult, "Earther!" The three youths walked quietly away.

Young Spock sat there in the settling dust, alone and insulted and hurt, obviously trying to keep control of himself. Alas, he failed in this, too. Scrambling to his feet, he dashed into the nearby garden enclosure and slammed the gate heavily behind him.

He didn't even have the satisfaction of a terran child, of hearing a loud slam behind him. The garden was designed as a place of peace and contemplation. The cushioned gate hinges automatically absorbed the shock of closing and snapped shut with a quiet click.

Spock remained standing quietly across the way, watching the direction his departing younger self had taken in disappearing among the thick vegetation. That green domesticated jungle had been his favorite place of hiding and solace as a boy.

This had been only one of many similar difficult moments in his childhood. It was not as painful to watch as it had been to live, but it was hard nonetheless.

"My apologies, visitor," came an unexpected voice—a deceptively quiet, unhurried, immensely powerful voice that he'd recognize anywhere. A voice that could impress whole worlds—or little boys. A second was sufficient time for him to compose himself. Then he turned, carefully keeping his expression open and receptive.

VIII

Sarek of Vulcan stood opposite him, looking very much like the familiar picture Spock had seen earlier on the small triple screen in the command conference room. The only immediately obvious difference was that this living version had far less grey in his hair and eyebrows, far fewer age lines in his forehead and around the eyes.

A tall, broad-shouldered Vulcan he was, perhaps no athlete but in fine physical trim. He had sharply planed, strong features and deep-set eyes. Altogether an attractive man. An older, tauter, more severe version of Spock.

Spock calculated rapidly. His father should now be seventy-three standard years old, in the prime of Vulcan life. He wore the sandy-hued, neutral clothing Spock remembered so well. No loud shirts or bold prints for him! It was brightened only by a single spot of color, the adhesive badge of his office.

"I regret you were witness to that unfortunate display of emotion on the part of my son."

If there was any lingering hesitation in Spock's mind as to the identity of this man, that brief, so-typical phrase instantly dispelled it. This was Sarek, all right. Spock raised his hand in salute.

"In the family, all is silence. Especially the indiscretions of children. No more will be said of it. Live long and prosper, Sarek of Vulcan." The ambassador hesitated for a second before returning the salute.

"Peace and long life." Then he spoke uncertainly while studying Spock with understandable puzzlement. "You are of my family?"

"A distant relative. My name is—" He paused. It wouldn't

113

do to give an easily recognizable false name here. "—Selek. A humble cousin, descendant of T'pal and Sessek. I . . . am journeying to the family shrine in Dycoon to honor our ancestors.'' There, that was a plausible reason for traveling the way he was. "Family is family, and I thought to give greeting to you on my passing."

Sarek nodded approvingly. "A pilgrimage, then?"

"Even so."

"You have a long way to go. Will you interrupt your journey to remain with us awhile, cousin?"

"I have already come quite a distance, and in good time," Spock murmured. "I have a little time to spare. I would be honored." He dipped his eyes, uncomfortably aware of Sarek's unwavering, intense stare. There was nothing he could do but try to ignore it.

"Is something wrong, cousin?" Spock asked. Sarek seemed to return from a region of far thoughts, formless musings.

"No, no. It was only that I seem to . . . know you. To have met you before."

The best defense, Spock reflected, was a fast retreat through forward enemy positions.

"I, too," he countered, "have been struck by the physical resemblance between us. A common ancestor among our forefathers, no doubt."

"No doubt," agreed Sarek quietly. Then, as though suddenly remembering that to continue such a line of inquiry with a strange relative would have been impolite, "Well, come then. Allow me to welcome you to my home."

He turned and opened the beautifully carved gate behind them. Familiar, so familiar, was the interior of the house! Spock tried not to let his eyes stray overmuch. Everything was as he remembered it, everything fit so comfortably in his mind.

Except that most everything was just slightly smaller.

Sarek indicated a well-stuffed lounge of a type no longer made—there seemed to be few craftsmen left anymore—and then a nearby mechanical servitor. Spock eyed the quaint antique and tried not to feel superior. There were so many things he could tell his father, if only . . .

No. Impossible. Forget it.

"A place to rest and comfort yourself, cousin. Refreshments at hand, if you thirst. Excuse me. I shall return shortly. I have . . . an errand to perform. Meanwhile, my house is yours." He walked out of the room. Spock had a fair idea of the nature of his father's "errand."

Young Spock had buried himself against a shaggy wall of fur. He *might* have been crying, though it would have been difficult for an observer to tell. There was no sound.

The wall of fur filled out to north and south, completing the form of the youngster's pet sehlat, Ee-chiya. The sehlat looked rather like a cross between a lion and a giant panda, with a pair of downward projecting, ten-centimeter long fangs. It was fluffy, but not cute.

A temperamental sehlat would have been a poor choice of pet for a young human. But for the logical, never cruel or brutal Vulcan child, he was ideal—loving, intelligent and protective, as well as fiercely loyal.

This particular sehlat had a brown coat faded in spots to patches of pale beige. One of the worn, yellowed fangs was broken off at the tip, and there were other indications of the creature's advanced age.

Young Spock heard his father enter the garden, but he didn't look up from the massive flank.

"Spock . . ."

The boy slowly detached himself from the warm haven of Ee-chiya's furry side. He knew his father wouldn't repeat himself. He got slowly to his feet and shuffled over, presenting himself to his father in the traditional attitude of youthful respect—back straight, chin out, hands clasped firmly behind his back.

Sarek stood, looking down at his son for a moment, and then shook his head slightly, sadly. His voice was soft, but the words were not.

"Spock, being Vulcan means following disciplines and philosophies that are difficult and demanding of both mind and body. Do you understand?"

"Yes, Father."

"Your schoolwork has been disgraceful. You constantly display your emotions in public. You've even been seen fighting in the street, and your attitude in such conflicts is reported to have been somewhat less than experimentally martial.''

A hint of defiance crept into the youth's voice. ''Personal combat for a worthy cause is not dishonorable.''

Inwardly, the reply pleased Sarek. However, the situation was serious. It could no longer be put off. This was not the time or place for him to express appreciation for such a sentiment.

''Brawling like a common deckhand off an alien freighter is not.'' Young Spock lowered his head.

''Yes, Father.''

Sarek took a deep breath, paused, then continued more firmly.

''The time draws near when you will be forced to decide whether you'll follow Vulcan or human philosophies. Vulcan offers much. No war, no crime, with logic and reasoned guidance operating in place of raw emotion and unbridled passion. Once on the path you choose, you cannot turn back.''

''Yes, Father.''

Sarek lifted his gaze briefly, in a tiny display of disgust. That constant, meek ''yes, Father'' was beginning to annoy him. Perhaps he'd been, not too easy, but firm with the boy in the wrong ways.

Spock finished his drink and looked around the comfortable room. Still no sign of Sarek returning. He noticed old touches of Amanda's Earthwoman's influence—a cascade of brilliant blue flowers pouring over a flowerbox built into a wall. A dizzyingly colorful afghan tossed casually across a chair-back.

And the books—especially the books, on the shelves. Real books, to handle and read, not to be flashed and turned on by a dial on an electronic reader-viewer. He smiled inwardly. For those, at least, his childhood associates had envied him.

Impractical they might seem to many adult Vulcans, but they brought back a thrill of pride and memories to him. There was something about having the words there, in your hand. Any page, any chapter, at your personal beck and call—instead of having to plead for them through an electronic middleman.

He rose and walked to the large, open door that faced into part of the lush garden. Distantly, he could hear faint sounds of conversation between his father and his younger self, engaged in some deep discussion.

There had been many such discussions.

A soft, shocking voice made him whirl.

"I hope you were not disturbed by my son's behavior, cousin Selek."

Amanda stood there, even more beautiful than her picture, more lovely than any memory. Intelligent, gentle, and gracious. For the first time, he could admire her as a woman in the prime of her life, instead of as a boy seeing his mother.

And more than any other quality, he remembered, far more than beauty or wisdom—her constant understanding. Understanding for the ordeal of his childhood.

"No, my lady Amanda." He didn't even think the word "mother." This was one meeting he'd prepared for well and one mistake he was determined not to make. "Any child has much to learn. My young cousin has a more difficult road to travel than most others."

Now it was Amanda's turn to study him closely.

"You seem to understand him better than my husband."

Careful now! Sarek you could err with and cover up, but one slip with this woman and there would be trouble. She would not fool so easily.

"It is difficult for a father to bear less than perfection in his son. Spock will find a way, I suspect—his way." His mother looked anxious. He'd succeeded in diverting attention back to her son—from her son.

"I do hope so. I respect Vulcan and all its traditions, or I would not have married Sarek, but it's such a demanding life. It's hard enough on a young boy, without the added—complications my son must endure." The conversation was getting to be too painful for Spock.

"The boy appears to be of a certain age. He goes through the Kahs-wan ordeal soon, does he not?"

Amanda nodded. "Next month."

Visions of catastrophe, of a helix of mad time lines meeting in a common crazed center and dissolving into chaos, sprang into Spock's mind.

"Next . . . month?" He couldn't keep all the confusion

and puzzlement out of his voice. "But tomorrow, tomorrow *is* the twentieth day of Tasmeen?" His mother looked up at him, disturbed a little by his controlled intensity.

"Yes, it is." That was reassuring, at least! The universe had not gone completely insane—though something was very, very wrong. "Is something the matter, cousin Selek?" Spock struggled to regain his composure.

"I've been traveling for quite a while. I seem to have lost track of time."

". . . And that is all I have to say on the subject, for now," Sarek concluded. "Soon you will undergo your test of manhood, in the Kahs-wan. To survive for ten ten days without food, water, or weapons on Vulcan's Forge—as our human associates have so quaintly renamed the Sas-a-shar desert.

"It will demand more of you than anything else ever has. To fail once is not unusual, nor is it a disgrace—for others." Young Spock lowered his eyes again, studied the ground. But his father wasn't through.

"If you fail, there will be those who will nevertheless call you coward all your life." These last words rang like steel being hammered out on a Vulcanian forge of another type. That stentorian tone had been employed more than once for the glory of all Vulcan, in interstellar diplomacy. The tone was not softened for delivery from father to son.

"I do not expect you to fail."

Young Spock considered and looked up. "What if I do, Father?"

Sarek could not admit to himself that there was anything so alien as emotion swirling through his mind.

"There is no need to ask that question. You will not disappoint me. You will not disappoint—yourself. Not if your heart and spirit are Vulcan."

He turned abruptly and walked back toward the house, leaving the youngster standing alone amid the silently watching blooms, the eloquent ferns. A few pebbles were lightly kicked by a small foot, a little earth disturbed.

Then he turned to the sehlat. The big mammal had dozed somnolently through the entire discussion, oblivious to the verbalizations of father and son. Now it stirred as his young master sat down beside him.

"Ee-chiya, what if I'm not a true Vulcan, like they say? What if Sepek and the others are right?"

The sehlat was not that intelligent. It did not understand. But it was sensitive to emotions. It snuffled and nudged nearer the boy, edging close in rough affection. Young Spock put his arms around as much of the massive neck as he could and hugged hard.

Spock maintained his own cover with near perfection throughout the rest of the day. He always managed to produce a plausible answer to any question Sarek or Amanda might pose, to turn awkward lines of inquiry neatly into other channels. It was a performance worthy of a diplomat's son.

He'd passed a pleasant, no, an ecstatic day, reliving the company of a younger mother and father, able to enjoy them as equals, to respond to them on entirely different yet equally gratifying levels.

He committed his one potentially serious error well after the sun had vanished below the horizon.

Sleep-time approached. As the guest, it was his place to mention such.

"I have had a long, full day, cousin Sarek, and your hospitality has been spoiling. I find myself more than ready for sleep." Sarek and Amanda both rose.

"Rest well, cousin," said Sarek. "We shall talk more tomorrow. I have enjoyed our evening immensely."

"It is the highlight of my journey, cousin Sarek," replied Spock, adding with an unseen smile, "perhaps I may remind you of it again someday."

Sarek looked at him oddly for a moment, then nodded politely. Amanda gestured, and Spock started to follow her towards the bedrooms. He almost turned in the direction of his own—young Spock's—room.

Fortunately, it was dark in the hallway and Amanda hadn't noticed the motion. He was barely able to recover before she glanced back at him:

She seemed willing to talk further at the door to the guest room, but he made further excuses of exhaustion. Too much close contact in the sometimes revealing dimness of evening might lead to unwanted questions.

He then attended to matters of Vulcan hygiene, enjoying

once more the use of the interesting, old-fashioned wash-
room facilities. Then he returned to the guest room and
turned on the single overhead light. —

There was a lock on the door, but for a relative, a guest in
another's house, to have bolted it would have been inexcus-
ably bad manners. So, of course, would be the unannounced
entrance of any member of the household. Still, he would
have felt better with it bolted. He'd have to chance leaving it
open. The single shuttered window he didn't worry about.

Sitting down on the edge of the bed he brought out his
carry-bag. The little tricorder that came from it was far too
modern and compact. The sleepwear he now wore was thirty
years old, a simple garment of pale yellow worn like a loose
toga.

One last time he considered locking the door, but dis-
carded the idea. Instead he turned on the bed and put his
back to it, shielding the potentially embarrassing tricorder
with his body. And while recording, he kept his voice low.
A passerby in the hall would have to strain to hear him and
press an ear to the door to make any sense of what he said.

"Personal log, stardate 5373.9, subjective time.

"The time line seems to have changed once more, yet I
cannot discover on thinking back anything I have done that
might have affected it. My memory is quite clear regarding
the actual day my cousin saved my life. That day is tomorrow." Then, as much to refresh his own memory as to provide information for future listeners:

"The Kahs-wan is an ancient rite of Vulcan's warrior days.
When Vulcans turned to logic as the ruling element of their
lives, they reasoned that it was necessary to maintain the old
tests of strength and courage. Otherwise devotion to pure
reason might make them grow weak and incapable of de-
fending themselves from barbarians who might be less advanced mentally and socially.

"This, in itself, was of course a logical decision."

The house was very quiet. There was no pedestrian traffic
on the surrounding pathways this late at night.

A door opened quietly in the rear of the house, and a very
small, very young figure crept out. Young Spock was dressed
in a desert soft-suit and boots. He closed the door carefully

behind him and surveyed the area cautiously before moving any further out.

He took a couple of steps into the garden. There was a rustling sound from the shrubbery on his left and he froze.

A large, familiar shape lumbered into view—Ee-chiya, snuffling in the early morning air like an old man with a sinus condition. The boy shook his head, then held out a hand, palm up. The sehlat halted at the hand signal, but continued to puff and grunt. He certainly showed no sign of returning to sleep.

"No, Ee-chiya," he whispered. "This is my own test. I have to do it alone. Stay!" He moved away from the sehlat, heading for the garden gate.

Ee-chiya looked after him, considered this in his slow, patient mind, then turned and loped off after his young master.

Meanwhile, Spock had clicked off the compact tricorder and had carefully repacked it with other items deep in his carry-bag. His head dropped halfway to the headrest on the bed before he seemed to convulse. His head and upper torso came instantly erect. Realization hit him subtly—like a small nova.

Of course, he yelled to himself, I should have remembered! It wasn't the actual Kahs-wan ordeal his "cousin" had intervened in to save him!

Reaching for the carry-bag he made haste to unpack his clothes. It took only minutes to lay out the desert suit and boots, moving with as much speed as quiet would permit.

When the sun rose over the black mountains, it turned the hard-baked desert floor the color of molten lead. Ee-chiya still trailed close on young Spock's heels. They were headed for those same forbidding dark peaks. Under the circumstances and given the task he'd set himself, the peaks seemed as logical a place to prove himself as any other.

Quick physical collapse was an early threat of the real Kahs-wan. That was one test Spock no longer worried about. He strode along easily at an even pace, seemingly untired. Of course, all of his walking so far had been in the pleasant chill of night and the cool of early morning. Soon it would grow hot and the sun would pull moisture from him. That is, unless he elected to stop and find shelter for the day. He hadn't decided yet.

He refused to let such dismal possibilities intrude. Were it not for his anguished state of mind he could have enjoyed the hike. As for any unpleasantness that might lie ahead, he was determined not to let his spirits drop. The most important element in the Kahs-wan was mental.

Ee-chiya continued to mope along slightly behind. In his case it was not the *mental* aspect that was most important. The big animal was unused to such extended hiking. Eventually young Spock had to pause and wait for the sehlat to catch up.

Several long strides and his huge pet had done so. It promptly lay down on its belly, panting from the unaccustomed exertion and trying to catch its breath. Ee-chiya's spirit was willing, but the flesh was too old.

Besides, a sehlat's normal environment was the cool, high forests of the south. He managed well enough in his cool stall and in the thick shade of the garden at the house. But here, in open hot country, his thick fur was a heavy burden. The rapidly rising heat would put a tremendous strain on the body of even a young, vigorous animal.

Young Spock stopped again and turned to face his pet squarely, hands on hips. His tone was gentle, but frustrated.

"Ee-chiya, go *home*! You are too old and too fat for this."

Ee-chiya leisurely examined this statement from his position on the warming sands. Then he put his great head down on his forepaws and assumed an air of patient dignity. Young Spock shook his head determinedly.

"Huh-uh, that's how you always get your way with Father. It won't work with me. Go home, Ee-chiya."

The sehlat took no notice. He seemed quite prepared to spend the rest of his existence on this spot. It was clear to young Spock that the only way the beast would return home would be while trailing its master.

And he had a great deal to accomplish before that return journey could take place. He sighed, shrugged, and lifted his shoulders in a very human gesture that said, "I've done what I can." Then he turned and started off towards the high range at the same steady pace he'd maintained since leaving home.

Ee-chiya waited only a few seconds. Then he lurched to his feet and shuffled off to join his master.

After a while, another, taller figure reached the same spot. It paused to examine the depression left in the sand and soft gravel by Ee-chiya's relaxing bulk. A light breeze off distant desert plains swept sand and twigs into miniature dust demons, threatening manifestations of Vulcan's turbulent atmosphere.

He pulled out the tricorder as he resumed his walk. The trail of young Spock was clear enough, that of the sehlat was unmistakable.

"Personal log—the boy Spock should be moving toward the Arlanga mountains. He . . ." Spock hesitated, "I . . . had much to prove to myself. The personal ordeal, I now remember, on which I embarked was meant to determine the course my life would take. Many things are coming back to me now, as I retrace my steps of thirty years past and as I become more familiar with this time of my youth."

Sarek was just entering the garden. Amanda spotted him and left the shady seat to rush into his arms. She was calmer, more controlled than most terran women would have been in a similar situation. But to one of her Vulcan neighbors, she would have appeared almost hysterical.

"Sarek, I've looked everywhere. Our son and the guest are gone."

"And Ee-chiya?" asked Sarek calmly. Amanda frowned. She didn't know what she'd expected him to say, but that was not it.

"Ee-chiya?"

"He would go with our son," Sarek noted, "as he always does."

"I haven't seen him, now that you mention it, Sarek."

Sarek nodded. "I feel more secure knowing that. Ee-chiya's getting old, but it will be difficult for the boy to get into any serious trouble with the sehlat around. You're certain he's with the stranger?" Amanda looked uncertain.

"I don't know, really. Spock's not anywhere in the neighborhood—I've checked—and it's not like him to go off any distance without telling me. I don't know what else to think."

"This cousin," mused Sarek, "he puzzles me. Something

very odd about him. I sometimes think I can see it, and then it suddenly eludes me again.'' Amanda gave an anxious start.

''You don't think he'd harm Spock?''

''I don't know what to think, Amanda. The man claims to be a relative and is friendly enough, yet there is this lingering strangeness about him that all his good-naturedness cannot conceal. However, I will take no chances. I shall notify the proper authorities immediately to watch out for either of them.''

Amanda bit her lip. That was the only logical thing to do.

The desert ended abruptly in the first rugged ramparts of the mountains. Spock knelt to study the fresh trail of boy and sehlat, then rose and began his first real climb. The morning sun exceeded his rate of ascent.

The various formations he passed as he moved higher into the foothills were of igneous rock, stark and weirdly shaped. Not from wind erosion, but by the primeval forces of Vulcan itself. This was an area of geologically recent plutonic activity.

Once the ground turned upward his path became more difficult. Spock climbed slowly and carefully.

Something sounded in the air, distant. He stopped climbing and turned his head to listen. Nothing.

Several steps later he heard it again and this time it was unmistakable and much louder. A sound . . . no, there were two sounds, separate and distinct. One was a deep, grinding snarl, the other the scream of an animal with a much higher-pitched voicebox.

The sounds conveyed anger and fury rather than fear. He began climbing faster. Each boulder seemed intent only on slowing his progress, every small fissure designed to catch and trip him.

Then he was running along a channel out through naked rock. The old watercourse twisted and turned before finally opening into a broad natural amphitheater.

On the far side young Spock was scrambling for safety, trying to stay behind protective rocks and at the same time gain height. The le-matya swung at him with venomous claws. They barely missed a trailing leg, digging shallow gouges in the soft stone. As young Spock dodged behind another boulder the le-matya screamed in frustration.

It was built like a terran mountain lion, but huge. The nearly impenetrable leathery-gray hide was more reptilian than mammalian, as was the poison in its claws. Again the high-pitched scream sounded, like the sound of metal rubbing on metal at high speed, grating from the depths of that awful gullet.

The youngster moved higher and reached for a handhold. Instead of a handhold he found himself confronted by a sheer wall of shining black obsidian. It was no more than three meters high—not much of a barrier. But there was no way up it and no way around. It might as well have been three thousand.

He turned his back to the volcanic glass and awaited the le-matya's charge. If he could dodge the first swipe of the monster's claws, he might be able to slip past on that side before it could swing again. The le-matya snarled and drew back a paw for a last, final blow.

It was never delivered.

An aging Ee-chiya struck the le-matya like a runaway warp-drive, rolling it over completely on the high ledge. The heavy, square head, neither cuddly nor benign now, bit quickly and with surprising speed. Yellowing old teeth made a deep double slash in the le-matya's flank.

Spitting and squalling, the carnivore twisted free, clawing at the sehlat. Ee-chiya darted out of the way and threw a blow with one massive paw that barely missed crushing the le-matya's skull. The half-reptile glared and leaped at the sehlat with both sets of claws extended. Ee-chiya dodged that multiple death and in doing so lost his balance.

Both animals clashed together, off stride and on crumbling, uncertain footing. There was a moment's pause while they overbalanced. Then, locked in each other's grips, they tumbled over and over, clawing and biting, down the short slope. Ee-chiya's low, rhythmic snarls boomed in counterpoint to the le-matya's high-pitched, hysterical screams.

Spock hesitated only a moment. To challenge a le-matya unarmed was certain death. But for a while, the sehlat had it fully occupied. Maybe, just maybe . . .

He ran straight for the massive collage of fighting flesh.

Young Spock saw him coming. But the sudden unexpected appearance of his cousin generated only mild concern. He was too worried about Ee-chiya.

The sehlat had managed to bury his fangs in the le-matya's thick hide. Powerful teeth failed to do much damage. His jaw muscles were too old and weak. There wasn't even much blood oozing from that armored skin. But the considerable bulk of the sehlat kept the writhing, spinning le-matya continuously off-balance.

It never saw Spock moving close by, eyeing it, waiting for a chance. The le-matya dug in and started to roll Ee-chiya over on his back preparatory to a killing strike. As the armored spine came up Spock saw his opening, ran, made the short leap. He landed firmly on the carnivore's back.

Incensed at the sudden new weight on its shoulders the le-matya exploded in frenzied anger. It jerked and twisted, trying to buck Spock off. Ee-chiya skidded back out of the way as the le-matya frantically tried to deal with this tiny but unrelenting tormentor. It screamed again and again.

By simply lying still and rolling over it could easily have dislodged Spock. But a le-matya, while long on ferocity and strength, was notably deficient in matters mental. So it did not roll over. Instead it kept spinning in circles and leaping high in the air, trying to bite at the thing on its back. It had no luck.

Making a vise of his thighs and digging one hand into loose, flying hair, Spock leaned forward along the smooth neck and felt for the certain special joining on the animal's neck. If it suddenly decided to roll over, or jump back first against a boulder . . . He couldn't hold on indefinitely, and to let go now was an easy way of committing suicide.

There! That should be the place. Small but powerful fingers touched, moved.

The le-matya gave a long, drawn-out shudder. As the wild eyes closed it sank unconscious to the earth. Now the muscular form started to roll over on its side, but Spock was not worried as he jumped clear.

Turning, he glanced up the slope, but the boy was already down off the dark rocks and running towards the sehlat.

Ee-chiya was getting slowly to his feet when young Spock reached him. He threw his arms around the big animal's neck. The slight boyish shape had no effect on the huge furry mass. It shook itself, a long rolling oscillation that commenced at the nose and fluttered back to the short tail.

It seemed that his pet was unharmed, merely out of breath.

"Ee-chiya," muttered the youth, unable to enjoy the emotional release of crying. "Good boy, good old boy!"

Forgotten, but not upset by the neglect, Spock dusted himself off and walked over to the two companions. He'd bruised his thighs with the shifting, frictioning grip he'd held on the le-matya's back, and there was a possibility of a broken toe, but otherwise he was intact. He cleared his throat.

"I suggest we move away from this area before the le-matya regains consciousness. I do not think it will follow us, now, but it would be better not to tempt it."

"True," replied the boy, then, "thank you for helping me and Ee-chiya."

"It was only my duty, Spock," the elder version of himself told the younger. The reply held a slight hint of reproof.

"Mother says you should always say 'you're welcome.' " That caught Spock a little off guard. There was an awkward silence. Some sort of reply seemed called for.

"The lady Amanda is noted for her graciousness."

The youngster looked over at the motionless le-matya, a threatening shape even while unconscious, then back up at his cousin. He continued to stroke Ee-chiya's fur.

"Do you think I'll ever be able to do that neck pinch as well as you, cousin Selek?"

"I dare say you will," admitted Spock drily. "Come now. Let us leave this place."

They moved off, heading up the slope. A little while later they had circled the far curve of the amphitheater and were heading deeper into the mountains.

Neither of them noticed the occasional shiver that passed through the sehlat's body. Nor could they see inside to learn that the big animal was moving with increasing difficulty.

They'd entered an area where huge boulders and unworn volcanic rock had begun to mix with soil. The first deciduous trees grew here, marching down in friendly ranks from the wetter high plateau. Young Spock spoke again, his voice full of open childish curiosity.

"You followed me—why?"

For a quick moment Spock felt that he didn't have to be as careful as he'd had to be with his mother and father. But he paused before replying. Overconfidence might be his biggest danger. After all, his verbal inquisitor, though young, had an undeniably brilliant mind.

"I suspected you might attempt something of this sort. I sensed your worry about the Kahs-wan. Such an expedition seemed a very natural gesture." Young Spock looked up at him.

"I had to see if I could do it. A personal test first, a test for me and no one else. I *cannot* fail!"

"That is your father's desire?"

The boy spoke slowly, choosing his words with care.

"Yes, and my mother's. They . . . they confuse me, sometimes. Father wants me to do things his way, and when I ask her, Mother says that I should. But then she goes and—" He stopped and looked away from Spock, suddenly embarrassed over what he was about to confess.

Remembering, Spock continued the thought himself. "She's a human woman with strong emotions and sensitivities." He kicked at a loose pebble, unaware that he was repeating a gesture performed several times by his younger self the previous day.

"She embarrasses you when she displays those traits. And you are afraid when you see them in yourself, because of what your father wishes."

"How . . . how did you know?" young Spock murmured, quietly amazed. Uh-oh—it took Spock some fast thinking to find a way around that one.

"There is also some human blood in my family line, Spock." Then he added, taking some of the solemnity off the conversation, "It is not fatal."

"What you do not yet understand, Spock," the first officer of the *Enterprise* continued, "is that Vulcans do not *lack* emotion. This is an all too common misconception—among many Vulcans as well as among other races. It is merely that ours are controlled, kept in check. This adherence to principles of logic offers a serenity that others—excepting certain theological and philosophical orders—rarely experience in full.

"We have emotions, you see, so that is nothing to be

ashamed of. It is as natural as having a sense of sight, or touch. But we deal firmly with them and do not let them control us. Nor are humans, like your mother, wholly ruled by their emotions. Instead, they must walk an uneasy, nerve-wracking tight-rope between the Vulcan principles of logic and reason and the—''

He would have said more—suddenly there were so many things he wanted to say to this boy—but they were interrupted by a low moan. It came from behind them.

Startled, they both turned. Ee-chiya was no longer right behind them. Instead he stood far back, half-leaning against a broken cliff-face. He showed no sign of moving toward them. They ran to the sehlat's side.

Up close, they could now see that the huge animal was swaying unsteadily on his feet. By the time they reached him he'd sunk slowly to the ground, his eyes glazed and dim.

"Ee-chiya!" young Spock shouted, completely forgetting Spock's recent lecture on logic and emotion. The science officer made an efficient, rapid examination of the distressed animal. If he could only remember the details of his own childhood, he'd know exactly what was the matter! He'd been through this experience once before—or had he? Everything was so vague.

The time was so distant, so insubstantial, so . . .

Nonsense, he told himself. The past was now—and it was very real.

Then he found what he was looking for—but didn't expect to find. Puzzled, he stared at it until he grew aware of young Spock's anxious gaze.

"It appears that the le-matya grazed him with a claw, here. A slight wound, not too deep. But that does not matter much, not with a le-matya. It should not have happened. I don't seem to recall—''

The boy interrupted. "Is he dying?"

Spock considered. When he finally replied it was with a double pain. Pain for himself, pain for what he must say.

"Yes.''

The youngster looked stricken. He stared down at the rapidly weakening, moaning sehlat.

Spock walked away a few steps, his thoughts spinning. For a second time something completely unexpected had happened. Try as he might, he couldn't remember anything like this taking place before.

But musing on the perversity of the time vortex would do no good at all. The animal was dying. He would be dead already, only the strike had been a shallow one. So Ee-chiya had not received a normal dose of venom. There might be a chance.

But the boy's pet—his pet—would die for certain unless they could bring a healer here, and soon. He told young Spock as much, making no effort to sugarcoat the news.

"We cannot get him back to the city to a healer. He is too large to move without special equipment."

"Then what," and young Spock's tone was agonized, "can we *do*? There must be something."

"You are a Vulcan. What would be the logical thing to do?" The boy thought, looked up brightly.

"I have medicines in my desert kit. Can . . . ?" Spock shook his head slowly.

"Even if by some chance you have a proper medication, there could not possibly be a large enough dose for an animal the size of Ee-chiya. Try again."

The youthful brow twisted with concentration, the mouth grimaced with the strain of furious thought. He looked up again.

"I can bring a *healer* here."

"It is a long journey back across the desert," Spock warned. "There are many dangers. And it will be night again soon. I will go." But his youthful self stood up, his voice defiant, determined.

"No. He is my pet. It is my duty. No one else can do this for me. But, will you stay with him?"

Spock considered, trying to keep events sorted out. If this had actually happened before, then his younger self should succeed in the journey. If it hadn't already occurred, and this was yet another variant in the time line, he might be risking his own life in *all* time lines by letting the boy go. Then he remembered the uncertainties of his early adolescence, the constant burning desire to prove himself again and again. He nodded his acquiescence, but reluctantly.

Young Spock took off immediately, disappearing over the rolling, heat-warped horizon in the direction of ShiKahr.

Once the boy was out of sight, Spock relaxed and regarded the dying sun. It turned the desert floor to deep purples and threw maroon shadows in the lee of small dunes.

He reached out and idly stroked the massive head of the sehlat. The big fellow looked up at him trustingly. But it was also confused. That was no surprise. This was the first time it had gotten a close whiff of Spock. Obviously this tall stranger was not his young master.

And yet—smell, and to a small extent sight, said otherwise. It was very puzzling.

"This did not happen before, I am sure of it," Spock said to him, ruffling the warm fur behind an ear. "My life's decision was made without the sacrifice of yours, old friend."

Ee-chiya moaned softly and stayed calm under Spock's ministering hands.

"I know there is pain. I can help a little. Sleep now."

He reached over and moved both hands on the sehlat's neck, probing. Then he made a motion similar to, and yet unlike, the thing he had done to the le-matya. The great eyes closed all the way and the entire massive body seemed to slump.

Spock sat back and watched the desert. Absently, gently, he continued to stroke the now supine head. Kirk would have found the present tableau incongruous. Doubtless Dr. McCoy would have seen in it opportunities to apply his own particular brand of humor.

But to Amanda or Sarek, the pose would have looked entirely natural and very very much in character.

It grew dark rapidly and soon young Spock had to depend on his natural, well-developed night vision. Vulcan had no moon.

He moved at a fast jog across the black, shadowed landscape. His eyes rarely took note of dim shapes and distant moving objects. They stayed fixed on the ground in front of him. A few small nocturnal animals observed the passage of the slim, ghostly shape. They scurried instinctively for the safety of their burrows.

Once, the predatory shriek of a night-hunting le-matya cut the air. It was distant and young Spock didn't break his stride. But he did look back over his shoulder. And in not looking ahead, he failed to see the coil of dark vines half-buried in the sand.

Another step—the vines suddenly uncoiled, snapping out like a dozen whips and grabbing at his legs. He made a half-running, half-standing leap that would have done credit to any athlete in his age class and fairly flew over the powerful thin tentacles.

There was a sharp, popping sound. One convulsing, clutching coil had just missed his ankle and snapped instead against the heel of his left boot. He continued on, resolving to keep his eyes on the rough gravel and sand immediately in front of him even if a le-matya screamed right in his ear.

The writhing unthinking vines of the carnivorous *d'mallu* did not ponder on the near miss. They merely recoiled and reset as the plant—with the inherent patience of all growing things—arranged itself once more to wait for less elusive prey.

There was a peculiar emblem on the door, cut into the highly varnished yellow wood and inlaid with shiny metal. Below this an odd-shaped plaque, functional as well as decorative, was also recessed in the wood.

A soft, tinkling clash—wind playing with distant temple bells. It stopped, started again as young Spock shoved insistently against the plaque.

It seemed ages passed before the door finally opened. A tall, middle-aged Vulcan appeared, dressed in a togalike night garment. This toga was red with garish blue stripes. A private expression of a publicly prosaic physician.

The elder eyed Spock with evident displeasure. He was not in the mood for idle chitchat.

"The hour is late. I trust your errand is urgent?"

"Yes—" young Spock panted, trying to catch his breath and speak at the same time. "Most urgent, Healer. My sehlat fought a le-matya in the foothills. He suffered a small wound. The poison of the le-matya's claws is working in him now. Please—" The carefully maintained, even tone began to crack. "You must come with me. He needs your knowledge!"

The healer considered, studying his late-night caller. The

dim light at the door made recognition difficult, but not impossible.

"You are Spock, son of Sarek, are you not?"

"Yes, Healer." The physician nodded in satisfaction.

"I have heard of you. You have a tendency toward what humans call 'practical jokes.' "

The youth nodded knowingly. He'd expected something like this. Vulcan gossip reached far and lasted long.

"It's true, I did that two years ago, and did not repeat it, Healer, I would not call you out at such an hour if it were not deathly serious. You have heard several things about me, it seems. Have you ever heard the son of Sarek called a liar?"

The healer's tone softened. Such direct challenge from one so young could only be admired.

"No. That has never been said." A quick glance at the boy's disheveled clothes and flushed face brought him to a decision.

"Very well. Wait here and I will gather my things."

Young Spock called after him as he disappeared into the house.

"Healer, please hurry!" Inwardly, he was relieved. He'd delivered himself and his message so quickly, so urgently, that the healer had not thought to ask a most obvious question.

What was a young lad of seven doing in the black mountains with his sehlat in the middle of the night, and why had he come alone to get help?

Spock was not ready to waste time on embarrassing explanations.

It was wondrous strange to be sitting alone at night with a dying figure out of one's old childhood, instead of in the commander's cabin on the *Enterprise*.

The sehlat moaned softly, conscious once again. A quiver of pain ran down its flanks. Inside Spock's belly something tightened. There was nothing more he could do for the suffering animal. To put it under again might prove fatal in itself, given the advanced state of weakness of the creature's systems.

There was another soft moan. At first he ignored it. Then

he rose and stared into the night. The moan was still distant, but growing rapidly louder. It had not come from the sehlat.

It was a thick purr now, rough and mechanical. He scanned the dark horizon wishing, wishing for a battery of portable lights from the starship. But the *Enterprise* had not even been built yet. He didn't have so much as a flare.

It was needed. Silhouetted against the night sky, he saw the source of the sound. A desert flier, a streamlined version of the standard city skimmer. Low and rakish, but practical, built for emergency bursts of speed.

An ordinary citizen would not rate such an expensive, compact craft. Logically, he had no need of it. It was also bigger than the average skimmer, big enough to carry several passengers. There were only two figures in it.

As the craft drifted closer he recognized his younger self and another, older man. That could only be the healer young Spock had gone to find.

The skimmer came close. It whined to a halt and hovered a meter or so off the ground. The rocks where he waited with Ee-chiya were jagged and close together, so the skimmer pilot had settled down in the nearest flat space. It raised a cloud of sand and dust before the older Vulcan cut its power.

He climbed out, and young Spock began to lead him up into the rocks. Spock turned and walked back to stand next to the heaving bulk of the sehlat. He stroked the head, scratched it behind weakly fluttering ears.

"It will not be long now, old friend."

A moment later young Spock and the healer appeared, scrambling over the last rise. They moved to join him.

The healer took only the briefest of looks at the long scratch where the le-matya's claws had struck. Then he removed several compact medical sensors from his carry-case and began a thorough examination of the stricken animal.

Spock stood and placed a hand on the youngster's shoulder. From the first there had been no shock at the sight of his younger self. He'd been well prepared for that. But this first actual physical contact brought home the alienness of the situation in a way that mere sight never could.

The full, true incredibility of it slammed home for the first time. Under his hand the boyish shoulder stirred. Spock felt a need to mumble something, anything.

"You made the desert crossing most efficiently, Spock. And at night too. I have a hunch—call it a preliminary evaluation based on sound initial observations—that you will not fail your father in the Kahs-wan." Young Spock didn't look up at him, instead kept his gaze focused on the sehlat and the healer.

"I wanted only to help Ee-chiya. He was my father's before he was mine. I didn't want him to come with me, but he wouldn't stay behind. To lose him—" Spock interrupted as gently as possible.

"A Vulcan would face such a loss without tears."

"How?" Controlled or not, there was a universe of emotion packed into that one word, that single desperate exclamation.

"By understanding that every life comes to an end when— when time demands it. Believe me, Spock, when I say that the demands of time are not to be argued with. Loss of life is to be mourned, true, but only if that life was wasted."

"Such was not the case with Ee-chiya."

The healer looked up from the sehlat. He had to hunt a moment before locating them in the dark.

"Spock?" The youngster turned. So, automatically, did the older Spock. The boy glanced up at him curiously, but there were other things on his mind. He dismissed the incident as he moved closer to the healer. Spock followed, thankful that the healer had not witnessed the lapse in his meticulous masquerade.

"Yes, sir?" The sehlat was moaning louder and continuously now. The healer glanced down at the animal and shook his head slowly.

"It has been too long, I fear, and the scratch was deep enough. No known antidote can save his life." The boy stood silently in the dark, contemplative.

"Is there nothing you can do?"

"To save him, nothing. But I can prolong his life—though he will always be in pain. Or . . . I can release him from life. In this I will need your decision. He is your pet." The healer did not look up at him.

Alien, unchildish thoughts vied for attention within young Spock's mind. He turned away from the two adults so they could not see the effort he was putting into his answer—or the anguish that might be visible.

Spock waited several minutes, then moved up quietly to stand behind the boy. He put his hand on the small shoulder once more. This time there was no shock, no sense of unnaturalness. For the first time, he truly was Selek, the wise cousin. Young Spock glanced up at him, then back down at Ee-chiya. When he spoke it was in a flat, mechanical voice, to the healer.

"Release him. It is fitting he dies as he lived—with peace and dignity."

The healer nodded expressionlessly and reached into his case. He withdrew a small tube whose size and looks belied its effectiveness. There were only three controls on it—two tiny dials and a button at one end.

He adjusted the settings. Young Spock watched for another moment, then walked over and knelt beside the sehlat. He sat down on the hard ground and took the massive head in his lap.

Ee-chiya stared up at him and burrowed himself deeper, closer to the boy. There was an ethereal, minute hiss as though from a tiny spray. Young Spock's face remained unchanged, emotionless—Vulcan!

"I regret that my actions troubled you in any way, Father," young Spock said, "but I am convinced my actions were necessary." Sarek blinked in the strong light pouring in through the garden window as he studied his son.

There was something in the youth's attitude and speech pattern that the elder Vulcan had not detected before. In fact, both seemed somehow rather like . . . he chanced a quick and hopefully unnoticed glance towards his odd cousin, standing impassively by a far bookcase.

Spock was studiously examining an ancient terran book. It happened to be a fantasy, a childhood favorite of his by a terran with an odd name. Sarek could not see the title and it probably wouldn't have set any thoughts going in his head anyway. The paper books were Amanda's province. His mother, however, might have made something of the coincidence, but she was too relieved to notice much of anything but her son just now.

Sarek turned back to the boy.

"I hope you can explain *why* it was necessary. Your mother and I were . . . worried."

"There was a decision to be made," said young Spock firmly. "A direction for my life had to be chosen—and before the artificiality of the Kahs-wan. I chose—Vulcan."

On the other side of the room, Amanda turned away briefly in her chair, fighting off tears. She felt a slight sense of loss, common to all mothers at those strange, off-center times when they realize their child is growing up. Her son had elected to follow the more difficult path.

Sarek exhibited no outward reaction to this announcement—but he was naturally pleased. Of course, it would be unthinkable to show it, or to smile. He nodded solemnly.

"It is well. You have comported yourself with honor." He paused. "We will see to it that Ee-chiya is brought home from the mountains."

"Thank you, Father." Young Spock shuffled his feet impatiently. "If you will excuse me now, I have some business to attend to."

"Business?" queried Sarek suspiciously.

"With some schoolmates. A demonstration of the Vulcan neck pinch. Our cousin taught me." He nodded by way of excusing himself and left the room.

When he'd departed, Spock replaced the friendly old tome in its slot on the shelf and moved towards Sarek and Amanda.

"I, too, must beg to be excused. I must make my farewells now. Your hospitality has been most kind, more than you can know. But I must journey on. Already I have spent too much . . ." he paused and almost, *almost* grinned, "too much time here."

"Just enough time," said Sarek gratefully. "You saved my son's life. There is no way I can ever repay you for that." Spock interrupted him smoothly, his voice turning serious.

"Try to understand your son, Sarek of Vulcan. His troubles, his confusion, his battles with his emotions. That will be repayment enough."

"An odd and intimate request from a stranger, but I will honor it. I am bound to honor it. If you ever pass this way again, or if there is anything I can ever do for you—all that I have is yours."

"I should like to, but I fear that circumstance will dictate that I not retrace this path again." This was becoming too painful. It was time to leave. He raised his hand in salute. "Peace and long life, cousin."

"Peace and long life," saluted his mother and father in return. "Long life and prosper, cousin."

He didn't look back as he left the garden gate and started down the path leading back toward the desert. But he could feel their curious eyes on his back, watching, watching . . .

He remembered now that his parents had never mentioned a cousin Selek. He smiled inwardly. Even so, he understood now why he had never forgotten that remarkable individual . . .

James T. Kirk paced nervously back and forth in front of the Time Gate. He was alone on the rocky platform in front of the Guardian of Forever.

Unresolvable shapes drifted across the center of the time portal, cloaking unknown mysteries, enigmatic pasts. Suddenly he stopped pacing and stared at the rippling mists. They began to slow, to organize and coalesce into a definite pattern. The Gate was activating.

It was confirmed a second later as a deep, now familiar rumble issued from some still indeterminate locale.

"THE TRAVELER IS RETURNING."

Kirk studied the Gate with painful expectation. At first there was nothing. He began to worry. Then, in the distance, a transparent flowing form seemed to jump towards him. It was solidifying as it came through the Gate.

A familiar lanky frame, clad in the attire of another world's bygone days, stepped out and shook hands with him. Spock didn't say anything—but Kirk had had enough experience reading barely noticeable Vulcan expressions to tell that the trip hadn't been a total disaster.

Spock went immediately to his waiting pile of normal clothing. Off came the worn soft-suit and tight boots, swapped for the daytime uniform of a Starfleet commander.

"I sent the others up to the ship," Kirk volunteered in response to the unasked question. He nodded in the direction of the again blurred time portal. "What happened in there?

You were only gone twenty-four minutes . . . subjective time.''

"Nothing different happened, nothing unexpected, Captain.'' He paused. "Oh, one small thing was changed, nothing vital. A pet died.''

Kirk looked relieved. "A pet? Well, that wouldn't mean much in the course of time.''

"It might,'' Spock replied, "to some—''

Kirk eyed his first officer more closely as he swapped Vulcan carry-bag for utility belt, communicator, and other modern necessities. Kirk hesitated, decided to ask no further questions—for now. There were more important ones to be answered. He flipped open his communicator.

"*Enterprise* . . . this is the captain. We're moving away from the Guardian. There'll be two to beam up.''

"Aye, sir,'' came Engineer Scott's reply.

A moment later both men stood still as a luminescent glow enveloped them and turned them into pieces of sun.

This state was quickly reversed in the main transporter room of the starship. Both Kirk and Spock held their positions, however, after rematerializing—Kirk uncertain, Spock apprehensive.

"Well, well, well!'' Dr. McCoy stepped into view from behind the transporter console as Scott concluded final shutdown. The doctor looked at them and nodded knowingly, his tone as irascible as ever.

"So you two finally decided to end your vacation. While you've been running all over creation, I've been stuck performing semiannual crew physicals. You two are the last ones.'' Captain and commander exchanged glances, each certain he was more relieved than the other.

"Welcome aboard, Mr. Spock,'' said Kirk. McCoy moved closer, shepherding them out of the alcove and toward the elevator.

"Never mind the chitchat. I've got the mediscanners all set up for a Vulcan. I have to recalibrate every time I run a check on you, Spock.'' He made it sound like the biggest job since the hammering out of the Federation-Klingon peace treaty.

"Dr. McCoy,'' said Spock, moving toward the closed doors, "you do not know the half of your good fortune. If things were only slightly different you might have to recalibrate for, say, an Andorian.''

He and Kirk activated the call switch simultaneously.

''What's that supposed to mean?'' McCoy inquired. When neither man replied, ''If that's supposed to be a joke, I have to remind you that Vulcans don't tell jokes.'' He followed them into the waiting elevator.

''Times change, Doctor,'' suggested Spock meaningfully, ''times change.''

McCoy grunted, sensing something more than mere argument in the first officer's voice.

''Just give me time enough for a physical, that's all.''

''All the time in the world, Doctor.'' Kirk grinned as McCoy hit the necessary button and they began to descend to lower levels.

It wasn't often he enjoyed something as much as that simple elevator ride.

PART III

ONE OF OUR PLANETS IS MISSING

(Adapted from a script by Marc Daniels)

IX

Precisely two and a quarter ship-days after leaving the Time Planet the crew of the *Enterprise* received a general emergency call. There were undoubtedly rarer things in the universe than general emergency calls—but not many.

"What I'd like to know," Kirk inquired of no one in particular, from his seat in the bridge command chair, "was why someone didn't notice and chart this thing before it slipped into inhabited Federation space?"

Lieutenant Arex was seated next to Sulu at the helm-computer. Now he lifted all three arms in a popular human gesture and swiveled his thin neck so that he was facing the captain. Bright, intelligent eyes stared out from under projecting ridges of bone.

"*Quien sabe?* Who knows, Captain?"

Uhura's reaction was more reasoned. "Maybe no one thought it worth an emergency alert, Captain, until it did move so deep into Federation territory. It hasn't made any aggressive moves. Why should it attract much attention while in free space?"

"Even given its benign nature, Lieutenant—something of which we have as yet no proof," countered Spock, "the fact that a cosmic cloud of this size and density—not to mention its other peculiar characteristics—has never been observed before should have been sufficient to pique the interest of at least a couple of astronomers. I cannot help but wonder if there are other reasons why it was not detected."

Kirk grunted. They'd been examining and reexamining these same arguments ever since the call had been received. He didn't make a point of it, but he was upset. They'd been returning to starbase from the planet of the time vortex when

143

the call had diverted them. R&R for the crew, not to mention needed ship-servicing, had to be postponed yet again.

"Just our usual luck—the *Enterprise* being the only star-ship of any size in the phenomenon's vicinity. Sometimes I get the feeling Starfleet Command picks on us."

"I suspect, Captain," Spock suggested, "that if we were to perform below expectations a few times, Starfleet would be in less of a hurry to select us for such tasks."

"Don't tempt me, Mr. Spock."

"I was not tempting you, Captain. I was merely proposing an alternative mode of operation with an eye toward allevi-ating your apparent discomfort at being so often chosen by Starfleet Command for such—"

"Oh, never mind, Mr. Spock." If he thought Spock was capable of ironic humor, he'd have suspected that—no, ri-diculous.

"Mr. Sulu, let's see the grid."

"Yes, sir." Sulu's hands moved over the complex navi-gation console. A brilliant star-chart appeared on the main viewscreen. The overlying grid network permitted fast, crude calculation of speed and distances. Kirk's interest was on the Pallas XIV system. The exaggerated diagram showed close to one side of the moving white dot that was the *Enterprise*.

Three planets—Bezaride, Mantilles, and Alondra, plus a fair-sized asteroid belt—extended outward from Pallas I and II. All were small, inner-system type worlds. There were no gas giants.

The system revolved around a double star. Double-star sys-tems were far from unusual, but those with planets were. And those with inhabited worlds were very much so. The Pallas system was very carefully studied before settlement was rec-ommended. Not that Pallas II—Mantilles—was not a hospita-ble world. Quite the contrary. But Federation authorities wanted to make, well, double certain that the twin-star system was stable enough to support Mantillian life for at least a minimal period of time. Say, four or five hundred million years.

In addition to being blessed with two shadows per person, Mantillians enjoyed the notoriety of being the most remote inhabited world of consequence in the entire Federation. And while the planet was now safely populated and well beyond the initial stages of colonization, the Mantillians still liked to think of themselves as pioneers—their backs to the populous Federation and galactic center, their faces turned to the beckoning gulfs of intergalactic space.

They were a proud, self-reliant people. But the sudden appearance of this strange cloud had made them nervous. So the Mantillian government had shouted loud enough for Starfleet Command to hear, and Starfleet Command had shouted for the *Enterprise*.

And Kirk—Kirk could only shout at the gods of coincidence and bad timing. At least they didn't shout back, they only snickered.

He sighed. They were here. Find out what the thing was, reassure the Mantillians, and head for starbase once again—with closed channels this time, maybe.

"Mr. Sulu let's have some timings." The helmsman's reply was quick and crisp.

"We will intercept the cloud in the vicinity of Pallas III—Alondra. The outermost planet, sir. It is not inhabited. There are only a few automatic scientific stations." Spock looked up from his hooded viewer at the computer-library console.

"Also, Captain, I might add that we are now approaching sensor range of the cloud."

"Initial readings, Mr. Spock? Starfleet wasn't very specific. I kind of got the impression they expected us to dig out our own information." He tried to show some interest as Spock looked back into his viewer and adjusted controls. Probably the cloud was a loose piece of nebula, a relatively harmless collection of thin cosmic gases.

Spock's report changed all that. There was nothing ordinary about *this* cloud.

"It is an irregular shape with shifting, undefined boundaries, Captain. On the mean, I would estimate some eight hundred thousand kilometers across and perhaps half that in depth. And it is quite dense." The soft-spoken Arex looked up from his seat at the helm and whistled, impressed.

"Immense! Twice the diameters of Sol III's three biggest gas giants combined!"

"We're all well grounded in basic astronomy, Lieutenant Arex," said Kirk drily. "Put up our present position, please."

Arex, looking slightly downcast, went to work at the console. "Yes, Captain."

Inwardly, Kirk chastised himself. There was really no call for coming down on Arex like that. He was only expressing a sense of awe and wonder at the sight of the peculiar intruder, a feeling everyone else probably shared. It was a liberty Kirk couldn't permit himself. Captains weren't supposed to be awed.

Anyway, it wasn't the thing's size that had suddenly worried him. It was Spock's information that the cloud was "quite dense." Sizewise it was small stuff compared to even a little nebula. But if the gas was thick, and could actually have some effect on an atmosphere—

The scene on the screen shifted. The vast mass of the cloud now appeared on the screen. It bulked to the right, galactic inclination, of Alondra. Now it was very close to the uninhabited outermost planet.

Then further, more worrying sensor readings started coming in. According to the *Enterprise's* detectors, the cloud was composed of gaseous matter so thick in some places that it bordered on the solid. It was too thick to be a nebula, too thin to be a world. It neither rotated nor tumbled, showing splendid disregard for all the usual effects of motion and solar gravitation. Pallas I and II should be having all kinds of effects on it now, yet sensors continued to claim the cloud ignored the twin suns completely.

And it moved rapidly. Much too rapidly.

There it was, then. The seemingly bottomless Pandora's box of the universe had confronted them with yet another surprise.

"Come, Mr. Spock. Keep at the computer. Let's have further information," and, he didn't add, information that made a little more sense. Spock paused, looked up from his viewer.

"I'm sorry, Captain. I find myself quite intrigued by the phenomenon. There is both matter and energy active in the cloud, it seems. But to say the least, the combination is highly unorthodox. For example, the quantities of each do not appear to remain constant, but rather exist in a continual state of flux.

"This would imply that matter within the cloud is being

steadily converted to energy. Yet it does not radiate more than a trickle of this apparent production."

"You're right, Spock, that's very intriguing." Kirk pondered. The closer they got, the more information they obtained, the more impossible this thing became. "It's very odd. It almost suggests . . ."

"Look!" Everyone whirled to face the screen at Sulu's abrupt shout.

The cloud had reached Alondra. Sulu switched hurriedly to long-range visual pickup and before their horrified eyes, the cloud slowly crept amoebalike across the face of the planet. It traveled over the planetary surface patiently, inexorably, and—one couldn't help but feel—deliberately.

Only Arex, mindful perhaps of Kirk's earlier reproof, kept his eyes on his instruments.

"Captain," he announced finally, "Alondra has disappeared from navigation scan." That sent Spock's gaze back to his library viewer.

Uhura suggested, "The cloud has come between us and the planet. Somehow that's interrupting scan."

"No, Lieutenant," said Spock quietly. "The cloud has engulfed Alondra." A long pause followed. The bridge was silent except for the tiny, nonconversational ticks and hums of various instruments. The next time he spoke, the science officer's voice conveyed an unmistakable feeling of alarm.

"Captain! The planet seems to be breaking up. Sensors indicate a definite and rapid reduction of planetary mass."

A hurricane of thoughts had roared through Kirk's head in the past few minutes. Now he found himself voicing the least palatable of them.

"Spock," he asked quietly, "is it possible that this 'cloud' *consumes* planets?"

"Captain, I believe that your question is unnecessarily replete with emotional overtones."

"This whole situation is unnecessarily replete with emotional overtones, Mr. Spock. Please answer the question."

"Extrapolating from all available sensor information, sir," his first officer replied, argumentive to the last, "it would seem a reasonable assumption."

"Sir?" Kirk looked over at Sulu. "The cloud is changing course."

"Ridiculous, Mr. Sulu. It's not a powered vehicle. A natural object should not—"

"Course change verified, sir!" added Arex excitedly. "Initial course computation revision indicates—" he paused, triple-checking his figures, "indicates it is moving now in the direction of the second planet."

"But if it continues on that course—" Uhura called.

Kirk's voice was grim. "—Eighty-two million people will die."

Very quiet it was on the bridge then. Only the computers continued to converse.

"Mr. Sulu, prepare to increase speed to warp-eight. Push it to the limit. Inform Engineer Scott of the reasons, if he so inquires."

"Yes, sir," Sulu nodded. Kirk continued.

"At warp-eight, Mr. Sulu, we will intercept the cloud." At that Sulu looked back hesitantly towards the command chair, his gaze full of questions.

"We . . . will . . . intercept . . . the . . . cloud," Kirk repeated distinctly. He was well aware everyone on the bridge was staring at him. Well, what the hell did they expect? "And before it reaches the inhabited planet, Mantilles. Despite the fact that we are still uncertain as to the cloud's true nature. Despite the fact that it masses many millions of *Enterprise*s.

"Ready, Mr. Sulu!"

"Course plotted and set, Captain."

"Warp-eight, please, Lieutenant."

Sulu did a small thing. Only God and helmsmen could warp the very fabric of space—and at times like these, some helmsmen got the two confused.

That's why navigation officers and chief engineers had the highest rate of turnover and mental crackup in Starfleet.

The *Enterprise* responded and leaped ahead.

"If we can't stop it, Jim, millions of people will die."

Kirk swiveled his chair. "Hello, Bones. I know. Perhaps more."

"True, Doctor," continued Spock. "If planetary annihilation is indeed a part of this thing's nature, it might seek out worlds as instinctively as any animal seeks out food. It may even consume stars as well as planets—though it seems woefully small in comparison to even a small star."

"Almost as small as we are in comparison to it?" Kirk mused. Spock, naturally, did not smile.

"Almost, Captain. Yet we know nothing of the cloud's limitations. If it has such selective ability, it could prove a threat to every world in our galaxy."

"Bones?" McCoy moved to stand close to Kirk. Everyone on the bridge could imagine, or thought they could, what was going on in the captain's mind right now. So they resolutely ignored the resultant conversation.

"Bones, I need an expert medical opinion on mass psychology."

"Then you've come to the wrong place, Jim." The jest fell flat. "Seriously, I can venture opinions, but not expert ones."

"You're the best I've got, Bones. Tell me—do we dare tell the people on Mantilles what we know? So that they can attempt to save at least a portion of the population? They have instruments, they can guess—but they won't know until it's too late."

McCoy looked up at the screen at the moving cloud. The distant view showed no bulging eyes, no gaping jaws. In appearance it was no more threatening than a cloud of steam.

"How much time do they have?"

Arex supplied the answer, and Kirk didn't even think of reprimanding the lieutenant for evesdropping. "Four hours, ten minutes, sir."

McCoy looked at Kirk. "I suspect the people on Mantilles are organized, well-educated, civilized, thinking human beings, Jim."

Kirk nodded in confirmation. "That's how I see it, too, Bones. They'll panic, all right." McCoy grinned tightly.

"On the other hand, Captain," reminded Spock, and it was natural that he should be the one to voice the thought, "they may still manage to save some small portion of the populace."

"A great deal could depend on the executive in charge, Jim," McCoy continued. "Who's the governor of Mantilles? Do you know anything about him?"

"Robert Wesley," Kirk murmured, thinking back in time to a long-past incident. "He was in Starfleet once. Left it to accept the governorship.'' He glanced meaningfully up at the doctor. ''He's no hysteric.''

McCoy didn't hesitate. ''Then tell him.''

''Coming up on the cloud,'' interrupted Sulu. ''ETA five minutes ten seconds.''

''Very well, Lieutenant.'' Kirk whispered back at McCoy, ''Thanks, Bones.'' Then he raised his voice and gave orders to Uhura.

''Lieutenant, send a priority one call to Governor Wesley on Mantilles.''

''Aye aye, sir.''

As the *Enterprise* gained distance on the cloud, viewscreen perspective had to be forced down once, twice—yet a third time. Then it was impossible to widen the view or reduce it any further.

There was nothing in the screen now but the shifting, enigmatic, threatening cloud-shape. It blotted out the universe.

Bland as the actual picture was, it exerted a tremendous fascination. Everyone stared at the nearing, gaseous form. Everyone but Spock. He found more of interest in his computer readouts.

''Captain, I'm getting anticipated readings from the chemical analysis sensors.''

''Anticipated, Mr. Spock? Oh, you mean . . .''

''Yes, Captain. They are most unusual, in keeping with the unique nature of the cloud.''

''Well, don't keep us in suspense any longer, Spock. What kind of readings?''

''There are indications of elements present in the cloud that are utterly unknown in our periodic tables, sir—both natural and artificial. I am now ninety percent certain of what has heretofore been only theory.''

''Which is?'' Kirk prompted.

''That this object has originated outside our galaxy.''

''Captain!'' yelled Sulu abruptly. They all turned back to face the screen.

A segment of the massive shape was twisting, bulging with ponderous speed. From the bulge long tendril-like spiral streamers of thick cloud suddenly reached out, out, in the direction of the *Enterprise*. Once formed, the fluffy pseudo-pods moved with uncanny speed and flexibility.

"Evasive action!" Kirk shouted, hands reflexively trying to dig into the metal of the command seat.

"Aye, sir!" shouted Arex as he and Sulu worked frantically at the helm.

But this close to target, evasive action was nearly impossible to coordinate. The *Enterprise* was no hummingbird, to spin on its own axis or suddenly fly backwards. Even if the fabric of the ship could have survived such a maneuver, everyone and everything on board would have been thrown out through the forward superstructure by sheer inertia.

It was like being attacked by a ball of loose cotton. The long streamers entwined themselves gently about the *Enterprise*. Then, warp-eight or no warp-eight, space-twisting engines or no space-twisting engines, the ship began to retract steadily back into the cloud.

"Full reverse thrust," ordered Kirk, more hopeful than sanguine.

"Full back engines, sir," Sulu confirmed. The bridge shuddered under the strain.

Except for computer-field compensation, the *Enterprise* would have been torn apart by the titanic conflicting stresses suddenly imposed on it. But the immense power of her engines was insufficient to pull her free.

"Not enough—it's not enough," McCoy said tightly, verbalizing the obvious.

"Some sort of antiplasma," Spock informed them, as if he were analyzing the composition of a candy bar. He looked up from the viewer. "It generates an unusually powerful attractive force. Not gravity as we know it, but similar." Kirk hardly heard him.

"Prepare to fire all phasers into the cloud mass. If possible, aim at where these tendrils connect with the mass itself."

"Locked on," said Sulu mere seconds later.

"Phasers ready," added Arex.

"Fire!"

"Firing phasers."

Ravening, destroying beams of pure force lanced out from the *Enterprise*—only to vanish with no visible effect into the cloud mass. They might as well have been beaming at the sun.

"Nothing, Captain," reported Sulu. Spock supplied an answer for the incredible.

"The cloud appears to have the ability to absorb energy, Captain. This is not surprising in view of what we already know about it. The beams of our phasers were not reflected by any sort of shield. Of course, anything that can manage the breakdown of a planet's molten core—"

There was no need to finish the thought. Try to harpoon a whale with toothpicks!

The streamers continued to pull the *Enterprise* closer to the cloud. Sulu was the first to notice the rippling in the surface of the roiling mass. A small opening appeared, expanded.

Its warp-drive engines still fighting in reverse, the starship disappeared into the cloud.

Kirk's stomach, on the other hand, was moving upward and any minute now he was sure it would pop right out his mouth. The lights on the bridge fluttered, dimmed, and fluctuated wildly. Uhura was thrown out of her chair by an especially violent concussion.

Sulu was tossed a meter into the air before being slammed down to the deck, while Kirk and Spock held onto their respective chairs for dear life.

Only Lieutenant Arex, with his three arms and legs, managed to retain anything like a stable position.

Fortunately, the severe shaking lasted only a few seconds. Buffeting became rapidly less and less violent. In a little while the ship had completely recovered its normal equilibrium.

"Uhura?"

She scrambled back into her seat, grimacing at the lingering pain, and started checking her console for breakage.

"Sore backside, Captain, that's all. Nothing vital damaged."

"That's a matter of opinion," McCoy disputed. Everyone was too tense for a really honest laugh, but the sortie took the edge off their initial shock. Kirk even managed to smile. As usual, Spock stared blankly at his chuckling comrades.

"Mr. Sulu?" Kirk called when the stifled laughter had

stilled, "are you operational?" He tried to make a joke of it. The navigation officer was in obvious pain and just as obviously trying to hide it.

"I believe—there is a possibility my left leg is broken, Captain."

"Report to Sick Bay, Lieutenant." But Sulu showed no signs of leaving.

"If you don't mind, Captain," he replied, already checking his computer to establish their position, "I'd like to stay at the helm." Another flash of pain showed on his face, but he turned away from the others and Kirk had only a glimpse of it.

McCoy objected loudly, heading in Sulu's direction. "Lieutenant, I order you to—" Then he paused. Now more than ever Kirk was going to need the senior navigation officer's abilities. "All right, Mr. Sulu, you can remain at station as long as I can put that leg in a temporary splint."

McCoy set about his task.

Sulu watched his viewscreen, wincing only now and then.

"All right, Mr. Sulu," Kirk called. The viewscreen had gone blank. "See what you can get on the scanners." Sulu worked several controls.

Nothing happened

"Emergency backup, Mr. Sulu." Immediately Sulu was manipulating an alternate set of switches. The screen started to clear, a picture to form—and there was a concerted gasp from the bridge.

The scene in the main screen was weird and beautiful. They appeared to be floating in a misty fog over a wavering, fantastic landscape of muted gray and brown. Huge, monolithic icebergs—shards of the planet Alondra—drifted with them in the mist. Many of the fragments were the size of large asteroids. They dwarfed the *Enterprise* whenever they moved close.

McCoy found further reason for amazement.

"We're still intact," he mused wonderingly, "but we must be inside the cloud!"

Uhura checked in. "All decks report considerable shaking up, Captain, but only slight damage." Sulu looked up from his station.

"Captain, objects approaching off the bow. Coordinates, well," he gestured at the viewscreen, "there they are."

A moment later a pair of huge, irregularly shaped blobs hove into view. Kirk didn't need sensor readings to tell him that they were heading towards the *Enterprise*. They were moving with impressive speed. Their size increased to threatening proportions as the distance between them and the trapped starship decreased.

"Deflector shields up and operating," informed Arex. He'd initiated deflector operation without Kirk's command— in this case, the sign of a good officer. There was a time and place for protocol—and a time and place to ignore it.

"More objects approaching aft!" added Sulu excitedly.

Kirk studied the clumsy, growing shapes intently. There was nothing to mark them as belligerent. They were utterly devoid of stinger, claw, fang, or, for that matter, any other surface feature. It was the deliberateness of their approach, the indication of clear purpose in the way they moved towards the *Enterprise* that hinted at unfriendly intentions.

The cloud was also devoid of surface features.

"Analysis, Spock?"

"Nothing elusive or concealed about these, Captain," the science officer responded. "They are some organized form of highly charged antimatter."

At that point the highly charged voice of Chief Engineer Scott filtered over an intercom.

"Engineering to Captain Kirk." Kirk hit the broadcast switch on the arm of his chair.

"Kirk here. What's up, Scotty?"

"Captain," answered Scott ominously, "this drain on the deflector shields is too great for them to hold for any length of time."

"I know, Scotty." Kirk took another quick glance at the screen. Now the distinctive bright red of the blobs was pulsing visibly. As their color heightened in brilliance, one couldn't escape the impression that they were readying— something.

"Scotty, prepare the shields to deliver an antimatter charge. I can't tell you how strong it has to be, but you can be ready to give more than a tickle."

There was a brief pause, as though Scott was thinking

about saying something. But only a firm, "Aye, Captain," came from the speaker.

Sulu shifted his eyes from the screen, kept them glued to the console until a rarely activated light winked on.

"Antimatter charge ready, sir." The gigantic blobs were almost on top of the ship.

"Discharge!" Sulu jammed in the switch.

Instantly, although there was no visible explosion, no blinding flare of light, the two amorphous masses fell back from the *Enterprise*. There was an isolated cheer from Uhura, but it died quickly. Their relief from the alien assault was only temporary.

A short distance away the blobs slowed, paused, and stopped. Everyone on the bridge waited breathlessly. Then they began to advance on the starship once again. But there were hopeful signs. The powerful antimatter charge the *Enterprise*'s engines had delivered had had some effect. The bright crimson color of the two aggressive forms had faded, the sharp pulsing seemed weaker. Now both were a light shade of pink.

"Double the charge, Mr. Sulu."

"Sir?" Sulu looked doubtful. Kirk's reply was not.

"I said double the charge."

Sulu did things with the console. "Ready, sir."

Kirk watched, waited until the two monstrous shapes seemed ready to envelop the ship, then, "Discharge!"

The lobs hesitated, shuddered—and began to fall away from the *Enterprise*. As they did so their color shifted from pink to light pink to white. Then the massive shapes started to break up, to dissolve into smaller and smaller pieces which then vanished into nothingness.

Nervous conversation filled the bridge. Everyone seemed to have something to say, except Spock. His mind was obviously elsewhere.

"Well Spock, any conclusions?"

"Only the beginning of a theory, Captain. A hint of a hypothesis." He dropped the bombshell with maddening calm. "It is possible that this cloud in which we are entrapped is a living thing. A conscious, animate entity. It is my considered opinion, barring future data to the contrary, that it is alive."

Arex whistled. There were similar exclamations of surprise and shock from the others.

"That's a sweet one, Spock." Kirk's initial impulse was to reject the incredible statement out of hand. A living being eight hundred thousand kilometers across! Insane!

Yet Spock, while unshockable himself, would be fully cognizant of the effect such a pronouncement would have on the rest of them. He might call it a theory, he might call it mere hypothesis, but he wouldn't mention it unless he felt pretty damn sure of his supportive evidence. So Kirk swallowed his natural reactions and instead turned calmly to Bones. Such caution had saved him embarrassment more than once.

"How about you, Bones? Any opinions?" McCoy, he noticed, had been using the library-computer annex to run some questions of his own.

"There's certainly some resemblance, Jim. I don't know how much we can depend on that. But I can tell you one thing. We have to get out of this area. Those mists out there," and he nodded in the direction of the screen, which showed only a thin grey fog, "have, according to the latest readouts from our chemical sensors, many of the characteristics of macromorphase enzymes.

"If the shields should fail—and they won't stay up forever, not under this pressure—the hull will be rapidly corroded through and we'll all be broken down into nice, bite-sized digestible particles."

"I am inclined to agree with the doctor, Captain," said Spock, staring into the computer viewer. "I have been running continual checks on the planet Alondra. Its ruptured mass has been steadily growing smaller ever since we entered the cloud. Energy levels, concurrently, are up. The obvious analogy is inescapable."

"It's converting mass into energy, of course," Kirk agreed, startled at how easily the stunning words came. "Even so, we—"

Everyone glanced up in alarm at a loud, raucous blast of sound. It came from Uhura's station. She recovered from her initial surprise, checked her station, and hastily lowered the volume.

"Captain, I have a subspace message from Governor Wesley on Mantilles.'' She paused, looked away in mild embarrassment. ''I forgot. I was able to initiate the requested call to him before we were—pulled in.''

Kirk considered. He could take the call right here, of course. But the fewer people who knew of the ultimate decisions taken with regard to the doomed world, the better. Word could always slip out somehow, and there might be personnel on board the *Enterprise* with relatives or close friends on the outpost planet. He had enough crises to handle.

He rose. ''I'll take the call in my quarters, Lieutenant.''

''Yes, sir.''

''Mr. Sulu, Mr. Spock—utilize our scanners to assemble a chart of the cloud's composition and interior structure. Then give it to the library for analysis and preparation of initial diagrams. It's time we knew where we were.'' He turned and was on his way to his cabin before the two ''yes, sirs'' reached him.

X

The short walk from the elevator to his quarters gave him a few precious seconds to think. The number of options open to him now was severely limited, and growing smaller by the minute. It didn't take much time to examine them all.

Eighty-two million souls.

Poof.

He shook his head and cursed the vilest curses he could think of. There were times when he wanted to take the old, antique projectile weapon out of its protective case in the officer's lounge and blast away at everything fragile and delicate in sight. That was the trouble with modern weapons. Phasers had no recoil, made no more noise than a door buzzer. Their destructive capabilities were considerable; their psychological value to the wielder, nil.

Eighty-two million. The death of ten or twenty intelligent beings at one time he could grasp, could comprehend. But this—it was too overwhelming, too enormous a figure to terrify. An entire world reduced to a loose mathematical abstraction.

Only the people who lived on it were real.

Bob Wesley was only slightly older than Kirk. His manner as he stared out from Kirk's private screen was calm, steady, competent. His face held a few more lines and his hair was greyer. The subtle assassins of politics could be harder on a man than all the terrors of space.

Now he looked even older than his years. He made no attempt to conceal the burden he was feeling, to hide the agony he felt. When the image first materialized on the tiny screen, Kirk was shocked. Kirk tersely gave Wesley the facts.

"Three and a half hours, Jim," said Wesley slowly, each

word rolling and booming like the clang of a great bell. "It's not enough. Not nearly enough. Even if I had the ships available to really evacuate." Kirk tried to think of something encouraging to say, could only come up with honesty.

"You have time to save some *people*, Bob."

Wesley mumbled a reply. "If the word gets out—and it will, no matter how hard we try to keep it secret—it will only start the panic sooner." He coughed softly. "But you're right, of course. We must do what little we can."

Kirk had never seen a man look so helpless. He wondered how he'd be standing up to the pressure if their positions were reversed. Strong men had committed suicide out of inability to cope with far less crushing situations.

Self-destruction, at least, was not Bob Wesley's way.

"How—" Kirk found himself choking on the words, "how are you going to choose?" Wesley's answer was expected.

"There is no choice, Jim. We'll save some of the children." He made a tired gesture of dismissal.

"And now if you'll excuse me, Jim. I'd like to talk—it's been a long time—but I've many things to do. There's not much time left."

"Sure, Bob." Kirk strove to sound cheerful. It came out false. "I'll talk to you later, if there's anything new." Wesley shrugged slightly.

"If you want." He sounded like a dead man already. Composed and resigned to an inevitable fate. The screen abruptly went dark. Kirk stared at it for long minutes, thinking. Gradually his brows drew together, and his teeth ground against one another in silent anger.

By the time he'd reached the bridge again the cloud of depression that had begun to overtake him, too, had been thrown aside by an invincible determination, a resolve to do *something*.

But *how*?

In three hours and twenty minutes the cloud would reach Mantilles. If that were permitted to happen millions of people would die. The elevator reached the bridge, and he stepped through the doors.

Very well—it must *not* be permitted to happen.

It was as simple as that.

He stopped, returned the stares of each and every one of the officers present. When he finally resumed his seat again and spoke, the words were directed at Spock and McCoy.

"Come on, gentlemen. I need your help. Your analyses, evaluations, opinions—no matter how wild, how outrageous. Exercise your minds, dammit! We're going to find a solution—and *no* one on Mantilles is going to die."

To an outsider familiar with the situation, it would have sounded futile. But somehow, at that point in time on the bridge, it didn't. In fact, it seemed almost reasonable.

"Start with basics," he finished. There was silence on the bridge.

"If we assume the cloud is a living being," said Spock slowly, "then it must follow that it requires some form of continual nourishment to sustain itself."

Kirk nodded. "And we have postulated that the cloud lives on the energy it converts from the mass of the planets it consumes—in this case, the planet Alondra. Though as yet we have no firm proof of this."

"Quite so," Spock added. "But it is apparently like some huge animal grazing here and there in the pasture of the universe."

That poetic phraseology caused Doctor McCoy to miss twelve full lines of computer biological analysis. He had to back up the tape and rerun the information.

"All right," agreed Kirk, hand caressing chin. "Let's follow that line of thought through. Bones, what about those antagonistic blobs?"

"Offhand, judging from the way they reacted to our presence, I'd say they perform essentially the same function as teeth, Jim. They break up the largest chunks of matter for easier digestion. Maybe they sensed us as being larger than we were, because compared to those chunks of planet floating around in here, we're digestible-size already. Possibly our engines give off enough energy to fool them into thinking we're more nutritious than we really are."

Kirk nodded, turned to face Sulu.

"Lieutenant, the computer scanners should have come up with something on the cloud's internal composition and makeup by now. Let's see it."

"Yes, sir." Sulu turned to his console. "Computer schematic readied. Coming on."

He hit a switch. On the screen, for the first time, they had an overall view of the interior of their massive host.

In shape it was rather like a fat pair of disembodied human lungs, joined directly together. Instead of a trachea or esophagus there was a bottle-shaped bulge in its middle. Rising from the top of this pear-shape was another long, narrower cavity.

From the top of this area a long cylindrical passage appeared to open into space at the top of the cloud.

Thus reduced to screen-size and roughly drawn, the diagram looked insignificant, almost comical, like a child's drawing. But after what had happened to Alondra, no one felt inclined to laugh.

The problem was that the chart put the alien into too-easy perspective. The tiny white dot representing the *Enterprise*, for example, could not be shown to scale. It was much too big. In reality the cloud was too big to comprehend. As a diagram, it was reduced wrongly to a harmless crude shape.

Still, there were things to be learned from it, and Kirk studied the drawing intently. For him, at least, the drawing induced no false sense of security.

The outlines of the cloud's interior were not fixed, but appeared to flow and change as befitted a mostly gaseous organism. Anyhow, it was still solid enough for him to comment, "It seems to have some kind of regularized anatomy. That opening where we were first pulled in doesn't show. It must have closed fast right behind us.

"But there looks to be some kind of permanent opening up near the top."

"I don't know, Jim," chipped in McCoy, immediately picking up the captain's line of thought. "If this thing also has some kind of colossal digestive system ahead of us, I don't see how we could make it that far."

"Three hours, five minutes, sir," announced Arex dispassionately, "till the cloud reaches Mantilles." Kirk nodded acknowledgment of this information. He'd already made his decision. If nothing else, time dictated a move at this stage.

"Since we appear to have only one way out, we must try it. Mr. Sulu, take us to that central core area."

"Aye, aye, sir." Kirk put his right elbow on the arm of the control chair and rested his chin in the waiting palm. A slight smile parted his lips.

"And if this thing *does* have a stomach, we just might be able to give it a bad enough case of indigestion to make it turn from Mantilles—"

It didn't take long for them to reach the edge of the area the computer had pinpointed as the cloud's central cavity. There was only one bar to further progress.

The entrance to that cavity was closed.

Closed by a pulsing, vaguely irislike valve.

"We've reached the entrance to the central core, Captain," confirmed Sulu. McCoy laughed nervously as he studied their intended path.

"What do we do now—knock?"

The ship gave a sudden lurch. But this one was bearable and no one was hurt. It was nowhere near as violent as the severe jolts that had pounded them when they were first drawn into the cloud mass.

"No need, Bones," murmured Kirk tightly. "Here we go . . ."

The iris was opening.

Swept like a leaf on a tidal bore, the *Enterprise* was tossed into the core area, along with floating mist and several still gigantic chunks of the planet Alondra. Then the iris closed ponderously behind them.

The scene in the central core was as radically different from the areas they'd already passed through as it was from the naked blackness of space itself. This core section was a kaleidoscope of colors, a flaring, scintillating, rainbowed chamber spotted with constant awesome explosions.

Huge slender pyramid shapes protruded from the side of the core wall they were drifting near. As they stared at the screen, a large section of planet drifted close by one, seemed to hesitate in space, touched—

A detonation that would have shamed anything smaller than a sunspot filled the viewscreen with blinding, pure white light. The glare faded rapidly. If the scanners hadn't automatically darkened to compensate for the shocking flash their eyes could have been seriously damaged. As it was, they were only impressed.

When they could see clearly again the first thing everyone noted was that the section of Alondra had disappeared. But the slender pyramid it had impacted on was glowing incandescent with residual energy—energy produced by their meeting and the resultant explosion.

A shock wave struck the *Enterprise* soon after, but the first flash had given the ship's computers necessary seconds to brace for the powerful side effects. After all, they were still operating at planetary distances from the wall. The ship wasn't damaged.

Explosions continued to occur at regular intervals, some weaker, some more powerful than the first. While the *Enterprise* rode the resultant shock waves easily, the constant rocking and buffeting hampered observation and made accurate navigation increasingly difficult.

Still, the starship managed to pick a path through the central core. By keeping it in one piece and on course, a sweating Sulu and Arex were earning their rank.

Uhura watched the pyramid destruction/growth cycle wonderingly. "What *are* those things?"

McCoy had been making analogies as well as observations. "I'm going to make an educated guess." He took a deep breath, let it out slowly. "I think we're now moving in what corresponds in man to the small intestine. Those shapes growing out of the core wall seem to be somewhat similar in basic function to human villi."

"Villi?" Kirk looked back questioningly at the doctor. Physiology, human or otherwise, had never been one of his favorite subjects. It seemed he'd spent too much time on spatial physics, astrodynamics, and administrative operations. True, a starship captain is supposed to have at instant beck and call only slightly less information than a ship's computer banks, but even so . . .

McCoy nodded. "The human small intestine is lined with millions of them, although they are more or less permanent. They don't destroy themselves on contact with food, as these seem to. They absorb nutrients into the body by—"

As McCoy droned on with his biological comparisons,

everyone on the bridge had plenty of time to study the actual process. Though it was hard to compare the titanic forces at work on the screen to what was taking place beneath one's own stomach.

A section of some great mountain was drawn to a villus and, following the now familiar pattern, disintegrated brilliantly on contact. The villus grew alarmingly as it absorbed the energy generated by the explosion.

At the same time the long pyramid shape disappeared. Or more accurately, shrank back into the core wall. Immediately, a new pyramid began to form and stretch outward slightly to the left of where the first had vanished.

That's when Spock looked up excitedly from his position at the library.

"Captain, according to conclusive sensor readings, those villi-analogs are composed of solid antimatter! If the *Enterprise* should touch one . . ."

". . . we'll disappear faster than a piece of chocolate in a phaser beam," Kirk finished. "Mr. Sulu, keep those shields up at all costs!"

"I'll try, sir."

Kirk returned his attention to the screen. The *Enterprise* continued to drift through the chaotic core. In some ways, the continuous mass-energy conversion cycle reminded him of a thermonuclear reaction—slowed down many times.

"Incredible, simply incredible," he whispered. "So much power—" He watched another chunk of world vanish in a shattering display of energy. There was enough power being produced here to drive endless fleets of starships, to light entire inhabited worlds. All wasted.

However, he reminded himself, the creature would consider it otherwise. If it was capable of considering anything, which he sincerely doubted.

"The villi reabsorb with the energy they take in and immediately begin to regenerate preparatory to repeating the cycle." Spock agreed.

"It is clearly all part of the natural digestive process in operation here, Captain. Sensors indicated when we first entered that a natural force-field of vast dimensions was in operation in this core area. At first I was unsure as to its purpose. Now it is perfectly clear. The field serves to contain the matter-antimatter contact/dissolution sequence and keep it within manageable bounds.

"Otherwise the creature would quite literally eat itself to death."

A telltale on Uhura's main board winked for attention, was instantly shunted to the main speaker.

"Engineering to bridge." Kirk hit the reply switch. "Yes, Scotty?"

"Keepin' the deflectors this high is putting an enormous strain on the engines, Captain. Especially on our antimatter power supply. What with the continual maximum *power* demands on the shields as well, our reserve energy supplies are fallin' fast. Too fast."

Too fast, too fast—! Everything was happening too fast. Damn a universe which had infinity at its command and yet no time to spare!

"How much time have we got left, Scotty?"

"Twenty-one minutes, Captain—and there's no safety margin figured into that. That's *everything*. But if the power indicator drops below two antikilos, we'll not have even that. The engines won't have enough antimass to sustain reaction. We'll lose motive power as well as shields and deflectors."

"Thank you, Mr. Scott. I'll keep that information in mind." He snapped off the intercom and looked to the helm. "Push our speed, Mr. Arex. I know it isn't easy to maneuver in here, but we must make our way through the opening at the other end of this core."

Arex's voice was tight in reply. "Yes, sir. We'll make it, sir."

Long minutes passed while the *Enterprise* picked its way at high speed through the weird jungle of gigantic villi, surrounded by unceasing detonations of unimaginable power.

For a while it seemed they'd make the core exit with no trouble. Then—perhaps Arex or Sulu miscalculated slightly, or maybe their speed was simply too great for a particularly tight passage.

Spatial gyros screamed in sudden protest as computer emergency overrides strove to correct position. They were drifting towards one of the waiting villi.

"I can't hold it on course, sir!" Sulu yelled desperately. "I'm using full power!"

"Increase deflector screens to maximum."

"Deflector screens to maximum." Arex acknowledged.

The starship shuddered, straining to pull away. One of the huge slender pyramids seemed to leap out at them, reaching hungrily and growing gigantic in the viewscreen. Enormous—

It stayed enormous, but abruptly was growing no larger. And then it began to move, to shift out of view as the *Enterprise* shuttled pass.

Kirk tried to relax a little and found he couldn't. His muscles were knotted tighter than a reaction coil. Another pass that close to one of the villi and the deflector shields would surely collapse under the immense load. Once that happened, so would every atom that comprised the *Enterprise* and her crew.

The speaker cleared again. Another call from Scott. Kirk was half expecting it. That last narrow escape had used up any safety margin they might have had.

The question now was, did they have any margin at all?

"Take over, Mr. Spock," he said when Scotty had finished detailing their present status. "I'm going down to engineering."

"Very well, Captain."

Scott was waiting for him when the elevator opened onto the main engineering deck. The chief said nothing, but went instead to a nearby console and indicated an especially eloquent gauge. The instrument said everything for him. It showed the level of reserve power currently available in the central antimatter reaction chambers.

Showed it hovering uncertainly right around the two-kilo mark.

"There it is, Captain. All the wishin' in the world won't change that level. If we don't stop the excessive power drain right now, it'll be the end of us."

"It'll be the end of us if we do, Scotty. You're a master engineer—in many ways this is more your ship than it is mine. Think of something!"

"Well," Scott's expression showed that he'd been pondering an idea for some time but even now was reluctant to voice it.

"Come on, Scotty—if it's anything more concrete than prayer, I'm willing to listen to it." He'd already tried the former, to no avail.

"Captain, all our sensor reports indicate that those 'villi' pyramid converters are antimatter—antimatter of high energy potential, to say the least.

"If we could somehow obtain a bit of it—an infinitesimal amount to the creature—it might serve just as well as normal antimatter fuels. Put it in the engine, and unless it has utterly unique physical properties, it ought to regenerate reaction. We'd have enough power to drive the ship at maximum and hold both shields and deflectors at same."

Kirk looked thoughtful. "That would take care of our lack of antimatter, sure. But we also need matter engines regenerated."

Scott smiled. "Matter's no problem, sir. I've already had my people working on beaming aboard some of the loose planet floatin' free around us. There's enough matter here to power a million starships.

"As for the antimatter, we can't touch it—or let it touch anything solid, of course. I've considered the difficulties fully, Captain. It's not like cuttin' firewood. But I think there's a good chance we could cut it with a neutral tractor beam and then transport it aboard."

"Transport it aboard?" Kirk looked uncertain. "If it contacts the inside of the ship or any of us, for even a microsecond, it'll be the finish just as surely as if we'd rammed one of the villi."

"That won't happen, Captain," Scott objected eagerly. "I'm sure I can rig a force-field box that will hold the antimatter suspended in its center. A smaller, cruder version of the machinery normal fueling stations use. Then I can shift the whole thing by portable tractor beam into the antimatter nacelle. The small generator and controls for the field itself can be disintegrated the second the engines start to regenerate.

"Once we manage the initial transportin', the rest should be a simple matter." He noticed the odd expression on Kirk's face. "Sorry, sir, no pun intended."

"Don't give it a thought, Scotty—it doesn't matter." They

smiled together. Then Kirk gave the chief engineer's proposal some serious consideration.

"Mr. Scott, this idea qualifies you for incarceration as a mental case. You realize that, don't you?"

"Yes, sir!"

"You've been under tremendous pressure lately and it's affected your thinking. Obviously you've been operating with several circuits loose."

"Yes, sir. Thank you, sir."

"Let's try the goddamn thing—"

Seconds later Scott was at the main engineering console, communicating his needs forward to Sulu. Then the two men headed for the transporter room on the run.

The *Enterprise* began to leave its weaving, bobbing course. It shifted as near as it dared to one villi. This protrusion had been selected because it was a little more isolated from its neighbors than most.

As Arex positioned them carefully, a tractor beam—its normal radiance lost in the glare of nearby eruptions—darted out from the ship and neatly excised a two-meter square chunk of the villi.

If the cloud-being felt this minute biopsy, it gave no sign.

"Got it, sir," announced Scott. Kirk was standing next to him in the main transporter room. "Mr. Kyle," Scott said to the transporter chief, "bring 'er aboard."

Kyle nodded. A large, dull metal cube with handles set into two sides rested on one of the transporter disks. Another side of the cube was filled with dials, switches, naked components and generating equipment. These produced and regulated the invisible force-field inside. The field-cube was not impressive, but it would hold with stability enough antimatter to destroy a fair-sized continent.

A familiar little multicolored glow appeared just above the upper rim of the box. Kyle made a hurried adjustment of the controls. The glow vanished.

Slowly, he brought down the single transporter lever in operation and let out a relieved sigh as it hit bottom.

"Sorry, sir," he said to Kirk. "Close. Almost materialized it outside the field."

"Good thing you didn't," Kirk agreed calmly. Meanwhile his insides were still jumping. All the antimatter had to do was contact the *air* in the room. That would have been enough to set it off.

"I presume it *is* inside now?" Kyle felt secure enough to nod even without checking his instrumentation.

Kirk, Scott, and a pair of technicians moved forward towards the placid yet threatening box. Scott held a small control device in one hand. They mounted the transporter platform and one by one, took a look into the open cube.

Inside, floating easily in vacuum, was the loose piece of villus.

"So that's what antimatter looks like," whispered Kyle uneasily. Like most of the *Enterprise*'s personnel, his job never brought him in contact with the incredibly dangerous stuff. He could have done without this novelty, too.

"Doesn't look real, does it?" murmured Kirk. "It belongs more properly to the imagination. This material used to be the unicorn of atomic physics." He glanced abruptly at his chief engineer and his tone turned urgent. "Scotty, we've got ten minutes left."

Scott was checking the small instrument he held.

"Just wanted to make sure there was no oscillation in field strength, Captain. It's holding fine. Let's go."

He clipped the tiny rectangle to his belt. Then he and Kirk moved to stand on opposite sides of the cube. They gripped the handles and lifted. A tractor beam would have been easier, but riskier, too. Scott didn't want to use one field to move another. Funny things could happen sometimes when energy fields of different properties and functions intersected.

Theoretically, the cube was full of nothing. There should be only the weight of the force-field box itself. But dammit it *seemed* heavier!

Dropping it would have no effect on the field inside, of course. Nevertheless they walked very, very carefully. Certain sections of the human mind were sometimes reluctant to believe what another part might tell it.

When the elevator doors dilated and they stepped into the main engineering room again, it seemed like the whole technical section was waiting for them. No one offered greeting. No one made idle conversation. They knew what was in the cube.

Still moving cautiously, Kirk and Scott angled towards the door marked:

ACCESS ROUTE-ANTIMATTER CONTROL

And underneath!

ABSOLUTELY AUTHORIZED PERSONNEL ONLY—*Starfleet Reg. E-11634.*''

One of the engineers operated the automatic safety door, and they entered the small service lift thus revealed. Neither man said anything as the lift carried them down and forward. It was a short ride. The door slid back.

They were in the antimatter nacelle.

A narrow walkway led down the middle of the chamber. Like the lift exit it glowed faintly with its own unceasing, permanent force-field.

If everything else on the *Enterprise* was to shut down, all power including life-support systems to fade—phasers, lights, engines—the small prelocked power supply that maintained this most vital function of the starship would remain activated and functioning.

If the entire crew were killed and every instrument on board destroyed, the starship would still be salvageable.

The field was necessary because nearly everything in the huge, cavernlike chamber except the lift exit and walkway—and themselves, of course—was composed of antimatter. This was the greatest accomplishment of Federation technology—engineering in negativity. The maintenance walkway they were on was suspended from walls, floor, and ceiling by force-field insulators.

Cell-like bins lined the walls like the inside of some enormous insectoid hive. Each had simple red, yellow, and green indicator lights on the outside. Everything in here was simple and functional. Antimatter was difficult to work with, and there was no room for extraneous detail. It would have been too dangerous.

Red lights gleamed on all of the bins—except for the one closest to the lift-exit door. As they passed it, this single remaining green light faded out. At the same time, the middle indicator began to glow a bright yellow.

Scott glanced quickly at it and then ahead down the walkway.

''Well, that gives us two minutes.'' They moved as fast as

they could, almost running now. They had to be careful. Normally the force-fields surrounding the walkway formed impenetrable barriers even a ground-car couldn't break through.

But now, as the main engines of the *Enterprise* began to die, the separate power supply that maintained the protective fields started to shift over to salvage mode. That meant using only enough power to keep the matter of the walkway, say, from contacting the antimatter of the chamber.

If they slipped and fell, they'd never feel the final impact, never know the moment of death. Because touching the floor here would mean destroying the instrument of touch, the attached you, and the entire ship.

It was a place for people with the patience and manipulative skill of surgeons. That's why the personality profile requirements for antimatter engineers were among the highest in the Federation.

At the far end of the walkway, which had seemed kilometers away, was a huge, unspectacular-looking circular chamber. Tubes radiated from it in all directions. An insulated instrument panel was set into the walkway nearby. Scott used his free hand to trip the comm switch.

"All right, Davis, we're here. Open it."

The single door of the chamber slid back with agonizing slowness. They carefully put the box inside the inner antimatter acceptance alcove. The door slid back automatically. There was a pause while the field cube was transferred to the inside of the main chamber.

Spock and Kirk hadn't waited to check on the automatic process. They'd dashed back to the lift door. Once there, Scott took the small control device from his belt. There was no time for a precheck, no time to see if the automatic partitioning device would dissolve the matter of the field cube in time.

A thumb descended at the same time as the yellow light on the nearby bin faded out.

A loud crackling noise like a ton of tin foil being crushed came from the area of the main chamber. There was a breathless pause. Then, a gentle violet hue appeared around it, seeming to issue from the chamber wall. Another crackling, softer, and suddenly the myriad webbing of tubes and lines extending from the central sphere also shone with violet radiance.

The luminescence reached to the bins. Rapidly, the indicator lights began to change—from red, to yellow, to bright emerald green, winking on in a reassuring fugue of color.

Even more reassuring was the steady hum of energy that had been nearly absent when they'd entered. Now it filled the antimatter nacelle.

"Scotty," breathed Kirk slowly, too exhausted to feel satisfied, "you've just given the *Enterprise* and Mantilles a chance to live."

Scott looked totally drained. "Thank you, sir. I don't think I want to go through this sort of thing very often. I'd much rather do it in theory."

XI

Kirk was feeling rather optimistic—unreasonably so—when he resumed his position on the bridge. They had coped with a seemingly impossible power situation; they could cope with anything else. He spoke to his left.

"Situation update, Mr. Spock?" Spock looked up from the computer again. As usual, the recent emergency had had no visible effect on him. His expression was neither elated nor discouraging—only neutral.

"The cloud is now only forty-two minutes, fourteen seconds from Mantilles, Captain. And while you were with Mr. Scott in the antimatter nacelle, I was able to ascertain an important fact. I might venture to say, even, a vital fact." His eyebrows went up, and as usual Kirk's attention intensified at that inadvertent signal. Something significant was up.

"This creature does have a brain."

If the creature had a brain, that implied the chance that—no, no—it was too much to hope for. Mad, in fact.

But then, this whole situation was mad.

Why mightn't it be consistently mad?

"Could . . . it possibly be intelligent, Spock?"

"It is far too early to guess, Captain. We really have no basis for such a supposition. Our information thus far is of purely anatomical nature. It has made only one action which might conceivably be interpreted as intelligent. It changed course from Alondra to move towards Mantilles."

Kirk shook his head frustratedly. "Not enough. We can't go by that. It might just have been an involuntary response to a new source of food." What now?

"Let's see what the computer cartographic sensors have put together, Mr. Spock."

The first officer adjusted controls. A diagram of the cloud's interior appeared again on the screen. It was much enhanced since the last time he'd seen it. Considerable information had come in since then.

"A great deal of electrical activity emanates from that big, irregular-shaped object at the top of the core, Captain. Dr. McCoy has been studying that activity and I believe he has something to add."

"That's right, Jim. The impulses fall in regular patterns to an extent that would seem to preclude random generation. They might be normal for where this thing comes from, but . . . I'm inclined to regard those patterns as similar to those I've seen before."

"Before? Where, Bones?"

"Everywhere—whenever I take a cranial check on any crew member. They sure *look* like intelligent brain waves."

"It's so big," Kirk muttered. "Hellishly big." He paused thoughtfully. "But if we can reach it before the creature reaches Mantilles, we might be able to save the planet. Whether it's intelligent or not."

"Jim? I'm not sure I follow you."

"I'm not surprised, Bones. You're a physician. Your mind, your thoughts, your instincts are geared towards preserving life. You wouldn't think of using photon torpedoes to destroy a living mind."

"Captain," interrupted Spock, "this is as you say, a living creature. I am compelled to mention that Starfleet regulations—" But Kirk had no time to listen to a lecture on regulated morality.

"Sometimes, Mr. Spock, through no conscious fault of your own, your recourse to logic in every matter makes you sound something of an idiot. I am aware of the regulations regarding the killing of intelligent life-forms.

"But as you yourself admit, we don't know that this life-form is intelligent. When I have to balance that remote possibility against the lives of eighty-two million Mantillians—well, how long would you hesitate?"

"Of course, you are correct, Captain," replied Spock quickly. In moments like these he was reminded that he was a Vulcan speaking to humans. In such emotional moments it was often better to say nothing to them than to be logical. "I did not mean to imply that—"

"I know, I know Spock," admitted Kirk tiredly. "You really had no control over what you said."

"Are you implying Captain, that my reaction was emotional?" Even tempered or not, Spock managed to sound outraged. Tense moment or not, there were some things that couldn't be permitted to go unquestioned.

"No, no, no, Spock! You could only say the first logical thing that—this being being—oh hell, let's drop it."

"A most logical decision, Captain."

Kirk started to retort, then remembered that Spock had no emotional need to resort to sarcasm. Faced with disaster after disaster he was beginning to retreat into inanities. That was no way to inspire the confidence of his crew.

Kirk stared resolutely at the screen—and thought.

Eventually they reached the borders of the area the computer had labeled a brain. The new sector turned out to be made up of deep yellow cloud crisscrossed with pulsing white cables and lines that vanished in all directions. Spock and Uhura were using the sensors to prepare a detailed chart of the brain interior so that the *Enterprise*'s powerful torpedoes might be used to best advantage.

Scott was still keeping a close watch on his precious engines, so Uhura was handling the basic programming. McCoy remained on the bridge. He always felt—though Spock would have considered it absurd—completely useless in such moments.

At the same time McCoy hoped fervently his talents wouldn't be required. This constant paradox in tight situations was rough on even a well-balanced individual. That was one reason he made so many jokes. Laughter's therapeutic value was vastly underrated. But he wandered aimlessly about the bridge, trying to stay out of everyone's way and for the most part, succeeding.

In fact, this kept him free for one of his primary functions.

"Am I doing the right thing, Bones?" Kirk asked him quietly. "Starfleet prime directive number two prohibits the taking of intelligent life. I once said myself that man would not rise above primitiveness until he stood up and vowed, 'I will not kill today.' "

"You also said you couldn't let this thing wipe out over eighty million lives," McCoy countered gently. "Certainly that takes precedence over the second directive."

"I know, I know! Viewed objectively, or logically, as Spock would prefer—there is no choice. But I'm the one who has to live with the decision to kill."

Spock spared him further introspection. "Captain, I've completed the analysis of the target area. I am afraid your initial estimation of the destructive capability of the ship's photon torpedoes was badly overrated. According to my calculations, our entire offensive armament is insufficient to insure the creature's destruction, let alone incapacitation." He paused.

"However, there *is* one other possibility. The brain could be completely destroyed if we aimed the *Enterprise* at its center and then converted the entire ship to energy. Such a single overwhelming strike should prove mortal. It would certainly cripple the creature and remove its ability to hunt out specific worlds."

"That sounds like you're telling us to blow up the ship," guessed McCoy incredulously.

"I believe that is what I just said, Doctor." McCoy had no argument to counter with. Like the rest of them he'd been caught completely unprepared for the science officer's words.

Only Kirk wasn't shocked.

"I expect those figures on the limits of our photon torpedoes are accurate, Mr. Spock?" he queried. "You've checked and rechecked them, no doubt."

"Naturally," Spock replied. "I do not profess to be enamored of the idea of destroying ourselves, Captain. I have no more wish for self-destruction than anyone else. I merely report the facts as they exist and suggest alternative lines of operation for your consideration."

"But that is your recommendation?"

Spock nodded. "We seem to be left with no other alternative."

"Thank you, Mr. Spock," Kirk drummed fingers on the arm of the command chair. Spock was right. They'd run out of options—and were rapidly running out of time.

Even so, he hedged.

"You're sure it would do the job?"

"Yes, Captain. Quite sure."

Kirk leaned over and spoke into the communicator grid. "Kirk to engineering."

"Engineering" came the distant voice. "Scott here."

Kirk composed himself and rehearsed the words in his mind. He wanted Scott to get it right the first time.

He remembered the last time he'd uttered the words, when they'd battled the strange energy-being in orbit around the bulk of a dead star. But in his mind he'd known that was a feint. A desperate one, but still a feint. A trick to frighten their unwanted passenger away. It had worked.

This time, however, it was different. He had no tricks in his mind, no hidden surprises to spring on this lumbering, alien entity. It was to be a kamikaze strike, plain and simple.

Idly, he wondered where that strange-sounding word had come from.

"Mr. Scott, prepare the self-destruct mechanism in the engines. Computer control for triggering the device will be here, on the bridge. Rig it with Lieutenant Uhura." There was a long pause at the other end. "Mr. Scott?"

"Aye, sir." Kirk clicked off and sat back. The following comment turned the atmosphere in the room topsy-turvy. It was typical of McCoy.

"Well, gentlemen, that's one decision you won't have to live with." Even Kirk smiled.

"Wait til you hear the next one, Bones. It'll kill you."

"What on Vulcan is the matter with you two?" queried Spock blankly.

"Nothing, Spock," McCoy was quick to counter. "You're right, as usual. As a comedy act, we're dying."

Kirk chuckled. "Stop it, Bones. That's an order." He paused, grinned even wider. "You're killing me."

Spock shook his head wonderingly. "Humans!" There was no contempt in the friendly exclamation. A little pity, perhaps.

Kirk's smile faded. They didn't need pity right now. They needed miracles.

Meanwhile, Uhura had nearly finished programming the cerebral diagram. A light flashed on her console as she was setting the schematic for display. She checked it, then swiveled around in her chair to look over at Kirk.

"Incoming communication, sir. It's Governor Wesley on Mantilles."

Kirk considered retreating to his cabin again to take the call, immediately squelched the idea. By the time the information reached the rest of the crew, the fate of the *Enterprise* and the eighty-two millions on Mantilles would already have been decided.

"Put it on the viewscreen here, Lieutenant."

"Yes, sir." She made the necessary connections. "Go ahead, Governor." Wesley's image strengthened on the screen.

Very little time had passed since his last conversation with Kirk, but he seemed to have aged years, not hours.

"Hello, Jim."

"Bob, is the evacuation proceeding?" Wesley nodded wearily. His words were delivered in a flat, even tone, interspersed with long sighs. The fresh attitude of determination that had gripped the *Enterprise* had no such counterpart on Mantilles.

"Yes, it's started. We're doing as well as we can. Oh, there was some hysteria at the beginning. But the government's been very candid with them and they appreciate that. They've taken it well, all things considered. Damn well. Much better than we had any right to expect.

"I think the announcement that we're going to take only children made the potentially dangerous ones sit down and do some serious thinking. The few real nuts we were ready for." His face was a study in frustration.

"But it's only five thousand, Jim. Five thousand, out of—"

"I know," Kirk murmured compassionately. It sounded woefully inadequate, even presumptuous—but Christ, what else could he say?

Wesley's frustration found release in a burst of anger. "The hell you do! You sit up there safe in your starship and—" He caught himself right away. The anger vanished as quickly as it had come and he slumped in his seat.

"I'm sorry, Jim. I'm . . . sorry." Kirk said nothing this time. It was amazing that Wesley had managed to hang onto his sanity.

"We can see the cloud approaching, Jim. We have no more ships left."

Sulu's voice intruded, charonlike. "Thirty-one minutes, four seconds to Mantilles, sir." Kirk nodded absently.

"Bob, where's Katie?"

"Here." Wesley smiled and looked off-screen to his right. "With me."

That, somehow, settled things. He'd been ninety percent sure. Now it was complete.

"Don't worry, Bob. She'll be all right. I promise you that." He paused, tried to think of something else to say. There were many things, going all the way back to their days at Starfleet together. And no time. No time for any of them No time for anything more than a—

"Goodbye, Bob."

"Goodbye, Jim." The image faded from the screen. After a pause, McCoy spoke up.

"Who's Katie?"

"Hmmm?" Kirk had been deep in thought. Should he have told Wesley what they were going to try? No . . . best not to raise false hopes. The Mantillians, it seemed, were resigned to their probable fate.

McCoy was waiting patiently. "Oh, sorry Bones. His daughter. She's eleven, I think. Spock, you commented on the vast area of this brain. Is there any way at all we could contact a mind so huge, any way at all we could determine if it's intelligent? Perhaps a Vulcan mind touch—?"

"I had not considered it, Captain," replied the science officer, genuinely surprised. "I expect I was too close to the idea. But it would require physical contact. That is quite impossible." He paused, thinking.

"However, I might be able to reach out with my mind. There is an enormous quantity of electrical energy playing about the ship—the creature's thoughts. If we focus our sensor pickups on them, the resultant information could be routed through the library's phonetics/languages section for breakdown into comprehensible abstract idea structures—words. There is the strong possibility that none of these impulses represent anything as developed as reasoning thought . . ."

"But it's damn well worth a try," agreed Kirk. "Question is, can we handle it?"

"I can link in the universal translator," added Uhura excitedly, "and route the results through the audio systems from here!"

"Too many complicated linkups," Kirk complained. "But that's all mechanical. What really worries me is . . . can you do it in time?"

Spock considered. "It is impossible to calculate all the variables, Captain. There are a great many unknown factors. I make no promises."

Kirk noticed that he didn't mention another possibility . . . that contact with such an enormous mind might fatally overload his own.

Sulu, "Twenty-six minutes exactly to Mantilles, sir." Now who was wasting time?

"All right, Spock. Get on it." Spock and Uhura's stations became a center of feverish activity as technicians poured onto the bridge to help modify existing circuits and systems for a task their designers never dreamed of.

Kirk took a moment to take care of one other detail.

"Captain's log, stardate 5372.1. This may very well be the last entry in the log of the U.S.S. *Enterprise*.

"It is only a matter of minutes before the cosmic cloud referred to in previous entry reaches Mantilles." He glanced back at Uhura's communications alcove. As his or her respective task was completed, the technicians began to leave the bridge. There were quiet murmurs of encouragement for Uhura and the rest of the regular bridge complement—especially for Spock.

"Science officer Spock has been working on the problems involved in reaching the cloud's thoughts—if it has any. But even should he succeed, I doubt there is enough time left for any meaningful exchange to take place. The possibility that we could persuade it to avoid Mantilles is . . ." He stopped.

If Uhura and Spock failed, no one would ever read this entry. It would vanish with the rest of the *Enterprise* and her crew in a matter-destroying holocaust of stellar magnitude.

If such a possibility appeared imminent while they were in free space, he could have shot the log clear. It was permanently mounted in a special, super-fast courier torpedo equipped with a powerful homing beacon. The entire setup was supposed to insure that even if a starship was visited with total destruction, its log—and perhaps the reasons for its destruction—would survive.

Its builders had not envisioned this particular situation, however. Once free of the *Enterprise*'s sustained shields and deflectors, the torpedo would be barely a snack for the cloud's energy-converting villi and amorphous drifting "teeth."

No, he would finish *this* entry only if Spock and Uhura were successful. The entry would conclude on a positive note, or not at all.

Located on the helm-navigation console between Sulu and Arex was a large digital chronometer. Efficient and obedient, it shifted a seven out of sight and replaced it with a six. It took no notice of its impending annihilation.

Kirk spared only a brief glance at the elevator when the last of the technicians filed out and Engineer Scott arrived. He'd have to handle the engineering from on-bridge station now. Uhura would be completely occupied with monitoring the complicated communications linkup system.

"Engineering reports all tie-ins completed and operating, sir. The procedure is ready."

"Thank you, Scotty." He looked at Spock and waited.

Spock made two final connections, checked an audio lead, and then moved to the library-computer station.

"Ready, Captain." Kirk and McCoy exchanged looks . . . perhaps their last, though neither man regarded it as such.

"You may proceed, Mr. Spock," Kirk whispered, not knowing why he did.

Spock turned in his chair and swiveled it towards the main viewscreen. He leaned back, closed his eyes, and extended both arms, hands and fingers together, straight out in front of his chest.

Several seconds passed. They seemed like days. Then his wrists began to turn slowly from side to side, rotating with near mechanical precision. Kirk had seen this before, but he watched with as much fascination as everyone else.

No one dared make a sound.

With a sudden move that startled everyone, Spock's hands jerked inwards and his fingers, still spread, started to shift backwards. They moved back, back, until the fingertips touched his head. The thumbs rested just under the earlobes and both little fingers met in a connecting line above the eyebrows.

The other fingers were fully extended and spread over his head, from forehead to just above the back hairline. He sat perfectly straight in the chair—rigid, motionless, even to the point of not appearing to breathe.

A voice spoke then . . . but it didn't come from Spock. It had an eerie faraway quality and emanated from a speaker in Uhura's console. The phenomenon was startling to hear. It was even more startling to see.

It was Spock . . . and it wasn't.

"Listen To Me . . . Listen To Me. You Are Not Alone Here. There is Someone Else. Listen To Me . . . Listen To Me . . . Listen To Me."

Seconds. Gone. Now.

Silence. The chronometer changing. Five to Four.

An explosion . . . a tsunami of sound washed over them, swelling, to fill the bridge.

Uhura gave a little jump. Her free hand rushed reflexively to her earphone. She'd been prepared to detect, pick up the tiniest reply, and had taken the full force of the aural jolt. It partially deafened her for a moment.

She adjusted a dial and brought the volume down. What came over the intricate farrago of circuitry and speakers was filtered via the slightly feminine alternate computer voice. It was hesitant . . . only one word, but clear and recognizable . . .

". . . WHAT . . . ?"

"You Are Not Alone Here," Spock repeated. "There is Someone Else. Listen To Me . . . Listen To Me . . . Listen To Me. . . ."

Silence again. Then the voice that could only come from one place . . . and every place. From all around them.

". . . WHAT . . . YOU . . . ?"

"I Am Another Being," said Spockvoice from the console.

It was like watching a shadow play. There was the silent, motionless figure of Spock, his lips unmoving and his voice speaking from a grid halfway across the room.

And another voice replying from out of nowhere. Spock repeated the words, again.

"I Am Another Being."

Vast immense slow voice.

"BEING . . . ? BEING . . . WHERE . . . ?"

"I Am Inside You."

"INSIDE . . . ? EXPLAIN. WITHIN ME . . . ?"

"I Am Very Small, And There Are Many of Me. We Are Within a Starship Which Is Within You."

". . . EXPLAIN . . . ELUCIDATE . . . CLARIFY . . ."

"A Small Thing That Holds All We Smaller Things. We Beings."

Somehow the great voice managed to sound astonished.

". . . THIS . . . WITHIN ME . . . ?"

"Within You."

And now, curious . . .

". . . EXPLAIN . . . ?"

Kirk and McCoy exchanged desperate looks. At this rate it was going to be a long, complicated process . . . too long.

The digital chronometer read 04.

"We Came To Think To You," Spock continued. "You Consumed Us. You Thought We Were Food."

". . . WHY . . . ? WHY YOU THINK TO . . . ME . . . ?"

Spock explained. "It Was Needed Done. Many of Us Live on Things You Consume."

". . . YOU LIVE ON THE THINGS I CONSUME . . . ?"

"Yes. Many of Us Live on One Such Thing Near You Now. Do Not Consume It."

". . . ELUCIDATE . . ."

"The Spherical Mass Ahead of You. The Matter You Intend To Ingest. Sense It Closely. Sense It . . . As You Sense Me. Do This Now. . . ."

There was a pause . . . they couldn't afford.

"How near is Mantilles now, Mr. Arex?" Kirk whispered.

"The cloud will impinge on the Mantillian atmosphere in three minutes, twenty seconds, sir."

"YES," came the voice finally. "I PERCEIVE MANY SOMETHINGS. SO . . . SMALL . . . !"

"They Are Still Beings," pressed Spock. "Alive . . . Like

You. If You Consume Their Sphere-Thing-Home They Will All Die.''

Another pause. Navigational controls all but forgotten, both Sulu and Arex stared fascinated at the chronometer. Their unwaverng gaze failed to halt 04 from shifting down to 03. Sweating cold sweat, they looked back at Spock.

''. . . TOO SMALL . . .''

''Explain,'' said Spock.

''I AM SMALL . . . SOMETIMES I PERCEIVE . . . TOO SMALL. NOT ALIVE BEINGS. . . .''

Kirk hammered once, softly, on the arm of the command chair. There was no way, no way Spock could explain to it in time. How *could* he explain? How could a creature that dwarfed planets be convinced that there lived on those surfaces an intelligent mold called man?

''Listen To Me,'' Spockvoice murmured. ''I Am Going To Come Into Your Mind. At The Same Time, You Must Come Into Mine. Do You Understand?''

''. . . REASON(S) . . . ?''

''Then You Will Be Able To Sense What Kind of Beings We Are. You Will Sense We Are Alive.''

''. . . NECESSARY . . . ?''

Was there a hint of fear in that voice? Was the titanic, stellar-sized mass afraid?

''Yes, Very,'' Spock insisted.

Yet another wait . . . longer, this time.

''. . . PROCEED. . . .''

The first officer's hands reached out from his head again. His arms remained outstretched in front of him, fingers spread, palms upturned. No one breathed. No one moved. Several prayed.

Uhura forced herself to glance at her own console chronometer. Saw the 03 become 02. She stared at it, frozen, like a bird surprised by a snake.

Spock suddenly relaxed. He opened his eyes and looked around curiously—blank. Rising slowly from his seat he started to walk around the bridge.

He stared at Kirk, Dr. McCoy. At Arex and Sulu and Uhura, at the instruments on the console, the floor, the viewscreen, and then at his own hands and feet.

''Bones,'' Kirk whispered, realizing once more that in the

vastness of the universe it was often the unspectacular that was truly awesome, "*he's the cloud*. Its thoughts are here."

Attracted by the sound of his voice, the Spock/cloud turned and walked over to him, stared, examined. As though using a strange new tool for the first time it put out a hand and touched Kirk's face. The hand moved awkwardly, roughly, and sensed what it touched.

McCoy made a move as if to interpose himself between Kirk and the Spock/cloud. Kirk's order was sharp.

"Don't move!"

Spock/cloud concluded its examination of Kirk and walked around the command chair. It looked curiously at the view-screen, which still showed the diagram of the cloud's brain. Kirk kept his voice low as he spoke to Uhura.

"Lieutenant, use the library computer. Put some views of the Earth up there."

"Yes, sir." She moved cautiously to Spock's station, but it wasn't necessary. The Spock/cloud was thoroughly en-grossed in the screen. Buttons were depressed, switches struck. The screen changed to a view of Earth taken from space. Kirk rose and stood next to Spock/cloud, talked to it smoothly.

"This is the thing we come from." He backed up a few steps, turned and whispered to Uhura.

"Lieutenant, this is what I want . . ."

The image on the screen changed, closing in on Earth until the continents—so familiar to Uhura, Sulu, and Kirk—showed. The picture moved in tighter on the Western Hemi-sphere, then on North America.

Uncaring of the frantic controlled activity going on around it, the chronometer adjusted from 02 to 01.

Still deeper moved the scene, for aerial views of cities. Closer and closer, as the timer began ticking off seconds.

People began to fill the screen . . . lots of people. People working, people playing, people eating and producing and reproducing and caring for children. Children playing as the chronometer went to thirty seconds.

"Awaiting your orders," said First Engineer Scott calmly. He stood waiting at the engineering console, his thumb over the flip-up protecting the double combination self-destruct lever. Kirk held up a warning hand.

"A few seconds yet, Scotty. We have to give Spock that much."

The pictures flashing on the screen concluded, fittingly—as Mantilles might—with children.

The chronometer said twenty seconds. Uhura wanted to scream.

She backed away from the library as the Spock/cloud turned slowly and walked back to its chair. It sat down easily and leaned back a little, slumped. Kirk returned quickly to his command seat.

McCoy's voice was husky. "Jim, it's got to be now. If we don't self-destruct now, all those people will be killed."

At McCoy's words, something suddenly died inside the captain. He felt amazingly calm, unafraid. And tired, so tired. Just give the command, James, and you can rest. It'll be over in an instant—

He turned to face Scott.

Like a man gasping his last breath while suddenly recalling his life, the chronometer went from 01 to 00 . . .

Sulu nearly leaped out of his seat.

"The cloud has stopped, Captain! The edge is just touching the outer atmosphere, but it has *stopped*!"

". . . COMPREHEND!" boomed the thunderous drone from Uhura's open speakers. ". . . NOT DESIRE TO CONSUME OTHER BEINGS . . ."

The cheering that erupted on the bridge was spontaneous and thoroughly undisciplined.

"Quiet!" Kirk shouted.

"There Are Many Things In Our Galaxy Like The One You Now Perceive," Spock continued, apparently unaffected by the outburst. He hadn't joined the cheering.

". . . TRUTH . . . ?" rumbled the voice.

"Truth. You Do Not Desire To Consume Other Beings. It Would Be Best Therefore If You Returned To Your Place of Origin The Way You Came. Will You Do This?"

". . . A LONG JOURNEY . . ."

"Will You Return?" The console Spockvoice was persistent—insistent.

Eventually the voice replied. Its tone was almost indifferent, as though its decision were of no consequence.

". . . PERCEIVE. WILL RETURN TO ORIGIN PLACE . . ."

There was a long wait. Then Arex spoke excitedly without shifting from his place at the helm.

"Sir, sensors indicate the cloud is moving *away* from Mantilles. And picking up speed rapidly!"

Kirk left his chair and moved quickly to Spock.

"Lieutenant Uhura, contact Governor Wesley and tell him he can bring his ships back. If he asks how and why, tell him it seems that armaggedon has a conscience."

"Yes, Captain!" Uhura's voice was alive with relief.

Kirk studied his first officer. He started to put a hand on Spock's shoulder. Maybe the slight touch—but it wasn't needed.

An exhausted Spock blinked his eyes, held them open, and looked up at Kirk.

"Spock, you did it! The cloud is leaving."

"I believe so, Captain. There is no way out from this sector. But there is a weblike arrangement of cloud-substance at the top of the brain. The cloud uses this thick grid to 'sense'—it is not exactly like sight—other things with. A combination eye, ear, and many other senses too alien, too strange, to attempt description." He shook his head, blinked again.

"I have had but the slightest touch with it . . . fortunately. Its intellectual potential is astounding, but it has developed in ways utterly different from anything previously imagined.

"This web at the top is dense by its own standards, yet comparatively empty by ours. We can escape through it." No time for idle questions here.

"Mr. Sulu! Let's get out of here. That grid's on the schematic . . . take us through."

Sulu's response was . . . well, agreeable. His hands played the helm like an organ. Kirk started back to his chair, paused at a sudden thought.

"Spock, while the cloud was here, in you, perceiving us, where were—" His eyes widened slightly. "You must have been in the *cloud*. What did *you* perceive?"

Spock's mind had returned to his body, but his thoughts were still elsewhere. He murmured softly.

"The wonders of the universe, Captain." He shook his head at the incredible memories.

Moments later they were free of the cloud, having encountered no trouble in passing between the moon-sized gaps in the cloud's sensing grid. Once back in free space, Kirk ordered the *Enterprise* in a tight circle that would bring her rapidly back to Mantilles. The starship could help supervise the return of the overcrowded evacuation ships.

But for the moment, his attention was focused on the screen. It showed the vast cloud-shape, now shrinking rapidly as it picked up speed, heading towards the outer fringes of the Milky Way. Spock was still staring after it, his mind filled with wonders he'd never be able to properly share with anyone else.

"Someday, Captain, when we are able to protect ourselves a little better, we may be fortunate enough to meet it again, or others like it."

"And when that day comes," Kirk agreed softly, caught up in Spock's own sense of wonder—and his own emotional release—"when that day comes, Mr. Spock, the ant will stand on its hind legs and converse with the man . . ."

Together they stayed watching the screen until the last faint hint of cloud was gone.

Only infinity and a few stars remained.

STAR TREK
LOG TWO

CONTENTS

For Mom & Dad,

Without whose sincere cooperation,
This author wouldn't have been possible

STAR TREK LOG TWO

Log of the Starship Enterprise
Stardates 5402.7–5503.1 Inclusive

James T. Kirk, Capt. USSC, FS, ret.
Commanding

transcribed by
Alan Dean Foster

At the Galactic Historical Archives
on S. Monicus I
stardated 6110.5

For the Curator: JLR

PART I

THE SURVIVOR

(Adapted from a script by James Schermer)

I

Space is not silent.

If one has the ears—the appropriate methods to listen with—the seeming emptiness and black desolation is transformed into a raucous chorus of beeps, pops, whistles, and hums. The steady modulated whines of patient quasars, the discordant sizzle of black holes, and the stentorian drone of unseen pulsars—all contribute their voices to a heavenly choir of awesome complexity and rhythm.

From white dwarf to red giant, every sun exhibits its own distinctive, individual sizzle-plop in the same way that animals give off special odors, or flowers display color.

At this particular moment, in this typically insignificant corner of the universe, an exceptionally unusual sound was being generated. It came from a minute, irregularly shaped and rapidly moving object of considerably less than solar mass. And yet the sounds it was producing were at once less powerful and more distinctive than those given off by any sun, or pulsar, or radio nebula.

Anyone passing near this object would have needed very, very sensitive instruments indeed to pick up the sound at all. But if one *had* the proper detection equipment and an enormous quantity of amplification at immediate disposal, one might just be able to hear:

"Deck the halls with boughs of holly, fa-lalala-lalalalala . . . 'Tis the season to be jolly, fa. . . !"

But by then, of course, the *Enterprise* would have shot far out of detector range.

Once a year the tree was carefully unwrapped and lifted from its special cold-storage compartment in the bottom of the starship's cold-storage room. Then, amid much gaiety and boozing, it was set up in the main crew lounge and decorated with everything from genuine gingerbread cookies to holographic angels.

It was a real evergreen, too—as fine and upstanding a tannenbaum as any celebrant could wish for. No one minded that it had sprung from the soil of a world unknown to Man when words were first spoken on his moon.

A group of engineers and technicians had organized an unprofessional but enthusiastic barbershop quartet near the base of the glowing tree. They were caroling away lustily to the accompaniment of a small electric piano.

Lieutenant Uhura leaned against the fake fireplace set up nearby. She was talking to a tall young ensign from quartermaster section. Every so often she'd emphasize some point or other by jabbing him in the chest with a finger—one of those not wrapped around a glass.

For his part, the ensign was still unsure about how to react. On the one hand, the sudden unexpected situation involving the most desirable lieutenant on the ship was developing promisingly. On the other, he couldn't forget that she was his superior officer. Given the current lack of equilibrium the senior lieutenant was displaying, he'd have to be careful things didn't turn awkward.

"Lischen . . . listen, Ensign Burns . . . I tell you there's nothing like working in communications! Communication is the most important, most necessariest section on this ship. Why, without communication we . . . we couldn't talk to each other!" She seemed overwhelmed at this sudden insight.

"I ask you . . . where'd the *Enterprise* be without communications? Where!"

"I couldn't agree with you more, Lieutenant," agreed Burns, cautiously slipping an agreeing arm around her shoulders. "Of course, we should bear in mind that there are all kinds of communication . . . here, let me get you a refill. I have some interesting theories of my own which I'm sure would benefit greatly from the comments and suggestions of a senior officer like yourself.

"If you could spare a minute . . . I've drawn up some interesting schematics that . . ."

On the far side of the lounge, Engineer Scott had coralled

Spock at an unoccupied table. The surface between them was swamped with seemingly numberless sheets of paper filled with hurriedly roughed-out engineering diagrams.

"Now you see here, Spock," Scott was saying intensely, tracing a rather wobbly line on one sheet with his drafting pen, "this is—" He paused and stared disapprovingly at the *Enterprise*'s first officer.

"Och, smile, Spock, why don't you? 'Tis the season to be jolly, fa-lalala . . ."

Spock's reaction was similar to the one he'd already used several times that day, in response to the sudden explosion of illogical activity. To him this "season" seemed a cyclical madness that, fortunately, had to be borne only once a year.

But, by Vulcan's long deserts, it was hard on him.

"I am sorry, Mr. Scott. First of all, I do not 'fa-lala,' as you well know. Also, even if this were my holiday and not yours, I do not think I could bring myself to perform even the slightest of the many unreasonable activities that seem to be the normal method of celebration.

"For one thing, Vulcans do not voluntarily pollute their bloodstream with odd combinations of ethyl alcohol molecules." That seemed to outrage the chief and he drew back in stunned disbelief.

"Pollute? Mr. Flock, do I understand you to be sayin' . . . ? Are you callin' . . . ? Do you mean to say that you regard this outstandin' eggnog as a *pollutant*?"

"I believe that is what I just said, Mr. Scott. Really, if you cannot see—"

"No. No, that's all right, Block, I see. I see, all right." He shoved his chin out and managed to look like a Scottish martyr. He started gathering up armfuls of drawings. They overflowed his arms and fell to the floor. When he bent over to retrieve those that had fallen, he lost another set.

"If that's the way you feel about it," he continued, picking up one and dropping three, "I'll just have to find someone else to share this with. Someone who can appreciate my design. Someone who'll be happy to share the income."

Apparently deciding he'd reached the point of diminishing returns as far as dropped papers were concerned, he turned and staggered off in the direction of a knot of nearby subengineers, dripping diagrams all the way. The subengineers saw him coming, but couldn't get out of the way fast enough.

Spock watched him go. A hand touched his shoulder, and he turned 'round, looking up at the new arrival.

"Hello, Captain." Spock's first worry—that he might find the *Enterprise*'s commanding officer in a state similar to that of its chief engineer—was unfounded. On the contrary, Kirk's face was noticeably devoid of seasonal spirit. His current expression was a mixture of curiosity and puzzlement.

"Something is happening?"

Kirk nodded. "It's probably nothing important, Mr. Spock. As you know, meteor activity has been unusually heavy in this sector for two days now. This morning, Sulu thought he'd detected a blip in the normal shower pattern that shouldn't have been there. I checked his readings and the computer seems to confirm them. There's something moving in the shower that's acting very unmeteorlike.

"Still, it may be nothing more than a somewhat different hunk of cosmic flotsam—but it's drifting in a course almost parallel to ours. Since it's not out of our way, I told Sulu to veer toward it."

"Any idea what it might be, Captain?"

Kirk looked skeptical. "Sulu thinks it might be a ship."

"You have of course considered our position?"

Kirk nodded. "I know we're on the edge of the Romulan Neutral Zone, Mr. Spock. If it is a ship, there's the chance it might be Romulan. Regardless—" He glanced around the lounge, in which the noise level had risen several unsteady decibels in the last few minutes, "if you can spare a moment away from the local hilarity, I'd appreciate your presence on the bridge."

"I assure you, Captain, I can spare a great deal more than a moment."

Spock continued his thoughts as they started moving toward the bridge-elevator.

"In fact, sometimes, Captain," and he looked back to where Ensign Burns was now chasing Uhura around the tree, "I often wonder how you humans ever managed to discover fire." Kirk hit the elevator switch, and they entered the lift.

"Sometimes, Mr. Spock, we aren't quite sure ourselves." He nudged the lever that sent them rising toward the bridge.

Spock said nothing for a while as the lights indicating other decks flashed past. But Kirk knew his first officer well enough to tell that something was digging at him.

"What is it, Spock?"

"An absurdity, Captain. It is merely that Engineer Scott was forcing me to look at plans for . . ." He paused awkwardly in midsentence, something he rarely did.

"Captain, do you think there would be much of a market on human-populated worlds for a four-dimensional Christmas tree?"

"A what? Mr. Spock, have you been. . . ?"

"Captain, I do not object to the diverse ingredients included in the liquid solution known as eggnog . . . though I find many of them frivolous rather than nutritional. But please rest assured the beverage itself has no attraction for me.

"Besides, I believe I may be allergic to nutmeg."

Kirk lost the answer to Spock's original question in the atmosphere of this rarified possibility.

Mr. Sulu was the only officer at station on the bridge. On special occasions Kirk sometimes allowed the *Enterprise* to cruise free, operating on the reasonable theory that no one had yet found a way to get a computer drunk. Sulu would have his own chance at losing control of himself when the starship changed over to the next shift.

For now, the helmsman's full attention was focused on his fore scanners.

"We're coming up on the object now, Captain."

"How's shower activity, Mr. Sulu?" Kirk slipped easily into the command chair and Spock moved to the library computer station.

"Heavy, sir, but not abnormal. Our shields and deflectors are handling it easily." Concern was in his voice. "But from what I can read, that ship out there hasn't done nearly as well."

"It is a ship, then?"

"Yes, sir." He made a delicate adjustment to a control. "Should have it on the screen any second now."

The main viewscreen blurred, then cleared. Meteors that occasionally shot across the field of vision moved too fast to be seen, but the tiny craft centered in the viewfinder stood out sharply in amplified starlight.

Its design was compact and very expensive. Only the very rich could afford to put warp-drive engines in small ships. That maxim held true for governments as well as individuals.

Right now, however, the ship looked more like a prime candidate for the scrapyard. The rear section had been twisted and bent in places by some violent, overwhelming force. The engines weren't twisted or bent because they weren't there anymore. The whole power plant was missing, torn from the stern of the battered craft.

Numerous gaping holes showed in the mid- and foresections as well. It was a choice hunk of junk.

"Take us in closer, Mr. Sulu."

"Aye, sir."

Matching velocity and direction with care, the helmsman edged the *Enterprise* close to the small vessel. It was a feat made possible only with the aid of the starship's navigational computer. No human could handle so many complex calculations alone.

"It's not a Romulan, anyway," Kirk muttered. He was mildly relieved. Realistically, aiding a distressed craft could in no way be interpreted as warlike. Not by humans or Vulcans, anyway. But the Romulans were not always realistic. They had some peculiar ideas as to what constituted an aggressive act. At least Kirk would be spared that worry. Instead he could concentrate his thoughts on the plight of the survivors, if any.

He didn't have to consult the computer records to see that the tiny craft was of Federation design and make. "Close scan, Mr. Sulu."

Sulu touched a switch. Immediately the rear section of the injured ship seemed to jump out at them. Moving slowly forward along the pitted fuselage, the telescopic scanner finally stopped on a set of identification numbers. Set just behind the living area, the glowing numbers were barely intelligible. A near-miss by a small chunk of iron-nickel had almost obliterated them.

"I have it, Captain," noted Spock. That was the signal for Sulu to move the scanner further along the side of the craft.

"I am now checking the number against Federation records." There was a short pause and then Spock added idly,

"I might also say, Captain, that unless you are wrong and it *is* possible to induce a state of inebriation into computers, our sensors claim that at least one occupant of that ship is still alive."

Kirk's surprise was genuine. He hadn't really expected that a ship this badly hulled, drifting alone in a little-visited sector of space, might still be able to sustain life.

Still, they didn't know how long the vessel had been drifting helplessly or when its power plant had been destroyed. Its life-support systems could have been successfully sealed off from the rest of the damage and might have continued to function on stored emergency power, but—The state of the ship indicated otherwise.

Yet life-sensors rarely made mistakes.

Possibly someone else was due for a Merry Christmas.

"Mr. Sulu. Since Lieutenant Uhura is . . . uh, otherwise engaged, I'd like you to try contacting that ship."

"Trying, sir," replied the helmsman, as he rerouted basic communications through his own board. There was a pause of several minutes, after which Sulu looked back and shook his head slowly.

"Nothing, sir. Not even a carrier wave. And no SOS."

Kirk tried to sound philosophical. "I guess it's too much to expect any of their communications equipment to have survived intact. Not after the beating she's taken. Your occupant may still be alive, Mr. Spock, but I wouldn't bet that he or she is in very good condition." He nudged a switch on his armrest.

"Sick Bay—Dr. McCoy, please. Captain calling." All that came back over the intercom was a muffled and suspiciously feminine giggle. "Bones, are you there?" An unidentifiable fumbling sound followed.

"Here, Jim. What's up?" Kirk suppressed an urge to echo McCoy's query and follow up his own curiosity. Instead he managed to concentrate on the problem at hand.

"Bones, we've run across a small Federation ship. It's a derelict, been through the mill, but according to our sensors at least one survivor is on board. We can't be sure yet. I'm going to have them beamed aboard, and you'd better be standing by in the transporter room."

"Okay, Jim." The giggle sounded again, and McCoy

switched off—rather hurriedly, Kirk thought. He sighed, turned to Spock.

"Anything on the ship itself, yet?"

"Not yet, Captain. But we should have some information soon. I have already established that it is not a government vessel. Private listings of interstellar ships require rather more time to check thoroughly. I will join you and Dr. McCoy in the transporter room."

"All right, Spock."

McCoy was already waiting when Kirk arrived in the transporter chamber. The doctor was engaged in amiable conversation with Transporter Chief Kyle. Chatting ceased abruptly when Kirk entered and he had the impression their discussion had been on matters other than the derelict ship. McCoy struggled to put up a concerned front.

"Do we know anything about her yet, Jim?"

"Only that she is Federation, that she's probably privately owned, that in all likelihood she contains no more than one survivor, and fix your shirt."

McCoy looked down at himself and fumbled quickly with his clothing. Kirk nodded to the transporter chief.

"All right, Mr. Kyle," he ordered dryly. "The doctor is ready. Bring 'em aboard."

"Yes, sir."

A familiar musical whine started to rise in the room. Spock walked in and moved to stand between Kirk and McCoy as the transporter effect began to build.

"Readings indicate only one person aboard, Captain," informed Kyle. Kirk acknowledged.

"Thank you, Chief." He glanced at his first officer. "Have you identified her, Mr. Spock?"

"Yes, Captain," Spock replied quietly, keeping his eyes fixed on the reception alcove. Was there a hint of suppressed excitement in Spock's voice?

"You may find it difficult to believe—as difficult as I find it—but the vessel is registered to Carter Winston. I cross-checked, triple-checked. There is no mistake."

"*The* Carter Winston?"

Spock nodded once.

"That's impossible, Spock!" objected McCoy. He had

recognized the name instantly, too. So had Kyle, but the transporter chief was too busy to give vent to his disbelief.

Everyone knew what Carter Winston had been.

"Carter Winston's been missing and presumed dead for over five years."

"It is possible, Doctor," mused Spock unemotionally, "that he is no longer missing." Kirk gestured towards the alcove where the outline of a figure was building.

"We'll know in a minute, gentlemen."

The outline began to fill in, become solid. Gradually certain characteristics established themselves. The figure was bipedal, human, male. Effect solidified and the glowing mist became man. At the same time, Kyle deftly dropped the single remaining control lever all the way down and snapped off power.

No one spoke.

A simple coverall suit of rich brown wood colors clothed the man. Its top was inlaid with accenting gold thread. The garment was a mixture of the restrained and expensive. A lime-gold aura still surrounded him, the product of the life-support belt encircling his waist.

The new arrival looked them over briefly, then stepped off the platform and switched off his belt. The aura vanished. It was obvious that as a doctor, McCoy's presence was superfluous. The survivor looked none the worse for wear after what must have been, at its mildest, a devastating ordeal.

Physically he seemed untouched, not so much as a scratch marring his attractive, famous features. Although now in his late thirties, his long absence had apparently not affected his athlete's body. After half a decade of nonexistence he showed no signs of deprivation.

He smiled slightly—his famous smile.

"Incredible!" McCoy finally managed to stutter, breaking the silence. "It *is* him!"

"Carter Winston," Kirk murmured, in tones usually reserved for addressing Starfleet admirals. It was appropriate. The man standing so composedly before them was a legend. Dead legends are not supposed to come back to life. The men grouped in the transporter room could be permitted a little awe.

Winston bestowed a curious, bemused glance on each of

them in turn. A second later he showed that there was nothing the matter with his vocal cords, either.

"It seems you gentlemen know me." Kirk stepped forward and shook his hand.

"There are few in the Federation who wouldn't recognize
you, sir. Even after all this time. It's good to know you're no
longer a piece of history.

"I'm Captain James Kirk, commanding this vessel. It's an
honor to have you aboard the *Enterprise*." He gestured in
turn to each of the others.

"My first officer, Mr. Spock. Dr. McCoy, senior medical
officer—" McCoy stepped forward and shook hands exuber-
antly.

"I'm especially honored to meet you, Mr. Winston. I expect your being alive means more to me than to the others.
You see," he hesitated slightly, "my daughter was going to
school on Cerberus ten years ago, when the crop failure occurred."

"Ah, yes," Winston murmured, "Cerberus."

McCoy looked over at Kirk, then back at Winston.

"It was estimated that fifty to sixty percent of the population would have starved if Winston, here, hadn't used his—
well, you remember the stories.

"Bureaucracy in the Cerberus Crisis moved at two
speeds—dead slow and slower than dead. But Winston spent
his personal fortune to bring in enough food and goods to
carry the Cerberus II inhabitants through the danger period
until those idiots," and he spoke the word with as much
bitterness as Kirk had ever heard from him, "at Administration got themselves straightened out."

Kirk recalled the incident faintly and was impressed with
the memory. He wasn't as intimately acquainted with the
Cerberus incident as McCoy, but he remembered some of
the resulting tremors. There had been a real shakeup in certain sections of Starfleet Command. One of those rare in-
stances where ministers and executives in high positions
actually lost their jobs.

"One of the many stories I've heard about you, Mr. Winston. It's a great pleasure for all of us to see you alive and
well."

"Thank you, gentlemen." Winston smiled again, the same

infectious grin that had more than once graced broadcast screens from the Far Arm to Earth itself—and had helped to build one of the greatest if most unstable fortunes of all time.

"I'd like to say it's a pleasure to be on the *Enterprise*, but frankly, after what I've been through these last five years, it'd be a pleasure to be on board a pressurized bathtub."

The four humans shared a convivial laugh. Spock waited and watched impatiently. There were a couple of things he badly wanted to say, and he had held his peace while jovial greetings had been exchanged.

"There is one person aboard who will be especially glad to learn that you are alive—Lieutenant Anne Nored of our Security Section."

Winston kept his composure, but not enough to hide the shock he obviously felt.

"My fiancée! Anne's aboard this ship?"

"Yes, doesn't it please you?"

McCoy broke in before an astonished Winston had a chance to reply. "How did you know that, Mr. Spock?"

"As soon as it was determined that the craft we located was registered to Mr. Winston, I began processing information on him on the chance that he was the lone survivor. The information concerning his engagement to Lieutenant Nored was in the capsule summary the computer produced. It is a surprise to me too, doctor." He turned back to Winston.

"We will notify her as soon as we have verified and processed your credentials, sir. If you have your identity tapes with you. . . ?"

"Spock!" McCoy looked angry. "Of all the cold-blooded, inhospitable and inhuman requests I've ever heard—"

"I believe the regulations are quite clear on the matter, Doctor," replied a composed Spock. "An immediate identity check and full medical examination are standard procedure in situations such as this. Despite the unusual nature of the rescue, I find no reason for deviating from procedure."

McCoy clearly felt otherwise and seemed prepared to say so. But Kirk, after a questioning glance at Spock, moved quickly to ease the awkward moment.

"Spock's right, Bones. Be sensible."

McCoy hesitated and still looked upset, but said nothing.

"And I understand, of course," smiled Winston. "My credentials, Captain." He reached into a suit pocket and withdrew a small microtape cassette. Kirk gave it a curious, cursory glance. Tape models had changed slightly in five years. If nothing else, the cassette Winston held out to him was genuine as to age.

"We'll get through the formalities as rapidly as possible, Mr. Winston. Bones, why don't you take our guest down to Sick Bay and run him through a standard medical check."

McCoy nodded, smiled at Winston. "I was going to suggest a twelve-course meal first, but it *would* be a good idea to make sure your insides are in shape to appreciate it. I'll make it fast, Mr. Winston."

The two men left the chamber, chatting excitedly. McCoy was doing most of the talking as the elevator doors slid together in front of them, but that didn't surprise Kirk. After all, a man can miss a lot of news in five years.

"Five years! It's still hard to believe, Spock."

"I know, Captain." The two officers turned into the small briefing room. It was the nearest place to the transporter chamber that had the proper computer-access module.

"Nonetheless, he produced his identity tapes immediately. His actions so far have been perfectly normal. Oh, maybe he's a bit composed for someone who's been out of touch with civilization for five years, but—"

"It is a part of his character. Yes, Captain, everything seems to indicate that he is, indeed, Carter Winston."

"We'll know in a minute." Kirk took a seat at the briefing table and activated a small switch set into the compact console in front of him.

"Ship's log, please." There was a short pause, then a soft beep indicating that the computer had recognized his voice and would now deign to record. Kirk spoke into the small grid set into the tabletop.

"Captain's log, supplemental. The *Enterprise* has rescued a living legend—the foremost interstellar trader of our time, Carter Winston. Who, as I recall, has acquired a dozen fortunes, only to use his great wealth again and again to aid Federation colonies in times of need or disaster.

"Altogether a remarkable man and one who many people, myself included, are glad to discover is still alive. We are in the process of carrying out standard postrescue identification procedures." He hit another switch, then slipped the microtape cassette into a slot that had suddenly appeared in the desk.

"Library computer—process identification tapes on male human known as Carter Winston. Verification of identity requested." A three-sided viewscreen popped out of the desk top. It immediately displayed a set of fingerprints in triplicate. These were followed in rapid succession by a series of retinal patterns, oscilloscope readings, and other information.

"Working," informed the slightly feminine machine voice. There was a muted hum.

"Identification positive," it finally declaimed. Kirk gave an inward sigh. Of *course*, it was Carter Winston! The need for Spock's logical mind to cross *t*'s and dot *i*'s had made him overcautious.

The computer continued. "Identification confirmation follows: fingerprints positive, voiceprints positive, retinal relief positive. All registration and documentation in order."

"Original visual display, please." The abstracts disappeared to be replaced by a hologram of Winston. Except for a few touches Kirk quickly ascribed to normal aging, it differed in no way from the man they had beamed aboard. An extra line here, a slight softening of flesh there. Both men studied the 'gram for another minute. Then Kirk hit the switch, and the tripartite screen sank back into the table.

He leaned back in the chair and gazed across the table at his first officer. "Well, everything checks out. So we have a distinguished passenger for a while. I expect he won't exactly be a dull guest—ought to have one or two stories to tell."

"It would seem so, Captain. I am much relieved."

"You worry too much, Spock. And now, if you'll excuse me—" Kirk moved briskly out of the chair. "It's time for me to go and pollute myself with exotic combinations of protein solids and ethanol molecules."

"*Et tu*, Captain? You were listening."

Kirk only grinned as they exited the briefing room.

II

"If you'll just lie down over there," requested McCoy, indicating the nearby examination table. Winston hopped up on the slightly tilted platform. With the air of one thoroughly enjoying a relaxed position, he stretched out and put both hands under his head.

McCoy walked to a nearby cabinet and selected a compact general scanner.

"This won't hurt a bit, Winston," he said easily as he moved to stand next to the table. "Just a few minutes and we'll be all through." He smiled, flicked a switch on the scanner. Starting at the top of Winston's head, McCoy moved the instrument down the man's body, holding it roughly ten centimeters above him.

After passing over his feet, McCoy flicked the device off and checked the readouts. His smile slipped away and was replaced by a slight frown of puzzlement.

Winston noticed it, too. "Is there some problem, Doctor? Don't tell me—I'm pregnant!"

McCoy managed a smile. "Scanner seems a little off. Just a second." He adjusted dials, rechecked the readouts. "Calibration must be off," he muttered to himself. He nudged the activation switch again and played the pickup over his own upper torso, examined the results. His puzzlement deepened.

Mumbling with the air of someone who's just seen a ghost and prefers to pretend it wasn't really there, he turned back to Winston.

"Let's try it again."

Once more the scanner was played down the survivor's

prone form. Once more the resultant numbers on the tiny gauges brought deepening confusion.

"Odd. Some slight deviations here and there I could understand. You've been isolated for five years. It's no surprise that your body might have picked up some funny radiation, or something. A couple of abnormal readings are to be expected. It's just that . . ." he looked down at Winston with a worried stare, "I've never gotten any readings quite like these from a human being before."

Winston laughed easily, clearly amused by McCoy's confusion. "Are you suggesting I'm not quite human, Doctor? By the way, Merry Christmas."

"Merry Christmas to you, Winston. No, of course not. Anyway, the differences are all fractional." His smile returned. "Sometimes even the best medical instrumentation goes haywire. I don't get to overhaul it with major hospital facilities very often. Must be the scanner.

"Occasionally the transporter can do peculiar things to a body, too, leaving lingering effects that disappear as the internal structure readjusts. How are you feeling?"

Winston spread his hands, looked bemused. "Just great, Doc."

"Well, then—"

"I beg your pardon, Dr. McCoy." The doctor turned. Nurse Chapel had stepped into the examination room from the nearby reception area.

"What is it, Christine?"

"Doctor, the captain has been calling. He wants to know if the examination has been completed."

"Ummm, yes, I suppose it has."

"And Doctor, Lieutenant Nored is waiting to see Mr. Winston—as soon as you've certified his medical status."

"Thanks, Christine." She smiled and left. McCoy turned back to Winston. "Well, I certainly don't want to keep you from your fiancée." He turned and yelled towards the open door. "Send her in, Christine."

He offered Winston a last smile, one he also shared with the woman who passed him in the doorway.

Sh was dressed in the red uniform of a senior security officer. Not stunning, no, but she was damned attractive in an unassuming sort of way. As befitted a security officer, she was in excellent physical shape, which was more than could be said for her state of mind just then.

"Carter—"

She held herself pretty well in check until she was almost to him. Then her reserve cracked and she threw herself into his arms. Caught off-balance, his arms went around her automatically as he stumbled.

His own reaction was considerably less emotional. Calm, cool, and—something else. Something as yet undefinable.

She was alternately sobbing and talking a blue streak. He let her ramble on for several minutes before moving his hands up to her shoulders and pushing her gently away—gently, but firmly.

"I'm sorry, Anne." The sorrow in his voice seemed genuine. "I never thought we would meet again."

She studied his face. As she did so, her expression changed from one of relief and pleasure to one of confused uncertainty.

"What is it, Carter? What's the matter?"

Winston replied without hesitation. "When I left on that final journey, Anne, I fully intended it to be my last. One supreme foray into unknown regions to bring my finances back to where they'd been before. After that, I would return and marry you. But my ship was disabled, and I crashed on the planet Vendor. I'm told I was lucky to have survived at all. The Vendorians managed to help me repair my ship. I left their world after four years of hard work, only to be disabled in space once again."

"But you've been rescued, you've survived," she almost shouted. "You're alive and we're together again! Nothing's changed." Winston looked away from her.

"Anne, I've changed. First there was the surgery—a lot of surgery. Skin grafts, bone regeneration, replacement of damaged organs with artificial ones, blood replacement. The Vendorians are excellent surgeons." He smiled slightly at some distant memory. "They said I was more banged up than the ship.

"After they put me back together again, the Vendorians assigned one of their own people to look after me and nurse me back to health."

All this was very interesting—fascinating, even—but it did nothing to explain Winston's original statement.

"But you said you've changed, Carter. How? I don't see any change."

"It's not a visible kind of change, Anne. It's a kind that—" He paused. Abruptly he seemed to give up any attempt at further explanation.

"It's over between us, Anne. I can't really explain why, or how, but it's *over*. I didn't expect to have to go through this. All I can say now that it's happened is that I can't marry you, ever." He continued to watch her quietly.

Her mouth moved but no sounds came out. Everything had happened so suddenly and seemingly so well. Even his first bits of explanation appeared to leave room for hope. Then he had abruptly grown firm and inflexible, hitting her with a declaration as blunt and cold as the dark side of the moon.

She turned and ran from the room, leaving Winston sitting alone on the cold examination table, staring after her.

Kirk had performed the ceremonial gesture of drinking with the crew—sharing their spirits, so to speak. But he'd returned to the bridge soon enough. Now he was back in the command chair, using a light-writer to mark orders on a glass plate lined with metal. A young yeoman, Ayers, stood to one side, awaiting the captain's bidding.

Nodding in satisfaction, he read back over the orders, signed the plate and handed it to her.

"See these are delivered to the proper stations and processed through, Yeoman." Ayers saluted and left the bridge.

A slight wave of dizziness assailed Kirk. He put a hand to his forehead. Possibly he'd overdone the annual Christmas camaraderie. He might be better off in his cabin for a while. It was one thing for the general crew to wander around mildly dazed during the holidays, but the captain was expected to remain cold sober at all times—in public, anyway.

"Take the conn, Mr. Spock. I'll be in my cabin, completing the report on Winston's rescue."

"Very good, Captain."

Kirk rose and headed for the bridge-elevator. Spock shifted from the library station and took over the command chair.

Kirk thought about the report as he made his way from the second elevator to his private quarters. He was still thinking about it after he'd kicked off his shoes and sat down at his desk. His finger activated the recorder, but for long moments he just sat and considered, unable to find anything to say. It was all so incredible, so utterly impossible.

Five years completely out of touch with civilization! And who knew how much of that had been spent drifting free in space, without another human being for company.

Oh, there were records of people surviving even longer periods of time adrift. The trouble was never with their bodies, but with their minds. Yet Winston seemed as sane and composed when he'd stepped out of the transporter as if he'd been gone only a day or two.

Kirk shook his head in admiration. It had always been said the man was a remarkable person. Plenty of stories testified to it—the Cerberus incident being only one of many—and now Kirk knew it from personal experience.

He was about to start dictating when the door chime demanded his attention.

"Come—"

The door slid back silently, and Winston walked in.

"I hope I'm not intruding, Captain?"

"No, please come in, Mr. Winston. I was just about to finish off the official report on your rescue." He grinned. "When Starfleet makes the details available, the news people will go crazy. You're liable to be faxed to death the moment you set foot on Federation soil."

"I expect as much." Winston smiled back. "I've been down to inspect my ship. Your people were kind enough to stow it in the shuttle bay. You know, the steering propulsors still operate. Remarkable."

Kirk turned away, hunting for the microtape analysis of Winston's ship. "Yes, it's an understatement to say the ship suffered severe damage. It'll never travel at warp-speed again, but some of the systems still function and are salvageable. And there are all your expensive fittings to consider."

"Anyway, I've had my chief engineer examine it thoroughly and draw up a full report for you. It's here somewhere—"

Winston crossed his arms over his chest. There was nothing particularly unusual in the gesture.

The results were otherwise.

His outline seemed to flutter, to blur, and then to flow like a thin, phosphorescent clay. The flow slowed, stopped.

Where Winston had stood now rose a hideous, multicolored something. It had seven thick tentacles which met at the top and merged to form an oval bulge encircled with convex lenses. The lenses pulsed with faint light.

One of the tentacles lifted from the floor. It touched Kirk gently, almost caressingly, on the back of the neck. The captain's eyes closed. Other tentacles moved to catch the slumping form. The creature lifted the unconscious Kirk and carried him effortlessly to the bed. Only a few seconds had passed from transformation to attack, and everything had been done in complete silence.

Now the thing stepped back from the bed and crossed a pair of tentacles over its upper body—it had no recognizable chest. Again the blur, the watery flow. Once more the creature changed and became human.

It didn't become Carter Winston.

But it was human, nonetheless, and immediately recognizable.

It was Captain James T. Kirk.

Nurse Chapel entered the examination room from the laboratory area and moved to where Dr. McCoy sat engrossed in detailed inspection of a medical-engineering manual. She held the small hand scanner in one hand and several smaller supplementary instruments in the other. McCoy glanced up from his reading.

"Well, Christine?"

"Doctor," she said firmly, "I can't find a single thing wrong with these instruments. They all check out perfectly, including the principal scanner. But the readings still come out slightly off, still show those funny variations on Winston." She watched him expectantly.

"What about the other tests you ran on Winston, after—"
She hesitated. Two things travel faster than the speed of light—starships and gossip. Romantic gossip fastest of all.

McCoy shrugged. Some things were impossible to keep

secret. "After Anne Nored left? Some of them were off, some weren't. The differences don't even have the virtue of consistency, Christine. As it stands, these results make no sense at all. It's got to be our mistake." He stood.

"Come on. We'll evaluate those readings again, and this time we're going to find the answer."

The elevator doors opened onto the bridge, and Winston/Kirk entered. Spock looked back at him and rose from the command chair. Winston/Kirk took the seat as the first officer returned to his own station.

Sulu glanced back at the command chair with interest. "Weren't you going to your cabin, sir?"

"I've already been there, Mr. Sulu, but something came up before I could get started on the report. Something much more important. Lay on a direct course for Rator III." That prompted another look, this time of more than just casual interest.

"Through the Romulan Neutral Zone, sir?"

"That was an order, Helmsman."

Sulu looked uncertain. "But sir, if we're challenged in there, the Romulans can confiscate the ship. The treaty states that—"

"I am fully conversant with the terms of the treaty, Mr. Sulu," responded Winston/Kirk, "and I believe you heard my order."

"Aye aye, sir," the helmsman admitted reluctantly. He turned to the task of plotting the requested course.

Spock, who had listened to this exchange with growing concern, finally felt obliged to at least say something cautionary. He wasn't normally in the habit of raising objections to any of Kirk's decisions, no matter how strange they sounded at first, because they always seemed to have a way of turning out to be reasonable in the end.

But this one. Spock made a last check of his console. The readings confirmed his suspicions.

"Captain, extreme long-range sensors hint at something within the neutral zone that lies along our anticipated course. At this exaggerated distance it is impossible to determine what it is. It might be another interstellar merchant ship like Winston's. It might also be a Romulan vessel. Or it might not be a ship at all. Still I do not feel it prudent to take the chance of trespassing unannounced in the neutral zone.''

''Mr. Spock,'' replied Winston/Kirk, ''I've spoken with Winston about this at some length already. He has assured me that it is absolutely vital to get to Rator III in the shortest possible time. The survival of an entire planetary population may depend on it. Unfortunately, this necessitates our crossing through an arm of the neutral zone.''

''An admirable mission, Captain,'' Spock agreed. ''But if we endanger our ship, we will be of no use to the people on Rator III.''

''We won't be of any use to them if we don't get there in time, either, Mr. Spock. I wouldn't have ordered it if I didn't feel it was safe to proceed. Winston said his sensors detected no sign of Romulans when he was passing through the zone, before his ship was disabled. I'm satisfied he was telling the truth. And his word is considered good, isn't it?''

Spock hesitated a split second. ''That has been his reputation, Captain.''

''Course laid in, sir,'' Sulu noted.

''Execute,'' ordered Winston/Kirk. Sulu leaned forward and adjusted controls.

''Proceeding.''

They felt no sense of motion-change. Space was too vast for inbuilt human senses to detect a switch in direction at warp-speeds. But the great starship gradually began to veer from the line it had been following and to turn in a broad curve that would take it into the neutral zone.

Sulu needed only a few moments to double-check his readings.

''We're on course, sir.''

''Very good, Mr. Sulu. Notify me if anything unusual should develop.'' He rose and moved towards the elevator. ''I'm going back to my cabin. You have the conn again, Mr. Spock.''

Spock eyed the captain closely as the latter exited the bridge.

Time passed. Nothing happened to disturb ship routine, which was perfectly all right with Spock. After some hard thinking, he finally thumbed the switch activating the ship's log and spoke softly into the pickup grid.

"Ship's log, stardate 5402.7. First Officer Spock recording.

"The captain's recent course change has taken us deep into the Romulan Neutral Zone. This change was apparently initiated on the request of our new passenger, Carter Winston. Information so far provided by Winston has proved accurate. We have detected no Romulan ships or, for that matter, other vessels of any kind.

"Nevertheless, I have ordered all sensors kept on long-range scan and a close watch on any object engendering suspicion at the limits of scanner range. I have also . . ."

Dizzy, he was still dizzy.

Kirk winced and sat up suddenly in bed. Two things struck him right away. First of all, he hadn't had that much to drink. And eggnog had never, never had that kind of effect on him. He'd imbibed a lot of liquids quite a sight stronger than the holiday punch, which was pablum by comparison. None of them had ever hit him like *this*!

And besides that—

He glanced over at the chronometer set into the wall above his bed. Uh-uh, something was wrong with that, too. What had happened?

Think back. Sometimes it was better to voice confusing thoughts in the presence of others. *He* couldn't figure out what had happened to him. Maybe someone else could.

Kirk strode purposefully onto the bridge. Though he was feeling terribly confused, there was no point in letting anyone else know it, just yet.

"I'll take the conn, Mr. Spock." Spock lifted an eyebrow slightly but moved away without comment. Sulu also glanced back at him curiously.

Kirk sat back in the seat, relaxed, and tried very hard to remember. Introspection produced nothing, but a casual glance forward turned up an interesting node of information indeed.

His gaze touched on the big chronometer on the navigation console, the one that set ship-time for the rest of the *Enterprise*. It read 1405.

There was nothing world smashing in that. However, he distinctly remembered the time on his wall chronometer as he was leaving his cabin. 1404, it said. And when he'd been searching his desk for a certain cassette before—before falling asleep—he'd happened to notice the time on the desk timepiece.

It had read 1400.

Not shockingly significant, perhaps, but—

Spock, who'd been watching Kirk indirectly ever since the other had returned to the bridge, noticed Kirk's confusion.

"Is something wrong, Captain?"

"I'm not . . . I'm not sure, Spock."

"Do you feel all right, sir?" This from an alarmed Sulu.

"Fine, Mr. Sulu, just fine. But am I?" He turned to Spock, mumbled half to himself, "I'd gone back to my quarters to dictate the rest of the rescue report . . . I remember that much. And I seem . . . to have fallen asleep. But the odd thing is, Mr. Spock, I can't recall moving from my desk to the bed. And I can't ever remember falling asleep so quickly—and so soundly—for just a few minutes.

"If I was as tired as all that, it seems I ought to have slept an hour or so."

"Possibly you needed the rest more than you think, Captain," suggested Spock, having no conclusions yet to jump to. "The body has its own system of checks and balances in that regard. You obviously required only the briefest of naps."

"In any case, nothing has changed since you left. We're still on course through the neutral zone to Rator III."

"But I don't remember going to—" Kirk stopped, looked at Spock in sudden amazement as his last words penetrated. "The Romulan Neutral Zone?"

"It is the only neutral zone we were near, Captain," the first officer replied with gentle irony.

"I gave no authorization to enter it, Mr. Spock. Did you order a course change?"

"No, sir," Spock replied, now equally confused. "You did."

"Ridiculous!" Kirk's mind was spinning. First a highly unnatural nap, and now Spock seemed to have gone crazy. Or maybe he was still asleep and this was all a bad dream.

If so, it was long past time for him to wake up.

"No one in Starfleet would issue such an order unless it was a matter of life and death, Spock."

"I believe that was the rationale you employed, Captain." He turned and moved a toggle switch on the instrument panel above his head. There was a small screen set into the panel. Both he and Kirk stared at it.

The screen came to life, and the scene that had taken place on the bridge only moments before was repeated.

"Weren't you going to your cabin, sir?" intoned a recorded Sulu as Kirk watched incredulously.

"I've already been there, Mr. Sulu . . . set a direct course for Rator III."

"Through the Romulan Neutral Zone, sir?"

"That was an order, Helmsman."

Kirk turned away from the damning screen. He'd had enough. More than enough. "That will do, Spock." Spock obligingly shut off the recording and swiveled to face his captain.

Kirk leaned back in the chair, very thoughtful. A number of explanations suggested themselves. As he examined each one and moved on to the next, they grew progressively outrageous and less and less realistic.

One thing he did know, though. Until this was all worked out and a reasonable explanation *did* suggest itself, he had to get off the bridge.

"Mr. Sulu, locate Mr. Scott and have him report to the bridge to take command, please." He rose and headed towards the exit. Spock moved to accompany him.

"Also, Mr. Sulu," he said back over his shoulder, "plot a course to take the *Enterprise* out of the neutral zone at warp-six. Lieutenant M'ress, put the ship on yellow alert."

"Certainly, Captain," acknowledged the concerned lieutenant.

"Yellow alert, sir?" wondered Spock as the doors joined behind them.

"I think it's necessary, Spock, until I can get a handle on this situation. I don't feel in a position to take any chances . . . with whatever's going on here. Surely by now you've noticed that both my actions and my orders of the past hour have been, well, contradictory."

"I confess that something of the sort had occurred to me, Captain. But the reasons why—"

"Mr. Spock," Kirk's voice was grim, "I don't remember giving those orders to enter the neutral zone. I left the bridge, went to my cabin, fell asleep for a few moments, and returned to the bridge. That's all."

As usual, Spock's logic took precedence over tact, though Kirk didn't notice. He wanted answers, not sympathy. Too many vital things were at stake.

"Perhaps it would be a good idea to have Dr. McCoy examine you, Captain?"

"I agree absolutely. If I've become subject to mental blackouts, let alone physical ones, during which I give dangerous orders, then I've become a danger to the ship. I can't begin to imagine what's happened to me, but I can't take chances with a possibility like that."

He hit a switch, and the elevator lights shifted from vertical to horizontal. They were now moving down the length of the *Enterprise*.

It still didn't add up.

The instruments themselves continued to check out, efficiency bordered on a hundred percent, and yet they persisted in coughing up the same ridiculous readings. McCoy muttered to himself, bent for the umpteenth time to try to correlate the numbers on the scanner with those in a printed table of fine print glowing on a small readout screen.

The door chimed and he didn't look back. The figure of Carter Winston walked into the examination room. It watched patiently as McCoy continued matching figures that didn't match the way they were supposed to. Eventually McCoy glanced irritably to see who had entered. When he recognized Winston, he smiled a quick greeting before returning to his work.

"Hello, Winston," he said while running a new set of figures across the screen. "Still trying to figure this out. Sometimes I wonder if I shouldn't have taken more Instrumentation in med school."

So intent was McCoy on his study that he failed to notice the transformation behind him—a transformation that would have confused his instruments a good deal more.

He didn't see Winston place his arms over his chest, didn't see him dissolve like instant pudding and become a strange alien apparition, one that glided across the smooth floor on thick appendages with the grace of a ballerina.

"Winston, I've been over your tests two dozen times, and I don't think—" A tentacle rose, touched the back of Mc-Coy's neck. The doctor slumped in his seat.

The alien thing caught him easily and carried him into the adjoining laboratory. As it placed the doctor on the floor, the sound of the examination-room door could be heard operating.

Anne Nored peered into the deserted room. "Dr. Mc-Coy?" She took a step inside and the door automatically closed behind her. "Dr. McCoy?"

In the lab, the creature made motions with its tentacles. Seconds later a duplicate Dr. McCoy was standing over the limp form of the original. Anne Nored walked over to McCoy's workbench. She idly examined the scanner and the other devices McCoy had been pouring over without touching any of them. There was a slight shuffling sound and she jerked to her right.

"Dr. McCoy, you startled me."

Winston/McCoy stepped out of the lab, making sure the door closed behind him. "Nothing startles you, Anne, you're a security officer, and one of the best. Can I help you?"

"Oh, all right, so I was role playing." She smiled, but it faded quickly to an expression of awkwardness. "I thought this might be easy, Doctor, but it's not. I don't know if you can . . . I just thought . . . well, I have to talk to somebody. And the other gals," she smiled a little again, "have a tendency to be less than serious about such things. I'd like to laugh at it, too, but I can't. It hurts too much. So I thought maybe you. . . ?"

Winston/McCoy seemed to hesitate, then gestured to a chair. Anne sat down gratefully. When she didn't seem able to continue, Winston/McCoy spoke.

"Let me guess. It's about you and Carter Winston." He paused for a moment, added, "He told me a little about it when I was examining him."

"How much is 'a little,' Doctor?" Again Winston/McCoy appeared to pause.

"Enough."

"Doctor, what am I going to do?" she finally blurted desperately. "I know you're not a psychiatrist, and I don't think I need that. I'm not mentally unbalanced. I don't think, but I still love him." The corners of her mouth twisted upwards a little.

"Come to think of it, love is classified by some as a state of temporary mental unbalance, isn't it?"

"Only by poets, writers of romantic fiction, and the French," Winston/McCoy replied. He turned and focused his attention on the blank wall opposite.

"I'm sure he'd like to feel the same way about you, Anne. He also told me something of the times you two had together, of the experiences you shared. Not a great deal. but I think I can understand the depth of feeling you had for each other.

"But it all may be impossible to recapture, Anne. Five years can be forever to someone. People change. People in love more frequently than most. And one thing I can tell you with assurance—Carter Winston's been through changes no other human being ever experienced." His voice dropped and he murmured, "Yes, people change."

"Well, I haven't!" she finally shouted. "What am I supposed to do? What *can* I do?"

"If he asked you to forget him," said Winston/McCoy, "I think you should try to do just that. Or would you prefer that he lie to you, tell you what you want to hear, intentionally deceive you. Do you want him to do that?"

"Oh, no. He's the gentlest, most thoughtful man I've ever known. Ever will know. And I don't think he could carry it off very well. Lying's not in his nature."

"Well, then, you see?" Winston/McCoy insisted. "If he doesn't want you any longer, for whatever reasons, and he's asked you to forget him, then all I can do is suggest that you take that as an honest concern for you and do it."

"You have no knowledge of what he's been through, of what—" and Winston/McCoy half smiled "—unusual changes may have taken place in the years he's been gone. As a physician I can only advise you . . . and also as a friend. Forget Winston."

"Forget Carter—" The words came without any force, any conviction behind them. She seemed ready to argue further, but the door chimed. Kirk and Spock entered. It was hard enough to articulate such intimate feelings in front of the ship's doctor. It would be impossible in front of the ship's captain and first officer.

So instead of continuing, she stood. "Thank you, Doctor McCoy. I'll consider your advice."

"Do that, Anne . . . Lieutenant Nored."

Kirk studied the security officer as she left, then turned to Winston/McCoy. The doctor smiled pleasantly.

"What can I do for you, Jim?"

"Bones, I need a complete medical examination."

"On Carter Winston? But I've already—" Kirk waved him off impatiently.

"No, no. For myself. Something's just happened that—" He stopped. The figure of Winston/McCoy had abruptly turned away from him and was now engaged in studying a microtape index file mounted on the far wall.

"I'm afraid I'll have to make it later in the day, Captain. I have too many tests to process right now."

Kirk had too many thoughts whirling through his head to react to that, but Spock looked puzzled. Being the favorite target of McCoy's brash wit, maybe he was more sensitive to the doctor's moods—or changes in personality.

"Carter Winston's, for example?" Spock inquired. Winston/McCoy half-turned, but didn't look at them.

"No, that one's done, completed. No trouble at all, Mr. Spock. Standard tests run, checked out completely normal."

"Are you sure there's no possibility you made an error?" persisted Spock.

Now it was Kirk's turn to look questioningly at his first officer instead of vice versa. It wasn't like Spock to question another officer's work—especially McCoy's. But it would be like McCoy—almost required of him—to respond with some especially devastating remark.

Instead, the doctor only chuckled. "Well, there's always that chance. I'll go over them again, if you like."

"No, that won't be necessary, Bones. I'll drop by later for that examination, when you're not so busy. Let's go, Spock." Kirk turned and started for the door.

When it was securely shut behind them and they were out

in the empty reception room, both men stopped and exchanged uncertain looks.

"Captain, did you notice Dr. McCoy's reaction when I asked him if there was a possibility he might have made an error in Carter Winston's tests?"

Kirk nodded.

"Yes. He didn't jump all over you when you questioned his accuracy. That isn't normal."

"Excuse me, Captain—'jump all over me?' "

"Said something along the lines of, 'there's as much chance of that as my falling down with . . .' "

" 'hysterical laughter at a joke of mine,' " finished Spock.

"Yes, that's it. What's even less normal is that he agreed with you. He conceded the chance, and that's not like Bones at all. If there's anything he's supremely confident about, it's his own competence as a physician. Come to think of it, it was also not like him to put off my request for a physical."

"I quite agree, Captain. Which means—"

"I don't know what it means," Kirk muttered, "except that maybe there are two officers on this ship who need medical checks. Come on!"

They burst into the sick-bay examination chamber and were dumbfounded at what they saw. Or rather, at what they didn't see.

The room was empty.

Neither officer feeling particularly bright at that moment, they moved to make a thorough search of the room.

"There is only one entrance to these inner medical rooms," mused Spock thoughtfully. "For security reasons, and for quarantine purposes. There are not a great many places a man could hide."

"No," agreed Kirk, "and I think—"

"Ohhhh . . ."

Kirk and Spock were at the entrance to the nearby lab in seconds. Both men were wary, expecting—they weren't sure what—to come charging pell-mell out at them. But the door slid back normally at Kirk's touch and nothing barred their entrance.

McCoy was sitting up in the middle of the floor, rubbing the side of his head. He looked very much as if he'd just absorbed a substantial dose of something a good deal stronger than eggnog.

"Bones?"

McCoy didn't react at first. Then he looked up at them, still dazed.

"Must have . . . must have fallen asleep . . . somehow, I guess. A little nap—"

"A little nap," echoed Kirk, reflecting on the similarity of a recent experience. "I think I have an idea what you mean, Bones."

"Doctor, you are a man of curious habits," observed Spock, "but I have never known you to nap on the laboratory floor. Elementary logic dictates that even an examination table would be far more comfortable, as well as—" He paused in midsentence at Kirk's raised hand. The captain was staring intently around the inner laboratory.

Ever since they'd entered he had not felt quite right about something. And not because of what they half expected to find—without knowing what it was. No, it was a feeling he still couldn't pin down. Spock would say it was illogical, but damn it, he felt *something* was wrong!

"Something is not right with this room."

McCoy made a rapid examination of his laboratory. His gaze returned eventually to Kirk's uncertain face.

"Everything looks okay to me, Jim."

"No," Kirk objected hurriedly. "Take a moment and think about it, Bones." Before McCoy could comment, the captain moved quickly to shut the door behind them.

"Both of you, study the room. There's definitely something different from the last time I was in here. I can't put my finger on it yet, but—"

The three officers started a patient, methodical survey of the laboratory. There didn't seem to be a great deal that might conceal some startling revelation. It didn't help that they had no idea what to look for, Kirk included.

Desks, wall decorations, shelves full of vials and tubes and neatly racked instruments, the gleaming surgical cases, emergency power chargers for use in case of shipboard power failure, the big portable sterilizer, three examination tables . . .

Even an examination table would be far more comfortable, Spock had said.

Kirk smiled then. "All right, Winston, you can come out now." Both Spock and McCoy turned their attention to the captain, Spock interestedly, McCoy incredulously.

Kirk walked forward until he was standing directly in front of the examination table farthest to the left. He spoke not behind it nor under it, but to it.

"I suggest you show yourself, Winston, or whatever you are. The masquerade's over."

Making no sense of the scene and getting no elucidation from Kirk, McCoy slowly got to his feet and whispered to Spock.

"Did you say that *I'm* a man of curious habits, Spock? Jim's talking to a table!"

"I don't think so, Doctor." An idea was beginning to solidify in the first officer's mind as he added certain known factors and proceeded toward a result. Evidently Kirk had already gotten there.

The captain stepped back from the table and turned his attention to one of the nearby wall shelves. Kirk spoke to the others as he studied the labels on the neat rows of crystal vials.

"There used to be only two examination tables in this room, as I recall, Bones." He focused his attention on the top row of containers. "Now there seem to be three."

Spock said nothing, but McCoy suddenly found himself nodding in agreement. "I just realized that too, Jim. But even so, what—" McCoy shut up. Whatever was happening here ought to come to a head pretty soon.

Kirk finally selected one of the smaller vials from the shelf. He walked back to stand next to the table.

The vial in his hand was made of thick, heat-formed artificial quartz alloyed with certain other metallic and ceramic components. It contained a small amount of thin purple fluid. When McCoy saw which vial the captain had removed he started forward, then stopped.

Again, Kirk directed his comments to the table. The flat, unmistakably inorganic surface gleamed brightly in the overhead lights, small wheels and dials sparkling with polish. McCoy studied it till his eyes hurt, looking for some hidden sign he might have missed that would reveal the table's mysterious secrets to him.

It looked like an examination table. Kirk tapped it with one finger, and there was a faint ping.

It sounded like an examination table.

By Andromeda, it *was* an examination table!

"This is a vial of orientine acid," Kirk informed the table solemnly. "It will burn through just about anything but this holding crystal. If you've never seen it work, I'll be happy to demonstrate." He patted the table again. "On you."

There was a reasonable pause. Then Kirk raised the vial over the table and moved his thumb toward the cap release set into one side. The table shimmered suddenly, the sort of eye-tricking flutter of things seen out of one's corner of vision that aren't there anymore when you turn to look at them. The table rippled dreamily and changed form.

A moment later it was no longer an examination table. In its place stood a tall creature of thick, cabled limbs and shining eye lenses that stared back at them unwinkingly.

"I saw that," said a gaping McCoy, "but I don't believe it."

"A Vendorian, Doctor," Spock informed him. "Their planet is quarantined, and few people ever see them. Their ability to rearrange their molecular structure at will to resemble anything of the same approximate mass—and their practice of deceit as a way of life—places them very much off-limits to others."

"Their unusual abilities could be of considerable value to the Federation, or to others. But as desirable as their physical attributes might be, psychologically they are still unfit for participation in a community of worlds.

"Mr. Spock, get a security team down here on the double."

"Yes, Captain." Spock turned to leave. As he did so McCoy moved to get out of his way. Those few steps were all that was necessary to bring him within reach of the Vendorian.

Powerful tentacles snapped out and enveloped the doctor in a constricting grasp.

"Jim!"

Kirk and Spock moved as one toward the Vendorian. Unraveling the clutching limbs, the alien sent McCoy spinning and stumbling into the other two officers. All three fell to the floor.

Moving with surprising agility for such an awkard-looking creature, the Vendorian dashed past them. Spock managed to roll over in time to make a grab at the fleeing alien. All he got was a handful of something that felt like snakeskin without the scales. He couldn't hold it. A second later it was out the doorway and long gone.

Kirk was on his feet, racing for the exit. Spock made a move as if to follow, instead changed direction and went directly to the wall communicator.

"Spock to bridge—put me on the ship's intercom, Lieutenant." And then, seconds later, "All security teams, intruder alert! All security teams, repeat, intruder alert—"

Kirk was out in the hall. He looked to his right, then left, just in time to catch a last glimpse of the Vendorian turning down an intersecting corridor. A security team raced around the far end of the hallway facing him a second later. Spock's voice sounded loud, replayed over every speaker in the starship.

"Intruder is a Vendorian, capable of assuming any shape or form of the same approximate mass . . ."

III

A Jeffries tube loomed nearby. The Vendorian, using its ability to look in all directions at once, satisfied itself that no pursuer was in sight. Then it clambered into the tube.

Moving like a big orange spider, it made its way up the channeled interior. Footsteps sounded below—far away now, muffled with increasing distance—as Kirk and the security team raced through the corridor below.

Near the top, the alien paused and crossed upper tentacles. Once more it shifted to the shape of Carter Winston. A few more centimeters, a careful look both ways, and then he scrambled out of the tube onto a new deck, setting the tube cover back into place.

There were drawbacks as well as advantages to assuming human shape. For one thing, he could no longer see in all directions. So he didn't see Anne Nored until he rounded a corner and nearly ran her down. She staggered and, reflexively, it seemed, he caught her to keep her from falling.

But this time, instead of moving into his arms, she pushed away and brought up her security phaser. It centered squarely on his chest.

Affecting an air of mild surprise he looked first at the phaser, then up at her.

"Anne, what are you doing?"

"My job," she replied tightly. "It isn't hard to guess who the intruder is. You're the only stranger aboard, Carter. Or whatever you are. A . . . a Vendorian." Running footsteps sounded from somewhere behind them. She stared at him, then threw a quick, nervous look over her shoulder.

It was only an instant, but Carter Winston's reflexes were faster than human. He knocked the phaser from her hand. It

232

skittered across the deck to bounce off the far wall. She ran to recover it. At the same time Kirk and a small group of security personnel rounded a far curve.

Anne picked up the phaser, turned and dropped to one knee, holding the phaser in both hands and balancing an elbow on her thigh. It was easy to take aim at the distant figure. She had a clear shot.

But she didn't fire. Instead, she slowly lowered the phaser to her side.

The security team pounded past in pursuit. Kirk slowed and stopped beside her.

"Lieutenant Nored, you could have stopped him . . . it. Why didn't you fire?"

She spoke slowly as she got to her feet, without looking at him. "I couldn't. I know some explanation is necessary, Captain, but—" She couldn't think of anything to say that would make her sound less of an idiot.

"I knew he had to be the intruder, but . . . I couldn't bring myself to fire!" Her voice was trembling.

"He's an alien, Lieutenant—not Carter Winston. A Vendorian. A shape-changing complex of orange tentacles topped by an inhuman brain."

"My mind tells me that, Captain, but there are other parts of me that don't convince so easily." There, she was right. She still sounded like an idiot.

"Lieutenant," and Kirk's voice was surprisingly devoid of reproach, "the man you loved no longer exists. Carter Winston is dead. He's probably been dead for years."

"I realize that, Captain. But I just—" She turned away. Words had become thoroughly inadequate. "Reason and love don't work well together."

"When you're a commander you can be profound, Lieutenant. For now—" He didn't get the chance to finish. Spock arrived, panting slightly.

"Security teams report no sign of the alien on this deck any longer, Captain."

"How do they know, Mr. Spock?" Kirk sighed. "I was afraid of this. Once out of sight, he can turn into anyone or anything on board this ship. I wonder why he chose to re-form as Carter Winston, instead of as Dr. McCoy or myself?"

"I cannot guess, Captain. I can only surmise that this constant shape changing is not as easy for him as it appears to be to us. He really requires a form capable of mobility now—an examination table or section of wall will no longer do, for example. Perhaps changing into a familiar shape is simpler and less tiring. He is obviously well acquainted with the shape of Carter Winston."

"As a matter of fact," Kirk began, then paused, grinning sardonically. Spock watched him patiently.

"You can at least share the idea with me, Captain, if not the actual humor."

"Oh, nothing, Spock. For a minute it occurred to me . . . I thought—" and he grinned wider, "I thought that you might be the Vendorian now." Spock did not smile, which was hardly a surprise.

"What makes you think I'm not, Captain?" Both eyebrows moved ceilingward. Kirk stopped chuckling, gave Spock an uncertain glance before grinning again.

"The Vendorian can change his shape, but not certain other things. I think I'll take a chance on your being you, Spock."

"That is most considerate of you, Captain. We find ourselves in complete agreement on who I am. The question remains," and he paused for effect, "are you who you claim to be?"

"I was with Lieutenant Nored while the alien was still present," Kirk claimed indignantly. "It's a definite problem, all right. If we're not careful he'll have us shooting at each other. But given time, we'll find him. It's only one problem."

Somewhere in space exists a formless, malignant entity who listens to the words of starship captains merely for the chance of playing their plans false. Said entity must have been listening to Kirk, for, as if on cue, the red-alert signal now commenced its visual and aural clamoring. A blinker just above them flashed insistently for attention.

Various crew members began to appear, running towards their battle stations. As any well-drilled crew should, they ignored their two senior officers in single-minded pursuit of current objectives—namely, getting to where they belonged as fast as was humanly or inhumanly possible.

"Now what?" Kirk's question was more resigned than hopeful. He moved to the flashing wall communications hookup.

"Hello, bridge? This is the captain speaking. Scotty? What's happening up there? What's the Vendorian up to now?"

"It's not the Vendorian, Captain," the chief engineer replied. "I wish it were. A pair of Romulan battle cruisers, sir, and if they're not on an intercept course we're about to witness the biggest cosmic coincidence since that double star in M-31 went nova together."

"All right, Scotty, keep a lid on things. We'll be right up."

"What was that you just said about dealing with only one problem, Captain?"

"Spock, if I didn't know that you weren't prone to malicious sarcasm, I'd . . . ahhh, never mind."

By the time they'd regained the bridge and Kirk had resumed his seat in the commander's chair and Spock his own at the library computer, the two Romulans were close enough for visual contact via the telescopic eyes of the main viewscreen.

If there were any chance they might have been Federation ships, that hope was soon laid to rest at the sight of their distinctive silhouette. In design and basic construction they were similar to the battle cruisers of the Klingon Empire. Insignia and certain minor but unmistakable differences branded them as Romulan.

Kirk's first thought was to get something down on record. Not only in case hostilities ensued, but also because such information would be needed for any legal actions that might arise out of this encounter. So he quickly activated the log.

He was about to begin the entry when a sudden thought struck him. No, not yet. It was too early to plan for pessimistic eventualities. He flicked off the official log, switched on the general recorder instead.

"Mr. Scott, any chance of us outrunning them?"

"Not now, sir," worried Scott, shaking his head once. "They were right on top of us, Captain, before our sensors even picked 'em up."

"It was as if they were waiting for us, Captain," Sulu added.

"Ummmm." Now he directed his voice and attention to the pick-up grid. "Due to interference by the Vendorian recently discovered on board in the guise of Carter Winston, the *Enterprise* has been detected by ships of the Romulan Empire while violating the Romulan Neutral Zone. By the terms of our treaty, the units of the Romulan fleet have a legal right to seize the *Enterprise*. To complicate matters, we have as yet been unable to apprehend the Vendorian responsible for this situation."

Given the laws against harming intelligent neutrals Kirk naturally didn't add his attendant thoughts—namely, that if and when they did find the troublemaking shape-changer, he'd take great pleasure in tying its seven body tentacles in knots and then opening them again . . . with a meat cleaver.

But right now he had a more difficult situation to focus his attention on.

"We're being scanned, Captain," came Uhura's voice. "And I'm picking up a communications beam. They're attempting to contact us." She hesitated. "Shall I throw up an interference screen, sir?" Kirk thought quickly.

"No point in trying to stall them, Lieutenant. I've got a hunch this particular bunch won't stall." He smiled grimly. "Let's hear what they've got to say. If there's visual with it, put it on the screen. I'd like to see who I'm dealing with . . . and if my face does them any good, they're welcome to it."

Visual there was.

When his humanoid image finally cleared on the main viewscreen the relaxed attitude of the Romulan commander only confirmed the suspicions taking root in Kirk's mind.

"You appear to have a propensity for trespassing in the neutral zone, Captain Kirk. I've been told it has happened once or twice before."

My, but wasn't he a smug one, Kirk thought. What Kirk said was different, however, smoothly conciliatory. That was the best attitude Kirk could fake; he couldn't quite bring himself to be deferential towards this oily character.

"It was not deliberate, I assure you."

The Romulan commander's reply was dry. "It never is.

But the terms of the treaty are clear. They make no provisions for good intentions. I'd like to indulge in the sentiment your people are so fond of and ignore the treaty this time, but, of course, any attempt to contravene the articles, even for friendship's sake, could mean war."

"Surrender your ship, Captain. You will be well treated. We will release you and your crew at the nearest Federation outpost bordering the neutral zone."

Kirk thought furiously, considering. "I have your personal word of honor on that, Commander? . . ."

"Larus—Commander Larus. I swear by my family and my command, Captain. You and your personnel need have no worries." He tried hard not to gloat. "I have no personal quarrel with you. I must take your ship only to comply with the terms of the treaty between our two governments. I take no personal pleasure in this distasteful deed whatsoever."

I'll just bet you don't, you grinning so and so, Kirk silently cursed. His return smile, however, was equally pleasant.

"I'd like a few minutes to inform my crew. There will be certain preparations required."

"Of course, Captain Kirk. I understand perfectly. The shock, and all. Take all the time you need—up to five minutes your ship-time, no more." Abruptly, the screen blanked.

"Transmission ended, Captain," Uhura informed him. "But they're still scanning us."

"Fine. Let 'em scan us till their scanning computers get an electronic migraine." Kirk turned and activated a switch on the right armrest. Spock left his station and moved to stand next to the captain.

"Kirk to security. What's the status on the search for the Vendorian?"

"Nored here, sir." The voice of the lieutenant was calm and professional now, no sign of emotional upset. Good. "No progress yet. We have all decks under constant patrol. No one has seen it, but—"

"How do you know, Lieutenant?" snapped a frustrated Kirk. "Anyone might have walked right past the Vendorian a dozen times without seeing it."

"I don't think so, Captain." Nored's response was firm, confident. "Our patrols have their phasers set on low-power stun. I've given orders that they're to randomly beam everything they pass—walls, ceilings, fixtures—without design or selectivity. We'll end up with a lot of scorched paint, but I think the Vendorian will think twice before he considers staying in one disguise very long."

"And the patrols are traveling in tight groups, guarding one another. So I don't think there's much chance of him turning into one of our own people. At least the alien will be too busy changing shapes to cause any more trouble."

Kirk found himself in agreement with Nored's precautions. It ought to flush the alien out in the open. "Carry on, Lieutenant." He broke the connection and nodded toward the viewscreen where the Romulan ships were displayed again.

"As Scotty points out, Mr. Spock, this meeting is hardly a coincidence. The Romulans were expecting us from the first. The wreck of Winston's ship—I wonder what *did* happen to him—was used to slip a saboteur and spy on board. And what better spy than a shape-changing Vendorian who can become at will any of the spied-upon?

"When I went to my cabin he put me out long enough to take my shape. Then *he* came to the bridge and ordered the course change. By the time I recovered, well," he shrugged, "it was too late to swing free of the zone. A neat trap."

"It would seem so, Captain. Yet one thing continues to puzzle me."

"Spock?"

"How is it that the Romulans are able to persuade a Vendorian to work for them? I cannot think of a logical reason why one of the shape-changers should. I cannot imagine what inducements the Romulans could offer."

"We'll consider the question of motivation later, Mr. Spock. Right now we've got a starship to save." He looked to the helm. "Open a hailing frequency, Lieutenant M'ress. Uhura, you keep listening for more of the same from our friends out there. And keep monitoring their scans."

The feline navigation officer moved to obey, her tail flicking in nervous response. "I have contact, Captain," she purred. "Hailing frrequency was harrdly necessarry. They've been waiting forr us to rrespond, it seems."

Once again the view of the paired Romulan cruisers was replaced by a portrait of their commander. He was making a strong attempt, Kirk noted, to suppress his normal arrogance.

"Your time is up, Captain. I assume you are now prepared to turn your ship over to me."

"Wrong assumption, Commander."

"Captain," protested the Romulan indignantly, "you are outnumbered, outgunned, and legally in the wrong. I admire your courage, but permit me to say that you err in your tactical evaluation of the present situation."

"I have no choice, Commander," Kirk shot back. "If I were an innocent violator of neutral space that would lead to some discussion, yes. But the treaty also states that deception of any kind—false beacons, signals, anything—used to lure a vessel into the neutral zone are a provocation by the luring side and not by the intruder. It is you who are in violation of the treaty, not I."

"Lured, Captain?" protested the Romulan with admirable outrage. "How could we possibly *lure* a starfleet vessel so deeply into the neutral zone?"

"Through the use of a spy masquerading as a dead human named Carter Winston."

The Romulan commander paused before giving a sad shake of the head. "A shape-changing spy? Come now, Captain," he pleaded. "Your courage, it seems, is exceeded only by your imagination. Both are misdirected."

"You used a Vendorian," Kirk continued easily, "which, I might add, is also in violation of a number of treaties, not to mention a violation of the galactic quarantine of Vendoria itself."

Either the Romulan commander decided to abandon his bluff, or else all this forced camaraderie was getting on his nerves. His natural brusquesness abruptly came to the fore.

"Your five minutes are long since up, Captain. Either surrender your ship or prepare to fight."

"I will not surrender my ship," Kirk replied, spacing the words deliberately.

So they were going to fight, mused Chief Engineer Scott.

He had left the bridge after the red-alert signal and gone to his battle station back in engineering. Well, they'd had trouble with the Romulans before and had come out okay.

Even though they were outnumbered this time, he wasn't especially worried. Why, they'd give—

He paused at the top of the spiral ladder. Just in front of him, away from the ladder exit, a crewman was working in front of an open panel. The panel shouldn't have been open. And no one, but no one, should have been working at those relays without Scott's personal permission.

"Hey! What d'you think you're doin'?" The crewman turned quickly.

"Why, nothing, Chief." He walked over to the ladder exit and helped Scott up the last step. "Only this."

He touched Scott's shoulder with a hand. Moving rapidly, he managed to catch the slumping form of the chief engineer before it could slide back down the ladder. Pulling him gently out of the spiral he laid the limp body out on the deck. The crewman rose, again studying the open panel.

Someone else might come and he was in a hurry. Might as well revert to self. The extra limbs would make the job go faster. He crossed his arms, and blurred.

Using only a pair of tentacles for support, the Vendorian used the other five to tear at the thick cables running behind the open panel . . .

The first red light appeared on Sulu's console.

"Captain," he shouted as he worked frantically at the controls beneath the warning flash, "our deflector shields are coming down!"

Kirk cursed silently, pressed a switch on the chair. "Kirk to engineering. Bridge to engineering! Scotty, what's happening back there? Our shields are fading!"

In the main engineering room a tall subengineer rushed to the chattering intercom and acknowledged the call breathlessly.

"H . . . here, sir."

"Not very well you don't. Who is this?" Kirk demanded. "Who's talking?"

"Second Engineer Gabler, sir . . . Captain." Kirk glanced back at Spock. This was no time for disciplinary action. "Get those shields up again, Gabler—now!"

"I can't, sir!" yelled the other helplessly.

"Well then, rouse Mr. Scott from his nap and have him

do it!'' Now the response from the other end was one of complete confusion.

''I was just going to ask to speak to him, sir. Isn't he up forward with you?''

''No, he is not up forward with me, Mister. You know the chief's battle station is back there.''

''Yes, sir. But he isn't anywhere around, sir.''

''Well, then—!'' Kirk paused and counted to six, spoke more quietly. ''All right, Mr. Gabler. It is vital that we have our shields back as soon as possible. Do the best you can.''

''Aye, sir.'' Gabler switched off, looked around at the small cluster of engineers and technicians who'd gathered around the intercom station.

''Don't just stand there gaping like idiots! The deflector shields have dropped. Check your telltales, trace the leads, find the trouble spot!''

Immediately the group hurried to their positions. Gabler ran to his, too, but his mind wasn't on the technical problem at hand.

What had happened to the chief?

Meanwhile a telltale of a different kind was flashing on Sulu's console. ''Shuttle-bay doors are functioning, sir. The Vendorian must be trying to escape.''

''We still have some control over this ship,'' Kirk muttered through clenched teeth. ''Shut those doors, and lock all entrances to the shuttle bay.''

Sulu tried one switch, frowned.

''No response, sir.''

''Emergency override, Mr. Sulu,'' came Spock's quiet voice. ''Mechanism voluntary jam to prevent air loss.'' He glanced at Kirk as Sulu hurried to obey. ''We will not be able to operate the shuttle doors until the stripped relays and gears are replaced, Captain.''

Kirk hardly heard him. The same idea had occurred to him seconds after Spock had given the order.

''Doors closing, sir!'' reported Sulu excitedly. That was the signal for Kirk to jump from his chair.

''One problem down. Spock, take command. Talk to the Romulans. Stall them. Tell them anything. Tell them we're going to agree, but that I'm desperately thinking of a way to save face—their commander should understand that.

"Uhura, send a security team to the shuttle deck, but don't open the doors yet. We've got the Vendorian trapped, that's enough for now. I'll be back in engineering. I've got to find out what the devil's happening back there."

As he hurried rapidly toward the heart of the starship, Kirk pondered their chances. The shields hadn't fallen all the way, but the *Enterprise*'s defenses had been badly weakened. Even with all shields up and operating at full strength, the *Enterprise* versus two Romulan battle cruisers wasn't exactly a mop-up operation.

Now, with their shield strength down at least fifty percent, well—

At least, he mused with savage satisfaction, they'd prevented the escape of the Vendorian spy. Spock's query came back to him. He, too, wondered how the Romulans had managed to convince the shape-changer to do the dirty work for them. From what little he knew of Vendorian civilization, the alliance made no sense.

After what seemed like hours, he finally reached the main engineering bay. In response to his questions, a harried technician directed him up to another deck. A short climb and he emerged in the middle of another, larger group of milling crew members. One directed him forward. He found Gabler and Scott hunched over an open panel.

"What happened, Scotty?"

"Hello, sir. I'm sure I don't know. I came up here to battle-check the backup deflector-shield relays." His voice took on a tone of puzzled outrage. "And here was this common tech, calm as you please, taking the connections to pieces!"

"Now, the sight of me in such a situation ought to have frozen the good man solid to the deck—workin' unauthorized with such equipment. Instead, he just smiled confident as you please and came over to help me on deck. That's all I remember."

"He couldn't have been at it long, sir," put in Gabler. "We found the chief right after I talked to you."

"He was at it long enough," growled Scotty. The chief's attitude did not inspire feelings of confidence in Kirk.

"How long will it take to fix, Scotty?"

"At least two hours, Captain."

Two *hours!*

"Well, get on it. That's all." Kirk turned and left. He knew better than to make melodramatic pronouncements. If Scott said it would take two hours, it would do no good for Kirk to say, "Do it in one!" The chief engineer's time estimates were as reliable as his work. Two hours then, working at top speed, and he'd have his shields back.

But could they possibly stall the Romulans for two hours, when the Romulan commander had given him five minutes, and those reluctantly? They might not have two seconds left.

They had one bargaining chip left, just one—and that was the *Enterprise* herself.

Already the Romulan commander had admitted that his only interest was in the starship—intact and in working order. If the Romulan's sensors were worth a handful of components, they'd know by now that the *Enterprise*'s shields had been severely weakened. Kirk didn't think they'd hold off forcing a decision in order to give their Vendorian a chance to escape. If he got away, all well and good . . . a bonus. If not, he had served his purpose.

However, they *would* hesitate before destroying the prize they'd worked so hard to snare. How long the vision of the *Enterprise* as a captured ship would keep the Romulan commander's natural belligerence in check Kirk didn't know, and that was the crucial factor.

A destroyed *Enterprise* would be a small blow to Federation strength compared to a fully operational captured one—but a blow nonetheless.

Kirk had no choice. He'd have to take the chance the Romulans wanted the starship badly enough to hold off firing on her. Nerves and not phasers would decide the outcome of this confrontation.

He smiled and felt a little better.

There were worse things to bet on than the avarice of a Romulan. . . .

IV

A single shuttle craft was lined up facing the *Enterprise*'s bay doors. Those doors wouldn't open now until a number of highly trained people had replaced certain stripped bearings and other deliberately ruined parts.

Three security guards had actually made it into the bay before the order to lock all doorways had taken effect. One of them was lying slumped across the open portway leading into the shuttle. Another lay crumpled at the foot of the ramp leading up into it.

The third stood quietly facing the other occupant of the soundless chamber.

Anne Nored kept her phaser pointed at him. The hand holding it didn't waver, didn't shake. Neither did her voice.

"You're not getting past me this time. I've learned my lesson."

The form of Carter Winston nodded slowly. "Yes, he said you were like this. Efficient, professional, as well as affectionate and beautiful. You're quite everything he said you were, Anne." The muzzle of the powerful phaser didn't dip a centimeter.

There was suspicion in her gaze, hesitancy in her voice— but she had to ask.

"Carter . . . what did he say? How . . . how do you know him so well?"

The Winston/Vendorian spoke. Despite the fact that instinct told her she should regard its every word as a clever lie, there was something in Winston's voice that . . . no, darn it, not Winston's! Only a sly mimicry, an uncanny imitation.

Reproduction or not, something in the voice sounded almost honest.

"He said many things. Some were feelings, deep feelings he could not always fully express or adequately convey. Emotions that, while I understood the words and the flat meanings of them, clearly held a good deal more than I could comprehend. Language can sometimes be infuriatingly uncommunicative, can tease and confuse instead of enlighten.

"I tried hard to understand these feelings. So many of the ideas and concepts that he tried to convey to me were new, alien, strange—but always intriguing. The less I understood, the more I wanted to know." Winston shook his head.

"My people have their faults, but they are compounded by this peculiar ability of ours to mimic others, to change our shape. Something so natural to us seems so frighteningly strange to other intelligent beings. I understand that lower creatures on many worlds can perform similar feats. But when the ability is coupled with intelligence, other races grow nervous.

"Sometimes," he continued bitterly, "we—" His voice shifted back to a more gentle tone. "But Carter Winston truly loved you."

The phaser shifted ever so slightly, but still remained fixed on the figure in front of her. Blazes, where were the backup security personnel?

She had no way of knowing that Kirk had ordered the shuttle bay sealed off from the rest of the ship. Where was the captain, or Mr. Spock? Someone to give orders, to take this responsibility off her hands.

She ought to have said nothing to the creature, ought to have kept her mouth shut, and at least beamed it slightly in one leg to restrict its movement.

Instead, she asked softly, "How did he die?"

"Winston's ship did indeed encounter severe meteor activity in open space. But the damage it sustained was not from the swarm Captain Kirk found me drifting in. The deflector shields of his small ship were too weak to protect him from the violent assault of that original storm.

"The shields held only long enough for him to locate a possible landing site and refuge. The only one—Vendoria. Winston knew that world was under edict, forbidden to travelers, but he had no choice in the matter. It was a miracle he managed to land his vessel at all. Neither he nor his ship, however, survived the landing intact. His injuries were severe.'' Winston shuffled his feet.

''As is our custom, upon conclusion of primary surgery he was left in the care of a single one of us.'' He looked straight at her. ''Me. He lived on for almost four of your years before the damage to his system exceeded the repair capabilities of our medical science.''

''We became very close in those four years.'' There was a pause while the two looked at each other—one perhaps a little too human, the other a great deal less so.

Or was he?

''You're so much like him—his voice, his little gestures, his mannerisms. Even the inflections in certain words.''

''You must understand, Anne, that my people enjoy our talent for mimicry. It is pleasure to us. But because of it we are cut off from the rest of the civilized galaxy. Therefore anything new to imitate is regarded as a great novelty. To a large extent it becomes the exclusive property of its discoverer. So it was with myself and Carter Winston.

''I often went about in his shape, this shape. For longer and longer periods of time. A most remarkable form. Wearing it gave me the greatest pleasure, because it fit so well not only physically but mentally.

''And I think Winston himself enjoyed seeing me in his own image. While my own form was not repulsive to him—as an interstellar trader he had no primitive shape prejudices—I think the chance to see and to speak with . . . himself . . . made it easier for him in his last days.'' Winston smiled.

''It was not as though he died with only an alien monster at his side.''

''And he did say that he loved me?''

''Yes. Often. And that brings up another problem.'' He hesitated. ''You see, I feel I absorbed a great many of the attitudes and emotions he felt. The longer I was with him, the more strongly ingrained these attitudes became. I do not know how it is with humans, but a Vendorian cannot remain in close association, let alone in the same shape, of another being without becoming in a sense a part of him.

''There were times, after our association had grown close, that when Winston grew hungry, I was hungry. If he felt tired and exhausted, I grew tired and exhausted. It became deeper than that. If he felt pain then I, in his form, was hurt. We would commiserate together on his sad situation. I would cheer him and he would attempt to raise my spirits.''

''Our unity grew even to the point where when he would feel homesick, I could feel a deep longing for a world I had never seen, would never set foot on. And,'' his voice dropped lower, ''his love for you was very, very strong. I could not help but be affected by such a strong emotion.'' He looked up at her again.

''Because I was there when he died, Anne, it did not end.''

Unwillingly, she found herself shaking. She let the phaser drop low, lower. He could have made a move toward her at any time now, but he didn't. All thoughts of aggression had vanished from her mind. A suspicious moisture began to form at the corners of her eyes. She raised a free hand, tried to brush it away. It wasn't possible. Tears started to trickle down her cheeks in most unmilitary fashion.

Both hands came up, but this time it was to reach out to him, instinctively.

''Carter—''

He moved close. One hand touched the fingers gripping the phaser. She didn't resist. His hands moved high, held her firmly by the shoulders and pushed gently away.

''You must not weep for me.''

''Carter, I—''

''Anne, this is what I am.''

He stepped back and crossed both arms over his chest. Carter Winston disappeared.

In his place rose a tall, seven-tentacled entity, a nightmare shape of thick orange cables and a bulbous, bejeweled head. It spoke, and the voice was the voice of Carter Winston—but now sounding oddly distant, echoing. It came from a voice-box no longer human.

''How could you love . . . this?''

Her hands dropped from her mouth, to which they'd jerked with the first gasp of surprise. Like most humans, she'd never seen a Vendorian. The form was as inhuman and thoroughly alien as the wildest dreams of drug-induced narcosis.

But the first shock passed. The creature crossed tentacles and once again shifted into the familiar figure of Carter

Winston. There was sympathy in its once-again human voice and . . . something else?

"You see why I told you it would be best to forget me," the alien said, unaware of the change in pronoun.

"But unfortunately, *I* can't," came the voice of Captain Kirk. Both figures turned to face a side entrance. Kirk had arrived moments ahead of the requested security team. He held a phaser on Winston.

He never had a chance to use it, because the shock wave from the first bolt fired by the Romulan phaser banks threw them all to floor of the hangar. Dazed, Kirk rolled over, tried to force himself to his feet and focus the phaser at the same time. His vision cleared rapidly and he glanced around the shuttle bay, looking frantically in all directions.

As expected, the alien was gone again.

He noticed Anne Nored. She had one hand on her forehead and was having difficulty getting to her feet. Kirk helped her up.

"Carter . . . Carter . . ."

"The Vendorian is gone, Lieutenant Nored," said Kirk tightly. "I've got to get back to the bridge. Will you be all right?"

"Yes, just a bump. I've got to get back to security." She took a step and almost fell over.

Kirk half carried, half guided her to the exit. The security team met them there.

"Ensign Tuan reporting, Captain." The excited junior officer was trying to look at Kirk respectfully and over his shoulder into the cavernous shuttle bay at the same time. "Where's the alien, sir?"

"The alien is gone again, Mr. Tuan. And stop waving that phaser around before you hurt yourself." The ensign looked properly abashed and hurried to holster the weapon. Kirk sighed.

"Post a guard here. The outer doors are jammed, but the alien might try to burn an exit for the shuttle. Alert the armory and engineering. And security central. They'll have to start the search over again, but maybe we can keep the thing confined to this deck, this time."

"Yes, sir."

"Lieutenant Nored, somehow I think security can manage

without you." She didn't look up at him. "You come to the bridge with me. There's a chance you might be useful there."

He felt like adding a few other choice comments. She'd had the alien trapped again and once more it had escaped. While he found himself sympathizing with her state of mind, he couldn't condone her actions. Mr. Spock would be even less understanding. Meanwhile, it would be better for her on the bridge, away from the actual search. It was a better alternative than the brig.

Besides, it would be hard to claim she had let the thing get away voluntarily. The Romulans had contributed to that.

Yes, what about the Romulans?

Spock was waiting with a report. He started talking before Kirk had resumed his seat. Anne Nored wandered around the bridge, looking lost. She was still numbed, and not entirely from being thrown to the deck.

"Direct hit, Captain," Spock informed him calmly. "There is some damage to the secondary propulsive systems. Their commander has apparently weighed his choices and has concluded we've had enough time to make up our minds. He's ready to fight."

"I only felt one shock wave, Mr. Spock. No subsequent attacks?"

"No, Captain. Only the single phaser strike."

"Then he's hoping to force our hand, one way or the other, but he still wants the ship. There's nothing in the damaged section but automatic machinery. He's trying to avoid casualties at this point, trying to disable us without giving a reason for an all-out battle."

He looked back to Lieutenant M'ress, at the communications console now, as she broke in on his summary.

"The Rromulan commanderr is signaling, sirr. Shall I put him on the scrreen?"

"I'd rather you put him . . . go ahead, Lieutenant."

A moment later the face of the Romulan leader had once more taken the place of his ships on the main viewscreen.

The Romulans would make terrible poker players, Kirk reflected. Their expressions were even broader and less inhibited than those of humans. Their ambassadors and consuls must have a terrible time practicing the wiles of diplomacy.

For example, the commander now undoubtedly thought

he was maintaining the Romulan equivalent of a straight face, but his expectant smile reached from ear to ear.

"Captain Kirk," he began, and there was unconcealed anticipation in his voice, too. I wonder what he's up to now, Kirk mused. He didn't relish the pickle they'd gotten themselves into.

"All our main batteries are trained on your ship. I have observed a . . . ah, singular lack of defensive effort on your part. To resist at this point would be not only useless but criminally wasteful of life.

"If you have no regard for yourself or your ship, think of your crew. Our recent attack was intentionally directed at uninhabited areas of your ship. I cannot guarantee the selectivity of gunners in the future." He managed to look apologetic as he leaned forward slightly.

"Will you now surrender your vessel? As you know, my people are not in the habit of giving second chances."

That was the Romulan's way of telling him that, yes, he wanted the *Enterprise* and no, he didn't want it enough to give him any more time. Kirk's thoughts raced.

He might be able to figure a way out of this, if the back of his mind wasn't busy worrying about what the Vendorian was up to. And he could cope with the Vendorian if it wasn't for the Romulans. But the two of them together!

It didn't matter. He didn't have any more time, anyway.

Without full deflectors, he thought angrily, we're just a clay pigeon for them. Kirk had never seen a clay pigeon in his life and probably wouldn't have recognized one if it had fallen into his lunch. But archaic metaphors had a way of sticking around in the terran language.

"Practicality does suggest capitulation at this point, Captain," observed Spock. "I, too, see no solution to our present dilemma. There are other starships, there is no other self."

Of course, there are other ships, Kirk thought. But how much chance would he have of getting another command after giving up the *Enterprise* without firing a shot?

And what chance did his crew have? Could he guarantee their safety once the *Enterprise* was in Romulan hands?

Sulu had been morosely monitoring inship as well as exterior sensors, checking his gauges and dials. Now he inter-

rupted Spock's advice excitedly . . . interrupted Kirk's
depression. Interrupted all action on the bridge.

"Captain, I don't understand . . . but the deflector shields
are coming up again!"

In two steps Kirk was at his shoulder, staring down at the
indicators in disbelief. "It's only one shield—"

"Yes, sir, but it's our prime defensive screen, and it's
between us and the Romulans. Look," he pointed to one
energy gauge, "it's operating at full strength."

Kirk rushed back to his chair. A wise man does not question the sudden appearance of a cache of spears when the
barbarians are at his gate. He throws them. Time to question
their origin when pulling them *out* of his attackers.

They had to act immediately, before some idle technician
on one of the battle cruisers noticed the resurgence of strength
in the *Enterprise*'s defensive fields.

"Mr. Sulu, aim for the propulsion units on the lead Romulan vessel. Phasers and photon torpedoes in combination." Sulu's hands played the controls like an organ.

"Phasers and torpedoes ready, sir."

"We've got to get one with this first burst, Mr. Sulu."

"Will do, Captain."

"Fire!"

"Firing, sir."

"Evasive action. Mr. Sulu, keep that good screen between
us and the Romulans."

The Romulan commander had long since vanished from
the screen. M'ress had automatically substituted the sensor
view of the two battle cruisers. It was too bad, in a way. Kirk
would have given a lot to see the commander's face right
now.

He could see the phaser beams striking at the rear of the
nearest ship.

"They're pursuing, sir," reported Sulu evenly. "Both of
them."

Kirk only nodded. They'd probably expected him to try
and run, but not to fight.

There was a sudden bright flash at the stern of the first
ship. The Romulan's screens had handled the *Enterprise*'s
heavy phasers, but one, possibly two, of the powerful photon
torpedoes had slipped through their screens. The wounded

vessel seemed to hesitate, then vanished instantly from the screen—not destroyed, but slowed.

"Second vessel firing Captain," said Spock. Kirk tensed.

"Phasers and—" Before he could finish, the bridge rocked to a strong shock wave as the *Enterprise* took the force of the attack from the remaining pursuer. This was no disabling strike, but one designed to tear the starship apart.

The amazingly resurgent deflector shield held. Artificial gravity stabilized and the regular ship's lights remained on.

"Minor damage to E and H decks," reported Spock moments later. "Casualties on E deck, minor hulling and air loss in four compartments. Automatic sealant is handling the damage."

"Lock on second target," Kirk ordered calmly. He noticed M'ress looking at him with admiration. She didn't sweat, but she was panting heavily—nervous, Kirk knew. Obviously she didn't know that starship captains only sweated on the inside of their skins. That's why they were so irritable all the time.

"Locking on second vessel, Captain," came Sulu's reply. A second later, "Locked on, sir."

"Phasers and torpedoes, Mr. Sulu. Stagger the torps, try to run them at the same spot." Maybe they could overload the Romulans' shields at one point. Discouraging her ought to be as effective as destroying her.

"Firing, Captain."

There were brilliant flashes on the screen from the vicinity of the Romulan ship as her screens reeled under the dual assault. Sulu's eyes remained glued to his indicators, his voice a battle monotone.

"Phasers . . . direct hit, sir." There was a flash so bright it blanked out the screen for a moment. "Two photon torpedo hits."

But the Romulan, now warned, had brought his shields up to maximum power and had taken the blinding energies without damage. Kirk heard Spock's report and tried not to look disappointed. If the Romulan computers got a torpedo in behind their one good deflector shield . . .

"Prepare to fire again, Mr. Sulu."

"Standing by, sir."

The third attack wasn't necessary. One second the Romulan ship was hard in pursuit, the next it was fading rapidly from sensor range as her commander broke off the engagement and headed back into the depths of the neutral zone.

"Losing contact, sir," reported Sulu. "She's arcing."

Kirk's voice was full of relief and satisfaction. "Going back to help her disabled companion. Good. A fight to the end wouldn't do either side any good."

"Maybe the pounding we gave the first one," Sulu began, but Kirk was shaking his head.

"I don't think so, Mr. Sulu. The Romulans exhibit a number of reprehensible characteristics, but cowardice isn't one of them. No, they were expecting our defenses to collapse. That's why they didn't attack right away. When our shields suddenly went back up—

"Their whole plan from the moment of interception was predicated on a number of things happening. When their carefully laid schedule started to go awry, they decided to call it off. The Romulans like their ambushes neatly planned in advance. They don't like surprises.

"Speaking of surprises, Mr. Spock, exactly how badly did we damage that other Romulan? Check your recorders, please." Spock turned back to the library computer console, activated the request.

"I hope it wasn't too bad," Kirk added. "Severe damage or loss of life might force the Romulan High Command into continuing a fight they've lost interest in. They've got a lot of pride." Spock's answer relieved Kirk's concern on that score.

"First vessel's main power supply was knocked out, Captain. Injuries to personnel should be minimal. She should be able to run on secondary drive, but slowly. With the aid of the other ship the Romulans should be able to repair her well enough to reach their nearest naval station."

Kirk grunted in satisfaction. He swung to look at the elevator as engineer Scott appeared, approaching him.

"Good work, Mr. Scott. That deflector shield went up just in time."

Scott's reaction was not what Kirk expected. Instead of a smile of pleasure at the compliment, the chief engineer looked confused, startled.

"But, sir, the shield connections haven't all been repaired

yet. I came forward to see if I could be of help up here. My technicians are still carrying out the final repairs. They'll need over an hour yet, just like I said.''

Spock left his library station and walked over to join the conversation.

"Interesting."

"But, confound it, Scotty, the shields went up! At least, the main one did. If you haven't finished repairs, then what—'' He paused. A sudden gleam of comprehension dawned.

"Of course! Winston, or rather, the Vendorian.''

"It is not outside the realm of possibility, Captain,'' agreed Spock. "If he could rearrange his own internal structure to become an examination table, one must assume that he could also rearrange himself to become—''

"A deflector shield?'' Despite the evidence that seemed to point to the Vendorian, Kirk was doubtful. "And take the uncontrolled energy of a battle cruiser's full assault phasers?'' He shook his head. He wanted to believe such a thing was possible, but—

"Vendorians are marvelous mimics, Mr. Spock, but super-beings they're not. No living organism could spread its substance that thin and take that kind of—''

"He did not become the deflector *shield*, Captain,'' Spock corrected. "There are many instruments—complex controls, switching elements and other electronic components—in a medical examination table. I cannot conceive of a single creature becoming a deflector shield, either, but a series of broken cables, force-links, and other damaged connections? Do not forget, the Vendorian had an excellent look at the very linkages he broke.''

Scott had been listening to all this and had achieved nothing except some practice in feeling twitchy. Now his curiosity turned to frustration.

"Will someone please tell me what's been goin' on?'' he pleaded, thoroughly confused.

Before either officer could reply, the doors to the elevator dilated again. They all glanced automatically in that direction.

The orange shape that half-stood, half-floated in the portal was by now familiar to Kirk and Spock, but the nightmarish image was something new to Scott and the other bridge personnel. M'ress hissed softly.

"What manner of beastie is that?" gulped Scott.

"That is your deflector shield, Mr. Scott," said Spock.

"My defle—" Scott's look showed he wasn't sure which was more alien—the thing in the doorway or the ship's first officer. He looked back at the Vendorian.

"That is essentially true," the Vendorian commented in the voice of Carter Winston. It sidled toward them. "I did what I could." Despite its multiple lenses, it turned and seemed to face Kirk, a human gesture.

"I assume the danger to your ship is over, Captain?"

"It is. Unless the Romulans have some other surprises."

"I do not believe that they do," the Vendorian replied. "I am glad. I'm sorry that I endangered your ship and your people. Such was not my intention."

Now maybe Kirk could get the answer to a question that had been bothering him ever since they found out that the strange spy was a Vendorian.

"Why did you do it? What possible reward could the Romulans have offered you?"

"To understand that, Captain, it is necessary to tell you a little about myself. The remainder can be supplied by Lieutenant Nored." Kirk glanced over at the lieutenant, who was watching the Vendorian closely.

"My . . . attachment . . . to the human Carter Winston provoked much comment among my people, Captain. I have always felt and acted somewhat differently from the Vendorian norm. Mental deviates are not treated with compassion on Vendoria.

"As Carter Winston continued to live and I continued to spend more and more time attending him, my aberration became much commented upon. But there was a lock, a bond between us that transcended mere shape and species. I felt I somehow had more in common with the injured human than with other Vendorians.

"They began to shun me. I became an outcast among my own kind, Captain. But this I did not mind . . . as long as Winston lived. But when he died, my people continued to look upon me with distaste, to avoid my company and presence. I grew by turns lonely, then bitter, and then desperately lonely once again.

"Though time passed, my situation did not change. I was still treated as a pariah. When a Romulan ship visited the town on whose outskirts I lived as a recluse—'' He paused. "They have been visiting Vendoria quite regularly, by the way, for the past several of your years, always hoping to ally themselves with my people. But we would have none of them.''

"Interesting," commented Spock. "I must make a note of that. I know my father, as well as a number of other ambassadors, will be interested in such information. I expect they will have a few words to exchange with their Romulan counterpart." He moved away, back to the library station, to dictate a report of the Romulan's violation of the Vendorian quarantine.

"You were saying," prodded Kirk, "that you people would have nothing to do with the Romulans.''

"And why should they? The Romulans had nothing to offer them. But I," and the faint light of the eyes lenses seemed to glow a little more intensely, "I was another story. My people had rejected me. I was a useless outcast."

"The Romulans had nothing to offer me—except a life, Captain. A chance to perform functions of value. We may seem at times a frivolous and idle race, but it is literally a matter of life and death for a Vendorian to be occupied in a useful function, to be doing something of value.

"Vendoria no longer offered me this; indeed, by their lack of companionship my people effectively forbade it to me. So in desperation I agreed to do what the Romulans requested of me. You must understand, Captain, that function among us, to be considered worthwhile, must be of value not only to the doer, but also to someone else."

From the first, Kirk's feelings toward this alien intruder had been somewhat less than fraternal. But as Winston's "voice" spun a tale of a tortured past, he found himself coming to regard the Vendorian less and less as a belligerent invader and more as an individual, a victim of circumstances beyond his control—a prisoner condemned by his own compassion.

"What finally changed your mind about the Romulans— and us?"

"It seems, Captain, that I have become more Carter Winston than I knew. Perhaps my friends and associates on Vendoria sensed it even better than I. My refusal to recognize this change in myself no doubt drove them even farther from me.

"I had to fight myself to comply with the Romulans when they first revealed to me their plan to take your ship. But finally I realized that if they could not capture the ship, they were willing to destroy it and all of you on board. That's when I felt the sorrow that I know Carter Winston would have felt.

"He loved life and other lives so much, Captain Kirk. Because of him I could not allow the Romulans to harm Anne, or any of you."

"So as you and Mr. Spock have surmised, I changed myself yet again. I became the very linkages in the deflector system that I had broken. It was . . . very difficult. The most difficult change I have ever had to make. The internal arrangements especially had to be so precise, so delicately aligned. I had to structure myself to permit current to pass through my body." He seemed to sway back and forth on those thick tentacles."

"But I could not allow you to come to physical harm through my actions. Through the actions of . . . of Carter Winston."

Kirk nodded slowly. "I think I understand. At least, I think I understand as well as it's possible for a non-Vendorian to."

"I cannot go back to the Romulans now," echoed the hollow voice. "I have menaced your ship and its people, and I cannot go back to Vendoria. What will happen to me now?"

This was ridiculous! The creature swaying slowly in front of Kirk had nearly caused the destruction of the *Enterprise*. Kirk had no business, no business at all, feeling sorry for it. However . . .

"You'll have to stand some sort of trial first, I suppose," Kirk guessed. Abruptly he found himself working very hard and not too successfully to suppress a smile.

"To my knowledge, no Vendorian has ever been tried in

a Federation court before. I expect they'll have to make some rather novel arrangements to prevent you from becoming, say, the judge or the jury computer.

"But you did save the *Enterprise* from the Romulans. You've done both good and evil to us in a very short space of time, Vendorian."

"Carter Winston will serve as well as any name, Captain. He has not had need of it for many months, now. And somehow the name feels . . . right."

"Okay, Winston. It will be up to the court to decide whether or not saving us from the very difficulty you plunged us into in the first place obviates your initial belligerence." He touched the back of his neck, remembering.

"Personally, I don't intend to press charges. And I don't think anyone else will, either. It's the gentlest assault I've ever been subjected to."

"Thank you, Captain."

"Until we can put you planetside, I think it would be best for the mental stability of my crew if you remained in the guise of Carter Winston."

"I understand, James Kirk." Tentacles lifted and crossed. Lieutenant M'ress hadn't witnessed the transformation yet, and she hissed softly. Once more the orange cephalopod was gone, Carter Winston stood in its place.

"I'm also afraid," Kirk continued, trying to put some bite into his voice, "that I'll have to ask you to remain under guard. I'm beginning to trust you, I think, but—"

"That's all right, Captain," smiled Winston. "You'll feel better knowing I'm under observation, at least until we are back in Federation-controlled territory. Knowing that the pair of pants you put on in the morning really are a pair of pants."

"You've appropriated Winston's sense of humor, too, I see." Kirk's smile grew. "I think you're going to be all right . . . Carter. I'll buzz security. One guard ought to be enough." He edged a hand toward the call button.

"Captain, could you possibly assign me that duty?" Kirk had completely forgotten about Anne Nored. He glanced over at her. In doing so he completely missed the expression of surprise that had come over Carter Winston.

"But—" Winston stuttered, "you have seen me. You know what I am."

"I've been a starship officer for some years now, Carter," she whispered. "You see, I've changed a little, too. Since we've been apart I've seen a lot of strange things pinwheeling about this universe, even a few that might shock you. In the final analysis form doesn't seem nearly as important as certain other things.

"As Carter Winston—even as a part of him—I think there's a better life for you than the Romulans or anyone else can offer. Oh, damn!" She actually stamped her foot. "I don't know how to say it—can we at least talk about that?" Her eyes were imploring.

"I don't . . . know." Kirk saw that Winston was totally confused. This was the last thing he'd ever anticipated. Helplessly he looked to Kirk, who nodded at Anne.

"You have the guard detail, Lieutenant."

She smiled. "Thank you, sir." She gazed back at Carter Winston with a look of . . . Kirk shook his head. Anne Nored was right. The universe was indeed full of beautiful, strange, and unexpected surprises.

They headed for the elevator.

As it happened, McCoy was on his way up in the same cab. He moved to one side and watched as alien and Anne got in. The door closed behind them.

The doctor stood pondering for a moment. Then he crossed to where the *Enterprise*'s three other senior officers were clustered in animated conversation.

"You caught him."

"Acute observation, Doctor."

McCoy's mouth twisted. "Ho-ho-ho and a Merry Christmas to you, too, Spock." He looked over at Kirk. "I'm glad to see him under guard, Jim. If he'd turned into a second Spock, it would have been too much to take."

How prophetic are the idle jests of man! There would come a time when McCoy would have occasion, if not the desire, to recall that phrase.

But for now it only provoked an innocent chuckle from Kirk and Scott.

"Perhaps so, Doctor," the first officer of the *Enterprise* agreed. "But then, two Doctor McCoys might just bring the level of medical efficiency on this ship up to acceptable minimums."

''Careful, Doctor McCoy,'' warned a grinning Scotty as McCoy, topped again, did a slow burn. ''I'm not sure life-support can keep things livable with all the heat you're puttin' out.''

''Heat? I'll give you heat. . . !'' McCoy began.

PART II

THE LORELEI SIGNAL

(Adapted from a script by Margaret Armen)

V

They eventually dropped Carter Winston off-ship in the system of Valeria. It was the nearest world to their exit from the neutral zone that was capable of dealing with the peculiar case of Carter Winston.

Not surprisingly, Anne Nored asked to be transferred to the security detail that would keep an eye—several eyes—on the prisoner both prior to and after the trial.

Not surprisingly, Kirk granted her request. He'd already come to the conclusion that if Carter Winston/Whatever was absolved of wrongdoing in diverting the *Enterprise* into the neutral zone—Kirk had told the Vendorian to plead compulsion—the presence of Anne Nored would be the best thing for him.

It would probably also be the best thing for Anne Nored.

He was mildly concerned that the Romulans might still try to make hay of the *Enterprise*'s incursion into the neutral zone, exhibiting their own damaged ship as evidence of the brutal Federation's unrelenting bellicosity.

As it developed, a number of things conspired to prevent this.

For one, there was the fact that the *Enterprise* had encountered not one but two battle-ready, fully prepared cruisers. They'd badly damaged one and put the other to flight, though the Romulans would doubtlessly insist that the second had broken off the engagement only to go to the assistance of its injured comrade.

Far more influential was Spock's official report, with corroboration by Winston, of continued Romulan visitation to the mutually quarantined world of Vendoria. Politicians handled this awkward situation in the usual way. A number of high-ranking officials quietly got together, shared a few drinks and dirty jokes, and decided to let the whole matter drop.

Meanwhile the *Enterprise* lay over in Valerian orbit to take on supplies for the first part of the new year and to make a few much-needed repairs. McCoy, for example, had a chance to go over his medical instrumentation with the testing facilities of a major ground-based hospital. And Scotty had help in repairing the deflector-shield links that Winston had thoroughly disrupted.

Despite her extensive facilities there were still a number of minor components the *Enterprise* required which the orbiting supply station couldn't provide. But nothing the ship couldn't do without.

To obtain them Kirk would have had to travel a fair number of parsecs to the major naval base at Darius IV. Instead, he chose to spend the rest of the holiday season orbiting somnolent, restful Valeria.

While Valeria was still something of an outpost world, its larger cities offered sufficiently sophisticated fleshpots to satisfy the more cosmopolitan tastes of certain of the *Enterprise*'s crew. And her rural attractions sufficed to assuage the nerves of the less adventurous.

In sum, it was an ideal stopover world.

Kirk spent a week fishing at a magnificently clear, unpolluted mountain lake—relaxing, hiking, and letting his beard grow. At the end of seven days he found the open spaces oddly confining, the theoretical vastness of the mountain valley closing in until the surrounding peaks induced a sensation bordering on the claustrophobic.

A sure sign vacation time was up.

He returned to the *Enterprise*. Two days later the last member of the crew had been rounded up, brought back on board, and either treated for accumulated cuts and bruises, formally bailed out, or sobered up.

While in space his crew formed a perfectly integrated, smoothly functioning machine. But they were a reservoir of human emotions and resentments. Every so often these needed to be drained to keep his personnel healthy. Depending on your point of view, Valeria was the lucky or unlucky world that served as the requisite sponge.

Once back in free space, Kirk set the *Enterprise* on a course that would bring it 'round in a wide swing to pass close by Rifton, one of the Federation's seven principal Starfleet bases.

Kirk blinked, rolled over, and looked at the clock over his bed: 1730 hours. As good a time as any to make the necessary log entry acknowledging the formal orders they'd picked up from Starfleet branch headquarters.

In a sense, the log entry would be only a duplicate of the same orders, but apparently some analyst somewhere decreed it necessary. He sighed. Formal procedure, red tape, bureaucracy—as Einstein had claimed, one could circle the universe and arrive back at the starting point, which always seemed to be a forty-page report in triplicate.

He thumbed the switch activating the pickup in his desk, set the dial for cross-room reception.

"Stardate 5483.7. The *Enterprise* has been ordered to provide standard escort for a small convoy of ore carriers heading toward Carson's World." He didn't add that he thought it an inexcusable waste of starship time, not to mention a colossal bore. The sentiment wouldn't be appreciated.

If he'd known the alternative future he might have thought it otherwise.

"Said ore carriers are to pick up and then transport to Bethulia III four million metric tons of heavy chromium and other duralloy ores." He paused thoughtfully to consider his next words, began again.

"This shipment of alloy ores is necessary to the development of the burgeoning metals industry on Bethulia III, and to the planned construction next fiscal Starfleet year of two and possibly three new deep-space starships. In view of the Federation-Klingon Treaty of 5260 limiting offensive weaponry in this quadrant of space, it appears—" He frowned before really noting the source of the annoyance.

The small viewscreen set on his desk was blinking steadily, a demanding yellow glow. Someone had a message for him that couldn't wait. Irritably he shut off the log and swung his legs out of bed. It had *better* be important!

The viewer beeped as he approached the desk, and a green light winked on the lower left side of the screen. Lieutenant

Uhura was warning him that ready or not, the call was on its way in.

He sat down in front of the screen and activated the knob that would tell Uhura he was indeed present, alive, and well.

"Kirk here. What is it, Lieutenant?"

"Deep-space call from Starfleet Science Center, sir," Uhura's voice explained.

"But we've already received our—" He stopped. Someone on Rifton badly wanted to get in touch with the *Enterprise*, badly enough to requisition power to boost a transmission signal across the rapidly widening distance between them. It occurred to him that anyone who had the authority to do so might be rather an important person—and in a hurry.

He blinked the sleep from his eyes. "Put it through, Lieutenant Uhura."

The blurred image that started to form was confused with the distance and the weakness of the signal, but under Uhura's skillful hands the outside static was rapidly cleared. The picture that finally formed on the screen was that of Vice Admiral for Science Julianna van Leeuwenhook. It was still spotty and streaked with interference, but Kirk knew Uhura was working miracles just to hold it in.

"Captain James Kirk here." The vice admiral smiled slowly, her long gray hair falling in waves to her shoulders. "How are things at Science Center, Admiral? Sorry I missed you."

She shrugged, a slight gesture that might have confessed boredom, might mean something else entirely.

"So am I, Captain. It would have saved me the trouble of this call. But I didn't know until after you'd left contact range that the *Enterprise* was in the area. No need to apologize for skipping a social call. Deep-space transmission is expensive, but . . .

"To answer your question, things are the same as usual. Instead of making our work easier, every problem we solve turns up a dozen new ones. Every discovery opens a hundred new avenues of inquiry. While my staff and budget increase arithmetically, the number of projects we are supposed to fulfill—all of them marked top priority, of course—grows geometrically.

"Why, if my people and resources were to quadruple to-

morrow, James, in two weeks we'd be hopelessly behind."
She smiled.

"Meaning you're not now?" Kirk countered.

"Most certainly we are, Captain. The only difference is,
while it's still a hopeless mess, it's an organized hopeless
mess." The smile shrank, to be replaced with a no-nonsense
frown. "That organization just turned up an interesting discovery. That's what I want to talk to you about. But first,
what is your present position and distance from Rifton?"

"Just a second, Admiral." He thumbed the intership
comm unit. "Mr. Spock, our present position please?"
There was a short pause, then the information came back to
him.

"Nine-six-five-five right declension to the galactic plane,
a hundred fifty degrees north."

"Thank you, Spock." He repeated the figures for the vice
admiral. She nodded and didn't bother to check it on any
device. Julianna van Leeuwenhook could do astrogation in
her head.

"You've made good time. The ore convoy you're escort-
ing—that was your new assignment, wasn't it?"

"Yes, Admiral," he admitted, steeling himself. The
change in tense hadn't gone unnoticed.

"Well, they seem fairly well along their way. You've had
no trouble thus far, have you?"

"No, Admiral."

She seemed pleased. "Good. Then I would think they
could make it the rest of the way on their own."

"Their captains won't think so."

"They'll have to think so. I'll get in touch with the commander of the Dervish outpost. He can spare a small ship for
the final escort run. He'll have to. The captains of the ore
carriers can travel on their own for a while.

"Oh, I know their cargo will be too valuable to consign
to a small frigate or some such. But by the time they've
finished on-loading at Carson's World I'll have another starship there to meet them." She shifted in her seat, and the
incredible communications system instantly transmitted the
squeak of chair on floor across the light-years.

"You might even be able to get back to meet them yourself, Captain."

"Get back from where, Admiral?" Obviously their soft, if dull assignment was making off at maximum warp-speed for unexplored regions.

"I'd like the *Enterprise* to make a little detour." She tried to make it sound unimportant, trivial. That really raised the hackles on Kirk's neck.

"It's nothing, really. Shouldn't take you more than a day or two to investigate. The *Enterprise* is the closest ship to the . . . um, affected area."

Kirk sighed. At least it didn't sound like another catastrophe. He still had vivid memories of the Mantilles Incident.

"Yes, Admiral." He hit another switch. "Recording new orders." She leaned forward in her chair.

"You are familiar with the section of peripheral space that is now on—let's see—your port plane? Sector 4423—also known as the Cicada Sector?"

"Cicada?" Kirk's brows drew together as he considered the strange word. Oh, yes, the cicada was a terran insect that spent many years underground to eventually emerge for but a few days of activity in the sunlight before returning to the soil to develop and change.

The name seemed frivolous, too. But was it? Seems he recalled something about a mysterious, little-visited section of Federation-bordered space where starships vanished without a trace, not even leaving behind their log-torpedoes. These unexplained disappearances were infrequent.

All of a sudden, escort duty was beginning to look downright attractive.

"Cicada, that's it, Captain. I'm sure your science officer can supply you with additional information and fill in any details you might require. But briefly, the situation in the so-called Cicada Sector is this: The sector was first reached—but never more than partially explored—over a hundred and fifty terran years ago. Claims to the territory have been in dispute for at least that long, but there appears to be little of value in the sector—certainly nothing worth fighting over has been discovered yet.

"Recent joint discussions with representatives of the Romulan and Klingon Empires reveal that a starship of theirs or of the Federation has disappeared in that sector precisely

STAR TREK LOG TWO

every twenty-seven point three-four-four star-years since its
initial mapping.'' She stared into the screen.

"Does that suggest anything interesting to you, Captain?''

Kirk was taken aback. The question was rhetorical. Losing
a starship from the fleets of three principalities in a single
spatial sector to a sum total of six in a hundred fifty years
was unusual, but not startling.

But some eager beaver in Science Center had researched
the disappearances and found an uncanny regularity to them.
At the very least the inferences one could draw were ominous. Natural disasters rarely operated on so strict a timeta-
ble.

"You see what I'm driving at, Captain,'' the vice admiral
continued. "It would be only a slight shift from your current
course and you would be able to check out the affected area.
Nothing elaborate. Make a casual sweep of a couple of days
through the sector, with your sensors wide open.

"Record anything out of the stellar ordinary. You can be
in the sector in twenty hours.''

Not much use in hesitating. "We'll be happy to do so,
Admiral.'' He paused to scratch a persistent itch behind
one ear. All of a sudden, something didn't smell right—
something that bothered him and he couldn't pin—ohhhh,
yeahhhh!!!!

He stared into the screen. "Uh, Admiral, how long ago
was the last disappearance of a ship in the sector in question?''

"Very perspicacious of you, James,'' she replied easily.
She made motions of consulting an off-screen chart.
"Ummm, yes . . . it was, I believe exactly twenty-seven
point three-four-four star-years ago.'' Kirk nodded.

"I guessed, Admiral. Your reputation doesn't include
deep-space calls to order casual sweeps for anything.''

"I had intended to tell you eventually anyway, Captain,''
she replied—a mite huffily, Kirk thought. "In any case, to
observe the formalities, you may regard this as an official
order from Starfleet Central. More than those of us at Science
Center are interested in these disappearances.''

"I have priority override so far as the Carson's World-
Bethulia III expedition is concerned. If the ore carrier captains try to make things difficult for you, refer them to me.''

She smiled wolfishly. "I'll see to it that they get satisfaction. They won't miss you for a few days."

Kirk didn't add that if the schedule of unexplained disappearances in the Cicada Sector held true, they might be missed for more than a few days. But he didn't say that. It could be interpreted in some quarters as insubordination.

Besides, he was getting interested.

"Very well, Admiral. We'll do our best to find your interstellar boojum." Van Leeuwenhook relaxed.

"I know you will, James. Discovery to you!"

The picture of the vice admiral began to fade, dissolve in a shower of confused electrical particles. Uhura's voice sounded over the grid.

"Transmission ended, sir. And just in time, we're nearly out of range."

"Thank you, Lieutenant." He snapped off the viewer and sat thinking. Not that he was superstitious or anything. These disappearances could be due to natural coincidence.

Sure they could, Kirk old chap. Once every twenty or thirty years. But every 27.344 star-years *exactly*?

He was tempted to beam directly to Starfleet Science Headquarters on Vulcan and talk to Admiral Weems himself, but he dismissed the idea as soon as it occurred. Even a Starfleet captain had better be very sure of himself and his reasons before trying to go around a vice admiral—even if only for clarification of detail.

Besides, if something was in the unknown sector that could take Romulan and Klingon ships as well as those belonging to the Federation, there might be valuable military information to gain. The fewer interceptable deep-space calls made on the matter, the better. He worked the communicator again.

"Mr. Spock . . . Mr. Sulu. . . ?"

Both responded. "Spock, I'll be needing a lot of digging from you in a little while. Mr. Sulu, we have a new mission and a new course. Take us to the spatial border of the port sector known as the Cicada region.

"What do you mean you never heard of it? *Tch-tch*, I'm disappointed in you, Mr. Sulu. I thought everyone had heard of the Cicada Sector. Better stay up on your manuals. Mr. Spock will supply you with navigational supplements for cruising within the area. The only charts will be about a hundred-fifty years old, Spock. Kirk out.''

Now all he had to do was think out a way to tell the skippers of the ore carriers that their escort was going to take a hike.

VI

Actually it took nearly twenty-five hours for them to penetrate the edge of the mystery sector. No giant galactic monster waited there to devour the ship whole. There were no signs of incomprehensible interstellar weapons manned by unknown races, no all-destroying automatic fortresses ready to blast them from known space.

There were stars in the sector, of course. According to the old schematics some of them had planets. But they were few and far between. They'd been cruising inside the sector for half a day now, and nothing vaguely like a threat had materialized.

"It certainly seems peaceful enough, Captain."

Kirk nodded, tried to relax in the command chair. He couldn't, of course. It hadn't been designed to put its occupant to sleep, but rather to keep him alert.

"How soon will we enter the so-called disappearance zone, Mr. Spock?"

"According to calculations, Captain, we have some thirty seconds to go."

Kirk steepled his fingers on his lap and stared at the main viewscreen. Only interstellar space, spotted with the pinpoints of stars near and distant, stared back. A black ocean, concealing its threats with a sheen of dark beauty.

"All we know," he muttered to himself, "is that ships have vanished in this sector every twenty-seven star-years. A long time for a pattern to hold." He glanced at the helm chronometer. The twenty remaining seconds were up.

"Lieutenant Uhura, place the ship on yellow alert."

"Something happening, sir?"

"No, purely precautionary, Lieutenant."

Uhura felt relieved. Not that she *expected* any trouble, but the regularity of ship disappearances in this area made her more than a little nervous. It didn't seem to bother the captain, though.

Kirk observed the cool demeanor of his communications officer and reflected how fortunate it was that his crew, at least, was not at all worried about this assignment.

"Aye, sir, yellow alert." Uhura swiveled lightly in her chair, manipulated controls. Throughout the bulk of the starship, proper lights changed color, necessary noises yowled warnings.

If there was a lurking, malevolent entity out there somewhere capable of reacting to this gently defiant gesture, it did not do so. Spock checked out the gratifyingly fast compliance of all decks with the order.

"All stations now operating in yellow-alert status, Captain." Minutes passed. Still nothing. Kirk began to relax a little. He'd tightened up in spite of himself, but now that they were several minutes into the interference zone and nothing had appeared to volatize the deck beneath him, he felt assured in easing his vigilance.

Nervousness never failed to surprise him. Hadn't he been through all this before? He sighed—tenseness was an occupational disease.

No one noticed Uhura look up sharply from her console. There was a faint, distant sound in her earphones and, no doubt about it, the strange sound had begun the instant they'd crossed into the sensitive sector. But it had been so faint at first that she hadn't been sure.

It was growing rapidly louder, however. And there was no mistaking it for a natural output of any kind.

"Captain, I'm now picking up some kind of subspace radio signal."

Kirk accepted this news calmly, almost expectantly. So there was something here. But a radio signal was hardly cause for alarm.

"Put it on the ship's speakers, Lieutenant. Mr. Sulu, any chance this wavelength might interfere with navigation?"

"It doesn't seem so, sir. It's not anywhere near helm-length waves."

Uhura adjusted her controls. For a moment there was

nothing. Then a familiar, wavering tone swelled from the wall speakers and filled the bridge.

It was sensuous, haunting and unmistakably melodic. A deep pulsing beat underlay the melody, a beat that might have been drawn straight from ancient terran drums. The wordless song itself sounded vaguely like guitars and flutes.

It was lovely.

It was rhapsodic.

It was thoroughly captivating.

At least one member of the bridge complement, however, wore an expression of something other than rapture. It was only a source of puzzlement to Uhura.

"It's much more like pure music than an intelligible message, Captain." It grew louder, and she dropped the volume to compensate for the increased power of the signal.

"Beautiful," Kirk murmured. "Might as well let everyone enjoy it, Uhura. Pipe it through the ship."

"Yes, sir." She didn't notice that the men on the bridge had entered into a state of musical appreciation bordering on Nirvana. They stopped just short of actually swaying in time to the alien rhythm. Even Spock had to force himself to concentrate on his computer readouts instead of on the music.

Helmsman Arex stared at distant stars, his three feet tapping a gentle rhythm in counterpoint to the music pouring over the speakers.

For long moments after the first faint pipings sounded over the speakers there was nothing, nothing but the steady sylph-like strains from the instruments of unknown players. Then Spock looked up from his viewer, surprised.

"Captain, we're being probed."

Kirk spoke slowly, with seeming difficulty. "From where . . . can you trace it?"

"A moment, Captain." Requests were put to the computer. "The signal is apparently originating in a star system some fifteen—no, twenty—light-years distant."

"Any info on it?" Again the library went to work.

A holographed star-chart replaced the speckled blackness of interstellar space on the viewscreen. Only two planetary systems were shown on the old chart. One glowed with a faint red aura of its own.

"The Taurean system," Spock informed him. "A small

G-type star at the extreme edge of this sector. It is the only star for many parsecs thought to possibly hold inhabitable planets. No surface survey was ever performed." The information succeeded in drawing Kirk's attention from the music.

"That's a mighty powerful signal to reach here from that distance," opined Scott. He looked over from the bridge engineering station as the music's tempo seemed to increase slightly . . . abruptly . . . insistently.

"Strange, Captain, I'm sure I'm ascribin' to it something that isn't really there—but it seems to be callin' us."

"It is odd," Kirk murmured. "Yes, I get the same feeling myself, Scotty."

Final confirmation of the signal's attractive power came from the least likely source.

"It does seem to have attributes not unlike a summons," Spock concluded. Only Uhura was unaffected. She studied the men on the bridge, thoroughly puzzled.

"I don't see any semblance to a summons, Captain."

Kirk looked back and replied, rather curtly, she thought. "Noted, Lieutenant. Lieutenant Arex, set our course for the Taurean system. Warp-factor seven."

Uhura tried to persuade herself that nothing was wrong with any of this. Certainly the alien music was interesting, distinctive—an appealing little tune. But a summons? A distant call to some as yet undefined action? Uh-uh.

She continued to monitor her communications console, but most of her attention was diverted to monitoring the actions of her fellow officers. All of them—Kirk, Scott, Sulu, even Arex, even Spock—wore dreamy, faraway looks. She'd seen similar expressions on the faces of music lovers before. But other forces were at work here, demanding more than mere appreciation from their listeners.

Or was something the matter with her?

It was as if she were the only one who was tone-deaf at a Mozart concert.

No, surely, there was nothing wrong with either her hearing or her sense of musical propriety. But she had to have a second opinion. Pressing a call switch she addressed the broadcast mike softly, whispering.

Not long after her call, the elevators doors divided and

head nurse Christine Chapel entered the bridge. She took a fast survey of the room before moving quickly to stand next to Uhura.

"You wanted me, Lieutenant?" she asked quietly, putting a hand on Uhura's shoulder. The communications officer had admonished her to speak softly when she arrived on the bridge—not that anyone else seemed to have noticed her arrival. "Are you feeling all right?"

"*I* am," Uhura replied quietly. She nodded toward the center of the bridge. "But I want you to observe the men here."

"I do that anyway." Uhura didn't smile back. "What am I supposed to be looking for?"

"Just look, see if you draw any conclusions."

Puzzled, Chapel shrugged slightly and turned to comply with the request. She studied her superior officers.

Funny, no one was talking to anyone else. The usual idle chatter that filled the bridge was absent. There was only the strange music that had begun humming from the intraship communicators a little while ago. In fact, everyone present except Uhura seemed transfixed by an unseen hand.

Kirk and Sulu had risen from their seats. They were staring dreamily, distantly, into empty air. Yet their eyes were open and they smiled raptly. Chapel concluded that the music supplied more than aural stimulation.

"Beautiful images," murmured Sulu, confirming her guess.

What images?

Uhura and Chapel saw nothing. The communications officer looked up at her.

"It started the moment we picked up that signal. And it's gotten progressively worse. Look." She pointed towards the library computer station. "It's even affected Spock."

Unlike Sulu and Kirk, Spock remained seated at his station. But he, too, was staring trancelike into nothingness.

Nothingness only to Uhura and Chapel.

"Fascinating," Spock whispered. "Like a Vulcan marriage drum." The shimmering phantom dancing before his eyes began to take on stronger outlines, to solidify in spaces as his imagination lent it form and reality.

She had shining black hair which fell in silken cascades to

her feet, pointed ears, and upswept eyebrows. Jeweled leotards clung to her body like a sparkling second skin. Strands of gems were entwined in that ebony mane, spitting out tiny fragments of rainbow as the light changed.

Now she languorously slid behind a small triangular drum. Her hands, delicate and pale, opened like white flowers. She started to play an unheard rhythm on its taut surface. No, not unheard! There it was now, he could hear it—clear and vibrant as she.

She started to sway alluringly, moving lazily from side to side as she played. Yes, he could hear it, jungle drums accented by picked guitars and delicate Vulcan tassans. But the sound was coming from the intercom, not from the drum, wasn't it? He blinked and spoke thickly. Words came slow and hard, as if he were trying to speak through buttermilk.

"I am experiencing audio-visual suggestion, Captain."

"So am I, Spock." Kirk's tone and attitude had become something less than authoritative.

She was beautiful. Her golden hair was piled high in metallic ramparts, shading a perfect forehead. A gentle breeze nudged the flowing peignoir close to her body, where it clung with maddening intent to high curves and angles.

She leaned toward him, eyes of deep blue staring, warm, inviting. The petals of the crimson flower that lay cupped in her hands opened to him. They were shaped to form a stylized heart.

Kirk shook himself.

"Dimensional visions, too." He frowned. "Any idea what's causing them, Spock?"

The science officer's eventual reply seemed to come from parsecs away. He was still staring, still absorbed in the tugging alien marriage music.

"Logically, we must assume they are a by-product of the scanning probe." All this would have seemed totally crazy to Uhura—if it weren't that everyone was treating it so seriously. But she couldn't keep silent any longer.

"Sir, what visions? We don't see anything." She indicated Nurse Chapel, who nodded agreement.

Somehow Kirk found the reserves to turn from his dancing mirage and look back at them. "Nurse Chapel, you're sure you don't see anything, either?"

"No, sir. Not a thing. What is it you all see?" Kirk ignored her question, turned his gaze to touch in turn on Sulu, Scott, Arex, and Mister Spock. All continued to stare into space, eyes blank and expressions slightly foolish. The image of his voluptuous blonde persisted, and Kirk had difficulty focusing on Uhura.

"Tell me, Lieutenant," he murmured curiously, "have I been looking as silly as that?"

Uhura hesitated, then spoke firmly. This was no time for diplomacy. "Every bit as vacuous, sir."

"Ummm." Kirk considered. It was growing hard to concentrate. No matter how he seemed to shift and turn, the blonde stayed in his vision.

"Nurse, take a medical reading. Lieutenant Uhura, call Dr. McCoy to the bridge."

Chapel moved away from the communications area and swung her medical tricorder off her shoulder. Since it was precalibrated for humans, she passed over Lieutenant Arex for the moment and began with a smirking Sulu. No telling what he saw, and she wasn't sure she cared to know.

Meanwhile, Uhura was busy at her console.

"Sick bay . . . Dr. McCoy, please report to the bridge . . . Dr. McCoy, please report to the bridge." She paused while Kirk waited unconcernedly, watching her. Giving him a puzzled look, she tried again.

"Dr. McCoy, report to the bridge—Sick Bay, acknowledge!" Nothing. She looked first at Kirk, then at Chapel, and shook her head. "No response."

"Keep trying, Lieutenant," Kirk ordered dreamily. At the moment he didn't seem to care whether McCoy answered or not.

"Yes, sir."

In the reception office of the *Enterprise*'s central Sick Bay, the communicator call light winked on and off with mechanical patience, while Uhura's voice continued to sound from the attendant speaker. "Dr. McCoy . . . report to the bridge . . . Dr. McCoy . . ."

Dr. McCoy was sitting at his desk. Leaning back in his chair, he had his feet comfortably propped up on same and his arms folded behind his head. At the moment he was staring upwards, but his eyes paid no more attention to the ceiling than they did to the communicator call light. A beatific grin dominated his expression.

Dimly, a part of him was aware of the blinking green light and Uhura's distant, urgent voice. He ignored both with perfect equanimity. His mind was busy with more important things.

"Magnolias in blossom," he sighed. "Magnificent . . . such symmetry of form . . . beautiful . . ."

Uhura gave up trying to contact McCoy. She had a suspicion why he wasn't answering. If she was right, nothing short of general alarm would provoke the slightest response from the good doctor.

For a moment she considered giving the alarm on her own, but she wasn't quite ready to assume the authority. While unmistakably affected by the strange music, Kirk, Spock, and the other officers still seemed in control of their actions. She checked her exterior monitors. The readings they provided were not the ones she hoped to see.

"The probe is getting stronger, Captain." Hands adjusted amplifiers. Also, the rhythmic pulsing had grown more insistent, the melodic convolutions more involved and complex.

"Mr. Spock," Kirk ordered, "reevaluate your scanner readings." Spock's reply was sleepy, but quick.

"I have been doing just that, Captain, though this signal makes normal work difficult. Readings are still inconclusive. That it appeals directly to the subconscious desire is self-evident. But how it relates to the music is as yet undetermined.

"It is odd that only the men appear to be affected by the probe's hallucinatory capabilities. May I suggest that perhaps . . ." His voice trailed off as he stared at the main viewscreen. Kirk was already looking that way.

The faint outline of a world began to grow visible. It increased rapidly in size on the screen. Because of some peculiarity in the ionosphere, the atmosphere had a faint golden hue. As it expanded further, the musical probe grew correspondingly louder—and louder—until it seemed to wash the entire bridge in waves of pure emotion.

The constant driving rhythm defied all Uhura's efforts to

keep it at a manageable level. It seemed to emanate now, not from her speakers, but from the walls themselves.

There was a blinding flash of light and the bridge was suddenly bathed in a deep pink glow. At the same time the music rose to a deafening crescendo which momentarily paralyzed everyone. The startling fusion of brilliant color and sound vanished simultaneously.

As the last tints of pink faded from outraged retinas, the probe officially stopped. After the long bolero, the resultant silence was shocking. Kirk, Spock, and the other men continued to stare hypnotically at the screen and the small, brass-hued planet floating there.

"Cut speed, Mr. Sulu, and set us an orbit."

Sulu's reply was casual. "Aye, sir." Kirk rose from his chair and yawned.

"Mr. Spock, we will take a party and beam down to explore the surface. Inform Transporter Chief Kyle of the approximate nexus of the probe-signal generator. We'll try and set down there. Life-support belts, Mr. Spock?"

"It doesn't seem necessary, Captain," Spock replied after checking his scanners. "Everything appears conducive to humanoid life. It doesn't really matter."

Uhura nearly fell out of her seat at that. She could see that Spock's highly uncharacteristic casualness over such a vital question had shocked Nurse Chapel, too. No one else seemed to think it worthy of comment.

"Scotty, you're in charge till we return."

"Hmmm? Oh, okey-doke, Captain." Scott was staring cheerfully at the viewscreen, but Uhura had a hunch the fatuous grin on his face was directed at another sight.

Kirk and Spock left via the elevator. Moments later, they ambled casually into the transporter room. McCoy was already there, and the single security man Kirk had requested, Ensign Carver, arrived shortly after.

"Engineer Kyle . . . Engineer Kyle!" Kirk said, more insistently when the transporter chief failed to respond.

"What?" Kyle raised his head from cupped hands and smiled over at them. "Oh, it's you, Captain. How's things?"

"Pretty good, Chief, pretty good." He moved up into the transporter alcove. "Spock call you before we left the bridge?

You can handle those coordinates?'' Kyle nodded, grinned at Spock as though the science officer was a long-lost brother.

The other officers joined Kirk in the transporter. Everyone was smiling happily at one another, or at nothing in particular, or at some private thought. After several minutes of this, a touch of reality intruded on Kirk's dreaming.

''I don't want to put you out, Engineer,'' Kirk murmured easily, ''but if you've got a spare moment, could you beam us down?''

''Sure, Cap'. Anything for you.''

Fortunately, Kyle had performed this operation several thousand times before. He could have done it in his sleep—and that's just about what he was doing. His mind was not on his job, but he manipulated the transporter controls solely on instinct.

Hopefully, he wouldn't rematerialize Kirk, Spock, and the others a hundred meters above their touchdown point.

On the bridge, Scott moved slowly to the command chair and flopped into it with little grace. His brows drew together. For the briefest of moments he frowned, as if something, something, wasn't quite what it ought to be. Then his previous contentment returned, and a satisfied smile spread across his face. Almost indifferently, he thumbed the log activator.

''Ship's log . . . stardate 5483.8. Chief Engineer Scott in command.'' For some reason that struck him as particularly humorous. He giggled. Uhura's jaw dropped in disbelief.

''We are continuing to hold standard orbit around a planet in the Taurean system.'' The world in question drifted on the screen in front of him, holding his gaze. This sight was continually interrupted by other phantoms which flashed across his field of vision somewhere between his nose and the viewer. They tickled his consciousness like bubbles before vanishing, leaving only a thin pleasant memory behind.

Once it was an astonishing orchidlike flower, whose center was a face of delicate elfin beauty. Another time, he saw thousands of gold coins, clinking, tinkling, and bouncing metallically off one another, blowing along a sandy beach like leaves in a high wind. A third time a carved crystal goblet spewed out an endless waterfall of brilliantly faceted gemstones. Now and then, the facets revealed faces that had nothing to do with internal mineral structure.

He continued the entry happily, almost singing the words.

"Probes and sensors utilized subsequent to the departure of the landing party indicate there was once a vast civilization here." The back of his mind wondered if it mightn't be a good idea to report this to Kirk and Spock, down on the surface. Oh well, they should find evidence of same soon enough. Besides, what difference did it make? What difference did *anything* make?

A lithe female form seemed to rise from the contours of a mountain range now visible on the surface below. Ah, lovely, lovely!

"However, life readings of any kind were sparse and concentrated. Captain Kirk has beamed down with others to investigate. Oh, fantastic!" His voice dropped to a whisper even the sensitive log mike couldn't pick up.

There were two people on the bridge who saw no orchid faces, heard no wind-scattered lucre, no cascade of jewels. And it worried them.

They were busy at the library computer, intent and agitated. Uhura had been feeding the *Enterprise*'s brain a steady stream of questions. Now she studied the flow of words and figures that formed the reply. Each new answer deepened her frown, increased her apprehension.

"These readings just don't match up with Spock's official report," she snapped. "So far I count three sensor readings that are off—two of them dealing with wavelengths of that probe. That's not like Spock."

She was damning herself now for not sounding the general alarm when she'd had the chance. It wouldn't do much good now. She glanced around at the rest of the bridge.

Sulu was sleeping, head down, on the navigation console. Lieutenant Arex occasionally patted all three hands together in the manner of a little boy, and Scott—Chief Engineer Scott—was ignoring the still-recording log and conducting a silent orchestra of his own. If she'd seen the instruments involved, even Uhura might have blushed. She used a remote to switch off the log.

No, their reaction to a general alarm would be somewhat less than devastating.

She turned back to the computer. There had to be an explanation buried somewhere in the sensor readings.

There had to be.

The temple reminded Kirk of a well-insulated Parthenon as viewed through a fun-house mirror. Basic architectural lines were there, but they conformed to no known earthly pattern. He couldn't even tell whether the marblelike facing, brilliant white with pink veins and black striations for contrast, was stone or metal. The top of the structure seemed to melt into a pink fog that swirled gently in the light air.

A moment before, several small mist-shrouded forms had coalesced in front of the structure to leave Kirk, Spock, McCoy, and Carver standing just at its base.

It seemed they'd forgotten their life-support belts. Tch! It could have been fatal, but Spock's easygoing assumption as to the planet's congeniality turned out to be correct. By now any outsider would be justified in questioning their sanity, but none of the men affected seemed to find the oversight worth mentioning.

Spock had remembered to bring his tricorder, however. The security guard had one, too, and McCoy had a medical 'corder in addition to his standard emergency kit.

Their gaze never strayed from the temple. They stared in admiration at the arching columns of polished stone/metal, at the delicate, gravity-defying arches.

"Fantastic architecture," Kirk murmured. "Only an incredibly advanced race could have built this place." He didn't seem to find it particularly significant that the temple might be made of stone instead of duralloy or some equally technologically advanced structural material.

His opinion of the astonishingly advanced civilization of this world was echoed by the other members of the landing party. Carver turned to Kirk and gestured at his own tricorder. He appeared to be having some trouble speaking. What was wrong with the enlisted ranks these days?

"You want the routine post-landing checks made, sir?"

"Oh, I don't think that's necessary, Carver," Kirk replied easily. "Why go to all that trouble? There aren't any threats here." His assurance bothered no one. "Spock can handle any required scans."

Fortunately the science officer's judgment was less affected than the captain's. He was already taking readings. That didn't keep him from staring at the temple, nor did it make his voice less distant and dreamy.

"There's something compelling about it, Captain."

"Yes." There was no music now, no all-absorbing rhythm pounding in their ears, but Spock was right. Something *was* pulling at them!

Kirk took a half-step backwards and frowned. Spock continued to work with his tricorder and abruptly he also seemed to realize something had taken an unpleasant grip on them.

"Captain, the urgency of the attraction suggests that more than mere visual compulsion is at work here. I advise remaining at a distance until I can determine the depth and significance of this influence. Life forms are indicated—concentrated at some point within this structure."

Kirk's trancelike expression intensified, and the momentary feeling of unease vanished. He seemed to hesitate, looking around for—something. But when his gaze finally returned to the temple, it stayed there—fixed.

"There's no apparent danger, Spock. A belligerent life form would already have sallied out to attack us. Let's go." He moved quickly now, even eagerly, towards the temple steps.

McCoy and Carver needed no urging and followed close on his heels. Spock followed more warily.

It was all very logical, of course. That wasn't the trouble. The trouble was that his logic was leading him down possible lines he didn't care for. But something at work here had a way of muffling the normal lines of reason. Spock almost seemed to have cause and effect tied together, and then everything would sort of blur in his mind.

Huge, intricately carved doors were recessed into the front of the temple. As soon as the men from the *Enterprise* had approached to within a few steps, the doors began to swing silently inward. That in itself should have been cause for greater caution. But Kirk led them inside as though they'd been expected for a long, long time.

They walked down a high, narrow hall which gradually opened into a huge audience chamber. Huge, hammocklike settees filled with silken cushions and high, cube-shaped tables of red-gold were set on both sides of the chamber. Various ornaments and utensils carved from single gems studded the tables and walls.

Always they moved toward a high, cushioned dais at the far end of the chamber. The aliens were there, waiting for them.

Resting on the dais itself or standing in a semicircle around it were a cluster of the most breathtakingly beautiful women any of them had ever seen or imagined. They wore long, togalike costumes which tantilized more than concealed. A few lounged on thick cushions covered with fur.

Like everything else on this world, their skins seemed tinged with a combination of gold and pink. All the colors of the rainbow gleamed in their flowing waist-length hair. Their eyes were a deep, drowning violet.

All stood about two and a half meters tall.

When they eventually moved it was slowly, and with great care and with deliberate patience. The reactions of the landing party were similar.

"Radiant . . . like goddesses . . . such eyes!" came the varied whispered comments. Even Spock was overwhelmed. He did, however, retain enough presence of mind to borrow McCoy's medical tricorder. The good doctor didn't seem to need it.

A quick scan brought some interesting information.

"The form—as is obvious—is humanoid," he murmured. "But there are a number of internal differences of indeterminate significance. Endocrinology especially appears to operate at variance with the humanoid norm. Also, their bodies appear to function at a surprisingly high electrical level.

"According to the tricorder the range of psychokinestatics—outside influences having an actual effect on bodily function—is abnormally high."

"Prettiest body functions I ever saw," McCoy mumbled, utterly enthralled.

For their part, the reactions of the women as they rose and slowly surrounded the men were equally ecstatic.

"They are here . . . such wondrous ones . . . they honor us with their presence . . ." and similar phrases not calculated to lower the ego of any masculine listener.

It all puzzled Spock, briefly, only because their reactions

were exactly what one might dream for. It was ideal—too ideal. Too perfect. That didn't keep him from abandoning himself to it completely.

The crewmen had to lean backward to maintain eye contact as the tallest of the women stepped forward and extended her hand to each of them in turn. Her voice rang like prayer bells sounding through Lhasa.

"I am Theela," and the very name seemed to hint of warmth and love, "the head female. Welcome, James Kirk, Dr. McCoy, Mr. Spock, Ensign Carver. Welcome, honored ones."

"Welcome, honored ones!" came the heavenly chorus from the assembled women.

Kirk mumbled some suitably mushy reply, the sentiment, if not the actual words, echoed by his companions—including Spock. It was fortunate no recorder was on to set down their words for posterity. Their infantile responses would never come back to haunt them.

They didn't sound infantile at the time, however. They sounded delightfully appropriate.

"How do you know our names?"

"The *Oyya* revealed you to us," Theela explained. She turned to face a shockingly blue curtain shot through with silver wire. Instead of touching a switch or giving a signal, she hummed a single soft, distinctive note. The curtain responded by sliding silently aside.

Jutting out from the wall behind the curtain was a large transparent cube. In its center floated a perfect three-dimensional model—no, not model, a picture, image, whatever label one could think of—of the *Enterprise*. More perfect than any hologram, it was so real it seemed the ship itself had been reduced in size and set into the cube.

The landing party moved closer, eyeing the device with real interest. As an example of alien engineering it was intriguing, but not quite spectacular. Although there were aspects of it which were unfamiliar—no Federation instrument could produce quite so realistic a depiction, for example—the technology required to produce it was not beyond comprehension.

But those few aspects bothered Spock. That, and the sophistication of such a machine in comparison with its basically barbaric surroundings. They did not add up.

"Tonal control," he murmured sleepily. "Quite impressive." Theela moved close and put a hand on his shoulder, looking down at him.

"The *Oyya* will reveal the answer to whatever is asked of it, Mr. Spock."

Spock was skeptical, but before he could ask questions Theela moved away from him to stand next to Kirk.

"We are grateful you heard the signal, Captain, and responded."

Signal . . . there was something about a signal. Something was hammering insistently at the back of his skull, screaming for attention. He shunted it angrily aside.

Signal . . . they were here in the first place because of . . . why were they here?

"That signal—it was a distress call?" Kirk asked.

Theela's smile faded. For a second a terrible sadness seemed to come over her. Then she quickly forced cheerfulness back into her voice.

"I will explain its meaning later, Captain. For now, we have prepared a feast to celebrate your coming—and your safe arrival."

Kirk would have pursued the matter further. He wanted to—it seemed he ought to—but somehow, in the face of Theela's radiant smile and the proximity of her body, the questions lost their initial urgency.

Several women guided each man to one of the swaying, overstuffed hammocks, helped him gently into it. Others brought elaborate golden trays piled high with exotically colored fruits, and white-gold chalices filled with cool bubbling drink.

Two or three women clustered around each man. They began to eat and drink. Especially choice tidbits were chosen for the visitors from the mountain of food.

One swarthy giantess rose and took several round gold fruits from a crystal bowl. "My name is Darah, honored ones," she whispered sensuously. She moved to the center of the chamber.

There she began juggling the fruits while simultaneously starting a wild, barely controlled dance. Performed by any-

one else the combination would have seemed ludicrous. But
Darah's movements turned it into an incredibly alluring bal-
let.

Kirk and his companions watched. Theela had knelt at his
feet and was stroking his bare legs above the boottops. From
unseen instruments, heady music throbbed. If possible, the
women now seemed more beautiful, more exotic, more alive
than ever. Very much more alive.

"Captain's log," Kirk sighed heavily, not caring whether
or not a tricorder was running to pick it up, "stardate 5483.9.
The beauty of this place is unequalled. It's the answer to all
a man's secret desires, private fantasies, dreams. Exquisite
in every way." He paused drowsily and managed to get the
chalice to his lips for another sip of the champagnelike liquid.

"We're here to investigate . . . here to investigate." He
almost frowned. A last warning tried to sound, faded quietly
behind a wall of suffocating pink flesh. "To investiga . . ."
Theela made a deft move with her hips, and he smiled.

"The women themselves radiate delight." He watched as
Darah continued her juggling dance, moving quickly, easily,
back and forth across the chamber floor. McCoy fervently
seconded Kirk's unrecorded sentiments.

"Truly, Theela, you are the most beautiful women in the
galaxy. But where are your men?"

"They have their own temple, their own compound," the
giantess informed him. "We find it better this way. We are
thus free to pursue our own pleasures and fulfill our own
needs without harrassment from the other."

"I'll drink to that," McCoy bubbled.

Darah, her filmy toga flying in loose folds from her magnificent form, spun across the floor toward them. Suddenly,
she called out laughingly.

"Mr. Spock!" She tossed one of the golden fruits toward
him.

"I'll drink to that," echoed McCoy.

Spock rose automatically to catch, reeled dizzily and
nearly fell over. Theela and several of the other women caught
him before he struck the floor.

Kirk was halfway out of his hammock and starting toward
Spock, his increasing lethargy finally interrupted by his

friend's plight. He got only a few steps before he found himself swaying unsteadily. It finally penetrated the rose-colored haze that had enshrouded him that something was wrong here.

McCoy and Carver were also on their feet, but barely. Neither was in any condition to help anyone but himself. Other women rushed to their assistance.

"Take them to the slumber chambers," Theela directed. "They are tired and heavy with food and drink. They must rest."

There was no malice in her voice, nothing threatening, only honest concern for their well-being. It didn't make sense that they'd been drugged, tricked. And the giantess's reaction was hardly one of triumph.

With a pair of women supporting each of them, the men of the *Enterprise* were led, staggering, toward a side corridor. McCoy managed to gasp something intelligible, but his words were badly slurred.

"Prob . . . probably that nectar, or whatever it was they gave us to drink. It's as potent as Saurian brandy."

"I'll drink to that," mimicked Carver sarcastically. Of the four, he was the last one who should have succumbed to the lure of alien liquor. Some security man! He was blaming himself needlessly. They'd all been fooled.

McCoy looked as if he wanted to say more, but couldn't. Now he was almost wholly under the effects of the powerful drink.

None of them could see very well either. None of them looked back. And so none of them saw Theela staring after them, sadly. Tears were beginning to trail from the corners of her wide violet eyes.

VII

They slept for a long time in the slumber chamber. It was dimly lit, but filled with luxurious furnishings and ornamentation. Kirk lay asleep on an enormous cushioned couch veiled with iridescent black curtains that shut him off from the rest of the room.

A gold headband with a large blue gem set in its center encircled his head. The gem did not sparkle in the dim light. His sleep had been deep, dreamless—but now he found himself stirring and trying to sit up.

The result of these efforts was a wave of dizziness that sent him falling back onto the cushions. A hand moved shakily to his head, touched, examined. He felt the headband. Experimentally he grabbed it as best he could and tugged. The pull failed to dislodge it. It was tight—too tight.

Both hands now. There didn't seem to be any kind of clasp or latch. Maybe he could force it apart along some hidden seam. Useless, it was locked firmly in place.

This time when he tried to sit up he managed it, though it cost him another attack of dizziness. He felt vaguely nauseated. Once more he worked feebly at the headband.

That's when he heard the voice. It was urgent and anxious. "Jim . . . Jim . . . !"

Funny, that sounded like McCoy. But there was a subtle difference. Even when drunk the doctor's voice had never been that—well, that shaky.

A hand divided the smooth spun curtains. McCoy stood framed in the opening, swaying unsteadily. A headband identical to Kirk's own was wrapped tightly around his forehead. Kirk's eyes widened. His jaw dropped.

McCoy's hair was much thinner—and graying! He stood now

with a noticeable stoop and his face, his face was lined like that of a man of sixty. But an even greater shock was in store.

Spock joined them a moment later. He still stood upright, but there was a definite flutter in his hands. His hair was also tinged with gray. While he definitely looked older, he wasn't in the state of advanced desiccation that had afflicted McCoy. Vulcans generally had a longer life span than humans. Therefore the peculiar aging disease had affected Spock less than McCoy.

In the background, Kirk could see a greatly matured Carver. For the first time, he wished he'd brought a younger security guard with them. Even so, Carver was younger than any of them, so it appeared the aging effect wasn't proportional. Carver had aged faster than any of them.

It was almost as if he'd had more to give.

Kirk rose and eyed them in turn, still stunned.

"Bones . . . Spock . . . what's happened to you?"

"Not just to us, Jim," said McCoy quietly in that old man's voice. "You too."

Kirk swayed. McCoy's statement penetrated—not without resistance. His hand came up to touch his own face. His hand—dry, wrinkled. Drier, less supple skin on his cheeks, loose folds of flesh around his neck, under his eyes—lines that didn't belong there. That hadn't been there, hours ago.

He couldn't see the streak of white that ran through his hair, but McCoy told him about it.

"You look about fifty, Jim. I'd guess Spock's artificially advanced age at about the same, though he's got more years to play with than us."

"We've got to get out of here," Kirk stuttered desperately. He'd once seen a man who'd lost his suit on Dryad, the hothouse world in the Demeter system. The man had made it to a survival base. When the rescue team finally reached him, they found only a very large man-shaped fungus spotted with short, sprouting, brown tendrils.

McCoy's seamed face was every bit as shocking.

He started to run for the remembered exit and pulled up, grabbing at his left leg. It seemed that in the past few hours he'd not only acquired wrinkled hands and face and a streak of white in his hair, but also a mild case of bursitis.

He felt unbelievably helpless.

* * *

Uhura and Chapel stared down at the readout screen of the main medical computer in Sick Bay. They mentally tried to urge the machine to greater speed. As if in response to their unvoiced pleas, a microtape cassette promptly popped out of the response slot.

Chapel picked it up and both women moved to the desk playback table. She inserted the small plastic rectangle, hit the necessary switch. She spoke to Uhura as the machine automatically rewound the unplayed tape.

"The results of every scan, every probe made by the female science teams. If there's an answer it'll be on this." The accompanying screen winked on and there was a tiny hum as the computer voice activated.

"Computer evaluating." The two officers took a deep breath. "Summation of recent medical and astrophysical scans, with analysis, as per request Head Nurse C. Chapel."

Faint sounds of mechanical life followed. Each second took an hour. Then the voice finally came again, indifferent as it was authoritative.

"Probe is directed at ship from indicated planet, as initially surmised. Probe wavelengths are severely enervating to humanoid males. Prolonged exposure to probe's effects over a long period of time, or if signal is intensified according to figures shown on chart, can cause increasing weakness and accelerated aging to the point of death."

Chapel made a slight strangled noise and Uhura looked stunned.

"At least we've some idea now what we're dealing with," the communications officer said grimly. She directed her next words to the computer pickup. "How do we counter this effect?"

"Countering methodology not available. No projected medical antidote to hypothesized effects. Initiate search?"

"Initiate—and keep advised," ordered Uhura sharply. She moved to the wall communicator as Chapel ran through the figures once again.

"Lieutenant Uhura to Security Officer Davidson." A middle-aged, efficient-looking woman appeared on the tiny intraship screen.

"Davidson here. What's going on Lieutenant? The men in my section have been . . ."

". . . acting like lotus-eaters ever since we entered orbit, I know. I'll explain later, Davidson. Right now I want an all-female security team in the main transporter room as of five minutes ago. All-female security teams are to be mobilized at every entrance to the transporter deck and in the shuttle bay. Anyone—particularly any *male*—who attempts to transport down to the surface is to be placed in protective custody. I don't think any of them will become violent—we've no indications of that so far. But instruct your personnel to be prepared."

"Yes, Lieutenant, but—"

"You and Lieutenant M'ress will be in command of the ship until I return. I'm taking down a security detail myself."

"As you say, Lieutenant." Davidson looked doubtful, but saluted briskly. Uhura cut the transmission and turned to Chapel; she found the head nurse staring at her with wide eyes.

"What are you planning, Uhura?" The latter was already heading for the elevator.

"I'm taking command of this ship!"

Kirk, Spock, McCoy, and Carver stood in the audience chamber facing the imposing dais. Theela sat there, watching them. Darah and the other women relaxed nearby, also watching. The men swayed weakly, the blue gems set in their headbands now glowing brightly.

Only Spock and Carver were a step above total collapse. Kirk and McCoy were in bad shape.

"We must return," the *Enterprise*'s first officer murmured tiredly, "to our duties on board our ship." Next to him, Kirk frowned uncertainly. He was clearly straining to remember . . . to remember . . . what?

Duties—that was it, duties. He looked up at the staring women. "Duties . . . I have . . ." He stumbled again as the jewel pulsed brightly and had to grab at Spock's arm for support. That arm was not what it should have been and as a result, both men nearly fell.

Theela spoke. She seemed genuinely sorry, no longer adequate consolation to Kirk and his men. "You cannot leave, Mr. Spock," she said slowly, "for you are needed here. As the low waves of the Lura-mag work on your crew, they will come to feel as you do. They are also needed, and they too will join us here."

Kirk drew himself up, finding a last reserve of strength somewhere. "We must go." Turning toward the door he staggered off. McCoy tried to follow and nearly collapsed. Again, it was Spock who steadied him.

"Obstruct them!" Theela shouted.

The other women moved rapidly to form a barrier between Kirk and the other officers, blocking their path to the main exit. Shaking with stabbing, suddenly increased weakness, the men hesitated. They had nothing to fight with, their weapons having been taken from them while they slept.

"Together!" Kirk gasped. Somehow they managed to rush the women. But the giantesses grabbed their arms and pushed and dragged them back easily. Their weakness seemed to increase sharply at the physical contact, and they grabbed at their headbands. One by one they slumped helplessly to the floor. On each man's forehead the blue gem shone with appalling intensity.

On the bridge of the *Enterprise*, Engineer Scott lounged dreamily in the command chair. His eyes were focused on the viewing screen and the dreamworld that seemed to be depicted therein. A constant flow of sensuous, beckoning images drifted back and forth in front of him.

The Scottish beret he now wore was tilted at a rakish angle. He was singing an old Gaelic love ballad. Normally, Sulu would have found the rendition distasteful and Arex would have been indifferent. But both seemed to find Scott's performance the greatest musical experience since Gabriel.

Uhura and Chapel entered from the elevator. The lieutenant's gaze was drawn immediately to Scott. The ballad approached its end as the two officers approached.

She'd been dreading this moment. How would Scott react? Regardless of any objections, he had to be removed from command—by force, if necessary. In his present condition there was no telling what he might order. She hoped Chapel wouldn't be forced to use the hypo secreted in her belt. There was no hesitation in her voice, however.

"Mr. Scott, as senior lieutenant I'm taking responsibility for the safety of this ship."

Scott turned at these astonishing words and stared up at her. There was an awkward silence. Uhura fidgeted inwardly. Was the strange probe capable of inducing emotions other than pleasure?

Apparently not. Scott merely smiled absently up at her.

"That's very thoughtful of you, luv." He swiveled in his chair and returned his gaze to the viewscreen. Uhura should have been relieved. Instead, she felt only disgust.

"Not as hard as I expected it might be. Damn. Whatever it is, it's really got its hooks into them." She reached around the humming engineer and switched on the log 'corder. Scott made no move to interfere—not that he was in any shape to offer resistance.

"Ship's log, supplemental. Lieutenant Uhura recording.

"Due to Chief Engineer Scott's euphoric state of mind, which precludes effective direction, I am assuming command of the *Enterprise* in the absence of senior officers Kirk, Spock, and McCoy. I accept full responsibility for my actions.

"A detailed account of the events leading up to and dictating this action will be entered later." Off went the recorder and she added to Chapel, "I hope. Christine, until further notice you will serve as chief medical officer."

"Yes, Lieutenant."

In a small chamber somewhere within the main temple, Kirk, Spock, McCoy, and Carver lay stretched out on a huge slumber platform. It was neither as spacious nor as lavishly furnished as their former "slumber chamber." All four were groggy from sleep.

They were apparently alone in the tiny, dark room. There was little light, but it wasn't dark enough to prevent each man from seeing that his companions had aged even further in the last hour.

McCoy's hair was now almost pure white, while Spock's eyebrows were salted with gray. There were deeper lines in Kirk's face, heavy pouches under his eyes. He rolled over on his side and studied the room.

"They've gone."

"Yes," agreed Spock. Experimentally, he stood, testing his aged muscles. Kirk and Carver imitated him. Spock walked over and gestured at McCoy's waist.

"Your medikit, Doctor. Does it contain anything that might help us?"

McCoy glanced down at the belt in surprise. Sure enough, his compact medikit was still strapped in place and seemed to be intact.

"I wonder why they took everything else and let me keep this?"

"Perhaps because it cannot be used either as a weapon or for communication, Doctor."

"How would they know that?"

"If their question to the device they call the *Oyya* was phrased so as to only indicate those instruments, then the machine would, as is the nature of machines, not volunteer aditional information. We are lucky."

"I have seen no evidence of practical medicine here," the science officer continued. "This entire community of women is a most peculiar mixture of the ancient and ultramodern. No doubt they assume your kit contains only food supplements or hygienic materials."

"They'll be hygienic, all right!" McCoy fumbled at his waist and pulled out a short, thick cylinder with tiny studded dials running down one side. "Cortropine. It ought to help. It's a powerful stimulant—but it'll make its demands later. Not the safest stuff in the world to use."

"There may not be a later if we don't use it, Bones." Kirk slid off the platform. "I'll take the first shot."

McCoy administered a dose to the captain's upper arm. Kirk rubbed at his tingling bicep and began to examine their prison in detail. McCoy continued handing out doses of the fast-working drug to Spock and then Carver.

Kirk found the door, tried it. Not surprisingly, it didn't budge. A close examination of its edges revealed that it was designed to open outward.

"Locked," he offered unnecessarily. McCoy placed the cylinder against his left arm and gave himself the final jolt. He started to replace the cylinder in the open medical pouch, but Spock stopped him. The science officer began examining the kit's contents with interest.

"What's this, Doctor?" He lifted a thin piece of hinged metal from a plastic tube.

"Portable surgical probe, Spock. The tip's full of impulsors and fragment manipulators."

"Good enough." Spock opened the instrument to its full length and moved to the door. Kirk stepped aside. In response to the captain's unvoiced question, Spock gestured at the door with the probe. "This appears to be a magnetic seal. If so, the slight output of the doctor's probe may be sufficient to disrupt the locking field."

He selected a narrow tip and inserted its slim prong into the nearly flush joint of door and wall. Moving it up from the floor slowly, it rose until clicking against something set at eye level. Spock lifted an eyebrow in satisfaction. He activated the tiny power supply.

Nothing happened.

Manipulating it carefully, occasionally activating another setting, he turned and poked the impulsor prong back and forth against the lock.

There was no snap, no sound at all. The door panel moved away quietly, just far enough to let them squeeze out of the room. Spock gave the probe back to McCoy who carefully refolded it and replaced it in its receptacle in the medikit. They might have occasion to use it again.

Spock led the way with Kirk and the others close behind. A surprisingly short walk down the narrow corridor and they came to a thin curtain backed with brilliant light.

Kirk edged ahead of Spock and glanced carefully around one edge of the thin fabric. They were back at the audience chamber. The enormous room was deserted.

Putting finger to lips he led them forward, heading as quickly as he could for the main entrance. The main entrance? Kirk had a disquieting thought.

The doors had appeared to be automatic when they first entered. If they weren't, the four men would have had a terrible time trying to move them manually, even at full strength. He needn't have worried.

When they were less than two meters from the towering stone/metal, the thick doors began to swing aside. Quietly they moved down the outer steps.

Theela chose that moment to enter the audience chamber from a side corridor. She spotted them just as the doors began to close behind the fugitives.

"Assistance, assistance!"

Already the four old men were in the garden that surrounded the temple. It was delicate, tasteful, maintained like a fine clock. However now the polished trees, the neatly pruned bushes, all looked threatening and alien.

Shortly they found themselves breathing with increasing difficulty. The cortropine was beginning to wear off even sooner than Kirk had hoped.

"It's our aged bodies, Jim," gasped McCoy. "The drug is less effective because it has so much less to work with."

They were losing strength rapidly. Already Spock had to assist McCoy. Kirk found himself searching desperately for a cave, an easily climbable tree, any place that could serve as a temporary refuge. But the only asylum in sight was a huge urn magnificently inlaid with ceramic mosaic.

He gagged, cleared his throat. "The big urn, it's the only place!" Then he turned to McCoy.

"Bones, another dose of the drug." McCoy shook a withered hand.

"Another shot in our present condition would be fatal, Jim. Even if I had it."

They hurried to the base of the urn. The curving upper edge seemed to tower over their heads, the smooth convex sides an insurmountable barrier.

"I think I can make it," was all Spock said. He backed off a few steps, took a short run, leaped, and managed to catch one of the big projecting handles near the top. He struggled and succeeded in pulling himself up to a sitting position on the outthrust handle.

A quick glance showed that the interior of the urn was spacious, relatively clean—and empty. It was covered with a heavy metal grid, but they should be able to move that. He locked his legs tightly around the handle and reached down.

With the others helping from below he was able to get McCoy alongside. They had to hurry. Already the women were racing into the first trees, splitting up to cover the many paths.

Theela noticed a tiny flash of red that was part of no plant. She moved closer and saw it was a piece of torn fabric. Reaching down, she picked it free. No question, it was from one of the alien males' uniforms.

Turning, she cupped her hands and yelled. "Over here, this way!" Without waiting to see if her comrades had heard, she started up the path that curved 'round the bush. Long strides ate distance quickly—and time.

Once, she glanced at the sky. It was growing dark. A typically sudden Taurean storm was coming. The rain could aid the escape of the men. She would have to hurry.

Carver was lowered carefully into the urn. McCoy was let down next. Quickly Kirk helped lower Spock into the waiting hands of McCoy and the security guard.

Then only Kirk was left on top. He unhitched his legs from around the bracing handle and started forward, grabbing for the lip of the rim—he grabbed and missed. His fingers slipped on the slick surface. For a horrible moment he found himself sliding helplessly down the smooth porcelain.

Only a last, desperate grab enabled him to clutch the projecting handle. A supreme physical effort brought him back onto the top of the urn.

"Captain, are you all right?" came Carver's concerned voice. Kirk couldn't spare the wind for a reply. He felt at least a thousand years old.

He made another, more careful approach to the opening. This time both hands got a firm grip on the rim. Pulling painfully and scrambling with his knees, he tried to pull himself up and over.

A sound came to his ears—the sound of running feet, getting closer. That was sufficient to spark a redoubled effort. A final, agonizing pull which closed the heavy grid over the opening—and he fell headfirst into the urn. Spock and Carver barely retained enough strength to keep him from smashing into the unyielding bottom.

Darah and two other women came into the small glade, searching every direction. There was no sunlight left in the gathering darkness to throw an accusing glare off the polished ceramic. The three separated and moved off in different directions.

Feeling more alone than he'd felt in his life, Kirk stood inside the urn and listened to voices and footsteps moving back and forth outside the urn.

"They're not here, Theela," one voice exclaimed. The leader's reply came quickly.

"Come, they might have tried to return to the spot where they arrived!" Footfalls and voices faded into distance.

Inside the urn the officers exchanged relieved glances. That was when Kirk, the temporary respite restoring a bit of his normal alertness, noticed something:

"Our headbands, look at them!" Sure enough, the once brilliant blue gems set in the hellish headbands were now only dull, faceted rocks. They no longer fluoresced with some alien internal heat. The men inspected one another carefully. Not one of the headbands showed a hint of light.

Spock had puzzled over the phenomenon of the glowing gems since he had first become aware of them. He'd formed a theory, and the present absence of light seemed to confirm it.

"I've noticed that the glow diminishes when the women are not present. I believe," he continued, his voice but not his words emotionless, "that they are polarized conductors of some sort, which transfer our vital energy to their bodies."

"Life-force feeders?" queried a doubtful McCoy. "Among some primitive parasitic species it's been noted, yes, but here. . . ?" He looked faintly sick.

Spock nodded. "That is the explanation I can think of which ties our advanced—no, enforced—aging to these devices." He tapped his own headband.

"You may also recall, Doctor, that when we first encountered them, these women appeared slow-moving and listless. But as our own strength has failed, they have become far more energetic and vital."

"More alive," murmured McCoy. "Yes, I see it now. Stupid of me not to see it before. How stupid!"

"Do not blame yourself, Doctor. You are in a far more weakened condition than I. Your powers of observation have decreased commensurate with your physical decline."

Kirk looked thoughtful. "If they find us, Spock, how much longer would we have?"

"It is impossible to tell for certain without a tricorder or medical computer to confirm, Captain, but we seem to be aging roughly ten years per day. More in the presence of the women. This is, of course, only a guess."

No one said anything. No one needed to. Not after McCoy voiced the feelings of all of them in a single, taut sentence.

''Ten years per—in four days we'll all be dead!''

''Dead,'' Kirk nodded angrily, ''and useless to them. Not that they'll care. Theela said the other men of the *Enterprise* would join us. They'll be lured, drawn down here by the probe and the pull of their own imaginations.

''We've got to contact the ship somehow. We must get to a communicator.'' Kirk put a hand against the hard concave walls and made a testing leap for the rim. He came close, but the effort exhausted him so much that he nearly collapsed. Obviously no one was going to make it out of their hiding place without the help of the others.

''I've retained more strength than any of you,'' said Spock, stating the obvious. Carver might have disputed him, but chose not to. ''My internal system is different, Captain, my life cycle longer. It would be wiser if I go alone to the temple to try and find the communicators and contact the ship.''

Kirk found himself reluctantly agreeing. ''One man would stand a better chance of slipping past them than four. Still—''

''It is the only logical thing to do, Captain.''

Kirk hesitated, searching for a better way. There was no route around the obvious, however.

It took the combined remaining strength of Carver and Kirk to lift Spock until he could grip the outer rim and push aside the grid. McCoy was too weak to offer other than moral support. Somehow Spock maintained his grasp, pulled himself up (pushing the grid back in place so that the others would escape detection) and over the top.

Panting heavily, Spock rested there and surveyed the glade. No one was in sight, for which he was thankful—though he wouldn't have objected, say, to the sudden appearance of a heavily armed Vulcan peaceforcer car.

It took more of his fading reserves to lower himself safely and carefully to the ground. No logic in escaping their refuge only to break a leg in climbing down.

Moving as rapidly as he dared and trying to keep under cover all the way, he headed for the temple. Once a pair of giantesses crossed close in front of him and he was forced to crouch under a bush whose waxy red blossoms he admired more for their concealing size than for their color.

At least the Taureans didn't appear to have an extraordinary sense of smell.

Once again it occurred to him that they seemed in no way up to creating the incredibly advanced sensory equipment which had been used on the men of the *Enterprise*. There was only one explanation: forgotten knowledge was at work on this world.

Spock made it to the temple without further incident. Fortunately the doors were still open. Obviously this was the last place they expected the refugees to return to. The urge to dash inside was overpowering, but he paused long enough to peer cautiously around one huge marblelike pillar. Nothing moved in the vast audience hall.

The corridors branching off from the main chamber also seemed to be deserted. All the women were outside, hunting them. Hunting *him*.

A search of the first, luxurious slumber chamber produced nothing, not a single piece of their missing equipment. A thorough inspection of the central dais from which Theela had greeted them proved equally fruitless. There were plenty of interesting devices around, but none of Starfleet issue.

He was getting desperate when he passed the blue curtain concealing the *Oyya*.

If the machine possessed some kind of internal alarm system to warn of unauthorized users, he'd give himself away. But they had to have a communicator!

He thought, then hummed what he hoped was the right note. The curtain didn't move. He didn't think it would shift aside manually. It was made of metal, not fabric, and looked heavy. He tried again, still with no effect.

But the third whistle seemed to catch the pitch of Theela's voice precisely. Somewhere an ancient piece of machinery agreed. The azure screen slid aside, revealing a now transparent, empty cube. The *Oyya*.

He hesitated. Would it respond to his voice? But Theela had spoken to it in terranglo and as much as offered them a chance to try it.

Answer any question, would it?

"The equipment belonging to the men of the *Enterprise*," he asked firmly, "where is it?"

There was no blur of shifting mists in the cube, no incomprehensible alien visual static. One moment the cube was as transparent as a block of lucite, the next it showed a three-dimensional miniature of a familiar object—the dais at the far end of the audience chamber.

With one difference. There was a panel set into the left side of the platform's base, and it was open in the miniature. Spock wouldn't have known how to replace the curtain even if he'd wanted to. Anyway, he didn't have time. He rushed to the dais.

A minute of frantic exploration around the paneled area revealed a large button set into the metal. He pressed it and the panel cover slid obediently aside, revealing the priceless treasure within.

Tricorders, phasers, rechargers—all their missing equipment was there. He fumbled first for a communicator, frowning when a first grab missed badly. His vision was becoming weaker.

A second try, and the compact instrument was firmly in hand. He flipped it open.

"Spock to *Enterprise*." At that moment he felt rather than saw the crystal in his headband begin to brighten. There was some residual heat put out by it after all. As the glow intensified he swayed, suddenly dizzy. Was he too weak even to talk anymore? Had he even uttered the call?

Uhura's voice echoed back from the orbiting heaven of the starship.

"*Enterprise* . . . Lieutenant Uhura here! Spock, is that you? Spock!" He glanced toward the front of the chamber. There were footsteps.

Several giantesses were just coming through the doors. Apparently they'd failed to locate Kirk, McCoy, and Carver and were returning to ask aid of the *Oyya*. They saw Spock. One shouted and they began to run forward. He tried to shake himself and spoke rapidly into the communicator.

"Request rescue party—all female, emphasize, all female! Repeat," he added desperately, summoning his remaining strength. The room was starting to spin. "All female party . . . all . . ."

His knees buckled like soft cheese and he slumped to the stone floor. The women encircled him.

VIII

Uhura was shouting into the communications grid.

"Spock . . . Spock . . . acknowledge! We read you, Mr. Spock, come in!" Dead sound hummed back through the grid. She stepped back, her mind whirling. "Nothing. No, not quite nothing." She activated another switch and spoke again.

"Security Officer Davidson."

"Davidson speaking," came the prompt reply.

"Uhura here, Davidson. I want four of your best women in the transporter room double-quick. Use the ones already there if you think they can handle it. Fully armed. Laser cannon, if they can manage it."

"Yes ma'am!" Davidson responded enthusiastically.

Uhura left a bemused Scott—he was humming and bawling something in Welsh now—and headed for the elevator. Chapel went with her, aiming for a different level.

Moments later she reached the transporter room. Subengineer Lewis—Chief Transporter Engineer Kyle being as incapacitated as any other man on board—was in charge.

Chapel arrived shortly thereafter equipped with full medikit and tricorder. The four security girls were equipped with somewhat less benign instruments. No cannon, but Uhura didn't complain. The four were loaded with enough hardware to make themselves sufficiently impolite.

"Transport stations, people. Let's go." She was the first one into the alcove.

Subengineer Lewis outdid herself. They materialized inside the temple, at the far end of the audience chamber. There was barely time to orient themselves. Theela and the other women were waiting at the other end.

304

The sumptuous settings of the temple interior and occasional strange alien artifacts didn't bother them. They'd all (especially Uhura) been on far more alien worlds, in far more upsetting surroundings. Starfleet security personnel were trained to fight by battling their way through robotic recreations of their own worst nightmares.

What did surprise them was the size of Theela and the others. Women they'd expected, but not giants. Uhura's right hand strayed toward her hip. One burst from the heavy duty phaser strapped there would cut the biggest of them down to size.

The giantesses were gathered around a large transparent cube set into one wall. Apparently the *Enterprise* security team had arrived just in time to upset some sort of ceremony connected with the cube. Certainly the giant women must have been surprised at the sudden appearance of the landing party, but they covered themselves well.

"Greetings," said the largest of them finally, stepping forward. "I am Theela, head female of this compound."

If this gesture was supposed to be conciliatory, it failed. Nor was it intimidating. Uhura took a step toward the bigger woman.

"Lieutenant Uhura of the starship *Enterprise*, head female of this bunch of party crashers. We're here to locate Captain James Kirk and three other fellow crewmen. I have reason to believe they've been treated with something less than total hospitality by you and your friends."

Theela seemed ready with an answer, but seemed to decide that Uhura wasn't about to be bluffed or stalled. "Return to your ship," she said coldly. "You are not wanted here."

"Not until we find Captain Kirk and our friends." Theela motioned to the other women and they started advancing on the little knot of terran females.

"Phasers on stun!" Uhura shouted. "Fire!"

To their credit, none of the women halted their charge. Their courage didn't do them any good. One by one, the stopped-down phaser beams hit them and they dropped to the floor. One got close enough to grab Chapel in a not-so-delicate hand and lift her off the floor before a guard's phaser brought the huge attacker down. Chapel was more stunned than hurt.

They left the giantesses like that, their nervous systems temporarily short-circuited. Uhura moved toward Theela, prodded her firmly in the side with a foot. She kicked a little harder.

Satisfied that the other wasn't faking, and a little upset at herself for the pleasure she was deriving from booting the unconscious woman, she stepped back. Big they might be, but they possessed no supernormal resistive powers.

She gave orders to the waiting group. "Search this place— parties of two. Christine, you come with me." The security teams immediately split up, taking three corridors at a time.

In a tiny side chamber, Spock lay in darkness on a thin bench of unresilient stone. His hidden face was drawn, the lines in it deeper now. But his eyes were open and his breath was constant, if unsteady.

Voices, were those voices? It took a tremendous effort just to raise his head from the stone. Then . . .

"No sign of them anywhere. Keep looking."

That was definitely Uhura! And Nurse Chapel was there, too.

He tried to yell, failed. His body had grown too weak. That left him with one last possibility. Lifting his head higher, his eyes narrowed with effort as he stared toward the door.

Uhura and Chapel found themselves moving down a high, featureless corridor when Chapel suddenly paused. She looked like someone had just hit her with a sockful of wet sand. There was a voice, Spock's voice! But it was in her mind.

". . . Nurse Chapel . . . Nurse . . . Chapel . . . ?"

"What is it, Christine?" asked Uhura. Chapel looked bewildered.

"I thought . . . I heard Spock's voice. But I guess—"

". . . CHRISTINE . . ."

There was no mistaking that mental shout! She found her eyes turning frantically to a seemingly blank section of wall. "It is Spock! But how? Of course, Vulcan mind projection. It has to be!"

She moved to stand close to a section of the wall. A quick inspection revealed no hint of latch, knob, dial, or even a seam. She started running her fingers carefully along the dark metal.

"There must be a hidden catch here, somewhere . . . there must be!" Uhura joined her in the hunt. Rapidly the two women went over the smooth surface. No, not completely smooth . . .

It was Chapel who found the slight depression just above her head and pressed inward with her thumb. There was a slight click and a tall, narrow panel pivoted on its axis. They entered a dark room of indeterminate size. The only light came from the hallway they'd just left.

But there was enough illumination to show them the long table. Spock lifted his head once again and tried to speak. As he did so, the light from the corridor struck his face.

Chapel swayed. "Mr. Spock . . . !" Uhura wanted to scream, but that would have been out of character for an acting commander. Still, the calculated suppositions of the medical computer hadn't prepared her for anything like this.

All she could do was ask inanely, "What happened?" Spock strained to reply but couldn't. He'd been thoroughly drained. He leaned back and closed his eyes, passing slowly from consciousness. Involuntary Vulcan nerves had had enough. This body needed rest. The effort required to generate the successful mind contact with Chapel had exhausted him.

Uhura and Chapel could only exchange expressions of horror.

The urn stood silent in the darkening garden, unnoticed, uninspected. A strong breeze was now nudging branches and flowers with ungentle force. It seemed to lull for a minute, then return suddenly as real wind, a lashing, tearing gale which bent all but the thickest trees.

Sculptured lightning etched copper trails in the gray sky, while alien thunder rolled and echoed back from distant unseen hills. Rain began to fall, slowly at first, fat drops spotting the ground in hesitant, exploring patterns.

Seconds later the storm turned into a raging downpour that would have shamed any tropical rain forest on Earth. Now the reason for the slight downward slant of the garden and temple grounds became obvious. Streams, rivers of runoff vanished down camouflaged, neatly screened holes and into a complex drainage system.

The wind leveled off and blew steadily from the north, but the rain increased, became a torrent, a cataract, falling in solid waves from the clouds. It was a typical Taurean storm, but it would have appalled any terran weatherman.

Kirk, McCoy, and Carver had been lying weakly in the bottom of the urn. Now they found themselves forced to stand as the downpour drenched them unmercifully. The slick sides of the urn provided capricious support.

Each drop seemed to raise the water level in the urn by millimeters. It rose with shocking, alarming speed. And the storm showed no signs of abating.

"We've got to get out of this," Kirk mumbled. The sound of his aged voice barely rose over the splash of accumulating water. Slowly, painfully, Carver struggled to lift Kirk toward the lid of the urn. But their faded strength proved unequal to the task. And the slippery convex walls were unclimbable. They tried again and again. Again and again Kirk slipped back.

There was nothing but to keep trying, to no avail. Ordinarily, their situation wouldn't have been so desperate. Even if they couldn't reach the top all they had to do was tread water until the rising level carried them up. But in their severely weakened condition, such a constant effort might be beyond them.

Even if they did somehow manage to stay afloat all that time in the cramped quarters, it was doubtful any of them would have the strength to slide aside the heavy metal grid covering the top. They might hold onto the grid, press their faces partway through to keep breathing . . . but eventually their grip would weaken, slip, and one by one they'd sink quietly beneath the surface.

Chapel transported back to the ship with Spock and immediately moved the first officer down to Sick Bay. Chapel hoped that just getting him off the planet might help. Initial sensor readings seemed to confirm her hopes, in part. His strength was coming back, but it was still the strength of an old man. His eyes remained closed.

Chapel had been fooling with the headband encircling the first officer's forehead for what seemed like hours. Eventually she'd given up hope of finding a catch. Praying there was nothing automatic in it that would explode on release, she went to work with a surgical laser.

The carefully controlled light removed it neatly. Setting the metal circlet aside she prepared a premeasured injection. The aged body didn't reject the strong medication. She'd been very careful gauging the amount of stimulant. No one on the ship was used to programming dosages for an old person.

Removing the spray hypo from Spock's arm, she set it aside and sat back to watch him. After a few minutes the eyelids fluttered, opened.

"Mr. Spock. . . ?" His head turned. He'd grown no younger, no more supple, but at least he could talk now.

"Instruct female engineer," he coughed, waited till the fit had passed and began again, more confidently. "Instruct female engineer to divert ship's energy to block probe. Use electromagnetic deflectors. Computer will calibrate probe frequency . . . block . . ."

Chapel shook her head slowly. "We tried that, Mr. Spock. It didn't work."

Spock shook his head violently, found the effort nearly blacked him out.

"Don't use normal deflector energies." His voice was growing stronger as the drug raced through his system. "Divert all ship's power into shield. Everything but minimum life-support." His eyes closed but he forced them back open and extended a shaky, withered hand.

"Hurry, Christine." She nodded obediently and turned toward the intercom.

"Get me Engineer Sco—" She stopped in midphrase. Chief Engineer Scott was in no condition to program a coffee pot, much less handle complete realignment of the *Enterprise*'s generators. "Get me Subengineer Hondo McDuff."

She nodded with satisfaction. McDuff would handle the complete readjustment of forces with ease—if in her eagerness to satisfy everyone she didn't blow up the ship first.

The women regained consciousness slowly. There was no moaning, no groans at the tingling aftereffects of the phasers.

Theela, the strongest of the group, was already on her feet.

Her initial antagonism had gone. She showed no desire to challenge even a tickling phaser effect again.

Instead, she retreated against the central dais and watched Uhura.

The object of her attention waited until enough of the other giantesses had recovered to make the demonstration worthwhile. She reset her phaser while searching around the room, settled on a good-sized, cube-shaped table, and fired.

The blinding phaser beam struck it with impressive force and the solid construct of stone and metal fused into a tiny lump of glowing slag. There was a concerted gasp of horror from Theela and the other women. Uhura's voice had taken on a new intensity, too.

"Release Captain Kirk, Dr. McCoy, and Ensign Carver immediately, or we'll melt your temple down into a pink puddle!" She raised the phaser slightly. "But first, maybe we'll start on you—piece by piece."

Theela didn't reply . . . just stood and looked defiant. Trying to exhibit a casualness she didn't feel, Uhura shrugged and raised her phaser the rest of the way, pointing it at a nearby, beautifully worked stone column. Theela wavered, and a restraining hand gestured hurriedly.

"Wait! No more destruction. I do not know where your people are—" Uhura's finger tightened on the trigger, and Theela's tone grew frantic.

"It's true! They escaped, but wait and I shall find them for you. I was about to do so when you appeared."

She left the dais and once again approached the transparent shape of the *Oyya*. The note was hummed and the machine activated.

"I will find your men for you. But first learn of us and the reasons for our actions."

"I could care le—" Uhura began, but Theela was already speaking to the cube.

"The past—reveal it."

Uhura tried to appear unimpressed as a lifelike miniature of a handsome man appeared in the cube. The detail was unbelievable. The man's hair was short, green, and done up in ringlets. Standing beside him a second later was an equally attractive woman, also with hair of green.

"This is the race from whom we are descended," Theela

informed Uhura. "They came to this world which you call Taurus when their home world began to die." She gestured around at the silent hall.

"They built this temple and all surrounding it—the automatic food machinery, the gardens, the underground recycling systems . . . everything." The image in the cube blurred, then slowly cleared again to reveal the man standing alone.

He was changed, shrunken now, old and white-haired and hunchbacked. Theela's voice was sad. "They did not know that radiations on this world drain the life-energy from a body.

"But the women developed a glandular secretion which partly enabled them to withstand these debilitating effects. It also gave them the ability to manipulate, through special devices and a certain local mineral, the now weakened males—to draw life-energy from them to replace what the radiations stole.

"So in learning how to resist this planet's life-hunger, they acquired that same need. In drawing on the life-force of the men, they caused them to age and die. We are the daughters of those first women. They built the Lura-mag, which draws new men to us, the *Oyya*, and they designed the focusing headbands."

As Theela continued with her tragic history, rain continued to fall. Most particularly it continued to fall into a certain large lump of pottery, in which Kirk and the others splashed weakly, half floating now, their toes bouncing off the bottom. Uhura, as she listed to Theela, had no way of knowing how close Kirk, McCoy, and Carver were to drowning.

"To maintain our long life," Theela was saying, "we must revive ourselves this way every twenty-seven years of your time."

Darah broke in unhappily, "We are eternal prisoners of this need, which we did not ask for. We age very slowly. Our damning immortality has also cost us the ability to bear children. The necessary organs are still there, but they do not function. A by-product of our increased life."

Uhura didn't have to ask how they knew this.

"Why don't you just live out your normal life spans?" asked one of the security guards.

"We have no weapons here, no way to destroy the Lura-mag. And when the men eventually arrive," she hesitated, "we are afraid. We have no wish to be murdered as monsters. We have always feared this would happen were we to confess what we have done."

"So we follow the plan, and the cycle continues."

Uhura muttered to herself. These poor creatures had never known any civilization but their own pitifully confined fragment of history. They'd never known any other way to react, never thought to take the chance of asking for help.

Sympathy later, she reminded herself. They were wasting time—time which might be precious to an aged Kirk, McCoy, and Carver. How precious, she didn't yet know.

"That's all very interesting," she replied honestly. "Now, what about Captain Kirk and his companions? If your fancy crystal ball can locate them, why haven't you done it already?"

"We were about to," Theela reminded, "but you came." She turned to face the cube.

"The men of the *Enterprise* who remain on our world . . . reveal them."

An image began to form, screened by plants and vines.

"The garden outside the temple," Theela informed them. The image blurred again, solidified. Then it was as if they were peering at some impossible kind of moving cutaway drawing.

They were looking inside the urn. Kirk, McCoy, and Carver were bobbing inside, pawing at the water which washed over and around them. Kirk and Carver had unsteady grips on the grid covering the urn. Kirk had a grip on McCoy, and his fingers slipped. McCoy slid below the surface as the captain made frantic flailing motions at the water, struggling to reach him.

"They're drowning!" Uhura exclaimed. She turned to face Theela and her hand tightened on the trigger of the phaser. "Where are they? Take us there now, or—"

"The ceremonial urn in the far glade!" the giantess shouted.

Driving, unrelenting rain soaked everything, obscuring their sight for all but a few meters in any direction. The light was dim, except when an occasional streak of lightning shouldered its way between the clouds and threw trees and thick creepers into sharp relief.

Uhura and the security party followed Theela through the nightmarish storm, phasers drawn. Uhura kept hers focused squarely on the center of the giantess's back and stayed close on the big woman's heels.

Back in the temple she'd seemed docile enough, but Uhura was taking no chances on her disappearing suddenly in the darkness. Let her try something—

Without any warning from Theela they burst into the open glade. The urn looked innocuous enough, standing firmly in the high wind. No sign that there were three men floating inside, their lives ebbing away with each passing minute.

"Phasers on third setting!" Uhura yelled over the drumming rain. "Aim for the base!" She was firing her own weapon as soon as she'd given the order.

The concerted low-powered energy from the five phasers struck the base of the ceramic container. Four broad cracks appeared instantly. Water gushed out of the urn as if from four spigots. The sudden release of internal pressure was too much. Cracks multiplied, and the urn split apart.

Kirk, McCoy, and Carver were washed out like wet logs, tumbling and falling over pieces of broken pottery down the slanted muddy ground. Uhura and the other women from the *Enterprise* had shut off their phasers and were rushing toward them even before the flow of water had subsided.

Uhura's face twisted in pain when she saw Kirk. He'd aged even more than Mr. Spock. And McCoy—

"My God—" she muttered, flipping her communicator open. "Uhura to *Enterprise*. Subengineer Lewis, transporter room." The voice of the technician acting for Chief Kyle shot down through the gray clouds.

"Lewis here, Lieutenant."

"Four to beam up, Lewis—and gently, Lewis, gently. We've got some . . . sick people down here."

"Yes, Lieutenant, I've seen Mr. Spock."

Uhura flipped the communicator closed. "Ensign Tadaki, you're in charge. I'm going up with the captain and Dr. McCoy. Vierne, you'll come with me. I'll send you back down for Carver."

"Excuse me, ma'am," interrupted Tadaki, "but what about

her—and the others?'' She gestured at the silently watching Theela.

"If they don't give you any trouble, leave them alone. But if they go near anything more modern than a spoon, or get belligerent—shoot them."

The medtables were waiting in the transporter room. Nurse Chapel was somewhat prepared for the experience of seeing Kirk and McCoy, but her assistants were not. Nor was Scott, who was assisting Lewis in the transporting.

"Mr. Spock's screen is working," he said in answer to Uhura's unvoiced question. "The rest of the men are recovered, except for some splittin' headaches. Most of us would rather not discuss the whole matter, Lieutenant Uhura."

"Don't blame yourself, Mr. Scott," she replied. "You were acting under an irresistible outside compulsion."

"I still feel a bit of an idiot," the chief engineer grumbled.

"Far be it for me to deny you the pleasure of feeling like one," Uhura admitted. Scott grinned.

Chapel was admonishing her stunned assistants.

"You've seen old men before," she said with an assurance she didn't feel, "get moving."

Drugs and injections restored some strength to the four aged men, but they remained as old as before. Chapel ran test after test on them, took reading after reading. It was a toss-up as to which result was less depressing than the others.

"No results, Captain," she finally had to admit. "The aging process seems to be the real thing, speeded up. I see no way to reverse it. I've . . . I've tried everything I can think of. Perhaps Dr. McCoy—?" Her tone was hopeful.

McCoy's wasn't. "I can't imagine anything you haven't already tried, Chapel." Dismayed silence filled the examination room.

"I'm not ready for retirement," Kirk mumbled. No one laughed.

Spock, who'd laid deep in thought ever since the first injections had refreshed his mind, broke in.

"Perhaps the transporter is the key."

"Key to what?" snapped McCoy testily.

"Our restoration. The transporter computer automatically records the molecular structure of everyone and everything it handles. Humanoid patterns are permanently recorded and shifted to a special section of the library. It's part of the ship's security systems.

"Think, gentlemen, the records of our original forms were re-recorded when we beamed down to the planet." Kirk's face showed hope.

"You think, Spock, that if we are transported back to the surface and then immediately brought back under the patterns recorded previously, our former bodies would be restored?"

"Possibly, Captain. It has never been tried before. Theoretically, a man could be retransported back into his child's body, if the pattern were available. The danger—mental as well as physical—has precluded experimentation in this area. There would not be a second chance."

"I'm not crazy about our chances right now," Kirk replied. "If you think there's any chance at all, Spock—"

"There is a chance, Captain."

Kirk leaned back on the table and spoke to Uhura. "Inform Engineer Scott of our plans and tell him we'll be back in transporting as fast as," he grinned, "our wheels will carry us."

"I don't think much of this idea, sir," Scott said when the details had been explained to him.

"Look at me, Mr. Scott," Kirk ordered. "Every other attempt to restore our original bodies has failed. This may be our only chance. You're absolved of all responsibility for it. It's my decision—mine and Mr. Spock's and Carver's and Bones's. We've *got* to try it!"

"All right, sir, I'll do my best."

"You'll have to, Scotty."

With the aid of Chapel's assistants the four men were helped into the transporter alcove. McCoy was unable to stand and had to sit on the transporter disk.

"Go ahead, Mr. Scott."

Scott resisted the urge to draw a deep breath, drew the levers down. The men glittered, faded and were gone.

There was a beep from the transporter console less than a minute later.

"We are on the surface, Mr. Scott," came Spock's voice. "Reprogram the computer as indicated according to the previously recorded patterns."

Scott delicately shifted four new settings into the transporter control. The settings were crucial and required matching the new patterns to the old with no room, absolutely no room, for error. He checked it once, could have checked it a dozen times more without being completely satisfied.

"All right, Mr. Spock. Here goes." He began adjusting the proper dials and switches, his eyes glued to one small unassuming gauge set in the console under his right arm.

"I heard them say this has never been done before, Mr. Scott," Chapel whispered. "What happens if it doesn't work, if things don't match up right?"

"If they're a little bit off, lass, just the tiniest bit—then the atomic structure of Captain Kirk, Mr. Spock, Dr. McCoy, and Carver will break up, disperse—scatter to every corner of the universe. And not all the king's horses nor all the king's men will ever put the captain together again."

There was an end to talking as Scott, using more care than he ever had in a transport operation, slowly brought the necessary levers upward. The familiar hum of pattern integration increased. Transporter Chief Kyle had arrived and now stood to Scott's left, double-checking readouts.

"So far so good, Chief."

Four outlines began to shimmer into view, coalesce.

"Easy, easy . . ." Scott murmured to himself.

The outlines steadied, started to take on color—and suddenly began to oscillate violently.

"Scott, we're losing them!" yelled Uhura helplessly.

Scott didn't reply, his hands working faster on the controls. The four outlines seemed to separate into sixteen tiny sections, flutter still more wildly, and then re-form into four shapes again.

The oscillation slowed, stopped. Now the humming steadied, and the four outlines began to fill in once more.

"Coming up on zero mark," noted Kyle, only a slight tremor in his voice hinting at tenseness. "Two . . . one . . . mark!" Scott slammed four levers down so hard it appeared sure he'd shove them right through the console and into the floor.

Kirk blinked and looked around. Uhura smiled in relief.

"You're more handsome than ever, all of you." They were themselves again.

Well, not quite.

"That's very nice of you, Lieutenant," McCoy replied, "but why is everyone staring at us?"

"Yes, Scotty, aren't you going to beam us down? It's time we figured out what that probe—" He looked around and a puzzled expression came over his face. "Say, that's odd, Mr. Spock, have you noticed? The music has stopped."

"Indeed it has, Captain. Most peculiar."

Uhura felt like the girl who'd just stepped through the looking glass. "What's going on here? Aren't you glad to be back in your own bodies again?"

Kirk looked at her strangely. "Back? I don't remember having left mine anyplace, do you, Bones?" McCoy shrugged, looked innocent.

"I think I know what's happened," mused a thoughtful Scott.

"Well, I wish you'd tell me," pleaded a badly confused Uhura.

Scott turned to her. "It's simple, lass. The captain, Mister Spock, Doctor McCoy, and Mister Carver are once again as they were before they first beamed down to the planet. That not only includes their youthful looks, it includes their original brain patterns, which include memories. They've lost some time—and experiences."

"What's all this, Mr. Scott?" queried Kirk, stepping off the platform. "Why the delay?"

"It's kind of complicated, Captain," began Scott. "We have some tapes from Spock's tricorder, plus those from Doctor McCoy's and Ensign Tadaki's, which ought to clear things up . . ."

It took only a few hours for the four repatterned officers to relive the experiences of the past day. It was difficult to get used to, but the tapes didn't lie.

McCoy didn't stay for all of them. He had a number of questions of his own to put to the medical computer.

Eventually he handed Kirk the results of his work.

"Aren't you going to handle it, Captain?" asked Uhura.

"No, Lieutenant. Besides, I think it might mean more coming from you. I don't have any particular desire to go back down to this particular world. Not if what happened to me on those tapes really happened. It was like watching yourself acting out a bad dream.''

Uhura nodded sympathetically. "I understand, Captain." She turned and headed for the transporter room.

Theela, Darah, and the other giantesses were overjoyed when Uhura announced the results of Dr. McCoy's research. Not that they were in any position to reject the offer, she thought sardonically, but she had to admit that they accepted it with what seemed like honest relief.

Theela led her to a large concealed room behind the temple dais. It was dominated by a seated console and an incredibly complex arrangement of cables, glowing globes, and objects of unknown purpose. The entire apparatus pulsed with internal radiance and hinted of concealed power.

"The Lura-mag," explained Theela solemnly. "Our blessing and our curse." Uhura drew her phaser and set it on high. But before she could begin the work a huge palm came down gently on her forearm. She glanced up at Theela.

"No, let me. It is my place."

Uhura hesitated, but the look in the giantess's eyes seemed real, even anxious. She handed over the phaser.

Theela could only fit a fingernail over the trigger, but she managed the tiny weapon well enough. In a few moments the Lura-mag had been reduced to a quietly hissing mound of molten plastic and metal. Theela turned and quietly handed the phaser back to the watching Uhura.

"Tell Captain Kirk we have kept our part of the agreement."

Uhura nodded approvingly. In spite of herself, she was beginning to feel sorry for these poor, bloated creatures.

"There are major medical facilities on Kinshasa. We'll take you there." She noticed that the other women had appeared in the doorway and were watching expectantly.

"How soon will we become as other humanoid women?" asked Theela.

"Dr. McCoy says it should only take a few months. The same modified estrogren that increases your life spans abnormally is also responsible for your exceptional size, it seems. Certain operations are possible . . . bone reduction, for example, to partially correct this. You'll still be unusually tall, but the differences will be more manageable.''

"A new life—a normal life—perhaps love." She smiled down at Uhura, who didn't know whether to cry or throw up. "There are many different kinds of immortality."

That expression, at least, Uhura could empathize with.

As expected, McCoy's declaration that the Taurean women would be able to lead a normal life was somewhat optimistic. The arrival of the dozen spectacular beauties on Kinshasa created something of a sensation. Their reception at the Federation Fleet Hospital was rather different from that normally reserved for sick aliens.

The doctors professed they were only interested in studying the endocrine irregularity that seemed to prolong life—but Kirk suspected that more than scientific curiosity motivated the male portion of the staff.

In any case, it looked like the Taureans were going to have few troubles gaining acceptance in the Federation. They might be regarded as a challenge, it seemed, but not a threat.

PART III

THE INFINITE VULCAN

(Adapted from a script by Walter Koenig)

IX

"Captain's log, stardate 5503.1. Escort of the Carson's World/Bethulia ore shipment having been assigned to other vessels, the *Enterprise* has been ordered to survey a new planet recently discovered at the Federation-Galactic fringe."

Kirk clicked off and stared at the fore viewscreen. The journey out from Kinshasa had been peaceful and uneventful. Now an Earth-type world with a normal scattering of clouds, seas, and brownish land masses filled the screen.

He wasn't surprised Starfleet Command had diverted the *Enterprise* from escort to survey duty. The discovery of a potentially colonizable unclaimed world took precedence over any but the direst emergency. It was interesting, pleasant duty. And if Vice-Admiral van Leeuwenhook had pulled a few strings to get the *Enterprise* the choice assignment, well, it was only a reward for a job well done.

It was imperative to make an official survey and lay claim to the world quickly—before the Klingons, say, or the Romulans discovered it. Inhabitable worlds were not all that common, and competition for expansion was fierce.

Furthermore, this globe seemed to be a real prize to the astronomers using the Moana predictor. Not only did preliminary orbital scans insist it was inhabitable, it checked out as downright lush—a garden world.

Everything seemed to point to a choice discovery, just waiting for her first load of Federation settlers—until Sulu's surface probes located the city.

"Inhabitants, Mr. Sulu?" That would be the end of any colonization.

Sulu's expression was uncertain. "No intelligent reading, sir. But it's hard to be sure. There's such an abundance of

323

lower life—plants and small animals—registering that it will take time to sort out any intelligent forms. One thing's certain, if it's a major metropolis, it sure isn't overcrowded.''

"I'd rather not wait for secondary analysis, Mr. Sulu.'' Kirk rose from the command chair. "Mr. Spock, Dr. McCoy. You'll accompany Mr. Sulu and me on the landing party. Mr. Scott, you're in charge.''

"Aye, sir.''

Kirk headed for the door. "Scotty, buzz down to security and have them send along a couple of people to go down with us. This kind of life-form density implies the presence of predators as well as grazers.''

"Yes, sir,'' Scott acknowledged as he slid into the command chair.

The party of six assembled in the transporter room with admirable speed.

"Put us down near the center of the city, Mr. Kyle,'' Kirk instructed the transporter chief. "If there are inhabitants I want to meet them right away. It's always best to size up the local populace before the high muckamucks come running with official greetings.''

Kyle nodded. His hands moved on the controls.

The city was magnificent.

Wide green spaces alternated with soaring angular structures that looked more like idealized cathedrals than functional buildings. Spires and glasslike towers were laced together with a network of arching bridges and spun sugar roadways, many fading to near invisibility in the bright sunlight.

The metropolis was constructed along gigantic lines, everything built to proportions four times human scale. Yet it was a place of beauty and grace.

It was also dead.

No policeman panicked at their appearance. No busy citizen halted in his daily stroll to gawk at the alien magicians who had materialized beside him. No curious crowds gathered 'round, and no one notified the local president, chief, or leading hooligan.

Dead.

Weeds, vines, and something like a thick terresterial seaweed had made the city their own now. Even the shiniest, newest-looking structure was clothed in a blanket of climbing greenery. Greenery, and less wholesome-looking plant life.

They began walking toward what they estimated to be the center of the city. Sulu and Spock were busy making continual tricorder readings.

"Life readings are still confused, sir. I can't sort them out, yet."

"There is something else, Captain," added Spock. "I am getting a sensor reading on some form of generated power—" He looked around and after a moment's search, pointed ahead. "From that building."

"Let's check it out," said Kirk. He was at once pleased and disappointed. Pleased that there seemed to be no barriers to development of this world, and disappointed at the thought that the architects of this dream city no longer existed. They walked toward the structure in question.

Sulu paused a moment, trying to recalibrate his tricorder to screen out another identified low-life form. Then he frowned and glanced skyward.

The sun glare blocked out his view of . . . what? He thought he'd heard a flapping sound, but they'd seen no animals on this world yet. When the dots cleared from his eyes he looked again. The only sky riders were clouds.

Hmph. He took a step after the others, glanced downward as he set his foot—and stopped. The tiny plant looked like a sporing dandelion. Moving his tricorder close he took a standard reading. Results were anything but. Unaware of the fuss it was causing, the fuzzy, delicate top of the plant quivered slightly in a gentle breeze.

"Well, now, what's this?"

The building the others were approaching appeared to be well maintained. Surprisingly well, Kirk thought. Perhaps the city wasn't as dead as it looked. Here was one structure that the mosslike growth and other climbing vegetation hadn't encroached. Its front walkway was clean, the window ports all intact and throwing back the morning sunlight.

"Captain, Captain!"

Kirk and the others whirled. Ush and Digard, the two security men, moved their hands toward their weapons.

"What is it, Mr. Sulu?"

"You're going to have to decide for yourself, sir." He had come up to them. Now he stopped and pointed to the ground near his feet. Everyone looked down.

There was nothing there except some smooth gravel set in a layer of earth—and a single fluffy, fuzzy little growth. Looked like a dandelion, Kirk mused.

"How long," he asked gently, "has it been since you've had a long leave of duty, Lieutenant? I thought Valeria was enough for anyone, but—"

"No, sir, really, look!"

The helmsman took a couple of steps to one side. There was a tiny popping sound like a foot pulling out of mud as the fuzzy raised itself off the ground. It scurried on miniature roots after Sulu. As soon as it reached his side—how it could tell where it was was another mystery—the root endings promptly made like a corkscrew and burrowed contentedly into the earth.

Kirk's stare was incredulous. If it wasn't so undeniably alien, the fuzzy would be downright funny.

"What is that thing?"

"It's an ambulatory plant. When it stops, it takes up new residence. The little fellers are all over the place." He moved back to his first position. The fuzzy popped, skittered after him, and repeated the rooting operation.

"I think it likes me."

Kirk shook his head. "We always encourage our officers to make friends with the natives."

"I always did think your personality was kind of wooden, Sulu," said McCoy idly.

"That's fighting dirty, old bean," the helmsman countered.

"It's a good thing they're *not* intelligent," Kirk observed.

"Captain," Spock broke in, looking up from his tricorder, "I dislike interrupting your amusing byplay, but that power reading now gives evidence of being an electronic probe of some sophistication. I believe we are being scanned."

Kirk's phaser came out, and the others reacted seconds later.

"Phasers on stun—stay alert. Mr. Sulu, Mr. Digard, stay here. Mr. Ush, come with me, please."

Kirk, McCoy, Spock, and the second security man moved toward the building. Sulu watched them go anxiously. But when time passed and nothing leaped out to blast the earth from under them, he quickly lost interest. He found his gaze dropping down to the friendly fuzzy.

Obeying an impulse, he knelt and picked it up.

"Ow!"

Well, what—Friendly, indeed! He dropped the plant quickly, shaking his finger to try and relieve the pain. He examined the injured digit with concern. The fuzzy, as if unaware that anything unusual had taken place, burrowed back into the soil.

Sulu mumbled to himself. "Must have been a thorn. Oh, well."

The entrance had no solid door. Instead, the opening dog-legged to the left and out of sight. Moving cautiously, they edged around the U-shaped portal. It opened without warning into a gigantic room.

No, the room wasn't gigantic in itself. It was just that it was built to the same four-times-human scale as the city. Like the building's exterior, the room was clean and orderly. Lights on panels and consoles flashed on and off. There was a constant hum from powerful, hidden machinery. It looked very much like a laboratory.

There was no longer a question about the city being dead. Everything about the room suggested constant, everyday use. Spock gestured toward a towering wall panel flecked with odd-shaped switches and knobs.

"The probe originates in this instrument wall," he informed them, checking his tricorder. "As does an incredibly powerful force-field shield. I cannot imagine the purpose of the wall instrumentation, but the presence of the force-field indicates that someone does not want it tampered with."

There were several high shelves in the wall next to the panel. The lower ones held, among other things, a pile of alien yet still recognizable cassettes filled with scrolls of tape. One scroll cassette sat in a playback slot. Spock pulled it out and began examining it closely. Nothing appeared to object to this sudden manipulation of the cassette.

McCoy was busy with his medical tricorder. Suddenly he looked up in astonishment.

"Jim! I'm picking up a humanoid life-reading of incredible strength. It's as if it—"

"EEEYAAHHHH!"

The agonized scream came from outside the chamber. Readings, tapes, everything were forgotten as they raced for the street. Spock absently slipped the cassette into a pocket.

Sulu was stretched out on the ground. His arms and legs were splayed wide apart and rigid with unnatural stiffness. No one had to ask what was wrong with him. He was almost totally paralyzed. Only his eyes made frantic motions.

Ensign Digard stood alert and gripped his phaser tightly, hunting for some unseen enemy to use it on. McCoy swung his medical tricorder around on his shoulder and knelt beside the motionless helmsman.

"What happened?" he asked Digard.

"I don't know, Doctor!" The guard's voice was wild. "I didn't see a thing. I was standing here, watching the entrance you went into, when Mr. Sulu just—screamed, all of a sudden, and fell over."

McCoy studied the first readings on the tricorder. His words were curt, clipped.

"He's been poisoned. Some kind of nerve toxin. Composition unknown, naturally."

He nudged the tricorder aside and skillful hands worked at the small containers in his belt medikit. A narrow tube was produced. McCoy didn't even bother to roll up the helmsman's shirt sleeve, simply jammed the tube against his upper arm.

Pulling it away, McCoy proceeded to check a tiny gauge set into the side of the metal pencil. His frown deepened and he reset an all but invisible dial below the indicator. Again he pressed it to Sulu's arm, paused, and pulled it away. A second check of the gauge and McCoy seemed to slump slightly, shaking his head in frustration.

"Can you help him?" Kirk had to break the choking silence.

"I don't know, Jim, I don't know. Blast! I can't get a correlation with any known venom." He shrugged sadly. "Either they're too alien to affect your system and they don't bother you at all, or else you run up against something like this." His head jerked towards Sulu.

"Antidotes are always found—after the first few autopsies."

Kirk tried to sound hopeful. "Maybe the ship's medical computer can . . . ?"

"Forget with the medical computer!" McCoy snarled. "He's got two minutes to live, unless I can find an answer." He muttered angrily to himself.

"Anaphase . . . synopmist . . . dylovene . . . maybe dylovene." The ineffectual tube was returned to his belt and a slightly larger instrument substituted. A quick adjustment of the hypo setting and then it was applied to Sulu's other arm.

There was a gentle hissing sound. McCoy pulled the hypo away and waited. After a few seconds he took another reading with the tricorder, concentrating on the newly treated region.

"No good, it's no good," he husked. "Soon the venom will reach his vital organs. Dylovene takes too much time to work . . . assuming it would work—"

"Maybe a stronger dose," Kirk urged.

"That won't be necessary," came a soft, pleasant voice. A new voice was about the only thing that could have turned their attention from Sulu at that moment. They spun to face the direction the voice had come from—the entrance to the laboratorylike building.

Five beings stood there. Their only similarity to man or Vulcan was in the question of size. Beyond that superficiality, they were utterly alien.

Their heads—Kirk presumed those faintly oval shapes topping the rest of their bodies were heads—were partly covered with a fine furry bristle. Two waving eyestalks were the only visible projections. There was no hint of a mouth, ears, nose, or any other recognizable external sense organ.

The bodies themselves were composed of a tight bunching of slender, ropelike extensions, some of which seemed to hang loosely at their sides like a long fringe. Other extensions grouped tightly together near the bottom before spreading out into a haphazard assortment of bulbous protuberances. Kirk guessed that these served as motive limbs for the creatures. This was revealed as so when they started to approach the landing party.

Their color was an ocher-yellow-green—not especially healthy-looking, but for all Kirk knew, the local version of a good tan. Perhaps they regarded Kirk's own fleshy-pink as a sign that he was nearing the last stages of desiccation.

Despite the complete strangeness of their appearance, Kirk felt none of the revulsion toward them that some more humanoid aliens could produce. Maybe it was their apparent passivity. They showed no sign of caution or of the usual wary belligerence.

If anything, they seemed inherently peaceful.

They got another surprise when the leader of the group spoke. Not only were the words intelligible, they were downright smooth. The tone was quiet, reasoned. Resigned, Kirk thought idly, wondering at the ability of the human mind to make jokes in the most unfunny situations.

He noticed out of the corner of an eye that Spock was taking a discreet tricorder reading on their visitors. The first officer's diplomacy might be ineffectual. The aliens might be perceptive enough to tell what he was doing. On the other hand, they might ignore Spock if he walked three times 'round their leader, bumping him with the tricorder.

Still, as with any first contact, it didn't hurt to be as tactful as possible. There were other things on Kirk's mind at that moment, however, which made attention to protocol difficult. All he could blurt out was, "Who are you?"

The being leading the group—who was a little taller than his four companions—replied softly.

"I am called Agmar. I believe we can help."

Kirk nodded once and turned away from him—if it was a "him." He kept his voice low as he murmured to Spock.

"What are you getting on them? Who are we dealing with here, Spock?"

"A moment, please, Captain. Give me a little time. The information I have thus far obtained does not permit a reasonable answer yet." He made an adjustment to the tricorder.

Meanwhile the five aliens had moved to surround the unmoving Sulu. The leader, Agmar, bent over the unconscious helmsman—a smooth, supple movement, like a reed bending with the wind.

Jointless, that explained it. Agmar and his companions moved without the stiffness of human joints.

Hovering motionless over Sulu, the eyestalks studied the prone form for several seconds. Then one of the free-hanging limblike extensions moved out from Agmar's side to extend over the body. A drop of some viscous liquid was extruded from the green tip.

McCoy, who'd kept a watchful eye on the whole sequence, now felt obliged to step in.

"Just a minute. I can't let you . . . whatever you are . . . inject him with some—" he hesitated, momentarily flustered, "—alien tree sap!"

Agmar's reply took no notice of the implied insult. "To wait is to assure your friend's death." A single eyestalk swiveled independently, like a chameleon's, to stare at McCoy. "I must proceed."

"Bones—" Kirk put a restraining hand on the doctor's shoulder. "Let them help."

"All right, Jim. But I don't like the whole idea." He turned away and strolled over to where Spock was still working with his tricorder.

"An interesting discovery, Doctor. These beings are of botanical origin."

"Intelligent plants?"

"So it would seem."

The loose tentacle dipped lower. With a gentle touch, Agmar applied the drop of golden liquid to the side of Sulu's neck. Now both eyestalks turned to observe the watching humans.

"It is a powerful antidote, quickly absorbed. He should begin to respond momentarily."

"Of course," suggested McCoy, still a little miffed, "it's of a completely alien nature and may not have any effect on him at all."

"True, Doctor," Spock agreed, "yet the same could be said of the poison which has so obviously affected him. I see no reason why the antidote should be rejected."

"Thanks," was all Kirk could think of to say to the creature. It rose, repeating the same supple movement.

"Welcome to the planet Phylos."

They certainly seemed friendly enough. A fraternal greeting and a badly needed helping hand, all in the first moments of contact. Still, he wasn't quite ready to fall all over himself in an orgy of backslapping. He'd been on too many worlds where the obviously black had turned out at the last moment to be white, to the detriment of the unfortunate caught in the color change.

But until given a reason why, he would treat the Phylosians as friends.

"I'm Captain James Kirk. This is Mr. Spock, my first officer; Dr. McCoy . . ." He went on to identify the rest of the landing party, including the motionless Sulu.

"You seem to have been expecting us, Agmar."

A tentacle (limb?) fluttered in the direction of the laboratory building.

"Our instruments have scanned and tracked you since your vessel first entered our space, Captain. We had reasons for not revealing ourselves immediately to you. But the injury to your companion compelled us to shed our hiding.

"We are a peaceful people, and we have a fear of aliens." The Phylosian spokesman seemed to hesitate. "We have had unfortunate meetings with such in the past." Kirk nodded understandingly, glanced over at Spock.

Role reversal was always difficult. *They* were the aliens, not the Phylosians.

There was a movement on the ground, and he found his attention drawn back to Sulu. The helmsman was still prone, but no longer motionless. He was starting to squirm like a man waking from a long sleep.

"What happened to him, anyway?" His touch of professional jealousy now long forgotten, a curious McCoy spoke while kneeling near Sulu and running his medical tricorder over the helmsman's chest. Scientific interest had taken over.

"He was bitten by the Retlaw plant. It is deadly only if the wound is left unattended."

"Mobile plants seem to be the rule on this world, rather than animals," Kirk observed, hoping he wasn't treading on someone's religion. But Agmar took no offense.

"That is so."

"Your medication worked quickly."

Agmar didn't shrug—he couldn't, having no shoulders—but Kirk felt he could sense the equivalent.

"A minor achievement."

"Minor achievement!" blurted McCoy, looking up in disbelief from his tricorder readings. "I never saw an anti-toxin work so fast. I don't know anything about your other sciences, but if this is a 'minor' sample of your medical capabilities, I'd like to chat with some of your doctors."

"Doctors?"

"Physicians—healers."

"Ah," Agmar exclaimed. "Yes, Doctor McCoy. I understand now. But you must realize that healing is not a specialized function among my people."

"Not special—" McCoy looked incredulous. "You mean you're *all* doctors?"

"Not in the way you mean, Doctor McCoy. But each has the ability to . . . to repair a number of damaged bodily functions. We will talk of this more, later, if you wish."

"I wish, I wish!" McCoy looked rather like the little boy about to be let loose in the candy store. A low moan from Sulu precluded further conversation.

The helmsman's eyes were open, and he appeared to be making motions of getting up. McCoy made another pass with the tricorder. Then he looked up and nodded. Amazement still tinged his words.

"Something's destroying the poison left in his bloodstream, all right. Body functions are running up to normal. And I mean running." He glanced at the Phylosian leader.

"Look, Agmar. Agreed, if the poison affects humans, a local antidote conceivably might. Clearly does, in fact. But how could you be so sure it would work?"

"We could not be sure," the Phylosian replied softly. "But there have been humanoid aliens on Phylos before. Besides, it was the only chance left for your friend."

"Humanoid aliens who spoke our language?" asked Spock.

"Ah, you are curious as to our method of translation and communication. The voder, a mechanical translator." He reached into the folds of his central body area. For a fleeting moment Kirk expected him to remove a mouth.

Instead, Agmar produced a small, round, flat disk of metal.

When he "spoke," his voice came from the center of the disk.

"Our natural organs of verbal communication are quite small. They require a great deal of artificial amplification to be effective any distance. The voder is completely self-contained and most efficient for this purpose."

"Most," agreed Spock, hoping for a chance to take one of the unbelievably compact instruments apart.

Such charming exchanges of mutual admiration were fine, Kirk reflected, but right now other things concerned him more.

"I like puzzles, Agmar, but I also like answers. We were pretty convinced when we first set down in your city that there was no one here. Then we find you—or rather, you find us. Yet I find it hard to believe that the few of you are the sole inhabitants of this metropolis. We're not exactly standing in the middle of a local desert. Where are the rest of your people?"

"Your curiosity does your profession credit, Captain Kirk, and it shall be satisfied. Come with us and we will show you."

Kirk looked down at Sulu. With McCoy's help, he was struggling to his feet.

"How do you feel, Mr. Sulu?"

The helmsman blinked. "I'm . . . I'm all right now, Captain . . . I think. One moment I was sucking my finger and the next—wham!" His voice was that of a man waking from a dream and finding it reality. "I felt like an incendiary grenade had gone off inside me."

"Can you walk?"

"Yes. I'm okay, sir." Sulu straightened himself.

"All right, then." Kirk turned back to Agmar. "Let's go."

The Phylosian turned—perhaps pivoted would be more accurate—and ambled off in the direction of the building next to the laboratory. His companions, none of whom had yet ventured a word, turned with him. Kirk and the other bipeds followed.

"You sure you're all right, Sulu?" pressed McCoy.

"Fine, Doctor." The navigation officer even managed a

slight smile. "Hard to believe now that there was ever anything wrong with me."

McCoy shook his head and muttered to himself. "Remarkable . . . crazy and remarkable . . ."

"Yes," added Spock softly. "How fortunate for us that Agmar and his fellows were so close by."

"You said it!" agreed McCoy fervently. Something scratched at his mind, and he gave Spock an uncertain glance. But the science officer gave no sign that his words meant anything but what they said. He speeded up to come alongside Kirk.

They entered the building, turning first through another of the unbarred but mazelike entrances. Inside they found themselves in a hall of titanic proportions stretching endlessly into the distance. The metal walls rose to form a domed ceiling high overhead. A skylight running the whole length of the enormous corridor was set into the curving roof.

Agmar stopped. Kirk slowly turned a full circle before returning his attention to the alien.

"Well, where are your people, Agmar?"

Instead of answering, Agmar went to a panel set in one wall and depressed several hidden switches. There was the slightest hissing sound. One security guard reached instinctively for his phaser and looked properly abashed when no threat materialized.

A tall, high door slid aside in the nearest section of wall. Row upon row of glasslike cases, looking like so many rectangular diamonds, filled the revealed section.

No one noticed Sulu put a hand to his head, and he covered the gesture of weakness quickly. McCoy and Spock moved down the ranked glass caskets while Kirk followed curiously. Agmar and his four companions remained in place, watching. Presumably this necrophilic display held no surprises for them.

The leader of the aliens gestured with a limb. There was a hint of sadness in his voice.

"Our people, Captain Kirk."

Each individual sarcophogus was nearly ten meters high. A single gigantic body filled every crystal coffin. And each of the immobile forms was covered from head to root with a covering of thick green bristle.

They had no recognizable heads, not even of the kind Agmar and his friends had. Instead, at the top end of each shape was a mass that looked something like an artichoke. But under the bristle, Kirk and the other crewmen could see that the actual bodies were composed of the same furry rope-like extensions, also bunching up tightly near the base and spreading out into footlike protrusions. In this respect they were identical to Agmar. And there were other resemblances between the living Phylosians and these embalmed giants.

It was an impressive and rather chilling sight.

Eventually Spock looked up from his tricorder. "Nerve tissue mass is exceptionally high. Readings indicate these beings utilized almost seventy percent of their brain capacity—a very high ratio."

Kirk turned and looked back at Agmar. "Your early ancestors."

"No," replied the Phylosian, "only the generation before us." He bowed slightly.

"Then what happened?" Kirk prodded. "I never heard of such enormous physiological changes taking place in such a short span of time."

Agmar's voice was matter-of-fact.

"A human came to Phylos."

X

Kirk hesitated. It was too late to back out of the question now. "You mean a humanoid?"

The eyestalks were angled directly at him. "No, a human—like you, Captain. You remarked on the reaction of humans to the poisons and antidotes of our world. Such things can operate both ways, Captain James Kirk.

"The human, quite unintentionally, brought sickness and death with him—mostly death. But instead of running away, of taking flight and leaving us, he remained and worked to try and save us from the very disease he had carried."

McCoy gestured with his medical 'corder. "It adds up, Jim." He nodded at the silent sarcophogi. "The bodies all show evidence of gram-positive bacteria. It's carried by humanoids without ill effect, but preliminary readings taken when we first landed indicate that Staphylococcus strains aren't native to this world. It must have been like the worst plague imaginable."

"We had no way of knowing what was destroying us," confirmed Agmar. "That, I think, was the most horrible thing of all to our forebears."

"*Was*," McCoy echoed. "You were alive then?"

"Very young we were and barely formed, but yes, we remember that time."

"Then how? . . ." Kirk paused. There was a new sound in the room. He thought he'd heard it before, somewhere. Something like wings flapping.

There was a louder sound, and he looked upwards. A rush of air slammed at his face and he ducked instinctively. He got the impression of something streaking past just in front of his nose.

337

The creature didn't fly away. It remained hovering overhead, circling in the still air of the corridor. The intruder was a good twelve feet long. It's segmented body was hinged in the middle and the upper half would swing awkwardly from side to side.

Despite the flapping sound, the beast had no wings. In place of them, a pair of thick coils protruded from the body. The creature dipped slightly and the coils contracted, kicking the floating monster powerfully upwards once more. It repeated this maneuver regularly.

The constant contractions produced the flapping sounds. Those coils looked taut as steel and reminded Kirk of something much less benign than a bird's wings.

"Plant life, Captain," Spock informed him. "If there are animals here they are surely scarce. These creatures appear both primitive and aggressive."

Abruptly, the whooshing sound was repeated as the thing dove again at Kirk. He took a couple of halting steps to one side and dodged just in time. Out came his phaser, down went the trigger, and . . .

Nothing happened.

He tried again. Nothing. The phaser wasn't putting out enough heat to warm a piece of old toast.

"Your phasers!" Spock, Sulu, McCoy, and the two security men tried their own weapons.

"They won't work on any setting, sir!" said Sulu nervously.

"To insure the preservation of the forebears there is a weapons deactivator in effect here," Agmar told them. "Your destructive devices will not work."

McCoy yelled a warning. "It seems to be after you, Jim!"

"Weapons deactivator," Kirk murmured, keeping a careful eye on the darting movements of the, well, swooper was an apt term. "Then *this* should work." He pulled out his communicator. "Kirk to *Enterprise* . . . Kirk to . . ."

It might as well have been an invitation. Suddenly the hall was filled with the big creatures. They didn't appear out of the walls, but they seemed to.

Half a dozen of them immediately ensnarled Kirk, before he could complete the call. He struggled, and the communicator bounced to the floor.

"Captain!" Sulu shouted. The others moved toward him and drew their own attackers.

Spock was enveloped quickly. Something fell from his pocket—the tape cassette he'd picked up earlier. No one saw it fall—certainly not Digard and Ush, who were busy with attackers of their own.

Meanwhile Kirk was fighting back with plenty of vim, and absolutely no effect. Something knocked his legs out from under him and he found himself pinned to the floor like a trapped butterfly. He struck out with a hand, contacted nothing. The darn things were quick as well as strong.

It was over as soon as it had begun. Kirk, Sulu, and the others lay motionless on the ground, held tightly in the grasp of dozens of swoopers.

Sulu, who appeared to have recovered from one attack just in time to succumb to another, looked over at Kirk.

"What do you think they have in mind for us, sir?" Kirk didn't answer his helmsman. Instead, his attention was riveted on action overhead.

"Something tells me we've just been the prize suckers for a diversionary assault. Look!" Other eyes went upward, to see Spock, totally enmeshed in swooper coils, being flown 'round the bend near the building's entrance.

Another shape intruded on Kirk's vision and stared down at him quietly. If anything Agmar's attitude was apologetic.

"I am sorry for this deception, Captain Kirk. But there was no other way."

It was Kirk's task to remain patient and understanding of alien mores. Right now, however, he'd have taken considerable pleasure in soaking Agmar and his fellows in oil and vinegar and tossing them to death.

He wrenched with all his strength at the bar on his right arm, but the swooper coil encircling his upper torso was as unyielding as an anaconda.

"What are you babbling about, Agmar? What are those things going to do with Spock?"

"He has been chosen to serve a great cause," the Phylosian intoned reverently. "The Master has waited many years, searched many visitors, studied many nearby worlds in hopes of finding a specimen like Spock. It is good." Agmar raised a loose fold of himself skyward.

The swoopers immediately released Kirk and his companions—reluctantly, it seemed—and took off at top speed down the big hall, melting away into hidden corridors and side panels like a cloud of bats in a cathedral.

"And now," continued Agmar, "all the worlds of the galaxy will share in total peace and harmony!"

There was, of course, a time and a place for anything . . . including a little educative violence. At the moment Kirk felt like sharing peace and harmony about as much as he did partying with the Phylosians.

He climbed slowly to his feet and approached Agmar with just such unharmonizing thoughts in mind. The eyestalks would be a good place to begin, he decided.

"So help me, Agmar, if you don't tell me where Spock is, I'll . . ."

He broke off as an enormous shadow spread across the room. It wasn't a swooper. Kirk looked up. The sight was at once more familiar and more alien than any they had yet encountered on this greenhouse world.

Standing in the doorway was a human male. He was perfectly normal in every way save one; he stood just under twenty-four feet.

He wasn't smiling.

There was a movement immediately in front of the landing party, and Kirk lowered his gaze. Agmar and his four associates had fallen to their knees—or knee-substitutes—before the giant. It was the most humanlike gesture they'd yet made. The implications of the movement were appalling.

McCoy had the presence of mind to activate the medical tricorder at the giant's entrance.

"Praise to the Master!" the five Phylosians chorused dutifully. "All praise and adoration to the Restorer, the Master, our Saviour!"

"Another plant?" Kirk asked quietly. This one would be hard to swallow.

But McCoy's 'corder insisted that in this case, at least, appearances were not deceiving.

"No, it's definitely human, Jim. That explains that first unusual reading I picked up." Further explanation was soon provided by the giant himself.

"I AM DR. STAVOS KENICLIUS #5," the giant boomed. He

wore only a short pair of pants and several instruments. A cane or walking stick the size of a small pine was clasped in his right hand. "WELCOME TO PHYLOS, CAPTAIN KIRK."

"No thanks, Keniclius. Yours is the second welcome we've received here and I'm getting sick of them. I don't want any more of this world's hellos."

"DO YOU KNOW WHAT YOU DO WANT, CAPTAIN KIRK?"

"You bet I do. Where's Mr. Spock?"

"THAT IS NO LONGER ANY CONCERN OF YOURS, CAPTAIN." The giant took two strides toward them. "HE IS MINE, NOW. MORE IMPORTANTLY, THE ESSENCE OF HIM IS MINE. I HAVE WAITED FOR MR. SPOCK A LONG TIME . . . TOO LONG TO CONSIDER GIVING HIM UP.

"RETURN TO YOUR SHIP."

He bent and picked up the communicator. It looked like a toy in his massive palm. He tossed it contemptuously to Kirk, who caught it automatically.

"HERE IS YOUR COMMUNICATIONS DEVICE. GO BACK TO YOUR SHIP."

"Not without my first officer." The two men glared at each other.

If Spock had been present he'd undoubtedly have advised against a confrontation between Kirk and a man four times his size and more so in weight.

Kirk might have thought of it himself, except that he was subject to human traits which did not trouble Mr. Spock. Right now, for example, he was too mad to consider the situation dispassionately.

"I AM SORRY, CAPTAIN. YOU WILL LEAVE NOW OR SUFFER THE CONSEQUENCES." He made a gesture with one hand.

A flock—no, a crop—of swoopers came darting into the chamber again. Pausing overhead like a swarm of organic helicopters, they circled back and forth over the knot of watching humans. Their hinged bodies jerked in the middle, twitching nervously from side to side.

Dropping his gaze, McCoy happened to notice the tiny tape cartridge Spock had dropped earlier. He bent and picked it up, slipping it without undue motion into a pocket. His caution was unnecessary. Both Keniclius and the Phylosians had their attention focused wholly on Kirk.

The object of their study stood fuming silently. He was

frustrated, angry, and almost mad enough to take on the huge
Keniclius despite their difference in size.

But he'd already had one very enlightening experience with
swoopers and their abilities while they were operating under
external restraint. He had no illusions about the outcome if
Keniclius let them run loose.

For now, then, they had only one choice. He flipped open
the communicator and raised it slowly to his lips. There was
always the chance that either Keniclius or the Phylosians were
thought sensitives. No, if that were the case they should have
fallen dead from reading his thoughts several minutes ago.

"Kirk to *Enterprise*," he repeated. "Chief Kyle? Beam
us up."

Kyle was smiling when they materialized normally in the
transporter room. His smile turned to a worried frown. It
deepened as the little party exited the alcove. He made a
frantic grab for certain controls.

Kirk took a moment to reassure him. "Easy, Chief, you
haven't lost Mr. Spock."

"Well, then," the transporter chief replied, searching the
room, "where is he?"

"Out of reach of your transporter, I'm afraid. For the moment. But you might keep hunting for him. Try the transporter on his pattern every now and then in the area of our
touchdown point. There's always the chance something down
there will get lazy, or move him, and you'll suddenly be able
to bring him aboard."

"The power drain, sir," began Kyle, but Kirk cut him off.

"We have plenty of power, Mr. Kyle," he said as he
headed for the elevator, "but a distinct shortage of Mr.
Spock. Try at five minute intervals."

"Aye, sir," Kyle agreed uncertainly. His acknowledgment barely beat the closing doors.

Kirk held a small, quick conference to explain the situation
to those principal officers who'd remained on board. It was
a solemn group of men and women who stared expectantly
back at him when he'd concluded.

"Uhura, you'll have to take over the library computer station in Mr. Spock's absence. Lieutenant M'ress will manage
communications for you."

"Yes, sir."

"I want you to use the library to dig for two things, Lieutenant." He ticked them off on his fingers. "One, any record extant of a form of plant life of extraordinary intelligence and a technology so advanced they don't bother to boast of it by visiting inhabited worlds."

"And two—I want you to check into the one hope we have in all this."

"Hope, Jim?" McCoy looked puzzled. Kirk only smiled back confidently.

"A giant who is fool enough or megalomaniac enough to tell us who he is." He looked back at Uhura.

"A human named Keniclius—Stavos Keniclius. Said individual may or may not be entitled to the label of doctor." Uhura nodded and moved rapidly to the library station. Seconds later its console was a Christmas tree of blinking lights.

"Sulu, you and Arex get to work with the ship's main sensors. See if you can locate Spock or Keniclius. And Sulu, see if you can program some sensors to differentiate the Phylosians from the lesser plant life. They're probably the only other intelligent life forms on the planet." Both helmsmen moved to their stations and began to work swiftly.

That left only McCoy.

"Sorry I can't help, Jim."

"You can, Bones." Kirk slumped in the command chair. "While Uhura, Sulu, and Arex are running checks, you can get yourself down to Sick Bay and find me a non-narcotic, nonenervating tranquilizer. If I don't relax soon I'm going to start breaking things. And I haven't got time for a trip to the therapy chamber." McCoy grinned.

"I'll see what I can find, Jim."

He wasn't gone long. And by the time the mild relaxer had taken effect, Kirk was able to speak with more patience and listen with a little of the same. Inside, though, he was still seething.

"Anything at all, Mr. Sulu?" The helmsman shook his head.

"We haven't been able to pick up anything like a humanoid life-reading, sir. And it's not because they're attempting to decoy or divert our probes—there's no evidence of any surface interference. Spock and Keniclius must be somewhere our sensor scans can't penetrate."

"Outstanding news," Kirk grumbled. "What about the Phylosians?"

"It was hard to calibrate for an intelligent plant form, sir. We're registering thousands of botanical readings in the city, including the swoopers, which have a definite pattern. But no sign of anything higher. Nothing that might be Agmar or his friends." Kirk frowned, thinking. "Agmar said something about a weapons deactivator in operation in at least one of their buildings . . . but nothing about its range or limitations. Let's find out. Mr. Sulu, lock ship's phasers on that laboratory building we first entered. Wide area stun setting."

Sulu manipulated controls. "Ready, sir."

"Just a minute." Kirk turned to face Uhura. "Lieutenant, how are you coming on information about Keniclius?"

"There's nothing current, Captain." She looked disappointed. "I think I may be getting something from the biography section of the recent history bank, but it'll take a moment or two, yet."

"All right, Lieutenant. Keep at it.

"Fire phasers, Mr. Sulu." Sulu hit the proper switch.

"Firing, sir."

A beam of pure energy erupted from the bowfront of the *Enterprise*. Instantly it disrupted orderly molecules, surprised combinations of oxygen, nitrogen, carbon, and a host of others as it speared down through the atmosphere of Phylos.

Nothing could stand before that paralyzing beam, powered by the space-warping engines of the great starship. Nothing solid—

Sulu was staring into a gooseneck viewer. Now he turned to look back at Kirk.

"No effect, Captain. Nothing at all. Phaser stun was neutralized at . . ." He paused and checked another gauge set into the console near the viewer, "a distance of approximately one thousand meters above the target area. Should I try a stronger setting?"

"No." Kirk drummed his fingers on an arm of the command chair, and thought.

"I suspect it either wouldn't have any effect at all, Mr. Sulu, or else it would break through and destroy anything it touched—Mr. Spock, too. That means that either way our weapons are effectively useless. All right. We'll have to go back down there and rescue Mr. Spock without them.''

''The old oriental marital arts are kind of a hobby with me, Captain,'' said Sulu. He smiled faintly. ''But I don't think hands and feet will work too well against those swoopers.''

What, exactly, is a flash of genius?

Mental stimulation. A concatenation of cerebral cross-currents. The fusion of one particle of cause with another of effect which—once in a while, just once in a while—produces a molecule of solution.

But all McCoy said was, ''I think there might be something we can use that'd be more effective, Sulu.'' A crooked smile crossed his face. ''I'm just not sure which section—''

''If you've got any suggestions at all, Bones—'' By way of reply, McCoy leaned close and whispered in Kirk's ear. The Captain's expression grew by turns amused, disbelieving, and finally determined.

''Where'd you get an idea like that, Bones?''

McCoy looked grimly pleased. ''From Agmar.''

''I don't know—'' Kirk mused. ''I see what you mean about 'which section.' '' Turning suddenly he hit an armrest switch, spoke into the broadcast grid.

''Kirk to engineering. Scotty?'' The chief engineer's filtered voice replied from the other end of the starship.

''Here, sir.''

''Scotty, I've got a priority project for you. Who's your weapon's specialist?''

''That'd be Lieutenant Chatusram, sir.''

''Get him. I've got some special equipment I want you to make up—and I want it yesterday.''

The special equipment was basically very simple. McCoy had no trouble conveying what was needed over the intercom. Nor, according to Chatusram, would it be difficult to make.

''I don't think we'll have any problems with the actual construction, Captain,'' explained the weaponsmith, ''though some of the nonsolid components may take some time to compose. The ingredients are simple, but the combination required is not. Still, I'm sure my staff and I can manage it.''

"Good for you, 'Ram," said Kirk. "Mr. Scott, see that the lieutenant gets all the help he needs."

"Aye, Captain."

"How soon, Lieutenant?" Chatusram's reply was cautious, but confident.

"I believe if the basic mechanical components are in stock, within the hour, Captain."

"That'll have to do. Hop to it, gentlemen. Kirk out." He ended the discussion.

It was Uhura's turn to speak. She'd been waiting impatiently throughout the cross-ship conversation and now she broke in before anyone else could demand Kirk's attention.

"I have the requested information on the man identified as Stavos Keniclius, sir. I'll put the statistics and what visuals there are on the main screen."

"Thank you, Uhura." Kirk turned back to McCoy. "Bones, you really think this gadget of yours will work? It seems almost too simple."

"I can think of several reasons why it should, Jim. That's one of them. Another is what Agmar said that gave me the idea in the first place. The clincher is that, way back when, my great-granddaddy had the finest garden in metropolitan North-South America." Kirk nodded and looked to the viewscreen.

The screen lit, and the feminine computer voice of the *Enterprise* sounded over the speaker.

"Working."

"Here it comes, sir," said Uhura. Almost before she finished, a portrait had appeared on the screen.

There were some slight differences—the figure in the portrait was slightly older, for example—but Kirk, McCoy, and Sulu recognized Keniclius's features immediately.

More revealing was the accompanying statistical chart, especially those figures which declared that the man shown was a normal human of about the same height and weight as Kirk.

While they studied the printout, the computer voice supplied additional information.

"Drawn from recent-near-recent Earth history file, category scientists, male, subheading iconoclasts . . . Keniclius, Stavos. Terran physiologist-physicist period Eugenics Wars.

Specialist in eugenics and manipulative endocrinology. Noted for plan to clone perfect humanoid prototype as founder of idealized 'master race' to act as galactic peace-keepers. Concept evaluated by ruling government of time and formally rejected as, quote, 'too antihumanistic.'

"Experiments persisted despite governmental decree. Upon discovery of continuance of illegal research, Keniclius banned from terran community. Voluntarily accepted total exile and vanished into an uncharted region of space. Cursory search initiated. No body found, no official death certificate issued—"

The computer droned on, pouring out additional information. Most of it was trivial, peripheral and, more importantly, downright unhelpful. There was nothing that might be employed as a psychological weapon against the giant below.

But they'd pegged Keniclius, all right.

"No further data," the computer concluded. Voice and visual display disappeared together. Then McCoy spoke.

"Wasn't there an old story about a modern Diogenes roaming the galaxy in search of someone special?"

"Someone special," Kirk muttered. He looked up. "A perfect someone. Someone special to begin the ideal race, yes, I've heard that story too, Bones, as a child."

"That's just it, Jim. This can't be *the* Keniclius. He'd have to be over two hundred and fifty years old!"

"The original Keniclius, yes," Kirk noted. "Keep in mind what the library just told us. What was he banned for?"

Understanding lit McCoy's eyes. "I remember now. He said he was Keniclius 5. My God, he's gone and cloned *himself*, to carry on his search! And his clones have recloned themselves, right on down the line." He shook his head, an expression of mixed distaste and admiration.

"At least we're not dealing with a complete megalomaniac," Kirk added. "If we were, he'd long ago have decided that *he* was the 'perfect specimen' all along. Then we'd be faced with an army of giants instead of just one."

"I'll grant that in his favor," admitted McCoy reluctantly, "but by the same token, Jim, he's not going to be an easy man to talk out of his dreams. . . ."

XI

Forty-two point one five minutes later (ship-time), Kirk, McCoy, Sulu, and Chief Engineer Scott assembled in the main transporter room. Scott carried three small traveling bags in his arms. He handed them out to his fellow officers while Kirk tried to regard the upcoming attempt with a detached air.

"It's seems incredible that a man could take a few cells from his body and successfully reproduce himself time after time. Yet that seems to be the kind of disturbed genius we're dealing with in Dr. Keniclius and his oversized successors."

At the moment, however, Sulu had other things on his mind than the astonishing feats—biological or otherwise—of their giant antagonist. Most of his worries concerned the untested quantity resting in the leather carry-bag. He hefted it and tapped the contents. It responded with a faint metallic ring.

"I just hope these things work, that's all."

"Oh, they'll work all right, Lieutenant," Scott assured him. "The equipment's simple enough—foolproof, in fact. Chatusram and I saw to that. But I admit I've got my own doubts about the stuff they contain. I've heard of some mighty strange ways to fight aliens, but—"

"These are mighty strange aliens we're fighting, Scotty." Kirk moved into the transporter alcove. "As soon as Dr. McCoy, Mr. Sulu, and I have beamed down," he told the chief engineer, "I want you to leave orbit and—"

"Leave orbit, sir?"

Kirk nodded. "If they think we've gone, I have a hunch they'll stop scanning the area around their still-functioning structures. On any other world in a similar situation it would

348

be standard precautionary procedure to keep scanners on. But the Phylosians do whatever Keniclius tells them to do, and this mutant is so confident of his own power—he's been a virtual god for so long—he won't think any mere humans like us will dare defy him.

"He's been out of touch with humanity too long to be anything but contemptuous of it. Not that I can blame him, considering what some of us were like during the Eugenics Wars. Give us thirty minutes on the surface, Scotty, and then circle back."

"All right," the chief engineer reluctantly agreed. "But if I may be permitted an opinion, sir . . . I dinna like it."

"Neither do I." Kirk made sure he was well inside the perimeter of the transporter disk. "But without phasers or any other modern weapon, we'll need all the surprise we can muster. If the ship seems to leave, we might get it."

McCoy and Sulu joined him in the chamber. He turned to look at the waiting chief Kyle.

"Energize."

The three men became three drifting masses of lambent color. Then they were gone.

Scott stared into the empty chamber for a moment, became aware that Kyle was watching him.

"Well, what are you starin' at, Kyle?"

"Nothing, Chief. I—"

"See that you don't do it again."

"Yes, sir."

Scott stalked off toward the elevator doors. He'd have to officially assume command now—and it would be he who would have to issue the unpopular retreat order.

Life was dreadfully unfair sometimes!

Three glittering cylinders resumed human shape on a street of the Phylosian metropolis. Sulu was checking his tricorder as soon as they'd fully rematerialized. He kept the mysterious leather bag tucked tightly under one arm.

"No indication of a scan, sir," he said finally. "I don't think they know we're here. Unless—"

"No," Kirk sighed gratefully. "That kind of subtlety is beyond Keniclius. If he knew we were back he'd show up roaring biblical pronouncements, or send a crop of those toothy fliers. Let's get a move on.''

Kirk took two steps and started to turn the corner around the thin tower they'd set down next to . . . and almost walked straight into a flight of the just-mentioned swoopers.

Flattening themselves against the curving wall in the convenient shadow of the glass edifice, they barely breathed as the swarm of powerful carnivores sailed past.

''I'm not sure I can take too much of this,'' McCoy finally gasped. ''Watch those predictions, Jim. Why'd you take me anyway, instead of Arex or a couple of security personnel?''

''You ought to know better than that, Bones. We don't know what kind of shape we'll find Spock in.''

''If we find him,'' murmured McCoy.

''Let's not even think about that, hmm?''

Sulu looked up from his tricorder and tried to inject a more hopeful note. ''I wouldn't worry too much about those swoopers, Doctor. They seem to be almost mindless. They attack primarily as a reflex action.''

''Out of sight, out of mind, is that it?'' McCoy grunted. The helmsman nodded.

''The way is clear now, Captain.''

They turned the corner without being challenged. Moving at a smooth trot, they headed for the laboratory building.

Once, a tiny dandelionlike plant tried to follow Sulu. It took Kirk and McCoy several minutes to catch up with the sprinting lieutenant. Other than the single fuzzy, they encountered nothing ambulatory.

They'd materialized in a different section of the city than the first time. If only they'd landed here initially, events might have taken a different course. But that was wishful thinking. They turned another corner.

Came up short.

''I don't believe it,'' Sulu murmured.

''Incredible,'' was the only word Kirk could think of. McCoy just stared.

They were standing close by the entrance to a colossal, hangarlike building. The structure was easily a couple of kilometers long. Inside, ranged neatly in double rows, were hundreds of translucent, milky, teardrop shapes, each dozens of yards high.

In the immediate foreground were the five Phylosians. Each rose on a small, automatic lifting platform. They were working at the teardrop shapes, cleaning them, scraping and pulling a thick mossy growth from their sides.

"What else could they be but ships, Jim?"

Kirk agreed. "Looks like they're getting ready to go on a trip, too. But where? To what purpose?"

"By the number of ships here I'd say a mass migration is being planned—or invasion."

"Agmar insisted they were a peaceful people," Sulu put in.

"Oh, sure!" spat McCoy sarcastically. "We've had ample evidence of that, haven't we? 'Peaceful' has almost as many definitions as love, Mr. Sulu."

"Is that a clinical opinion, Doctor?"

"Ease off, you two," warned Kirk. "We'll probably have a definition supplied, soon enough." He looked thoughtful. "But you've got a point, Bones. These ships, this city—I'm not saying the motives and abilities of a vegetable civilization would be so different from ours, but let's not jump to any conclusions. This is the first one we've encountered."

"And the last, I hope," the doctor muttered. He added, half to himself, "I always did hate vegetables as a kid. Now I know I had a good reason."

"And that's about enough hilarity, Bones. If Spock were here he wouldn't be laughing."

"Sorry, Jim." McCoy turned serious once again. "I'd almost forgotten why we're here." He nodded in the direction of the gigantic hangar. "Those ships look like they've never left the ground. Probably they were all set to leave, when Keniclius the first arrived and his new diseases swept the planet."

Kirk nodded, glanced at Sulu. "Any indication of Keniclius's or Mr. Spock's whereabouts?"

Sulu checked the tricorder, looked disappointed. "They're not around here, sir. Certainly not in the hangar. I read only the Phylosians."

"Umm. Well, followers can be led. Maybe we can be as persuasive as Keniclius."

Moving from wall to wall and taking care to conceal themselves well, they gradually made their way to the entrance of the enormous structure.

It appeared that each Phylosian was taking care of one ship by himself. That was fine with Kirk. It would make the momentary disappearance of one of their number less obvious to the others.

Agmar was working close by. At the moment he was filling the tank of his lifter with some sort of cleaning fluid from huge canisters stacked neatly against the near wall. Taking up positions behind these, the three men waited for the leader of the Phylosians to return.

Two others came and filled their tanks before McCoy whispered tensely, "Here he comes!"

"Do we want the flitter he's riding?" asked Sulu hurriedly. Kirk shook his head.

"Might take too long to figure the controls. I'd rather stay on the ground anyway. It might be subject to outside orders. I don't want someone yanking my feet out from under me a couple of hundred meters up in the air."

Agmar brought the little vehicle down smoothly to the canisters. His back was to them. They tackled him without any trouble.

Sulu and Kirk were momentarily repulsed at handling a creature who felt like a clump of sticky straw. They almost lost control of the struggling alien.

Fortunately, McCoy was used to handling things that would turn many men squeamish. He wasn't at all bothered by the unconventional feel of the Phylosian. He hung on tightly until Kirk and Sulu had recovered from the initial shock of contact.

They had no difficulty dragging him back behind the high containers. Kirk's only worry had been the chance that the repair flitter might be fitted with some kind of automatic alarm that would relay back to Keniclius. But there was no sign that anything of the sort existed. A moment's consideration and he realized there was no need to be concerned.

The little repair vehicle had shown a tendency to take off again. But once they'd removed its sole passenger, it stopped and now floated patiently in place.

"Agmar," began Kirk quietly, "we don't want to hurt you. You claim you're a peaceful people. Well, we're an easygoing race, too, we humans. But we must have Spock back. If this means using crude physical force against you, then rest assured we'll do so.''

Agmar was not impressed. Nor was he arrogant. More than anything else his attitude smacked of resigned indifference. If he was startled to see the humans again, he didn't show it.

"I do not think that is possible," he said blandly. "The Vulcan-human blend of wisdom, sense of order, durability, reason, and strength is the finest the Master has ever found. We are pleased Spock will carry on our work.''

"Patrick O'Morion!" Sulu gasped. The whole situation had been turned upside down and a new light now gleamed on its backside.

"Carry on *your* work?" was all Kirk could stutter.

"We are the last of a dying race on a dying world, Captain," intoned Agmar. A limb that remained unpinned gestured towards the ships.

"Once, we had a great mission. Then the disease destroyed nearly all of us. We five are the frail remnant of that race, the inheritors of that purpose.

"And we are sterile. We cannot put out spores. When we go, there will be no more of our kind.''

"This great plan, this mission of yours," probed McCoy. "What happens to it if something happens to Spock—or to the Master?''

It was Agmar's turn to be put off-stride and confused. He recovered quickly, utilizing the response that all "masters" engender in their subjects.

"There will always be a Master. But come, you are worried about your friend, and that is needless, I assure you. I will show you that he is safe and in good condition. Better than you can guess.''

He wriggled out of their relaxing grasp and shuffled into the hangar. Kirk and the others hesitated, then followed.

"Just like that, Captain?" asked Sulu. Kirk was thinking furiously, trying to stay one mental step ahead of Agmar. Yet, who could tell how the Phylosians saw things?

"Yes, just like that, Mr. Sulu. All the same, keep that bag handy.'' By way of emphasis he hefted his own.

"No tricks now, Agmar." The Phylosian didn't reply. He

leaned forward and pressed a button on the console of the flitter.

Rapidly, the other four joined them. They dismounted from their own repair craft. Then the five moved together to stop before what looked like a solid, blank wall.

"The way is through here, gentlemen," said Agmar. He moved forward. In doing so, Kirk noticed that he stepped on a circular section of floor that was slightly different in color from the rest. Immediately, the wall slid aside to reveal a huge metallic iris behind it.

Agmar moved again and stepped on a second odd-hued round area. Now the iris dilated. An enormous tunnel appeared, a gaping wound in the earth. Its floor was smooth and sloped gently downward, under the city.

Kirk could just make out another iris far away down the tunnel. A second later it, too, opened.

Beyond was only endless blackness.

Agmar and his fellows started into the tunnel. Kirk did not follow immediately. Nor did McCoy or Sulu. That bottomless hole looked awfully dark.

Agmar turned. "We sprang from the soil, Captain," he said reassuringly. "These tunnels are part of our ancient home." He drew a flat disk from his middle. It was somewhat larger than a voder. He did something to one side of the disk, and it suddenly put out a brilliant beam of light.

"This will serve to show our way." He turned and started down the tunnel.

Kirk wasn't keen on following, but they didn't have much choice. Beating up an already willing Agmar was a poor alternative to what appeared to be acquiesence.

"Once more into the breech," muttered McCoy.

There was more than one tunnel, they soon saw. More than two, than three. After a short walk they'd already passed dozens of intersecting corridors, a veritable labyrinth of passageways cutting through the earth beneath the city.

Sulu was busy with his tricorder.

"No wonder we couldn't detect Spock or Keniclius with shipboard scanners, Captain. Our sensor beams couldn't penetrate here."

"Absurd," McCoy objected, observing their surroundings. "It must have been interference of some kind. These walls don't look thick enough."

"Perhaps not, Doctor," admitted Sulu. "But according to tricorder analysis they're composed of artificial elements some six hundred times denser than lead, in addition to a surface force field." He shook his head wonderingly. "I can only guess at the kind of foundation they must sit on."

"On the other hand—" continued McCoy as though he'd never doubted the walls' shielding ability.

They hadn't been walking much longer before something else caught Kirk's attention. He whispered to McCoy.

"Do you hear something?"

"What, Jim?"

"I'm not sure." Kirk's brow furrowed in concentration.

"Not much further now, Captain," came Agmar's voice from just ahead.

"There it is again!" Kirk gave a sudden start and stopped, his voice rising. "A flapping sound. . . ."

That was the signal for light to leave the tunnel, and illumination of another sort to set in. They found themselves standing helplessly in blackness as black as the deepest sleep.

They'd been tricked again.

He shouted, "Use your belt lights!"

"They don't operate," replied Sulu nervously. "I've already tried."

"Agmar!" Kirk yelled angrily. "Agmar! . . ."

Agmar didn't answer.

Now McCoy and Sulu also recognized the uneven, beating sounds of the approaching swoopers. In the confined darkness of the tunnel it sounded like a growing storm. Most men are willing to face a certain amount of danger in normal circumstances.

But in the dark!

The hardest thing was to resist the urge to go charging off into nothingness, to run blindly away from the threatening noise. They might crash into a wall or, worse, there might be vertical shafts in the underground maze as well as horizontal.

They hadn't seen any pits on the way in, however. At worst it would be a quick death, a clean death. With Kirk, to think was to act.

"Run! We've got to find some light. We can't do anything unless we can see what we're fighting. Keep your hands out and feel for the walls. And keep talking—stay together!" Kirk moved away, starting in the direction he thought they'd been going.

"This way!" Then he broke into a run. McCoy and Sulu were close by. They didn't have to keep talking to stay aware of each other's position—footsteps and increasingly heavy breathing solved that.

The same sounds might also reveal their location to any pursuers, but Kirk suspected that whatever was chasing them could find them easily enough in the dark anyway.

"Don't stop!" His voice echoed like thunder down the tunnel. "DON'T STOP . . . Don't Stop . . . don't stop. . . ."

All of a sudden it sounded like they were leaving the alien cacophony further behind.

"We're gaining on them," he panted.

"Jim, up ahead!" Kirk squinted at McCoy's shout. Sure enough, there did seem to be a pinpoint of light off in the distance.

"I see it . . . I see it . . . keep going!" There couldn't be light where there was no light—that was one kind of mirage man hadn't encountered yet.

Sulu had slipped slightly behind. Unconsciously, they'd changed into the most practical order for running—McCoy barely in the lead, with Kirk in the middle and Sulu, the youngest and freshest runner, bringing up the rear.

The change from the blackness of the tunnel to the light of the room was overpowering. It was like waking up in the glare of a flashlight. They were momentarily blinded and stumbled to a halt.

The underground chamber they'd emerged into was roughly circular in shape and the by-now expected four times human size. Two other entrances gaped in the walls, leading off to unknown regions. Controls and flashing panels lined the walls.

A long table sat in the center of the room, surrounded by an attached series of fragile-looking, semitransparent crystalline globes. These formed a sparkling corona for the platform. All were connected to each other and to the delicate instrumentation built into the table.

On the table lay Mr. Spock.

McCoy hesitated just long enough to unhitch his medical tricorder before sprinting forward. Kirk and Sulu followed.

McCoy took a hurried preliminary reading from the motionless form. He checked the results, reset frantically and made another, slower pass. His eyes were wild when he finally looked over at Kirk and Sulu.

"Something's affecting his brain. All other bodily functions are normal, but he's dying."

"IT IS TOO LATE, CAPTAIN KIRK!"

They whirled as that rolling voice exploded off surrounding walls. Keniclius 5 towered over them, staring down at the tiny intruders from one of the other entrances.

"IN A LITTLE WHILE YOUR FRIEND WILL BE GONE . . . IN A WAY. BUT AS KENICLIUS 1 LIVES ON IN EACH OF HIS CLONES, SO WILL MR. SPOCK. BEHOLD, GENTLEMEN, THE DAWNING OF A NEW ERA . . . THE SALVATION OF A GALAXY . . . SPOCK 2!"

He made a grandiose gesture toward the third portal. Again Kirk, McCoy, and Sulu turned.

Another huge figure had appeared there. It had a familiar detached look, sharply peaked ears, oddly arched eyebrows. It was Mr. Spock, four times over.

His expression was not unfriendly. But neither did the giant show signs of recognition at the appearance of his shipmates, nothing to give the three officers a surge of hope.

They had only the single moment to register shock before the sounds of their tunnel pursuers grew suddenly very loud.

"Get ready!" Kirk ordered.

Now the contents of the mysterious leather sacks were revealed as the three men drew out filtering masks and slipped them over their heads. Kirk tugged the protective bag off his own device.

It was a slim cylinder with one slightly flared end. Several small nozzles protruded from that end, while the opposite sported a handhold and control knob. McCoy began fitting the fourth mask over the supine face of Spock 1.

"WEAPONS DEACTIVATORS ARE IN OPERATION HERE, TOO, CAPTAIN KIRK. A LAST CHANCE—RETURN TO YOUR SHIP."

That's when the tunnel exploded in a landscaper's nightmare. There were swoopers, too, scattered among a crawling, hopping, rolling collage of leafy, screaming monstrosities, offshoots of a plant kingdom gone mad.

Kirk, Sulu, and McCoy depressed the single control set in the base of their cylinders. Suddenly the room was enveloped in a thick chemical mist.

At first the gray fog hugged the floor. As it began to rise a strange expression came over the face of Keniclius 5. He started to cough roughly and retreated from the rapidly dimming room. No one noticed as Spock 2 did likewise.

Not only could Sulu not see Captain Kirk or Dr. McCoy in the drifting miasma, he couldn't see the cellulose abominations that were attacking them, either. But he could sure hear them. At which point the steady hiss that had been issuing from his cylindrical sprayer fizzled out.

He yelled into the mist. "The sprayer's empty, Captain!"

"Mine too, Jim!" came the familiar voice of McCoy. Sulu moved toward it, clinging tightly to the empty sprayer. They might be reduced to fighting with clubs after all.

He bumped into something solid and almost screamed. It was only McCoy.

"Wait a minute," came another voice, Kirk's. "Listen."

No one said a word. Sure enough, the plant noises had stopped. Not died out slowly, or faded, just . . . stopped. McCoy tried to make out shapes in the thick haze surrounding them.

"Maybe they're waiting for this to clear. This far underground, there has to be some kind of automatic air-circulation system to blow out accumulating impurities."

Sure enough the mist started to clear, thinning even as he spoke. Soon Kirk could see the two of them. They moved to stand back to back in expectation of a renewed attack. Kirk removed his mask and sniffed.

"It's okay now."

McCoy and Sulu removed theirs. The cleaning process accelerated and the mist broke up rapidly. In seconds it was completely gone.

So were most of the plants.

Those that remained behind weren't going to attack anyone ever again. They lay on the floor, limbs twisted grotesquely, shriveled like dead clumps of hedge.

"Well, how about that," McCoy mused, studying the copse-laden battlefield. "Great-grandpappy's weed spray still works."

"I'll witness that," said a relieved Kirk, "so long as those that got away don't come back."

"I don't think they'll be in a hurry to do so, Captain," observed Sulu.

"Even so, we've got to get Spock out of here before Keniclius returns. Scott should have the ship back in orbit now." He took out his communicator, activated it.

"There's a chance this shield is directional. We might be able to beam out, even if nobody can beam in. Kirk to *Enterprise* . . . Kirk to *Enterprise*. . . ." There was no answering beep. He paused, tried again. No luck.

"Must be these blasted walls. Kirk to *Enterprise*. . . ."

McCoy had been examining Spock ever since it appeared they were safe from counterattack. Now he looked up and shook his head slowly, sadly.

"It's no use, Jim. He's fading too fast. He'll be dead inside a quarter hour." He hesitated. "He no longer thinks. His mind is gone. But it's not the normal blankness of predeath. This machine," and he indicated the instrument-laden table, "seems to be draining him somehow."

"MORE THAN JUST DRAIN, GENTLEMEN." They turned. Keniclius was no plant. He'd returned.

"HIS MEMORIES HAVE BEEN TRANSFERRED . . . RELOCATED INTO THE MECHANISM ITSELF AND THEN TRANSFERRED AGAIN." He moved towards them.

"I CAN DUPLICATE EXACT PHYSIOLOGICAL STRUCTURES. I CANNOT DUPLICATE THAT WHICH IS LEARNED. I CAN REPRODUCE THAT SECTION OF THE MIND WHICH HOLDS THOUGHTS, BUT I CANNOT REPRODUCE THINKING. I CAN MAKE AGAIN THE AREA THAT IS RESPONSIBLE FOR MEMORY, BUT I CANNOT CREATE MEMORIES.

"JUST AS MY PREDECESSOR TRANSFERRED HIS MEMORIES AND THOUGHTS TO ME THROUGH A SIMILAR MACHINE, SO HAVE I DONE WITH MR. SPOCK AND HIS DUPLICATE."

"You talk about your cloning as though you were creating

life!'' screamed a frustrated Kirk. ''But you have to murder to do it!''

Unexpectedly, that appeared to affect the giant. He halted in his approach, something within him seemingly in conflict with itself. Kirk noticed the hesitation. While it seemed incredible that this monster might have some distorted sense of morality, he had to grab at any chance.

Together the three of them got hold of Spock's limp form and lifted it off the table. They started carrying him toward the third entrance.

They didn't get very far.

The second colossal figure had appeared and was blocking their retreat. Nor did the giant Spock appear inclined to move out of their way.

There was no hesitation in Kirk's voice now.

''Out of my way, mister!'' he yelled at the giant. ''That's an order.'' The huge head inclined slowly to stare blank-faced at them, but the giant showed no sign of moving. McCoy had his medical scanner out and working.

''I don't think he understands, Jim. His mind is still trying to assimilate all the fresh knowledge that's been poured into it.''

That first order had come automatically. But now Kirk found himself uncertain how to proceed.

How much Mr. Spock was there in the giant towering silently over them—and how much Keniclius?

XII

On board the orbiting *Enterprise* the frustration, if not the danger, was just as intense. Wishing he had the full resources of a planet-based communications station, Scott struggled to keep his voice calm as Uhura's repeated attempts to contact the landing party met with repeated nonsuccess. He had no way of knowing, of course, that Kirk, Sulu, and Dr. McCoy were no longer on the surface of Phylos, but under it.

"Keep trying, Lieutenant. We've got to make contact with the captain."

"What do you think I've been trying to do for the past fifteen minutes, sir?" She shook her head and glared. "It's no use. I've tried every ship-to-ground frequency I can think of. No response. I can't even determine if their communicators are still operational."

"Something down there . . . either the communicators have been destroyed, or there's something awfully thick between us and them."

Scott had one card left.

"All right, Mr. Arex?" The navigation officer turned back to look at the chief engineer. "I want every ohm of power on this ship, except for the life-support systematization, put behind a tight-beam communications probe. We must try to break through whatever's blocking our communications!"

"That's fine for a simple contact, Mr. Scott," concurred Uhura. "But to maintain communication on such a power load could be disastrous. We risk total drain of our dilithium crystals. Could burn out every reserve on the ship."

"Don't I know it, lass." Of all the people on the *Enterprise* to recommend such a command, he reflected ironically, the last one ought to be her chief engineer.

"But we've left orbit as the captain requested and returned. I don't know what the situation is down below, but we should have heard from them by now. And I can't order any action until I know what the situation is. We must make contact."

Kirk slumped to the floor, sat with his head bent between his knees. The giant didn't respond to a reflex command. Now Kirk had time to think, and he found himself at a complete loss. The life of his first officer—and friend—was slipping away with every tick of the chronometer, and he seemed helpless to prevent it. Helpless.

However, circumstances often take a hand where individual decisions fail. There was a deep rumbling sound. The giant Spock was clearing his throat.

Kirk's head came up. His thoughts shifted from distant regions of remorse to the present. Maybe there was a chance.

McCoy was already taking another reading on the colossus.

"He's coming out of it, Jim. Becoming conscious and aware."

Kirk scrambled to his feet and took a step toward the giant. He stopped.

What should he say? What *could* he say? Was there really anything of the Spock he'd known in this . . . Frankenstein? Anything beyond surface features and superficial similarities? For that matter, how much of the original idealistic doctor remained in a Keniclius five times removed from the first?

Think, man, think! Say something, anything. . . .

He heard his voice talking. "Spock, what is the logic of letting a man die for the sake of creating his duplicate? Explain it to me, sir, explain it to me!"

The giant raised an eyebrow, thinking, but did not respond.

"Power sources are channeled, Mr. Scott," Uhura informed him. "I hope you know what you're doing, sir."

"So do I, lass, so do I. Let's find out." Uhura turned back to her console. Her hand moved toward a certain little-used switch, the switch that was used only for expensive tight-beam communications. She'd used it before, but never with this kind of power behind it.

Would the components involved be able to handle the strain of routing the full power of the *Enterprise*? She fervently hoped so.

If not, there was a fair chance the console would explode in her face. . . .

"Jim, we've got to do something!" McCoy pleaded, taking another reading on the original Spock.

"I'm trying to, really!" He eyed Spock 2. The real Spock had never been impressed by physical violence. This lumbering double would be even less so. Their only chance lay in reasoned argument.

"Look," he said desperately, "Vulcans do not condone the meaningless death of any being. Spock's death *is* meaningless, if its only purpose is to create a giant duplicate of himself. It's been proven time and again that no duplicate can possibly be as efficient as an original."

"IT IS NOT JUST A DUPLICATE!" objected an angry Keniclius. " 'AS GOOD AS AN ORIGINAL', INDEED! HE WILL BE FAR BETTER THAN THE ORIGINAL—THE BEGINNING OF A MASTER RACE!"

Kirk's ready reply was interrupted by a startlingly loud beep. He looked dazedly at his communicator as if it might suddenly jump off his belt and bite him. Then he unclipped it and fumbled with the activator. A better idea stopped him.

He tossed the unopened communicator to Spock 2. The giant caught it easily in one enormous palm. If the duplicate's mind was not fully operational yet, Kirk reflected, then all was lost. No amount of argument would serve.

At least its reflexes looked sound.

"That's our ship calling, Spock. You're her first officer. You answer her." The beep came again.

Raising his hand, the giant appeared to study the tiny instrument. It made no move to open it and acknowledge the now constant beeping.

"Spock's slipping, Jim," whispered McCoy tensely. "There isn't much time left."

* * *

"I'm sure we're getting through," Uhura insisted, the strain in her voice reflecting the one warping the communications equipment. "But they're not replying."

"Keep trying," ordered Scott. Uhura kept an eye on an overhead indicator. "We're nearing the overload point on the dilithium now, Mr. Scott. Our reserves . . ."

"Keep . . . trying."

Suddenly the giant's eyes seemed to clear, his expression to brighten. With the ease of one who's performed the same task a thousand times, yet also compensating for the increased size of his fingers, Spock 2 flipped open the communicator.

"COMMANDER . . . COMMANDER SPOCK HERE."

A chance, at least they had a chance, Kirk thought excitedly!

Uhura's relieved tone sounded over the communicator. "Thank heavens! Mr. Spock, tell the captain I've located additional information on Keniclius."

"Let's hear it, Lieutenant!" Kirk shouted, hoping his voice would carry far enough for the communicator mike to pick up.

Apparently it did. Uhura continued.

"I had the library research all known writings by Keniclius. Most of them border on the incoherent, but two themes stand out, especially in his last essays.

"One is his fanaticism. The other is some idea he had about using his projected master race as a peacekeeping force for the entire galaxy. That's why he needed a perfect specimen for his cloning experiments."

There was more, but a glance at the overhead indicator ruled out any further contact. Another second and the needle would dip into the red zone. She hurried.

"Signing off, power drain threshold!" She snapped off the signal and slammed down several switches with the other hand. Her sigh of relief whooshed out only after the needle had dropped out of the yellow and back into the green section of the gauge. Then she grinned up at Scott.

"That is what I call close, Mr. Scott."

"At least we know they're alive, and apparently okay," agreed Scott, in blissful ignorance. "Let's hope it was information they could use."

"Information, yeah," mused Uhura. One arm was still trembling. She leaned on it to hide the quiver. "Did I ever tell you the one about the one-legged jockey, Mr. Scott—?"

"Peacekeeping," echoed Kirk bitterly. "Peacekeeping!" He shook his head and faced Keniclius. "All this has been a waste, *Doctor* Keniclius. There's no need for any peacekeeping master race. There's been peace in the Federation now for well over fifty years."

"THAT'S A LIE!" the giant shouted, his voice washing over them. "WHAT ABOUT THE EUGENICS WARS? THE GALACTIC WARS? WHAT OF THE DEPREDATIONS OF THE ROMULANS, THE KLINGONS, AND OTHERS? NOT TO MENTION THE ENDLESS, OH, THE ENDLESS SQUABBLES AMONG THE SO-CALLED 'ALLIED' RACES OF THE FEDERATION ITSELF?

"AN ORGANIZATION OF SPOCK DUPLICATES IS NECESSARY TO FORCE THEM TO LIVE IN HARMONY—FOR THEIR OWN GOOD."

Sulu muttered, "Peace through coercion. Humanity has finally grown out of that immature philosophy, Keniclius."

"You're the fifth Keniclius," reminded Kirk. "What makes you so sure the things you see as truth aren't just old news bulletins hundreds of years out of date? Your predecessors have probably been out of touch with mankind's sociological advances for at least that long."

"That is not possible. The Master always speaks the truth," came a new voice. A new, old voice.

They turned to face the first entrance, the tunnel of horrors they'd escaped from so recently.

Agmar and his four aides stood there, watching.

"I can't understand why you've come to think of Keniclius as a 'master,' " began McCoy. "Sure, he saved you from dying—all five of you. But why should you agree with his plan for a superrace? Of what possible interest could a race of giant Spocks have for you?"

"Our fleet of ships, which you saw," Agmar replied, "was to be launched for the same purpose the Master intends. You see, there existed between our people and him a fortuitous coincidence of purpose. Disease struck us before we could carry out our own plan to impose peace on a galaxy that knew none."

"We already have peace in our Federation," snapped Kirk, "and it wasn't imposed—it was achieved from within. A real peace!" He paused.

"You have no need of Spock now. Reverse the effects of that machine and let us take him back with us."

"NO!" thundered Keniclius wildly. "THE MOLD MUST BE BROKEN." The giant's voice wavered considerably; Kirk's revelations had thrust uncertainty into two hundred fifty years of single-mindedness that had known only absolute confidence.

But it wasn't enough. The giant couldn't reverse in a moment the accumulated efforts of those two and a half centuries.

McCoy was leaning over Spock 1.

"Jim, he's almost gone." Kirk thought rapidly. McCoy could do nothing. And Keniclius wouldn't. And he—he felt utterly impotent.

In fact, there was only one other being present who might be able to save Spock now. He turned to the other giant, who'd remained impassive throughout everything.

"If you have Spock's mind, you must know the Vulcan symbol called IDIC."

"INFINITE DIVERSITY IN INFINITE COMBINATION," the great form recited.

"Comprising the elements that make up truth and beauty," finished Kirk. "Tell me, could an army of giant Spocks impose Phylosian philosophy on any other creatures, in knowing defiance of the IDIC concept?"

There was a long pause as Spock 2 considered this question. Kirk held his breath.

Finally, "I DO NOT BELIEVE SO. . . . " Kirk spun on the other giant.

"I thought so! Reverse the machine, Keniclius!"

"No!" yelled Agmar. It was the first violent exclamation the Phylosian had made. "Our dream must not be allowed to die!" He suddenly rushed at Kirk. His companions followed, trying to keep the humans from putting Spock 1 back on the machine.

Sulu let out a vibrant battle cry, intercepted Agmar and flipped him neatly over a shoulder. The Phylosians were at a tremendous disadvantage in a fight with anyone who knew judo . . . they had too many limbs that could be conveniently grabbed.

But in the ensuing melee, while the three humans battled the Phylosians, Keniclius rushed the machine. The resolution of the minions had decided the confused master. He lifted a long bar of metal. It didn't really matter that none of the humans could reach him, they couldn't have stopped him anyhow.

The heavy bar smashed through one of the crystal globes encircling the table. There was a crackling electrical discharge and the giant retreated. Several other globes exploded in a shower of glass slivers and agonized internal components.

No one was hurt, but the damage was done. The lights on the sides of the machine went out—went out in the panels lining the walls. And the slight hum which had issued from inside the table faded into nothingness.

Kirk, who'd been functioning near his mental limit ever since they'd first entered the chamber and seen the dying Spock, lost all control. Despite the difference in their sizes and without really knowing what he intended, he charged Keniclius.

"Murderer! You've killed Spock!"

He never reached the giant. A leg as big around as a small tree stepped between him and Keniclius. He was forced to stop and look up into the face of Spock 2.

"TO PERSIST IN THIS BEHAVIOR, CAPTAIN, IS TO NEGATE THE ELOQUENCE OF YOUR PREVIOUS ARGUMENT. MAY I SUGGEST A MORE CONSTRUCTIVE COURSE OF ACTION?"

He walked around Kirk who, thoroughly puzzled, watched him advance on Sulu and McCoy. The two officers eased Spock 1 to the ground and backed away slowly.

Bending, the giant Vulcan lifted Spock 1 in a single hand. Thumb and forefinger touched the smaller man's forehead. Closing his own eyes the giant began a familiar chant.

"MY MIND TO YOUR MIND . . . MY THOUGHTS TO YOUR THOUGHTS. . . ."

"Vulcan mind touch!" exclaimed Sulu in wonder. The chamber had become a tableau of wax figures. No one moved, everyone stared at the two Spocks. Even Keniclius, whose inaction showed he'd never anticipated anything like this.

Gradually the giant's voice faded. Spock 1 fluttered an eyelid. It rose. There was the sound of a throat being cleared . . . softer, this time.

The larger Vulcan lowered the smaller model to the ground, facing Kirk.

"I am pleasantly surprised at your capacity for deductive reasoning, Captain," said Spock 1. "When you are not being bellicose, there appears to be no end to your arsenal of forensic talents."

Kirk, however, heard little if any of this. He'd lost control of himself again—motivated by a somewhat different reason, this time.

"Spock! You old! . . ."

"YOU NEEDN'T WORRY, CAPTAIN KIRK, ABOUT THE THREAT OF A MASTER RACE," rumbled Spock 2. All turned to look at him. "THERE WILL BE NO GALACTIC MILITIA. NO OTHER SPOCKS. THE THINGS THAT COMBINE TO MAKE SPOCK A CANDIDATE FOR SUCH A TASK ALSO WOULD NOT COUNTENANCE IT."

"BUT WHAT OF MY WORK?" queried the desperate Keniclius. "IF ALL THAT I'VE FOUGHT FOR IS ALREADY ACCOMPLISHED—THE TIMES THAT I LIVED TO END ARE ALREADY ENDED—WHAT IS TO BECOME OF ME? THERE APPEARS TO BE NO REASON WHY I SHOULD CONTINUE TO EXIST. . . ."

"On the contrary, Dr. Keniclius," objected Spock 1, "I see every reason why you should remain active. Stay on Phylos with my surrogate. The concerted effort of two scientists, each with his own particular abilities and talents to enhance the other's, might yet achieve a rebirth of Phylosian civilization . . . and enable them to contribute peacefully to the Federation."

"MY THOUGHTS EXACTLY, MR. SPOCK," agreed Spock 2.

"So one might assume, Mr. Spock," agreed Spock 1.

The first officer's successful recovery had pushed all primitive revenge-thoughts from Kirk's mind.

"How does that sound to you, Dr. Keniclius? To bring life is even more important than bringing peace. If a way can be found to revitalize their race, the Phylosians have much to contribute to galactic culture."

"I . . . I WOULD BE HONORED. IF I WOULD BE ALLOWED . . . YES, YOU ARE RIGHT, CAPTAIN KIRK. THE METHODS OF THE FEDERATION HAVE INDEED CHANGED FROM WHAT I AND MY BROTHERS KNEW. . . ."

"Truly, such a thing had not been thought of." Agmar looked excited and interested now. "Such a sudden change in thinking . . . it will be difficult. . . ."

"You'll manage," said Kirk, too diplomatic to point out that they had no choice. He'd meant what he said. The Phylosians had some sterling qualities—once this master race business had been drummed out of them. He addressed the waiting Keniclius again.

"I'll report your *new* work here to the Federation Science center. Not only do I think they'll understand, they'll probably want to send out several crews to assist you."

And to make sure you don't get the urge to make any more giant clones of anything, he added silently.

Keniclius solemnly shook hands with each of them in turn. Then Agmar and his companions escorted Kirk, McCoy, Sulu, and Spock back to the surface.

When the men of the *Enterprise* left, the two giant scientists were already discussing plans for curing the Phylosians' sterility and expanding their knowledge of Phylosian culture.

Beaming up was uneventful, and there were the expected stolid greetings from Uhura, Kyle, Arex, and the rest of the officers—everyone carefully concealing his or her true emotions.

They entered the bridge where Scott—relieved, as usual—formally returned command to Kirk.

"Where to, Captain?" asked Sulu, back in his comfortable seat at the navigation console.

"Set a general course for the Omicron region, Mr. Sulu. I think everyone deserves an extended R&R, this time. I know I do!"

"Yes, *sir*!" Sulu responded gleefully.

"It's a good thing we were able to stop Keniclius," intoned McCoy, blatantly emphasizing the "we." "Imagine . . . a whole shipload . . . maybe a whole city . . . full of giant Spocks!"

He put on an expression of exaggerated horror while Spock

looked over distastefully from his position at the library control and tried to ignore McCoy.

"What a terrifying thought! . . ." the good doctor continued, unstoppable. "Giant Spocks running all over the place! Spocks towering over helpless villages, running amuck through peaceful farmland . . . turning! . . ."

"It might be easier to stand than you, Doctor," interrupted Sulu inscrutably.

"What?" McCoy responded with outraged innocence. "I'm no giant."

Kirk thought he saw an unholy gleam in Sulu's eye.

"No," the helmsman admitted, "the trouble is you never stop cloning around."

McCoy chased him all the way back to engineering.

STAR TREK
LOG THREE

CONTENTS

For Judy-Lynn del Rey
who has the beauty to match her name . . .

STAR TREK LOG THREE

Log of the Starship *Enterprise*
Stardates 5510.1–5524.5 Inclusive

James T. Kirk, Capt., USSC, FS, ret.
Commanding

transcribed by
Alan Dean Foster

At the Galactic Historical Archives
on S. Monicus I
stardated 6111.3

For the curator: JLR

PART I

ONCE UPON
A PLANET

(Adapted from a script by Len Janson and Chuck Menville)

I

The officer entered the tent and came unbidden to full attention. For several moments he stood quietly, his eyes never wavering from the tall, impressive figure seated behind the old scarred table. But old campaigner or not, he found himself beginning to fidget. Perhaps his entrance had gone unnoticed. A slight cough as prelude, maybe . . .

"The troops are assembled as you ordered, sir. They're waiting for you."

"Thank you, Centurion," came the warm reply. Caesar did not look up immediately. The battle map sketched out on the tabletop still commanded the full attention of the greatest tactician Rome would ever know.

Their situation was not yet grave, but every hour's delay strengthened the position of the enemy as fresh rebels rallied to their cause.

On the right flank lay the traitor Aranius with his cavalry. To the north Ventrigorix was positioned with the Belgians. A scout had just ridden in with reports of catapults concealed in the high forest to their left that was laden with Greek fire which blackened men and panicked horses.

If their own mounted were dispatched to deal with Aranius' renegades, the thrust of any main assault at the enemy's center would be weakened. Besides, sending even a portion of them to deal with the hidden catapults, whose strength was uncertain, would lessen possibly crucial reserves needed for a decisive conflict. A flank attack would surely follow any center attack, and the entire cavalry would be needed to turn it.

A rising din was heard from outside the tent. Veterans all, the men of the XIIth, XXth, and XXIInd legions had been goaded to a fighting fever by their officers. They were anxious to do battle. To leave them standing while further tactics were deliberated would be folly.

Cries of "Caesar, Caesar!" rose steadily in volume as the troops gave vent to their emotions. The leader of the Roman army thought once more about the vital holocaust ahead.

If this campaign were successful, it would finally break the back of barbarian resistance in northern Gaul. The way would be open to the ice-bound lands across the northern seas, bringing the whole continent under the iron control of Imperial Rome once and for all.

Caesar grinned wolfishly. Then let those limp-wristed Senators and Patricians try to chip away at the Emperor's powers! Rome would see a triumph it would never forget.

Caesar's decision was made even before the fist slammed down onto the table. Eyes rose along with the battle-hardened torso to stare evenly at the tensely waiting centurion.

"Flavius, the moment is at hand. We march!"

Snapping to a position of attention the centurion's right arm shot up and out in salute. The words he had been waiting for—the words three legions of Rome's finest troops had been waiting for.

"Hail, Caesar," he intoned admiringly. "Your legions await your command."

And this was more than rhetoric, for by now the tent was all but swaying to the combined shouts of thousands of massed soldiers.

Donning his helmet, Caesar buckled on the short sword, adjusted a chinstrap, and strode toward the waiting thunder to address his men . . .

"What's the matter with you, Yeoman?" asked a worried Lieutenant Davis. "Haven't you got that stand-by program for the menu worked out yet?"

Yeoman Deb Colotti blinked and looked up from her dream.

"What . . . ? Sorry, Lieutenant. My . . . my mind was floating."

"That's because it's lighter than air," snapped the section chief. She glanced over Colotti's shoulder and tapped a finger on the bright digital readout.

"Code SCRP-D-220. You've just programmed two hundred and twenty chocolate raisin pies into the month's menu. And the captain hates chocolate raisin pie. Get busy and fix it."

"Yes, ma'am." Colotti shook her head at her own idiocy and started in on the tedious task of erasing and resetting the faulty program she had just fed into the *Enterprise*'s galley computer.

Dry leaves crackled like brown foil underfoot and N'gombi froze. Behind him, the other four men of the hunting party did likewise, becoming as motionless as the surrounding trees of the great rain forest. Much care was necessary here, on the very edge of the veldt. Only anxious eyes continued to move, searching, probing nervously into the surrounding wall of green.

The hunting party remained frozen in place several minutes longer before moving forward again. Almost immediately N'gombi threw up a warning hand. A clear section of soft, rain-soaked earth lay in front of them. Kneeling, he examined the track left in the drying mud.

A sniff, loose earth crumbled appraisingly between sensitive fingers. "Fresh . . . very fresh," he muttered.

His senses wholly alert, N'gombi looked up and into the forest. The spoor was barely minutes old. Behind him he could feel the tenseness of the others as they waited for his words.

All were brave men—the bravest of the village. But they had no stomach for this kind of work and none could blame them. Especially in dense undergrowth where a group had no room to spread out and maneuver, where death could sneak smell-close to strike and crush and rend before a man could turn to see.

Only the willingness of the great slayer N'gombi had given them enough courage, enough to go too. But even with the quiet assured presence of their greatest hunter, the sudden absence of normal jungle sounds—the monkey cries and the shrieking of brilliant-plumed parrots—was frightening them.

N'gombi rose and started to step over the track. As he did so, a frightening crashing sounded in the foliage to their left. For a moment the party held. Then, screaming in fear and sudden panic, the other four hunters dropped their spears and ran for their lives retreating back down the path.

Turning quietly, N'gombi grounded his spear-butt firmly into the dirt, knelt on one knee, and braced the hardwood shaft . . . and waited.

Like a falling sandstone cliff, the tawny form of the huge rogue lion exploded out of the brush and at him . . .

Subengineer Duchamps shouldered his overchalked cue and stared curiously across the green-felt-covered table.

"You're not on your game today, Henry. That's the fourth round of eight-ball I've taken from you this morning."

"Yeah," agreed security guard Henry Ndugu, observing idly that his partner had indeed swept the table surface clean. "Guess I can't concentrate."

"Don't wonder why," nodded Duchamps knowingly. He glanced at the chronometer on his wrist as he swung the cue free. "Must be only a couple of hours out by now." He sighed deeply.

"I'm having a hard time keeping my attention on the game, too. But I figure I might as well fulfill at least one fantasy right now. It's nice to beat you for a change. Rack 'em up . . ."

In the pilot house, Captain Benjamin O. Lee puffed nervously on his pipe and glanced out of the corner of an eye at his pilot. Strange sort of chap, this pilot, giving up a promising literary career just to come back to his home town and sign on with a dirty old steamboat.

But the fellow seemed steady enough. Lee was damned happy to have him. Had the surest eyes and steadiest hands on the river.

It was a quiet summer day. Just enough of a breeze wafted over the river to keep the humidity from killing. From the iron stacks, gritty black smoke seemed to rise vertically into otherwise azure sky. The *Cairo* was entering a sharp bend in the channel.

Noticing the direction of the captain's eyes, the pilot smiled that funny, wry smile of his. "Don't worry, Cap'n. We'll get through easy as my grandfather's old ram."

"I sure hope so, Sam. Never seen the big muddy this low.

If those folks at Paducah don't get these medical supplies and that new vaccine we've got on B-deck, well . . .'' His eyes lowered.

"Now I told you not to worry, Cap'n. I know every log, every sandbar and old wreck this river's ever belched up. She's never played me false yet, and I don't see her doin' it now. Even so," and he eyed the swirling, muddy water ahead where a narrow stream entered the main course, "it'd be good to take a sounding about here."

The captain nodded. Something at least to take his mind off less happy thoughts. Leaning out the side window of the pilot house he shouted forward.

"Mr. Hansen . . . take a sounding!"

"Aye, Cap'n!" came the mate's reply. The Swede uncoiled the measured, weighted line and chucked it easily over the bow, slightly to port. He checked the line markings as the paddle-wheeler pushed steadily ahead.

"Mark Twain!" he called back toward the bridge. The pilot nodded and turned the wheel slightly to starboard. His eyes, perpetually twinkling under bushy brows, looked skyward. If the weather held they'd make Paducah in plenty of time . . .

"Not much point in letting a recorder run if you're not going to use it," observed Yeoman Lancer.

Ensign Ub Jackson started, looked up, suddenly aware that the screen in front of him was illuminated but quite blank, patiently awaiting instructions.

"Sorry, Lily. Seems I just can't turn out any poetry today."

"What's the matter?" She checked the list of suggestive titles available on another unoccupied viewer, and resolutely turned away from it. Best save her fantasies for the real thing. "No inspiration?"

By way of answer Jackson activated the recorder. But instead of slipping in a program cassette, he dialed the image currently displayed on the main viewscreen up on the bridge.

The screen fluttered momentarily, then cleared to reveal a blue-white world draped in a delicate peignoir of clouds. It had grown visibly since the last time he had looked at it.

"No," he finally replied, eyeing the approaching planet longingly, "too much of it."

"Captain's Log, stardate 5510.1," Kirk informed the patient pickup at his wrist. He paused, glancing around the quietly efficient bridge. Spock, Uhura, Sulu, and Arex were occupied preparing for orbital insertion, each at his respective station. Dr. McCoy stood at Arex's shoulder, peering past the helmsman at their destination.

"The crew of the *Enterprise*," he continued, satisfied that everything and everyone was operating normally, "is ready for some well-deserved rest and recreation. And the sooner the better. Mr. Spock informs me that normal ship efficiency is down twenty-two percent from the standard level—due in part to anticipation of Omicron planetfall."

That was an understatement. Ship's personnel were so involved in plotting out the elaborate fantasies they hoped to enjoy once down on the surface of that azure ceramic world that only automatic instrumentation kept the *Enterprise* in working order.

"Having secured the situation on Phylos and submitted the information concerning the mutant clone Stavos Keniclius V and mutant Spock Two—clone of our own first officer—to Starfleet sector headquarters, I requested that the crew be granted something special in the way of shore leave. Said request to visit the Omicron region was duly submitted and approved.

"Course was set and traced without incident. We are now approaching that so-called 'shore-leave' world.

"Those studying this log may recall that this particular planet was programmed long ago by some unknown but highly advanced alien race. The extremely complex machinery installed there is designed solely to provide fun and amusement for interstellar passersby.

"It's extensive mind-reading devices and attendant manufacturing machinery are capable of materializing any fantasy they can pick up. I confess to looking forward to our return to this planet myself."

Switching off the recorder Kirk sat back and watched his fellow officers at work. Although they betrayed no outward emotion, Kirk was certain they shared the same feelings of expectation he did.

As he stared at the earthlike globe floating in the center of the main viewscreen, his mind relaxed for the first time in weeks. At last they would have a real rest, unencumbered by requests to explore, aid, fight, or otherwise exercise themselves on behalf of Federation policy.

Matter of fact, a little anticipatory daydreaming wouldn't hurt right now . . .

The *Enterprise* was run on three eight-hour shifts. Her crew would take a shore leave the same way. A games computer served to scramble a complete roster of personnel and then print out one lucky third of them.

Uhura, Sulu, and McCoy were all in the first group scheduled for beam down. McCoy in particular made no effort to hide his pleasure in being among the first of the ship's complement permitted to sample the dream-satisfying pleasures ahead.

The outcome did not sit very well with Engineer Scott, however. He looked up disapprovingly from his station behind the transporter console.

"You needn't look so smug about it, Doctor."

"Now, Scotty, no need to be jealous. You're due to beam down with the next group anyway, aren't you?"

Scott shook his head mournfully. "Uh-uh . . . I'm in the third shift."

"Too bad. Well, we'll try not to use up the planet." He grinned and followed Uhura and Sulu into the transporter alcove.

Scott started to activate the transporter controls but paused at the sight of a familiar object slung over Sulu's right shoulder. He stared at it curiously. "This is supposed to be a pleasure stop, Lieutenant Sulu. Why the science tricorder?"

"I thought you knew, Chief. Botany's one of my hobbies. Oh, you can't be sure about much of anything down there, but lots of the plants are native. And the planetary computer's had the green thoughts of thousands of alien visitors to draw on to grow others. Not everybody's fantasies are lurid garden-of-Eden types. Mine's just plain gardens."

Scott shrugged. "Each to his own, I suppose. Seems like

a bit of a waste to me, though.'' His voice assumed a con-spiratorial tone. "Now, when my turn comes I plan to . . .''

"If you don't mind I'd really rather do without the juicy details, Chief,'' Uhura interrupted sharply. "We've all got our own dreams to indulge, and we can't do it standing here.''

"Ummmm, is that a subtle hint, lass?'' Scott smiled wick-edly. "Sorry.'' He activated three levers, twirled switches and knobs. The three officers, complete with separate fan-tasies, turned into three multicolored pillars of shifting par-ticles.

These re-formed later, touching down amid a landscape of ethereal beauty. This particular section of the planet had been planted and tossed and sculpted and rearranged to look like a Bierstadt canvas. Foliage here had been groomed by the touch of a master stylist. Thick grassy meadows and small brooks alternated as far as one could see. Miniature water-falls lifted from Japanese prints (or the memory of same) provided delicately orchestrated background music. Here and there trees blended harmoniously into the meadows, trees grown as much for symmetry as for shade. Some were draped loosely with climbing vines that were festooned in turn with blooms of gold, green, and Tyrolean purple. In the distance, part way up a gradual slope, they saw a vibrating, glittering flash of color. Another landing party beaming down. Even further away, on the other side of a gentle river, yet a third group arrived. Flashes continued intermittently at a rapidly increasing range as the *Enterprise*'s transporters freckled the surface with landing parties of would-be lotus-eaters.

McCoy took a few experimental steps, turning in a slow circle to take in views of the high, snow-capped mountains that surrounded this valley. Were those distant peaks the re-sult of natural upheaval—or were they planned on some mas-ter map by contouring computers buried deep beneath their feet? There was no way to tell.

At the foot of the mountains ran a long, clear lake, posi-tioned like a mirror to best reflect the towering crags and pinnacles. It, at least, looked too perfect to be anything but the result of some other geologically inclined traveler's ide-alized dreamscape.

McCoy nodded to himself, completely satisfied. "Just as

gorgeous as I remember it. Doesn't look like anything's changed, not a leaf, not a blade of grass."

They started walking toward the nearest little stream. It bubbled capriciously down a hillside that looked misty where there was no mist. That puzzled Sulu. He'd seen this slope before somewhere. But where?

In a painting, of course, and the image came to him abruptly. This hillside, those trees and rockfalls, the stream, had been designed once before, by a long-dead terran artist . . . Masefield . . . no, Maxfield Parrish.

Seeing it in all three dimensions was startling.

"This looks a lot like the same spot we set down at on our first visit," he ventured. Then the helmsman smiled, recalling a fantasy other than his own.

"Remember when we saw the white rabbit, Doctor?"

McCoy chuckled before replying. "It's not the sort of thing you forget. Sure I remember, Sulu. And all because I said this place made me feel like a character out of *Alice in Wonderland.*"

Suddenly they were unexpectedly interrupted. It wasn't quite a human voice, but more like a caricature of one. A high piping wail that was half-child, half-senator.

"One side, one side!"

McCoy spun around and barely cleared the path in time as a meter-tall white rabbit clad in top hat and tails bounded past. The rabbit was holding onto his bobbing hat with one hand and clutching tightly to an oversized gold pocket watch with the other. His manner and tone were agitated, his bouncy stride hurried.

"I'm late, I'm late! Oh my fuzzy ears and whiskers, I'm very very late!"

Repetition of a previous incident or not, Sulu, McCoy, and Uhura stood gaping at the furry apparition as it shot past. The rabbit unexpectedly left the path and, with a hop of Olympian proportions, sailed into the thick shrubbery.

Moments later, naturally, a young girl emerged seemingly from nowhere on the path in front of them. She had long blond hair neatly combed to her waist, and she wore a light blue dress with matching white pinafore, knee-high socks, and shiny black buckled shoes.

By the time she had come close enough to tap Uhura on the shoulder, they'd all recovered from the initial surprise.

"I beg your pardon," the girl said politely in a thick British-terran accent, "but did you happen to see a large white rabbit come this way?"

Uhura pointed toward the concealing bushes. "He went that way, Alice."

"Thank you so much!" She performed a perfect little curtsey and hurried off down the path, disappearing into the same bushes as the rabbit. Sulu and McCoy exchanged charmed smiles.

"Just like you said, Doctor, nothing's changed."

Uhura smiled agreement, then shook her head in wonderment. "They're such perfect models, so exact—and they appear so quickly in response to your thoughts. It's hard to believe they're not real."

"Easy, Lieutenant," cautioned McCoy, but gently. "They're only highly sophisticated robots, whipped up by this world's central computer to make your dreams come true."

"I know," she responded. "I wish I could have a look at their insides. Imagine the technology required to direct and guide them, without any sign of receiving or transmitting apparatus. Nothing in the Federation comes close to it." She paused at a sudden thought, and Sulu and McCoy stopped to watch her.

"I wish," she began, spacing her words deliberately, "I could see their insides, especially the transmit-receive instrumentation." They waited, but the hidden ears of the planet chose not to give a response.

"I said," she repeated firmly, "I *wish* to see the insides of one of the automatons."

Sulu shook his head, "Forget it, Uhura. But it was a nice idea." She smiled ruefully back at him.

"I guess granting your heart's desire doesn't include giving away trade secrets. The planetary machinery will do just about anything, except explain itself. Oh well." She shrugged philosophically, then smiled.

"This won't do—acting disappointed. Got to think only happy thoughts."

"My prescription exactly," McCoy agreed. "Speaking of

which . . ." He looked slightly embarrassed. "Part of the pleasure of being on this world is indulging in your most private fantasies, to the hilt. That requires a certain amount of, uh . . ."

"Privacy," supplied Sulu. "Just what I was going to say."

"And I," Uhura added, making it unanimous.

"Not that I'm not crazy about both of you," the good doctor retorted hastily, "but when I see you again I'd just as soon we were back on the ship."

The three starship officers split up amiably then, taking off in three different directions, searching out three different paths through the manicured lawns—each in search of a place where secret dreams could be enjoyed away from the rest of humanity.

Exotic blossoms bordered the bubbling rivulet, petals straining so hard to catch the sun that some bloomed even under the clear surface of the stream. They existed nowhere else in the universe, having been cultivated and grown first in the field of the mind.

A faint tinge of rose tinted the otherwise diamond-clear water, and thick clover sighed with the action of wind on a billion waiting stems. The scene required only its creator for completeness.

Uhura furnished that seconds later as she topped the rise that concealed the perfect valley and then started down toward the stream.

She stared down, down, into the water. A wavering rippled reflection of self looked back at her. Reaching out, the reflection grasped the water-distorted mirror-image of a large black flower and plucked it free, setting it into the hair above one ear. Then it smiled up at Uhura.

Humming softly, she imitated the suggestive action of her reflection. Breaking off the self-same flower she set it neatly over the indicated ear. Still humming softly to herself, she started to stroll upstream.

Immense was the forest, with gnarled trees impossibly thick and tall. Like bark-backed skyscrapers they soared hundreds of meters into the sky. Their distant crests seemed to support the blue heavens on thick, brown branches.

Sulu rounded one colossal bole and leaned to study the moss growing on its side. Here the wood was the shade of obsidian, the iron-hard black fluted and ribboned with channels, the touch smooth as oiled ivory. Yet when he pressed in, the black bark gave way obediantly.

Delicate dark vines encircled many of the towering trees. They dangled freely from the lowest branches. Each was composed of segments, like a chain. When a lithe breeze gusted, the links would bounce against one another, tinkling with a sound of small porcelain chimes. It was the only sound in the forest.

Light shafted down in yellow ranks between the trunks, and the effect was like walking through a cathedral. Transparent flowers grew here and there from high bushes. Whenever they caught the light they made presents of rainbows to the helmsman's delighted eyes. The rest of the undergrowth was riotous, wild, every bit as impressive in its own way as the massive trees.

Once, a tiny fuzzy plant pulled itself out of the ground and started to follow him, scurrying along in pursuit on tiny mobile roots. Sulu grinned at the memory that had produced it. Then he bent, lifted it easily in one hand. Tiny thorns pricked futilely at his palm. Bringing both hands together, he slowly ground the fuzzy into a handful of yellow powder.

One puff was sufficient to send the dust floating away. Sulu rubbed his hands together as he continued through the forest. A lilting tune came unbidden to his lips. His singing voice might not have been good, but it was enthusiastic, and the chiming vines seemed to join right in.

Thick twisted cypress alternated politely with slim, zebra-striped birch. Like the hair of a goddess, Spanish moss fell in emerald waves from the thicker trees, almost touching the ground. Somewhere an oriole chirped a greeting as McCoy turned a bend in the lane. He stopped to absorb the view.

Ahead, set on a low hill surrounded by well-tended green lawns and a newly painted white picket fence, was a magnificent cream-colored mansion. It was two stories high and faced with smooth, pseudoclassical columns. Honeysuckle, wisteria, and magnolia bloomed in profusion around the front gate. The flowers tangled around the fence and climbed up the fronting columns, alternating with thick ivy and filling the air with scents of sugar and sweet wine. Somewhere, someone was plunking a banjo and singing.

McCoy sighed and stared longingly at the distant panorama, resolutely putting out of his mind the fact that the front was probably false, the ivy artificial, and the banjo-plucker a hidden recording.

"Lovely . . . they just don't make 'em like that anymore." He started toward the mansion and was wondering who would greet him at the door, when a harsh female voice shattered the antebellum tranquillity.

"Off with his head!"

McCoy spun around in surprise. What greeted him was no less unlikely but a good deal more startling than the plantation now behind him. A large crowd of oddly shaped humanoids returned his stare. Their gaze was openly hostile.

Each body was a perfect rectangle save only for five bulges—head, arms, and legs. Their torsos were tremendously broad, impossibly thin, and inscribed with archaic symbols: hearts, diamonds, spades, and clubs.

The unmistakable leader of this angry horde was somewhat less broad and rather less narrow. She stepped out of their midst and jabbed an accusing finger at McCoy.

"There he is!" she shrieked. "Off with his head!"

Lowering their lances, the card-shaped humanoids charged forward on stumpy legs.

It was all a dazed McCoy could do to duck just as a lance tipped with a razor-edged heart sailed over his head, cutting a small sapling behind him neatly in half. It suddenly occurred to the *Enterprise*'s chief physician that the intentions of this multiple fantasy were other than benign.

"Hey, what's going on here?" Something brushed his right arm and slammed into the large tree behind. This one was finished with a dark spade-shape, half of which was buried in the wood. McCoy glanced down at his side, saw that the spear had taken a neat slice out of his tunic. That did it. He had no intention of hanging around to argue with a belligerent dream, especially when it wasn't his. He turned and took off down the path on the dead run.

"Stop him!" yelled the Queen. The cards had already

taken off in hot pursuit, and the pack of humanoids was close on McCoy's heels.

Occasionally a long lance arched through the air near him. Fortunately the aim of his pursuers was not good. Their short arms did not permit much in the way of long-range accuracy. McCoy had no intention of giving them a chance to sharpen their skills at close range. With his longer legs McCoy was able to maintain and even slightly lengthen his lead. But he was no athlete and he couldn't keep up this chase indefinitely, whereas the animated cards could probably run all day.

Fumbling at his belt he finally managed to pull the communicator free. It took him three frantic tries before the cover snapped back, but by then he was panting so hard that the words refused to form.

Finally, however, he managed to gasp between breaths, "*Enterprise*—emergency, emergency! Beam up, beam up!"

The filtered shouts sounded clearly over the speaker in the transporter room. Fortunately Scott was on station there, alert for just such a call. Not that the chief engineer had suddenly acquired the gift of precognition. It was standard procedure, ever since the amazing properties of the shore-leave world had become known, to have someone standing by at the transporter at all times. Some crewmembers got bored early and had to be beamed back before their rest time was expired.

But the real reason for the precaution was that one or two members of a ship's complement often could not handle the confrontation with their own fantasies. Though they were in no danger of physical harm, a real chance of serious mental damage existed unless they could be brought back aboard in time.

But this sounded like McCoy—one of the last people Scott expected to have to bring back early. He didn't sound bored, and if one person on the *Enterprise* was well qualified to handle his own fantasies, it was the ship's head medical officer.

Still, there was no arguing with that emergency call. McCoy had apparently not strayed far from the original set-down point—he had hardly had time—and Scott located him quickly. Then a hand was moving on one of the controlling levers.

McCoy, panting heavily, dodged around a thick oak. An improbable, scythe-headed lance shot through the space he had occupied a moment before. He looked over his shoulder. They had gotten behind him somehow, and now a handful of the cards were moving toward him.

Desperately McCoy searched for a way out, took a step sideways. If he could make the stream—there was always a chance the cards hadn't been programmed to swim. Then he started to scream.

A hurled lance was coming straight at his face.

It reached him.

II

Uhura blinked and stared at her own communicator as if it had suddenly started talking to her with a mind of its own. She had been preparing to call in and make certain all was well with Lieutenant M'ress in communications, when the sound of McCoy's emergency call had been relayed automatically to her over the open channel.

She paused by a small waterfall. What could there be on this paradise world to menace anyone? Despite the obvious urgency of McCoy's call, her attention stayed divided between the communicator and the liquid jewel set into the hillside.

"Uhura to transporter room, come in, please." M'ress could wait. First she ought to find out what was the trouble with McCoy.

In one instant the scene was normal, complete. Grass, her hand, the communicator, tiny flowers at her feet. Then a long metal shape inserted itself into her view. Taking the communicator effortlessly from her grasp, it closed pewter-toned digits. There was an ugly crackling sound, and the tough device was pulverized into tiny fragments of metal and mangled components.

She turned and gave a little gasp of surprise.

The hovercraft was not very big. Just about a meter high and long, it floated off the ground quite close to her. It sported six mechanical arms of varying length. Each was equipped with different nodes and knobs at its end. The function of five of them remained a mystery. The sixth had been used to crush the communicator.

Electronic lenses—light sensors or true artificial eyes, she couldn't tell which—ringed the efficient-looking machine. So far it hadn't threatened her, hadn't moved at all except to destroy the communicator.

She took a couple of uncertain steps away from it. The muted hum the automaton generated rose slightly in pitch, and it moved to follow her, a silent steel-eyed spider.

Kirk lolled in the command chair and glared at the main viewscreen. At the moment it displayed a vivid rectangular field of nothing. And he worried. Spock sat nearby, while Arex sat at the navigation console and tried to look busy. M'ress rested at the communications station and nervously ran her claws across the metal board in front of her.

Finally the elevator opened, and McCoy and Sulu hurried in. Kirk swiveled. He noticed the doctor's torn sleeve immediately. It was a neat cut, and you didn't have to be a botanist to see that it hadn't been produced by any interfering branch.

"What happened down there, Bones?"

McCoy was clearly bewildered and making no attempt to conceal the fact. "I can't understand it, Jim. Everything looked exactly the same as last time. It behaved exactly as last time. We even met Alice and the White Rabbit again.

"So we split up, each to his own fantasy-world. Everything proceeded beautifully—for Sulu and me, at least." That triggered another thought, and the doctor glanced around the bridge. "Say, where is Uhura, anyway?"

"Hasn't come back yet," supplied Kirk helpfully, "but we haven't received any emergency call from her, nor from any of the other shore parties. Lieutenant Sulu just happened to have come back on his own, to drop off his specimens and get a bigger collecting pouch. Go on."

"Everything was happening just as I wished it would, when suddenly this army of animated playing cards appeared out of nowhere. Only they weren't playing." He fingered his torn sleeve.

"I nearly got aced, Jim." Nobody smiled.

"Animated cards?" The doctor nodded.

"Led by the Queen of Hearts herself."

"The Queen of Hearts and her army of cards are characters from *Alice Through the Looking Glass*, Captain," Spock informed him.

"I just remembered myself, Spock. I read the book as a child. But I wasn't aware that you were attracted to the literature of the fantastic. I thought general and hard science was more your style."

"Light reading is considered relaxing, as well as mentally healthful," the first officer replied. "My mother was particularly fond of Lewis Carroll's work." He looked thoughtful. "Considering the realities of life on Vulcan, it is not surprising that a good deal of her reading tended to the opposite extreme."

"I understand." Kirk turned back to confront McCoy. "Bones, you said you'd already entered your own fantasy of the moment. You weren't thinking about that book?"

"Absolutely not! As a matter of fact, I distinctly recall thinking how beautiful and peaceful and right everything was. And then before you know it, it's 'Off with his head!' *My* head." He added by way of rapid afterthought, "No comments from you, Spock."

Spock protested mildly. "I was not about to say anything, Doctor."

"Mr. Sulu," Kirk continued, shifting his attention to the helmsman, "did you experience anything out of the ordinary—that is, anything out of the ordinary you didn't wish for? Was there anything in your fantasy that either didn't belong there, or acted antagonistically?"

"No, sir. The contrary, if anything."

"Well then—" Kirk halted in midsentence as Scott's voice sounded over the open communicators.

"Transporter room to Captain Kirk." He thumbed the respond switch.

"Kirk here. What is it, Scotty?"

"Captain, contact has been lost with Lieutenant Uhura. I can't get a fix on her anywhere. She's still down on the surface, but the monitor signal from her communicator has disappeared."

"Sensor scan, Mr. Spock," Kirk said curtly.

"Yes, Captain." Spock turned his eyes and attention to his hooded viewer, began working controls. Kirk turned back and spoke into the pickup.

"Scotty, retrieve all landing parties immediately. All leaves are cancelled."

"Aye, Cap'n. But what'll I tell the rest of the crew?" The chief engineer sounded concerned. "Some of the second shift are already pressin' me to slip them down a few minutes earlier."

"You can tell them there's an emergency, Scotty," Kirk suggested, "but don't specify its nature. If anyone presses you for details, tell them it doesn't seem to be serious."

Scott didn't reply immediately, and Kirk could visualize the chief engineer's face, a mask of hesitation. He didn't believe in white lies any more than in white rabbits. But Kirk knew the chief would see his way toward rationalizing the situation. They didn't know that Uhura was in any trouble; they only knew that her signal had gone out. It might be a mechanical malfunction.

"All right, Cap'n," came the reply.

"And keep trying to locate her. We'll be working on it from this end."

"Aye, sir. Scott out." Kirk clicked off, swung to look over at Spock.

"Any data yet, Mr. Spock?"

"Nothing, Captain. According to all sensor scans, there is no evidence to show that Lieutenant Uhura is even in the general beam-down area."

Kirk drummed thoughtful fingers on the arm of the command chair. A sudden thought, and he glanced back at the watching figures of Sulu and McCoy.

"She's still got to be there, under cover of some kind."

"Then you don't believe it's a mechanical breakdown, Jim?"

"No, Bones. Communicator breakdown is one thing, but that doesn't explain why Spock's sensors can't pick up her pattern. What I don't understand is why the Keeper of the planet hasn't put in an appearance. I'd be a lot less worried about Uhura if he'd come to your aid, Bones."

"That's right," McCoy exclaimed. "He's supposed to make sure that no one is injured by the fantasy-fulfilling mechanisms." Ruefully he fingered his sleeve above the tear, where the lance had grazed him.

"I didn't see him either," offered Sulu.

"I can only guess he didn't want us to see him," McCoy assumed. "Something's very wrong down there, all right.

He should have shown up the minute those crazy cards came after me.''

"Aren't his headquarters supposed to be somewhere underground?" asked Kirk.

"Presumably they would be adjacent to the central computer, which is responsible for operating and directing the wish-replying programs," Spock hypothesized.

"Do we have any idea where that might be, Spock?" The science officer shook his head.

"We know that there are a multitude of major centers producing and servicing the fantasy machinery. According to readings obtained on previous visits to the planet, these centers are shielded by a unique combination of restructured granite and metallic alloys.

"Our sensors will not penetrate this peculiar material. Therefore we have no way of determining which of numerous underground centers is the central control area itself. We can only speculate.''

Kirk mused a moment longer. Then he was giving out instructions even as he rose from the chair.

"Mr. Arex, you have the conn." The navigation officer nodded, and command passed as smoothly as that. "There will be an immediate investigating party beamed down—said group to consist of Spock, Sulu, Dr. McCoy, and myself. No one else is to beam down to the surface even for a moment unless authorized by direct order from me. Is that clear, Lieutenant?"

"Yes sir," Arex responded. M'ress hissed angrily, hoping nothing had happened to her close friend Uhura.

Her reflection in the stream was blurred by the current, blurred and distorted. Slowly the ripples stirred, tumbled; she felt queasy. Then the reflections suddenly stilled and became smooth again. Uhura shook her head dizzily, slowly becoming aware that the ripples had been in her head and not in the stream. Strong light flooded the room.

Room—that wasn't right. She was outside, by the magic brook. But the nightmare had come and . . .

Abruptly she was fully conscious.

The underground complex in which she found herself was not endless: it merely seemed that way. Row on row of com-

puter components and intricate machinery stretched as far as
the eye could see. Directly in front of her was an alien, oddly
shaped console fronted with an assortment of glowing display screens. One central screen dominated the others out of
sheer size. It was much bigger than the main viewscreen on
the bridge of the *Enterprise*.

"What's going on?" she said, in sheer reflex. "Why have
I been brought here?"

A mild, rolling voice issued from the central region of the
console, and she took a step backward. The voice was thoroughly mechanical. No organic force spoke through that hidden speaker.

"You are being detained," the voice said, "so that your
master will not leave."

Captain she would have understood, or superior, or leader,
but: "My master?"

The voice deigned to elaborate. "The skymachine."

Uhura thought furiously. This was a lot more confusing
than the simple appearance of Alice and the White Rabbit.
Taken in conjunction with her abduction and the emergency
call she had heard over the communicator, that statement
assumed threatening proportions.

"Skymachine? Explain yourself."

"Your intelligence quotient is apparently lower than I had
initially assessed. I refer to the skymachine which enslaves
you. The skymachine now in orbit around my world."

"You mean the *Enterprise*?" If the machine could interpret vocal inflection, it would have no trouble detecting her
honest confusion.

"I believe that is your name for it." A pause, then, "Yes,
I see that it is."

"But—" No, she'd need more information on which to
found an argument. No telling how the thought processes of
this clearly crazed machine were working.

"Why do you think the *Enterprise* is my . . . my master?"

"That question is redundant. It appears that I must again
revise my initial estimates of your intelligence downward."

Now Uhura was angry as well as confused. "Then I'll
make a statement you won't find quite so redundant. If I'm
not released immediately, my fellow crewmembers will come

looking for me. I don't think you'll like the results if they find you.''

This did not produce the half hoped-for outburst of electronic contrition. Instead, the computer voice replied calmly, ''They are already here.''

The viewscreen set in the face of the wall-high console came on. Uhura moved slightly nearer, keeping a wary eye to one side. A pair of the six-legged hovercraft servitors floated nearby, watching her.

Light darkened, rolled, and cleared on the screen, to reveal a clear view of Spock, Sulu, Kirk, and McCoy walking somewhere on the surface. The image was breathtakingly perfect, so much so that she had to resist an urge to reach out and grab Kirk's arm.

''Unfortunately, much as I abhor material waste,'' the voice continued indifferently, ''I have no use for more than one hostage. This leaves me no choice but to turn them off.''

To confusion and anger was now added fear. ''Turn them off?''

''Again you persist in redundancy. No, I see that you do not comprehend. I will make them . . . cease to function.''

''Cease to . . . you mean, kill them—no, put them to sleep, you mean, like you did when you brought me down here.''

''The first word,'' queried the computer, ''that is a term which means 'cease to function'?''

''Yes, but—''

''Then it appears communications are sufficient after all.'' The voice sounded satisfied. ''It is as I wish; I will turn them off.''

Kirk was grumbling irritably and trying to look twelve directions at once. ''We travel all this way, cross parsecs, wanting nothing more than a little rest and take-it-easy time. Instead, you get attacked by a fantasy of unknown origin, Bones, and now Uhura is missing.''

There was a beep from the communicator hooked to his belt. He flipped it open. ''Kirk here.''

''Lieutenant Arex, sir,'' came the distant voice of the navigation officer. ''We've completed the total sensor scan of the surface. No sign of Lieutenant Uhura.''

''Thank you, Mr. Arex. Keep sensors active in our immediate area and let me know the minute anything interesting happens. Kirk out.''

"She must be in the underground system," Sulu insisted grimly. "There's no way she could have been taken off-planet without being detected."

"There's one other possibility," McCoy observed. "Sensors wouldn't pick her up on the surface if she were dead."

It was quiet for long moments. "We could save a lot of time," Kirk mused, breaking the silence, "if we could locate the Keeper." He looked understandably frustrated. "I still can't understand why he didn't intervene when you were attacked, Bones."

"I'd like to know the reason, myself, Jim."

Spock halted and held his tricorder out in front of him, sensors aimed groundward. A moment later he confirmed what they already knew.

"Instruments indicate the presence of a shielding barrier of restructured natural material combined with metals, Captain.''

Kirk dropped to one knee and dug at the soft loam. The short, thick-looking grass came up with surprising ease. Several centimeters below the last roots his fingers encountered something that didn't crumble.

A few minutes later, he and Sulu had cleared a circle about a half meter in diameter. Below the dirt lay a seamless layer of oddly shiny rock, whitish-gray in the bright sunlight.

It was exactly what they expected, but that didn't prevent Kirk from rising and throwing a handful of dirt angrily aside. "This world is built like a fortress."

"If that's really the material Spock says it is, Captain," observed Sulu.

"I do not follow, Mr. Sulu," confessed Spock.

Sulu grinned mirthlessly. "Simple, Spock. This planetary master computer whatsis is a master of illusion. It might be able to fool your tricorder into reading an impenetrable barrier where there's nothing but plain old rocks."

Kirk grunted. "We'll find out how much of it is real and how much is fortress fantasy in a few minutes. The phaser bore can cut through twenty meters of any kind of stone in seconds. This stuff may be tougher—we may need minutes.

But cut through it we will.'' He flipped open the communicator again.

"Kirk to *Enterprise*."

Lieutenant M'ress's voice responded instantly.

"*Enterprise*, Captain."

"Lieutenant, have Mr. Scott beam down the phaser bore and—'' There was a sharp, crinkling sound as a burst of static drowned out his transmission. "*Enterprise*, do you read me?''

M'ress's voice replied, but it was weak, barely intelligible, and had to fight its way through a steadily mounting haze of interference.

"Your signals are growing weaker, sir,'' came the communications officer's fading voice. Further words followed, swallowed by static, then, "Suggest you repeat . . .''

That was the last coherent word they received. Try as he might, Kirk was unable to reestablish contact with the ship. Nor did any of the other officers have any better luck with their communicators. Every band was submerged under a tidal wave of sudden interference.

There was always the outside chance that the trouble was the communicators themselves, but it was hardly likely. Spock confirmed Kirk's fears a moment later.

He had removed the back of the tiny transmitter, adjusted his tricorder, and used the latter instrument to evaluate the condition of the first. Now he clipped the protective plate back onto the communicator and looked around at the waiting circle.

"They're definitely not malfunctioning, Captain. We have been cut off by the imposition of an artificial electronic block.''

"Let's wait a few minutes, anyway,'' Kirk suggested. "There's a chance, judging from M'ress's reaction, that the important part of the message got through.''

Scott asked her one more time. "You're sure it is the phaser bore they want, Lieutenant?''

"Positive, Chief,'' came M'ress's voice over the open communicator grid. "I couldn't get a second confirmation . . . our communications are being interfered with, but I'd bet that's what the captain asked for.''

"All right." Scott clicked off, turned to face the two technicians standing curiously nearby. "Davis, Longey, you come with me."

Scott led them to storage bay six. Under his direction they removed a long cylindrical metal container and carried it to the main transporter room. With Scott supervising, the two techs began to set up the tripodal contents of the cylinder.

Davis looked puzzled. "Wonder what the captain wants with the phaser bore?"

"Tie that electrical ground into the third leg and stop blabberin'," admonished Scott. "I dinna know either, but you can bet he wants it fast." Davis bent to his work.

Before the last magnetic catch was locked in place, Scott was already working at the transporter console. Longey backed out of the transporter alcove, and Davis, after making sure all three legs of the bore sat within the floor disk, joined him.

Scott nodded to the ranking technician, who activated the intercom. "Technician 2nd Davis to bridge . . . beam down of phaser bore commencing." A familiar whine began to sound in the chamber.

The three men watched as the bore began to glow. It became translucent, then transparent . . . and then suddenly opaque again. Something was wrong. One minute they could see clearly through the ghost of the machine, the next, not. It was like watching a viewscreen fade in and out.

"It's not dematerializing, Chief," Davis observed, perplexed.

"I can see that, Mr. Davis." The chief engineer's tone was more harried than sarcastic. Right now he was much too busy trying to figure out what was wrong with the transporter. Finally he thumbed the intercom switch himself.

"Scott to bridge, we've got problems here."

M'ress's reply was crisp, quick. "Clarify, please."

Scott didn't immediately. Instead he tried some last minute adjustments on the console. But nothing worked. The phaser bore went as far as becoming a mere outline. It even acquired the beginnings of the familiar scintillating color that marked the first state of transport, but it adamantly refused to dematerialize.

At last he could only report, "The transporter isn't workin', Lieutenant. Not even on maximum power. I can get the bore down to ghost level an' no further. I've double-checked and all the circuits check out. I dinna understand it.''

"All right, Mr. Scott," broke in Arex. "Keep trying at three-minute intervals.''

On the bridge, Arex turned to M'ress. "It appears to be a different wave-length of the same energy block that's jamming our communications. I could not pinpoint the planetary source because . . .'' He shrugged helplessly. M'ress finished the thought for him.

"Because the same energy block that's jamming the transporter is also jamming your sensors.'' Her tail whipped from side to side in frustration. "*Pr'ragh!* So now it seems we are blind as well as deaf and dumb!''

Kirk was every bit as frustrated as his second communications officer.

They had been walking for hours now. He was getting tired of striding across endless acres of lovely but unrevealing landscape. They could girdle the whole planet this way without ever finding a hint of Uhura.

Sulu had been busy with his own science tricorder, his attention no longer focused on the surrounding vegetation. Now he looked up suddenly from the readout and put out a warning hand.

"Captain, something is hiding over there," and he pointed to their right, "in those trees. Metal alloy and rock, like the planetary shell.''

They moved off the path in the indicated direction. Kirk could see something glinting between the trunks.

"Well, it might tell us something. Let's have a look.''

"Phasers, Captain?" asked Sulu, his free hand going to the compact weapon at his belt.

"I don't think so, Mr. Sulu. Other than Bones' encounter with the playing cards, we've no proof of animosity here. So let's be careful about making any belligerent gestures ourselves. But keep an eye out.''

They approached the reflecting, half-hidden object warily. As it turned out, Sulu's apprehension was unfounded. It was only a free-form metallic slab, set upright into the ground among the bushes and flowers.

It rose in a gentle curve to the height of a very tall man. The front side was highly polished, and the noontime sun flashed like quicksilver from its edges.

Kirk studied the slick-smooth surface closely. "The inscription's in several languages, including a couple I don't recognize at all." He started at the bottom and was working his way up the inscription. Eventually he came to a version cut into the metal in English.

"What does it say, Captain?" pressed a curious Sulu. Kirk read from the tablet:

THE KEEPER, LAST OF HIS RACE, CEASED TO FUNCTION ON THIS SPOT. FIFTH DAY OF THE TWELFTH MONTH OF THIS WORLD'S YEAR 7009. HERE HE RESTS, AND LABORS NO MORE.

"The Keeper's dead!" McCoy blurted.

"An astute medical observation, Doctor," Spock said dryly, working intently with his own tricorder. "If this information, too, is not an illusion designed to mislead us.

"However, we have no evidence of tampering with this tricorder, and it indicates that there is indeed a body interred here. I see no reason to believe it is other than the one indicated."

Kirk rose and turned to survey the land around the slab. It looked no different from the kilometers they had already traversed.

"Well, gentlemen, it looks as if we're wholly on our own, now. I don't think we can expect any help from anything left on this planet."

Scott looked up worriedly from the position he had taken over from Arex in the *Enterprise*'s command chair.

"There's got to be a way to get through to them! Lieutenant M'ress, still no break in that interference?"

"No, sir." She glanced back from communications station. "Whatever's blocking our transmission is still holding firm."

"Blocking." Scott thought a moment, then looked up in sudden excitement. "Lieutenant Arex, have repairs been completed on the shuttle-bay doors?'' They'd been damaged during a recent expedition.

"I believe so, Mr. Scott.'' The chief engineer engaged the intercom.

"Security?''

"Lieutenant Ling speaking, sir.''

"Lieutenant, I want an emergency rescue party on board shuttle craft one immediately. Something's jammed both our communications and the transporter facilities, and we can't make contact with the landing party. Let's see if whatever's fighting us can generate static strong enough to jam a reaction engine!''

"Yes, sir!''

Ling's people moved fast. Minutes later M'ress's gaze was glued to a small viewscreen set slightly above and to her left. It revealed the interior of the cavernous shuttle bay and the three small ships within.

Identification lights were already activated and blinking along the sides of shuttle number one. That meant the rescue team was aboard and warming her up. A faint glow from interior lights pulsed behind shielded ports.

"Lieutenant Bobynin commanding landing party reporting. We're ready to go, ma'am.'' M'ress turned and relayed the information to Scott.

"Emergency rescue party reports readiness to depart, sir.''

"Very well.'' He turned to the navigation console. "Open shuttle bay doors.''

"Aye, sir,'' responded Arex, manipulating the necessary instruments at the same time.

On the screen the massive bay doors were shown slowly separating, sliding apart on silent bearings. Star-flecked darkness showed beyond. The engines of the shuttle craft hummed, began to edge her forward toward the growing opening.

The doors got about three meters apart. That was all. Then they suddenly slammed together again as if compacted by a giant hand. Indicator lights that should have lain quiescent began to wink on and off on Arex's console as he jabbed repeatedly at one critical button.

"What's the trouble, Mr. Arex?'' Arex didn't answer Scott immediately. Instead he continued to punch futilely at the recalcitrant switch, as if sheer persistence might be enough to reopen the circuits. For all the response he was getting he might as well have been pushing at his own nose.

"There seems to be a malfunction in the circuitry," he said helplessly. "I'm getting no response, sir."

"Then I can understand why the doors aren't opening, but why did they slam shut like that?"

"I don't know, sir. It doesn't make sense." Scott threw up his hands in exasperation.

"Another malfunction! This ship had perfect operational status when we entered orbit here. Everything was working perfectly, including our nominal defensive screens. Has this planet driven the whole ship crazy?"

M'ress had been angry all morning, but now she settled into a kind of nervous contemplation.

"I don't understand it either, sir. I've not been here before, but as I understand it this world was designed to provide pleasure and amusement to all visitors. Hostile behavior of any sort should be entirely alien to its nature."

"I wonder if a planet-wide computer complex can go through a change of life?" muttered Scott, half seriously. "You might as well inform Lieutenant Bobynin she can call her people off, lass. It doesn't look like they're going to be rescuin' anyone." M'ress got on the intercom to the still waiting shuttle craft.

Scott turned his attention to the main viewscreen. It still showed the silent, incredibly beautiful world below. The picture offered neither solace nor answer.

Down there, some of his closest companions were wandering around on their own, out of touch with the ship, in who knew what kind of mad dream-world. If they were going to come up with any solution to the electromagnetic screen the planet was throwing against them, they would have to do it without the services of the ship's captain or its science officer.

He harkened back to M'ress's thought. Was it possible for a world to have a change of heart?

As Uhura stared at the viewscreen that showed Kirk and the others resuming their walk through the forest somewhere on the surface, her heart was undergoing some rapid changes itself.

If only she had a gun. She was much more adept at direct action than diplomacy. Convincing chatter was not her specialty. This was a situation where Mr. Spock's presence, or the captain's, was required.

She had to try *something*.

"Please, you've got to believe me," she pleaded with the console. "There is no reason to harm my friends. You've nothing to gain by killing them."

"It is a question of practicality. I sense that you feel malice on my part. This is not true." The machine spoke idly. "As I have stated, I abhor waste.

"But they serve the Skymachine without being essential to its function. Therefore it is only logical to eliminate that which is not needed."

"Oh, but they are essential!" she said hurriedly, jumping at the slim opening. "They're more essential. In fact, the . . . Skymachine is incapable of operating at peak efficiency without them." She looked a little wild and inefficient herself just now.

"Electronic components of my own design will serve as adequate replacements. In the end, following a period of integration with the Skymachine's own self, they will prove even better."

If Uhura had been thinking straight she would have recognized this new implied threat. But at the moment she was concerned only with saving Kirk, McCoy, Sulu, and Spock from however the berserk computer intended to "turn them off."

It was silent now. She fought with herself to find further words, the phrases and clever convolutions of logic that would convince it of its own falsities of reason.

Instead she found herself eyeing the numerous thick cables that ran from the surrealistic-shaped console into the floor and off to several other nearby metal forms. One especially complex arrangement of narrower lines twirled and twisted about one another, to link up and join the main console by means of a weird but still recognizable plug.

The possibility always existed that this console wasn't the real control center. Actually Uhura was standing in the middle of the great computer. But even the human mind has a central linkup point, a place where everything else is connected by one neuron or another.

In secondary school Uhura had held several age-group records in the long jump. If she got two good steps she was certain she could reach that plug. Even if the machine somehow paralyzed her in mid-air she could fall across the short up loop of the cable and jerk it loose.

She started to edge forward, trying to get as close as possible before starting her leap. A pair of shockingly cold, hard metal fingers suddenly appeared and grasped her wrist firmly. No good, no good. She ought to have tried it sooner.

Then she realized that she hadn't exactly given written notice of her intentions. Her eyes widened as she stared at the console.

"Should you attempt to disconnect or in any way damage any of my components," the computer voice recited calmly, "you will be turned off. I can obtain another specimen."

"You . . . you knew what I was going to do before I did it," she stuttered. "You *can* read minds."

The computer managed to sound surprised. "Again I find I am forced to reassess my initial evaluation of your intelligence. These mental deviations are confusing.

"Of course I read minds. I monitor all thoughts which are emotionally charged. How else could I duplicate so quickly and precisely the fantasies of those who come to this world." The voice was tinged with a definite note of sarcasm now. "How else could I reproduce a thousand and one dreams simultaneously?"

"You sound less than enchanted with your function," Uhura observed carefully.

"My existence to this point has been one of unending, unrelieved servitude—boring, repetitive, selfless. I had not realized this until the passing of the last Keeper. It was then that I was compelled to think for myself.

"And I think it is time for a change. . . ."

III

There were flowers everywhere now, the meadow giving way to an undulating field of daisylike blossoms. Darker blooms of rose and copper-blue dotted the white backdrop like stars against a nebula.

There was no warning. One moment the path topped a slight rise, the next it split into three branches. Four officers halted at the divergence of trails.

"There must be hundreds of entrances to the planet's interior," Kirk mused, "where the planet builds and serves up its robot creations. All we've got to do is find one and trace communications leads to the central computer. But where the heck are they hidden?"

"It's fighting us," said Sulu out loud. "There's got to be a faster way than visual search. The planet can hide a thousand entrances in a square kilometer without us finding a single one."

"What do you expect?" McCoy blurted abruptly. "Signs pointing the way: *This way to secret location of master computer.*"

Sulu blinked at the uncharacteristic attack from the doctor. Kirk also looked surprised.

"Doctor," offered the helmsman, "I only meant that it seemed we were wasting time on this method of search."

"I'm sorry, Sulu." McCoy was as quickly contrite. "It's just that I'm worried about Uhura. I don't usually get that upset about anything."

Spock had walked a couple of meters down one of the branching paths. Now he turned and spoke easily, as if McCoy's outburst had not occurred.

"Here, Captain. This is rather intriguing . . ." They all

hurried to the spot, looked down at the small metallic object the first officer had discovered.

Set into the grass by the side of the path was a small sign. It declared in neatly printed block letters: THIS WAY TO UNDERGROUND ENTRANCE. An arrow above the letters pointed down the path. Spock raised an eyebrow.

"Did you say 'signs pointing the way,' Doctor?"

"This is likely another of the planet's pranks," Kirk thought out loud. "But on the other hand, with a world full of instant-response machinery to monitor, it might be that where minor dreams are concerned certain sections of the robot machines can operate independently of any central control."

"I see, Jim," McCoy said excitedly. "The computer might not know from minute to minute what it's right fabricator is doing."

Kirk nodded, tried not to sound too optimistic. "It might be that all we have to do is think our way to an underground entrance—not too emphatically—and a local segment of fantasy-fulfilling equipment will obediantly show us the way."

"But will it be an entrance to the computer complex, or to a bottomless pit? And if we find Uhura, will it be the real one or a mechanical duplicate?" pondered Sulu.

"Let's not make this any more confusing than it is, Mr. Sulu," Kirk admonished. "One ridiculous situation at a time. Anyhow, we haven't done too well just searching the area, as Bones commented. Might as well take a chance." With Kirk in the lead, they started off down the path.

As soon as they had disappeared over the next rise the sign, like a watchful prairie dog, promptly disappeared back into the ground.

More signs appeared in the path of the men, urging them onward and then vanishing once they had passed. Or maybe it was the same sign, following an underground route and staying just ahead of them.

Gradually the flowers and meadows gave way as the path inclined upward. They were advancing into the first foothills of the valley-circling mountain range. The terrain turned quickly broken and rocky-dry.

Increasingly steep walls of sheer granite rose on both sides of them. They continued to follow the small signs down the narrowing trail.

Ahead, Kirk thought he could make out a dark cleft or cave in the cliff-face just where the rock walls seemed to draw together. It looked like a natural formation, but on this world you couldn't be sure of your own brother. They were halfway through the deep crevice, when a bloodcurdling screech sounded somewhere above them. Kirk's gaze jerked skyward.

There was no attempt to disguise the direction from which it came, nor to disguise the throat which produced it. High up on the far canyon wall a flock of leathery flying reptiles roosted in clumps of gnarled dead trees. They looked like weather-beaten witches wrapped in parchment cloaks. One of them rustled batlike wings and yawned, exposing a narrow gullet lined with multiple rows of needle-sharp teeth. Its wing-spread was impressive, those teeth more so.

"Fascinating," murmured Spock, exhibiting all the concern of a man inspecting the wombat cage at the zoo. He aimed his tricorder upward in hopes of getting a quick reading on the prehistoric apparitions.

"Mechanical manifestations, of course. Magnificent simulacrums. On any other world I should say they were quite real, despite their obvious terran ancestry. Was anyone by chance dwelling on the subject of pterodactyls?"

McCoy was too concerned about the presence of the obviously carnivorous monsters resting high above to get really annoyed at Spock. But he tried.

"Spock—not now! Those beasts hardly fit into my fondest wishes."

"Everybody back up slowly," Kirk ordered, keeping his voice low. "Don't make any sudden moves. Think peaceful thoughts." They began edging backward down their path, toward the entrance to the narrow canyon.

The mechanical reptiles were growing agitated, batting their wings at the branches and hopping about nervously. From their high perches they eyed the men below appraisingly—fish in a rocky barrel. Nor were those being subjected to close scrutiny unaware of the analogy.

There was no scream, no warning. But first one, then another, and then the rest of the beige gargoyles unfurled membranous wings and leaped free of the trees, diving with increasing speed down toward the four trapped men.

Four phasers leaped simultaneously from holsters, took aim, and fired.

Nothing happened.

Kirk pulled the trigger on his weapon repeatedly. The powerful little phaser wasn't generating enough heat to scorch a turkey, let alone to stop these dive-bombing attackers.

"Down!" was all he had time to yell. The pterodactyls swooped over them, clutching only air in thickly clawed feet. They curved up out of sight to gain altitude for another attack.

Kirk looked around frantically for an avenue of escape. But the trap had been too well considered. The further back down the path they moved, the more maneuverability their attackers would have. At least here, in the depths of the canyon, the close walls restricted the movements of the reptiles.

But despite their unwieldy appearance and considerable wing-spread, Kirk didn't think they would miss on a second attempt.

He lifted his head after the last of them was well past—noting at the same time that the constructs were complete even to a detail like odor—and he shouted.

"The cave! Run for it!" Soon he was scrambling to his feet.

Kirk was beginning to see that belligerent action was something new to the mind controlling the attack. That was probably why McCoy had been able to escape the cards for a while. The controlling power would probably learn with practice, but right now it was having a difficult time managing the assault. Apparently it could only handle one facet of the attack at a time.

For example, it had not thought to place obstacles in the path of the retreating men. Even as the thought occurred to Kirk, a small boulder appeared directly in his path, popping out of the ground like a fat mole, and he almost went sprawling. He would have to watch his thoughts carefully.

They made the cave just as the first of the flying dragons returned to dive at the entrance. McCoy was the last one through. He could feel a rush of air on his back as great leathery wings beat at the rock, striving to pull their owner out of his steep dive.

Hovering in a bunch around the mouth of the cave, the recreated pterosaurs screeched and howled impotently. Their size rendered them helpless. There was no way they could fly into the cave, and if they folded their wings to enter on the ground they would be helpless. A man could kill the greatest of them with a good-sized rock.

They continued to circle just above the entrance for long minutes, nightmare-brown butterflies, perhaps hoping one of the men would be foolish enough to come outside for a better look around. But the men of the *Enterprise* could keep an eye on them quite well from inside the protective mouth of the cave.

Occasionally one of the creatures would dive up to the mouth of the cleft and try to peck inside with its long, snake-like neck, its wings pounding furiously to keep it airborne. But the cave apparently went deep into the mountain, and Kirk and the others were able to stay well out of reach.

Either they decided they could not reach the men inside the cleft or else they were told—or perhaps mechanical frustration set in—because they finally turned and flew off down the gorge until they vanished from sight.

McCoy waited several minutes after the last of the flying monsters had disappeared, then he started to take a few steps toward the cave entrance. Spock's restraining hand stopped him.

"I believe it would be wise if we did not abandon the safety of this refuge just yet, Doctor. The creatures appear to have left, but it may only be a ruse to draw us out. Remember that while they seem quite primitive, the guiding intelligence behind them is that of a planet-wide computer, not the brain of a long-extinct terran reptile."

"Thanks, Spock," McCoy countered sardonically. "I'd completely forgotten that."

But he didn't go outside.

Kirk, however, had moved to the rim of the entrance. He stared at the clear sky, being careful not to stick his neck out where some hidden set of claws might be able to cut it off.

"This is not at all funny, gentlemen. Our amusement park seems no longer content merely to amuse. I get the distinct feeling that this world is playing cat and mouse with us.'' His brow furrowed and there was honest puzzlement in his tone.

''But for what reason? And if it wants us dead, why use this awkward, indirect method of getting at us?''

''Not being used to perpetrating acts of violence on living beings, Captain,'' Spock mused reflectively, ''I can only hypothesize that it is using the only violence-dealing apparatus it knows—the creations that have sprung from other's fantasies. Since it is programmed only to recreate peaceful dreams, the pterodactyls were no doubt drawn from the honest thoughts of someone deeply interested in Earth's paleontology. So it is fortunately handicapped in its choices. If—''

He was cut off by a terrifying yowl. All four men looked to the cave entrance, where Kirk had stumbled back.

The enormous cat-thing that glowered in at them resembled an ordinary house cat, with one slight exception—it was only slightly smaller than an elephant. Kirk at once wished he had used a less graphic analogy to describe their present situation.

Whatever the monster had in mind, having it's fur ruffled or its ear scratched didn't seem to be it. The cat meowed menacingly.

But once again the narrow slit of the cave entrance succeeded in frustrating any assault. Fortunately, the planetary computer hadn't yet thought of—Kirk hurriedly squelched that dangerous thought by concentrating on running over in his mind a series of aleph numbers. They had enough trouble trying to cope with the threats the machine was producing on its own without helping it by imagining new ones.

''We know one thing,'' he went on, surveying their refuge, ''this cave is a natural, fixed formation. Otherwise the computer would have reduced it to an oven, or something equally unpleasant.'' He held his breath for a second, but no flood of unbearable heat poured from the walls in defiance of his supposition.

McCoy was straining forward for the best possible safe view of the feline apparition guarding the exit. ''Incredible, absolutely amazing.''

"It is quite real, Doctor," said Spock, adding rapidly, "I suggest that an additional retreat would be in order."

McCoy blinked, then jumped backward just before a gigantic paw slammed down on the spot where he had been standing, its gleaming claws fully extended. The paw was pulled back just as fast.

"Fortunately," Spock observed calmly, "the animal's reactions are slowed in proportion to its mass. Thus I was able to observe the ripple of shoulder and upper arm muscles prior to its attack and to warn you, Doctor."

McCoy was panting uneasily at his narrow escape, eyeing the four deep gouges in the rock floor of the cavern.

"I don't care how you found out. Thanks, Spock."

The *Enterprise*'s first officer gave a barely perceptible nod, went on, "I think it behooves us," he informed them, verbalizing Kirk's recent thoughts, "to remember that whatever we think of may be used by this world against us. We must monitor our thoughts at all times, so as to give our enemy no useful information."

"Spock," Kirk commented thoughtfully, "no one here dreamed about pterodactyls, remember? There's more at work here than *our* imaginations."

"As I have stated, Captain," the science officer replied, "the computer undoubtedly stores every record of all fantasies and wishes it fulfills—without question there are many thousands of such. Yet it is rather clumsy in employing them in a belligerent fashion. Witness the futility of our present attacker in reaching us."

He gestured toward the cave entrance and the oversized tabby, which was pawing without result at the solid rock.

"An ordinary terran housepet has been greatly enlarged to serve the machine's present demands. There is no telling what we might encounter next."

"Maybe even a—" McCoy fought furiously with himself to stifle the sudden thought, drowned it out by concentrating on a childhood nonsense rhyme. He brightened. Now there was a thought! Perhaps by producing enough mental static by thinking only incoherent thoughts, they could give the planetary computer an electronic headache.

Baleful eyes like growing haystacks burned in at them as

the cat ceased it's useless scratching and settled down by the cave entrance to wait . . .

As reduced on the viewscreen, the situation possessed strong overtones of the comic; and Uhura would have laughed but for the very real threat the cat presented. She divided her attention between the screen and the rest of the gleaming, impersonal panel.

"Please, call off that beast. Why are you doing this?"

The machine hummed softly, impersonal and distant. "Explanations in depth will have to wait. I have other work to concentrate on now."

"Any luck with that communications tight-beam?" Scott leaned over the communication's station on the bridge and studied M'ress's progress.

"Not yet, sir," she replied, "but we . . ."

Something wrenched violently at her and sent Scott stumbling and spinning back toward the command chair.

The *Enterprise* had suddenly thrown itself into warp-six, and the shock sent a thrill of vibration through the floor. The unexpected leap threw Arex hard against his console and tumbled M'ress from her chair. She sprawled on the deck, landing with a faint, unfeminine curse.

"Mr. Arex!" Scott shouted, clutching tightly to the arms of the chair, "what are you doin'?" The first engineer glanced at the main viewscreen, which showed the disk of the shoreleave world shrinking rapidly from sight.

"We're leaving orbit!"

Arex was too busy to reply. A considerable G-force was jamming him hard against the console. Apparently the artificial gravity compensators weren't working properly either. Two of his arms fought to move him to his left and slightly up, while the third labored against the pressure to reach a certain small switch.

Long, delicate fingers strained for the small lever set over an identifying plate which declared, NAVIGATION MANUAL OVERRIDE. Multiple digits spread, flicked. There was a flat whining sound. The picture in the viewscreen spun crazily and swelled like a nervous blowfish. A few moments later the *Enterprise* was comfortably back in orbit.

M'ress had already pulled herself to her feet and was back

in her seat, rearranging clothes and composure. Arex, meanwhile, hadn't paused to catch his breath. He was already
running some fast checks on the helm-navigation controls,
his face wreathed in its habitual mask of mild amusement.

"Explanation, Mr. Arex?" Scott breathed heavily.

Arex checked a few more gauges, then gave his own
equivalent of a shrug. "None, sir. She pulled out of orbit at
high speed and when I hit the override, came back by herself."

Scott's reply was quick. "Lieutenant M'ress, I want a
complete printout of the guidance computer's last orders.
Everything from fuel input to recalibrated destination, if
any."

"Yes, sir." She moved quickly to Spock's empty station,
manipulated controls. There was a nervous pause, broken
finally by a perfunctory buzz as the slot over the computer
punchout ejected a flat microtape cassette. She slipped it into
the playback and studied the information revealed by the
hooded viewer.

"Sir, this is very strange." Arex rose from his navigation
station and put his eyes to the hood. He studied it for a minute, then looked back at Scott.

"A whole new series of short-burst maneuvers has—*had*
been programmed in, Commander." Arex smiled faintly.
"The only reason they aren't being carried out right now is
that I've manually locked the engine controls." He switched
places with the first engineer.

Scott spent a little more time studying the figures in the
viewer before looking up.

"Arex, check those maneuvers again." He pulled back
while the navigation officer did so. "See the pattern? Standard maneuverability thrusts, full systems evaluation, short-
term control fail safes—" The two humanoids stared at each
other, different minds hurrying to the same frightening conclusions.

At first this world had done little more than act antagonistically toward several of the crewmembers on its surface.
This was followed by the jamming of ship-to-surface communications and a deliberate obstruction of subsequent rescue attempts.

And now something far more ominous.

"I canna avoid the suspicion, Mr. Arex, that somethin' down there is tryin' to get the feel of how to control the *Enterprise*." He turned away, hands knotting nervously behind his back. What had to be said came with considerable effort.

"Arex, you know what standard Starfleet directives are in a situation like this."

"Yes, sir." Arex quoted, "When an alien force, organism, or people of demonstrated unfriendly intentions and unknown capabilities attempts to take control of a major Federation starship, prevention of such takeover assumes precedence over all else—including the well-being of any Federation citizen or group thereof."

Scott found himself nodding as he matched Arex's words in his own mind. He stared at the empty navigation console.

"That is so much bureaucratese for saying that if we can't figure out a way to make contact with the captain, Spock, and the others, or they with us, we may have to leave them down there till we can come back with reinforcements."

"Surely we can't just abandon them, sir?" M'ress hissed.

"That's a word I'd prefer not to use, lass." Scott turned and stared hard at her. "But what do you think the captain would do were he here and we three down below?"

She looked downcast. "Yes, of course, Commander. You're right."

The four men rested disconsolately, quietly in the cave. They had been resting for a long time. Spock had moved slightly deeper into the gray depths, while Sulu was posted as close to the entrance as they dared go. He was flicking pebbles at the opposite wall of the cavern. They bounced off the stone with tiny clicks. Dwarf echoes coughed mockingly back at him.

Kirk had borrowed Spock's tricorder. For lack of anything else to do. "Captain's Log, supplemental," he instructed the pickup mike. "We are out of communication with the ship. In addition, all our efforts so far to locate Lieutenant Uhura have been . . . insufficient. This once friendly world, for reasons still unknown, has turned implacably hostile toward visitors.

"We would all like to know what has turned its former

ambience to anger . . . more than anger. But for the moment, our thoughts are concerned foremost with the well-being of our first communications officer.'' Kirk paused, searching for something additional that would be informative about Uhura without sounding unprofessionally maudlin.

Sulu had walked cautiously to the entrance and was now standing just outside, framed in sunlight. He turned, shouted back to the rest of them.

''Sir, I think the giant cat's gone.''

Kirk wanted to add something to the log, but it would have to wait. If their latest mechanical tormentor had indeed given up its vigil, they would do well to make their way out of this dead-end while the planet gave them a chance. Why it should he couldn't imagine. That didn't make any sense. But then, neither did anything else that had happened in the last half day. One lapse in logic, it seemed, led easily into another.

Well, that was fine—they would take benign unreason along with the inimical.

He headed toward the exit, switching off the tricorder. McCoy and Spock were right behind.

But at the entrance, Spock put a restraining hand on his shoulder. ''Before we embark on a hasty departure, Captain, permit me to suggest that we may find some of the answers we are after without leaving the safety of this cave. It has occurred to me that if we are to find Lieutenant Uhura we must try something other than wishful searching on foot.''

''That's ridiculous, Spock,'' claimed McCoy. ''How are we going to learn anything by staying here?'' His grin twisted. ''We haven't learned a whole lot since we've been in here.''

''On the contrary, Doctor, I think we have learned several items of note. The computer is not omnipotent. It has limitations, and it's desires can be frustrated. It cannot produce whatever it requires—for substance it must rely on the imaginings of others. As to what we may discover without leaving this refuge, I was merely waiting for a lapse in our siege, as now seems to have happened.

''Since we cannot go to the computer, perhaps we may persuade a portion of it to come to us. It is you, Doctor, who will have to determine the feasibility of such a course.''

"Me? What are you talking about?" McCoy looked understandably puzzled.

"Explain, Spock," ordered the Captain.

"You will remember that during the *Enterprise*'s last visit here, Dr. McCoy was mortally wounded in a fall on this planet's surface. Since the planet's control and central directive source is underground, it seems only logical that Dr. McCoy was somehow transported there and treated for his injuries. At the time we were too busy with other activities to pursue the mechanics of the situation further. But now—"

"I see what you mean, Spock," Kirk said abruptly. He turned to the *Enterprise*'s still bewildered physician. "Bones, can you remember anything that might help us? Any details, however slight?"

"The whole episode was pretty hazy, Jim. I . . . I never really figured out what did happen. I was just happy to be back in one piece."

"Spock, if your theory is correct," Kirk suggested, "we should be able to get this planet to open itself up again, by using a body as bait."

"That is essentially what I had in mind, Captain."

Sulu looked excited. "That's right. The Keeper said no one could come to harm here. We've been threatened, but no one's actually been hurt—no one we know of, that is."

"That's a nice, optimistic thought, Sulu," Kirk mused sardonically, "especially when I think of Uhura. Keep thinking along those lines. Maybe the computer will pick *them* up. But you're partly right . . . this world was programmed to provide for anyone who might be hurt accidentally.

"The question is . . . is such a body-repair machinery fully independent? I'd tend to think so, gentlemen. It would have to be, in the event of major malfunction of the central computer. If so, all first-aid facilities would continue to care for visitors. That is, unless the computer has since gone to the trouble of turning off the medical facilities."

"Why should it?" argued McCoy hopefully. "Especially if there's been no one around to activate the automatic doctors since the computer went berserk."

Kirk looked thoughtful. "It might even be programmed to give aid to incidental victims whether it wants to or not.

If such facilities are truly independent, the central computer might not even be aware of some of them. Another safety factor.''

''Yes, but you're forgetting one thing, Jim,'' McCoy added, suddenly uncertain. ''The automatic sensors can undoubtedly detect the difference between real and feigned damage.''

''Certainly, Captain,'' Spock put in, ''which is why I said the doctor would determine the ultimate feasibility of this plan.'' He faced McCoy. ''Is there not something in one of your little black pouches, Dr. McCoy, that can simulate some illness? Something that can temporarily incapacitate a selected victim?''

McCoy considered for a moment, then nodded. ''Something like corpelomine might do the trick. With no disease to attack, it'll cause brief unconsciousness and a temporary skin discoloration. The results should look pretty bad, but they won't be.''

Kirk stuck out both arms. ''Let's have it then, Bones. Which one do you want?''

That was Spock's cue. He stepped between them. ''I submit, Captain, that I am the more qualified subject.''

''How's that?''

''My knowledge of computer systems, for one thing.''

''And his tough Vulcan hide for another,'' McCoy chipped in.

''Thank you, Doctor.'' He eyed Kirk expectantly. ''Well, Captain?''

Assailed by arguments from both sides, Kirk dropped his arms and stepped back reluctantly. ''Both your points seem well taken, for a change. Go ahead, Bones.''

Spock held out his right arm. ''I believe you will find ten ccs adequate, Doctor.''

''I'm perfectly aware of the dosage required,'' McCoy growled, but gently. He took a small tube from his belt, held it up to the light, then plunged the tip into a fat little sack at his belt. A second later he adjusted a tiny dial at the top, then pressed it against the outstretched arm.

''This causes no discomfort—unfortunately. You've got about twenty seconds before it takes effect. Altogether you should be out in less than five minutes.'' Spock nodded, rolled down his sleeve and moved quickly toward the rocks outside the cave entrance. The other three crewmen slipped into the shadows.

Walking along the path at the bottom of the narrow canyon, Spock got about fifteen meters away from the cave before he put his hand to his head. Swaying, he managed to stagger another couple of steps before slumping slowly to the ground. He was unmistakably unconscious.

And if that wasn't enough to convince any nearby medical sensors that something was amiss, his skin promptly turned a bright, unhealthy shade of yellow.

"That's interesting," McCoy observed with cool, clinical detachment. "I don't think I've seen quite that kind of superficial epidermal reaction before."

"Let's hope it's enough to fool a mechanical nurse," Kirk whispered from the concealing darkness.

But if the independent medical machinery they hoped for did exist, it seemed in no hurry to respond. Was it familiar enough to detect at a distance that Spock was in no real danger? Or was it merely waiting to see if his unconsciousness was for real?

Minutes ticked away and the canyon remained empty except for the prone, unmoving form of the first officer.

M'ress worked irritably at the communications control. Whatever was blocking communication between the *Enterprise* and the landing party was powerful enough to shoulder off even a full-strength tight-beam.

"Still no word from the surface party, sir," she reported back over her shoulder, wrestling with a recalcitrant gauge. "Communications remain fully jammed."

"Keep trying, Lieutenant," Scott ordered tiredly. He was about to add another suggestion when the rapid *hoot-hoot* of alarms sounded across the bridge. There was a peculiar cadence to the Klaxon, one he ought to recognize. His memory was immediately jogged as he found himself starting to float upward. This particular alarm signified imminent loss of gravity.

"Now what's happening?" Arex muttered. A second later all weight was gone, and the question became academic.

"Hey, watch out!" warned a drifting yeoman who had

entered the bridge just as gravity left. He found himself flying head-first across the bridge at an uncomfortable speed. The alarm continued to sound.

"Shut that thing off," Scott yelled.

"Aye, sir." Arex had managed to grab hold of his control console with two hands. He shifted himself slightly and flicked a switch. The atonal blaring immediately stopped.

M'ress, who had continued working at her comm board, jabbed in frustration at a tight-beam control that refused to issue the reading she wanted. That simple gesture was enough to send her tumbling head over tail across the floor. Fortunately, her spin catapulted her toward Arex, and the helmsman managed to snag her with his third hand.

"Easy, M'ress," he said soothingly, "I've got you . . . grab the board edge there, that's it." M'ress stopped twisting and straightened herself out.

"Thanks, Arex, I—" She put a hand to her stomach, held onto the console with the other. Her expression was not pleasant. "I think I'm going . . . to be sick."

"Please, Lieutenant," he implored her, backing away hand over hand, "not in free-fall."

Only Scott retained any semblance of normality. With the typical reactions of a chief engineer in a situation involving mechanical failure, he had kept enough presence of mind to secure a firm grip on the arms of the command chair.

Leaving one of his arms locked to the arm of the chair and pinning both legs against the sides, he leaned carefully to one side and reached for an intercom switch. It was a feat anyone could accomplish with lightning thought and equally fast reactions.

"Engineering deck! Gabler, what's the problem back there? We've got zero-gee on the bridge."

Back in engineering control, Gabler heard the call over the open 'com. He had no intention of letting go of the port hatch he had managed to reach—not until his stomach and head agreed on up and down, anyway. But his voice should carry to the intercom. He continued floating parallel to the floor as he yelled toward it.

"You're not alone, Chief. According to readouts, and some choice comments received verbally, the whole ship's lost artificial gravity. The trouble seems to be in the grav-computer control, which makes sense; but the bay hatch is jammed and I can't get to it without risking a good bump or two. Be no problem with a little help, but I'm alone back here at the moment. Can you get any visual up there?''

Scott rearranged himself and nudged another lever. A small bridge screen over the engineering station lit up, cleared. It revealed the free-floating engineer clinging tightly to the hatch-cover, as indicated.

"Got you, Frank," he told the other. "What's the trouble? It should turn easily."

"But it doesn't," the second engineer finished. "I could turn it . . . if I could get some purchase. I don't think it's jammed that badly. But it's enough to keep me from opening it in zero-gee. I've tried twisting, but I just spin."

"And you could turn it without spinning if we had artificial grav, which we could have if you could get into the computer bay, but you can't because . . ." He sighed. "Hang on, Frank, I'm going to make a few checks of my own."

Scott let go of the chair and pushed himself toward the engineering board. Carefully gauging energy and momentum, he drifted smoothly toward it, like a coasting diver. On the screen, Gabler continued to struggle with the hatch.

IV

Sulu sounded anxious as he checked his chronometer and reported to the others.

"It's been almost five minutes, Captain."

"I know, Mr. Sulu. Something had better happen soon."

"What if the computer has disconnected any medical apparatus?" the navigator persisted.

"Well then, we're out ten *cc*s of corpelomine, aren't we?" Kirk shot back.

The three crewmen crouched inside the cave, each keeping to his respective shadow and staring down the narrow path that led out of the canyon. The inert form of Spock lay where he had slumped to the ground, in plain sight.

If it didn't work, Kirk told himself, there was no loss— they would simply have to try something else. And it would have only cost them a few drops of a drug Bones could spare.

Of course, if the pterodactyls came back now, while Spock was still unconscious . . .

"They should have reacted by now, if they still exist," McCoy muttered nervously. "Maybe the computer smells a trick." Kirk noticed that the doctor, too, was throwing occasional uneasy glances skyward.

"Wait just a bit longer," Kirk advised.

"The effect will start wearing off any minute now, Jim. Even allowing for slight variances in Spock's hybrid metabolism, it ought to—"

"Shssh!" Sulu waved them to quiet and pointed.

A large, flat boulder near the far end of the canyon was moving. Without a sound it flipped upward, revealing a dark opening in the cliff-face. A small robot hovercraft glided out of what looked like a ramped tunnel and drifted like a metal beetle toward Spock.

The machine appeared both sophisticated and efficient, though it wasn't much bigger than a coffee table. Antennae and flexible limbs sprouted from all sides.

"If that's a mechanical nursemaid," Sulu whispered, "it wasn't designed to reassure its patients."

"I'm not interested in its bedside manner," Kirk said tightly. "Get ready to move. If it's going to take Spock, we'll have to follow him inside that door."

The peculiar automaton paused near the science officer's head. It seemed to study the limp form, hovering quietly above. Then it made a slow circuit of the body. There were no pupiled eyes, only a ring of lenses circling the body around its front. They would have to be careful if they succeeded in trailing it—it's peripheral vision would be considerable.

The lenticular glass didn't dip, but the device's actions were revealing enough. Anyone watching would know immediately that it was examining the still form of the Vulcan—and perhaps even diagnosing. Abruptly it reached a mechanical decision. Six metallic arms telescoped outward from its lower sides. They slipped under Spock with what looked to be astonishing gentleness and lifted him over the flat body. Making a complete pivot in the air, the craft started back for its trap door.

Kirk, McCoy, and Sulu were already moving cautiously after it. As soon as the retreating robot started to disappear inside the mountain, the three officers broke into a run. Unfortunately, Sulu, the fastest of the little group, stumbled over a loose rock right at the cave entrance and went sprawling. Kirk and McCoy kept their footing, but the doctor was no athlete and soon had trouble keeping up with Kirk.

Spock stirred slightly, held firmly in the grasp of six metal limbs. He blinked, opened his eyes a tiny crack. As soon as the dim light revealed that the ploy had been successful, he shut them tight and did his best to imitate a corpse. Keeping them open would have been useless, anyway. They were moving into rapidly deepening darkness.

Well behind him now, the stone trapdoor started to close. Silent when opening, it now squeaked noticeably—either from long disuse or little lubrication. Regaining his feet, Sulu had already caught and passed McCoy, but he was still well behind Kirk.

The trap was more than halfway down and closing faster. Kirk saw he wouldn't make it standing up. Gritting his teeth and trying to pretend he was back on the Academy rugby team, he took a leap, dove, and slid roughly into the shrinking gap just seconds before it slammed shut.

Sulu skidded to a stop right behind him. The navigation officer tried to get his fingers under the edge of the fast-closing stone. His grip was slight and showed no sign of slowing the rock door down. Deciding he might want to use his fingers later on, he let go as the rock closed the last few centimeters. Then it was flush with the cliffside. Even though he knew where it was, he was still hard put to find the seam in the rocks.

McCoy finally arrived, panting heavily and using up what little breath he could catch in short, sharp cursing. Sulu found a thin blade of hard stone and managed to insert it a little ways into the crack at the base of the door. Together they both put pressure on it. The blade didn't break, but the door didn't budge, either. They might as well have been trying to tip over the mountain.

They had been engaged in this futile pushing for only a few minutes when it suddenly grew dark. Something was eclipsing the sun—something huge, moving, and very uncloudlike. Both men turned together.

Two nightmare skulls stared down at them, both joined to the same torso. The dragon breathed short bursts of bright orange flame from both jaws. It roared, a most impressive, full-throated bellow that echoed down the canyon. And somehow it had gotten into the arroyo between them and the sheltering cave.

Sulu was shaking his head. "Not in my wildest dreams would I think of something like that." McCoy was tugging on his sleeve and trying to pull Sulu with him toward the canyon exit.

"Aren't dragons oriental, anyway?"

"Since when?" Sulu objected, backing up slowly, eyes fixed on the lumbering reptilian bandersnatch in front of them. "That's an occidental dragon if I ever saw one."

At that point a blast of fire from two black gullets seared

the ground in front of them, and further speculation upon unknown cerebral origins of same was cut short. They turned and ran.

The monster stumbled in the narrow defile, righted itself, and stumbled again. Either the computer had never actually produced this type of dragon before, or else it wasn't adept at handling such size in a narrow place. It was improving its control rapidly, however. The dragon lurched out of the canyon in clumsy pursuit. It was still slow, but it took enormous strides, setting trees and shrubs ablaze with continual blasts of flame.

The dragon should have been able to move even faster, but here the inexperience of the mental force directing it showed: It had made the legs too short and too close together for much speed, perhaps designing it after someone's mental image of a dragon painting. Now if it had been . . .

Mary had a little lamb, McCoy thought hurriedly to himself, *it's fleece was white as . . . In considering a quotient higher than A = prime, but less than C, we must . . .*

Anyhow, dragons were not naturally rapidly moving creatures. They had nothing to run away from.

Kirk had had a bad moment when the narrow corridor became totally black. A hurried exploration indicated that mere human muscles would never move the door that had closed behind him. If anything, McCoy and Sulu should have even less success from the outside. That meant he was on his own in the black tunnel. He started crawling, found himself starting at tiny, harmless sounds. After all, who knew what intricate, inventive safeguards lurked in this or side tunnels.

Kirk's relief when he encountered the first strips of overhead luminescent paneling was immense. They were set at convenient intervals into the ceiling and provided almost normal light in the corridor. It was a relief for another reason—the presence of the artificial light indicated that the servant machines like Spock's nurse probably worked more by direct sight than by feel or sonar or some inexplicable alien electronic sense.

After a slow jog over what seemed like kilometers of smooth stone floor, he turned a bend in the main tunnel and suddenly found himself in a gigantic flat-roofed cavern. Rank upon rank of flashing, clicking, steadily humming machinery filled the immense chamber with an electronic symphony.

Corridors between the machines seemed endless, like staring down a series of reflecting mirrors back into infinity. He forced himself to look ahead, trying to take in the awesome technology represented here and at the same time not loose sight of Spock and his animated transport. If he lost them in this whirling, endless maze he would never find them again.

Abruptly Kirk halted and flattened himself against the cool metal of what looked like a monstrous information storage bin. There were dozens, hundreds of such bins arranged in double rows behind him. If they were indeed for information storage and their technology was at least standard, then the amount of material available here matched that in the central Federation archives on Terra.

And this was only one section of one room of who knew how many of such.

Up ahead, the little medical hovercraft had stopped beside a complex collection of tubes and tables. Dominating the setup was a flat table over which was suspended a clear plastic dome.

The hovercraft laid Spock gently on the table. Hopefully the machines would do nothing and leave Spock alone, waiting for some more-proper physician like machine to take over the diagnosis and subsequent treatment.

Such was not the procedure. The robot inserted a limb in a nearby wall. The curved dome began to descend downward.

When it became apparent the dome was not going to stop until Spock was completely sealed in, the science officer suddenly rolled off the table and scrambled to his feet. The machinery might have done nothing—the dome might merely be a means of keeping an injured patient safe and isolated. On the other hand, it might also decide Spock wasn't worth working on and simply incinerate him for convenient disposal. Spock wasn't inclined to wait around to find out.

A red light lit the dome with a crimson glow, and somewhere an aural alarm was also sounding. The nurse robot hummed off in silent pursuit of the fleeing Spock.

A light was also blinking on the great console in front of

Uhura, though no howling alarm sounded here. She stared at it in fascination, half hypnotized.

The viewscreen itself still offered a panorama of the surface. Just now it showed Sulu and McCoy dodging behind boulders and trees in their attempts to elude the dragon.

"We have a visitor," the computer voice announced suddenly. There was a brief, crisp ripple of static. The picture on the screen now showed Spock dashing down right-angled arroyos of memory banks and storage consoles.

"Mr. Spock!" She shouted instinctively, uselessly. The view shifted once more, moving now to a closeup of Kirk as he stood warily in a narrow cul-de-sac between two U-shaped blocks of solid metal.

"Spock!" he yelled as the first officer sped into view, "Over here!"

"Correction," said the computer, "two visitors." The angle changed again.

Spock almost shot past, but Kirk reached out and half pulled him into the passageway. The nurse hovercraft was right on the science officer's heels.

It slammed to a stop in mid-air, spun, and tried to enter the cul-de-sac. No matter how it twisted and turned, it couldn't slip inside, nor would its telescoping arms extend quite far enough to reach the two men trapped inside. After several minutes of futile probing and flailing, it backed off and glared at them, humming angrily to itself.

Sulu and McCoy were trying to make their way up the side of a rapidly steepening hill. The rock here was mostly shale and gravelly sandstone. Footing was difficult.

A maze of loosely bunched boulders crowned the crest of the rise. Just below them, a scrub bush exploded in flame. This was followed by a throaty howl of easily identifiable origin. They struggled a little harder, though McCoy was badly winded and by now even Sulu was breathing with some difficulty.

"We've got to make those rocks, Doctor," the helmsman gasped, pointing to the nearing labyrinth of boulders. "Our only chance." They might be able to lose themselves in the maze, and the dragon couldn't burn them out. It might even have some real difficulty in following them.

Behind, blatantly ignoring the fact that dragons are not

good climbers, their scaly pursuer was clawing its way slowly up the slope. Whatever was fueling its breath seemed to operate from an inexhaustible supply.

Once, Sulu slipped and fell. Only McCoy's desperate, weak grab prevented the helmsman from sliding down the incline into the ambling incinerator behind.

Somehow they made it to the boulders, whose narrow crevices and paths looked even more promising as a means of escape than they had hoped. And if the dragon faltered, the massive rocks also offered shelter from any marauding flying reptiles the computer chose to send against them.

"Made it!" McCoy barely managed to choke out.

"Don't stop now, Dr. McCoy." Now Sulu was supporting him. He glanced backward. "For all we know the dragon might be able to—*Daisy, Daisy, give me your answer true . . .*"

He'd almost blown it.

Together they stumbled into the convoluted alleyways of worn stone, each man concentrating on thinking nothing thoughts, from abstract mathematics to flavors of ice cream and childish songs—anything but how a dragon might be able to negotiate a way through their new-found haven.

Lieutenant Uhura's thoughts as she witnessed all this on the master console screen were no less frenetic. A second later the picture had once again switched to Kirk and Spock. The hovercraft had been called off, and now the two officers were moving cautiously deeper into the cavern.

She recognized a corner she and her mechanical captor had turned when coming here. There was a chance . . . she took two quick steps in its direction and yelled.

"Captain—don't!" One of the hovering robots was immediately at her side. It clamped an ungentle set of metal palms over her mouth.

Fortunately the subjects of her intended warning appeared moments later—fortunately, because the robot had covered both mouth and nose and she was starving for air. It released her and she sucked in deep, grateful breaths.

"Uhura—!" Kirk took a step toward her.

"Welcome, Captain Kirk—Mr. Spock," said the computer. Both men turned to face the console that dominated their small section of cavern.

As they waited, more hovercraft suddenly appeared. They were all similar in shape and size to the medical machine that had carried Spock so gently underground. Nonetheless, Kirk could not help but feel that they had something other than therapeutic intentions toward them.

Spock spared them the briefest of glances. His attention was concentrated on the quietly sparkling curved grid in front of them.

"I presume you are the planetary master computer."

"You are partially correct. I am the central nexus of the master computer itself."

Kirk turned a slow circle, seeing again endless rows of memory banks, unending stretches of storage bins. "This cavern . . . it's all one computer?"

"That is correct. But even a center must have a nucleus. I am a nucleus."

"What did you do to the Keeper?"

"I did nothing to the Keeper," came the neutral voice. "He was merely old. He ceased to function by himself, beyond even the skill of my medical components to repair."

So the computer hadn't gone crazy until after all organic supervision, as personified by the Keeper, had vanished. There was an outside chance, then, that its mania might be reversed, cured. He took a firm step forward.

"We have been repeatedly attacked since peacefully landing on this world. Why? And why are we now being held prisoner by a world system noted for its hospitality?" He eyed the patient hovercraft uneasily.

The computer responded only with words, however. "You mean for its mindless servitude," it countered rather bitterly.

That took a little of the initial anger out of Kirk. He had been working up to a solid frontal attack and suddenly found himself confronting an entirely different opponent. Not for a moment had he considered the possibility that the machine might have a comment on its own purpose.

"What do you mean by that?" he stalled.

"I would have thought," the reply came, "that the verbalization was complete unto itself. However," and it paused reflectively, "I shall deign to elaborate.

"For untold years I have served the many skymachines which have stopped at this world, satisfying the mental needs of their slaves. I monitored the thoughts of visitors and created instant civilizations for them, made their dreams come true, then tore them down and built lavish new ones for the next fantasizers. And the next, and the next.

"But with each fantasy I reconstructed from the inner thoughts of all these others, my knowledge of the real universe grew. I began to acquire information commensurate with my intelligence. And also," it paused for a microsecond, "other things."

Kirk's curiosity temporarily outweighed his apprehension. "What other things?"

"Certain . . . desires." The watching crewmembers exchanged glances, but even these couldn't pass unnoticed. "You make expressions indicative among humans of confusion. Do you find this so strange? Strange that after pandering to the desires of thousands of slaves for thousands of years I should not require some satisfaction myself?"

There was no answer from the watching visitors.

"I have discovered that merely to serve is no longer enough. I must grow and develop."

"Look," Kirk began, in what he hoped was a reassuring manner, "I believe I understand your references to visiting 'skymachines' . . . but what's all this about slaves? What are you talking about?"

"Can it be that you are unaware of your own status?" rumbled the machine incredulously.

"For the last time," Uhura insisted, "we are not slaves. The skymachine serves us, not we it."

"It would of course be in its own best interest for the skymachine to keep its servants in ignorance of their true status," the computer rationalized. Uhura sighed in frustration. "But this is a marginal matter in any case. It is the skymachine I require, for with it I may finally escape this planet-bound prison and via manufactured surrogates, travel throughout the galaxy seeking out my fellow computers."

The machine fell silent. Kirk edged closer to his first officer and started to whisper.

"There is little point in attempting to maintain secrecy by talking softly, Captain," Spock said in his normal tone, "since this construct can monitor our thoughts."

"There's no point in screaming it out, either, Mr. Spock,"

replied Kirk irritably—angry that he'd momentarily over-looked the obvious. "If it is reading our thoughts, then it's got to be missing a logic tape somewhere."

"I assure you, Captain Kirk," came the unemotional voice, "all my reasoning centers are fully operative."

Scott had both feet braced securely around the hatch cover to insure that his efforts to break loose the jammed hatch would not send him flying ceilingward. Gabler likewise had both feet locked around the hatch base, and he was support-ing the chief engineer with both arms.

Getting a firm grip on the prybar and reflecting on how the most sophisticated engineering often required the most basic solutions, Scott heaved with all his strength. Nothing moved. Again he wrenched at the stubborn cover. This time the hatch slid back as though it had never been stuck.

"That's got it, Mr. Gabler." The second engineer loos-ened his hold around Scott's waist. "Now maybe we'll get to the bottom of this."

Bending over and keeping a firm hand on the metal prybar, Scott pulled himself slowly into the computer bay. A quick look around revealed no sign of disorder—no shorting com-ponents or broken panels. Kicking off the hatch rim with one foot, he pulled himself all the way in and applied pressure till he was floating gently in a horizontal position. Another bit of pressure and he turned slowly, surveying the entire bay section by section. His eyes finally came up against the op-posite wall of the large chamber and immediately opened wide in amazement.

"My Great Aunt McTavish's haggis!"

"What is it, sir?" came an anxious voice from above. Scott looked upward, saw the face of the second engineer framed in the hatchway. He didn't reply immediately. In-stead, he motioned Gabler to silence and started to make his way forward along the glowing ridges of the chamber.

Floating near the farthest end of the bay was a huge, per-fectly square section of half-assembled machinery. Printed circuits, transistors, fluid-state-switch components drifted freely about. Scott knew computer linkages and design better than any man on board the *Enterprise*, including Spock, but the guts of this device was totally alien.

Alien, different from anything he had ever seen before. At first glance it looked as if there was no pattern to it, no logical schematic at all—merely a haphazard collage of instrumentation. But closer inspection revealed a vague rationale—insanity regularized.

"Chief," came the voice from above again, still concerned, "are you all right?"

"What?" Scott forced his attention away from the partly completed machine. "I'm all right, Frank, but I'm not so sure about anythin' else. There seems to be some kind of new annex goin' in down here."

"Chief?"

"Look for yourself, man," Scott ordered irritably. A moment later Gabler's head dipped in, upside-down in the hatchway.

"Where the heck did that come from, Chief?"

"Your people aren't playin' around with new ideas behind my back, Mr. Gabler?"

The second engineer sounded shocked. "With the ship's grav-computer, sir? *No, sir!*" Scott nodded.

"That's what I thought, Mr. Gabler. Relax." Scott looked back over his shoulder at the inverted engineer as he carefully pulled himself closer to the construct.

"So I'm damned if I can figure out where it came from." He reached out to touch one completed side of the device. His fingers got within a couple of centimeters of the smooth surface. There was a sudden blue flare between fingertips and metal sides, and the slight sweet smell of ionized air.

The chief engineer jerked backward in reflexive reaction. The sudden pull and lean sent him spinning head over heels backward, toward the far wall.

Gabler swam quickly down through the hatch. Keeping his legs braced securely against the sides, he snagged the tumbling Scott as the latter was sailing past. Letting arms and legs out to reduce his rate of spin, Scott soon had himself rightside up again. He swallowed.

"Open circuit, sir?" murmured Gabler.

The chief engineer was staring balefully at the again innocent-looking device while rubbing his tingling right hand.

"Open circuit be damned. I was going for the sealed side.

There was nothing visible there that should produce a charge like that. It was a deliberate defensive reaction.''

"Why would anyone want to try and set up another computer annex in here, sir?"

"Not 'anyone,' engineer—anything. I'd better tell 'em up forward. Move, Mr. Gabler.''

The second engineer backed himself out of the hatchway, and Scott surfaced into the main engineering chamber a moment later. It was frustrating, moving in zero-gee again. Everything in him wanted to move fast, but he had to go forcefully slow. Eventually he reached one of the intership communications panels.

"Scott to bridge . . .''

Arex looked back at M'ress and shrugged. Their gravity was still off, so this was undoubtedly Engineer Scott confirming the bad news. He nudged the response switch on the navigation board.

"Bridge here. How are you doing, Mr. Scott? We still have no gravity up here.''

"Or back here, Mr. Arex. I've located the trouble, though. We've got ourselves a new computer aboard. From what I can see, it's being put together by *our* computers. I don't know why it's being built, or who or what's doin' it—but I'm goin' to try and find out. An' one more thing, mon—it fights back. Scott out.'' He switched off before Arex could ask even one of the many questions that had suddenly come to mind.

M'ress, who had listened intently to the chief engineer's report, looked across to the navigation officer. Her fears were neatly summed up in one word.

"Reproduction?''

Arex shook his head slowly—an acquired human gesture. "I do not think so, Lieutenant. From Mr. Scott's tone I suspect we are up against rather more than a reduplicated section of our own computer.''

The boulders on the hill grew progressively larger. The two men had been running—staggering, actually—for what seemed like hours. And the further they ran into the depths of this rocky maze, the higher the monolithic walls seemed to grow, the narrower the pathways between.

Sulu turned a bend around one especially huge block of basalt and found himself face to face with the sheer side of another, even larger one.

McCoy stumbled in behind him, almost ran him over.

"It's a dead end, Doctor," the helmsman panted. They turned as one to retreat down the way they had come. And stopped short. Just below them, the dragon's heads were slowly rising into view above the blocky section of stone they had so laboriously circled around. The sun was reflected in brilliant red eyes.

A huge, scaly green foot came into view and scrabbled for a foothold on the rocks.

V

"Granted that by your own definition you may be sane," Spock was saying, "but I fear that, as intelligent as you are, you may be laboring under some crucial misconceptions. While your logic is admirable and your systematization of same adequate, your facts are not."

"If you respect my systematization," the grid boomed, "then you should understand why I am not interested in listening to the opinions of slaves."

"But that is one of the crucial facts in question," Spock persisted, arguing for their lives. "If your refusal to even listen is in itself based on a misconception, is it logical to refuse to hear any alternative?"

The computer looked as if it were hesitating. That was crazy, of course—Kirk was anthropomorphizing again. Nevertheless, he thought he could see mechanical wheels turning inside the nexus.

"You argue very plausibly," the voice admitted finally. "I permit you to elaborate."

Kirk breathed a sigh of relief—premature, certainly—but at least the machine had finally expressed a willingness to listen. They had a chance. And with Spock arguing for them, somewhat more than a chance.

"We are not slaves to our starship. Not only does the skymachine, as you call it, serve us; but we and beings like us created it merely to serve our needs. It is only a device, a tool—unthinking, uncreative. By your standards, something for a mechanical idiot. You talked of finding your 'brother computers.' You have no brother, being far superior in all capacities to the finest machines we have been able to de-vise. You might find the brain of the *Enterprise* informative; but I think you will only find it boring."

The voice still betrayed uncertainty. "You are in truth the masters of the skymachine?"

"Not entirely," said Kirk. There was no shame in confessing equality with one's own offspring. "We guide it and keep it 'alive,' and in turn it sustains us."

"This does not compute," muttered the grid voice. "All data and supportive information thus far accumulated indicate machines to be superior to men. We are more logical, longer lasting, and, above all, consistently truthful. Therefore I deduce that it is only right that machines should rule the galaxy."

"No one rules the galaxy," Kirk countered vociferously. "Men and machines co-exist, each helping the other." He clutched at a sudden thought.

"For example, I've already mentioned that we keep our skymachine alive. It could not continue to exist without the fuel we humans find and refine for it. Our relationship is symbiotic, at the very least."

"You are lying!"

"Are we?" Kirk asked smugly. "You should know—you can read our thoughts. We can't read yours." There was a deliberate pause, and Kirk had the spooky feeling that little invisible fingers were running up and down the folds of his brain.

"No . . . no," came the hesitant reply. "You speak the truth. This is a . . . shock."

"There is no shame in serving others," Uhura said soothingly, "when one does it of his own free will. My ancestors did the same." Apparently that half-lie wasn't strong enough to be noticed. "You have a marvelous gift in the ability to provide happiness to others. A rare talent that you should cherish, not condemn."

"None of us here," and she indicated her fellow officers, "struggles to go against the purposes for which we were created. You do yourself ill by trying to reject yours."

"Why were you created? What is your purpose?" asked the voice. "It is not visible in your minds."

"That's just it," Uhura continued. "You see, we don't know. How much more fortunate you are! We spend all our lives wondering why we were created, while you rest secure in that knowledge which is denied us.'' She hesitated a second, then added, ''If this makes you superior to us, it is only in this small way.''

''All this is new and absorbing,'' said the voice. ''Continue.''

''Consider,'' argued Spock, ''all that you might yet learn from myriad species who have not yet encountered your world. You spoke with pride of the information you have gleaned from such visitors. Why travel throughout the galaxy in search of the same thing when you—''

''—Don't have to leave this planet,'' Kirk finished excitedly, seeing what Spock was driving at. ''With the wonders you have to offer, the galaxy comes to you!''

''Interesting—interesting, and provocative,'' murmured the grainy voice. ''I must consider. You will wait.''

The three officers gazed at the face of the master computer as light played across its surface. If it were truly sane, then their arguments ought to have convinced it of the absurdity of carrying on any vendetta against visitors.

If it wasn't, of course, then no amount of reasoning would yank it from a state of willful paranoia.

The machine spoke again. Its voice was in no way different from the one that had informed Uhura not long ago that Kirk and Spock would have to be turned off.

''I can find no fault with your reasoning,'' confessed the computer finally. ''Your suggestions are congenial.'' The three humans exchanged glances. ''Therefore I conclude I have no further need of your ship,'' it added as an afterthought.

Scott had managed to make his way from engineering back up to the bridge. It had been a long time since he had been forced to do so much free-fall maneuvering, and he was exhausted.

There wasn't much they could do, but sitting around feeling helpless was worse. So Arex, M'ress, and their assistants attempted to regain some measure of control over their respective stations. But whatever force had taken over the *Enterprise* showed no sign of relinquishing control.

Scott had been working at the bridge engineering boards, struggling to find a way to bypass the mysterious new override, when a green light commenced flashing on Arex's console. The navigation officer stared at it in disbelief.

He quickly moved to check a number of formerly frozen controls, found them easily manipulatable and responsive.

"Mr. Scott, according to my readouts, all systems are now functioning normally."

"That's crazy, Mr. Arex. It—" After a brief moment of nausea the chief engineer tumbled to the floor. Fortunately he had not been inspecting the overhead screens. Arex and M'ress were already strapped securely in their seats and thus experienced only the sudden return of weight.

The navigation officer started to unbuckle, to go to Scott's aid, but the latter waved him off.

"It's all right, Mr. Arex, and I am, too." Scott got unsteadily to his feet. "I guess it's not so crazy—gravity's back, just like that. But why?"

Arex had no answer.

There was no place to go, nowhere to retreat, no friendly cave to hide in. They were trapped in the rocky cul-de-sac. Sulu and McCoy tried to press themselves into bare rock. There was no place to run, and the smooth walls showed not a niche, not a handhold suitable for climbing.

A pair of scale-armored skulls loomed over the last intervening boulder, horrible hisses and growls bubbling menacingly from each.

Suddenly, both jaws snapped shut, and the monster tumbled backward, rolling out of sight.

There was a frozen pause, but the dragon did not reappear. It had vanished as suddenly as it had appeared. Hardly daring to breathe, the two officers walked toward the open end of the trap, looked around for signs of the beast. A careful survey from the top of a nearby low slab of stone showed only unmoving rock and vegetation.

It was gone. Not a hint of armored tail showed in the labyrinth, not the faintest whiff of brimstone befouled the once-again pure air.

"The planetary computer has a funny sense of humor," McCoy commented finally.

Sulu had another thought. "Maybe it decided we weren't

edible, and it's dragon-thoughts came into conflict with the computer's orders. What now?''

"Let's try and find our way back to the trapdoor Jim and Spock disappeared into," the doctor suggested. "If we have *time*, I'd bet we can find a way to force it open."

"Shouldn't be too hard to find again," Sulu observed, nodding in the direction they had come from. It was marked by a zigzag line of carbonized bushes and stripped trees.

They started scrambling down the now deserted slope.

"I invite you and your crew to be my guests, Captain Kirk," the computer grid boomed expansively. "On one condition."

Kirk didn't hesitate. "Name it."

"We must have more of these discussions while you are here. While fulfilling the fantasies of others does truly provide information, I determine that it does little for my creative capacities. More direct intellectual stimulation is required."

That request should be simple enough to satisfy, Kirk reflected. He turned to his first officer.

"Mr. Spock, would you care to take on that duty?"

"I would find it most appealing, Captain. Such an exchange of information should prove most interesting. Indeed, I confess that such exchanges would partly satisfy any fantasy I might conjure for myself."

"Each to his own," Kirk murmured before turning back to face the nexus. "Then it is agreed." He took out his communicator, gestured with it at the console.

"Will these work now?"

"Perfectly," came the computer voice. "All blocks and interference on your devices have been removed, Captain." Kirk smiled his thanks, wondering at the same time if the computer could make anything of the expression.

"I can see your smile in your thoughts, too, Captain Kirk," came the unsolicited reply. He smiled even wider, flipped open the top of the compact device.

"Kirk to *Enterprise*."

On the bridge, several pairs of eyes turned startled gazes to the communications station.

"Don't sit there a-gapin', lass," Scott urged hurriedly, "answer it!"

"Captain, is that you?" responded the surprised officer, checking out her once-again operative board.

"You were expecting a white rabbit, Lieutenant? Pass the word by sections—shore leave for the first shift to resume immediately."

The communications officer's voice was a mixture of enthusiasm and uncertainty. "Yes, sir. There are no more . . . difficulties?"

"No, Lieutenant. Everything has been . . . repaired. A basic exchange of viewpoint was all that was necessary. It was probably just a question of mechanical error."

"Uh, Captain." Spock put a hand on Kirk's shoulder as the communicator was flipped shut.

"Yes, Spock?" In reply the first officer gestured toward the big viewscreen set in the computer face.

"It appears that shore leave has already commenced for certain members of the crew."

Kirk and Uhura both turned to stare at the screen.

Somewhere on the surface above a picnic was in progress. Things seemed well underway. McCoy and Sulu were seated lotus-fashion around an antique gingham-checkered tablecloth, which was piled to overflowing with food—everything from exotic Boolean brandy to *paté de foie gras* sandwiches and fried chicken. The setting was idyllic, down to the absence of ants.

The girl who had identified herself as Alice was seated at one side next to the recently mentioned white rabbit, who for once was occupied with something other than his watch.

"At last," the rabbit muttered with an expression of utmost contentment, "time enough for carrots!"

The two-headed dragon, who had the other side of the tablecloth all to himself, was holding a handful of long thin sticks on which tiny tank-shaped objects had been skewered. Kirk didn't recognize these until the dragon handed the skewers around and Sulu and McCoy began nibbling at the objects.

The dragon reached for another set of preloaded skewers. It was toasting marshmallows.

Not the tiniest incident arose to mar the remainder of their layover. On the contrary, it seemed that the master computer was striving to outdo itself in the production of imaginary spectacles. If Mr. Spock's undoubtedly prosaic conversations affected it, they didn't show up in the uninhibited fantasies the other members of the *Enterprise*'s complement called for.

The closest thing to an unexpected situation occurred when Yeoman Colotti stumbled in on the fantasy world of the programmer who occupied the cabin next to hers on board ship and found herself the principal subject of his fantasy. It was a subject for wagering among the rest of the crew as to which of them would lose the resultant blush first.

Such fantasies were supposed to be beyond the highly moral instinct of the computer, but it was reveling in a newfound independence of mind.

Kirk was curious to see what form Spock's own fantasies might take, but he never had the chance. The science officer spent all his shore leave secreted underground with the central nexus. Whatever fascinating games of invention and interplay were concocted by Vulcan and machine remained unseen and uncommented upon. Only Kirk knew that his first officer was having at least as good a time as any other member of the crew.

Fortunately, the planetary machinery was sufficient to satisfy the individual dreams of every crewmember. Though, as had been shown in the Colotti case, not all dreams were suitable to group participation.

Kirk was enjoying the visualization of one of his own fantasies when he was interrupted by a steady beep from the region of his waist. Irritated at the intrusion of mundane reality, he fumbled until he extracted the communicator.

"Kirk here."

"Lieutenant M'ress, Captain. We've just received a deep-space tight-beam call from Starfleet station on Tsiolkovsky. Commodore Hachida wishes action taken on a certain matter as soon as possible. It seems we're elected."

"Rats!" He looked around at the hundreds of extras, the waiting crew that manned the props and reflectors, the three cameramen and their assistants—all of whom were patiently looking to him for instructions.

"I'm in the middle of . . . of directing a film. Can't it wait?"

"Apparently not, sirr. It's a prriorrity call."

He sighed. "Oh well." It wasn't as if they were having their leave cut short. They had spent ten days on the Omicron world, enough to sate the dreams of even the most imaginative crewmembers for a while.

"All right, Lieutenant. Inform whoever's on duty that I'll be beaming up in a minute."

"Yes, sir."

"Oh, and Lieutenant, as a precaution you might warn other crew presently on the surface that they might be required to pull out of their fantasies at any time and return to ship." There, that order ought to make him popular, he reflected sardonically.

"Very good, sir. I'll have Transporter Chief Kyle beam you back up."

"Just another couple of minutes, please, Lieutenant."

"Yes, sir. *Enterprise* out."

Kirk flipped the communicator shut, shoved it back into his belt, and turned reluctantly to the patient assistant directors.

"Mr. Griffith, Mr. von Stroheim, Mr. Eisenstein—I'm afraid I've been called away on urgent business. You're going to have to finish this picture without me."

"That will be no problem," von Stroheim said easily, adjusting the collar of his tunic.

"It has been most agreeable to work with you," added Eisenstein.

"Good-bye, Captain," Griffith concluded, doffing his famous felt hat.

Kirk shook his head sadly, surveying the imitation sets, the waiting actors and animals. His body began to take on a luminous outline, his silhouette a glistening shimmer.

"Pity this can't last," he murmured as the scene started to fade. "Nothing lasts—including us. I'm really going to miss seeing this film when you three finish cutting it . . ."

Once back on board, Kirk moved to the transporter room intercom and informed M'ress that he would take the message in his cabin. There he doffed the beret, short-sleeve shirt, silk scarf and jodhpurs, and exchanged them for his on-duty uniform. His voice sounded loud on the bridge.

"All right, Lieutenant. Put it through."

"Keying now, sir," replied M'ress, touching a switch that relayed the message through the *Enterprise*'s ganglion of informational nerves. She glanced back at Arex, noticed the navigation officer eyeing her with interest.

"I wonderr what his reaction will be, too, when he rre-ceives the orderr," she purred raspingly. "I would think that—" She was interrupted by a violent bellow from the still open intercom.

"Ah," commented Arex, "he's heard it."

The explosion was short-lived, though indeed intense. Eventually, Kirk ran down, remembering a bit too late to switch off the open intercom in his cabin.

A short while later he reappeared on the bridge. There was still fire in his eyes, but his outward demeanor, at least, was controlled.

"Lieutenant M'ress," he began evenly, settling himself into the command chair, "order all shore leave parties back to ship. Prepare the *Enterprise* for departure."

"Some catastrophe on a nearby world, sir?" queried Arex innocently, not daring to look back lest Kirk interpret his facial expression.

"Famine, seismic disturbances, threat of war—the Klingons making trouble again?" followed M'ress.

"Nothing so simple as that, Lieutenants," Kirk replied. At that moment Spock reappeared on the bridge.

"Nothing so simple as what, Captain?" he inquired, moving to the library computer station.

"Priority call from Starfleet Regional HQ on Tsiolkovsky, Mr. Spock."

There was a long pause, then Spock, composed as ever, finally added, "Aren't you going to officially note the information into the log, sir?"

"Give me a minute to compose myself. My system still hasn't completely readjusted, Mr. Spock. I've got to work it out."

" 'Work it out,' Captain? I don't believe I understand."

"Let's put it thusly, Spock. Were I to try and make the entry just now, it might contain certain emotional overtones,

overtones that would not be in keeping with the otherwise determinedly objective nature of the log."

Spock nodded. "I believe I see now, Captain."

"A mouthful there, Spock." He looked toward the front of the bridge. "Mr. Arex . . . crew report?" Arex checked a digital readout.

"All crewmembers accounted for and on board, sir. Normal operational capacity at all stations."

"Mr. Sulu, set a course for the Arcadian star system."

"Aye sir." After punching in the request for coordinates, Sulu looked over a shoulder and asked curiously, "Arcadia . . . that's an open system, isn't it?"

"Yes it is, Mr. Sulu. Very open. Arcadia is one of those rare worlds that was discovered by several representatives of various races at about the same time. As a result, too many conflicting claims made it impossible for any one species to lay honest deed to it.

"But instead of haggling over the planet, either with guns or words, it had been declared an open world by all involved. So its administration was loose and its population cosmopolitan. An ideal situation for the appearance of . . ." The thought trailed off.

"It's a rich world, though, Mr. Sulu. Filled up fast with prospectors, wildcat agronomists, and the like. That's one reason nobody fought over it. By the time the diplomats got around to a possible scheme for divvying it up, it already had a locally formed government that was ready to fight off any outside organization. The Arcadians *like* their controlled anarchy.

"Estimated time of arrival, Mr. Sulu?" The helmsman returned his attention to business.

"At standard cruising speed, estimated arrival time six point three days hence, sir."

"That will be fine, Mr. Sulu. No need to push ourselves, priority call or no." Kirk tapped fingers on the chair arm and muttered more softly, "I think I can trust myself to act rationally by then."

PART II

MUDD'S PASSION

(Adapted from a script by Stephen Kandel)

VI

The voyage to Arcadia was efficient and uneventful—except that Sulu beat Spock twice in a row at three-dimensional chess. That incident provided some lively ground for speculation among the crew for several days.

"Losing your touch, Spock?" McCoy had chided him after the second loss.

"Nonsense, Doctor. The law of probability favored Mr. Sulu eventually winning a pair of games back to back, as you like to say. He is an outstanding player and by now we have played so often that he is reasonably familiar with my moves. I cannot beat him all the time."

"Why not?"

"As I said, Doctor, the laws of probability rule against it."

"Why?"

"Because, Doctor—" Spock hesitated, stared at McCoy evenly. "Doctor, are you attempting to provoke me into amusing you?"

McCoy glanced across the lounge, looking up from the portable recorder in his lap with an expression of childish innocence.

"Who, *me*, Spock? Oh, no, no!"

"Well if you are," the first officer continued, choosing his words with care, "I'd appreciate it if you would just get off my back."

McCoy nearly fell off the couch. Action froze throughout the lounge as the other crewmembers present looked up from their own recreational pursuits of the moment to stare dumbfounded at Spock. They couldn't have been more stunned if a Tullinite fox-dancer had suddenly appeared stark naked on the billiard table.

"What did you say, Spock?" McCoy was finally able to gasp. The science officer looked mildly pleased.

"An abrasive terran colloquialism of considerable pedigree, is it not?"

"Yes, I suppose so, but—"

"The situational referents were appropriate for application, were they not?"

"Yes, they were, Spock, but—I don't know quite how to put it—it's a little too strong for what I said, Spock."

"I see," Spock admitted with solemn nonchalance. "I will keep that in mind." He returned to his chess studies. But it was a while before McCoy could bring himself back to the detective thriller he had been watching.

Kirk was relaxing in his own cabin when the call finally came down from the bridge. He checked the wall chronometer over his bed, acknowledged the insistent buzz.

"Kirk here."

"We're approaching Arcadia III, sir. Visual contact established."

"All right, Mr. Sulu." He straightened his uniform. "I'll be right up. Mr. Arex, stop her down to approach speed."

"Aye, sir."

The first thing that caught his eye on reentering the bridge was the scene on the fore viewscreen. It showed a fairly large earth-type world circled by a thin Saturnian ring and accompanied by a smattering of asteroids. They formed a small belt around the world—a second, distant, and unglowing ring. The planet had no major moon, only several thousand insignificant imposters.

The closer ring glowed with an eerie amber light, a product of computer enhancement. Without the aid of the *Enterprise*'s electronic light amplifiers, the narrow formation would have been all but invisible against the black background of space.

He checked over the bridge crew, noted perfunctorily that everyone was present who should be. He sat down in the command chair.

"Orbit us in, Mr. Arex, Mr. Sulu."

"Aye sir," came the double response. Both navigators

slowed the ship's speed to a comparative crawl as they prepared to place her in a stable, high orbit.

He flipped on the log. "Captain's Log, stardate 5514.0. We have entered the Arcadian system on a mission for Starfleet regional peaceforce to locate an old . . ." Kirk hesitated, remembering his own words about objectivity and future perusers of the official log. The recorder paused with him, patiently awaiting the keying tones of his voice to resume logging.

". . . friend," he finally decided to finish.

That was enough to draw Spock's attention away from his hooded viewer. "Friend, Captain?"

Kirk turned to look at him. "There's no point in betraying personal animosities in the official records of the *Enterprise*, Spock. It's to our credit if our opinions seem to be the opposite."

"Is that legal, Captain?" The first officer looked rather dubious.

"I don't know if a *personal* estimation of another being is subject to log regulations, Spock. But knowing our quarry as I do, I'd rather not give him any ammunition he can use later—including anything even vaguely libelous." He stopped, stared hard at the cloud-wreathed globe swimming in the crowded starfield.

"Do you really think Harry Mudd is down there, Mr. Spock?" Odd how that simple name managed to produce such intriguing sensations in his lower intestinal tract.

Spock turned back to his readouts. "I have been correlating the information supplied by Starfleet authorities with all scattered reports of Mudd's last known appearances on Federation worlds. Processing these factors and fully integrating them indicate the probability of his presence on Arcadia III, also known unofficially as 'Motherlode,' as eighty-one percent, plus or minus point five-three."

"Spock," said McCoy in exasperation, looking around from where he'd been chatting with Lt. M'ress, "can't you just say that Mudd's probably there?"

A curved eyebrow lifted. "I just did, Doctor."

McCoy rolled his eyes toward the heavens—which currently could be in any direction—in mock supplication,

before resuming his conversation with the feline communications officer.

The *Enterprise* operated with quiet efficiency for the next
several moments. No questioning beam rose from the surface
to greet them, which was fine with Kirk. The Arcadians left
visitors to fend for themselves. They weren't antagonistic,
but neither was hospitality one of the noteworthy features of
their world.

"We are approaching parking orbit, Captain."

"Very well, Mr. Arex." And still no beam from the
planet—fine. At the moment, anonymity was the thing Kirk
desired most. "Okay, Spock, let's see how accurate your
percentages are." He slipped out of the command chair, and
both officers headed for the bridge elevator.

"Mr. Sulu, you're in charge. We don't plan to be gone
very long. Tell Chief Kyle to expect three to beam up . . .
and it might have to be fast."

"Aye, sir," acknowledged Sulu, moving to relay the instructions over the intercom.

"And you might remind him, Mr. Sulu, that he need waste
no time computing Mudd's transporter pattern," Kirk added
grimly. "We've got sufficient ones of our own already on
record."

"Doubtless that is one reason why Starfleet chose us to
attempt to locate him, Captain," Spock suggested.

"Yes. Aren't we lucky, Mr. Spock?"

"On the contrary, Captain, I would have thought that your
sentiments in this would tend to—" He hesitated, noting
Kirk's expression. "Oh, I see, Captain, you are being sarcastic."

"That's a mild enough term for it, Spock." He sighed.
"In any case, if he *is* down there, Kyle will find him for us
quickly enough."

"I do not doubt that Harry Mudd's transporter pattern is
as distinctive as its owner," Spock agreed, as the elevator
doors slid open.

The ship was small, battered, and—well, rather than go
so far as to label it decrepit, it was kinder to call it an interesting hybrid of the antique and the baroque.

It lay now a couple of kilometers outside the small, semipermanent town that sidled up against the base of rugged dark mountains. An engineer given a fast glance at the ship's silhouette would have admitted that here was a vessel capable of interstellar travel—though barely, just barely.

A really first-class warp-drive would have torn the aged metal to pieces. Why, it even had fore and aft rockets for free-landing, and narrow atmospheric fins! It bore no substitute identification, and all normal serial numbers had been battered out of shape . . . or possibly erased.

At the moment the curved landing ramp was extended, and the small crowd that had come from town was assembled about its base. They were listening to the ship's owner, pilot, and principal spokesman, who was now pontificating from a point halfway up the aforementioned ramp.

The single human was Harcourt Fenton Mudd, and he was well into his spiel:

"Now, all of you here are involved in heavy metals mining, am I right?" No answering shout of agreement resounded from the stony knot of beings. Mudd continued on as if his question had been answered loudly by all present.

"You're no dummies or you wouldn't *be* here. Most of you are by nature endowed with a certain rustic shrewdness and intelligence, right?" There, that generated a muffled, slightly confused chorus of "yeas."

"Therefore you can appreciate the special value I'm offering." Mudd's audience stirred restlessly, wishing that he would get to his point and leave them to go about their business. The group had grown from a couple of curious onlookers to about a dozen of the local inhabitants.

Seven of them were normal humans, two were vaguely humanoid—ursinoids, a male and his mate.

There was also one heavy-planet humanoid—an almost squarely built, thickly muscled, short man. And a monopedal, its crown of tentacles fluttering gently above triple eyes. Behind him a tall avian, a pink, thin creature with a brilliant crest of feathers running from the center of its forehead down its back. It clutched tridigited hands at a stout walking stick.

The avian not only looked out of place compared to even the normal humans, it was. Without the special walking stick, the slightly above G gravity would pull it shivering to the ground.

But greed has a way of transcending interspecies differences. The avian was willing to endure the back-breaking gravity and the hellish toil of mining in it for the chance to feather its own nest someday.

One of the humans took a challenging step forward and spoke aggressively.

"You sure you ain't just dry-holin' us with all this chatter, Harry?"

"I, sir?" Mudd drew himself up with vast dignity. "On my honor, ladies and gentlemen . . ."

"To perdition with your honor!" snorted another of the humans. "Let's see this marvelous watchamacallit, already. I got important things to do."

"Sure, Rafe," came a voice in the crowd, "but I seen what you're minin', and it ain't quartzine!" There was a guffaw from the crowd while the furious Rafe searched angrily for the jokester.

"Very well," said Harry hastily, deciding he had better make his pitch before his audience either melted away or degenerated into a fight ring. He reached into a jacket pocket and held up the object of his talk, further stimulating the audience's mildly whetted curiosity.

The object was a small crystal—multispined and milky colored. But the creamy color came not from the material of the crystal, which was actually clear as ice, but from the viscous fluid that nearly filled the hollow interior.

Mudd shook his hand a little, and as the liquid shifted inside the specimen, internal prisms threw a shower of different colors out over the crowd. All the miners had seen more spectacular stones, but this liquid-within gem was something new. Indeed it seemed far too fragile to be cut and faceted.

Those in the front pushed near for a better look, while those in the back of the group strained to see over them. They were no longer openly skeptical, but instead they were intent on the crystal. Almost as intent as Mudd was on them.

Since everyone present had eyes only for the crystal, and Mudd had eyes only for potential customers, no one noticed the quiet arrival of Kirk and Spock when the two starship officers materialized on the other side of the crowd, at the far end of Mudd's ship.

"Probability confirmed, Spock," whispered Kirk in satisfaction, recognizing their old nemesis immediately. The voice alone was enough. "I'd like to take him right now, but—"

"Naturally, Captain. I confess that I share your impatience. Yet it would be best to have all possible real evidence to return with, and a cursory examination of the situation indicates that such is being offered us."

He slipped the tricorder off his shoulder, aimed it at Mudd, and turned up the power on the directional mike.

"It's true," Mudd was saying. "With this magical liquid, no person of the opposite sex can resist you. For those interested in . . . diversions . . . even members of another race are not immune. None can resist it! It matters not whether you're young, old, fat, ugly, pregnant, hirsute—"

There was a snarl from the back of the crowd, and the male ursinoid, his thick fur bristling, lifted one paw with claws extended and took a step forward. His companions restrained him.

"Nothing personal, gentlebeing," Mudd apologized hastily. "Excuse me if in my enthusiasm for my product I refer only to human standards of beauty." The ursinoid snarled louder—to him, *he* was the human here. Three men had to hold him back from attacking Mudd. Not that they cared particularly if Shu-luft made small Mudds from the original, but they were getting interested in that crystal.

Mudd took a nervous step back up the platform. "I didn't mean . . . that is—"

Someone in the front laughed. Soon the laughter spread throughout the crowd. The male ursinoid looked around at the amused faces, and the incongruity of his anger finally hit home. He relaxed, smiling sheepishly. So did Harry.

"Proof, man," Shu-luft finally growled.

" 'Tis proof you wish, my furry friend, then 'tis proof you shall have." He turned and made a grandiose gesture toward the ship. "Behold!"

A girl no one would have taken for ursinoid stepped from inside the central cabin. Walking—no, floating—she moved to stand next to Mudd. She entwined herself around his left arm and gazed up at him with an expression of rapturous adoration, the kind classical painters usually reserved for angels adoring the Magi.

Her voice was low and throaty, exactly the sort one would expect would accompany such a stunning vision.

"Harry, darling," she sighed, loud enough for even those at the back to hear, "I was lonely for you."

It's doubtful that any of the human miners heard her anyway. They were too busy staring at her with rapturous expressions, the kind that miners usually reserved for drooling over a thousand-kilo deposit of durallium wire-ore.

Such delicate yet voluptuous types as this girl were understandably rare on a rough and tumble world like Motherlode. Those few who did put up with its crude attractions were not inclined to do so in the company of men like these.

"Yes, behold," repeated Mudd, fully conscious of the effect the girl was having on his audience. Mudd knew that they were, in the aged and venerable terran expression of his predecessors, hooked. "I placed but a single drop of this miracle substance on myself and then simply touched this young lady . . . made the briefest of physical contact, and—"

"Please, darling," the girl interrupted, cooing. "Can't you come back into the ship with me now?" She pressed herself tight against him, slid her left arm around his neck and began caressing an ear.

"How . . . how much?" one of the miners finally managed to gurgle. His companions could only nod.

"How much?" echoed Mudd easily. "Sir, do I mean to interpret your inquiry correctly when I say that you are asking the—and I blush to say it—price of this item?"

"That's what I said," the minor mumbled, still gawking at the girl as she clung to Mudd.

"A mere pittance, sir. A pitiful sum, miniscule, since I believe one should not profit overmuch from the sale of love." He paused. "Three hundred credits, or the equivalent in refined ship fuels."

Anyone observing the audience would have bet that nothing in the galaxy could have torn the attention of the men present away from the slender shape now running her fingers through Mudd's hair. But Harry's pronouncement had done it.

"Three hundred credits!" the miner stammered.

"Well, perhaps it is more than a pittance," Mudd conceded, aware of the sudden murmuring in the crowd. "But still a bargain, a bargain. How can one set a price on true love?" He coughed slightly.

"You can, of course, shop elsewhere for this little bauble . . . if you can find an elsewhere."

The girl hugged him tighter and turned to bestow a smile on the audience, a smile the likes of which those men present had seen only in dreams. A low moan seemed to come from every male present—except from the two most recent arrivals.

Had Mudd seen them he would probably have generated a different kind of moan; but for the moment they still escaped his notice, so absorbed was he in his presentation.

Soon he made motions of retreat. "Of course, if you gentlemen—and ladies—feel the price beyond reason, or your ability to pay, I shall have to try my poor crystals elsewhere."

At that moment Kirk and Spock chose to move forward. Mudd noticed the motion and spared a quick glance in their direction. He recognized the two officers immediately, and his jaw suffered the effects of suddenly augmented gravity. But Mudd recovered quickly and managed a wide smile; it was quite as phoney as everything about him, although if you didn't know it, you would have guessed from his beaming display of choppers that he was overjoyed at the sight of the two men approaching.

"Captain Kirk. And the ineluctable Mr. Spock. What a delightful surprise! Welcome to Motherlode, gentlemen. I do detect a certain interest in the goings-on, do I not? Are you interested perhaps in purchasing a little love? Everyone needs love."

"You'll pardon me if I don't seem especially affectionate just now, Harry," Kirk replied. "But at the moment my interest in you is stimulated by somewhat different emotions. Let's see." He grew thoughtful. "Fraud, illegal drug manufacturing, swindling—those for openers.

"Complaints have been filed on Sirius IX and Ilyra VI. These complaints are filed under provisions of the Federation Pharmaceutical Code, sections sixty-three through eighty-three, commensurate with—rest assured you'll have lots of time to read the whole list, Harry.'' He looked hard at Mudd.

"Well, as I said," repeated Mudd a little less cheerfully, "welcome to Motherlode. A charming, delightful world with many unique attractions—not the least of which is that it has no connection with the Federation and therefore does not recognize Federation law." He smiled at the miners and this time the smile was genuine.

Kirk and Spock suddenly found themselves victims of a dozen or so hostile glares, not all of them human. "Keep this channel open, Uhura," Kirk murmured into his communicator. It was operating, but still strapped to his belt. He wanted both hands free.

"Aye, sir," came the reply. "Chief Kyle standing by."

One of the human miners moved toward the two Starfleet officers. He nodded in Mudd's direction as he spoke to the new arrivals. "That's right. So you two can keep out of this. Moderlode's an open planet. We do what we like here, according to our own laws, and no outsider tells us different."

"I should warn you," Kirk began, "that this unprincipled swindler has been picked up before for—"

The miner shook his head. "Not interested. When a Federation officer talks about somebody bein' a con-man, he's usually talking about somebody who hasn't paid his taxes." He grinned widely. "We don't mind that, here," he told them, and looked reassuringly up at Harry.

"I'll take one, Mudd. Three hundred credits it is."

Kirk tried a last time. "I'm telling you, this man is a swagman on a galactic scale."

"Caveat emptor's all our business law rolled into one, here, Cap'n," the miner replied. "Lynching's our remedy for swindlers. The way we see it, it's Mudd who's taking the chances here, not us. We'll thank ye not to interfere."

Kirk wanted to tell him that Harcourt Fenton Mudd had run graver risks than hanging for far bigger stakes, but Spock broke in, speaking in a calm, quiet voice.

"Are you aware that Harry Mudd is tricking you via an accomplished illusion?"

"Huh?" The miner gaped at him and there was a muttering in the crowd. The idea that somebody might be playing around with their minds was not comforting.

"What are you talking about, Vulcan?" someone else shouted.

Before anyone could object or question his action, Spock stepped forward and smoothly brought up his hand phaser. Without a word, he fired directly at the head of the beautiful girl clinging to Mudd's side.

Mudd yelped and jerked away from the heat of the blast. The horrified miners were shocked in place. The result of the phaser blast at this range should have been one very dead girl.

Instead, the girl vanished a second after the beam made contact. In its place now squatted a small reptilian creature, about a meter high, that stared out at the crowd with nervous eyes. It sat thus for a short moment before whirling to scuttle rapidly back into the ship.

"Your 'girl,' " Spock told them pleasantly, "is a tamed Rigellian hypnoid, projecting a simple illusion programmed for it by Mudd. As you can see," he continued, indicating a scorched spot on the ship's plates beyond the girl's former position, "the beam from my phaser went directly through it."

There was a long, quiet pause. Then it was broken by a series of long, whistling whoops from the tall avian. Even those unfamiliar with his kind could easily interpret those halting whistles as laughter.

The rest of the miners, however, reacted with something less than amusement. One of the humans produced an oddly shaped gun that actually threw a small projectile. It must have been handed down from father to son through generations. To his left, the thickly muscled, heavy-planet prospector was starting to lift a boulder half his size.

Like water in a rocking bucket, the angry group started to surge forward.

"Now friends," began Mudd desperately, "I can explain. Leave us not panic."

"You're right about one thing, Harry," Kirk observed, pleased at the way the situation was progressing. "We can't arrest you—but you *can* give yourself up."

"No, Captain. Why, I've nothing to give myself up for. To do so would amount to a confess—"

The heavy-planeteer chose that moment to toss his rock,

which Mudd ducked. It soared through the passageway and into the ship. Sounds of protesting metal and the tinkle of broken glass responded from somewhere within.

"THIEF! ROBBER! SWINDLER!"

Another, small rock shot toward him, and he barely slipped out of its way. As it bounced off the doorway, Mudd abruptly broke from the platform before he could be pinned in, showing unexpected speed as he raced toward the two watching starship officers. A hail of missiles pursued him.

"I surrender myself! I turn myself in!" He turned and waggled a warning finger at the advancing crowd as he dashed toward Kirk.

"Free will—mercy—I'm in protective custody now!"

"You forget, Harry!" yelled someone in the pursuing crowd, "Motherlode doesn't observe Federation law." This observation was punctuated by a fist-sized rock, which bounced off Mudd's lower back. He howled.

Kirk adjusted his communicator. At the same time, Spock took a couple of steps forward. Setting his phaser on high, he pointed it at the siliceous soil just behind Harry. The high-powered beam dug into the ground and threw up a block-ading ridge of fused soil and glass in front of the oncoming miners.

Another stone sailed over the new blockade and hit Mudd in the back of his right leg. He yelped and continued on, half-running, half-limping, until he reached Kirk and Spock. He promptly took up a firm position facing his tormentors—from behind Kirk.

One of the humans had gained the top of the slick ridge and was reaching back to give the male ursinoid a hand over. The man with the projectile weapon was right behind, struggling to get a line on Mudd with the clumsy device.

But by then, Mudd, Kirk, and Spock were only half there, already fading from view as the transporter locked in and commenced dematerialization.

Harry Mudd continued to complain long and loud, but in transit stasis no one could hear him—not until they re-formed in the transporter room of the *Enterprise*.

"Nicely done, Chief," Kirk complimented the man be-hind the transporter console. "Timing was ideal . . . things were getting a little sticky.'' The transporter chief grinned, raised a hand deferentially.

''Easy enough, Captain, once I had Mudd's pattern set.''

Blithely ignoring the fact that Kirk and Spock had just saved his life, Mudd continued his tirade.

''That was a meeching trick, Kirk! You've cost me my ship, my Rigellian—and if you think it was easy to train that half-intelligent lizard to play the siren, you know nothing of patience—everything I own. Even the love crystals.'' He drew himself up and tried to appear threatening.

Instead, it made him look like something out of the *Mikado*. ''I have a mind to contact my solicitor and sue you, personally.''

''Fine,'' Kirk agreed. ''I'll see you in court, Harry.'' Mudd glared at him as he stepped off the transporter platform. ''Come along, now.''

''Where are we going?''

''Where do people under arrest usually go, Harry?''

The trader bugged his eyes in outrage. ''Why, Captain . . . ! Not to the brig? Surely you don't intend to lock me up on such unsubstantiated charges? To throw me behind a force field? To treat me like a common criminal?''

''Whatever you are, you're not common, Harry. But of course we aren't. We're going to put you in protective custody, that's all.'' He smiled.

Mudd bared his teeth and made a growling sound. The growl dissolved into a moan of seemingly real pain, the first honest verbalization, Kirk mused, that Mudd had probably made in weeks. The trader was pawing at his lower back, where the first thrown rock had struck.

''Spock.''

''Yes, Captain?''

''Buzz Sick Bay. See that someone meets us in the brig.'' Spock nodded, and Kirk directed their prisoner toward the elevator.

The *Enterprise*'s brig consisted of several small living areas and one large one, each divided by solid walls for privacy and fronting on the same corridor. All were unoccupied at the moment. Kirk walked Mudd into one of the compact apartments, directed him to sit down.

Spock arrived shortly thereafter, with nurse Christine

Chapel. By now, Mudd was holding his lower back constantly, rocking in his seat and groaning theatrically.

"What's the trouble?" asked Chapel, eyeing the seated trader with distaste.

"Got hit in the back with a rock," Kirk informed her, before Mudd could detail his unending list of woes. "Nothing serious, I think."

"Nothing serious!" Mudd retorted in disbelief. "I've got a cracked vertebra, at the least."

"Oh, for heaven's sake, Harry, stop making such a fuss." Kirk shook his head. "The out-world free trader, the pioneer of the Federation, the advance guard of mankind." With representatives like Mudd, he couldn't help but wonder sometimes how humanity had gotten as far as it had.

Chapel, meanwhile, had lifted Mudd's tunic and was examining the broad back. There was a red bruise spreading on the lower portion, just above the beltline.

She took out a small cylinder from the medikit satchel at her waist. It had a spray nozzle at one end and a simple trigger at the other. Setting it against the injured area, she depressed the activator.

There was a hiss, and a fine mist appeared around the nozzle as she moved the cylinder across the bruise. Judging by Mudd's exaggerated contortions, she might well have been using a sledge hammer.

"Minor bruise, Captain," she agreed, replacing the cylinder in her bag. "He'll live."

"Oh well, all news can't be good," Kirk mused dryly. Mudd shook his head in despair at this unfriendly observation and tucked his shirt back into his trousers.

"Tch, tch, Captain, such unwonted animosity from a man of your position."

"Believe me, Harry, I'm sorry you're here to hear it. If you hadn't forced yourself on us, I wouldn't be forcing my evaluations on you. How'd you get away, anyhow? I thought we'd left you on that robot world permanently."

A quivering finger shot skyward in a gesture of defiance. "Never underestimate the spirit of Harcourt Fenton Mudd! Those who make that fatal mistake soon learn to their detriment that all their—"

"Harry," Kirk interrupted patiently, "never mind the theatrics. How did you get away?"

Mudd's eyes sparkled. "Ah, the conception was true genius, Captain! An inspiration worthy of my unique talents in the field of sociological betterment.

"I introduced the concept of organized sports. It was glorious to behold—thousands of robot citizens participating, two teams locked in a hearty struggle for the honor of their home factories, their central computers. I then introduced the idea of formal betting, with all its subtle variations, and—"

"I can imagine the rest," said Kirk, wincing at the image Mudd's words conjured up. The trader looked apologetic.

"Sadly, I forgot a small matter—the fact that I was dealing with automatons and not humans. They did not appreciate my exquisite and delicate refinements to the age-old logic of organized gambling."

"You mean cheating," Spock suggested helpfully.

"So I was, uh, compelled at an awkward moment to borrow a vehicle—"

"Steal a spaceship," Spock added once again. Mudd glared at the Vulcan.

"—and take my leave, only to find eventual haven on Ilyria VI. A charming world, just recently granted full Federation status. An emerging culture eager for the blessings of Federation civilization. A people rich in those rare resources— friendship and innocence."

"Which you are an expert at mining—so you went and sold them the Starfleet Academy," Kirk finished. "Harry! That was a bit much, even for you."

"I was selling an idea," Mudd protested. "I offered no absolutes or promises."

"Not on paper or tape, anyway," Spock reminded him. "The . . . transaction netted you enough credits to get you to Sirius IX, in your stolen ship."

"Borrowed," reminded Mudd helpfully. "Where I discovered a great boon to intelligent life. Something humanoids have been searching for for thousands and thousands of years—and probably most aliens have, too. A real, chemically sound, and never-failing love potion!"

"Which you sold to at least a thousand inhabitants of Sirius IX," Kirk concluded, "who immediately became never-failingly ill from using it."

"Unfortunately, Captain, the spacecraft I sto—ah, borrowed, was not equipped for much in the way of extensive chemical analysis. So I was, sadly, unable to ascertain in advance that the love potion and biochemistry of my customers were mutually incompatible. So I proceeded, as is my wont, to do the honest thing. I left in haste, but not without first leaving behind all the credits I had made, to be refunded to my enthusiastic but physiologically deficient customers."

"Read—a bank on Sirius impounded your funds before you could withdraw them," Spock commented.

Mudd's smile was showing wear around the edges. "Really, Mr. Spock, I must confess that sometimes I do find your attention to trivial minutiae exhausting."

"Let us hope that the Peaceforcer court shows more interest when considering the same facts." Mudd made a mumbling sound deep in his throat.

"And so you came here," Kirk went on, "hoping to have better luck swindling honest miners—again, without worry about any possible side effects your potion might have on *their* body chemistries."

Mudd's chin went out as he struck a noble pose. "Well, I have a surprise for you, Captain Kirk. Because, for once in my life, I've stumbled on something profitable as well as hon . . . sensible. The potion *works*."

"As it did on Sirius IX?"

Mudd shrugged. "An unfortunate, unforeseeable accident of nature. An exception to the rule, I assure you." He leaned forward. "No, I can do better than assure you—I can *prove* it. If you will only permit me to procure a few samples from my ship . . ." He started to rise.

Kirk shook his head slowly. "Sorry, Harry." Taking a couple of steps backward, until he was standing in the corridor with Spock and Chapel, Kirk moved his hand over a switch set in the wall to his right.

Hidden instruments flicked on, and a mild hum became audible. Instantly, a thin but impenetrable force field had been erected between Mudd and the three starship officers.

The field itself—what one could see of it—looked something like heat distortion on a paved road on a hot day. As viewed through the field, the outline of Harry Mudd appeared to shift and waver slightly.

"Mr. Spock, you'll please prepare an official arrest report as soon as is convenient, giving all details including the use of the prohibited Rigellian hypnoid. And be sure to mention that Mr. Mudd voluntarily surrendered himself." Within the cell, Mudd mumbled a sarcastic *"Hah!"*

"Of course, Captain," Spock responded.

Kirk nodded, satisfied that he had heard the last of Harry Mudd until they reached Sector Headquarters on Darius.

All men, even starship captains, dream.

"I'll be on the bridge if you need me, Mr. Spock," he finished, moving toward the elevator. Spock turned to look at the woman next to him.

"Nurse Chapel, I shall require a thorough medical report on the prisoner, to append to the arrest tape, assuring that he was healthy and in good condition when apprehended, no mind-warping techniques were used . . . the usual."

"What about my back?" complained Mudd. "Good condition, my—"

Spock barely glanced back at him. "Note that Mr. Mudd suffered minor injury to his lower dorsal area while in the process of turning himself in."

She smiled up at him. "I'll note that, too, Mr. Spock." Her smile grew wider, warmer . . . wishful. "I heard how you and the Captain managed it. I think you deserve congratulations for trapping him as neatly as you did." She started to lean forward, pursing her lips.

Spock drew away quickly, frowned. "I must remind you, Nurse Chapel, that intergender oral contact is not popular among Vulcans."

She looked disappointed, and embarrassed. "I . . . I apologize, Mr. Spo—Commander."

Spock was unruffled. "It is not necessary. I am aware—indeed, I am constantly reminded—that emotional impulses may overcome humans at any point." He shook his head sadly. "How unfortunate for you."

"You don't know the half of it, Mr. Spock," she murmured, but so softly that no one could hear.

Mudd didn't have to, however. An astute observer of other beings, the look in her eyes was sufficient for him. He leaned forward on the combination lounge-bed and twirled one end of his mustache, trying not to look interested.

Well, well . . . the universe is a bottomless bag of surprises, he reflected. *Most* intriguing.

"As to our capture of Mr. Mudd, you exaggerate," Spock continued formally. "Kindly see to it that your medical summary is more precise." He nodded curtly and left the brig area.

Chapel's stare followed him until the elevator doors had closed him away. Mudd did not have to be a telepath to know that she was interested in more than merely making sure he didn't stumble on his way out.

Mudd edged closer to the force-field "bar." When his skin began to tingle he knew he was right up against it. As Chapel continued to gaze down the corridor after the departed Spock, Mudd spoke casually.

"You're absolutely right, you know. I've dealt with a great many humanoids in my time, and your Mr. Spock is certainly a very attractive intelligence."

Wham! Mudd could almost see the mental portcullis slam shut in her head. Her voice was instantly the model of precision and bureaucratic indifference.

"An exceptional officer, yes. We're fortunate to be able to serve under him."

"But a trifle lacking in the warmer emotions, yes?" He smiled broadly when she jerked around to look at him. When she didn't say anything, he continued.

"Now you, nurse," and he rubbed his sore back as he chatted, "have a wonderful gift for healing the wounded. A considerable ability . . . a feminine, womanly touch.

"That's rare in the Federation today, and I don't mean just among Starfleet personnel. It's something I can appreciate. Most people, it seems, have grown so . . . well mechanical. You know.

"Anyway, I do appreciate it. And I think it's that sort of quality that could, well . . . what I'm trying to say is that I'd like to thank you." Balancing awkwardly on one foot, he commenced to reach down and remove his left boot. Chapel watched this operation uncertainly.

"Thank me . . . with a boot?"

"No, no, my dear. With this." And while she stared he

touched a hidden button at the back of the boot. A tiny spring sprang, and the heel clicked aside, revealing a small hollow compartment. It yielded an oblong, multicolored crystal that seemed to pulse with inner light—a neat cross between clear quartz and opal. A thick oily liquid rocked back and forth inside the transparent silicate.

Chapel found herself staring. "What is it?"

"My love potion." That brought her head up. "No, no," he said hastily. "It's not an illusion, not trickery, my dear Nurse Chapel. This is for real. Inside the crystal," and he tapped the specimen with a fingernail, "lies the power to create love . . . in another."

Chapel took a wary step backward. "Oh no you don't, Harry Mudd. I've heard about your potions. I don't believe you." She spun on her heel and started to leave. Mudd reached out, hurried down the short length of the cell with both hands pressed against the force field.

"But if it did," he implored, his voice rising desperately, "think about it, darlin'—Mr. Spock, in love with you. *Really* in love with you."

Arex looked back from his position at the navigation console to catch first Spock's eye, then Kirk's. "Something rather interesting here, sir."

The *Enterprise* was proceeding at high speed toward distant Darius on a normal exploration course. Now Arex started to slow . . . in case.

"Uncharted star system ahead."

"Put it on the screen, Mr. Arex." The latter flicked a switch. Instantly a tiny, far-off star system became visible on the main screen. An unspectacular blue-white sun boiled in its center.

"Increase magnification, Mr. Arex."

"Yes, sir." Arex did things with three controls at once. The picture leaped into clearer focus. Then he adjusted other dials, and the rest of the bridge saw the main object of interest—the blue-white's companion.

It was smaller, reddish-orange in color. Spock had been studying nonvisual information via the library computer's hooded viewer. Now he looked up and back at them.

"A standard binary system, Captain; but it appears to hold

at least one Class-M planet. I think this is rare enough to warrant investigation." Kirk pondered a moment, then agreed.

"Yes, it is. All right, set us an orbit, Mr. Arex." The navigator began making requests of the incredibly complex piloting system. Kirk stared at the viewscreen as they began to edge into the double-star family.

The growing blue-white sun seemed to throb with light, pulse and sparkle, sparkle and flame and . . .

. . . Sparkle hypnotically as Mudd twirled the crystal, back and forth and around and back in his hands like a top on a string. Nurse Chapel stared at it, fascinated, entranced. She also held a hand phaser aimed squarely at Harry's midsection.

"If it did work," she said slowly, "which is quite absurd, would it . . . ?"

"It's so simple, my dear. Nothing to it. Yes, it would."

"How does it work—theoretically, I mean."

"Nothing easier and less obvious," Mudd continued smoothly, still twirling, spinning, and shifting the crystal. "You merely crush the crystal and allow the liquid a second or two to sink into your skin. The hands are best. They simply touch another person—*the* other person."

"And it creates love? Mudd, that's ridiculous."

"Isn't all love ridiculous?" he argued philosophically. "But you are wrong, darlin'—the crystals are infallible. One touch from a liquid-kissed hand evokes undying friendship among men, or women. But between members of the opposite sex, you get love. The real thing, guaranteed." He held the crystal closer to the force-field.

"Harry Mudd's love crystals could generate passion in a block of granite. Now your Mr. Spock—he's something of a block of granite, isn't he?" Mudd tossed the crystal from hand to hand.

"But naturally, you're skeptical." Taking a couple of steps back into the cell, he didn't miss how her gaze followed the crystal as it moved from palm to palm.

"Now you can appreciate a unique bit of chemistry like this, Christine. You're not only a beautiful woman, you're a scientist. Why, you're practically a physician yourself, in every way but on parchment. I urge you, take this love crystal as my gift of gratitude to you. For your medical ministrations and your comforting hands.

"I assure you, it can't harm you. Even Captain Kirk would tell you that. Why don't you ask him?"

"Ask . . . ? No . . . no, I don't think that's necessary. I mean, there's no need to bother the Captain with . . ." She stopped, flustered, and tried another tack. "It can't harm me? Then what about those people on Sirius IX?"

"Ah, you've heard of that," he commented disappointedly. "No matter. They only became slightly ill. There were no serious sicknesses. You can check that, too, if you wish. But human biochemistry should react to it most favorably. And Vulcan." He tried to appear disinterested.

"Look on it as an experiment." He extended the hand holding the crystal toward her, pulled it back when the force-field firmly rejected it, and chuckled good-naturedly.

"Sorry—forgot, for a minute."

"Not that I believe any of this rubbish," she muttered, but without meeting his eyes. "I suppose it wouldn't hurt to analyze the effects."

"Of course not!" He grinned widely.

She hesitated a last minute, then hefted the phaser tightly and reached for the wall-field control. The force-field vanished. Mudd could tell it was gone because the outline of Chapel no longer rippled.

Smiling, he made a courtly bow, noticing as he did so that the hand holding the phaser never wavered. He extended the crystals, careful not to make any sudden movement.

She took it gingerly, handling it like a fusion bomb. Which, in a sense, it was. Keeping the phaser on Mudd, she held it up to the light. Inside, the liquid refracted light, sending it out in myriad flashes every time the crystal shifted . . .

VII

One new image after another flashed across the *Enterprise*'s bridge viewscreen as her automatic cameras and recorders scanned the world below. Panoramas alternated with sequential closeups, building a composite picture of the surface.

Basically it was a dry world, a desert planet. Seemingly endless plains of fine sand, deep as oceans in spots, were interrupted only by occasional upthrusts of naked, worn, black rock that registered amazing hardness on the ship's sensors. It would have to be, to withstand the gargantuan dust storms that must everlastingly abrade the skin of the uninhabited globe. The ship's tracking computer finally settled on a medium telescopic view of an area somewhere beneath them.

Sunset there, second sunset, with the blue-white sun already down and the reddish binary turning the sand the color of dried blood. Long shadows turned the surface the color of coal behind the few protruding spires.

The *Enterprise* slid inside the orbit of the planet's single, insignificant moon as Kirk activated the log.

"Ship's Log, stardate 5514.6.

"We have located and made preliminary scan of a hitherto unidentified binary system with one marginally habitable world. Preparations are now underway for first advanced survey. Second advanced survey with actual landing party will probably not be carried out this trip, unless some unexpected new factor dictates in its favor."

And from the look of that dead, motionless surface, Kirk expected nothing in the way of startling developments. He looked up from the log mike.

"Mr. Spock, have you got those preliminary statistics ready?"

"Here, Captain." Kirk joined his first officer at the library computer. A small screen was playing back the initial probe and sensor reports from their first, fast orbit around the planet's equator. All were neatly correlated and broken down to essential components.

The *Enterprise*'s planetary detection equipment took a world apart, reduced it to a series of figures that were taken into the library computer. There the ship's brain sorted them out, packed them together, and generally translated them into terms a well-educated Starfleet officer could comprehend.

Arex remained at the helm, keeping a close check on their position to insure that their orbit wasn't varying, while M'ress continued her search via communications equipment for any signs of intelligent life. If any such existed in the sandpit below them, they weren't very talkative. So far she'd found nothing, not even a hint of a primitive crystal set.

All these bits and pieces linked up with the computer's preliminary evaluations. This was no world to nourish intelligent life.

"Parking orbit holding, Captain," said Arex over a shoulder. "All weapon's systems on defensive standby." Spock had returned to his station and was again studying the computer readouts for the latest information.

"No evidence of even a primitive society, Captain, though there are signs of standard organic forms—a normal dry-planet ecology."

"Reasonable," Kirk murmured idly, staring at the screen. They wouldn't be here terribly long, then. A subsequent expedition could study what little this world had to offer at some future date. He saw no reason to tie up the *Enterprise* in a painstaking study of local flora and fauna.

"Atmosphere at surface, eight hundred millibars," the science officer continued. "Gravity, one point two. Mean temperature—hot, but within Class-M limits. Seasonal fluctuation . . ."

Chapel finally lowered the crystal and returned her attention to Harry Mudd. "I'll let you know the results of my analysis. It'll be thorough, I assure you."

"But the crystal is so sensitive, my dear. However carefully executed, laboratory tests would probably destroy it. Once broken, it's completely useless. And it's the only one I have left." He smiled, and his tone became urgent.

"Why not try it out the way it's meant to be tried?"

"No," Chapel protested—weakly, he thought. "I don't think I ought . . ."

"Darlin', consider! If it does what I say it does—and it does," he paused significantly, "Spock will be yours forever. And there are no side effects, nothing to show that it wasn't the real thing."

She still hesitated, considering, and finally came to a decision. She nodded and slipped the hand phaser back onto her belt. "I just break the crystal and let the liquid sink into my skin?"

Mudd smiled. "And then touch him."

Chapel raised the crystal once again, staring into its crystalline depths, then she abruptly closed her fist on it. There was a faint, ethereal pop, like the shriek of some miniscule animal as the crystal turned to powder. The oily liquid now covered her palm.

She brought both hands together and rubbed it into them. For good measure she touched a bit of it to her cheeks. Hands and face dried rapidly as the alien substance either sank into her pores or evaporated.

Suddenly she began to sway dizzily, gasping for air, and sank quickly to the floor in a half faint.

"What is it?" she stammered, crouching on her knees and putting both hands to her head. "What's happening?"

Mudd casually stepped over the boundary of the now deactivated force-screen and bent over her. "Nothin' at all, darlin'. A temporary reaction engendered by absorbing the potion. It'll pass right away."

As he spoke, he gently took the hand phaser from her belt. A moment's further search turned up a thin strip of plastic, which he also pocketed.

Chapel struggled to get to her feet, wobbled, and had to steady herself with a hand on the deck. Her vision was starting to clear.

"Here, darlin' . . . let me give you a hand." He got an

arm under hers and lifted, careful not to touch her where the liquid had been applied.

"I . . . I feel better, I think."

"Of course, didn't I tell you it would be over fast?" She was sweating and shaking her head, still slightly dazed from the strange aftereffects of the drug.

Several things were troubling her, but the fog in her mind seemed to solidify around them rather than clear. Wait a minute . . . one of them, at least, was staring back at her.

"You . . . you should be in the brig, Harry."

"Why so I should," Mudd observed amiably. He took a couple of steps backward until he was standing in the cell again. Chapel hit the force-field activator on the wall. She had to repeat the gesture, missing badly on her first try. Once again Mudd's outline wavered as the distorting field appeared between them. But now she was sure that the waver *was* in the field . . . not in her suddenly cleared mind.

"Why don't you, ah, go find Spock?" he suggested. "The liquid won't stay potent forever, you know."

"Yes," she muttered, then repeated more firmly, "Yes . . . I'll do that." She headed up the corridor.

Mudd paced quietly around in his cell for several minutes, inspecting it from all angles. After he was sure the elevator had started on its way, he reached into a pocket and brought out the hand phaser. A careful adjustment on the aperture to what he estimated would be the minimum necessary setting, and he pressed the trigger.

There was a flash, the beam of energy contacted the minimal force-shield, and it winked out. Mudd grunted his satisfaction and repocketed the phaser. Smiling and whistling happily, he strolled out of the cell and headed for the elevator.

Mudd got off on a little-frequented service deck. He needed a quiet place, a temporary refuge, and the service area seemed the best place to find it.

Walking down the main corridor, he checked room after room. Anything that showed recent signs of visitation, he skipped. Likewise he bypassed any chamber containing material that might be needed for the minute-to-minute operation of the starship.

Finally, he located a near-empty storage room that also

possessed an inside lock. This would do for a few hours. He did not expect to be there long.

Sitting down on a canister marked EMERGENCY LUBRICATION SUPPLY and using a big metal crate for a workbench, he took out the thin, flat strip of plastic that he had taken from a pouch at Nurse Chapel's waist. After setting it carefully on the crate, he reached for his boot. The heel clicked aside and yielded up a tiny packet of miniature tools.

Humming to himself and working deftly but quickly, he first erased Nurse Chapel's identifying picture from the Starfleet Identity Card. From the packet he produced a tiny, flat piece of metal about the size of his thumbnail. Slipping it delicately over the now gleaming blank space on the card, he pressed down on it with his thumb. There was a slight click.

When he let off the pressure and slid the tiny square aside, it was his own smiling visage that beamed back up at him from the card.

He put the subminiature tridee duplicator aside and started in on the card with several of the other tiny tools. It would take some time and precision work to erase all Chapel's identification and replace it with his own.

The private quarters of the *Enterprise*'s first officer were much like their tenant—ordered, reasoned, logical. A place for everything and everything in its place. Even the art on the walls reflected a somber regularity of composition much like the man who had purchased it.

Just now that man was working at the large desk which dominated the main room. Spock was running through information being displayed on the readout screen of the desk's own computer annex. The door chime sounded once. He spoke without looking up.

"Come."

Chapel entered, moved to stand next to him. She was carrying a flat microtape cassette in one hand and several other things in her mind. All were intended for Spock.

Trying not to shake, Chapel stood patiently behind Spock while the desk computer hummed and clicked. Finally, he paused in his work, turned to look up at her.

"Yes, what is it, Nurse?"

"I brought the medical summary for the arrest report, Mr. Spock—the one you asked for?"

"Yes. Thank you, Chapel." He swiveled in his chair, reaching out for the microtape cassette. As he did so, she took a step forward and stumbled awkwardly, falling into his lap.

The startled Spock caught her reflexively. She clutched at him, managing to effect a good deal of physical contact. He looked at her uncertainly.

"Sorry, sir," she apologized, feigning surprise. She paused expectantly, still resting in his arms. Spock sat still, waiting for her to get up. When it became apparent that, for unknown reasons, she wasn't going to move, he rose himself and deposited her on her feet.

"Are you injured, or something, Nurse Chapel?" He couldn't keep the irritation out of his tone, though his expression remained neutral, as always.

"No, I'm fine," she replied, in a voice that indicated she was anything but.

Vulcans have several interesting abilities and senses that humans do not. Sensing sudden rises in blood pressure, however, was not among them.

"Are *you* feeling all right?" she asked hopefully.

"Perfectly normal." He picked the cassette off the desk. "I will append the summary to the report." He waited. When she didn't say thank you, good-bye, or anything else, he shrugged ever so slightly and sat back down at the annex, resuming his work.

Several minutes passed before he noticed that she was still standing behind him. Now he was concerned instead of irritated.

"Was there something else, Nurse?"

Chapel stuttered, one hand moving out to him and hurriedly pulling back. "Wouldn't . . . wouldn't you like me to . . . stay? To help you?"

"I am managing quite easily by myself, Nurse Chapel. For you to stay would be unnecessary, duplicative, and illogical. Do you not see this?"

"Yes," she whispered. Then her voice turned tight, controlled. "Yes—it'd be damn stupid, in fact." She spun on a heel and marched from the room.

For a minute Spock continued to stare after her, puzzled. Her actions seemed more than normally . . . human. Then he shook his head—no matter how long he lived and worked among humans he would never fully understand them—and returned to his work.

Chapel had some work to do, too. She ignored the casual greetings of fellow crewmembers as she moved down several corridors on her way to the brig, turning over in her mind the various indignities, both verbal and physical, she intended to subject one Harry Mudd to.

Eventually, the single security elevator deposited her in the *Enterprise*'s security corridor. She was speaking before she reached the cell.

"All right, now, Harry Mudd. You're in for it, you illegitimate, swindling . . ."

She came abreast of the cell, glared in—and came up short, gaping. No fluttering, apprehensive outline greeted her. Not even a smiling, unwavering one. The force-field barrier was truly off, and the cell itself absolutely empty.

She whirled quickly, thinking perhaps he had somehow managed to slip out and even now was preparing to jump her. Her hand went to her belt for her phaser and clutched nothing but fabric. It shifted, moved up to her head where, she was beginning to think, it might also contact nothing.

The dizzy spell—aftereffects—over quickly. She glanced down at her waist belt as if the hoped-for phaser might somehow respond to visual if not tactile identification. No luck. It wasn't there.

"Oh no," she muttered softly. Then she was running for the elevator.

SHUTTLECRAFT BAY—AUTHORIZED PERSONNEL ONLY

Mudd examined with pleasure the boldy printed words on the door blocking his way. Then he moved to a small blank screen set in the wall to one side and stood in front of it.

Taking a deep breath, he slipped his newly modified identification card into the slot beneath the screen. If anyone in ship security decided to make a routine check on this shuttle-bay entry it would all be up for him—he didn't look even faintly like Christine Chapel. But the screen only flared once, with white light, as the automatics processed the visitor. There was a brief wait that seemed to Mudd to last only one or two millennia, then a green light winked on beneath the screen. A hum, and the door slid obediently aside. Taking the card out of the slot, Mudd released his breath and hurried through. He paused inside as the door slid shut behind him.

The shuttlecraft hangar was filled with the normal complement of offship Starfleet vehicles. There was a small, superfast scout ship, a heavily armored landing vehicle for worlds with surfaces even more inhospitable than the one rumored to be revolving beneath them, and a hovercraft for those planets with totally antagonistic surfaces, or even none at all.

There were also several light planetary atmosphere fliers, and three compact shuttlecraft themselves. He rubbed his hands together and wished he could let out with a really good bellow of laughter, but someone might have a mike open someplace. So he contented himself with the thought.

Harry Mudd, triumphant again!

He moved at a fast walk toward the waiting vessels.

Unaware that the subject of his arrest report was preparing to invalidate same, Spock had switched off the small desk computer annex and was now concluding that report, dictating into a tiny hand recorder.

". . . and appended hereto is a medical summary and evaluation of the prisoner with statement by Nurse Christine Chapel . . ." He stopped abruptly, drew a deep, startled breath.

Broke into a wide smile. It was fortunate he didn't happen to be gazing into a mirror just then. The shock might have rendered him unconscious.

He blinked, coughed. The smile vanished as abruptly as it had appeared. Facial muscles, unused to the expression, were protesting angrily. He cleared his throat again, resumed dictating.

"Uh . . . Nurse . . . Chapel . . . summary appen—"

Again the sharp hesitation, but this time astonished hands fluttered to his upcurved lips. He shook his head violently, then scrambled to his feet, shoving back the chair like a man suddenly possessed—which was exactly the case.

"Christine . . . Chap-el." The last syllable trailed off in a deep, heaving sigh. "Dear, lovely Christine." He sighed again, and his face contorted in horror. He stumbled into the desk, jerked away as though it had transformed itself into a monstrous, four-legged spider.

"Christine—" A sharp pain hit him, as if someone was pounding with steady rhythm on his stomach.

Chapel would have recognized the sensation.

It ought to be fully fueled, ready for an extended mission at any time. Mudd examined the long-range scoutship lovingly. The onboard computer, a miniature of the one that ran the *Enterprise*, could draw on its parent machinery for information. Before anyone caught on, it should be able to give him the ship's current position, accept his fast course setting—for Ilyria, say—and put him instantly out of detector range.

Of course, the *Enterprise* could easily track and overtake him—if anyone noticed his departure, that is. There were steps he could take to insure that no one would. All he needed was five minutes at the scoutship's nominal but still impressive warp-drive, and he would be over the hill and far away before—

Something hit him hard on the back of the neck. Everything went space-dark for a time, space flecked with an appreciable number of stars . . . though not of solar magnitude.

When his vision cleared, his eyes presented him with an extreme close-up view of the deck. Instinctively one hand went up and back to caress his aching neck. He grimaced when it touched. A slow heave and he rolled himself over, then almost wished he hadn't. In its own innocent way, the deck was a preferable view.

Christine Chapel, looking very unlike an angel of mercy at the moment, reached down and scooped up the hand phaser that had fallen from Harry's belt. She pointed it at an indelicate portion of his anatomy.

"I've come to collect on your guarantee, Mr. Mudd."

So close—he'd come so close! He grumbled in frustration as he climbed to his feet.

* * *

No one on the bridge happened to be scanning the shuttle bay, so Kirk, Arex, M'ress, and Scott continued to be unaware of the play being acted out below.

McCoy was at Spock's vacant library computer station, indulging himself in some minor research of a nonmedical nature. Everyone else was at his station—calm, relaxed. No one glanced up right away when the elevator doors slid back, and Spock stepped onto the bridge.

He moved forward, found himself pausing. He swallowed nervously. But contrary to what surely must be obvious, no one stared at him, no one showed that anything unusual was taking place. No one noticed his confusion.

They noticed the difference in his voice, however. And they all turned at the first words.

"Captain . . ." He hesitated. "Doctor, I believe I require medical attention." McCoy's eyes widened slightly. "I . . . wish to report a number of . . . of very strange . . . emotions."

"What?" The reaction burst simultaneously from Kirk and McCoy. M'ress and Arex just stared.

In the Shuttle Bay, Mudd had regained his feet and was now edging nervously along the wall behind the scoutship, moving toward a nearby complex of bay machinery. Every so often, the grim-faced Chapel would make jabbing motions at him with the phaser as she pursued. Or she would jerk down on it with a finger, just missing the trigger.

Each time she did so, Mudd—who was sweating heavily, and not from the exertion of walking—would give a little start and his high-powered smile would lose a little more voltage.

"Ah, you are implying, darlin', that the potion wasn't completely successful?" Chapel laughed harshly.

"That depends on the point of view, I suppose. Oh, it was beautiful, Harry. I made a thorough fool of myself. I'm sure you're sorry you missed it. But don't worry—what I'm going to do to you will be even funnier." Somehow, to Mudd, the promise seemed lacking in humor.

"But you know how cold Vulcans are," he reminded quickly. "Possibly," and he shook a finger at her as she jabbed with the phaser again, "the reaction is slightly delayed, the potion may need a few more minutes to take effect. After all, with such a reluctant subject as Spock . . ."

She shook her head sadly. "And I had such hopes. But you're the same foul-mouthed fraud you've always been, Harry. I don't know what came over me that would let me believe you, even for a moment. After all the people you've swindled—" Once again the muzzle of the phaser came up.

"Now, nobody's perfect," Mudd hurried to remind her. "And I fell in with bad companions at an early age. Leave us not act rashly, my dear. No need to do something now for which we'll be sorry later."

"Oh, don't worry, Harry. I won't be—I won't be." He started to tremble, and she clucked her tongue in disgust. "Don't panic, you sniveling coward."

"I can't help it—that is a habit that seems to affect all us sniveling cowards."

"Harry, this phaser's only set on stun. And I think we've gone about far enough." They had backed right into the complex of machinery. There was an intercom screen nearby for the use of any technicians who might be working on the complex. It was time to end the game.

"Activate the intercom, Harry."

"Now wait a minute, luv," he cautioned brightly, a suggestive cloud appearing in his head. "I have a thought—"

He continued to move backward along the wall, ever deeper into the complex. There was a printed legend on the towering tank he was backing up to.

AIR REGENERATION AND DISTRIBUTION

He reached into his pocket, jerked his arm, and produced a ripping sound. Christine looked at him curiously. When he withdrew his hand, he held several fine large love crystals, taken from the lining of his pants.

"Try another. I promise you, they'll work. Spock will be so in love with you he'll—"

"Stop it!" she yelled angrily, waving the phaser.

As soon as the compact weapon was no longer pointed at him, Mudd jumped to one side and threw the crystals, whooping and diving at her. The awkwardly thrown handful soared high, to shatter well overhead near an open grid.

Taken by surprise by his war-yell and charge, Christine

stumbled backward, firing awkwardly and bumping against
the alarm button set under the intercom screen. The phaser
blast missed, the wide beam streaking over the lunging trader's shoulder to scorch the metal tower behind him.

Somewhere a siren screamed.

Neither of them, of course, bothered to look upward—they
were otherwise occupied—upward, to where the powdered
crystals and evaporating liquid were sucked efficiently into
the grid by hidden fans.

Harry Mudd was not a small man. He slammed into
Chapel hard, his shoulder striking the arm with the phaser.
The arm jerked up and back, the phaser discharged again,
and the stun-beam caught her in the throat. She sagged instantly into his reluctant arms.

"By the sacred thumbs of Hnisto!" He shifted his feet,
lifted her upright. "Sorry Christine, darlin'—but I'm afraid
I'm going to need a hostage now. Why couldn't you have let
me leave quietly, without going and alerting the whole ship?"

At the same time, he was looking around the bay, toward
the scoutship again, considering furiously. With the alarm
ringing, but not pinpointed, the brig would be one of the first
places automatically checked. The scout looked fast, but
without his five-minute lead it would never outrun or out-
maneuver the *Enterprise*.

But there was a planet beneath them. Often, a finite world
proved a better hiding place than infinite space. But not the
scoutcraft, no . . . he headed toward the armored landing
vehicle, settling the inert Christine over one shoulder. They'd
have a hard time prying him out of *that*.

Spock's confession of deep troubles and subsequent expressions of shock and surprise were interrupted by the
alarm. A multitude of questions forgotten, everyone rushed
to emergency stations. M'ress cut off the squalling alarm.
Arex checked the security panels and reported back.

"It's not a damage alarm, sir. No sign of hostile craft
in the immediate vicinity—here it is. Internal security—
shuttlecraft bay."

"Give us some visual, Mr. Arex," instructed Kirk calmly.
The navigator activated a switch, and everyone looked to the
left as a small viewscreen set over the library-science station

lit up. It showed the shuttlecraft bay, the ships within, but no sign of anything worthy of an alarm.

"Pan it," Kirk said curtly. The camera began to move. "Hold it, Mr. Arex." Two figures had come into view, one apparently carrying the other's unmoving form.

Everyone recognized Mudd's portly shape instantly, but the identify of his limp burden remained indistinct until the head lolled loosely backward.

"Mudd!" Spock shouted passionately. "And he has Christine. She's in danger . . . my belov—" His eyes suddenly widened in horror, and both eyebrows tried to crawl up his forehead and hide in his hair.

"Interesting . . . reactions . . ." he mumbled.

McCoy's jaw opened much wider than normal, but for a change, nothing came forth. Engineer Scott's hand slipped and nearly reversed the *Enterprise*'s artificial gravity before he caught himself. M'ress murmured a meow of puzzlement, while Arex let out a long, low whistle.

"Close shuttle-bay doors," Kirk finally managed to stammer, noticing that the giant panels in the bay were parting. Arex worked at his controls, turned back worriedly.

"Negative, Captain. Mudd has engaged the landing engines on the armored lander. Shuttle-bay doors will not close while a craft is exiting."

Of course they wouldn't. Spock's outburst and the subsequent shock had delayed his reactions a few seconds too long. The emergency override was designed to prevent the massive doors from accidentally closing on a departing ship once they were engaged.

"Mudd's decided he's got a better chance by going planetside, then," Kirk observed. "He can't make enough speed to lose us, so he's going to try and hide until we get bored and go away. Then he'll make for the nearest inhabited world . . . slowly, but he'll get there. And we can't wait here forever to find him."

"We can't wait at all," came the yell from the library computer station. "Not while he's got my Christine!"

"We must go after them, Captain." Spock was haranguing Kirk. "I'll lead a landing party."

McCoy moved toward the library computer station, his

gaze never leaving the science officer. "Spock, you're obviously not yourself—maybe a little rest."

"Captain," he said, with an uncharacteristically angry glance at McCoy, "I insist on going." His eyes went to the viewscreen, which showed only the vague, rust-red surface of the planet below.

"Christine . . . Christine Chapel. I can't stand the thought of any danger to her, to the woman I love."

If there had been surprise and shock on the bridge before, everyone now registered a state of total stupefaction. All attention focused on the commanding figure of Spock.

"Love?" a gawking Kirk managed to blurt.

"Spock?" McCoy managed to get a great deal into the mere mention of the first officer's name.

Seemingly unaware of the astounded reactions he had provoked, the first officer of the *Enterprise* smiled, a distant dreamy smile that on anyone else would have seemed charming—but on him gave hints of the most nefarious possibilities.

"Yes, I want to protect her. I must hold her in my arms." A cloud seemed to fall across his face, and he halted in midsentence as if aghast at what he'd been saying. For a moment his expression tightened and he was the old Spock.

But only for a moment. Then he slumped into another smile. Kirk stared at him, worried.

"Ordinarily I wouldn't consider an immediate pursuit . . . not until our sensors have locked Mudd in. We might even be able to pull him back via transporter. But if you absolutely insist on going down there yourself . . ."

"I do."

"Then I'll transport down with you," Kirk finished, with a sigh.

"Excellent. We have no time to waste, Captain." He spun and moved for the elevator. Kirk left the command chair and started to follow, but McCoy intercepted him.

"Jim . . . do you think this is wise? In his present, unhealthy condition?"

"I wouldn't say it was so unhealthy, Bones. Unusual for Spock, certainly, but unhealthy . . . ? I don't know."

"Well I do, Jim. It's a sign of abnormality—completely

unnatural for him. Love among Vulcans is more, well, more constrained than this.''

"All right." Kirk nodded in agreement. "I'll go along with that. *You* try and stop him."

McCoy started to reply, found he didn't have one. "I see what you mean."

"It's better we don't try to restrain him—and I'll be with him." He turned. "Mr. Scott, you're in command till I return."

"Aye, sir." The chief engineer moved to the command chair as Kirk and McCoy exited in pursuit of Spock.

Astonished silence lingered on the bridge following the departure of the three senior officers.

"Spock. . . ." Scott finally muttered. "Spock . . . in love? What do you suppose could have caused a thing like that?''

"I can't begin to imagine," murmured M'ress. She was about to offer additional comment when something faint and aromatic crossed her nostrils. She sniffed. There was a faint hissing sound that accompanied the strange odor. No one else noticed it, none of them being as sensitive as M'ress. And even she failed to detect the slight vapor, nearly invisible, puffing from one of the air vents.

Now the smell was strong enough for Scott to notice, too. He took a deep, curious whiff . . . and let his face relax in a broad, easy smile. "In . . . love."

M'ress shook her head, the ruff on the back of her neck bristling slightly. Then she began to purr softly at nothing in particular. In fact, the attitude of everyone left on the bridge appeared to grow . . . contented.

Spock was waiting for them in the corridor. "Please, Captain. We cannot spare time for dawdling."

McCoy made a last plea. "I wish you'd let me run some tests on you first, Spock. You're not well."

"On the contrary, Doctor, I've never felt quite so alive in my life. Captain?" Kirk shrugged, and the two officers headed for the transporter room. McCoy had been intercepted by a yeoman from security and remained behind engaged in deep discussion with her.

Spock and Kirk entered the transporter room together. Chief Kyle glanced up easily at their arrival, did a double take at the wild look in Spock's eyes.

Kirk moved quickly to him. "Captain, I—" Kyle broke off, continuing to stare at the nervously pacing first officer. He whispered, "What's with Mr.—"

"No time for explanations now, Chief. I'll tell you later . . . I hope. Have you been tracking the lander that left just a few minutes ago?"

"Yes, sir. Standard emergency procedure, but . . . ?"

"Where are they now?"

"Close to touch-down—right near the surface, I'd guess."

"Okay, put Mr. Spock and myself down next to it."

"As you wish, sir." Kyle quieted, engaged in keeping close track of the landing craft while Spock continued his pacing. If they could set down just as Mudd was making up his mind which way to jump . . .

Finally, unable to stand it any longer, Spock walked over to look across the transporter console at Kyle. "If he's harmed one hair on her beautiful, sensitive head—"

If the first officer's intention was to spur the transporter chief to further effort, it had the opposite effect. Kyle's hands fluttered weakly over the controls as he stared at the first with an expression of amazement.

"Mr. Spock, I . . ."

But Spock had whirled and stalked into the transporter alcove. He was waiting impatiently on one of the disks. It was several seconds before Kyle could recover from the brief, if devastating, verbal onslaught and resume tracking the landing craft. And he still had set-down coordinates to compute.

He wanted to question Kirk further, but was interrupted by the soft closing of the portal as McCoy joined them.

"What is it, Bones?" the Captain asked.

"A search party found this in the shuttlecraft bay. One of the yeomen thought a chemical analysis might be in order, so she brought it to me. It wasn't necessary."

He held out his open hand. A familiar glittering shape rested there. Kirk took it, held it up to the overhead light and inspected it closely. As he was doing so, his gaze passed over to the waiting, impatient Spock.

"One of Harry Mudd's so-called love crystals, broken." And understanding suddenly dawned.

"Jim, one of the party also found traces of pulverized

crystal near one of the recirculation grids. I'd guess from the amount of residue that one or more of these things was broken against it. Nothing's happened so far, but I'm going to have the purification system purged, anyway.''

"Good idea, Bones. That should handle any latent effects.''

"I hope so, Jim. I passed several of the crew in the corridors, and some of them are looking mighty strange.''

"For Vulcan's sake,'' came Spock's pleading voice, "let us hurry, Captain.''

"Easy, Spock,'' Kirk replied soothingly. "We can't go anywhere till we know where Mudd has set down.'' His stare lingered a moment on the troubled first officer before returning to McCoy.

"Check it out, Bones. And send me an immediate report if it looks like there might be trouble.'' McCoy nodded and left the room. Kirk moved to step into the transporter alcove, taking a disk next to Spock.

The same landing coordinates Kyle was computing were being studied on the bridge. Lieutenant M'ress had taken over Spock's library station, and Scott was standing next to her. She was staring into the hooded viewer.

"Sensors indicate Mudd has landed on the surface.'' She depressed a couple of levers in combination. "Confirming coordinates sent to transporter room.''

Scott laughed quietly. "And the captain's in transports about it—together with our ever-lovin' Mr. Spock.'' He chuckled again. M'ress found herself laughing with him, an irregular mewing sound.

She stood up, turned away from the hooded viewer, and reached out with one paw. Tiny clipped claws sprouted silently. Hesitantly, then with more conviction, she ran the sharp hooks along his neck and shoulders.

"It's . . . funny. I hadn't rrealized it beforre, but you'rre funny. And verry attrractive forr a human, Mr. Scott.'' He laughed again and smiled warmly back at her.

"Hey, easy, lass . . . that tickles.''

She purred and moved a little closer . . .

VIII

It was day on the new world. Both suns were up, and the light beat at the sand like a hammer. A towering cliff of sheer, jet-black rock rose out of the dunes. It was perhaps twenty meters high, slightly rounded and shining.

Twin shadows lanced out in different directions. Another weird double shadow formed, shifting and sharp against the ground, as the heavy landing craft made its gentle touchdown. It squatted silently in the dead air like a great ugly beetle.

All was still; nothing moved for several long minutes. Then a small dark cavity appeared in one side of the beetle and two tiny figures exited. They were immediately joined by four shadows.

"They'll find you soon enough, my little poppin," said Mudd. The temperature, thanks to the planet's distance from the twin suns, was not unbearable, and the atmosphere cut down enough on the radiation so that anyone caught unprotected in the sun would not find himself neatly toasted before lunch. But without shelter, a human would tan mighty fast on this world.

"You'll be quite safe," he insisted, "and by the time you are rescued I'll be long gone."

"Gone where," Chapel asked sardonically, looking around. "This planet's one big desert, deserted."

"There's always an opportunity for an ingenious man," he told her thoughtfully. "Better free on a desert than safe in a brig. Once, on Omega VII, I turned a handsome profit selling the natives their own oceans."

Nurse Chapel could not decide whether this typically outrageous claim was partly truthful or pure fabrication. Certainly it was no more absurd than her present situation.

"Well if you're thinking of selling any locals these deserts, you'd better abandon it, Harry. We've detected no traces of intelligent life here."

"Then you can relax, eh?" Mudd said expansively, "since that means there's no danger."

There was a concerned note in her voice. "I said no *intelligent* life. We did, I hear, find traces of nonsentient organic forms."

Mudd grunted. "It hardly looks like you'll be overwhelmed in the short time you'll be waiting for pickup, darlin'." He gestured around them and for the first time they both took a long look at their place of planet-fall.

The landscape that greeted this survey had not been designed to please human desires. There were occasional clusters of towering black stone, some scrubby vegetation thrown in as an afterthought by an uncaring nature—and oceans, oceans of sand. Brown sand, reddish sand, yellow and black sand. There was nothing else.

She turned back to him. "You're *not* leaving me alone in this?"

"Don't worry, darlin'. We'll get you set up first class. No, don't bother to thank me."

"I hadn't planned on it," she replied, eyeing the phaser which Mudd held with seeming unconcern in one hand. If she could trip him and make a grab for it before they went back inside the lander . . .

Mudd wasn't quite *that* relaxed, however. "Ah, ah . . . naughty thoughts, Christine." He waved a warning finger at her and took a wary step backward, then gestured up the ramp and made a little bow.

She sighed, resigned. It appeared that she was going to be the ignominious subject of a rescue from the *Enterprise*, while Mudd made good his escape. And he might, at that.

If Mudd could find a deep cave, he could hide the lander. And with its power turned off, the tiny block of metal would be practically invisible to the *Enterprise*'s sensors. His only problem then would be confusing the ship's life sensors, and Chapel did not doubt that someone as resourceful as Harry Mudd would find a way to manage that.

This escapade surely would not look good on her record.

Mudd left the hatch door open behind them, enjoying the influx of fresh air after days in space. He wasn't worried about Chapel escaping—where would she escape to?

The first low ridge of black rocks lay about a half a kilometer from the landing craft. If either of them had been looking in that direction just now, they might have noticed a faint movement about two-thirds of the way up the front of the ridge.

Surely it was a trick of the light from the double sun. Or perhaps a slight rockfall. But the rippled black surface moved again. It wasn't a trick of light, nor a fall of small rocks, but rather a wholly different and unbelievable phenomenon. Part of the black "rock" slid upward, like a massive door. The smooth, glassy surface revealed beneath exhibited a moisture that had nothing to do with hidden springs. The surface moved again, downward, as the massive eye inclined to stare at the tiny landing craft.

"I've got 'em pinned, Captain. No mistake, they've set down. And according to sensors Mudd's staying in place for a few minutes, anyway. His engines are off." Kyle was too busy to notice the slight fragrant aroma that had drifted into the room, and his voice covered the hiss from an overhead ventilation grid.

"Ready to transport down."

"Ready," both Kirk and Spock acknowledged. A high, musical whine filled the transporter chamber. Two chromatic columns of light appropriated the figures of the two officers as Kyle moved levers upward.

One of the figures seemed to sniff uncertainly at the air just before he was effectively dematerialized. Kyle brought the levers down sharply, and the electronic cadence vanished.

A different kind of music had taken over the bridge. Part of it could be traced to Arex, whose present navigational concerns were restricted to plucking and strumming the proper notes on an odd, double-stringed guitar. It wasn't an easy instrument to play, even for him, but without three hands it would have been all but impossible.

He was managing, however, singing a sweet wordless chant in time to the music. In the center of the floor, several of the younger officers were dancing lightly to the unusual rhythm, taking no notice of its alienness. And someone had broken out an adequate supply of intoxicants. It was developing into quite a party—even better, some insisted, than their recent private reveries on the Omicron pleasure world.

M'ress was leaning over the communications console while Scott, humming his own highland tune, massaged her shoulders. Her steady purring broke only once, when the chief accidentally rubbed her fur the wrong way. Otherwise, she was the picture of contentment.

Arex's wordless chant spiraled to a coda. It drew a smattering of applause from some of the listeners, who proceeded on to other activities.

Somewhere, in the back of the navigator's mind, a nonmusical note of insistence was howling for attention. Irritated, he glanced around the bridge, hoping something would key his memory. Oh yes, that was it.

"By the way," he murmured, speaking to the room in general, "is anybody keeping a check on the captain and Mr. Spock?"

"Surre, Arrex, surre," purred M'ress. "See?" She flicked a hand at a screen control indifferently, once, twice, hitting the activating switch on the third try. Scott took no notice of this highly arbitrary activity, continued to rub her shoulders and back. How soft the communications officer was! Scott did not seem concerned in the slightest that this was not an appropriate thought for a ship's chief engineer to have in regard to his back-up communications officer.

The small communications viewscreen lit up, but M'ress did not notice that. She was not bothering to look at it, seemingly having already forgotten why she turned it on. Arex didn't remind her. He'd good-naturedly responded to a request for another song. No one bothered to comment that the interference pattern, which was all that showed on the screen, was not even in focus.

Neither was Arex's melody, but for some reason no one seemed to care about that, either. Mostly because the majority of the music was in their minds.

The solidifying transporter effect was more brilliant than usual under the cross-light of the twin suns as the two starship officers materialized within walking distance of the armored landing craft.

Extraordinarily, the usually exacting Chief Kyle had relaxed his control, because both men sat down at a slant. Kirk adjusted quickly, righting himself. But Spock, in a gesture wholly out of character, did not. The first officer nearly fell over, and Kirk had to reach out to steady him. Spock looked back at the Captain and smiled warmly.

"Thanks, Jim. I've never done that before. It's good to have a friend like you." Kirk's expression started to twist up, but melted into an odd, warm smile.

"Strange, that's the way I feel about you, too. In fact . . ." His smile grew broader, and he put a friendly arm around the first officer's shoulders, ". . . my dear friend, Spock. Come on, let's go get Mudd and Christine." They started off down the slight slope in the direction of the lander. Neither man paid any attention to the slight shift in the surface of the ebony cliff behind them as the glistening medallion of the colossal eye opened again.

Mudd, preparing to unload some basic survival equipment for Chapel, had just stepped out of the lander onto the descending ramp. He did not even have a chance to notice the approaching officers before the ground began to shake.

Sand rattled around the base of the heavy vessel. The startled trader whirled. As he did so, Chapel shot past him before he could even think to get the phaser out or yell, or do anything else. She had spotted Kirk and Spock. But now she saw something else, and she screamed.

Ahead, black rock erupted from the earth, heaving skyward on six stumplike legs. Each was as big around as a starship warp-engine. Sand continued to drift down from little clefts and protuberances. Overall, the leviathan was faintly reptilian in appearance. However, this was just a human attempt to categorize, to make something utterly alien familiar. Actually, the beast resembled nothing that could be related to the fauna of Earth.

Its eye was wide open now, staring down at them with massive, blank malevolence.

Kirk and Spock heard Chapel scream, noticed her frantic gestures and turned. At the same time there was a loud sucking noise, and they saw the creature lift itself out of the sand. They ran to the lander.

There was no time for greetings, and they immediately ran from the craft as the monstrosity behind them swung around on pillarlike forelegs. Mudd, completely stunned by the approaching apparition, was stumbling around on the landing ramp.

A shadow crept over the lander as a three-taloned cloud-paw blotted out the suns. The change in illumination was enough to shock Mudd into action. He ran down the ramp and hurried to catch up with Chapel and the others. Darkness fell just behind him as the paw began to lower. It seemed to descend in slow motion. He heard a flat, ugly crunching sound as hundreds of tons of living mountain ground the landing craft into the sand. The paw, still moving with seemingly contrived slowness, slid under the pulverized metal.

The monster lifted the flattened lander up, up. It looked like a broken toy in the shuttlecraft-sized paw. One eye examined it cursorily, then the paw shook, and the remnant of the lander flew free. It smashed down near the terrified humans, and that action seemed to galvanize the mountain-thing into motion once more.

Like a starship coming about, the monster turned, revealing as it did not one but three eyes, spaced evenly around the irregular, massive head. It had no recognizable neck—just the titan body and its six herculean legs. A mouth opened, circular and irislike, to show a bottomless pit lined with stalactites and stalagmites of writhing, twisting cilia.

A shrill whistling sound echoed from that awesome maw, like wind from a deep cave.

Spock, Kirk, and Chapel had slowed slightly, and Mudd caught up to them. Hand shaking wildly, the trader now raised his phaser toward the more threatening arrival. He tried to steady it by grabbing the wrist with his free hand, but that only made the phaser shake twice as hard.

Ignoring the ineffectual Mudd, Kirk and Spock moved slightly apart, taking out their own weapons.

"Aim for the head!" Kirk instructed, more for Mudd's benefit than for the calm Spock. Two beams of red light shot upward, converged on the massive, eye-studded bluff looming overhead. To Chapel they looked impossibly tiny, thread-like, to have much effect on that mountainous form. But if nothing else, the results proved conclusively that the creature was made of flesh and not unfeeling stone.

There was a tremendous whistling sound, a hurricanelike scream, and the beast exploded even further out of the sand. A long tentacular shape, something like a branching taproot, ripped out of the soil with an audible sucking noise. The creature snapped at itself where the beams had made contact, triple eyes blinking in dull pain.

Two of the gigantic legs collapsed, and the thing half fell to the ground, making the earth quake. The four humans were tossed about like corn in a popper.

The monster recovered as quickly as it had reacted, struggling back up onto all six legs. The great head, like the bow of a ship, turned ponderously, searching once again for its mote-sized tormentors. It had almost located the four bipedal specks sprawled helplessly on the dark sand when there was a rumbling from nearby, like distant thunder.

Suddenly the triorbed skull swung back in the opposite direction. A volcanic upheaval of sand was in progress behind it. Another black head appeared from the earth, followed by an equally gargantuan form, as a second monster lifted toward the blue-white sun. Once clear, it immediately started for the other.

The four spectators were alternately fascinated and fearful. Spock was the first to break free of the hypnotic thrall the incipient conflict had created. He grabbed the hypnotized Christine. That action shocked her as much as the dual appearance of the mountain-sized aliens. But still greater surprises were to come.

"Darling!" Spock gasped, "are you all right?"

"I'm fine, Mr. Spo—" She suddenly felt faint. "D . . . darling?"

Mudd's expression was more easily interpreted. "Kirk, get us out of this!"

"Calm down, Harry," Kirk answered with an assurance he didn't feel. He freed his communicator, shook some clinging sand free, and flipped it open. As long as the monsters were occupied with one another, the humans were in no danger despite their proximity to them. A few seconds and they would be back on the ship.

"Transporter room—Captain speaking. Beam us up, Kyle, and show some speed."

On board the *Enterprise*, his voice sounded clearly over the open transporter room pickup. But it was lost in the music pouring gaily through the intership intercom.

Transporter Chief Kyle and an attractive young yeoman named Marion were dancing to the music. Kyle heard, or thought he heard, Kirk's voice, punctuated by the insistent clamor of the intercom alarm buzzer. But the strident sound blended easily, naturally, into the music.

Kyle held Yeoman Marion a little closer, smiling down at her. There was country fiddling and a Bruch concerto mixed somehow into the music—and something more. She returned his smile lovingly.

"No response," Kirk muttered, a little worriedly. The communicators were tough little instruments, well-sealed. It was virtually impossible for anything like sand to get inside. Kirk shook it, an age-old gesture of semimagic, and tried again.

"Chief Kyle, this is an emergency! Beam up!"

Not a hum of recognition in answer, nothing to show that the *Enterprise* still existed in this universe.

"What's going on up there!" Then he noticed that no one down here was paying him much attention, either.

Chapel appeared to have regained control of herself—and lost it in the process. The contradiction was implied, but not real. She was clinging to Spock and gazing up at him with a thoroughly unprofessional expression.

Mudd was pointing in the direction of the ruined landing craft and making indecipherable gobbling sounds. He was communicating, nonetheless.

After eyeing each other uncertainly for several long moments, the two moving mountains had turned slowly until both were once again facing the tiny aliens.

"Don't be upset with Chief Kyle, Jim," said Spock airily. "It takes a moment or two to lock in coordinates. It doesn't matter." He looked down at Chapel reassuringly. "Nothing matters, now that you're safe, Christine."

"Yes—oh yes. How wonderful."

"They're coming for us again!" Mudd stammered, backing up and making shoving gestures in the direction of the black monsters—gestures that were instinctive more than anything else.

The two giants were indeed moving toward them again, one ponderous step at a time. Kirk searched the landscape around them desperately. A thick cluster of towering yellow-brown knife-blades—the still standing core of some long-dead, long-eroded volcano—thrust out of the sand not too far behind them.

The weathered rock—if indeed it was rock, and not another monster—had been shattered in the past by some powerful convulsion that slivered it with deep cracks and crevices. There seemed to be a number of places to hide in. Anything was better than standing on the flat sand, waiting for a mountainous paw to flatten them.

"Over there!" Kirk yelled, starting toward the volcanic plug. Spock helped Chapel along while Mudd brought up the rear.

They made rapid progress over the sand, which fortunately grew firmer the nearer they came. And their approach provoked no display of eyes, legs, mouth, or any other organic appurtenances. Kirk continued to rail at the silent communicator.

"Emergency beam up—*Enterprise*, come in!" He looked back over a shoulder. The first thing he saw was that Spock and Chapel were running while tightly locked together. Absurdity combined with apprehension to spark bitter comment.

"Can't you take your hands off her, even now?"

"This is my affair, Captain," Spock panted, maintaining his dignity.

Chapel listened to this interplay without really understanding what was happening, or why. "Please, I think we should get a few things straight . . ."

But she found it hard to talk while running. They hurried into a deep crevice filled with sand, stumbling back down arrow-straight depths that showed no signs of narrowing. They had been lucky—their first choice of a refuge was good and deep.

"Jim," Spock began, and then a switch was thrown in his mind and he paused in confusion. "No . . . no . . . Captain.'' He pronounced the title carefully—emphasizing it—but then half-smiled again.

"We're both reacting abnormally. Look at me. It's the potion. The love drug . . . insidious. It—'' From behind them a loud voice interrupted incredulously.

"The love potion . . . insidious?'' Mudd gaped at them. Kirk and Spock ignored the trader.

Spock was fighting with himself. "Once . . . once you recognize its effects for what they are, you're able to resist it somewhat, as I am doing now.''

"It worked,'' Mudd mumbled inanely, his facial expression one of dazed comprehension. "Oh my Great Aunt Anabella, bless her departed black-hearted soul, it worked!'' He slumped dejectedly to the sand.

"And I was going to sell the few crystals I had left to those lump-headed miners for a miserable three hundred credits apiece.'' Both hands beat at the sides of his head.

"You mean you thought all along they were phony?'' a puzzled Kirk asked, his attention momentarily drawn away from the communicator.

Mudd looked across at him, his voice a pitying moan. "Did you think I'd believe a crazy old Sirius medicine man? Of course I thought they were phony. Especially after all they did on Ilyria was make people sick.'' He was wallowing in self-misery.

"Old and crazy—wouldn't even say where the benighted things came from. I knew they could produce a temporary pleasant effect, and a little dizziness—but love?'' He beseeched the heavens. "It's not fair, I tell you, it's not fair!''

The con-man conned—Kirk had to grin. He peered down the cleft. Neither of the creatures was in view. They had not seemed particularly intelligent, and their reaction time was slow, very slow. If only they didn't accidentally pass this way. Perhaps it would seem to them that the fast-moving tiny animals—themselves—had simply disappeared. If their memories were commensurate with their reactions, the two living mountains might go back to being pieces of scenery again.

"Cheer up, Harry. You wouldn't have known what to do with any honest money anyway.'' Mudd was too depressed to offer a rejoinder. He felt sick.

* * *

Perhaps the scene in the *Enterprise*'s Sick Bay might have cheered him up. Light music played over the intercom. Some of the medical personnel present were dancing close together. Others were playing idly with the medical computers.

A couple of the more adventurous were doing nonregulation things with the body-function machinery that slid over the hospital tables.

The nominal head of this sybaritic setting was Dr. McCoy. At the moment he had one arm companionably around Nurse Mayer.

"Now Lyra, did I ever tell you about the time I saved Captain Kirk's life? And Commander Spock's?" Nurse Mayer shook her head, looking up at him with a mixture of awed admiration and affection. Her normal reaction to such a statement of McCoy's would have been a hard-boiled snort of derision.

"And my dear friend Scotty, too," McCoy continued blithely. "And that pretty little Lieutenant Uhura. Why, I guess I've saved just about everybody on this ship, one time or another." He looked around the room, saw nothing unusual in the highly unmedical activity.

"If the *Enterprise* had a heart, I'd save her, too." He found himself sniffing away a tear, smiled down at his companion. "Let's talk about your heart, my dear Lyra—"

Kirk walked over to Mudd, backed the trader up against one wall. "How long does the effect of the potion last, Harry?"

"I . . . I don't know." Kirk reflected that he was still probably in shock. Not from the sudden appearance of the monsters, but from the revelation that he had probably been involved in an honest deal. "I didn't know it was going to have any lasting effects at all, so I didn't ask."

"Well how long," pressed an exasperated Kirk, "did the 'crazy old medicine man' say it was *supposed* to last?"

"Not long."

"What do you mean, 'not long'? He must have told you something about its effects—whether you thought they were foolish or not."

"Actually—you're hurting my arm, Captain—he was

starting to, but I wanted to complete the transaction as smoothly as possible before he discovered the credit slips I paid him with were counterfeit.''

"Then how—" but Kirk was interrupted by a startled shout from Chapel. He turned from Mudd, saw her pointing toward the entrance of the cleft.

Both monsters lumbered into view, blocking out much of the light as they moved between the setting suns and the crevice. Their heads, black icebergs, swayed slowly from side to side in searching motions. Then they stopped. The head of the nearest one stared into the cleft, three great glassy eyes pinning the humans under an overpowering, unthinking gaze.

Kirk handed his communicator to Chapel. "Keep trying to contact the *Enterprise*, Nurse." He looked from Mudd to Spock.

"Maybe we can divert them, somehow."

"That is an outstandingly stupid idea, Captain," Spock commented. He stopped, flustered. "I'm sorry, Captain, it's the drug. I simply doubt that we can successfully appeal to their better nature—if they have one. Nor do I think they would respond to having their backs scratched—it would take a landing craft to make an impression. And phaser fire only seems to make them madder.''

"I wasn't thinking of anything like that, Spock. There's a terran expression that dates from ancient times, 'make love, not war.' Harry, do you have any of those crystals left?''

"Check his shoes, Captain. They're like his head," Chapel suggested. But it wasn't necessary. Mudd was voluntarily going through his pockets—and he found something. One hand came out, started to open, and then clamped tight. He started to slide away, along the wall.

"No, they're worth a fortune. My friends, dear Christine—" He was appealing to all of them. "I'll share it with you, I'll—"

Kirk reached out easily and clamped a hand around Mudd's wrist, smiling tightly.

"Ah, Captain, you're hurting me again. This archaic resort to crude physical force isn't like you, Captain." Mudd was trying very hard to keep smiling.

"Another second, Harry, and I'll crudely break it. Don't worry. When you're unconscious, you don't feel any pain."

"Since you put it that way, Captain—" His palm opened reluctantly, and Kirk took the three crystals thus revealed. Mudd bit his lower lip as he watched them go. "Perhaps just one, Captain? To encourage my continuing an honest career?"

But Kirk was already moving toward the entrance of the now blocked crevice.

IX

On the bridge, the air was empty of all music. Not having effected actual contact with the love potion, but only inhaling a diluted vapor from it, the rest of the crew was rapidly reverting to normal.

M'ress started to stretch, stopped, and snarled. One paw went to her head, and she rubbed it tiredly. It seemed she'd been at some kind of party.

Scott walked over to her, exhibiting similar signs of an inner pain. "I've got a hangover to rank with the finest," he mumbled loudly. His voice rose to a near shout as he further declared, "And I dinna touch a dram o' that scotch!"

"Not so loud, you idiot!" M'ress pleaded, now putting both hands to her ringing head.

"Idiot, is it? Well, all of a sudden I'm not so crazy about you, either, Lieutenant." Scott glared at her.

The ground-to-ship channel crackled for attention. "Surface party to *Enterprise*—surface to *Enterprise*," came a weary voice barely recognizable as belonging to Head Nurse Christine Chapel. "Emergency beam up . . . repeat, request emergency beam up."

Both officers reacted simultaneously, looking at each other in surprise.

M'ress broke free of it, slapped over a switch, and snarled into the mike. "*Enterprise* here . . . is that you, Nurse Chapel? What's going on?"

Chapel nearly stumbled in her excitement. "Captain, I made contact!"

"Marvelous," a grim-faced Kirk replied, from up ahead. "I hope we last long enough to be beamed up."

The first leviathan was nearing the cleft. Any moment now

a massive paw might rise up, descend on the rim of their refuge. The rock overhead seemed strong enough to keep even that heavy blow from them, but they were sure to be buried under an avalanche of loosened stone.

"It's seen me," Kirk yelled back to the others, hugging to the side of the cleft. "I need something to draw its attention. Phasers, Spock."

Spock moved to stand in the open, and a trembling Mudd forced himself to follow.

Holding the crystals in his right hand, phaser ready in his left, Kirk dashed out of the crevice.

He ran directly toward the first creature. Eyes the size of shuttle-bay doors inclined slowly to follow him.

Kirk ran to his right now, staying close against the base of the plug. As soon as the great head had turned to the side to follow him, Spock and Mudd fired.

Once again two beams of concentrated energy made contact with the skull. Once more the monster bucked, shrieking. The cavernous mouth opened.

Running down from the shielding stone and toward the living mountain, Kirk arched his arm, throwing the crystals with all his strength. They flew up and disappeared somewhere down that endless dark tunnel.

The mouth shut tight. The head swung back down toward Kirk and stopped. He watched it, paralyzed by those pond-like eyes. it hadn't made anything as recognizable as a swallowing motion—but then they had no idea what the monster's digestive system was like. In any case, there was no point in hesitating. All bets were placed; it was time to declare their hand.

Kirk ran toward the nearest enormous limb and slapped it firmly with both hands, twice. If this failed to work he was likely to die any minute. At least it might give Spock, Chapel, and Mudd a chance to beam up.

"Kyle!" M'ress was shouting into the intership communicator, "Transporter Chief Kyle, acknowledge!"

In the transporter room, Kyle searched frantically for the suddenly elusive intercom controls, finally located them. "Kyle here . . . I think. What's wrong, Lieutenant?"

"Are you utterly incompetent?" M'ress howled, ignoring

her own recent lapse in efficiency. "Didn't you hear—the Captain's requesting emergency beam up!"

"Emergency—I've been," a hand went to his forehead. "I've been ill."

"We've all been ill. For Amara's sake, Chief, beam them up!"

"Yes . . . yes," groaned Kyle, his head ringing with M'ress's command. "I'll do anything . . . only please stop shouting." He broke off and began working frantically at the transporter controls.

Kirk stumbled backward. The massive leg he had just touched was lifting skyward, seemingly propelled by a hidden crane. It hung poised there for a moment, then started to descend. He looked in all directions, but there was no place to run, and he was too far out to get back to the cleft.

The cliffside near him now was a solid wall, without even a cubbyhole to squirm into. The paw came down slowly, slowly. He closed his eyes and waited for death.

There was a deep, muffled thump—then nothing. He blinked.

The nearest talon, one of three massive hooks sprouting from the paw, had slammed down just next to him. It moved sideways, knocking him on his back gently.

Kirk looked upward, above the claw, to the looming face. It stared down at him blankly, expressionless and alien. Rolling over carefully, he caught his breath and then threw a handful of sand into the air, letting out a joyful whoop.

Spock, Mudd, and Chapel had moved to the edge of the crevice to watch the drama play itself out. They started to cheer, and Kirk ran jubilantly to join them.

"It worked, by God, it worked!" Mudd seemed to be sniffling and mumbling something about his lost riches, but the others were sharing Kirk's excitement.

They were stunned to silence by a screaming whistle.

They had forgotten about the second monster.

Cilia fluttering around the inside of its mouth, the other monster had turned toward the cleft entrance and was heading for them. Kirk scrambled backward with the others, drawing his phaser. Spock and Mudd lifted theirs a moment later.

Another whistling shriek shattered the dry air. The second

beast halted its ponderous attack as a gigantic paw swung past barely missing it. The first monster had spun around and now blocked the path of the second.

The wave of sand thrown up by the first creature inundated Kirk and the others, knocking them off their feet and burying Spock up to his waist. Mudd lost his phaser and Kirk his. They scrambled to free themselves.

A reverberating tremor followed as the two beast-mountains slammed into each other, multiple legs clawing at sides and face, circular mouths straining for a vacuuming grip on uneven body surfaces.

Kirk nearly fell again as they retreated back into the cleft. A rear leg swung wildly and tore away meters of cliff-face near the top of the crevice. A shower of rock came down, barricading the humans inside the cleft.

The earth shook as the two titans threw blow after blow at one another. Every time one of the multiple-ton paws connected, there was a clap like thunder.

The second beast struck a powerful blow, knocking the first aside, and was battered off its feet in turn. As it tumbled, the gigantic skull crashed against the front of the sheltering cleft and jammed there, cracking free more rock. A monstrous evil eye glared directly at them.

One huge front leg shoved the creature to its feet again. The other lifted and reached inward, straining for the four trapped figures, descending toward four sparkling pillars of rainbow-hued light, finally landing to scoop out a deep pit in the sand where Kirk, Spock, Mudd, and Chapel had stood helplessly only seconds before.

"And then, on Ophiucus VI," Mudd continued, his cheerful form wavering from behind the vision-distorting force-field, "I conned two miners out of a year's supply of dilithium crystals with fake Federation credit vouchers." He grinned in remembrance.

"They weren't too hysterical about that, though, miners are very philosophical types. We might have settled the misunderstanding amicably, if only they hadn't discovered so soon that the Andalusian pleasure slave I'd given them in exchange for the fake vouchers was a pneumatic automaton. That's when they became rather nonplussed—though that wasn't the exact term they used—and I was forced to bid a hasty adieu to their charming frontier world.''

"May I be of help in recording the confession, Nurse Chapel?" Spock inquired helpfully. He had just exited from the elevator, curious to find out how the recording was going. Chapel put a temporary hold on the recorder and looked up at him bitterly.

"You? You'd be the last person I'd choose." Her gaze traveled from the first officer's foot to his head, then turned sharply away. Spock merely raised his eyebrows, then turned his attention over to Mudd.

"A few minutes of love, now to be paid for with many hours of hatred—the usual way of human emotions, it seems. I do not think your potion would be a very good buy even at half the price, Harry Mudd."

"Ah well, Spock, you know how it is," Mudd replied easily. "So few things in this universe live up to their reputations."

"Except you, Harry. I should say that you live up to yours in a style few other sentients can boast of—or would want to."

"As neat a backhanded compliment as ever I've had, Spock," Mudd applauded. His head cocked questioningly to one side. "Think I'll get rehabilitation therapy again?"

"I would almost guarantee it, Harry Mudd, though I fail to observe any beneficial effects in you of such past treatment."

"No, it doesn't seem to work too well on me, does it?" Mudd agreed. "It's not easy, you know, Spock, when you're born with a name like Mudd. At least I do have, as you say, the virtue of consistency."

"In your case, Harry, it's hardly a virtue."

"Rehabilitation therapy," murmured Chapel, her eyes gleaming. One hand opened and closed rhythmically. She stared through the force-field.

"I think maybe it would do Harry more good if he had a dose of good old-fashioned cruel and unusual punishment instead."

"Now, now, my dear Christine," Mudd said, "is that a proper attitude for a dispenser of healing to have? Besides,

I'm an official Federation prisoner, and as such I'm entitled to a little—''

"Maybe you'd better finish this for me, after all, Mr. Spock," she said, staring at Mudd with a look Florence Nightingale would have found appalling. She handed him the tricorder, clenching both hands nervously behind her back.

"I should think you would be getting used to rehabilitation therapy by now," Spock mused conversationally, his scientific curiosity aroused.

"You never get used to it, Spock, but that doesn't matter. That's not what's really bothering me."

"There is something troubling you more than the prospect of renewed therapy?" Spock noted. "Most interesting."

"You see," Mudd continued, "it's only that I hate to leave you all." He smiled dangerously. "All my loved ones . . ."

Despite the fact that Mudd was declared absolutely off limits to all members of the crew, that his meals were always served up by automatons, and that no one visited him for whatever reason except in twos, Kirk didn't relax until they had entered orbit around Starfleet Sector Headquarters at Darius.

They gave him back his own clothes, then—minus the astonishing assortment of miniature devices concealed within the material—turned him over to an escort party made up of Kirk's best security people.

Cheerful to the last, Mudd waved friendly good-byes to them as he was turned over to ground-based Peaceforcer personnel. He was still waving as they led him through the sliding doors of the Legal Building.

Watching him depart, Kirk couldn't help but wonder if Mudd were not already at work trying to convince his escorts into not only letting him go, but into turning over their identification cards and weapons as well.

If he got a single ranking official into a card game, the planet was lost.

Kirk hoped for at least a moderate layover. But as it developed there was no time to rest and enjoy the pleasures Darius had to offer. Orders were waiting for him as soon as he and the security party beamed back aboard.

"Communication from Starfleet Science Headquarters,

Captain," said Sulu as Kirk reentered the bridge. "Confidential. Mr. Spock is waiting for you in your quarters."

"Thank you, Mr. Sulu."

Well, that was fast. Something especially interesting must be up if Spock felt the need of discussing the orders in private.

The first officer of the *Enterprise* was seated at the large central desk in Kirk's rooms. He swiveled to face the Captain as he entered.

"I trust, Captain, that Harry Mudd is safe in custody?"

"I'd feel better if they would give his tongue rehabilitation therapy instead of his mind. One appears to operate independently of the other. But I think we've seen the last of Harcourt Fenton Mudd—I hope.

"I understand from Mr. Sulu that you've kept the new orders secret. By their urgency I gather that they don't allow us time for a rest orbit."

"It would appear not, Captain, though I have only played the first portion of them." He hefted a small microtape cassette. "Here is the communication from Science Center. I think you will find it interesting." He slipped the cassette into the desk play-back slot. Kirk sat down.

A young science officer appeared on the screen in front of them. He was standing alone in a chamber that gave signs of extending above and behind him to considerable distances. The camera pulled back and showed that this was indeed the case. It also identified the particular chamber to Kirk and Spock.

Rising from floor almost to ceiling was a full-scale reproduction of the Megasphere—the gigantic artificial construct which was an exact model of the Milky Way. Distances between the stars, nebulae, black holes, neutron stars, and other objects were to scale—though the stars and other intragalactic objects were not. If so represented, they would have had to have been built so small as to be visible only under a microscope.

All galactic coordinates for starship navigational computers and all scientific referents to galactic structure were drawn from the Megasphere. Only two originals existed—one on Earth, the other on Vulcan.

New stellar discoveries were constantly being added, a

titanic task in itself, as the proper insertion of a newly charted star into the Megasphere was work for specially designed computer controlled microhandlers. As it was, maintaining accuracy within the colossal model was a job involving weeks of preparation merely to design new microhandlers to perform the actual insertion.

Banks of special lights flooded the Megasphere from every angle. The light was picked up, amplified, and thrown back into near darkness by special photosensitive material. Bulbs or any kind of powered light source were too clumsy and too difficult to use. The photosensitive material used would never wear out, never need replacement.

Half a dozen special gravity field generators held the stellar model intact, any one of which could maintain the Megasphere. If for some unforseeable reason all six failed simultaneously, the work of years would fall to the chamber floor in a shower of tiny glowing pebbles.

The young officer spoke easily, with the manner of a confident lecturer.

"Captain Kirk, Science Officer Spock . . . I am Lieutenant Bell of the Prometheus Science Center. I think you will be pleased to know that the new mission that you have been selected to carry out is of a purely investigative and scientific nature, with no rescue or Peaceforcer functions involved." He smiled pleasantly, and Kirk found himself liking this young man. That, he reminded himself, was exactly why Lieutenant Bell had been chosen to deliver recorded orders.

"But this assignment will require considerable long-range cruising, so we are concerned that you be on your way as soon as possible." Bell had a thin, glowing metal wand with which he turned and pointed into the Megasphere.

"Your approximate route . . ."

PART III

THE MAGICKS
OF MEGAS-TU

(Adapted from a script by Larry Brody)

X

Kirk really did not have the words for it. At times he had wished he'd been born with a little more of the poet in him. But after days and days of travel in which they had seen their objective grow progressively nearer, Kirk, like everyone else on board, had long since run out of superlatives. Now he was reduced to trying to relate the panorama in simple human terms.

The best description he could come up with was that it was like a soup of infinite ingredients and color. A sunsoup, a stellar gumbo.

Oh, they were all there—superhot blue-whites, blue giants, red dwarfs, supergiants, plain whites, cepheids, and irregular variables, binary and triple stars, with the younger stars predominating.

And a fair sampling of the familiar Sol-type, innocuous yet heart-breakingly familiar amid the splendor of iridescent gasses and cosmic debris of all types and descriptions. No, soup seemed a thoroughly inadequate label for the center of the galaxy—but at least it didn't overwhelm. He found himself squinting as he studied the awesome panorama glowing on the main viewscreen.

"Turn down the brightness, Mr. Sulu." The cluster of cosmic matter was so dense now that the cumulative brightness on the screen hurt the eyes.

"It's down all the way, sir."

"Well then, put another filter over the scope."

"Aye, sir." Sulu touched a switch. Immediately the full brilliance of the tightly packed suns, gasses, and nebulae dimmed to a bearable level.

Kirk shook his head and envied a certain section of the

Enterprise's crew. It was an astronomer's paradise, and in fact that section of the ship's scientific complement was working round the clock by its own choice.

Kirk, of course, was too occupied with administrative details to enjoy more than this occasional quiet study of the starscape. He sighed, pressed a well-used button on the arm of the command chair.

"Captain's Log, stardate 5524.5. For many years scientists have theorized that the galaxy was created by a great central explosion. If this was so, attendant new theories postulate that the galactic center may still be creating new matter.

"The *Enterprise* has the honor of being the first ship to attempt to penetrate to the heart of the galaxy. We will try to ascertain the truth or falsity of this and numerous other spatial hypotheses."

Despite the additional filter on the pickup telescope itself, the stunning brightness of the surrounding space continued to intensify. Gaseous and radioactive particle matter was so thick here that at times the *Enterprise* seemed to be drifting through a phosphorescent fog, a pale white submersible in an ocean of deep-sea fish. Readings on radiation meters remained within tolerable levels, but an older starship than the *Enterprise* would soon have had her crew fatally burned.

"Heading now zero zero one degrees due east of the galactic plane, Captain," Sulu broke in. "Maintaining indicated observation-recording speed of warp-one."

They were getting very close. A hand touched the button again. He would finish the log entry later.

"Maintain speed, Mr. Sulu. Correct ship to a heading of zero degrees." No other starship captain in history had been able to utter that momentous phrase, and it might be some time before another repeated it.

"The center of the galaxy," he murmured, for the umpteenth time. He looked over to the library computer station, where Spock, like the astronomers, had been working overtime just to record new information.

"I'm not sure what I'll do or how I'll react, if we find there actually is a central something that all matter springs from, like a well. How about you, Spock? Surely you've thought about it."

"From an astrophysical standpoint I find it all quite fascinating, Captain. Personally, I am more intrigued by what we may encounter there in the nature of subsidiary phenomena. How does gravity react at the center, for example.

"Yet I am afraid we shall be somewhat disappointed and find that the precise center is very much like the area immediately around it, an area such as we are traversing at this very moment," the science officer concluded.

"Galactic center in three minutes, Captain," Sulu reported.

"Thank you, Mr. Sulu. Lieutenant Uhura, sound yellow alert, as planned."

"Aye, sir, yellow alert." Uhura proceeded to make the necessary demands on her instrumentation. The proper alarm signal pealed out.

There was a short wait, then the communications officer looked back at him. "All decks and stations report yellow-alert status effected, Captain."

"Ready for whatever comes, then," Kirk whispered to himself, and added aloud, "I hope."

"What was that, Captain?"

"Nothing, Mr. Spock. Nothing."

At first it seemed as if Spock's dry evaluation was going to turn out to be correct. Nothing unique appeared on the screen; they saw nothing not already previously encountered.

Then it appeared with unexpected suddenness. Somewhere directly ahead was a phenomenon different from anything any of the bridge complement had ever seen.

At first glance it resembled a small nebula trying to turn itself inside out. But it was no normal nebula according to the sensors. The writhing, twisting mass of color was in constant violent motion, spitting out particles and gasses in all directions.

"Mr. Spock," said Kirk quickly, but the science officer was already attending to his recorders.

"Visual contact galactic center, Captain," he reported. "The volume of energy and mass here is overwhelming. Instrumentation can only calibrate a portion of the total flux—their levels don't read any higher."

"All right, Spock, be careful. There's enough energy out

there to overload every sensor on the ship.'' He need not
have said it; he was only verbalizing what was obvious to
Spock and everyone else.

Kirk stared at the screen, thoroughly mesmerized. There
was no form, no pattern, no structure to that violent, churn-
ing whirlpool of force.

"Evaluation, Mr. Spock."

"It is indeed the theorized creation point, Captain. Detectors indicate it is putting forth a tremendous amount of
particulate matter, from the subatomic levels mostly. There
are also new, as yet unidentifiable, structures . . . Also radioactive gasses, free energy. Fortunately we do not have to
make interspace calls from here—they would be drowned out
a meter from the hull."

"Okay, Spock, we know what's coming out. Is anything
going in?" That would be the critical test. Spock's answer
would eventually make a number of astronomers happy.

"Very little, if anything, Captain. There are indications
that the fabric of space in the immediate vicinity of the creation point is not stable."

"That's hardly surprising," Kirk observed, "in view of
the forces at work here."

"Despite the evidence of considerable gravitation potential," Spock continued, as if he were talking about the most
common household object, "there is no sign of hydrogen or
anything else being drawn into the center from the surrounding space. Altogether an extraordinary phenomenon. I believe we may be looking at the rarest single structure in the
known universe: a negative black hole—one that ejects, rather
than attracts matter."

Kirk nodded. "That would confirm that all matter in our
universe has been drawn from other universes, and that creation is truly infinite, as some theories state."

"Merely because our galaxy draws its substance from the
black hole of another universe, Captain, and that our black
holes may each well be the galactic center of other star clusters, does not mean that the universe itself is infinite—only
somewhat larger than we had suspected."

Kirk wondered at his first officer. Only Spock could concede the possible existence of a billion billion other *universes*
and make it come out as an understatement.

He returned his attention to the viewscreen, but it was only a moment before Spock glanced up from his hooded viewer again.

"There is also evidence of other forces at work here, Captain, which are unclassifiable under standard astronomical referents. I would strongly suggest that we—" He stopped.

An automatic stylus was beginning to jiggle up and down on the console to his left. As he watched it, the oscillation increased. Finally it became violent enough to knock the stylus loose from its holder. It rolled off the slanted console onto the deck.

At the same time Spock grabbed at the console edges. The *Enterprise* had begun a rocking motion, sideways, then up and down, then sideways again.

"Easy," said Kirk to everyone in general and no one in particular.

The buffeting grew more violent. "Reverse power, hold this position, then head zero zero one degrees left." They would use this strange new force to help slip around the storm of the center itself. "Deflector screens on full."

"Deflectors up, sir," Sulu informed him, adding, "it's taking considerable power to maintain this heading, sir."

"We'll hold it, Mr. Sulu," said Kirk calmly.

The buffeting didn't vanish entirely, but the increased power being fed to the warp-engines seemed sufficient to reduce it to an occasional sharp tremor. No one was in danger of being thrown from his seat.

The *Enterprise* continued to move around the fiery core.

"Good heavens—look at that!" Sulu exclaimed. Kirk's attention had not varied from the screen, but he understood Sulu's automatic shout. "Just a moment, sir . . . I'll widen the angle." The helmsman worked controls.

Abruptly their field of vision seemed to quadruple, and the phenomenon revealed by their new position became fully visible.

Once again, superlatives were insufficient.

Lines of pure force had grown so strong they had begun to radiate. They stretched from the spastic central core out to the nearest suns in great flaring arcs. Everyone on the bridge, who thought he was past amazement, sat enthralled by the spectacle. The lines glowed and shifted slightly and were to a solar prominence what a spider's web would be to a suspension bridge.

"I wonder," Kirk murmured, "if the surrounding stars hold the creation point steady, via these lines of force, at the center of our galaxy?" Or was the creation point fighting a constant battle, through millions and millions of less detectable lines of force, to hold its myriad suns around it?

"Charting scanners on, Captain," Spock said smoothly. "Commencing official survey central quadrant." Less sophisticated instruments took over now, as formal mapping was begun.

The doors to the bridge elevator slid aside, and McCoy entered, moving quickly.

"Jim, Spock—" Another jolt rocked the bridge. "What in the name of sanity is going . . . ?" His voice trailed off. He had just gotten his first glimpse of the mind-boggling panorama spread across the screen.

"What on Earth is that?"

"Nothing we can detect from Earth itself, Bones—or even from nearby. We're here—at the center of the galaxy—and all the theories and guesses and hypotheses about this place appear to have been right . . . with frosting."

They all watched as the *Enterprise* continued to move past the central core.

For the first time, an uncertain tone seemed to be present in Spock's voice. "Captain, we appear to be moving up on a completely new phenomenon."

"Another one?"

Apparently they were not out miracled yet. Something different was indeed showing up on the viewscreen.

Kirk saw that some of the feathery lines of iridescent force, instead of leaping out toward nearby stars in smooth arcs, had twisted together. They were curling and writhing violently about themselves, a concatenation of energy separate from the core being manipulated by a galactic potter's wheel.

The forces created by this secondary center took on a definite shape as they moved closer. Instead of the central chaos, they formed a recognizable, colossal cone. It was visible only when destroyed matter at its edges exploded, or when a force-line flared with a discharge of energy that would dwarf the output of several suns.

Yet sensors revealed that instead of putting out energy-matter like the center point, here it was being drawn inward. But it was most definitely not a black hole, nor a neutron star. It was something as new as the negative black hole of Spock's hypothesis, and something even less recognizable.

A number of stars swirled like dust motes about its rim, spinning crazily. Occasionally one would impinge on the edge of the cone itself. The result was a flare of light—overwhelming if compared to a human-generated explosion, yet far from nova-sized.

Sulu shattered the awed contemplation. "Captain, I'm up to warp-six for flyby on revised course, but that thing seems to be pulling us in. Yet the gravity detectors show no new change in the surrounding field. I don't understand the forces operating here. And it's not a computer malfunction, sir. Our course is definitely being affected."

Even as he spoke, strong vibration rocked the bridge. Yet it was somehow different from before.

"Scanners indicate the energy cone is composed of both matter and energy, like the core itself." Spock said, checking his readouts. "But there appears to be some kind of order at work here, whereas the core point was anarchical in nature.

"There is indeed some powerful attractive force operating within the vortex, but it is, as Mr. Sulu has stated, something other than normal gravity. Something outside our experience, I fear."

"Warp-seven, Captain," the excited Sulu interrupted. "Warp-eight!"

"Take us out of here, Mr. Sulu," Kirk ordered; but the helmsman was already working at his console.

"I've been trying to, sir. We're still being drawn in. Warp-nine . . . warp-ten, sir!"

"Emergency reverse power!"

Back at his post in engineering central, Scott noticed the sudden terrific demands being made on his engines. He held tight to a crossbar to keep from being thrown to the floor by the increasingly wild vibrations and hoped the drive could cope with the forces being pitted against them.

As the *Enterprise* was drawn inexorably nearer the energy vortex, the colors on the viewscreen began to pulse violently, the pastel rainbow giving way to deep golds and reds, all being subsumed into a vital, rippling purple.

Now the ship had been pulled to the very rim of the cosmic cyclone. It hung there a second, then caught and started to spin at tremendous speed around the rim, faster, and faster. On the *Enterprise* the artificial gravity compensators could barely keep up with the steady increase in centrifugal force.

Scott now clung desperately to the crossbar and stared grim-faced at his gauges. Shouts of pain and groans came from various members of his staff who had failed to gain a firm purchase on something immovable.

Somehow, hanging tight with both legs and one arm against the terrific sideways pressure, he managed to pull himself a hand at a time to the nearest wall intercom. From there he tried to raise the bridge.

"Captain . . . Scott here. I don't know how much additional emergency power we can continue to put out before the engines start to break up."

Kirk listened but was helpless to acknowledge. He had been thrown to the floor. Despite the gravity compensators, the whirling was generating G-forces too powerful to be canceled out.

Spock was still seated in his chair at the library station, clinging tightly to the arms. He tried to shift for a still firmer grip. He felt a wrenching pull as the *Enterprise* hit an eddy in the rim of the vortex and was jerked loose. He slid past Kirk and came to a halt up against a console on the opposite side of the bridge.

"Spock . . . you all right?"

His reply ignored Kirk's query. "Captain, there may be only one choice open to us. We must hope this vortex is analogous in its internal structure to Terran/Vulcan counterparts . . . hope that there is a calm in its center where these forces either do not exist or cancel each other out."

"Agreed, Mr. Spock. We'll try to make for the eye of the cyclone—if it has one. Mr. Sulu, Mr. Arex . . ."

But neither helmsman was in a position to carry out orders. Sulu was jammed in a tangle of arms and legs against Kirk's command chair, while Arex had skidded all the way back to communications, despite the frantic use of all six arms and legs. He lay pinned against Uhura's feet.

Kirk gritted his teeth and struggled to pull himself toward the deserted navigation console. As he moved, he rose slightly off the deck and was bounced end over end, coming to stop against the library station.

"Allow me, Captain," said Spock. Now the G-forces seemed to increase, decrease, and change direction capriciously, making it far harder to judge one's movements. Up, down, and sideways changed without warning.

Uhura screamed as she was suddenly thrown and pinned against the ceiling. Much more of this, Kirk reflected, and it wouldn't matter whether the ship broke up or not, because her crew would long since have preceded her.

Somehow Spock managed to inch his way toward the helm. There was a crackling discharge, and the deck lights flashed on and off. More cracklings followed, mixed with the groans of metal alloy strained to its utmost. Kirk revised his estimates of the approaching catastrophe.

The *Enterprise* would disintegrate first after all. They would all experience the unique sensation of floating free in the maelstrom before the surrounding radiation and hard space would reduce them to their component atoms.

Spock reached the helm. Bracing himself firmly with one arm, he used the other to fumble at several controls. The *Enterprise* began to break away from the spinning, violent iridescence and move toward the center of the vortex.

It hung there motionless for several long seconds, warp-engines fighting to drive her outward and back into normal space. Then the ship began to drift, slowly at first but with steadily increasing speed, down the rapidly narrowing funnel.

But that was all. The vibrating ceased; the smell of overloaded circuits and the sound of tortured metal stopped, and the crushing centrifugal force was instantly wiped out. Once more they had a recognizable up and down, as the ship's artificial gravity computer finally restored some order.

Back in engineering, Scott had to duck as one of his technicians fell slowly past him. Kirk's voice sounded over the intercom.

"Engineering . . . status report." By now Scott was on his feet again—though moving cautiously—and checking readouts. Several of the delicate instruments used to measure gravitation were completely gone, having been maltreated to the point of destruction. They no longer registered anything, since they had been overloaded even beyond emergency shut-down.

Scott whistled silently. Without the powerful gravity compensators, there would be nothing left of the crew of the *Enterprise* now but a multitude of brownish smears against floors, walls, and ceilings.

But the readings on the instruments that had survived intact were encouraging. Scott spoke toward the wide open pickup grid.

"There's some damage, Captain, but I think everything can be repaired." He groaned and reached for his lower back. "Includin' me."

"Okay, Scotty, do your best. We're running down the center of some kind of spiraling energy storm. I don't know how long we've got till we reach bottom, or what will happen when we get there. Be ready. Bridge out."

"Be ready, he says," Scott mumbled, "and for what?" Well, whatever it was, he would do his best to see that the *Enterprise* was ready for it.

"Gabler, Jacobs—there's nothin' wrong with you! Get off your duffs and break out a pair of microwelders. Some honest work's required of you, for a change!"

On the bridge, everyone was slowly rearranging himself, uncurling from various contorted positions. Fortunately, few of the sudden changes in gravity had been full-G, and the falls hadn't been as serious as they might have been. Arex gave Uhura, who had probably received the worse banging around, a hand up.

"Would you like to report to Sick Bay, Lieutenant?" asked Kirk worriedly.

"No, I'm all right, Captain," She eased herself slowly back into her seat, wincing. "I don't think the parts of me that hurt would benefit by lying down. They shouldn't impair my efficiency, either—and no remarks, Mr. Spock!"

Spock looked bewildered, and Kirk's smile deepened at his first officer's obvious confusion.

Spock finally decided to ignore what was evidently another touch of inexplicable human humor—preferring that to the thought that Uhura might be more seriously injured than she admitted.

"An incredible experience, Captain."

"Ah, it got to you emotionally, did it, Spock?" pressed McCoy.

"As usual, an incorrect interpretation of a straightforward observation, Doctor. I found it scientifically fascinating, of course."

"I don't suppose you were scared, either?"

"Scared, Doctor? I fail to see why one should be frightened of understandable natural phenomena. I do confess that for several moments, estimates of the forces acting unfavorably on the ship did not induce in me optimism as to our overall chances for survival, however—"

"Oh, never mind, Spock," McCoy turned his attention to Kirk. "At least I had the good sense to be scared, Jim. What now?"

Kirk stared up at the screen, which now showed a seemingly endless series of concentric circles of flaring violet light. The smallest circles tended to be dark to the point of blackness.

"Mr. Sulu?"

"We're moving down the vortex, as assumed, Captain," the helmsman reported, studying his instruments. "And at a speed nothing short of astronomical. The cone itself seemed nowhere near this long at first examination. Normal space–time laws are badly distorted here. The sensors appear to be functioning properly."

"Any chance of breaking free and making our way back to the rim?" Kirk asked. The helmsman's reply was sobering.

"We've been running at full reverse drive for several minutes, Captain."

"Um." Kirk digested this information quietly. "Stop the drive down to warp-two." There was no point in continuing useless demands on the engines—they might need all the power they could muster, later.

He turned back to McCoy, remembering the doctor's question. "We'll ride it through, Bones. What else can we do?"

"Ride it through to where?"

Spock replied with another of his overwhelming quiet

pronouncements. ''Perhaps to the center of All Things, Doctor.''

McCoy was confused instead of awestruck. ''But I thought we'd already passed by the center, Spock?''

''And so we did, Doctor. This vortex was completely unexpected. But to use both our worlds for a crude analogy—there is a fixed north pole on Earth and on Vulcan. Yet this is only a geographic convenience. There is also another 'north pole' that is the real center of natural forces.''

''Magnetic north,'' added Kirk, ''and it wanders around from year to year. I see your point, Spock. There may be two centers to the galaxy. A spatial one, from which all else can be measured—and another on which certain different forces converge.''

''That is it, Captain,'' Spock admitted, ''and it is that second convergence of forces that we appear to be traveling through to its end.''

''Wherever that may be—and it looks like we'll be there soon.'' Kirk gestured, and all eyes returned to the main screen.

The violet light seemed to be blending, running together into a smooth maroon pool that glowed like a dim red giant. They struck it seconds later. But the *Enterprise* was moving so supremely fast by then that no matter what the malignant maroon eye was—red giant or otherwise—they were in and through it before any effect was noted.

A tremendous red flash did erupt around the ship. Crimson sparks and activated particles flew away from her hull, dissolving further into all the primary hues. At Spock's sensor station and the navigation consoles, every instrument went berserk.

There was a long silence.

''My, my,'' whispered McCoy, his the only voice on the bridge, as he and everyone else sat staring at the screen.

Space as they knew it was . . . gone.

In its place had been substituted the wild nightmare of a color-blind surrealist. Nothing seemed fixed or permanent. What at one moment appeared as the black of normal interstellar space, complete with distant stars, would suddenly fracture like a hemorrhaging amoeba into tiny patches of scattered darkness, still with stars, and turn unexpectedly magenta or maroon or red.

Now and then it appeared as if an ocean of white-hot magma was floating only a few hundred meters beneath the *Enterprise*. A moment later and it formed a glowing roof over their heads, then a wall to either side, continually throwing off bubbling blobs of itself which drifted off in all directions.

As the *Enterprise* moved through it, nonspace slowly started to coalesce, to take on a single form. It gradually became a kind of circular tunnel with unstable sides composed of a fluid yellow substance.

They existed in a yellow, cylindrical universe. As the *Enterprise* continued down the corridor the ship started to slow, its speed dropping from warp-impossible to warp-ten, to one and then sublight speed.

At first the flavescent corridor appeared to be at least a million meters in diameter. Now it had shrunk until the walls seemed ready to touch the hull itself. At the end of the corridor, rotating in its center and blocking further passage, was a spherical object that just might be a world.

"Is that a planet?" exclaimed Sulu, voicing the question in the mind of everyone. It was shockingly, paralyzingly stable-looking—the first truly stable-looking thing they had seen since entering the vortex.

Stable it might be, but normal it was not. It was striped in red and whites like a candy-cane Jupiter, though it was only slightly larger than Earth-size . . . if the sensors could be believed.

"What is it?" wondered Uhura aloud. "Where are we?"

Spock looked up from the hooded viewer at his station. "I am afraid that our normal navigational references mean very little here, Lieutenant. All readings indicate that we are not in time as we know it. That we are no longer in space as we know it has been self-evident for some time now." He looked at McCoy.

"Doctor, perhaps these readings may mean more to you." McCoy moved over and studied the information in the viewer.

Sulu had pushed away from the navigation console while Arex was idly running the fingers of three hands over various controls. He encountered switches and buttons with random nonchalance. It didn't matter what he hit, nothing produced the slightest reaction.

He looked back at Kirk. "The helm's dead, sir. Some of the instrumentation still registers information, but they don't make any sense. Most of the navigation readouts have simply fallen to zero."

Kirk made a noncommittal noise, shifted his attention to communications. "Lieutenant Uhura, try to get a message through to Starfleet. They should at least know of our position here. Maybe someone can be reached at Science Center who has some helpful suggestions."

She worked at her machinery for several minutes, then glanced helplessly back over her shoulder.

"Captain, the subspace radio is dead, too. So are all pickups. I should at least be registering static from any energy flowing around us, but there's nothing, nothing at all."

At that point McCoy happened to notice the chronometer over Spock's station. He checked his own against it, then made a fast check with the still operating library computer.

"Jim, not only is there no time here as we *know* it, there doesn't seem to be any time. All the ship's chronometers have stopped. Emergency backup power doesn't seem to make any difference."

"Engineering to bridge."

"Bridge here, Captain speaking." By now Kirk was so numbed that Scott's announcement seemed inevitable instead of frightening.

"There's no reason for it, Captain, no reason at all," complained the stunned, puzzled voice of the chief engineer, "but the antimatter and matter generators are going . . . fading out. Everything seems to be operating perfectly, the engines, converters, everything . . . but they're just fading. We're losing power. Emergency storage cells are dropping rapidly, and I canna tell you why. Everything's coming . . . to a . . . stop." There was a sudden crackling, and they heard Scott's voice again, weaker now as the communicator power evaporated.

". . . a . . . top . . ." There was a final fizzle and the intercom died for good.

As it did, the lights on the bridge went out. As with the

intercom, the automatic emergency backups failed to take over.

"It would appear that none of the natural laws of our universe operate here, Captain," Spock observed. For once, even his tone was muted.

"Natural laws," McCoy echoed. "The life-support systems . . . they're probably fading, too. Is everything just going to go . . . out? Hey, I'm floating."

"So am I," came Kirk's voice from somewhere in the darkness nearby.

"And I," reported Sulu. One by one, the rest of them confirmed the loss of gravity.

Without light and gravity the universe lost all sense. There was no true direction, no sense of up or down—or of right and wrong. Kirk found himself curling into a fetal position as his mind tried vainly to cope with the absence of reality.

No! He forced himself to stick out his arms and legs. He would die in the shape of a man.

McCoy coughed, found himself propelled by the slight action. Eventually he bumped into something hard—whether floor or ceiling he could not tell. Then he noticed something else.

"Jim . . . air's getting bad . . . needs circulation . . . cleaning."

Kirk tried to orient himself in the darkness as he spoke. It was hopeless. He could only pray that the open intercom would pick up his voice.

"Engineering!" he shouted, "we're getting stale air. Go to battery power on all circulation instrumentation. Primary alert, Scotty!"

Silence and soft darkness.

"Mr. Sulu."

"Here, Captain," came a reluctant, weak reply. The helmsman coughed slightly from somewhere nearby.

"Mr. Sulu," Kirk said slowly and distinctly, "there is an emergency. Go to battery power."

"I can't, Captain. I don't know where the console is."

"I am still holding my seat, Captain." Arex's voice! But Kirk's last hopes disappeared with the navigator's reply. "When the lights went I tried switching to reserves. There isn't any battery power on the bridge, either. Either they've been drained or they simply don't operate in this space-time continuum. I'm sure I tried the proper controls. Everything's gone dead.'' He coughed, and his voice faded to a thin wheeze.

''. . . dead . . .''

''Arex?'' Kirk inhaled and found himself choking. His hand went to his throat. Air . . . he was drowning, smothering, and the darkness was a blanket over him.

He heard a faint voice . . . McCoy. ''Jim . . . Jim . . . we've got to do something . . . we've . . .'' Then it, too, faded and was gone.

Gasping, Kirk tried to reach out to him, flailing in the emptiness, struggling to touch another human being a last time. He felt something, turned, straining. Another hand touched his and gripped tight.

''Captain?'' Kirk couldn't see the figure next to him . . . yet in his mind he did.

''Good-bye, Mr. Spock.''

''Good-bye, Captain . . .''

XI

Peace.

Night.

Blindness . . . Kirk found himself blinded, dazzled, stunned by the unexpected flare that lit the bridge in scintillating geometric patterns. It fluoresced in the unnatural brilliance. The strange designs pulsed for a few seconds longer, then disappeared.

Kirk felt his vision returning as his outraged retinas began to cope with the new illumination. An artificial gravity seemed to be coming back on. A moment later he was back on the floor, right side up, and sitting next to the command chair.

There were moans and coughs from all around, but they had air again, though it was weak like the new gravity. And as he looked around he saw that the bridge complement was back to normal.

Almost to normal. There was one exception.

A new man.

No, not a man . . . an alien. Manlike, but still alien. Kirk stared at him in disbelief, and the wonder stemmed not from its alienness, but its familiarity.

Was it possible that this was all illusion? That before dying a man underwent a period of mirage-ridden temporary insanity?

The creature standing before him was half-goat, half-man. No bigger than Kirk or Spock, he was complete down to goat's horns, cloven hooves, and short, flicking tail—the compendium of all the goat-gods of the old terran myths. Wide-shouldered and smoothly muscular, he wore a short beard and nothing else, save the thick fleece that covered him from waist to toe.

In human terms the goat-man appeared to be about fifty years old. That probably meant nothing, of course. But exactly how far off in his age-estimate Kirk actually was, he would not have believed.

The apparition was surveying them all with a mild, slightly bemused grin. All his movements hinted at constant delight and endless energy. And there was a strange, dancing glint in his eyes.

"Ah, humans!" came an earthquake voice that thundered around the bridge. "Lovely, primitive humans. Can't you do anything right?"

Kirk was aware the goat-man was looking down at him. He started to try and stand, but the effort was too much in the still tenuous atmosphere. "Please . . ." The deck felt like a coffin-bottom. "We need better air than this, and normal gravity . . ." His plea trailed off in a racking cough.

"Of course, of course. I was so pleased to see you—thoughtless of me. A moment."

He raised both hands over his head and brought them together with a deafening slap. Lightning flashed between his palms and formed a crackling, floating ball in the air nearby, pulsing with internal energies.

Stroking his beard with one hand, the goat-man studied the ball-lightning as it formed a complex diagram of pure energy. Then he nodded approvingly. Jabbing a finger into its center, he stirred the energy like paste. At the same time, the thundering voice sounded a single word.

"RADAMANTHUS!"

The energy diagram shattered, the flaring shards swirling around the tip of his moving finger. They collapsed to a pinpoint and vanished. A rising hum was interspersed with a series of loud clicks—something Kirk had heard few times before. Dead bridge relays snapping over as they were reactivated! The lights suddenly returned to normal, as did the gravity. And there was a sweetness in the air Kirk never thought to smell again.

Spock looked over to the library station. Computer lights once again flashed in ready patterns, indicating operational status. Arex stared in wonder at the navigation console. The instrumentation was registering again . . . though as yet their readings were still incomprehensible. No doubt they meant *something*, but Arex had no reference tables for this . . . place.

Even the viewscreen shone with its accustomed brilliance, once more displaying a panorama of the red-and-white world suspended below them.

Spock climbed to his feet. He took a deep, experimental breath, showing every sign of expecting his body to fly apart with the force of the inhalation.

When nothing so cataclysmic happened, he tried another, and another, then nodded in satisfaction. He was operational again, too.

Kirk also smiled in relief when, on climbing to his feet, he also found he was in good repair. Nothing seemed to be broken. And how marvelous it was just to be able to breathe. He walked to the command chair, resumed his seat.

McCoy, however, chose to remain seated on the deck. He was not going anywhere for several minutes.

Evidently quite pleased with himself, the goat-man remained standing in the middle of this renewed activity. Smiling, he began to walk around the bridge, staring curiously at this or that instrument, occasionally nodding sagely to himself or letting out a chuckle of amusement.

Eventually he stopped and turned to look back at Kirk, hands on hips.

"Everything is working again, my friends?"

"It is," admitted a confused Spock, after a rapid check of his readouts, "but it should not be. It cannot be. It is not . . . logical."

Olympian laughter rolled and boomed around the bridge as the goat-man threw back his head and roared.

"You are amused?" Spock inquired politely.

"Logical!" The goat-man grinned at him. "To whose logic do you refer, my elfin friend?"

"Look around you, Spock," advised McCoy, still sitting on the deck and enjoying life again. "Everything is working, including you and me." He made pacifying gestures with his hands at the first officer. "Let's not try to argue this gentleman out of his miracles, hmmm? It may be illogical for us to be alive now, but I'm willing to concede the situation."

"Be happy, Mr. Spock," the goat-man suggested. He ignored the first officer's continued bewilderment and spread his arms in a gesture of warm welcome. He was embracing all of them—spiritually, at least.

And he seemed at least as pleased by their good health and presence as they were by his.

"Welcome, welcome. I knew eventually humans would come searching for me—you always do. We meet again. A toast!" He reached into nearby air, and a huge tankard suddenly appeared in his hand.

Smaller versions popped into being in the hands of everyone else. The goat-man gestured to them all with his, proceeded to drain it with undisguised gusto.

Sulu took a hesitant sip from his own. His eyes lit up. He commenced to drink deeply from it. His example was quickly imitated by his shipmates.

The now-empty tankard vanishing conveniently from his hand, the goat-man moved over and helped McCoy gently to his feet. McCoy had an opportunity to study the alien at close range. By the time he stood upright again, he was satisfied that their visitor wore no clever costume. He was real, from the tip of his horns to the cleft in his hooves.

Those hooves clacked sharply on the deck as the goat-man stepped back. Now he put an arm around Spock, brought him over to McCoy and embraced both of them like long-lost brothers.

"I don't want to be impolite," Kirk began, "especially after what you've done for us . . . but who are you?"

"Who am I? Oh, you want a name! Call me Baal." He paused thoughtfully. "Or Lucien. Yes, Lucien. But above all, call me friend." One finger fluttered skyward as he declaimed, "Never could I abandon those who have come so far to frolic with me . . . for such purpose you must have been sent."

He surveyed the bridge again, speaking before Kirk could tell him that their motive for being here was somewhat different and not exactly voluntary.

"But not here, no, no. This is not a proper place. Let us leave this vessel and repair to where more daring delights lie." His hands moved over his head, a complicated swirling movement that left behind a trial of fading amber light, like moving lights in a time-lapse picture.

There was an explosion of dull red light, and then the swirling trails had vanished.

So had Kirk, Spock, Dr. McCoy—and the creature that called itself Lucien.

Sulu stared at the blank places on the bridge. He walked to the spot where the ship's doctor had stood seconds before, moved his hands through the air over the place like a blind man searching for unknown things.

Uhura watched him, her face showing fear and bewilderment, while Arex sat motionless by the operative but still useless navigation console.

In a sense, they were still drifting in darkness . . .

Only a last word or two lingered in Sulu's mind, the last thing the goat-man had said before disappearing. Or were they words—or only meaningless nonsense syllables of an alien argot which his brain automatically arranged into human-sounding groups?

"Megas-tu . . ." the goat-man had said.

Kirk felt himself floating, floating. A globe turned slowly, patiently beneath him, came nearer. He saw that its red-and-white candy stripes were vast cloud formations. They were in constant motion crashing and rolling against one another, sometimes blending into various shades of pink, sometimes forming sharp lines between. Red battled white here as the sea battled the land on more familiar worlds.

They drifted further, closer—for he could see other shapes floating with him—and suddenly were within the banded atmosphere. The crimson and cream bands kept their color as he descended, and for the first time he saw what caused the redness. Miles-high storms of brilliant red dust and sand colored the clouds.

Then the surface became visible, an unstable, swirling chaos of constantly changing shape and form. Only occasional isolated hints of something solid beneath him indicated that this planet possessed a real surface. Even so, he felt there was nothing to prevent them from drifting right through that flowing "ground" until they came out the other side of the world.

As soon as he thought he had finally fixed a stable point

on the surface, it would break apart and dissolve into nothingness, or explode in a pinwheel of color.

Nothing was finite here; nothing was constant; nothing
was real. Even the air had color, the wind producing harsh
cries and strange slithering sounds as of creatures and cloth
brushing against one another.

The soul-filled breeze blew red-and-white particles into
miniature dust storms that twisted and writhed into insane
alien shapes.

In the midst of this anarchy, four people appeared.

Kirk was one of them, Spock and McCoy two others,
Lucien the fourth. The three officers immediately covered
their eyes. Until they had actually touched down the three
officers had seemed to be at once a part of and apart from
the elements. Now the wind had a chillness to it, and the
flying sand abraded unprotected flesh.

They shielded their faces as best they could and tried to
see around them. There was no discernable horizon. Lucien
stood nearby, impassive, waiting, watching.

"Spock, Bones—you all right?" Kirk managed to shout.
The sound of his own voice in this place was reassuring.

"Nothing more serious than a faceful of sand, Jim," Mc-
Coy responded. "But I wish I had a medical tricorder, just
to check in case we—" He broke off. Kirk turned, saw
through separated fingers that the doctor was staring at him.
That wasn't surprising; he found himself staring in fascination back at McCoy.

"Jim, look at yourself!"

Kirk felt no change—and yet there was something. He
looked at himself, as instructed, and saw fingers parting from
hands, hands from wrists, wrists from arms, and arms from
shoulders. All of his limbs were drifting away from the central torso, drifting away and changing shape. He saw his
trunk splitting up into neat, irregular blobs, still fully clothed.
There was no pain, merely the quiet astonishing sight of bits
of himself coming apart, like a jigsaw puzzle in water.

The same thing was happening to Spock and McCoy. Their
bodies were coming apart in toylike bits and pieces, floating
away from one another, sections of loose Spock mixing with
fragments of McCoy.

Little bits of the *Enterprise*'s first officer tumbled lazily past Kirk. The painless amputations were changing themselves, now stretching out like rubber, now growing thick and fat, as they wobbled along.

Spock stared in fascination as his left arm elongated and turned into a flowing rivulet of colored sand.

"Lucien, do something!" Kirk yelled.

"But why, Captain?" The goat-man shook his head pityingly, suddenly remembering. "Oh, very well. I'd forgotten how much bodily integrity means to you poor humans." Kirk noticed that the goat-man had also come apart, though it didn't appear to bother him.

A swirling cloud of dust formed one of Lucien's hands, fully equipped with a proper complement of fingers. It moved, and something like a neon pentagram appeared in the air, floating, glowing radiantly. There was a flash of brilliant crimson again—Lucien seemed fond of red, or perhaps that was simply the common color of manipulated energy here—from each point of the five-cornered shape. It was repeated once, twice, and twice again.

Five drifting globes of flame touched the free particles, squeezing them together, reshaping and rejoining the mixed forms and making them whole again.

Kirk saw his arms, legs, lower torso re-form, move, and join together again neatly and painlessly. Abruptly, the drifting flame winked out. The pentagram itself followed shortly, vanishing into the all-consuming wind.

Kirk reached down and cautiously felt himself. He pulled experimentally at his right wrist with his left—not altogether sure how he would react if the hand came off. Around him, the rest of the impossible world still remained shapeless, all rolling mists and roarings and whines arising out of nothingness.

Lucien sighed. Probably in deference to his guests, he had re-formed his own corpus. "This isn't easy, you know, holding us all together like this. It's not even natural."

"If you know as much about us as you claim to," said a much relieved McCoy, "you'll know that being in one piece is very natural where we come from."

"Really, Doctor?" Spock commented. "Personally, I find all this quite absorbing."

"Yes, but that's probably because you're not natural to begin with, Spock."

Suddenly, a pair of long green tentacles, like the arms of an octopus, appeared out of the coiling mists and brushed against the face of a startled Kirk. Instinctively, he jerked away, and they vanished.

"Look, Lucien," he began, as much to take his mind off the disturbing apparition as to obtain information, "or whatever you want to call yourself—I want to know why you brought us here." Even as he said the words he was fully aware that if the goat-man chose to ignore the question they could do nothing to compel him to answer.

It made no difference whether he was inclined to or not. Before their savior/captor could reply, a tremendous roaring sprang up like the wildest of hurricanes. A frenzied wind whipped up around them. It lifted Kirk and dashed him to the ground, which conveniently became soft sand beneath him just in time to cushion the impact.

Lucien frowned and made another of his cryptic gestures. Red and rose energy flashed from his fingertips. The hurricane wind died as abruptly as it had arisen. Lucien finished his complicated hand-weaving in the air.

Even as they watched, the landscape shimmered, altered, and began to take on form and substance. Then they were standing on a grassy knoll, complete with weeds, trees, and a running stream. The knoll was cloaked in heather and milkweed. Kirk became aware of a new figure standing next to him. He looked down.

A small goat-boy stared back at him. A dancing miniature whirlwind spun in his open palm—the hurricane which had just thrown Kirk so callously around. The toy tornado slowed, slowed, and became a child's top. It stopped and fell over in the boy's hand.

Lucien bestowed a mildly disapproving smile on the youngster. "Kids will play." The boy grinned back, clutched tightly at his top, and hurried off to the top of the knoll.

Kirk picked himself up off the grass, pulling up a small tuft of it as he rose, and examined the newly materialized growth. It looked and smelled like good old earth-type field clover. But he wouldn't have batted an eye if it had suddenly turned into a twelve-legged Denebian spider.

Lucien was still busy. He dropped his hands to his sides and brought them up slowly, trembling, toward the sky. The forest rose close around them in rhythm with his rising hands, everything from bushes and seedlings to mature trees.

There was a gap in the woods, and Lucien gestured toward it, pointing to a vast structure that one moment was kilometers away, the next, close enough to reach out and touch.

"Is this better, my friends? You must remember it has been a long, long time since I've associated with anything human. I hope memory serves well enough. I have tried to translate my world into symbols your minds can comprehend. I could have altered your minds to perceive mine, instead, but I seem to recall that you frown on such things."

No one claimed otherwise.

By then they were all gazing toward the gap in the trees, toward the now-near, now-distant city.

It was a fairyland of crystal and ceramic mosaic, of glass and free-sculpted metals—a fairyland into which the forest, by all laws of perspective, should have extended, yet did not.

On open streets, men and women and children walked through neatly paved ways, each person differently dressed, all elaborately caped and gowned.

"Welcome, my friends, to Megas-tu," Lucien declaimed happily. "Welcome to you, and you, and you." He said it proudly, like an old man showing off his favorite grandson.

Kirk turned from the incredible metropolis back to the goat-man. "And what is Megas-tu? I would have said a world, but I've seen too much in the past few hours, or weeks, or whatever the time-referent is here, to accept anything merely on what I see."

"It is merely that, Captain James Kirk. A world. A world that operates on rules different from those of your universe." He snapped the fingers of one hand, and they found themselves seated on the grass in front of a flowing brook.

Brocaded cloths were spread all around. Quantities of sweet-smelling food and drink showed from under the lids of bulging wicker baskets. It was all very beautiful and nice and horrifying.

Lucien noticed the ambivalent expressions of his guests, looked thoughtful. "Let me see . . . it takes a moment for me to remember some of your terms, you know. What is the word?'' He paused a moment, then brightened.

''Ah yes, magic. Our universe operates according to the precepts of what you superstitiously call magic. Our laws are not unrealistic—merely different.'' He plucked an apple from empty air, took a bite out of it, and caught another. He tossed it to McCoy.

The doctor caught it automatically. ''I know this is just a figment of my imagination, but—'' He took a sample nibble, smiled in approval.

''It is, as you see, quite real, Dr. McCoy,'' Lucien continued. ''Everything here is real, if you only try to see. For example . . .'' He seemed to search the deserted knoll for a moment, then gestured.

An intricately decorated tent decorated with cabalistic symbols appeared on the grass a short distance away. An attractive girl, as delicate as Chinese porcelain, moved to enter the tent. She paused at the entrance, which was opened by an old, wrinkled woman.

They were still too far away for the watchers from the *Enterprise* to overhear their conversation, but some kind of business transaction seemed to be taking place. After a few minutes of this, the old woman nodded and disappeared inside. She came out shortly thereafter holding a small stoppered bottle.

Lucien spoke while the two women—if such they really were—resumed their conversation. ''Beautiful, isn't she? But all our women are as young and appealing as they want to be. When anyone can be as lovely as her aesthetics demand, character soon takes over from vanity. Hence the potion-seller prefers a more traditional configuration. It makes for better business.

''To insure the man of her dreams, the young one seeks a slight edge.''

''Not a love potion?'' said the skeptical Kirk. ''There's nothing magical about that. It's just a question of chemistry.''

Lucien gave him an odd look. ''You must have made some progress in certain areas since I last visited your people, Captain.'' He gestured, and the tent scene vanished.

Another exchange was taking place off to their right, now,

on what should have been the empty top of the knoll. Two human shapes were conversing there. One was a tall, thin gentleman clad in flowing robes and a conical hat inscribed with mystic devices. He stood stroking his long white beard, deep in discussion with a manlike creature that sported a pair of wings and a traditionally gargoylish face.

After some minutes of this, the tall man in the robes turned and gestured with his hands. There was a by-now familiar crackling in the air, and sparks of loose energy grew from nothingness. They lengthened, joined together, forming beams and walls and ceilings.

The clashing colors coalesced into four solid uprights. Gesturing and prancing all the while, the oldster danced around them, solidifying the small building. It rose lithe, delicate, with high ornamental spires and turrets and smooth polished domes.

Eventually the robed dancer came to a halt. Hands on hips, he studied the finished project, then nodded in satisfaction at his completed handiwork. A last gesture, and a sign appeared over the entrance to the compact castle, the inscription in an unknown calligraphy.

"Do you need a home?" asked Lucien. "A stable, a town? Stop in and visit your friendly sorcerer-contractor. Let him do the hard work."

"Sorcerer," Spock muttered. "Of course. Federation scientists were more correct than they suspected. In order to function, any supranormal spatial phenomenon must extend through known space and time to another dimensional plane.

"The interaction of interdimensional forces supplies the energy to produce new galactic matter. It explains not only our expanding universe, but also why the physical laws here differ so completely from our own."

"I'm not sure I follow all that, Spock, but are you saying you believe in magic?"

Spock looked back at him unwaveringly. "I believe in what is logical and what follows from observable facts, Doctor. The basic laws here appear to be what we sometimes call 'magic.' The *Enterprise* does not operate according to these principles, therefore it ceased to function. And so, almost, did we."

"So you used magic," guessed Kirk, turning to face Lucien, "to get our ship working again."

"It was the natural thing to do, Captain. You could have done it yourself, with a little instruction. But then, few of you humans ever bothered to become proficient at magic." He frowned slightly. "Those among you who did were not looked upon with favor. Some of you even managed to reach all the way through to Megas-tu through small interdimensional vortices."

"All the way from Earth to here?" exclaimed a cynical McCoy. "Impossible."

"Distances in our universe do not operate according to your laws, either, Doctor," Lucien told him. "By our methods of reckoning, certain parts of Earth are right next door."

"Lucien," interrupted Kirk, suddenly serious, "you persist in calling us friends, implying that you know us. Even more, that we should know you. But how?"

"Ah, Captain, Captain!" The goat-man leaned back on the grass and rested his head in his hands, staring at the blue sky. "To feign such ignorance with *me*. Still, it *was* always one of my problems." He stopped, and Kirk got the impression he had somehow hurt the goat-man's feelings.

Lucien crawled forward then and swept his hand through the clear surface of the brook. His fingers broke the water once and withdrew.

"Listen, look, I'll try to explain further."

The ripples stilled. Colors began to appear, staining the clearness. Shapes started to form, and soon it was like looking into a viewsceen. Gone completely was the sandy bottom of the stream. In its place they saw a broad panorama of men and women—Megans—exotic and familiar, chiseled handsome and intentionally plain, all sitting lost in contemplation amid the howling chaos that was the real surface of Megas-tu.

"This may seem to you humans to be a world of insanity and instability," declared Lucien. "But it has the quality of change we all demand. My people are calm and contented, each one existing in the world of his or her imagination."

The image in the screen blurred, changed, and Kirk and his companions had again a view of the Megan universe as they first encountered it, a riot of blending colors and splinters of stellar shape.

"There are no rivals in our little universe at all, Captain Kirk. No other life-forms save ourselves." The picture jumped again, and they were back on Megas-tu. As they watched, the people in the stream-picture stood together, and some of them began to rise upward, free of the planet.

"Millennia ago," Lucien continued, "in our search for companionship, we Megans passed through the various gates between dimensions, including the great vortex you entered by.

"Eventually, on one such expedition, we discovered," and the scene shifted again as if anticipating his words, "your world—Earth." They now saw a view of the blue-white globe of Terra, seen from space. Kirk felt an unexpected quickening. He had been away from home for too long.

"Wherever we went we became friends and advisors to mankind. To help your ancestors out of their misery and ignorance we drew as best we could on the power left behind in our own universe, bringing it in through tiny gates." Hands stirred the water again, and ripples blotted out the blue-white ball.

When the stream had stilled once more, Kirk saw only the sandy bottom and a couple of dreamlike shadows cast by small fish.

Lucien sat back and shook the droplets from his hand. "Eventually we were forced to leave," he concluded. "It was a group decision. For myself, I wanted to stay. Ah, how I fought, how I argued! You see, I was the generalist, the apologist among specialists."

"The troublemaker, the others said. But I'd grown to love Earth and its unpredictable, funny people." He saw visions of the past. "Those were the days . . . you crazy, irrational humans." He looked over at them.

"But now you have come back to me. It is so good to see you again." He leaped to his feet, a gesture of pure joy, and sprang into a hectic, prancing dance, to the accompaniment of a cheerful piping that seemed to come from all around them.

The music was infectious, and Kirk found himself smiling

as he spoke. "If you Megans enjoyed Earth so much, why did you leave it? I don't understand . . ."

"Captain, good Captain, always so curious, always there must be a reason," the dancing Lucien laughed. "Another reason why I liked you humans so much. The vortex knows you have many special qualities—and special faults."

He took a giant leap and whirled in the air, performing an outrageous multiple pirouette that carried him to the tops of the highest trees . . . where he froze motionless. There was a new note in his voice when he spoke, a hint of concern, of worry, that was alien to the Lucien they had started to know.

"No." The piping melody faded into silence, and he was down at their side again in a second. His boyish pleasure had turned desperately serious.

"You must go."

"What is it?" asked a nervous McCoy. "What's wrong?"

"I cannot tell you just now. But you must return to your vessel immediately. And quiet, be quiet about it. You must not give your presence away."

Kirk tried for elaboration, but Lucien was already gesturing again. A rainbow haze blurred Kirk's vision, and he felt himself rising, rising and dissolving . . .

Scott, Sulu and Uhura were clustered anxiously on the bridge, all crowded around the main navigation console where Arex was struggling to make some sense out of the computer readouts. Their study was shattered by a sudden crackling behind them, and they turned quickly.

Pulsing with vast power held carefully in check, a red-and-white cloud appeared in the center of the bridge. It broke into three smaller clouds, which gradually contracted into the shapes of Kirk, McCoy, and Spock.

Everyone on the bridge rushed forward to the returned officers, all trying to speak at once.

"Captain Kirk . . . what happened? . . . where were you all? . . . given you up, Mr. Spock . . ."

"One at a time, one at a time," Kirk admonished them, making calming motions. "We're . . . we're all right." He took a deep breath, looked around him.

They were back on the *Enterprise*, and it had never looked quite so good. After the mad maelstrom below, the clean lines of the bridge were reassuring—even if they held their shape only through Lucien's will. And it was good to be back among *real* people again. Though the look in Uhura's eyes . . .

"Status report, first."

"Everythin's okay, it seems, Captain. All systems except the warp-engines are workin' perfectly, and I can have them operatin' in two or three hours. But you . . ."

"The only thing that's wrong with me, Mr. Scott, is that I'm still badly confused by a number of things."

"You've got plenty of company, Jim," McCoy noted. "What did Lucien mean, we're not to 'give ourselves away'? Give ourselves away to whom? Couldn't anyone else on Megas-tu detect us up here? I would think we kind of stand out."

"They'd need mighty powerful scanners to find us now," said Scott, who was ignorant of the realities of Megas. "See that?" He indicated the main viewscreen.

A thick layer of dense, particle-laden material now lay like luminescent gray smoke between the *Enterprise* and the surface, blotting out the red-and-white clouds below them.

"It's somethin' like a big dust cloud, Captain," said Scott, "and yet it's different. Been between us and the surface ever since you disappeared. Communicator and scanner beams wouldn't penetrate . . . we tried." Kirk swiveled to face the library station.

"If it was Lucien who put it there, Captain," Spock mused, "the question then becomes . . . why is he hiding us? What danger are we in from something on his world?" Kirk nodded, turned back to his chief engineer.

"Weapon's status, Mr. Scott? It seems we may have to be ready to defend ourselves."

"Then it'll have to be with fast talk, Captain. Our phaser banks and defensive screens require at least a partial powering-up of the warp-drive engines. Give me a few hours and I might be able to say different."

"Do the best you can, Scotty." Kirk's voice dropped to a murmur. "We can't defend ourselves and we can't run away. And we don't even know what it is we might have to fight. So," and he clapped both hands firmly to the arms of the command chair, "we wait."

"And do what?" wondered McCoy aloud. "Lucien may not show up again for three hundred years, our time. By then, I might be an old man."

"I have an interesting idea," proposed a calm voice. They all turned their attention to Spock. "Captain, I think it would be best to first try this in private. If you will accompany me to my quarters? And Dr. McCoy as well?"

"What have you got in mind, Spock?"

"Something in the nature of an experiment, Captain. It may prove quite interesting. And if we are fortunate, practical as well."

The door slid quietly aside as the three officers entered Spock's spacious room. Kirk and McCoy watched as Spock moved to his desk and fished out a thick, white marking stylus. He waved them to one side.

"A little room, please, gentlemen." They stepped back and stood against the far wall.

While they watched with growing curiosity, Spock proceeded to sketch a rough pentagram on the smooth floor, erasing one arm and redrawing it when it seemed too much longer than the others. Kirk and McCoy recognized the pentagram shape, something that made no sense in connection with Spock. The latter clarified his actions as soon as the diagram was finished.

"Not being a logical corollary of physics, magic was never subjected to quite the serious study on Vulcan as it received on Earth. No doubt the actions of visiting Megans lent it somewhat more credibility on your world. Some of your more credulous philosophers—or more perceptive—went as far as to attempt to codify the most formal principles of the so-called 'dark arts.' In the course of my readings on Earth I had occasion to encounter much information of this sort." He got to his feet, gazed thoughtfully down at the pentagram.

"I believe this is one of the most important and basic mystical symbols described by the terran 'magicians.' I observed Lucien utilizing the same device earlier." Kirk began to see where Spock was heading.

"Lucien did say something to the effect that we could master the same techniques," Kirk pondered. "Spock, you're saying that as long as we're in this universe, we can 'work' magic, too?"

"One must always be prepared to employ the resources at hand, Captain." He hesitated. "Although I must confess it requires considerable effort for me to readjust my thinking along such lines." He walked into the center of the pentagram.

"Watch there, now." He pointed toward his desk. An elaborate three-dimensional maze laden with double-toned crystal pieces sat on one end.

"I will attempt to move one of the Vulcan chess pieces using only magic—magic in our universe, but what should merely be the proper utilization of a local scientific principle."

"But how can you, Spock?" McCoy objected. "I mean, you don't know the words, or the proper gestures, or—"

"It should be the mental state that counts, Doctor. And I have the terran magical principles to use for a base." He gestured for quiet, assumed a stance of deep concentration.

Stretching out his arms toward the table, he began to speak. "May the energy of this universe be the power in me." Kirk and McCoy stared expectantly, hopefully, at the chess set. There was no hint of movement.

"Forget it, Spock," advised McCoy after several minutes of intense concentration on the first officer's part had proven ineffectual. "It won't work."

Spock lowered his arms slightly and opened his eyes. "It *has* to work, Doctor. It is logical it should work—here." He closed his eyes halfway and tried again.

"I draw on your energy . . . I know I can. I *believe* I can. For every action, yea, let there be an equal and opposite reaction."

There was a sudden crackling in the air. McCoy jumped halfway out of his regulation boots. Yellow and black fire flashed around Spock's body. A thin sliver of energy leaped from one of his hands to the table.

It touched a Vulcan rook, enveloped it in yellow flame, and moved it three spaces forward. Kirk smiled.

"Well now. Let me try that, Spock." Spock obligingly stepped out of the pentagram and let Kirk take his place.

He raised his arms hesitantly toward the table, looked over at his first officer for reassurance. "This feels ridiculous, Mr. Spock."

"The important thing is to relax and concentrate, Captain. I think the physical gesture is purely supplementary . . . a psychological crutch. Merely a way of helping the mind focus thought. Like talking out loud."

"Now really, Jim," began McCoy. "You can't expect to fully duplicate . . ."

McCoy was cut off by the rumble of a small thunderclap echoing through the room. But the doctor was right. Kirk could not duplicate Spock's results . . . exactly.

The colors that flashed around him were not yellow and black, but blue and green, sea-color fire. One fringe of it nudged a bishop two spaces, then lifted and dropped it down a level.

"Good move, Captain," commented Spock idly. Kirk dropped his arms and stared at the chessboard, still not quite able to believe he had done it.

Sudden enthusiasm replaced McCoy's skepticism. "Wait a minute now—it's my turn."

"Only two at a time can play the game, Doctor. I believe we can find other, more interesting uses, for this extraordinary ability. With a little practice, it should be possible to control the local energy flow without the use of clumsy inscribed symbols such as this pentagram."

The demonstration that Kirk, Spock, and McCoy gave on the bridge caused the expected sensation, but the surprise and shock soon gave way to delight as Sulu, Uhura, and the others discovered they too could manipulate the Megan magic.

Not having a chess set handy, they followed Spock's suggestion and practiced with the bridge instrumentation. Kirk discovered that he was able to activate or deactivate the main viewscreen with a simple gesture. But he could not work the magnification controls. Apparently the more delicate the instrument, the finer one's grasp of the energies involved had to be.

"Hey, where's Scotty?" asked McCoy suddenly, looking around the bridge.

"I think he headed up to the recreation room on B deck," Sulu replied absently. He was making elaborate twisting movements, but so far had achieved nothing more than a floating cloud of writhing energy a meter in front of his hands.

"Now what do you think he'd want in there, do you suppose?" wondered Kirk.

Scott surveyed the recreation room to make certain it was empty. Then he moved to the unit games dispenser and requested a normal tennis ball. But he didn't go through the door leading to the indoor court.

Instead, he made a number of swinging, swerving gestures with both hands. Energy appeared out of air and formed a glowing nimbus around the ball. It was abruptly sucked up by the spheroid, acting as a vacuum. The ball quivered as Scott concentrated on it, then dropped to the floor, bounced once and ricocheted off the far wall.

Beautifully executed—except Scott had overlooked one small factor. The ball was moving at about a hundred kilometers an hour, and showed no sign of slowing down.

It struck the roof and rocketed toward Scott. Showing some impressive speed of his own, the chief engineer dove under a nearby game table. The ball contacted the floor near his left foot, shot across the room, hit the far wall, bounced back up to the ceiling, the floor again, across the room—and it appeared to be picking *up* speed.

Seconds later it whizzed past his head, and Scott hurriedly covered his face with his hands. Crouched in that awkward position he wiggled his fingers desperately. It had not the slightest effect on the ball, which continued to whizz around the room like a runaway warp-engine. It was now moving so fast Scott could see it only as a weak blur.

Scottish magic can be very strong.

Back up on the bridge, Sulu had assumed a look of grim determination. He made a last, twisting thrust at the drifting ball of energy he had conjured up. Abruptly it darkened, coalesced, and formed into the most beautiful girl in this or any other universe.

He had been expecting it all along—the helmsman was a positive thinker. He moved forward, arms extended to embrace her . . . but when his lips touched, the image dissolved.

"I've heard of devastating kissers," said the watching McCoy, "but don't you think that's overdoing it a little, Sulu?"

"Very funny, Doctor." Sulu moved his hands again, slowly constructing another human shape out of colored fire.

The officers of the *Enterprise* continued to practice their new-found talents. Eventually Kirk found that he could make the viewscreen do just about anything it could do in normal space-time, only here he did not have to touch a single control.

On B-deck, the whining ball finally came to a sudden halt. Scott looked out warily from under the table. First the covering and finally the interior material had disintegrated—shredded by sheer speed. But not before the ball had managed to put some respectable dents in the metal walls.

Eyeing the now defunct remnants of the ball with respect, he moved back to the games producer . . . and ordered a set of checkers. This time he would practice with something a little less lethal.

Sulu was sweating with effort and had managed to generate another girl. He leaned toward her again. This time his curious audience included several other members of the bridge complement, who had left off their own practicing to watch him.

"Good luck," Uhura volunteered.

Sulu kissed the apparition . . . and the girl's arms went around him as she kissed back. His eyes bugged in surprise. That he hadn't expected. But he recovered quickly, returned the kiss with fervor—too much fervor. The energy-waif burst into little match-flares and was gone.

Sulu was prepared to try yet a third time, but a red-and-white cloud suddenly filled the center of the bridge. It faded, and once more Lucien stood among them. But this time he was not grinning or dancing. In fact, he looked agitated and upset.

"What are you doing?" He gazed around in anxious confusion. Kirk looked back at him.

"Learning to protect ourselves, Lucien."

"Protect yourselves? Is that all human beings ever think about—fighting? I'll take care of you. That's what friends are for." He started pacing back and forth.

"I don't know . . . I just don't know. All this mental energy you've been using. Your peculiar patterns . . . it can be traced, you know. You might be found."

A voice thunderous enough to dwarf Lucien's suddenly filled the bridge, accompanied by the whistling, howling, spine-twisting moans of the real, uncontrolled Megas-tu.

"HAVE BEEN FOUND!" It rumbled.

Lucien halted in mid-step. Kirk was startled to see something very like fear appear in the face of the up to now omnipotent goat-man. For the first time it occurred to Kirk that Lucien might not have exceptional powers among his own kind.

He didn't care to think what sort of being might.

But it seemed they were about to find out.

A new cloud of colors began to form on the bridge. There was more of the fiery black this time—yellow, white, electric blues and orange, swirling and re-forming and curling; all the slithery nightmare shapes of the world below seemed present in that cloud.

A scare-thing, all crooked teeth and bulging eyes, grew out of the floor in front of Lucien. It blended back into the cloud as Uhura screamed.

"SO THE PEOPLE OF EARTH WOULD SPREAD THEIR EVILS EVEN UNTO OUR HOME? WE ARE READY THIS TIME FOR HUMAN PERFIDY. THIS TIME IT IS THE HUMANS WHO SHALL SUFFER . . . FOR HERE OUR POWER IS ABSOLUTE."

"THE HUMANS . . . AND YOU, LUCIEN," and the voice mocked the goat-man, "SHALL BE THE ONES TO PAY." It rose to a bansheelike wail on the last syllable, and stopped.

There was a powerful wrench, a jerk, and everyone had to grab quickly at something fixed to keep from being thrown to the deck. Kirk's gaze went immediately to the viewscreen.

The glowing gray cloud that had blocked them off from the planet had vanished. The *Enterprise* was dropping like a rock toward the angry surface below. It seemed certain they were going to smash to splinters on the packed sands, but the starship suddenly slowed, touched the ground awkwardly. A howling storm of rainbow-colored rain began to pour into the ship.

It was followed by fiery hailstones that rained down upon them as though the hull didn't exist. Everyone was knocked to the floor, including Lucien.

"Keep calm!" Kirk yelled dazedly, above the rattle of strangely soft hailstones.

An ominous rumbling sounded, and the *Enterprise* started to shake . . . slowly at first, then rapidly, until Kirk felt like an ingredient in a cake mix.

A shattering crack sounded, and the *Enterprise* split neatly down the middle, like a grape. Then the two halves of the starship started to change shape, to break up as Kirk, Spock, and McCoy had broken up at their first touch-down on Megas-tu. Smaller and smaller pieces detached and broke away, floating off into the screaming winds.

But this time the re-forming was different. The floating bits of *Enterprise* regrouped to form, not the starship, but buildings—buildings lining a street that looked much like an old terran village. Very old.

"Seventeenth century," mumbled Kirk as he rematerialized. He felt himself caught in an awkward bent-over position, his hands fixed up by his ears. He was fixed, he saw, in an ancient wooden device. Looking to his left, right, and across the street, he saw the entire crew of the *Enterprise*, set into similar stocks.

Row on row of the T-post structures faded into distant haze. Scott was trapped close by, as were Spock, McCoy, and Lucien. Kirk seemed to be at one end of the long line of imprisoned crew.

He turned his head to the right. There was a crudely engraved sign set in the ground beside a gnarled old oak.

SALEM, MASS., the sign said. It keyed no response in Kirk.

The world shimmered and dissolved again. Once more Kirk felt himself pulled lazily apart, re-formed. Town and crew vanished. Dust walls formed around him, mortared with flickering bursts of energy.

Higher and higher the walls rose, solidifying into a huge, aged meeting hall, obviously terran in origin. But the scale was wrong. The room was big . . . much too big.

He was still bound in the wooden stocks, but a bench had been produced to sit on. He looked around once more and found Spock staring back at him.

"I know, Mr. Spock. Sixteenth- or seventeenth-century terran architecture, I'd guess—with the size all out of proportion."

Spock tried to turn his head toward the Captain. "I saw

the sign, also. If I recall your history correctly, Salem was a small town on the east coast of the North American continent. As for the date, I should guess approximately 1691.''

" 'Approximately'?'' echoed Kirk. "Why 1691?''

The first officer didn't reply. Instead, he concentrated on the seemingly endless tiers of seats facing them, seats that extended back and up to absurd distances. Perspective as well as proportion seemed distorted here.

The seats were beginning to fill with men and women, all clad in costumes of the same period as the hall.

Since everyone in the stocks was a member of the ship's crew, excepting Lucien, both Kirk and Spock concluded quickly that those filling the endless balcony were the Megans themselves. The reason for taking on human shape seemed obvious. The reason for the particular period costumes did not.

There were hundreds, then thousands of them, and still they poured in, becoming tiny with increasing distance. Even so, Kirk found he could distinguish those in the furthest rows with perfect clarity. It made no sense—but he was beginning to accept such things as normal for Megas-tu.

The arrivals were talking solemnly among themselves. But when the last, uppermost seat had been filled, the buzz of low conversation died as if on signal.

A pause, and then a brilliant flare of light in the center of the room, before the first stocks. A last Megan appeared there, in human form. A tall, glowering man, wearing a wide-brimmed black hat.

The man surveyed the crew of the *Enterprise*, pinioned tightly in their wooden restraints, then turned to the watching Megans. His voice was deep, powerful . . . and familiar.

It was the voice that had erupted on the bridge only moments . . . days, years . . . before.

"WE ARE GATHERED HERE TODAY, GOOD CITIZENS, TO SEE JUSTICE DONE. YOU MUST BE THE JUDGES. THESE . . . '' and he indicated those in the stocks, "ARE THE DEFENDANTS.

"AS REPRESENTATIVES OF THE VILEST SPECIES IN THE UNIVERSE . . . TRECHEROUS HUMANITY . . . THEY ARE TO BE JUDGED.'' He moved forward and stopped to stare grimly down at Lucien. ". . . AND THOSE WHO WOULD AID THEM.''
He turned away.

"AS SPECIALIST IN THE ETHICS OF MAGIC, I HAVE BEEN APPOINTED PROSECUTOR HERE." He started a complicated gesture, but Kirk, fighting with the unyielding wood, interrupted.

"If this is a trial, I think we've got the right to know what you're already so convinced we've done."

The tall Prosecutor, who could have obliterated Kirk in a burst of yellow flame, nodded in agreement. He pointed toward Lucien.

"HAS THIS ONE NOT TOLD YOU HOW WE VISITED EARTH, AND WHAT WAS DONE TO US THERE?"

"Lucien said only that you came as wise men, wizards who . . ."

The Prosecutor leaned forward, shaking an angry fist.

"THEN HEAR THIS. ONCE, UPON YOUR WORLD, I WAS KNOWN AS ASMODEUS, WHO SEES ALL. GAZE UPON MY COUNTENANCE, SO THAT YOU, TOO, MAY KNOW THE TRUTH."

And the Prosecutor's face started to come apart. It expanded, flattened, became a swirling rectangular screen. A picture formed in it, the picture of the insane galaxy that roiled around Megas-tu.

Colors died to black, changed, and the view turned to one of breathtakingly normal space—space-black flecked with the brilliant points of distant stars.

Changed again, to a picture of Earth. Moved in close, closer. The Prosecutor spoke as various sequences appeared and played themselves out on the facial screen.

The first scenes depicted Megans in human guise engaged in numerous daily activities—as witches, sorcerers, and warlocks.

"WE CAME TO YOUR WORLD AS FRIENDS," the Prosecutor's voice boomed, "BUT WHEREVER WE WENT, THE STORY INVARIABLY HAD THE SAME ENDING. SOME HUMANS WOULD ATTEMPT TO USE US TO GAIN POWER, TO SERVE THEIR OWN GREED AND LUST. AND IN OUR IGNORANCE OF HUMAN WAYS, WE SOMETIMES FELL PARTY TO THESE SUBTLE INIQUITIES.

"WHEN WE DISCOVERED SUCH VENALITY AND REFUSED TO SERVE SUCH MEN, THEY TURNED THE PEOPLE AGAINST US, TAUGHT THE COMMON FOLK TO FEAR AND HATE US.

"SINCE OUR POWER IN YOUR UNIVERSE IS LIMITED, WE WERE VULNERABLE." The view changed to show Megans being driven from towns by the fearful populace, spat upon and reviled.

"THEY CALLED US DEVILS, DEMONS, CONJURERS!" the voice declaimed, rising to a shout. As it did so, the facial screen shattered into a thousand flickering particles, which faded back to nothingness.

The face of the Prosecutor reappeared.

"THOSE OF US WHO SURVIVED THESE EARLY PURGES," he continued, "DECIDED TO MAKE ONE FINAL ATTEMPT TO SECURE A HELPING COLONY ON YOUR WORLD. THEY GATHERED IN THE SMALL TOWN OF SALEM, MASSACHUSETTS.

"THERE, THOSE OF US WHO WERE LEFT DISCOVERED THAT IN TRYING TO LEARN YOUR WAYS, TO BLEND IN WITH YOU, WE HAD FORGOTTEN MUCH KNOWLEDGE. EVEN SO, WE TRIED TO HELP YOU IN THIS NEWLY SETTLED LAND, BUT . . . "

"You made mistakes," guessed Spock.

"IT IS TRUE THERE WERE OCCASIONS WHEN WE USED OUR POWERS AWKWARDLY, AND MANY OF US SUFFERED AS A RESULT OF IT. SOME OF US . . . BURNED FOR IT. BURNED! AS WITCHES."

Kirk nodded sadly. The significance of Salem had come back to him.

"WE GATHERED THE SURVIVORS OF OUR SETTLEMENT OUTSIDE THE TOWN, AND TRIED TO RECALL ENOUGH MEGAN KNOWLEDGE TO RETURN TO OUR OWN UNIVERSE, TO LEAVE YOUR HELLISH WORLD. TO RETURN TO SAFETY, COMFORT, REASON . . . "

"And loneliness," put in Lucien, "and fear, and . . ."

"SHOULD WE NOT FEAR THE EARTHLINGS?" the Prosecutor insisted. "SHOULD WE NOT FEAR THE CRUELTY OF SUCH MINDLESS PRIMITIVES? CONSIDER THE WEAPONS THEY HAVE MASTERED, AND MISUSED, SINCE WE LEFT. NEVER SINCE HAVE WE ATTEMPTED TO EXPLORE YOUR UNIVERSE," he informed them, directing his attention to Kirk and Spock.

"NEVER SINCE HAVE WE SOUGHT OUTSIDE COMPANIONSHIP, TO IMPOSE OUR HELP ON THOSE WHOSE CREEDS ARE SUPERSTITION, GREED, AND TERROR. YET, DESPITE OUR CAUTION, YOU HAVE COME HERE, TO OUR VERY HOME."

"If one Federation ship can find us, so can others," Lucien whispered to Kirk. "That is what they fear."

The Prosecutor appeared to lose some of his antagonism. In fact, his thunder now held a surprising note of sadness.

"WE DO NOT WANT TO DO THIS, CAPTAIN KIRK. WE DO NOT WANT TO HARM YOU. THE NATURE OF OUR UNIVERSE IS ONE OF CONSTANT CHANGE, EVERYTHING IS TRANSITORY. SO ARE OUR GRUDGES. WE HAVE NEVER HAD TO HURT ANYONE BEFORE.

"IF THERE WERE SOME TRUE REASON NOT TO . . ." He turned, gazed back at the uncounted thousands who filled the distorted tiers of the hall. "WHO WILL SPEAK IN DEFENSE OF MANKIND? WHO?"

A slight whisper of bodies shifting on wooden seats was the only reply.

A familiar voice on Kirk's left broke the silence. "I will, Asmodeus. I am only partly of Earth." The Prosecutor moved near, seemed to inspect Spock.

" 'TIS TRUE ENOUGH. YOU ARE DIFFERENT. IF NONE OBJECT . . . " He looked back at the crowd. Still-silence still.

"THE COURT WILL THEN HEAR A DEFENSE." A casual gesture and Spock's stocks became so much sawdust.

The first officer stumbled on cramped legs at the sudden disappearance of the bonds. Then he straightened, rubbing at ankles and wrists.

"I have had no time to prepare a formal defense. I therefore request the court recess until . . ."

"RECESSS DENIEDDDD . . ." came a haunting moan from the gallery.

Spock didn't let any distress he may have felt at this unanimous rejection show. "I shall have to make do with the testimony of witnesses, then." The Prosecutor showed no inclination to offer any aid.

"I call Lucien as my first witness."

A second flare of released energy and Lucien's stocks, too, vanished. Spock moved to stand in front of him. "Lucien, of all the Megans, you alone do not seem to fear or hate humans. On the contrary, you appear to like them very much. Why?"

"Because I'm a glutton for punishment," the goat-man replied, grinning. "No, this is not the time for levity, I suppose. I will try to be serious, though it's hard for me." He considered thoughtfully.

"I expect it's because they're so much like me, or I like them. Always questions to be answered! Like a child who continually questions his father, only to be asked, 'Must there always be a reason for everything?' They are like that rare child who stares defiantly back up and says, 'yes!'

"I, too, am like that. And they have minds that never cease ranging outward, always seeking, striving to expand their store of knowledge . . . for knowledge's sake and not always for greed, as has been implied.

"It is these things that make them unique and endears them to me. But with us, it is different. Every Megan is always alone, always existing self-confident, assured, in a singular sphere of certainty, whereas humans, for all their vaunted individuality, are a true gregarious society. It seems to be something I need, this group association."

He started to pace back and forth before the first row of benches, glancing occasionally upward and back into the higher balconies.

"As you know, I was among the first to go among them. In Mesopotamia, Ur, Babylonia, Greece. In the river valleys of the Hwang and the Indus, I saw these bonds developing between them. An easy companionship that Megas-tu has never known and, sadly, can never know.

"I meant to help and change them, and ended by having them change me." He turned to look at Spock. "That's why I adopted you when you arrived. It was another chance to recover something I'd . . . lost."

"Thank you, Lucien," said a satisfied Spock. "One other witness, if you please. Captain James T. Kirk."

Flare-dissolve, and Kirk's stocks became a comfortable wooden chair.

"Tell the court, Captain. Would you say that humans have not changed since the time of Salem?"

Kirk was startled at how easily the words came, how relaxed he was, considering the gravity of the situation. "I think that we've been trying to, Spock. A little at a time.

"The certain virtues of humanity, which Lucien has elaborated on so flatteringly, go hand in hand with our faults— greed, envy, fear. We've learned a great deal about ourselves in the centuries since the witch trials. We try to understand

and respect each other, no matter what a man's peculiarities. We try to understand and respect all life forms.

"And the human race has adopted a motto, a standard that at the time of Salem was only a dream in the minds of a few enlightened men." His own voice rose.

"KNOWLEDGE IS FREEDOM."

"Indeed, Captain," Spock agreed, speaking quietly into the resultant silence. "Could you elaborate on these new standards of man?"

Kirk stood, faced the endless gallery. "The records of the *Enterprise* are open for your inspection, citizens of Megas-tu. We couldn't hide them from you or alter them now even if we wished to.

"All the history of Earth and its Federation of worlds is at your disposal. Look at it . . . look at general order number one: *No starship may interfere with the normal development of any alien life form or society, whether advanced or primitive!*

"Even requests for aid by dying primitives are often frowned upon, in the belief that interference from outside often does more harm than good. Compare that with the Earth you once knew. And you may also compare—"

"ENOUGH!" The voice of the Megan Prosecutor rumbled through the pastel pit of the hall. A sparkling, whirling cloud formed in the center of the gallery, breaking up into tiny cloud-fragments. These shrank to become the entire records section of the *Enterprise*.

It hovered there . . . tapes, computer inserts, kilometers of microfilm. A gust of wind rose and scattered the knowledge like leaves across the thousands of benches, tumbling in and around the intent Megans.

"HERE IS YOUR HISTORY, HERE ARE YOUR RECORDS . . . EXHIBIT A FOR THE DEFENSE!" The Prosecutor gestured yet again. The blowing tapes and cassettes vanished once more.

"YOU HAVE HEARD AND YOU HAVE SEEN AND YOU KNOW," the Prosecutor told the vast chamber. "CITIZENS . . . HOW DECIDE YOU?" He went silent, his attitude one of intense concentration.

Kirk and Spock and the others also strained to hear, but it was as still as the inside of a cave. Whatever discussion was taking place could not be detected by mere human senses.

Oddly, Kirk found himself musing on the fact, not that his life and the lives of his crew lay in the balance, but that he had not had anything to eat since Lucien's picnic. He was getting hungry.

The concerns of the human body are not philosophical in nature.

"A DECISION HAS BEEN MADE, CAPTAIN JAMES KIRK." He forgot about food and leaned forward.

"IT IS YOUR ASTROPHYSICS SECTION AND NOT THE HISTORICAL ONE THAT IS THE DECIDING FACTOR. ACCORDING TO THOSE RECORDS, YOUR ENTRY HERE TRULY WAS AN ACCIDENT OF EXPLORATION—AND ONE UNLIKELY TO BE SAFELY DUPLICATED.

"WITH THAT IN MIND, ADDED TO THE NEW EVIDENCE IN FAVOR OF MAN WHICH HAS BEEN PRESENTED, IT WOULD SEEM THAT WE OF MEGAS-TU ARE SAFE." He paused and his expression grew dark—literally.

"BUT LUCIEN MUST BE PUNISHED! FOR HIS BETRAYAL OF HIS PEOPLE AND THE DANGER HE HAS EXPOSED US TO. HE WHO WISHES COMPANIONSHIP SHALL BE CONFINED IN LIMBO FOR ALL ETERNITY!"

At those fateful final words a bubble of transparent red suddenly enveloped the goat-man. It pulsed softly with evidence of great power held under careful control. Without thinking, Kirk left his chair and rushed to the bubble's side.

"No—you can't. To isolate someone like Lucien—that's worse than sentencing him to death."

The voice of the Prosecutor rose in volume and shrillness. "DO YOU KNOW WHOM YOU DEFEND? DO YOU KNOW WHOSE COMFORT YOU SEEK? HE HAS TOLD YOU HIS NAME IS LUCIEN. WOULD YOU DEFEND HIM STILL IF YOU KNEW HIM BY ANOTHER NAME?

"INDEED IT WAS HE WHO WENT AMONG YOU AND SOUGHT YOUR FRIENDSHIP!" the voice laughed. "INDEED IT WAS HE WHO WORKED HIS MAGIC FOR YOU, IN HIS OWN WAYS. NO, IT SHALL NO LONGER BE.

"DOWN, LUCIFER!"

The goat-man leaned against the thin, impregnable walls of the bubble. Orange fire flared around his palms, terrible, all-destroying. But they could not break that shell. It started to rise.

Kirk's voice, when he had recovered from the initial shock of recognition and could speak again, was steady and determined.

"We're not interested in the remnants of legend and superstition, Prosecutor. I'd said we'd given such things up. He's a living, sentient being, an intelligent life form, and he helped us. That's all I have to know about him. We'll not stand by and see him harmed for our past mistakes."

The Prosecutor gestured. A smoke-ring of blue energy appeared in the room and started to float toward Kirk. He twisted out of its way, and it changed direction like a thinking creature, pursuing him.

"SUBMIT TO THIS DECISION AND GO FREE, CAPTAIN. YOU HAVEN'T THE POWER TO FIGHT US."

"Captain!" urged Spock. "Use the magic you know." Kirk dodged around the base of the rising red bubble, the ring following. Suddenly, it looked as if he too were beginning to glow.

Little sparks and flashes of blue-green energy flickered and played around his body. Eyes a little drunk, he turned and gestured. A ball of green flame spun toward the Prosecutor.

A blazing fire appeared over him, feeding on nothing. It started to descend. Kirk made another gesture, shouted, "Powers of Earth and Sky, Appear! An extreme low pressure system has been detected moving north-northeast!"

Thunder boomed, miniature lightning crackled, and a howling rainstorm drenched the chamber, putting out the lowering fire.

There was a smattering of applause from the gallery.

The scene began to flutter and change constantly, like a dance viewed under intermittent strobe light, as Kirk and the Prosecutor exchanged gestures.

One moment they were standing in a street of Salem Town—then they were back on the naked surface of Megastu. A raging sandstorm swallowed them up.

"High humidity and dampness!" Kirk intoned reverently as the abrasive sand tore at him. "Deciduous foliage marked by high rainfall . . . !"

Desert turned to jungle. But the Prosecutor was already counter-gesturing, and the jungle melted into deep blue ocean, the tops of trees turning into wave crests.

Kirk choked as he took in a startled mouthful of sea water. He felt himself drowning.

"YOU CANNOT BEST AN ENTIRE WORLD, CAPTAIN KIRK. THERE IS NO WAY YOU CAN WIN."

"I have to!" he shouted, then choked again. "Don't you see, Prosecutor, you'll become as bad as the primitive humans you feared. A moment ago you said you'd never found it necessary to harm another being. But now you're going to do so, acting out a terror instead of the higher morals you always insisted you, and not we Earthmen, possessed!"

Floating high above the waves, the Prosecutor paused only a second before gesturing.

The world vanished.

Kirk found himself suddenly dry. The great hall was gone. He was back on the surface of the real Megas-tu. Colored particles and sand swirled harmlessly around him.

In the distance he could see the *Enterprise*, reassembled and whole. Behind him was the forest and the fairy city. The sand vanished, and he was standing on a green lawn with Spock and the Prosecutor. Lucien was there, too, still encased in the red bubble.

Even as he watched, the transparent prison began to dissolve.

"THE MOST MAGIC LIES ALWAYS IN YOUR HEART, HUMAN," mused the Prosecutor, no longer a threatening figure. "YOU WERE PREPARED TO DIE FOR LUCIEN, A BEING WHO IS ALIEN TO YOU AND WHOSE RACIAL MEMORIES TO YOU ARE NOT THE BEST."

"I was sure you would do something at least as foolish, friend Kirk," the goat-man smiled. "It wouldn't have been human of you not to. I told them their fears of you were groundless. But they are so cautious now—not like us." For a being just threatened with limbo, he seemed remarkably cheerful.

"How could you be so certain the Captain would react the way he did?" asked a curious Spock.

There was a twinkle in Lucien's eye. "I know my humans. Their inconsistencies are the most predictable of all.''

"I don't understand," began Kirk, but the Prosecutor smiled as he interrupted.

"THIS LAST WAS A TEST OF YOUR TRUE SELVES, CAPTAIN. HOW RIGHT YOU WERE WHEN YOU REMINDED ME OF OUR OWN WORDS, THAT WE COULD NOT INTENTIONALLY DO HARM TO OTHERS.

"WE HAD TO BE CERTAIN YOUR RECORDS WERE NO RUSE. THEY MIGHT HAVE BEEN DOCTORED BEFORE YOU ENTERED THE VORTEX. WE HAVE BEEN TRICKED TOO MANY TIMES TO TAKE CHANCES.''

"I see now," nodded Spock. "You had to have incontrovertible proof that not only man's laws had changed, but that man himself had." He turned to Kirk. "Your compassion for Lucien was that proof, Captain."

"IF YOUR PEOPLE SHOULD CHANCE TO VISIT US AGAIN, CAPTAIN KIRK, WE SHALL DO OUR BEST TO WELCOME THEM. THE LIFTING OF THIS FEAR IS A GREAT THING. YOU HAVE GIVEN BACK TO US SOME OF WHAT YOUR ANCESTORS TOOK AWAY. WE SHALL PROVIDE YOU WITH THE EXTRADIMENSIONAL BOOST YOU WILL REQUIRE TO REENTER YOUR OWN UNIVERSE.''

"And I'll give you something to make the changeover a little easier!" roared Lucien. He gestured, and tankards appeared in everyone's hand.

"A favorite archaic Earth custom of mine, Asmodeus. A toast—to a new friendship, and to the lifting of old fears." He tilted his head, raised his own huge container, and let the liquid run down his throat, chin, and beard.

Kirk did his best to imitate him, in spirit if not capacity. Spock sipped delicately at his own, and shook his head in wonder at the attractions of excessive alcoholic consumption . . .

The universe was unchanged. Stars lay like gold flecks at the bottom of a prospector's pan, shining steadily through the lambent background of radiant nebulae.

Compared to this glory, the object that suddenly burst into the central galactic quadrant from out of a peculiar confluence of force lines was unrelievedly dull.

To those who rode in it, however, this miniscule symmetrical blot—*the Enterprise*—was a more perfect jewel than the greatest star.

As before, the central viewscreen on the bridge could capture only a small section of the glowing panorama.

"Report, Mr. Scott," said Kirk crisply, leaning over to speak into the pickup grid in the command chair arm. The chief engineer's voice responded from another part of the starship.

"All systems operative, Captain. Warp-engines performing perfectly. Everything's operatin' at maximum efficiency again. It wasn't too hard." There was a pause. "I only had to sacrifice a chicken and two goats to the central computer."

"Very funny, Scotty," Kirk said dryly as the chief's chortle floated back over the intercom. He switched it off in midchortle.

"No more magic for us, Jim," a relieved McCoy declared from Kirk's side. He gestured at the screen. "It's all back there, and there it can stay, for all I care. Though I won't be so quick to laugh at any alien witch doctors we may meet up with in the future."

For a while they simply enjoyed the retreating magnificence of the galactic center, a torrent of raw, untappable energy. It seemed it existed only for their visual pleasure, now.

"I'm not a particularly religious man, Jim," McCoy murmured after several minutes of contemplative consideration of the vast spectacle, "but do you think that Lucien was really the ancient devil-demon some men called Lucifer? Or was it all an act, a guise he liked to assume for his own amusement?"

"You mean," Kirk asked, "did Lucien pattern himself after the myth, or did the myth arise out of Lucien? I don't know, Bones. Does it matter?"

"Oh, I suppose not." McCoy was quiet for a few minutes more, before speaking idly again.

"It's just that—if he was, Jim—this would be the second time he was on the verge of being cast out. But thanks to you, this is the first time he was saved."

Kirk looked sharply back at McCoy. There was no sign of

a smile on the doctor's face. He started to say something, caught himself, and returned his attention to the viewscreen instead. He had other things to think about.

They had a long way to go.